WYOMING

Four Novels of Love in Frontier Forts

COLLEEN COBLE

BARBOUR BOOKS

An Imprint of Barbour Publishing, Inc.

Printed in the United States of America.

COLLEEN COBLE

Colleen and her husband, David, have been married thirty years this October. They have two great kids, David Jr. and Kara. Though Colleen is still waiting for grandchildren, she makes do with the nursery inhabitants at New Life Baptist Church. She is very active at her church, where she sings and helps her husband with a young adult Sunday school class. She enjoys the various activities with the class, including horseback riding (she needs a stool to mount) and canoeing (she tips the canoe every time). A voracious reader herself, Colleen began pursuing her lifelong dream when a younger brother, Randy Rhoads, was killed by lightning when she was thirty-eight. Since that time, Colleen has published eight novels and five novellas.

WHERE LEADS
THE HEART

In memory of my brother, Randy Rhoads,
who taught me to love the mountains of Wyoming,
and my grandparents, Everett and Eileen Everroad,
who loved me unconditionally.
May you all walk those heavenly mountains with joy.

Chapter 1

"Well, I think it's just disgraceful." Anne Drake sniffed behind her lace handkerchief and rearranged the folds of her long skirt as she sat against the wall on a crude wooden chair. Above her head hung an assortment of bridles and farm implements. Her foot tapped in time to the music as her pale blue eyes followed Sarah Montgomery's figure around the floor. She perched her glass of iced tea on a weather-gray wooden barrel, then turned to watch the dipping couples. "First she snatches Rand out from under poor Sally's nose, and now she's taken up with Ben Croftner—with Rand scarcely a year in his grave."

Her companion, Nora Cromwell, nodded, twisting her thin, colorless lips into the semblance of a smile. "I've never understood why all the fellows are attracted to her, anyway. That mass of hair—it looks quite messy most of the time. And those eyes—I declare, they put me in mind of a cat. That shade of green is quite peculiar."

"It's probably all Ben's money." Anne sniffed again, the lines of petulance and discontent deepening around her eyes as she saw the way Sarah's hair caught the light from the dozens of lanterns strung around the barn.

Sarah couldn't help noticing the spiteful looks the young women kept sending her way as she whirled around the barn floor on Ben's arm, but she was used to it by now. Ever since she'd become engaged to Rand Campbell, the best-looking bachelor in the county, she'd been subjected to gossip and tittle-tattle behind her back. But it hurt just the same—especially on top of the anguish of losing Rand a year ago.

Rand. Just the thought of him still brought almost unendurable pain, and she steered her thoughts away from the painful past. It was over and done with, and no amount of wishing or crying would ever bring him back. She knew she would never get over his death.

She felt Ben tighten his grip around her waist as if he sensed her sadness and discontent, and she forced the fake, brittle smile to her face again. She wondered fleetingly if her face would crack before she could murmur her apologies and go home. It seemed that all the entire county of Wabash had done in the past few weeks was party. The dreadful Civil War was finally over, and the Union was preserved, but at what a price. Scarcely a family in the county had been spared the loss of one of their loved ones. And she had lost the only man she had ever loved. She had tried all evening to find a last remnant of her old gaiety and join in the festivities, but it was just a mask.

Ben tightened his grip on her waist as the song ended, and she tried to pull away. "Come outside a minute. I want to talk to you." His firm voice brooked no objection as he pulled her toward the big sliding door at the front of the barn, past the wooden tables piled high with cakes and pies of every imaginable flavor, past the rows of seated older women who watched their exit with tolerant, reminiscent smiles.

Sarah fought the feeling of impending doom that rushed up into her throat at his words. *He's going to ask me tonight,* she thought in panic. *I'm not ready yet.* Her steps faltered as she hung back. "Le—let me get my shawl." Her hands shaking, she grabbed her blue shawl from a peg on the wall and threw it over her shoulders.

"Come on." His voice impatient, Ben tugged on her arm and drew her outside into the crisp autumn air. The sunset was still a faint pink glow in the darkness, but the most light came from the lanterns strung around the graying barn and through the muddy yard. They swung in the light breeze, their lights dipping and swaying like some giant form of firefly. The air was moist and tangy, a mixture of ripening grain and the smoke from a bonfire in the adjoining field. Sarah pulled her shawl more closely about her shoulders as insurance againt the chilly September night.

Ben pulled Sarah down onto a wooden bench away from the rest of the couples who watched the fire shoot sparks high into the dark sky. His eyes were dark, unreadable pools in the moonlight, but his voice was tender and earnest. "It's time we talked about our future, Sarah." He hesitated as if gauging her reaction. "I want to marry you. You know how I've felt about you for years, and now that Rand's gone—well, you need to get on with your life."

Sarah raised a trembling hand to her throat and felt her pulse fluttering under her fingertips. *No, I can't marry you,* she wanted to scream. *I still love Rand.* But the words stuck in her throat. She had to marry Ben. She'd watched her father's health go downhill ever since the news of Rand's death came. Wade said it was because their father was so worried about her future. He said she owed it to Papa to get her life settled, and she could see the sense of her older brother's words. How could she be selfish enough to refuse to do whatever it took to get Papa better? And besides, what else did the future hold except to be someone's wife?

She took a deep breath and said, "All right. I'll marry you." She winced inwardly at the flat tone of her voice.

Ben's smile of self-satisfaction deepened in spite of her less than enthusiastic response. "Wade assured me you'd be agreeable. I'm so glad, my dear. You won't be sorry."

I already am, she thought, her stomach sinking as she twisted her icy hands in the folds of her skirt. *I already am.*

"Let's go announce our good news." He drew her up and tucked her hand into the crook of his elbow. "Your family will be so pleased."

She pinned the smile back on her face as they walked into the barn. Ben pulled her with him to the front of the room and waved his hands. "Ladies and gentlemen, may I have your attention?"

The music stopped with a last, dying squeal of the fiddle, and the flushed couples stared at them. Sarah felt the heat in her cheeks and took a deep, calming breath. She caught her best friend Amelia's horrified look and smiled encouragingly. Amelia wouldn't be pleased at the news, but she'd accept it eventually.

Sarah glanced up at Ben and straightened her shoulders a little in pride. He was certainly very good-looking, but in a different way than Rand had been. Ben's hair was very blond, almost white, and he had gray eyes the color of the Wabash River on a stormy day. His pride at his own accomplishments gave him a self-confident, almost arrogant stature, and his self-assurance smoothed most obstacles he encountered. Like Wade said, she would never want for anything as Ben's wife. *Except for love,* an insistent voice whispered.

"You all know how long I've tried to get Sarah to agree to be my wife." Ben's voice interrupted her thoughts.

"I always thought she showed a lot of sense," called Jason Maxwell from up in the haymow where a group of young men had been playing checkers. A group of adolescent boys lounging in the hay of the loft as they watched the game hooted with laughter.

Ben laughed too, but there was no humor in the look he threw Jason. "Well, you can all congratulate me—she finally gave in! You're all invited to the wedding—and it'll be a humdinger!"

Their friends and neighbors crowded up quickly to congratulate them, and Sarah was hugged and kissed as she fought to keep her smile from slipping. She saw Wade's complacent grin and the smile on her father's face. Then over her father's stooped shoulder, she saw the two Campbell boys, Rand's broth-ers. Her heart skipped a beat, and she pulled her arm out of Ben's possessive grasp to intercept them.

They stopped beside the heavily laden tables and waited for her. Jacob was home on leave for about a month. He had to report for duty at Fort Laramie about a week from now, after his own wedding to Sarah's friend, Amelia. Jacob took her hand, his dark eyes, so like his older brother's, sad in spite of his smile. "No need to worry, Sarah. We saw it coming. And Rand wouldn't want you to grieve forever. We just want you to be happy. Right, Shane?"

Shane, the youngest, pushed his blond hair out of his face and turned sober blue eyes on her. "Ri–right. The only thing is—" He hesitated and looked from Jacob to Sarah. "What if Rand's not really dead?"

Sarah gasped. "What do you mean?" She looked from one to the other in shock, unable to still the small, faint flutter of hope. Did they know something they hadn't told her? "What does he mean, Jake? Ben saw his body in the prison camp. We got official notification from the army, and his name was on the list in the newspaper."

"But we never got his body or his things," Shane insisted stubbornly. "There could still be some mistake. Maybe he was wounded real bad. Ben could be wrong."

"Shane, it's been over a year since he was reported dead!" Jacob said. "Don't you think Rand would have written or the army would have contacted us? Thousands died with no one to mark their graves or send their belongings home, both Union and Rebs. I know—I was there too. Rand is dead!"

Tears welled up in Shane's eyes, and Sarah blinked back moisture in her own eyes as that glimmer of hope died. She didn't think she would ever get used to the reality of Rand's death, but she understood why Jacob was being so brutal. Shane couldn't begin to heal until he accepted it. Just as she was finally begin-ning to accept it.

Jacob threw a comforting arm around Shane's shoulders as tears trickled down the youngster's cheeks. "I'm sorry, Sarah," he said. "I had no idea such a notion was brewing in that brain of his. Forget what he said and just be happy." He reached out and touched her cheek. "Ben's a lucky guy. But remember, you'll always be a part of us too."

"I'll remember," she whispered as she watched them thread their way through the throng. How she still loved Rand! Would the pain never go away? Every time she closed her eyes, she could see his square-jawed face with its deep dimples, the warm brown eyes so alight with joy and love of life, and the thick dark hair that fell heavily across his broad forehead. And he had been the kindest man she'd ever known. She'd helped him take food to needy families many times, and once he'd even given his new coat to a drunk shivering in just a ragged shirt. It was such a huge, tragic mistake for him to be lying in an unmarked grave somewhere.

There was a soft touch on her arm, and she whirled, afraid it was Ben, that he would see her tears and demand to know why she was crying. But it was just Amelia, her dark blue eyes anxious. "Amelia! No, don't say it," Sarah interrupted her friend's beginning protest. "I know you don't approve, but I really didn't have a choice."

Amelia McCallister sighed and tears hung on her long lashes. "Yes, you do. Can you look me in the eyes and tell me you love him?" She stared into Sarah's eyes.

Sarah bit her lip in frustration. Amelia always cut right through to the heart of the matter. "N–no. Not like Rand. But I'll be a good wife to him. I have to marry someone, and Ben loves me." The excuses sounded weak, even to her own ears. "I have to get on with my life. It may not be the life I'd dreamed of or hoped for, but Ben will make sure it's a secure one."

Amelia hesitated, eyeing her friend. "I just don't trust Ben," she said finally. "I know I should, and it shames me I feel like that. I've prayed and prayed for more patience and compassion for him, but I just don't think he's all he seems."

"Well, you're the only one who seems to feel like that. Since he's gotten back from the war, everyone seems to think he's just wonderful." Sarah smiled and nodded toward the cluster of young ladies hovering around Ben in the middle of the floor. "I know a couple of girls who would give anything to be in my shoes. You must not have seen all the nasty looks flung my way tonight."

Amelia followed her gaze and gave a sigh. "They're just a little jealous," she said gently. "They haven't found the one God has for them yet. Why can't you wait for the right person?"

"You mean like Rand? There won't be that kind of love for me ever again. Anything will just be second best. Be happy for me, Amelia. Please? Be my bridesmaid?"

Amelia sighed in defeat. "You know I will if we're still here. When is the wedding?"

"We haven't set a date yet, but it probably won't be for awhile. Don't worry—you'll still be the first bride." Sarah didn't know how she could stand to be separated from her best friend. She saw Ben motion with an imperious gesture. "I've got to go, but I'll let you know. We'll get together tomorrow and make some plans." She hurried off, pinning her smile back in place and wishing for the evening to be over. But now they'd have to stay for hours yet and accept everyone's congratulations.

By the time all the well-wishing and hugging were over, the rest of Sarah's family had left to go home. She'd hoped they'd all be in bed by the time Ben dropped her off, but a dim light still shone through the parlor window's lace curtains as he helped her down off the buggy. The parlor window was open, and she could smell the aroma of fresh-brewed coffee. Evidently, no one was planning on going to bed anytime soon.

"You've made me very happy tonight, my dear," Ben said as he leaned down to kiss her.

She couldn't help the involuntary flinch as he bent his head, but she forced herself to accept his kiss.

Ben was aware of her recoil, and his grasp tightened around her waist as he frowned slightly.

In spite of her resolve, Sarah quickly pulled away from his possessive grip. "I'd better go in. I'll see you tomorrow." She rushed up the steps without waiting for a reply, her heart lightening with every step she took away from Ben.

She could feel his gaze boring into her back as she rushed up the step.

The speculation in Ben's eyes frightened Sarah a little when she looked back. *He looks almost, well, evil,* she thought with a shiver as she dragged her eyes from his strange gaze and hurried inside.

She heard the murmur of voices as she stepped into the hallway and sighed in resignation. She hung her shawl on a hook on the wall and walked into the parlor. The thick rug muffled her footsteps, but Wade looked up from his seat in the overstuffed chintz chair beside the fireplace as she entered. Her father lay on the matching sofa, his breathing labored and his face pale in the dying light from the fireplace. "Papa, are you all right? Should I call Doc Seth?" She rushed to his side, her heart pounding.

"No, no. I'm fine. Just tired." William's breathing eased as he smiled up at Sarah. He took her hand and drew her into an embrace. "You remind me so much of your mama tonight, Sweetheart. Her hair was the exact same shade as yours the night I met her. And her eyes—just like yours. I had a marble I kept for years because it was just like her eyes—deep emerald with gold flecks." He released her then closed his eyes and laid his hand against his chest. "I just realized how much I'm going to miss you. It will be almost like losing your mama again."

Sarah's heart thumped in sudden hope. Could Wade be wrong about how Papa felt? "I don't have to get married, you know. I'd rather stay home with you and Joel, anyway." She was the only mother her young brother had ever known. Their mother, Kate, had died giving birth to Joel. She didn't know how she and Joel could bear to be separated.

"No, no, Sweetheart. You've been too self-sacrificing already, and I should never have been selfish enough to let you. You were only eight when your mama died and much too young to take over the household and the new baby the way you did. I should have hired someone." He wiped a shaking hand across his brow, beaded with drops of sweat. "But I just wasn't thinking clearly. And all these years you've managed our home like a grown woman. It's time for you to step out on your own and have your own life, your own home." He sat up and swung his legs off the couch. "You get on up to bed now. That's where I'm headed."

Relieved at the way his voice seemed stronger, Sarah stood up as Rachel, Wade's wife, came into the parlor carrying a tray laden with cups of steaming coffee. "Here. Let me take that. It's much too heavy for you in your condition." Sarah eyed the gentle bulge under Rachel's skirt.

Rachel handed it over with a tired smile of thanks and a glance at her husband.

As if aware of the censorious look his wife gave him, Wade's gaze sharpened, and he smiled at his sister. A self-satisfied smirk. "I'm glad to see you came to your senses. Ben is quite a catch. Just see you don't forget your family when you're rich."

Was money all he ever thought about? Sarah bit back her angry words. She didn't want to upset her father. "That's not important," she said in a quiet voice.

Wade gave a cynical laugh. "It's the only thing that's important. I always thought you could do better than Campbell."

Her father squeezed her arm. "Why don't you go on up to bed, Sweetheart? You can tell us all about your plans tomorrow."

Her anger died, and she nodded wearily. It didn't do any good to argue with Wade anyway. He had never liked Rand, probably because he was one of the few people Wade couldn't dominate. Rand had been a strong man, in body as well as spirit. She kissed her father good night and walked upstairs, running her hand along the smooth oak banister. She looked back down into the entryway as she thought about her father's words. She was going to miss her home more than she'd realized.

Once in the sanctuary of her room, she pulled off her dress and reached for her nightgown. She caught a glimpse of herself in the oval oak mirror. Goodness, but she'd lost weight in this past year! Her ribs were prominent stairsteps up her chest, and her neck looked positively bony. She'd always been tiny, barely five feet tall, but now she looked as though a strong wind would blow her away. Her green eyes were enormous and stood out in sharp contrast to the honey golden skin stretched over her high cheekbones.

She looked around her familiar bedroom. The large room was furnished with dainty white furniture stenciled with pink. A lacy coverlet topped the feather bed, and dozens of pastel pillows offered a plump, safe haven to curl up and read. She pulled the coverlet back and crawled beneath the smooth sheets, pulling her feather comforter up to her chin. Foreboding filled her as she remembered Shane's words. What if Rand wasn't dead? She bit her lip at her foolish thoughts. She'd indulged in such daydreams in the first months after his death. But the feeling persisted as she drifted off to sleep.

Chapter 2

B en swung off his horse and walked quickly toward the house. Life was good and all his plans were falling into place. As he approached the stately brick two-story, he was struck again with his usual sense of pride in all he'd accomplished. He, Ben Croftner, son of the good-for-nothing drifter, Max Croftner, had pulled himself up by his own bootstraps out of the dirt and lived in a house that was the envy of everyone in Wabash—and Indiana, for that matter. And if some of his business dealings didn't bear close scrutiny, well, that's just the way it was in the world of high finance. You did what you had to do to get to the top. There had been much opportunity since the war, and he had discovered he had an aptitude for exploiting it. And now Sarah was finally his.

He wiped his dusty shoes on the rug by the door, then stepped into the parlor. His pride rose again as he saw the elegant appointments in the front parlor. Velvet drapes, fine walnut tables and Dresden figurines, a plush rug imported from France, and an overstuffed horsehair sofa and chair. He frowned as he saw the figure on the sofa. Too bad he couldn't just leave his family behind the same way he'd left his old life. Although his brother *had* been useful this past year.

Labe swung around at his entrance and jumped up, an envelope clutched in his hand. "I ain't goin' to do it no more, Ben." His voice quivered with fear and outrage as he thrust the envelope into his brother's hand. "My boss almost caught me takin' it. And I ain't goin' to jail for nobody. Not even you."

But even his brother's fear failed to mar Ben's satisfaction with life. He patted Labe's shoulder. "You don't have to do it anymore. Sarah finally gave in last night. By the time the next letter comes, she'll be my wife."

Labe's mouth dropped open. "I never thought you'd really pull it off. When you come back from the war with that crazy scheme, I thought fightin' them Rebs had done made you loco."

Ben's grin widened as he sank into the plushness of the high-backed chair and took off his sweat-stained Stetson and wiped his face. His voice grew soft with reminiscence. "When I got back and found out they all thought Rand was dead, I knew it would be an easy matter to let them go on thinking it. All I had to do was burn the letter I was supposed to give Sarah from Rand. Lucky for me I had such a faithful brother working in the post office. I always knew she belonged to me."

"Easy for you, maybe," Labe burst out. "You're not the one who had to steal six letters with a boss like mine around. That Jack don't miss nothing that goes on. I don't see how I got away with it this long."

"I know, Labe, and I appreciate all you've done." Ben said impatiently. "Like I said, it's all over. Now all you have to do is keep your mouth shut." He dismissed his brother's worries and looked at the envelope in his lap. "I suppose I should read what this says." He grinned as he ripped open the top and took out the single sheet of paper. "Won't Mr. High-and-Mighty Rand Campbell be surprised when he gets back and finds out Sarah is married to me?"

He settled more comfortably in his chair and quickly scanned the sprawling lines. His smile faded and a scowl twisted his face. "He's coming home in a couple of weeks!" He ripped the page to shreds and jumped to his feet. "But he's going to be too late!" He strode out the door without another word to Labe.

"Just like Rand Campbell to spoil things," Ben muttered as he strode toward the barn. "But he's going to be too late this time." He flung the harness over his horse's still-damp neck and hitched up the buggy. As he flicked the buggy whip over the horse's head and headed toward the Montgomery farm, he clenched his teeth with determination. He'd come this close—he wasn't about to let it all slip away now. Not even if it meant Rand really had to die.

He hadn't kept up a charade for five months to lose Sarah now. He'd been really clever, telling her how he'd found Rand in the prison camp and got him to the hospital, only to see him die while holding his hand. And Rand *should* have died. He'd been just a shell of a man with his skin stretched over his bones when he was finally liberated from Andersonville prison camp. It was the most hideous thing Ben had ever seen. But he had rallied, much to Ben's dismay. Ben really hadn't expected him to recuperate as fast as he had, and now he threatened to spoil all Ben's carefully laid plans.

Sarah was sweeping the front porch when he stepped down out of the buggy. She looked up with a start, afraid for an instant it was Wade back from the fields. *That's one good thing about getting married,* she thought. *I'll get out from under Wade's thumb.* She relaxed and lifted a hand in greeting when she saw him. His blond hair just curled over his collar, and his gray eyes were gentle and tender. She dispelled her misgivings from the night before. The strange look just had been a trick of the moonlight. She was doing the right thing.

"How's my lovely lady today?" Ben bounded up the steps with a smile and took her hand.

"A little tired," she admitted. "Everyone has been stopping by to congratulate me. News travels fast."

"Especially good news." He guided her down onto the porch steps and sat beside her. "I was talking to Labe this morning, and he was saying how good it would be to have a real woman doing for us once you and I are married. You know we haven't decided on a date yet, and I was hopin' to make it on my birthday next weekend. Could you be ready?"

"Bu–but, Ben! That's only eight days." Panic rose in her throat, and she tried to keep the dismay out of her face as she stared at him. "There's such a lot to do. I–I have to make my dress. And—"

He gripped her shoulders, and a note of impatience crept into his voice as he stared into her eyes. "You can be ready, I'm sure. If you really want to be. Don't you think you've made me wait long enough? I surely don't care what you wear. Your Sunday dress will do just fine."

She dropped her eyes, ashamed. Why did he always make her feel so guilty, so indebted to him? "I can be ready," she whispered. She allowed his hug, then watched him ride away with something that felt like relief. What difference did it really make anyway? One date was as good as another if she was really going to go through with it. And besides, if she wanted Amelia to be her bridesmaid, the wedding needed to be before Amelia left.

She untied her apron and started toward the McCallister farm. She paused at the knoll overlooking Amelia's home. It was so pretty from up here. Doctor Seth and his family still lived in the log home he'd built when he first arrived twenty years ago, although with his burgeoning practice he could well afford an elaborate home in town. But she was glad the McCallisters had never moved. It was her second home, and she ran over the meadow that separated the two properties nearly every day.

The house had been added onto over the years and now sprawled carelessly in several directions. Their two families had been best friends ever since Sarah could remember. At one time there was hope that Amelia would marry Wade, but that was soon dashed as Wade grew to manhood and became the arrogant, self-righteous boor he was. Amelia felt sorry for him, but she had never had any romantic interest in anyone but Jacob Campbell.

Amelia was on the wide front porch, churning butter. "I was just coming to see you as soon as I was finished," she said, smiling, her face flushed with exertion. Tendrils of dark hair clung in curls around her face. "I have some ideas for the wedding."

Her smile faded as Sarah explained Ben's plans. "Eight days! Isn't that too soon to get everything ready?" she asked hopefully. "And you said I would be the first bride."

"It has to be enough time, and if we wait until after your wedding, you might have to leave too soon." Sarah avoided her gaze. "Ben wants to be married on his birthday. It's the least I can do after all I've put him through these past five months. You know how patient with me he's been—" Her voice faltered as she saw the skeptical look Amelia threw her way. She shrugged. "What difference does it make?"

"I suppose you're right," Amelia said slowly. "One time is as good as another to ruin your life. And I've never understood why you think you owe Ben anything. He hasn't done anything special for you. He was just determined to capture you, and it seems that he has."

"Don't start, Amelia. Please." Sarah's tone was uncharacteristically sharp, and she saw Amelia's blue eyes glisten with quick tears. "I'm sorry." She hugged her friend. "It's just that I have to go through with it. Papa would be so disappointed. And besides." She gave Amelia a wink. "I was thinking last night how nice it will be to get away from Wade."

Amelia smiled and blinked away her tears. "He just needs the Lord in his life."

Sarah just smiled. She was a little envious of her friend's faith. No matter what happened, Amelia seemed to trust God. She never had a bad word to say about anyone.

That's why her attitude toward Ben was so perplexing. Sarah knew her friend was just concerned. But this was really for the best, if Amelia could just see it. Sarah would make a fresh start with Ben, and as the years passed and she had children to occupy her time, maybe she could numb the pain in her heart.

The next few days sped by as Sarah threw herself into marriage preparations. She fell into bed at night too exhausted to think or even to dream. Papa had bought her a new machine called a Singer treadle sewing machine. Her dress, even with its yards and yards of soft, creamy lace, quickly took shape under its whirring needle.

Friday afternoon she sat back and massaged her aching neck thankfully. It was finally finished. She stared out the living room window at the weeping willows swaying along the riverbank. The soft breeze, laden with the rich scent of the Wabash River, blew through the sheer curtains and caressed her hot face. Unbidden, a memory of walking hand in hand with Rand along the riverbank hit her, and she clutched her skirt in anguish. *I won't think about him anymore,* she told herself. *I'll be Mrs. Ben Croftner in two days.* Then all the ghosts would be laid to rest.

She jumped nervously as the knocker on the front door clattered. She jumped up and hurried to the front hall. Pastor Aaron Stevens stood on the front porch, turning his hat in his hands. "Pastor," she said in delight. "Come in."

"I was out calling on the new family by the river, the Longs, and just thought I'd stop in and see how you're doing," he explained as he followed her into the parlor. His deep blue eyes were concerned.

"I just finished my dress." She pointed to the heap of cream material on the sewing machine.

"Are you all right, Sarah? You look—" He hesitated as he sat down on the sofa. "Well, troubled. Not quite the picture of a joyous bride-to-be I expected."

She smiled wearily. Pastor always seemed able to sense her moods in a strange way. She sighed and nodded. "I guess I am troubled. More than I've admitted to anyone else. And I don't *want* to be! This is for the best—I'm sure of it."

Pastor Stevens pushed his heavy black hair away from his forehead. "Are you *really* sure about this marriage, little sister? Have you prayed about it?"

Sarah lifted her chin mutinously. "Not really. And I know you're going to say I should. But God didn't seem to be listening all those months when I prayed for Rand's safety." There. She'd finally admitted the thought that had been nagging her for over a year. Did God really care about her?

Pastor Stevens frowned as he leaned forward. "I had a feeling you blamed God for Rand's death. I'm glad you're finally admitting it." He took her hand, his dark blue eyes warm with concern and compassion. "Sarah, please listen to me. It's hard, I know, but we can't always see God's plan in our lives. I remember when I was a little boy, I was lying on the floor at my grandmother's feet. She was doing some embroidery work, and I looked up at the underside of the hoop. The yarn was all tangled and gnarled. A real mess. But when I climbed up beside her and looked down at what she was working on, it was a beautiful garden. That's the way our lives are. We're looking at the picture from underneath, but God is working out a specific plan from above."

"No plan could be right without Rand in it! I don't think God really cares about me anymore." She didn't care if the words shocked Pastor; it was how she really felt. If God really cared, He wouldn't let her go through this heartache.

Pastor Stevens got up and knelt beside Sarah's chair. "God still loves you, Sarah. He didn't promise we'd never have trouble or heartache. In fact, He assured us we would. But He's given us His Word to go with us every step of the way. Can't you just trust Him like you used to? I remember the old Sarah and how she believed God for every little thing in her life. Wouldn't you like to be that same young woman again?"

"I just can't!" she said, standing up and moving to the window, her back to the young pastor. "Maybe someday when the wounds aren't still so fresh, I'll be able to trust Him like I should. But nothing has turned out like I expected. Every time I see the knoll on the other side of the woods, I remember it's the spot where Rand and I meant to build our home. Everywhere I look there are reminders of how my life is in shambles." She turned. "If you don't mind, Pastor, I have a lot of things to finish up." She knew she sounded abrupt and rude, but she just couldn't talk about it anymore. It hurt too much.

Pastor Stevens stood reluctantly, frustration etched on his face. "If you need to talk, you know where to find me," he said as he left. "Please pray about this before you go through with it, Sarah."

She didn't answer him, and he left after gazing at her for a moment. She breathed a sigh of relief when she heard the front door shut. She pushed away a stab of guilt as she went to the kitchen to start supper. She'd chosen her course, and she'd stick with it.

Chapter 3

The train shrieked a warning of imminent arrival, and Rand Campbell jerked awake, his heart pounding. He licked dry lips—how he'd love a drink of his ma's iced tea. The thought of sun tea brewing in a glass jug on the back step at home caused a fresh wave of homesickness to wash over him. It wouldn't be long, though.

Then the fear he'd tried to keep at bay for the past three days flooded back. What would he find at home? He'd passed mile after mile of war-ravaged scenes. Homes burned, fences torn down, hopeless looks on the faces of women and children. What if he arrived and found his home gone and his family missing? And Sarah. What if she were dead? *What if she didn't wait for you?* a part of his mind whispered. He pushed the thought away impatiently. His Sarah would wait no matter what. *Then why didn't she write? Why didn't Ma write?* The unanswered questions made him feel sick.

The train whistle blew again, and he peered out the soot-streaked window. He was almost home; eagerly, he scanned the rolling pastures outside the window. There was the Johnson place; it looked as neat and well tended as usual. The Larsen farm looked unharmed. The train slowed as it began its descent into the valley. Through clearings in the lush canopy of glowing leaves, he could see the sparkling river and the town just beyond.

The town of Wabash nestled between two steep hills, with the courthouse on the far hill overlooking the sprawling brick and wood buildings that clustered neatly below it. He drank in the familiar buildings and the glimmer of water that ran in front of the town like a silver ribbon. During the heyday of the Wabash-Erie Canals, the river had bustled with boats of all types and sizes, but since the railroad came, the canal traffic had slacked off, and the river once again resumed its placid course. Hungrily he watched for a familiar face. But the streets and boardwalks were almost deserted. The few people he saw hurrying along were strangers.

But the town looked just the same. The ravages the war had left behind seemed very far away from this peaceful town. There was Beitman and Wolf's. And Martha's Millinery, her fly-specked window crowded with bonnets. Several old-timers in bib overalls lounged outside Lengel's Gun Shop.

Do the younger members of town still patronize the Red Onion Saloon? he

21

wondered. He grinned at a sudden memory of the last ruckus he'd gotten into at the saloon, much to his grandma's dismay. She was always quoting Proverbs to him after an escapade at the Red Onion.

Those Bible verses he'd memorized at her knee were a big part of what had gotten him through the horror of prison camp. He didn't really understand some of them very well, but they were somehow very comforting. Maybe when his life settled down a little, he could study the Scriptures for himself.

His smile faded. He knew the war had changed him and not for the better. Something inside him had turned hard and cold, and he realized that in reality he had little desire to study the Bible. After what he'd seen in the war, the existence of God didn't seem too likely. He pushed his grandmother's memory away and gazed out the window intently.

The train gave one final, wheezing bellow, then came to a shuddering stop under the overhang of the depot. Rand took a deep breath and stood up, pulling his haversack out from under his seat. His heart pounded as he limped toward the door. Wouldn't it be grand if Pa or Jacob were in town? No chance of that, though. For one thing, he was here a good week earlier than he'd written he'd be. Lot more likely to find them in the field on the way home, if Jacob were even here. *And if he survived the war,* an inner voice whispered.

His weak leg, cramped by the long trip, gave out as he stepped down, and he fell into an elderly, stooped man's surprised face. "Why—I—I cain't believe it! Rand Campbell, is it really you?" Liam, who had run the train station for as long as Rand could remember, grabbed him by the shoulders and peered into his face.

His hair was even more grizzled than Rand remembered, but his breath stank of garlic like usual, and Rand suppressed a grin. Liam's wife believed in garlic's medicinal qualities, so most folks steered clear of her specialties at the church picnics. "It's me all right, Liam."

"Rand," the old man gasped again before enfolding him in a bear hug. "We heered you was dead, Boy."

Rand hugged him back until his words penetrated, then drew back in shock. "What do you mean, dead? I wrote my folks and Sarah every few weeks. I've been in the hospital in Washington."

Liam pulled a filthy handkerchief from his pocket and wiped his face shakily. The surprise was almost too much for him. "Wait 'til Myra hears 'bout this!" He put the dirty cloth back in his pocket. "Don't know nothin' 'bout no letters. No one here got no letters, I'm sure. Yer folks been grievin' themselves to death over you. Had a memorial service at church for you last spring, and I ain't never seen so many people at one of them things." He stared in Rand's puzzled face. "I'm tellin' ya, we all thought you was dead, Boy!"

Rand felt like he'd been punched in the stomach; he couldn't catch his breath. How could something like this have happened? "I–I sent a letter with Ben Croftner to give to Sarah," he stammered. "Didn't he make it back here?"

A look of surprise and something else Rand couldn't identify flickered across Liam's face. "Yeah, he got back—let's see. Must be pert near six months ago." He paused and glanced quickly at Rand's face before continuing. "But he didn't say nothin' 'bout no letter."

Rand stared at him. There was something odd in Liam's manner. "What aren't you telling me?" he asked.

The man flushed. "Well, now—I–I guess you have to hear it sooner or later," he stammered. "Ben's s'posed to marry Sarah tomorrow. Right after church. Whole town's been invited. Ben's been struttin' 'round all important-like."

The strength left Rand's knees, and he sat down on the passenger bench outside the depot. The implications of what Liam said began to sink in, along with a bitter anger at Ben's betrayal. And Sarah's. "He let her go on thinkin' I was dead," he said slowly. He stood up angrily and slung his haversack over one broad shoulder. "He let my family go on grieving and suffering. He'll pay for this," he spat through clenched teeth. Abruptly he turned south and strode off without saying good-bye to Liam, his slight limp more pronounced because of his fatigue and agitation.

Rand clamped down on the rage that was building in him. How could Ben do such a thing? And Sarah. How could she be so fickle? Why, he must have been declared dead only a few months before she took up with Croftner! Was that all the time she mourned someone she was supposed to love? His emotions felt raw, and he just couldn't seem to make any sense out of it.

By the time he made his way to the livery stable, paid for a horse, and swung up into the saddle, he was shaking with fury. He dug his heels into the mare's flank and set off toward home.

Being astride a horse again for the first time in a year cleared his thoughts, and he was more in control of his emotions by the time he pulled the mare off the road and headed up the deeply rutted track that followed the river. The fields were tawny with drying corn. Harvest would be in a few weeks. His heart quickened as the white two-story home on the hill overlooking the river came into view. Home! How he'd longed for this moment.

He pulled the horse up sharply, undecided. Should he go home first or go see Sarah and demand an explanation? He could just see the roof of the large Montgomery house over the next rise, and he let the horse prance on the path for a moment as he decided what to do.

No, he decided. He'd see his family first. At least they'd mourned for him.

By the time he reached the front yard, his heart was pounding, and his palms were slick with sweat. A nagging headache persisted just behind his eyes. He pulled his horse to a stop and dismounted, a little disappointed no one was outside. As he approached the back door that led to the kitchen, he could see his mother washing dishes. A wave of love welled up in him as he saw the new gray in her hair and the fine web of wrinkles at her eyes.

His mother's back was to the door, and he watched her a moment as she picked up a dish and proceeded to wash it. "I think I heard a horse," she said to the little brown dog lying on the rug by her feet. "Probably one of the men-folk home." The little dog pricked up her ears and whined as she looked toward the door. His mother dipped the soapy plate in the pan of rinse water and laid it to drain on the wooden chopping block beside her.

Rand let the screen door bang behind him, but she didn't turn. "Don't bang the door," she said automatically just as Jody yipped and launched herself in a frenzy toward the door. She wiped her soapy hands on her apron.

"Ma." Rand knelt and picked up the little dog as he stared at his mother.

She froze, and Rand saw one emotion after another chase across her face. Uncertainty, disbelief, hope. She clutched her hands in the folds of her apron and swung slowly around to fully face him.

"Ma, I'm home." Rand patted Jody and laughed as the dog wriggled in his arms and licked his face joyously.

Her mouth gaping, his mother stared at him as if he were an apparition.

"It's me, Ma. It's really me. I'm not dead."

"Rand?" she croaked as she took a faltering step toward him. "Rand!" With a noise something between a cry and a croak, she threw herself into his arms as the tears started down her cheeks. After several moments, she drew away. "I can't believe it! Let me look at you." She held him at arm's length, then hugged him, laughing and crying as Jody licked both their faces and whined and wriggled in ecstasy.

Rand clutched his mother so tightly he was afraid he might hurt her. For over a year, ever since he was captured, he'd longed for his mother's gentle touch on his brow. At night when he awoke bathed in sweat from the pain, he had ached to lay his head on her breast and hear her soothing voice as she sang to him. He had been so hurt and bewildered at her silence after his release. Every time the door to the hospital ward opened, he had expected to see her anxious face.

He swallowed hard then drew away. "That coffee smells good." He settled in the chair with a contented sigh. Home, he was finally home.

He was on his third cup of coffee when the sound of horses and voices came to his ears.

"Sounds like your pa and your brothers are home." His mother's face shone with joy as she looked at him.

Rand rose and stood as his brother came through the door, Jacob first followed by Shane and their father.

"Jake," Rand said.

His brother froze, his dark eyes widening. Jacob opened his mouth but no words came out.

"Rand!" Shane shrieked his brother's name and flung himself into Rand's waiting arms. A moment later all four men were hugging and slapping one another on the back, Rand was unashamed of his wet cheeks.

"It's really you, it's really you," Jacob said over and over as he stared at his brother as if memorizing his features.

"The good Lord answered our prayers after all." With a shaking hand, Jeremiah wiped at his eyes with his bandanna. He was breathing hard, as if he'd just run all the way from the back pasture to the house.

They sat down around the kitchen table as Margaret hurriedly poured them each a cup of coffee and joined them. Just as she sat down, they heard the front door slam.

Hannah, the eldest and the only girl, hurried into the kitchen. "Sorry I'm late, Ma," she panted. She stopped short and looked at the group clustered around the table. Her puzzled stare stopped when her eyes met Rand's. She opened and closed her mouth several times, but no sound escaped.

"What! My gabby sister with nothing to say?" Rand stood. Hannah looked older, more settled than he remembered.

Hannah screamed and dropped the basket she was holding. Potatoes rolled across the wooden floor, and she almost tripped on them as she rushed toward her brother. She threw herself into Rand's arms, and he picked her up and swung her around, kissing her soundly before setting her on her feet again.

"Let me look at you!" She held him at arm's length and frowned as she saw his thinness. "What's happened to you? We thought you were dead!"

She hung onto his arm as he limped back to the table and sat down. "I was just about to explain when you so rudely interrupted," he said with a grin. "Of course, that's nothing new—you've never learned how to be quiet."

"Very funny!" She punched him on the arm and sat down beside him.

"Ouch." He rubbed his arm, then grinned at his family. "Now, as I was about to say, I was captured outside Atlanta in August of '64. I'd been on reconnaissance trying to see where the heaviest troops were. That's how I spent most of the war, slipping back and forth through enemy lines. The Rebs took me to Andersonville prison camp—"

"Andersonville!" Jacob interrupted, his voice filled with horror. "That camp is notorious. I heard the Union army found 12,000 graves there when the war was over."

25

Rand nodded. "I was lucky I wasn't one of them. You can't imagine how bad it was. We had to build our own shelters, usually just a lean-to made with whatever we could find. Blankets, clothing, sticks. Some of the men could only dig a hole in the ground and cover up with a single thin blanket. There were so many of us we just barely had enough space to lie down. And the food—"

He broke off and took a deep breath. "Well, it wasn't like yours, Ma. We were lucky if they gave us a little salt, maybe a half a cup of beans, and about a cup of unsifted cornmeal. A lot of men died from the inflamed bowels the stuff caused. One day I helped bury over a hundred bodies in a common grave."

Margaret laid a trembling hand on his arm. "I just thank God you survived it, Son."

He covered her hand with his and smiled before continuing. "I was delirious by the time we were freed, a combination of dysentery and malnutrition." He smiled grimly. "The doctors tell me I weighed less than a hundred pounds when I was brought to the hospital. A skeleton really. I've spent the last six months at Harewood Hospital in Washington recuperating."

"Why didn't you write?" Hannah burst out.

"I wrote several times. At least once a month."

"We never received a single letter. Just a notification from the army of your death about the same time you say you were captured." Jacob's look was puzzled.

"I knew you weren't dead. I just knew it," Shane put in excitedly. "I told Sarah just last week!"

At the mention of Sarah's name, Rand looked at Jacob. "What about Sarah, Jacob?"

Jacob just stared at him.

"I already know she's going to marry Ben Croftner. How could she do that—didn't she mourn me at all?" There was a bitter taste in his mouth as Rand spat the words out.

"Mourn you? You idiot!" Hannah interrupted, standing up and raking a hand through her mane of chestnut hair. "We all feared for her sanity! She refused to eat for days. Even now she hardly smiles. And you know what a perky, bubbly little thing she has always been."

"Then why is she marrying Ben?"

Hannah hesitated, her eyes searching her brother's face. "William is dying." She sighed as she sat back down beside her brother. She took his hand gently. "Sarah doesn't know, but William and Wade have pushed her to marry Ben right away. And Ben has promised Wade that fifty acres of prairie he's always coveted as a marriage settlement, Rachel told me. Wade's taken advantage of Sarah's apathy since the news of your death to convince her she owes it to the family to do this."

"Wade's always thought of himself instead of his family," Rand said angrily. "But there's something else you don't know." He stood and paced over to the window at the front of the kitchen, then wheeled to face them. "Ben has known all along I wasn't dead."

"What!" Margaret stood in agitation. "Are you sure?"

He nodded grimly. "Ben was with the troops who liberated the prison. I even gave him a letter to give to Sarah."

"Maybe he thought you died after he left," Margaret offered.

Jacob shook his head thoughtfully. "He knew we read it in the paper last fall—before he got home. And that we received an official notification shortly after that. I'm positive he never gave Sarah any letter."

"What about all the letters I wrote from the hospital?" Rand sat down and stretched his aching leg out in front of him, rubbing it absently as he tried to figure out how Ben had pulled his little drama off.

"The mail service has been wretched," Jeremiah said. "Maybe they were lost."

"All of them?" Rand shook his head. "Not likely. Ben must have gotten ahold of them somehow."

"Labe works in the post office," Shane said in a small voice. "But he's really nice. He wouldn't do anything like that."

His announcement silenced everyone. Finally, Hannah spoke up in a soft, hesitant voice. "Surely Labe wouldn't tamper with the mail." But her tone indicated her own doubt.

"What other explanation is there, Sis?" Jacob jumped up angrily, his fists clenched.

Rand got to his feet. "I'm going to see Sarah," he announced. "Then I'm going to get to the bottom of this."

Margaret held out a placating hand. "Let it go for now, Son. Try to get a handle on your anger before you talk to Ben."

Rand shook off her hand. "Let it go! After all I've been through, you want me to let it go? Ben needs to find out he can't treat a Campbell like that."

Margaret touched her son's cheek gently. "The war has changed you, Rand." She paused, as if searching for the right words. "You seem so harsh and headstrong. You've always been the even-tempered, rational one in the family."

Her criticism stung. "What do you expect, Ma? For me to just forget how Ben lied and deceived the people I love? Well, I just can't do it. Maybe if I hadn't been through so much the last few years, I could. But I thought Ben was my friend. I trusted him. I think I deserve an explanation for what he's done."

Margaret bit her lip, and her hand fell away from his arm. " 'Vengeance is mine; I will repay, sayeth the Lord,' " she quoted softly.

Rand looked at her for a long moment, then grabbed his hat and strode toward the back door. Easy enough for her to talk of forgiveness. She hadn't been the one confined to Andersonville all those months.

"Don't go see Ben without me," Jacob called after him.

Rand nodded without looking back. He strode into the barn and grinned at the welcoming nicker. At least Ranger didn't think he was dead. He patted the horse's white nose lovingly, then saddled him and headed first toward the Montgomery farm. Then he'd settle with Ben Croftner.

Chapter 4

S arah took a sip of tea and tried to drag her attention back to Myra's conversation, but her thoughts kept whirling around. Tomorrow she would be Mrs. Ben Croftner. She thought she knew just how Joan of Arc must have felt the night before she was burned at the stake, and her spirit recoiled at the thought of what tomorrow would bring. The last few days had swept by in a daze, and now her future was hurtling toward her at breathtaking speed. The lighthearted chatter of her friends around her, the brightly patterned quilt still attached to the quilting frame, the gifts heaped beside her, all served to deepen her sense of impending doom. She didn't want to leave her home, her comfortable, predictable life. And how well did she really know Ben? What if her new life was so different she couldn't adjust?

Suddenly aware of a strange hush in the room, Sarah looked around at the other ladies. They all wore the same look of shock and disbelief, as they stared toward the door. Sarah frowned and turned to see what had caused such consternation.

She blinked at the figure blocking the sunlight as his broad shoulders spanned the doorway. Her eyes traveled up the gaunt frame to the face staring back at her intently. She gasped and began to rise to her feet. Was she dreaming? She put a hand to her throat.

"Sarah."

The voice was so familiar, so beloved. She gasped, then took a step toward him and reached out a trembling hand.

Rand caught her hand as she reached toward him. "Hello, Sarah."

"Rand?" Sarah could barely choke out the name. Was he real? "Rand, is it really you?" Hesitantly she touched his square jawline and felt the rough stubble on his chin. "It is you!" She buried her face against his chest and burst into tears. If it was a dream, she didn't ever want to wake up. But this was no dream. The rough texture of his uniform under her cheek, the familiar spicy tang of his hair tonic, and most importantly, the touch of his hands on her waist were all too vivid and real for it to be a dream.

She was barely aware of the room clearing as the ladies left them to a private reunion.

As soon as the door shut behind them, Rand pulled her away from his chest, and she stared up into his brown eyes. "Where have you been? We thought you were dead!" she whispered, blinking back the tears. "You're so thin!"

"I know you were told I was dead. I stopped home first, and Jacob told me." He explained all the events of the past year, while Sarah absorbed every detail of his appearance. He was too thin, but he looked grand in his blue uniform with the brass buttons gleaming and the cap perched on his dark hair.

"Why didn't you write?" she said when he paused for breath.

"I did."

She suddenly realized that he hadn't really embraced her yet, and his shoulders were tense. "What is it?" she asked, her throat tight. "What's wrong?"

He picked up her left hand; the diamond engagement ring Ben had given her only days before sparkled in the afternoon sun streaming through the lace curtains. "Why didn't you wait for me like you promised?" He dropped her hand and took a step back. "How could you do it, Sarah? I trusted you. The thought of you waiting here—loving me, I thought—was the only thing that kept me alive during those long months at Andersonville. The only thing that kept me sane."

"But, Rand—"

He interrupted her with a fierce look. "Some of the other men got thrown over, but I never worried about that. Not my Sarah, I thought. She would be true no matter what happens. Sometimes I questioned why I was allowed to live when I saw all my friends die, but I knew it was because you were waiting on me. Depending on me to come back to you. Did our love mean so little to you?"

What was he saying? She began to sob again, only now the tears were of sorrow instead of joy. "We—we thought you were dead," she whispered. "Don't you understand?"

"All I understand is that you forgot me in only a few short months. And your wonderful new fiancé knew all along I wasn't dead."

"No, Rand, he told me—"

He seized her trembling shoulders, his face white with rage. "He knew, I tell you! I gave him a letter to give to you. Did you get a letter?"

"No, but there must be some mistake. Ben cried when he told me about how he found your body—"

"Yeah, I'm really dead, aren't I?"

"Bu–but Ben *saw* your body." She felt idiotic repeating herself, but her mind felt somehow sluggish and stupid. She couldn't seem to reconcile the two totally different stories.

"I tell you he knew all along I wasn't dead! He was with the troops who rescued me!"

"But we saw in the paper—"

"It was wrong, and he knew it was wrong. And how do you explain the letter he neglected to give you?"

She suddenly understood he was accusing Ben of deliberately keeping the truth from her. "There must be some explanation. Ben wouldn't do something like that," she insisted stubbornly.

"And I've written you and my folks many times while I was recuperating in Washington. You didn't get any of those letters, either. And you know why? Labe works at the post office! How can you even stand there and defend what Ben's done?"

His words finally penetrated the fog encasing her. What a fool she'd been! How gullible she was! All that phony sympathy—and the details he'd offered to prove to her Rand was really dead! "But we didn't know! How can you blame me for it?"

Rand took a deep breath, and she flinched from the pain and anger she saw burning in his brown eyes. "I reckon what really hurts the most is just how quick you took up with Croftner. I didn't realize until now how little you loved me. And that hurts, Sarah. That really hurts." He wheeled to the door, wrenched it open, and stalked out.

"Rand!" she cried after his retreating figure. "Don't go. I do love you!" She ran after him, but he ignored her pleas and stomped down the porch steps. "Wait. Please, wait." She caught his arm, but he shrugged it off and swung up onto Ranger's back.

He gazed down at her, the muscles in his throat working. "Maybe we can talk again in a few days. I just can't right now." He took a deep breath, then his jaw hardened as he stared down at her for one long moment. He shook his head slightly as though to clear it, then dug his heels into the gelding's flanks and turned down the lane.

She stared after him in horror and disbelief. He had to listen to her—he just had to! She sank down on the porch step and buried her face in her hands. The diamond ring Ben had given her just last week was a little too big, and it scratched her cheek where it had twisted toward her palm. She pulled her hand away and stared at the ring in rage and revulsion. Wrenching it off her finger and standing up, she threw it as hard as she could toward the woods to her left. She could see it winking in the sunlight as it arced up, then disappeared into the burnished canopy of leaves. She couldn't stand to have it touch her or to even see it. It was just a reminder of her gullibility.

The buckboards and buggies were gone, and the house was quiet when she walked listlessly back inside. The ladies had all discreetly gone home, but the clutter left from the quilting bee was still strewn about the parlor. Rachel had left to go pick up Wade in town. Sarah kicked aside a pincushion and sat down. She felt numb, drained. There had to be some way to make Rand see, but she was just too tired to find it right now. She curled up on the sofa, her knees drawn up to her chest. She was so very tired— When she woke up, she'd think of some way to get through to Rand.

Chapter 5

Rand paused for a moment on a knoll overlooking the Campbell home sprawling below him. What a homecoming. He had so many conflicting emotions. His love for Sarah told him to forgive her and understand the situation, but his overwhelming disappointment just wouldn't let him. He'd always thought they had a love to last a lifetime, but it had been a figment of his imagination.

He urged Ranger down the lane toward the house. He had to see Ben—as soon as he stopped to get Jacob. His wounded pride demanded a face-to-face explanation from Ben for his treachery.

He was reasonably certain where Ben could be found too. Unless he'd changed a lot in the past two years, he'd be at the back table at the Red Onion. Ben was certainly going to be surprised when he walked in. Or maybe not. Maybe he had read his letters before he destroyed them.

The family was sitting around the kitchen table when he stepped in the back door. Pa was saying grace, so Rand stood silently, his head bowed. As soon as he heard the amen, he limped to the table and dropped into the empty chair beside Jacob.

"You still want to go with me, Jacob?"

Jacob stared at him and his face darkened. "I'll get my hat."

Margaret laid a hand on his arm. "Wait 'til tomorrow, Son. Think it over with a clear head."

"Think about it! That's all I've done for the past three hours. Ben is going to have to explain what he's done." He hated the way his voice shook with emotion. "I can't even enjoy being home until I see him." He stood abruptly as Jacob came back into the kitchen.

The two young men mounted up and rode out silently, the stillness broken only by the clopping of the horses' hooves and the croaking of the frogs along the riverbank. The fecund smell from the river wafted in on the breeze.

"You know where Ben lives?"

"He bought that fancy brick house on Main Street. You know the one Judge Jackson built?"

Rand looked at him in surprise. "How'd he ever afford a place like that?"

"Land speculation, mostly. And investments after the war, I guess. He's pretty closemouthed about it."

Rand followed his brother as they cantered up the steep Wabash Street hill and turned down Main Street, dimly illuminated by gaslights. His anger against Ben deepened at this new revelation. *God never promised life would be fair,* he could almost hear his grandma whisper. He shook his head to clear the thought out and clenched his jaw tighter.

When Sarah awoke, the situation seemed even more dreadful to her. The hardest thing to accept was her own naiveté. She surely hadn't shown much of the clearheaded thinking she'd always prided herself on, she thought wryly. And the realization of how easily she'd been deceived really stung. The clock chimed, reminding her how late it was, so she hurriedly threw more wood into the cookstove and sat down at the table to peel potatoes. Papa would be back from town anytime, and Wade, demanding supper, wouldn't be far behind with Rachel. There was a heavy cloud cover, and the smell of rain came through the open window. It was already dark although it was barely six o'clock.

"Sarah."

She jumped at the sudden sound. She had been so lost in thought she hadn't heard the knock on the door. She turned when she saw Ben. She clenched her fists, then rose and took a step toward him. "How dare you come here after what you've done! How could you do such a thing to me—to Rand's family?"

"Rand, always Rand! Don't you care about my feelings at all?" His eyes narrowed, and he nodded at her left hand. "Where's your ring?" he demanded hoarsely, grasping her shoulders in a painful grip.

Sarah stared at him. "You can't possibly think I would marry you after all you've done?" She couldn't stand to have him touch her, but her twisting to escape his grip was useless.

Ben ignored her retort. "Where—is—your—ring?" He punctuated every word with a shake, and her hair tumbled out of the pins and down her back.

"I threw it into the woods," she said with a defiant toss of her head.

His fingers bit deeper into the soft flesh of her arms, and she winced. "Do you have any idea how much that ring cost?" he shouted.

"Is money all you care about? Don't you care about the pain you've caused?" She couldn't believe how quickly his tender, well-mannered facade crumbled.

He saw her appalled expression, and his own face hardened. He seized her elbow and yanked her toward the door.

"What are you doing?" Panicked, Sarah tried to free herself. "Let go of me!" She heard the fabric rip under her elbow as she tried to wrench her arm out of his grip.

"You're mine, Sarah, and no one else's. You're coming with me, and Campbell will never find us."

She fought him as he dragged her through the door and toward the buckboard. Her strength felt puny as he tossed her up beside Labe like a gunnysake of flour.

Labe's gaze skittered over her, then he looked away. "I'm sorry, Sarah," he whispered. "I tried to talk him out of this, but there was no stoppin' him."

"Shut up. Tie her up and be quick about it," his brother snarled as he crawled up beside Sarah. "Everything arranged?"

Labe nodded as he wrapped rope around Sarah's wrists. "Bedrolls are in the back, 'long with everthin' else you said."

Fear raced through Sarah as she saw the strange glint in Ben's eyes. She lunged backward, intending to crawl over the bedrolls and out the back, but Ben was too quick for her.

He sat her back in the seat with a bone-jarring thump. "If you don't sit still, I'll truss you up like a chicken," he warned.

And he would too. She sensed the pent-up rage strumming through him. Shivering from the cold needles of rain that pelted down in earnest now, she huddled in the seat and tried to think of how to get out of this mess.

Ben picked up the reins, but before he could slap them against the horse's flanks, two riders came around the curve of the lane. Sarah recognized the broad shoulders on the nearest rider.

"Rand!" Sarah cried in relief. She started to clamber over Labe, but Ben grabbed her arm.

"Let go of her, Ben. This is between you and me." Rain dripping from the broad brim of his army hat, Rand slid to the ground and walked toward the buckboard, skirting the widening mud puddles. Jacob followed close behind, his fists clenched.

The click as Ben drew back on the hammer of his pistol was muffled in the pattering rain. "Don't come any closer, Campbell."

Rand stopped. "Why'd you do it, Ben? Why did you lie to everyone?"

Rage and hatred burst out of Ben like a torrent of pus from a festering wound. "It was always you! Even my pa thought the sun rose and set with you. Ever since you stopped and helped him mend our fence and round up all the escaped cattle. It was always, 'Ben, why don't you study as hard as Rand,' or 'Ben, I hope you turn out as well as that oldest Campbell boy.' I got so sick of being compared to you. I don't know why he expected so much of me anyway. He was just a no-account drunk all his life."

He sneered and aimed the gun at Rand. "Then there was Sarah. You never noticed how she mooned over you for years. Instead you chased after that Baxter girl, and I hoped Sarah would come to care for me once you were out of the picture. But, no. You had to finally set your sights on my girl."

"I was never your girl!" Sarah leaned toward him slightly, her eyes on the gun.

Ben continued as if he didn't hear her. "But when I got back from the war five months ago and found out they all thought you were dead, I thought fate was finally smiling on me, and Sarah would be mine at last. But you had to come back early and spoil everything, just like you always have. But you're not going to ruin things for me ever again." He bought the gun up higher.

Just as he pulled the trigger, Sarah leaned against him with all her strength, and the shot went wild. "Run, Rand!" she screamed.

But instead of running, Rand launched himself at Ben and dragged him down off the buckboard seat. The two men thrashed in the muck. Rand threw a hard right swing that connected solidly with Ben's cheek. Ben reeled back and hit his head on the wheel of the buckboard as he fell. Rand pushed his hair out of his eyes, and with an unsteady hand he stepped away from Ben.

Shivering and soaked to the skin, Sarah climbed awkwardly out of the buckboard on rubbery legs and almost fell. "Thank God, you're all right!"

He untied the ropes on her hands gently, then stepped away. "What were you doing with Ben, Sarah?"

She stared at him in dismay. Surely he didn't think she was running off with Ben willingly? She raised her chin defiantly. "I was eloping, of course. Don't all eloping brides allow themselves to be tied up?" She expected him to laugh, but instead he drew back from her. She caught his arm again. "Rand, surely you don't believe—" She bit her lip as he turned away, his eyes hooded.

Jacob touched his brother's arm as Ben drew a groaning breath. "Rand, I think one of us had better ride after Doc Seth. Ben doesn't look too good."

"I'll go." Rand shook off Sarah's restraining hand and mounted his horse.

She stood looking after him in dismay. He had to listen to her eventually. He just had to!

Chapter 6

Rand could sense Sarah's gaze as she stood beside Doc Seth, but he resisted looking at her. The rain had soaked through every scrap of his clothing, and he shivered as a buggy came sloshing around the corner and a slight, frail figure painfully clambered down.

"William."

Sarah's father turned as Rand stepped out from the shadows. Shock raced over William's face, then he drew Rand into an embrace. "My dear boy, I heard the news in town. What a happy day this is for all of us."

Rand was shocked when he saw William's condition, even though Hannah had warned him. William had always been frail but vibrant in spite of it all. Where was the man he'd idolized all his life? He didn't recognize him in this stoop-shouldered man with deep lines of pain around his mouth. Tears stung his eyes as he hugged William. The older man's frailty reminded him of a dying baby bird he'd found once, its bones thin and brittle. "It—it's good to see you, Sir," he stammered, trying to hide his dismay.

"You too, Son. You too." William drew back and wiped his eyes shakily with his handkerchief. "What's going on here?"

"I gather that Ben was trying to force Sarah to go off with him," Rand said, then went on to explain Ben's deception.

"I can't believe it," William said, shaking his head. "I really liked that boy. He seemed so ambitious and honest. I really admired the way he pulled himself up out of his family circumstances. Wade will be very upset."

Doc Seth straightened up and stepped over to Rand and William. "He'll be all right. But he's sure going to wake up with a sore head tomorrow. I told Labe to take him home and put him to bed, and I'll look in on him tomorrow." He thrust out a hand to Rand. "Good to have you home, young Campbell. Amelia told me the news."

Rand shook his hand. "Tell her I'll stop by and see her soon."

He broke off, and they all turned as they heard another horse and buggy canter into the yard.

Wade slid down from his buggy, his jowled face florid with outrage. "What's going on here?" he demanded. He didn't bother to help his wife down but stomped over to where his father stood.

Joel slid down from the buggy eagerly and bounded into Rand's arms exuberantly. "Rand! Oh, Rand!"

Rand laughed and hugged him tightly. He loved Sarah's little brother as much as his own. "How you doing, Half-Pint?"

"Great. I've missed you so much. When can we go fishing?"

Rand grinned at the familiar question. He'd always felt sorry for the lad. William's health prevented much of the usual father-son relationship, and Wade was too self-centered to take any of his precious time for such mundane things as fishing. "Soon," he said.

He pulled a hand free and thrust it out as Wade stomped up. "Hello, Wade."

Wade ignored the outstretched hand. "I thought we were rid of you for good! I want you off my land, Campbell. Now!"

Rand lowered his hand and put it back in his pocket. "I was kind of hoping you'd changed, Wade. I should have known better."

Wade took a step toward Rand, his face reddening. "You—"

"That's enough!" William's voice boomed out in a sudden surge of strength. "Your treatment of a guest in our home is unacceptable, Wade. And as long as I own this property, no friend will be turned away—least of all Rand. You have no idea of the wrong that's been done to him over the past few months."

Wade glared at his father, his massive hands clenched. "Who cares? I was just glad to be rid of him. I don't want him showing up now to spoil all our plans."

"What you want doesn't matter to me. And you know as well as I do that Sarah would never marry Ben now, anyway."

Wade's color deepened. "How do you know her feelings haven't changed? Ben would make a much better husband than Campbell."

William sighed. "Money isn't everything. I wouldn't want my daughter to marry someone who could deceive her the way Ben has." William directed a slight smile Sarah's way. "Ask your sister if she would marry him now that Rand is back."

Sarah shook her head. "You know I wouldn't."

The muscles in Wade's face worked as he clenched his jaw. "But what about the land?"

"Is that all you care about? More land, more money?" William shook his head wearily. "I'm telling you right now, if you do anything to hurt Sarah or Rand, you won't have *this* land or house."

Wade stared at his father. "You'd cut me out of your will?"

"Don't push me or you'll find out. Now get in the house until you can get a civil tongue in your head."

Wade glanced angrily at Sarah, then swung his massive head toward Rand before stomping into the house. He let the screen door slam shut behind him.

Rachel sighed and followed him.

"Good for you, Papa." Sarah slipped her small hand into his.

"Wade's had it coming for too long. I should never have let him get away with his arrogance for so long." He suddenly looked smaller and even more frail. "Come in out of the rain, Sweetheart. You and Rand can have the parlor. I'm just going to have a bite to eat and go to bed." He shook Rand's hand. "Stop by tomorrow, and we'll talk. I'm just as eager as Joel to hear the full story." He walked into the house, his shoulders stooped.

But an order from their father wouldn't stop Wade for long. Why did he hate Rand so? She shook her head in puzzlement. Ever since she could remember there had been an unspoken antagonism between the two men.

She pushed the disturbing puzzle out of her mind and turned back to Rand. "Rand, we need to talk?"

"There's nothing to say right now." His tone was abrupt. "I still don't know how I feel about you or anything else." He took off his sopping hat and ran a weary hand through his wet hair. "And Wade has a point. Maybe your feelings *have* changed."

"Campbell!" Ben's hoarse cry interrupted them.

Ben raised his head from the back of the buckboard and gave Rand a long look filled with hatred. "This isn't over, Campbell. You'll never have her. Never. You just remember that." His head fell back against the floor of the buckboard as Labe slapped the reins against the horse's flanks, but Ben watched them until he was out of sight, a burning hatred in his eyes.

Sarah shivered. "I think he means it," she said. "Watch your back, Rand."

"I can take care of myself." He saw her shiver again. "You're soaked to the bone," he said. "I'll come back and talk in a few days. You go on in now. Just give me some time."

Sarah hesitated, her eyes searching his sober face. Time? How much time? But she left the questions unasked and walked wearily up the porch steps, her spirits as low as her wet skirt dragging in the mud. She turned to watch Rand and Jacob mount up and ride down the lane and around the curve. Didn't he realize how much time they'd wasted already?

She was shaking uncontrollably by the time she dragged herself up the steps and into her room. She pulled off her dripping clothes and left them in a puddle in the middle of the floor. Her teeth chattering, she climbed into bed and pulled the down comforter up over her shaking shoulders. How did she get through to him?

❧

The next morning, Rand woke disoriented. The familiar clanging of trays in the hallway and the squeak of nurses' shoes hurrying with breakfast trays was missing. Sunshine streamed in the window and illuminated suddenly familiar surroundings. The toy soldiers Grampa had carved for him when he was five were lined up on a battered chest against the wall. His fingers stroked the brightly colored quilt, soft and faded with numerous washings. The rug on the unpainted wooden floor was as threadbare as he remembered it. He glanced at the space next to him. Jacob was nowhere to be seen, but the familiar indentation on the pillow brought a lump to Rand's throat. How good it was to be home!

He jumped out of bed, suddenly eager to get downstairs. He wouldn't worry about anything today, he decided as he splashed cold water on his face. He was just going to enjoy being with his family again after three long years. No uniform either, he thought, opening his closet. He grabbed a pair of overalls and his favorite plaid shirt and pulled them on. The pants hung around his waist, and they were too short, but they would have to do.

By the time he pulled on socks and boots, the aroma of coffee and bacon filled the air and made his stomach rumble hungrily. The low murmur of voices quickened his steps as hurried down the stairs.

His mother spun around as he stepped into the kitchen. "I was just coming to wake you. I fixed ham and eggs, grits, flapjacks, and coffee. I'll have you fattened up in no time." She stepped into his arms for a quick, reassuring hug.

Rand grinned as he squeezed her, breathing in the faint fragrance of roses that clung to her. He dropped his arms as she bustled over to the cookstove and offered him a plate piled high with food. His mouth watered as he took it from her and sat down between Shane and Jacob.

Hannah came hurrying in as Rand took his first sip of strong, hot coffee. Her face brightened as she saw Rand shoveling another forkful of eggs into his mouth. "Now I am sure it's really you," she said as she slipped into the chair opposite him. "The brother I remember was always eating."

Rand, a wicked grin on his face, caught Jacob's eye and gave a meaningful nod. "How come you're still here, anyway, Sis?" he asked. "I thought you would have been successful in trapping a husband by now."

"Come on, Rand, be realistic." Jacob poked his older brother with an elbow. "Who would have her? She has always been the ugliest Campbell."

Rand stared at his sister thoughtfully. "Yeah, I forgot about that big nose of hers. And all that hair."

"Not to mention her temper! Her tongue could cut a man to ribbons." Jacob grinned at the rising color on Hannah's face.

Rand knew they'd get a reaction when they hit on her sore spot. She was always moaning about her nose. Personally, Rand didn't see anything wrong with it, but she seemed to think it didn't match the pert ones described in her favorite novels.

She flushed a deep red, then burst into tears.

"Hey, I'm sorry, Sis." Rand hadn't expected this much of a reaction. He slid over and put an arm around her. "You know we were only teasing. I've always liked your nose."

Hannah just cried harder. "It's not that," she finally sputtered as Rand handed her his bandanna. "It's just so wonderful to have you here, to see Jacob smile again, to hear your voice—" She stopped and gulped.

A lump formed in Rand's throat, and he swallowed hard. "I'm home now," he said.

His Pa cleared his throat gruffly. "You're just in time to help with the farming too," he said heartily. "It's almost more than Shane and I can handle. I've tried to talk your brother into staying home, but he won't listen. Now I'll have some help come spring."

Rand glanced at Jacob apprehensively. Hadn't Jacob told them of his plans? He and his brother had laid awake for hours talking last night. He'd been hoping that by now Jacob would have broken the news to their father. His brother shook his head slightly.

Jeremiah saw the wordless exchange. "What is it?" he asked, his eyes traveling from one to the other.

Rand hated to disappoint his pa. "I–I won't be able to stay long, Pa," he stammered. "I'm in the Third Cavalry. I can stay for about a week, then I have to report for duty." He winced at the stricken look in his mother's eyes. "I've been garrisoned at Fort Laramie."

"Not you too!" Hannah stood twisting her hands in her apron. "The Indians have been rampaging for months out there. Isn't it bad enough we're losing Jacob?"

"That's why so many of us are being sent out there. And I've found out in the past couple of years how much I enjoy the cavalry. I've always wanted to see the frontier. Maybe I can find my own spread while I serve my country a few more years. Besides, it's what I want—I volunteered."

"You can't!" Jeremiah rose to his feet. "Why do you think I've worked so hard on this farm? Always expanding, always looking for ways to make more money?" He put an arm around his wife. "It's been for you! For you and your brothers. I agreed to let Jacob go against my better judgment, but you've always been the one who had a feel for the land. I forbid you to go!"

Rand saw his mother flinch as the words echoed in the warm kitchen. He stood and faced his father. "You forbid? You forget I'm a grown man, Pa."

Margaret laid a gentle hand on her son's arm. "Your pa is just concerned, Rand. Can't you think about staying home now and letting us all begin to heal? You can raise horses right here on land that's been in the Campbell family for twenty-five years instead of fighting Indians to gain a small piece of land in some godforsaken wilderness. You haven't been with us for three years."

His mother had always been able to change his mind in the past, and he fought against the soft persuasion in her voice. "I can't, Ma." He raked a hand through his hair. "I've fought worse than Indians in the last three years. And I know what it's like to be hungry and alone. It's something I have to do. Maybe it's just because I need to prove something to myself, to build my own dreams with my own sweat, but I have to go."

His Pa wheeled then stomped from the room. His mother stared at him, then her eyes filled with tears and she rushed from the room.

Always the peacemaker, Hannah cleared her throat and laughed self-consciously. "Land sakes, who could forget the way you've always had with horses and cattle? When Ma was carryin' Jacob, she asked you if you wanted a baby brother or sister. You looked up with those brown eyes of yours all serious and said, 'If it's all the same to you, Ma, I'd just as soon have a horse.' "

Laughter diffused the tension as they heard the familiar story. Jacob punched Rand in the arm. "Yeah, and you've been treating me like a beast of burden ever since!"

When the laughter faded, Hannah said softly, "You are taking Sarah, aren't you?"

Rand looked quickly at her expectant face. "No," he said finally. "Not right now. I need some time to accept all that's happened. I'll keep in touch, and down the road, we'll see if we can work things out." He folded his arms across his chest. "And anyway, that area is no place for a woman. Sarah would soon get sick of being confined to the fort. You know how independent she is."

"Jacob is taking Amelia. It must not be too dangerous," Hannah said.

He saw the mutinous expression on Hannah's face as she opened her mouth to argue further. "Don't push me, Sis. I know you're concerned, but I have to be sure in my own mind why she took up with Ben. She was mighty young when I left for the war—only sixteen. I need to be sure she knows her own mind."

Hannah sighed impatiently. "Why are men so thickheaded?" she asked, rolling her eyes in exasperation.

Rand grinned and pushed away from the table. "It's the only protection we have against you women." He stood up and stretched. "Better get to the fields. I'll help all I can while I'm here."

"What about your leg?" Hannah asked anxiously.

"I feel fine, Sis. And I need to work at getting my strength back." He pushed back his chair, grabbed his hat, and followed his brothers out the door. As he worked beside his brothers, he thought about Sarah. Maybe he was wrong.

Sarah sighed as she stared across the river. What could she do to change Rand's mind? She hadn't heard a word from him all day. Should she just swallow her pride and go find him? But he'd said to give him some time. Tears welled up in her eyes as she leaned down and picked up a flat rock. She skimmed it across the water. It only skipped three times. She must be losing her touch.

"The last time I saw you do that, it skipped six times."

She turned immediately, and a bright smile lit her face when she saw Rand. It was almost as if her hopeless wishing had conjured him up. "Oh, Rand, I'm so glad you came," she said as she scrabbled to her feet and hurried toward him. He held out his arms, and she rushed into them.

She buried her face in his broad chest and clung until he lifted her chin and kissed her. As his lips touched hers, she wrapped her arms around his neck and kissed him back with all the love in her heart. She wanted to hold onto this moment forever.

"I tried to stay away, Green Eyes, but I couldn't," he whispered. He loosed his grip on her with obvious reluctance.

"I'm so sorry about Ben," she began.

"It's not your fault," he interrupted. "I realized it as soon as I cooled down enough to think. I can't blame you for wanting to go on with your life."

"You are my life. Nothing seemed real with you gone. I knew I couldn't be happy, so I thought if everyone else were happy, it would be enough. But I was already beginning to regret promising to marry him."

"Then you still want to marry me?"

She smiled. Didn't he know without asking? "More than anything in the world." She stopped and looked up at him, her eyes sparkling with joy. "James Benson left on the wagon train last May, and his cabin is still empty. We can live there until our place is built on our knoll."

Rand's smile faded, and he looked away. "I can't stay, Sarah. I'm still in the cavalry. I'm heading out west in a couple of days."

Not staying here? She stared at him as his words soaked in. "But we've always planned to build on the knoll and help Papa with the farm. He's not well, Rand. I can't go running off out west and leave him."

"Your pa will understand. He came here with your ma and settled just like I want to do. He wasn't content to stay in Philadelphia."

"That was different. He was poor and had no prospects. You have land here, both mine and yours from your pa. I can't believe your pa will let you do this. He was very upset about Jacob's plans to leave." Surely Rand wasn't serious about this scheme. They'd made too many other plans.

"It's not different. Your pa wanted to build something on his own just like I do. I don't want to take something another man built. There's so much opportunity out west, Sarah. Land for the taking, gold, new businesses. It will be a great life. Besides, do you really think Wade and I could get along well enough to work together?"

"I *can't* go," she said frantically. Couldn't he see that? "I couldn't leave Papa. You haven't seen how ill he's been. He seems to go downhill every day. It would kill him for me to leave."

"I know he would understand. Let's go ask him." He took her arm and started purposely toward the house, but she pulled away.

"No! I don't want to upset him. I just can't go now. Can't you wait a few years? Just until he doesn't need me?"

"*Now* is the time of opportunity, Sarah. Besides, I have my orders and a letter to deliver for General Sherman. I have to go."

Sarah took a deep breath and stepped back from him. "And I have to stay." Tears filled her eyes as she saw Rand's face harden. She *couldn't* leave Papa. Why couldn't he understand that? He just didn't seem to be the same man who'd left three years ago. He was harder, more unbending.

"That's your answer then? After all we've been through? After all your protests of how much you love me, that's your answer? You're not the woman I thought you were, Sarah. Not the woman at all." He turned and left her standing on the path.

She opened her mouth to call him back, but the words died in her throat. What was the use? She couldn't go and he wouldn't stay. It was as simple as that. He didn't really love her or he wouldn't ask her to leave Papa. Not as sick as Papa was. Couldn't Rand see that? She choked back the tears in her throat and rubbed at her dry eyes. Her life was in shambles, and there seemed to be no solution.

Chapter 7

T he train shrieked and puffed out a billow of soot as Rand, Jake, and Shane climbed down from the buckboard. Leaving his mother and father had been rough. Ma had cried, then pressed his grandma's Bible into his hand before hurrying away, and Pa wouldn't even come out of the barn to say good-bye. Shane snuffled, and Rand ruffled his hair, then hugged him. "I'm counting on you to take care of the family, Squirt."

Shane bit his quivering lip and nodded, straightening his shoulders. He trotted around behind the buckboard and, heaving the saddle over one shoulder, led Ranger to the waiting train. Rand's horse would accompany him west.

Rand hefted the haversack over his right shoulder and picked up the hamper of food and his satchel. He hesitated, suddenly indecisive. Why not stay for awhile longer? General Sherman had told him to take more time to get back on his feet if he needed to. The letter would wait a few days. Maybe he should go see Sarah just once more and see if things could be worked out.

"All aboard!"

The conductor's shout broke his mood, and Rand shook himself mentally. Of course, he was going. This was what he wanted. With one last look at his brothers, he raced toward the slowly moving train and jumped up the steep steps. He caught one last glimpse of Jacob, standing alone with one arm upraised, his arm around his younger brother. Rand waved until the buckboard with the two figures beside it was no longer in view, then took a deep breath and made his way to a vacant seat. His great adventure was about to begin.

He sat next to a man, obviously a pig farmer from the odor that hung about him, who talked incessantly. Rand would just be dozing off into a fitful sleep and the man would ask him a question. By the time the thirty-six-hour trip was over, his eyes were scratchy, his throat was sore, and his chest hurt from coughing the black soot the small potbellied stove belched out. His leg ached from being in the narrow, cramped seat, and he limped heavily as he made his way to the door and out into the fresh air.

Kansas City was a sprawling assortment of wooden shops and storefronts. The streets teemed with horses and cattle, buggies and buckboards. And people. Everywhere people hurried across the muddy streets and crowded the uneven boardwalks. Rand felt invigorated by the hustle and bustle, despite the smell of manure and the distant lowing of cattle from the stockyards. *Someday I'll bring my own cattle to Kansas City or a cow town like it,* he thought with a thrill.

Across from the depot was the Holladay stagecoach station, and he walked across the street and stood in line behind another soldier. "Heading to Fort Leavenworth too?" he asked him.

The other man turned with a friendly grin. "Sure am. Been on leave and kinda hate to go back. You new?"

"Lieutenant Rand Campbell." He thrust out a soot-streaked hand. "But I'll just be there a few months. Until the snows pass. Then on to Fort Laramie—at least I think so."

"If that don't beat all. So am I! Lieutenant Isaac Liddle." He shook Rand's proffered hand and, taking off his wide-brimmed hat, wiped his forehead with a bandanna. "What unit you with?"

"H Troop, Third Cavalry. You?"

"Third Battalion. You're going to like Old Bedlam. You heard of it?"

Rand shook his head, liking the looks of his companion. Isaac reminded him in some way of Jacob. Unlike Jacob, he had auburn hair and a dusting of freckles, but he had the same muscular build and quiet but friendly manner as Jacob. Strong, capable hands. A man someone could depend on. And from what he'd heard of the Indian Wars, he wanted that kind of man around.

Isaac grinned. "It's what we call the single officers' quarters. It came by its name legitimate. A lot of loud shenanigans goes on at all hours. At least I assume that's where you'll be quartered. I don't see a pretty lady with you. You're not married?"

A shadow darkened Rand's eyes. "No," he said shortly, pushing away an image of Sarah's heart-shaped face and dancing green eyes.

"I was hopin'. Fort Laramie doesn't have many women right now. Where you from?"

"Wabash, Indiana. Born and raised on a farm about two miles out of town." Rand was grateful for the change in topic. "Where you hail from?"

"El Paso, Texas." He held one hand out in front of him hastily when he saw Rand's eyebrows raise. "But I fought for the Union."

That explained his accent. The line moved forward, and they followed. "What brought you so far from home?" Rand asked.

"Always hankered to see the West for myself. Figured joining the army was going to be the only way to do it. I'm the youngest in a family of seven boys, so I knew I'd never have anything for myself back home. I've asked the good Lord to help me find a place to settle down and raise racehorses."

"I aim to have cattle and stock horses someday. But I like the army for now. It's a good way to see the frontier." Rand continued to become acquainted with his new companion as the line moved slowly forward, until finally they had their tickets. Rand only had to pay for his luggage since he was riding Ranger instead of traveling on the stage.

Isaac crowded in with eight other soldiers, with three more squeezed outside on top. When Rand saw the bouncing, lurching ride, he was thankful to be riding his bay gelding.

Every ten miles or so they stopped at a way station for a break. Each one was the same. A small adobe building, a hut really, where they drew water to wash away a little of the dust and bolted down a nearly inedible meal of beans and hard, moldy bread. He was glad to see the small encampment of Fort Leavenworth by the day's end.

Rand had been at Fort Leavenworth only two weeks when he and Isaac were unexpectedly ordered to proceed on to Fort Kearny, then to Fort Laramie. The weather had been unseasonably balmy, and the army wanted some reinforcements at Fort Laramie as soon as possible. He was a little sorry to leave the jolly little community behind, but he couldn't still a thrill of excitement as he fell into place behind the long column of men and supplies plodding toward the west.

By the time they arrived at Fort Laramie, Rand felt like he'd known his comrades all his life. He settled into Old Bedlam happily. The officers were a congenial group who loved a good time. Most evenings they gathered in the game room for cards or checkers. His days were full and his duties varied. He was sure he had made the right decision.

He'd been at Fort Laramie a week when he was ordered to lead a detachment to meet a column from Fort Kearny. Major DuBois and his retinue were expected to be in the column, so Rand wore his dress uniform. His brass buttons and buckles glimmered in the sunshine, and Ranger's sleek coat shone. He and his detachment met the major about three miles out from the fort. There was no mistaking the major. He sat on his black horse with stiff military bearing, and his uniform was precisely brushed and neat.

Rand saluted. "Good morning, Sir. I'm Lieutenant Campbell, and I'm pleased to escort you to Fort Laramie."

The major saluted smartly. "At ease, Lieutenant." He dismounted and motioned for Rand to do the same. "How's the situation with the Indians? Any trouble brewing?"

"Nothing I can put my finger on, Sir. But I have an uneasy feeling that something's going on we can't see right now. There have been grumblings about the miners tramping through the Sioux hunting grounds on the Bozeman Trail. Red Cloud hasn't come in for rations, and some of our tame Oglala say he's calling for a fight to the knife. I don't trust him."

The major waved his hand dismissively. "We'll deal with him if he steps out of line."

The flap to the ambulance behind them opened, and a young woman stepped through the opening. "Good morning, Daddy. Why have we stopped? Are we there?"

The major smiled indulgently. "Lieutenant, I'd like you to meet my daughter, Jessica. And my wife, Mrs. DuBois. Jessica, Letty, this is Lieutenant Rand Campbell. He has come to escort us into the fort."

"Call me Letty, Dear," the older woman, a softer, plumper version of the daughter murmured as she placed her round hand in Rand's.

Rand gripped it briefly and muttered some response, but his gaze was on the major's daughter. She was the most beautiful woman he'd ever seen. Her fiery red hair was arranged in a mass of curls that framed her delicate face in a halo of color. She smiled at him as though he were the first man she'd ever seen.

"I'm *very* pleased to meet you," she said softly. Her soft hand lingered on his.

Rand was aware he was staring, but he couldn't seem to stop. She really was the most amazing looking woman. He helped her back up into the ambulance. He told the private driving the ambulance to take Ranger, and he would drive the ladies into the fort. All the while he was conscious of Jessica's blue eyes fastened on him.

❧

Sarah sat by the gurgling water with the autumn sun warm on her arms. In spite of the mild temperature, she couldn't seem to feel anything but a cold deadness inside. She threw stale bread to the ducks along the riverbank as she stared across the water. Why had God allowed this to happen to her? Did He really not love her as she'd told Pastor Stevens? She slid to the ground and lay back in the grass. Gazing into the sky always filled her with a sense of God's power. Tears leaked from her eyes as she thought about the mess her life was in. "Are You there, God?" she whispered. Taking her life into her own hands had certainly left it a mess.

Pastor Stevens's sermon from that morning echoed in her head. *"Come unto Me, all ye that labour and are heavy laden, and I will give you rest."* She rolled over onto her stomach and didn't try to stop the tears from flowing. She wanted rest so badly. "Forgive me, Lord," she sobbed. "I've been so pigheaded and willful. I know You want only what's best for me. Help me to always see Your hand in my life. Restore me and give me Your peace. I know I fail You so many times, but I want to serve You. Let me start fresh and anew with You again."

As she prayed she felt His gentle touch in her heart. The lethargy and deadness fell away, and for the first time in two weeks, she felt hope. God was in control. Whatever He wanted was for her own good.

She sat up and wiped her eyes. She should have swallowed her pride and turned to the Lord months ago. She smiled and lifted her heavy hair from her neck for the cool breeze to caress before settling herself on the large rock again.

She sat there in quiet joy for some time before she realized she was being watched. "Papa, you startled me." She looked at him with new eyes, seeing his frailty and the yellow pallor of his skin. She hadn't realized how old he'd gotten.

Her father was wheezing by the time he reached her. "Room for two?" he asked.

She moved over, and he dropped down beside her. He took her hand, and they sat for awhile in companionable silence. "Is that a smile I see on your face, Sweetheart?" he said finally. "I don't think I've seen you smile since Rand left."

Sarah kissed him on the cheek. "I've just taken Pastor Stevens's advice to heart," she said. "I've been blaming God for everything that goes wrong, and I finally saw how wrong I was. God's forgiven me, though."

Her father hugged her. "I knew you'd been bitter, but I left it for God to deal with you. That pride of yours always trips you up. You should have gone with Rand, you know. I love you, Sweetheart, but you must ask God to channel that stubbornness of yours."

Sarah looked at him in shock. "I couldn't leave you!"

"You're not a little girl anymore. And there comes a time in every person's life when he has to step out and stand on his own feet. Rand was ready, and I think you are too. We both know I won't be around much longer."

"No, Papa—!"

He held up a hand at her protest. "You just don't want to admit it, my dear girl. I would rest easier if I knew you were settled and happy. I never expected you to give up without a fight! You had to fight to get him in the first place. Remember all the tears until I let you put your hair up and wear your mother's green satin dress for Christmas dinner with the Campbells the year you turned sixteen?"

Sarah smiled at the memory. "It worked too. That was the first time he saw me as anything but a pesky younger sister. But he's half a continent away now. What can I do?" Tears started into her eyes, and she brushed them away angrily.

William stood up. "I don't know the answer, but I'm sure God will tell you if you'll listen." He patted the top of her head and turned to walk back to the house.

Sarah was barely aware of his departure as a seed of an idea began to take shape. She could follow Rand. She almost gasped aloud at the daring thought. Women went west all the time. She could take a train to rail's end in Omaha. Surely there would be a stage or a wagon train she could catch on to Fort

Leavenworth. Amelia said Jacob had told her Rand would be there until spring came. Maybe then Rand would realize how much she loved him and she could talk him into coming back home. Just for awhile, of course. Just until Papa didn't need her. With Rand around to talk to, Papa would soon recover his spirits.

She shivered at the thought of the rough men she might encounter. She wouldn't have a protector. She smiled. Yes, she would. God would go with her.

She spent the next two hours in feverish plans. She wished she had a pencil and paper to make a list of what she wanted to take. How long did it take to get to Fort Leavenworth, anyway? But it didn't matter. Nothing mattered except finding Rand and persuading him to come home where he belonged. She almost skipped as she hurried back to the house to begin packing. God would work everything out.

When she reached the front yard, she heard shouts and almost collided with Wade as he rushed through the door. "What is it?" She blocked his path and clutched his burly arm.

He shook off her grip angrily. "It's Pa. I hope you're satisfied. You've finally managed to kill him! I'm going after Doc." He glared at her one last time before continuing his headlong flight to the barn.

Her heart in her throat, Sarah ran into the house and found Rachel kneeling beside William's crumpled form. With a cry, Sarah flung herself down beside her father and took his hand. "Papa, it's me," she whispered. "Don't die, please don't die. Just hold on. Wade's gone for Doc."

At her voice, William's pale lids fluttered, and Sarah felt his cold fingers move. She leaned closer. "Don't try to talk. I'm here with you."

With an effort he opened his eyes and tried to smile. "Don't cry, my dear girl. Jesus is waiting for me, and I'm going to be with your mama at last," he whispered. His gaze seemed vacant, then his eyes cleared and he smiled into her face. "Just be happy, Sweetheart. You fight for your Rand, if you must, and don't let Wade bully you into anything." He coughed weakly. "But don't leave Joel with Wade. Promise me." His voice grew stronger, and he raised his head slightly. "Promise!"

"I promise," Sarah whispered as she felt his icy fingers loosen.

His eyes widened. "Kate!" he gasped. His chest hitched once, then was still as the last of his breath sighed out his slightly open mouth.

"Papa!" Sarah stared at him. This couldn't be real. He'd just been talking with her! She clutched his hand tighter. "Don't leave me, Papa!" She kissed his cheek and gathered his head into her lap. "Dear God, no," she sobbed. "Don't take him. This can't be happening." She looked over at Rachel kneeling and weeping on the other side of William's body. "He's just unconscious, Rachel.

He can't be dead." She spoke through numb lips. Surely, he would open his eyes and smile at her again.

Rachel just shook her head and cried hard. "I'm so sorry, Sarah. We all loved him. He was a good man." She scooted around and put her arm around Sarah's shaking shoulders. "He never got over missing your mama. Just be happy he's finally with her again."

"But I still need him." Sarah's voice was bewildered as she stared down into her father's peaceful face. "He can't leave me now." She touched his grizzled cheek, already cooling.

They both turned as Wade and Doc Seth rushed in the door. "Help him, Doc," Sarah pleaded as Amelia's father knelt and put his stethoscope to her father's chest. She clenched her fists in the folds of her skirt.

There was a long pause, then the doctor straightened up. "I'm sorry, Sarah. He's gone." His voice was hoarse with emotion.

The words hammered into Sarah's brain with a stunning force. Wade's accusing stare was the last thing she saw before she whirled and ran from the room, keening in grief.

The next few days were hazy with anguish. There was the preparation of William's body, the ordering of the casket, the sitting up with her dead father three nights in a row, as well as the hordes of mourning friends who came to pay their last respects. William had been a much loved and respected man in the community.

Sarah thought if she heard just one more time how wonderful it was that William was finally with Kate, she would have a screaming fit. She knew she was selfish, but she wanted him here with her. Amelia hovered anxiously near her every moment, but there was nothing anyone could do to ease her grief. Pastor Stevens tried to comfort her, but she just brushed his words away.

Finally the crowds were gone, and William was laid to rest next to his beloved Kate in the meadow beneath the weeping willow tree. Sarah performed all the usual tasks of homemaking, somehow managing to get through each day. The thought of following Rand was distant and unreal. It took all her strength just to survive the heartache.

As the days passed, Sarah found herself leaning on her faith in a way she'd never known. Instead of questioning God's hand in her life, she felt His presence in a very special way. She spent many hours beneath the willow tree talking to Him as she kept vigil beside her father's grave. A week after his death, she knelt beside the grave and planted bright cushions of mums over the mound of dirt. They reminded her that her father was more alive than he'd ever been here on earth. There was no more pain for him. Only peace and love and wonderment as he beheld heaven and his Lord. *Guide me with*

Your Holy Spirit, Lord, she prayed. *Don't let me stray from the path You have chosen for me. Keep watch over Rand and send someone to speak to him about his need for You in his life.*

Sarah's twentieth birthday came and went with little festivity, just an aching sense of loss. The Montgomery home had become a solemn place where no one smiled or laughed. Jacob and Amelia slipped away and were married quietly instead of the big celebration they'd planned. Sarah stood up with Amelia, but she was still in such pain she didn't remember much about the wedding.

Six days after the wedding, she sat peeling potatoes for supper. The weather was still unseasonably warm, and the breeze blew in through the open window with a hint of rain in it. The kitchen door banged, and Wade stomped in.

"Supper's not done yet?" he growled as he hung up his red plaid jacket. He turned and saw her strained face. "I think it's time you and I had a talk."

She didn't trust his mild tone. He wanted something from her, and she had a sinking feeling she knew what it was. He'd brought up Ben's name several times over the past few weeks. "What about?" she asked quietly.

"Your future." He stared at her challengingly. "I saw Ben in town today, and for some reason he still wants to marry you. I told him I didn't see any reason why you wouldn't. That good-for-nothing Campbell went off and left you in the lurch and—"

"No." The short, clipped word cut him off just as he was picking up steam.

"You will do what I say. You're under age and my ward." Wade compressed his lips and glared at her.

"I will *not* marry Ben. Rand and I belong together. That was Papa's last words to me. I won't marry anyone but Rand. I'll never marry Ben."

"Well, that's just too bad, Missy. You'd better get used to the idea because you will do as I say. Campbell has run off to the frontier, and you'll never see him again anyway." He pulled her to her feet and shoved her toward the door. "You'll stay in your room until you agree to abide by my decisions." He grabbed her arm and dragged her roughly up the stairs and into her room.

He thrust her toward the bed, and she stumbled then fell. Wade slammed the door, and Sarah ran to it. She heard the lock click on the other side, and she pounded her fists against the door. "You can't keep me in here, Wade," she shouted. "This isn't the Middle Ages! Let me out of here. I'll never marry Ben—never!" She twisted the latch to no avail, then kicked at the solid oak door in a helpless frenzy of rage. Minutes later, she had nothing to show for her efforts except a sore foot and a splinter in the palm of her hand.

She sat down on the bed to think. Joel would be home soon, and Rachel would be back from the market. Surely one of them could be persuaded to let her out. But what then? What could she do? She bit her lip. The idea of going to Rand revived suddenly. Jacob and Amelia were leaving tomorrow. Perhaps she could convince them to let her go out with them. Jacob would surely be glad of a companion for Amelia. She'd find Rand and confess how wrong she'd been. He would forgive her. They could make a new life away from Wade's meddling.

Instead of asking to be let out, she spent the night planning her escape and was pale and drawn from lack of sleep by the time morning came. She packed a suitcase of essentials and hid it under the bed just as she heard Wade's heavy tread outside the door.

The lock turned, and he stepped into the room. She wanted to throw something at him as soon as she saw his smug face. "Ready to be reasonable yet?"

"Do I have a choice?" she kept her face averted so he couldn't see her eyes. He smiled. "I knew you'd come around. I had Rachel save you some breakfast."

The exultation in his voice caused her to clench her hands to keep from screaming at him. "I'm not hungry," she said quietly.

She met his probing gaze without flinching until he smiled. "Fine. I'll go talk to Pastor Stevens, and we'll discuss when the wedding can take place." He left the door open behind him and tromped back downstairs and out the door.

She sprang to her feet as soon as she heard the buggy rumble down the rutted track toward town. She pulled her suitcase from under her bed and turned toward the door. She froze at a sound in the hall until she realized it was just Joel.

"What are you doing?" Joel's face was pinched and drawn with misery. His red hair didn't look as though it had been combed for days. She'd been too overcome with grief to pay much attention to him, but he had lost his father too.

Sarah stared at him in consternation. She had forgotten about Joel and her promise to her father. She couldn't leave him here with Wade. She knelt and put her arms around him. "I'm going to find Rand, and I want you to come with me."

His pale face brightened. "Honest injun?"

"Honest injun." How she was going to manage it, she wasn't quite sure, but she'd find a way. It would be hard enough to slip away by herself, but encumbered by an eleven year old, it would be much harder. "Let's hurry and pack your things before Wade gets back."

They went to Joel's room, and Sarah threw three changes of clothes for him in the only suitcase small enough for him to handle.

"Can I take my rifle?"

Sarah hesitated as she looked into his pleading face. The less baggage the better, but the rifle had been Papa's, and she didn't have the heart to make him leave it behind. She nodded, and he slung it over his shoulder and picked up his suitcase. They slipped down the steps and came face-to-face with Rachel.

She looked from the suitcases to Sarah's face. "You're leaving." It wasn't a question. "I knew Wade would never force you to fall in with his plans—but who has ever been able to tell him anything?" She pushed her hair back from her forehead and held out her arms.

Sarah put down her suitcase and went to Rachel with a sigh. "I'll miss you, Rachel. But I have to find Rand." Her words were muffled against Rachel's shoulder. She drew away and looked into her sister-in-law's eyes. "Don't tell Wade I've gone."

Rachel smiled faintly. "No problem. He won't be back 'til suppertime. If you hurry, you can catch the afternoon train and be long gone before he knows you've left." She hugged Sarah fiercely, then shoved her toward the door. "Write when you get there. And don't forget about me and the baby. We love you."

Sarah gulped and wiped her eyes. "I know, Rachel. And you've been a real sister to me. Make sure you write us when the baby's born."

Rachel nodded and made a shooing motion with her apron. "You'd best get going. You have a lot to get done today."

Joel hurried ahead to hitch up the buggy, while Sarah took one last look at the home where she'd been born. The sun shone through the bare trees in dappled patterns on the front porch roof. The solid two-story seemed so safe and familiar. She could see the red barn just behind it where she'd played in the haymow as a child. The chicken coop off to the east, the pasture beyond that, and all around the gently rolling hills of Montgomery land; it was all so heartbreakingly beloved.

She'd never had any plans of leaving her home. At least not any farther than the knoll beyond the pasture. Would she ever see it again? And who would tend Papa's grave?

She choked back tears and climbed up beside Joel. This was no time for tears, for second thoughts. Wade had left her no choice. She waved one last good-bye at Rachel, then stared firmly ahead. She couldn't think about what she was leaving or she wouldn't be able to go.

Chapter 8

Sarah stared unseeingly out the window of the stagecoach as the barren landscape swept by. Would this trip never end? Jacob and Amelia had readily fallen in with her plan. They had assumed she was arriving to say good-bye, and Amelia's sad little face had flushed with joy when she realized her best friend would be coming with them. By ten o'clock, the four of them were on the train headed west.

When they arrived at Leavenworth, they'd found Rand had gone on to Laramie. It was just a temporary setback, though, as the commander readily agreed to allow them to accompany a troop of new recruits heading out to Laramie. Four days later, they squeezed about the crowded stagecoach and started the last eighty miles of their journey.

Sarah's teeth chattered as the unheated stagecoach lurched and bounced its way across the frozen prairie. They were all crammed together so tightly she couldn't move anything except her head, and every bone in her body ached. She could no longer remember a time when she wasn't cold and sore.

The smell bothered Sarah more than anything. The stagecoach reeked of dusty leather, hair tonic, horse, and underlying everything else, the unlovely aroma of unwashed bodies. Occasionally, one of the soldiers traveling with would try to strike up a conversation but soon fell silent under Jacob's glowering gaze.

The frozen landscape rolled past all that day and through the night. The next morning was colder, and a hint of moisture was in the blustery wind. The soldiers predicted a blizzard but not until the next day. They should all be safe and snug in Fort Laramie by then.

"I can't believe we missed Rand. He wasn't supposed to come out to this wilderness until spring," Sarah moaned.

"It won't be long now," Amelia said soothingly.

Sarah sighed again, and her breath steamed. "I hope I get a chance to bathe before I see Rand. I must look terrible." She could feel her hair hanging in straggly wisps against her cheeks. The last time she pushed it out of her face, her gloves had come away smeared with dirt. Rand would take one look at her and send her home.

Jacob shuffled his feet on the other side of Amelia as the driver gave a shout from topside. He grinned at Sarah. "Sounds like we're there."

Sarah moaned and tried to pat the strands of hair back into some semblance of order as she lifted the leather covering and peered out of the window at the famous fort. Surrounded by rocky soil and sagebrush, it sprawled across the Laramie River, its frame and adobe buildings lining a wide parade ground fortified with mountain howitzers. But it was all so barren. The fort seemed a tiny oasis in a vast plain of frigid wasteland.

She gave an involuntary gasp when she saw the Indians encamped all around the fort, their tepees gleaming in the sunshine. Hundreds of them. Squaws squatted around open fires; children shouted and played in the dust.

"The fort's been overrun with Indians." She gulped.

The garrulous old soldier across the aisle chuckled. "Fort Laramie's the headquarters for the Sioux. There's always a passel of redskins round here. You'll git used to it."

"But there's no stockade," she said with a shudder. "What if they turn hostile?"

"There's always plenty of hostiles around, but they know better than to attack a fort as well garrisoned as this one. You don't need to worry none, Missy. The most them savages ever done was run howling through the pasture to stampede the horses."

Several soldiers manned a ferry, and the trip across the river was accomplished quickly. Sarah's heart pounded as the horses pulled the stage up the hill and it rolled to a stop. The driver threw open the door and helped the two ladies down before climbing on top and tossing all the luggage down to the eager hands waiting below.

Sarah stared all around in dismay. It was not at all as she'd imagined. The adobe buildings sat in neat rows along a barren parade ground. They looked cheerless and unwelcoming. A U.S. flag whipped forlornly in the wind atop a flagpole on the far side of the parade ground. The fort seemed to be stuck out in the middle of nowhere with the wilderness all around. She could feel all the soldiers milling around the fort staring at her and Amelia.

"It'll look better come spring," the old soldier consoled.

Jacob piled their luggage together in a heap, then accosted a nearby soldier. "Could you tell me where we might find Lieutenant Rand Campbell?"

"Well, don't this beat the Dutch." The soldier had a friendly, smiling face. "You've gotta be Jacob. You look enough like your brother to be two peas out of the same pod." The soldier stuck out a large callused hand. "Isaac Liddle's my name, and Rand's my bunky."

Jacob shook his hand vigorously. "Mighty glad to meet you. Got any idea where that rascal brother of mine is?"

"Probably at mess. Bugle sounded a few minutes ago. I was headed there myself. Just follow me."

Shivering as much from nerves as from the cold, Sarah took Joel's hand and trailed behind Jacob and Amelia. She felt as though her entire future hung in the balance. She could hear shouts of laughter emanating from the officer's mess hall, and her stomach rumbled hungrily as the wind brought a mouthwatering aroma of stew to her nose.

The room was brightly lit with dozens of lanterns, and the general feeling of high spirits and fellowship warmed her as much as the heat rolling from the pot bellied stove in the center. She scanned the room quickly as their presence caused the babble of voices to soften, then still. She caught sight of Rand sitting at the far table next to two women. Her first impulse was to call out his name and run to him, but the expression on his face as he gazed at the young redheaded woman stopped her. Sarah didn't like the dazed smile on his face or the possessive hand the woman had on his arm. She gulped as he looked up and saw them.

Rand rose slowly to his feet as the small party neared. "Sarah? And Jacob! I didn't expect you, Jacob, not for at least another week or two." He grabbed his brother's hand and pumped it, then hugged Amelia and Joel but didn't touch Sarah. "Hello, Sarah."

"Who are all these folks, Rand?" The redheaded woman stood and slid her hand into the crook of Rand's arm, and Sarah caught a whiff of her perfume. Some exotic flowery scent she couldn't place. "Introduce me to your friends," the woman purred.

"Jessica, this is my brother Jacob, his wife Amelia, and," he hesitated, then continued. "And some friends from back home, Sarah Montgomery and her brother Joel."

"Pleased to meet you all," Jessica said with a seductive smile. "I've heard all about you, Jacob. Rand tells me you're the county boxing champion." Her smile deepened into a dimple as she looked at Jacob. "I'm Jessica DuBois, and this is my mother, Mrs. Major DuBois."

The address sounded strange to Sarah, but she was aware that was how wives were addressed in the army. And Sarah thought she'd never seen anyone more lovely than the young woman on Rand's arm. Jessica had deep blue eyes and dark red hair that shimmered in the candlelight. Her skin was almost translucent, with a pale peach tint to her high cheekbones and lips. Jessica's mother was a blurred image of her daughter with softer, plumper lines and a gentle expression.

"Please call me Letty," the older woman murmured. "Everyone does." She smiled at Amelia and Sarah. "I'm so glad to have two other women here at Laramie. We must get together for tea tomorrow. We ladies have to stick together. It helps the time go by. And you all are here just in time to help plan the wedding."

"Wedding?" Sarah looked at Rand. "Whose wedding?"

"Why, mine and Rand's, of course." Jessica hit Rand on the arm with her fan. "Why, you bad boy, haven't you told your family about us yet?"

"They had probably left Wabash by the time my letter got there," Rand said, his eyes on Sarah's face.

Sarah felt as though she were falling. She couldn't catch her breath. How could he? How could he come out and get engaged in less than two months? She fought down the tight tears in her throat as she gripped Amelia's hand. She didn't want to give the other woman the satisfaction of seeing her cry. Did she know Sarah had once been engaged to Rand?

"Congratulations," Jacob said after an awkward pause. "I had no idea you were seeing anyone, Rand."

"I think a kiss for your new sister-in-law-to-be is in order," Jessica said. She stood on her tiptoes and kissed Jacob lingeringly on the lips. Sarah saw Amelia clench her jaw.

"Rand, we're really tired," Amelia said through tight lips. "Could you see about finding us a place to stay tonight?"

"The quartermaster is by the door. Come with me, Jacob, and we'll get you all fixed up."

"I'll come along," Mrs. Dubois said. "A woman's touch is always better." She followed the men.

"My goodness," Jessica said. "You and I are certainly lucky ladies, Amelia. Those are some men we have." She didn't seem aware of the undercurrent of tension as she turned to Sarah. "Have you known Rand long yourself? I knew as soon as I set eyes on him, I was going to marry him."

"All my life," Sarah said, ignoring her last statement.

Joel tugged on Sarah's arm. "How can Rand marry that lady when he's going to marry you?"

Jessica choked on her coffee. "Why, whatever does the boy mean?" she asked.

Sarah went scarlet with mortification. She had wanted to preserve her dignity if she could. "Rand and I were engaged before the war," she admitted.

"Oh, I see," Jessica said with a long look at Sarah's face. She narrowed her eyes. "You lost him. Well, let me tell you, I don't intend to lose him. Don't think you can waltz in here and take him back. We're getting married in June, and I won't allow anyone or anything to interfere with my plans."

Sarah gasped and choked back an angry retort. She was a new creature now, she had to remind herself. God was in control of this situation too. "Rand and I have been friends all our lives," she said quietly. "If you are the woman he wants, I want to be friends with you too." She could sense Amelia's silent approval of her soft answer.

Jessica frowned, uncertain how to respond to the gentle answer. "Well, uhm, that's fine then," she finally muttered ungraciously as Jacob hurried back over to them.

"We're all fixed up," Jacob announced. "Let's go get settled. Rand is going to bring us over some stew after we get cleaned up."

"You just remember what I said," Jessica murmured as Sarah turned to follow the men out of the mess hall. "I never give up anything that belongs to me." She flounced away to meet her mother by the door.

Sarah felt numb as she held onto her skirts and followed the little party across the windy parade ground. How could all her hopes and dreams end like this? What could she do? Was this God's plan?

Rand led them to an adobe building. "Captain Leeks lives on the other side with his family, but his family never stays here in the winter. His wife and two sons will be back in May." He opened the door and led them into a narrow hall that opened onto a small, cheerless parlor. The room was cold and barren with plain plank floors. It smelled musty from disuse but had a lingering odor of smoke and soot. Rand knelt at the fireplace and poked at the logs. "I'll have it warmed up in no time." He got the fire going, then stood. "You can all get cleaned up, then I'll be back in about an hour with some supper for you." He grinned. "Cookie likes me. When he hears we have two new ladies, he'll be glad to whip up something."

"We need to talk," Sarah said.

Rand avoided her gaze. "I'll be back later. We'll talk then."

"Now, please." She didn't know how she could rest until she heard his explanation.

Rand sighed and ran his hand through his hair. "Sarah, you need to unpack and get settled in. And we need to talk in private."

He was right. She sighed and turned away. She knew it was a vain hope to think there might be some good explanation for what had happened. Rand was engaged to another woman. What was there to explain? No wonder he wasn't anxious to discuss it with her.

In the tiny kitchen there was a Sibley stove that Jacob soon had blazing. The warmth crept into the room and seeped into Sarah's cold skin, but nothing could reach the icy despair in her heart. A battered kettle sat on the stove. Sarah rinsed it with water from the bucket a private brought to the back door. First they'd have a cup of tea, then see to bathing the road dust off their sore bodies. She felt as though the fine yellow grit was in every pore of her body. She could even taste its gritty presence in her throat. She looked around the small quarters. Only one small bedroom opened off the kitchen. Where could they all sleep?

"I'll bring over a couple more bunks," Jacob said. "We can put one in the parlor and use it for a sofa during the day. You can sleep there, Sarah. I'll put another one in the entry for Joel, and everyone will have a little privacy. Just for tonight, you and Amelia can sleep in the bedroom, and Joel and I will put up in the barracks." He hauled the hip bath down off its peg on the wall and set it in the small bedroom. He sent the private down to the river to haul some more water for bathing.

Even with several kettles of boiling water added, the bathwater was barely tepid, so they all bathed quickly. Sarah was by the time Rand brought over a steaming kettle of stew and bread. They wolfed down their supper in ten minutes.

Jacob yawned. "I'm beat. I think the rest of us will turn in if you and Sarah want to talk, Rand."

Rand nodded reluctantly. "See you in the morning," he said.

"Can I look at your saber?" Joel asked between yawns.

"In the morning." Rand grinned at Joel's crestfallen expression and ruffled his hair. "You guys get some sleep. When you're rested, I'll show you around your new home tomorrow."

Joel and Jacob said a quick farewell and headed out for the barracks. Amelia smiled encouragingly at Sarah before slipping off to the bedroom. Sarah waited until the door to the bedroom was closed, then turned to Rand. "How could you do this, Rand? It hasn't even been two months since you asked me to come out here with you. Does your love die so quickly?"

Rand's lips tightened. "I like army life, Sarah. The adventure, the sense of doing something worthwhile with my life. Something that affects other people besides just my family. I want to be part of taming the West for my country. And Jessica will make an excellent army wife. She's lived on frontier forts most of her life. It hurt when you didn't love me enough to leave your family for me. Jessica will go wherever I'm sent without a complaint. She understands soldiers and their duties."

"You can't tell me this is just a marriage of convenience! I saw the way you were looking at her when we arrived. And if you are just using her, what kind of a man have you turned into, Rand?"

"I care about her," Rand admitted. "She was here when I was hurting over your rejection. She let me know right off how she felt about me. I needed someone, and she was there. And like I said, she'll make a good army wife. What are you doing here, anyway? You said you'd never leave Indiana."

"Papa's dead." She regretted her bald words as soon as she saw the hurt and shock register on his face. She softened her tone. "His heart just—gave out."

"Oh, Sarah." His eyes looked stricken. "I really loved your pa. He was like a father to me."

"He loved you too," she said softly. "He spoke of you just before he died."

"He did?"

She nodded. "He was gone just a few minutes after we'd talked. He told me—" She broke off and bit her lip.

"He told you what?"

"He urged me to fight for you."

Rand sighed. "Is that why you're here? Now that he's gone and you don't have anything else to do?"

Sarah bit her lip. What should she tell him? Slowly she nodded. "I was coming before he died. I was making plans when I heard the shouts at the house. His death actually delayed my arrival by several weeks."

"You're a little late."

"So I see," she said. "You're not the same man I've loved for so long. Where did he go?"

"He died in the war," Rand said stiffly.

Sarah laid a hand on his arm. "Rand, you won't be happy with this kind of life. I've discovered in the past few weeks how important it is to let God lead me. If I hadn't been determined to run my own life, I wouldn't have been deceived by Ben."

"You sound like Isaac," Rand blurted.

"Isaac is a Christian?" she asked.

He nodded. "He's been a good friend. He talks about God a lot, but I don't think God bothers with our daily lives. I believe He's out there somewhere, but I don't think He cares what we do. We just use our own ingenuity to live our lives as best we can."

Sarah shook her head. "Your grandma would wallop you if she heard you say such a thing."

Rand grinned. "Probably. But it's how I feel. If God ever speaks to me directly, maybe I'll listen."

"It may be too late, then."

"I'll just have to take that chance," he said firmly.

"Do you love Jessica?" Her face felt so stiff she could barely move her lips. She had to know the answer, but her heart pounded with fear.

"Not like I loved you. But she's been good to me. And she's very sweet and kind. I can't just throw her off like a busted saddle."

Sarah stared at him incredulously. Sweet and kind? He must see something she didn't. "Then there's nothing more to say. I'll try not to bother you too much. You'd better go now." Her eyes burning with tears, she stepped away.

He hesitated, then nodded. "I guess you're right. I'm sorry, Green Eyes."

Don't call me that, she wanted to shout. *You're not the same man who nick-named me that.* But she said nothing. He picked up his coat and left silently. As the door shut behind him, she let the tears fall.

Chapter 9

Reveille sounded at five, but Rand was already awake. Jacob and Joel were sleepily pulling on their overalls and boots when he strode in to check on them. "Hurry up, or you'll miss the cold slop we call breakfast," Rand said with a grin.

"How's the Indian situation?" Jacob poured icy water out of a battered tin pitcher into a chipped bowl and splashed his eyes.

A group of soldiers had been up playing cards all night, and their loud talk and laughter had made sleep difficult. Most of them had already cleared out of the long room lined with bunks, but the odor of hair tonic and dirty socks still lingered.

"Bad. And likely to get worse. The Bureau of Indian Affairs has really botched things. Every agent they've sent sets out to line his pockets with what belongs to the Indians. Once one gets rich enough, he goes back east and another comes to start the same process all over again." Rand shook his head. "And it's really explosive up in the Powder River area. Quite a few miners have been killed trying to get to the gold fields."

"Much hostility around here?"

"Not really. A few skirmishes. There's mostly tame Oglala Sioux and friendly Brulé. Most of the wild Oglala are with Red Cloud at Powder River."

"The girls will be relieved to hear that."

"I was just about to check on them." Rand paused. "I'm sure glad you're here, Jake. You're going to love this country."

The smell of impending snow freshened the air, and the frigid wind stung Rand's face as they hurried across the parade ground toward the light spilling out the front window of the house. It looked warm and welcoming in the somber darkness of the predawn morning. Their breath made frosty plumes in the air, and their boots crunched against the frozen ground as they waved and called morning greetings to the soldiers heading toward the mess hall, most of them shrouded in buffalo robes against the cold. The trumpet's call to breakfast carried clearly in the cold, crisp air.

Sarah's heart was heavy as she finished dressing. Rand and Jacob should be here any moment, and she didn't know how she should act. She wasn't sure what she should do. She couldn't go back home. Wade would just get up to his old tricks again. She turned as she heard the men thump up the porch steps and ran to unlock the door. "Good morning," she smiled, anxiously searching Rand's face.

Rand didn't look at her. "Breakfast is going to be over if you two don't hurry up."

"We're almost ready. Let me finish my hair. Jacob, why don't you take Amelia and Joel and go on ahead?" Sarah's words were mumbled through a mouthful of hairpins. She had deliberately dawdled over her toilet so she might have a few moments alone with Rand.

With a quick, understanding glance, Amelia drew on her navy cape and followed Jacob and Joel out the door. Sarah finished her hair with a few quick thrusts of well-placed hairpins, then looked up at Rand. "Have you thought about what we talked about last night?"

"Sarah, what do you want me to say? It's too late. All the regrets in the world won't change the situation." He stood with his back to her, staring out the window. "We both know it's over. Unless of course you're looking for a new fellow. There's plenty willing I'm sure. It's so rare for the men to see any unattached women—you'll probably have a dozen proposals before the week is over."

Stung by his words, Sarah tossed her head. "Don't worry that I'm going to embarrass you with unwanted attentions. I had hoped we could at least be friends."

"As long as you don't expect anything more from me. Jacob said he'd probably be sent to one of the northern forts come late spring or early summer, so I reckon we can be civil to one another for a few months." He picked up her cloak from the foot of the bed and held it out to her courteously. "Now I think we'd best be heading over to mess. As I recall, you're always hungry in the morning—unless that's changed too."

Red spots bloomed in Sarah's cheeks, and her lips tightened. "I'm not the one who's changed—you have! Traipsing off to the back of beyond was never in our plans. Where's the gentle farmer I used to know? The Rand I knew wasn't a glory-hungry warrior." She drew her gloves on with angry jerks and tied her bonnet under her chin.

Rand shrugged. "Maybe so. But I'm not the same person I was before the war. And neither are you, in spite of your not wanting to admit it."

She swished away from him without another word. The wind struck her as she stepped out onto the porch, and as she staggered, Rand caught her arm and steadied her. She was very conscious of his strong, warm fingers pressing her arm through her cape.

His dark eyes were impersonal as he gazed down on her. "The wind is ferocious out here. Watch your step." He led her across the parade ground toward the mess hall, the soft glow of lamplight shining out its windows and a lazy curl of smoke rising from its chimney.

With an effort, Sarah controlled her hurt and anger. She forced a smile to her face and laid a hand on his arm before stepping into the mess hall. "I'm sorry I lost my temper. Friends?"

Rand hesitated, then smiled. "Friends." He closed the door against the rising wind outside.

The mess hall was a big open room filled with long wooden tables that seated eight to ten men. The tables closest to the stove in the center of the room were all filled. "Rand!" Jessica, clad in a green dress, was seated across the table from Jacob, Amelia, and Joel at the table closest to the stove. She waved to them.

Sarah stifled a sigh. She hadn't thought she'd have to face Jessica quite so soon. The other woman's shining red hair was elegantly piled high on her head, and her pale complexion was flawless. Her mother had the same cool loveliness, but where her expression was serene and gentle, her daughter had a petulant twist to her mouth and an acquisitive look in her blue eyes.

Jessica nodded coolly at Sarah, then turned adoring eyes up to Rand. "Don't forget the new play at Bedlam is tonight. You did say you'd pick me up at seven, right?"

Rand nodded, and Sarah clenched her fists in the folds of her skirt until the overwhelming jealousy subsided.

"You must come, Miss Montgomery. You and your friends." Mrs. DuBois fluttered her plump, white hands. "My husband has the lead role, and you'll be able to meet all the officers."

"Please call me Sarah," she said automatically, her eyes on Rand and Jessica.

"You can call me Letty. Everyone does, my dear. It will be so pleasant to have other ladies at the fort." She shuddered delicately. "One gets so lonesome for the refined company of other women in this primitive place. Perhaps we can get together for tea tomorrow?"

Sarah forced herself to smile and accept Letty's invitation. She strained her ears to listen to Jessica's monopoly of Rand's conversation. Obviously, Rand had spent considerable time with this girl and enjoyed her company. Did Rand really love her? No. Sarah refused to believe that. They had shared too much, and their love was too strong for it to just die like that. She *would* get through to Rand; she wasn't too late. Sooner or later he would realize he really loved her. God wouldn't have brought her this far for it all to end.

But what if He had? Maybe He had other plans for her. He certainly wouldn't want her to marry Rand when he held beliefs so contrary to God's Word. She felt weary and defeated as she settled down to eat breakfast.

The breakfast lasted an interminable amount of time as they ate the nearly cold flapjacks and grits and washed it all down with strong, hot coffee. Nearly every officer in the place found some excuse to stop at their table for an introduction. Jacob glowered at the attention Amelia received, but Rand just looked on impassively as the younger officers flirted with Sarah and paid her extravagant compliments.

Jessica made no attempt to hide her disinterest in any man except for Rand. She glared after them when Rand told them he was taking the new arrivals on a tour of the fort and took his leave of her and her mother. Sarah resisted the urge to give Jessica a triumphant smile. She felt anything but triumph. She wanted Rand's love, not his duty.

After breakfast, the quartermaster gave them rough woolen blankets, a couple of crude wooden beds with straw mattresses, and a water bucket. Amelia had brought a trunk packed with kitchen utensils and plates as well as some bright calico and gingham material, several sets of muslin sheets, and some quilts she'd made over the years.

As they carried their booty back to their quarters, Sarah was able to take a good look at their new home. Darkness had fallen so quickly last night she hadn't really noticed much about it. A front porch ran the width of the house with wide front steps. Two doors opened off the unpainted porch.

Rand opened the main door, and they stepped inside the wide, bare entry hall. The first door led to the tiny sitting room that looked out on the front porch. Sarah stood looking around with her hands on her hips. There were definite possibilities. She walked through the narrow door in the small kitchen and surveyed the Sibley stove in the middle of the tiny room. There was just enough space in the corner for a small table. Hooks could be hung from the low roof for pots, and a small corner cupboard could be built in the corner adjoining the parlor. "What do you think, Amelia?"

Amelia brushed a stray wisp of hair out of her eyes. "I don't know where to begin," she faltered. "You take charge, Sarah. You're so much better at decisions than I am."

By midafternoon, the tiny rooms had been scrubbed, Jacob had tacked the wool blankets to the floor in the sitting room and bedroom, fires blazed in all three fireplaces, and the beds were set up and ready for occupancy. Sarah and Amelia each had a lapful of material as they stitched curtains for the windows and cloths to cover the crates that would suffice as tables. Sarah could hear the thunk of axes behind the house where Joel and Jacob were chopping more wood. Isaac had told them to let the wood detail bring them more logs, but

Jacob insisted he needed the exercise after being cooped up in the stage for so long. She glanced around the room in satisfaction as she sewed. They could write and ask Margaret to send a rug for the sitting room, she decided. With a few trinkets and pictures, it would be quite homey. At least it was beginning to feel like home.

Chapter 10

Sarah awoke the next morning with a sense of foreboding. She and Amelia had promised Mrs. DuBois to come to tea around eleven. She groaned and pulled the blanket over her head. Maybe the weather would still be too bad to get out, she thought, remembering the fierce snowstorm that had blown in late last night. She could hear the bustling as the fort awakened for a new day. The wind no longer howled, and she could see a glow as the sunrise began to peek over of the eastern hills.

She groaned again. The last thing she wanted was to hear details about the wedding. And Jessica was cruel enough to delight in seeing if she could make Sarah squirm. Sarah sat up and swung her feet to the cold floor. She lifted her chin and pressed her lips together. She'd be cool and calm. No matter what Jessica said or how much it hurt, she wouldn't let her see her pain.

By the time Amelia and Jacob opened their bedroom door, Sarah had already gone through her trunk and decided on a dress. It was a deep green poplin trimmed with black velvet and edged with lace. A sleeveless jacket of black corded silk went over the dress and cinched around her waist. An intricate design of velvet ribbon adorned the skirt and sleeves.

"Good morning," she called when she saw Amelia and Jacob. She tested the curling tongs on the kitchen stove with a wet finger. It sizzled. Almost hot enough.

"You're up early," Amelia yawned. "What's the occasion?"

"Have you forgotten we have a date for tea?"

Amelia eyed her uncertainly. "You seem almost pleased. I thought you were dreading it." She put a skillet on the stove and turned to mix up a batch of biscuits.

"Don't bother with breakfast for me," Jacob interrupted. "I'm running late. I'll grab something at officer's mess." He kissed Amelia and grabbed his coat off the hook by the stove.

"Be careful," Amelia called before turning her attention back to Sarah.

"I was really hating the thought of having to be nice to the ice queen," Sarah continued. "Then I decided it would just be a challenge. God promised us that we would be conquerors in all things. This is a chance for me to put my faith into practice. Besides, there must be some good in her or Rand wouldn't care

68

about her."

Amelia smiled. "I wish you luck finding it. I haven't seen it yet."

"My, that doesn't sound like you. I've never known you to have a bad word to say about anyone but Ben. You're always telling me to have more patience with people."

Amelia colored. "I know I shouldn't feel that way, but she makes me uneasy, just as Ben did."

"Well, she's not married to Rand yet. Could you help me with my hair? I want to look my best."

Amelia nodded, and the girls spent the next hour curling Sarah's hair. They pulled it back from her face and let the back cascade down in tight curls. After pulling a few curls forward by her ears, Sarah was finally satisfied.

Amelia looked pretty and demure in a deep blue silk dress with a lace collar and lace around the sleeves. Her dark hair was pulled back in a loose knot at the nape of her neck with a few curls escaping at the sides.

Sarah threw her best cloak of brown wool with bands of velvet fringe over her shoulder, tied on her green silk bonnet, and walked confidently toward the door with Amelia in tow. Knowing she looked her best helped calm her agitation.

But when Mrs. DuBois opened the door and Sarah saw Jessica standing behind her, she felt dowdy and plain. Jessica wore a lilac-colored silk dress with an intricate pattern in the skirt. Rows of lace ruffles cascaded over the skirt and sleeves, and her lovely white shoulders were bare. Her hair was braided and looped in an intricate way Sarah had never seen. The style accentuated Jessica's high cheekbones and big blue eyes.

But Mrs. DuBois was easy to like in spite of her daughter. "Come in, come in, my dears." She fluttered her plump hands as she drew them inside the warm hallway. "We've been so looking forward to this, haven't we, Jessica dear?"

"I certainly have."

Sarah thought she detected the hint of a sneer in Jessica's smooth voice. She squared her shoulders as she handed her cloak and bonnet to Mrs. DuBois.

Jessica led the way into their cheerily decorated quarters. Since Major DuBois was a senior officer, he received more deluxe accommodations than a lowly lieutenant. The parlor was large with a soft flowered carpet on the wood floor. Dainty tables and a horsehair sofa and three chairs furnished the room. Garden pictures and gold sconces adorned two walls, while the fireplace dominated the third. Sarah could see the dining room through the arched doorway. A walnut table and chairs on another beautiful carpet occupied the center of the room. A young, attractive black woman hovered near the table.

"Rose, please pour our guests some tea," Mrs. DuBois called. "Sit down, ladies, and tell us how you like our little garrison."

Sarah sat on the sofa, expecting Amelia to sit next to her, but Jessica quickly settled there. With a quick glance at Sarah, Amelia sat down on one of the chairs, while Mrs. DuBois took possession of another one.

"What do you think of Fort Laramie so far? Are you ready to return to Indiana?" Mrs. DuBois asked.

"It's much more primitive than I expected," Sarah admitted. "And so cold. It seems very isolated."

"It's really very jolly in the summer. More ladies are here, and we have dances and parties almost every night. Wait until then before you decide to leave us."

"They'll be gone by then, Mother. Won't you?" Jessica addressed her last remark to Sarah.

Sarah forced herself to smile breezily. "Who really knows with the army? We're hoping to stay near Rand as long as we can." She heard Jessica's sharp intake of breath.

"Excuse me for a moment, ladies," Mrs. DuBois said, seemingly unaware of the awkward pause. "I just want to peek in to see how our refreshments are coming." She scurried away and disappeared behind the door on the far side of the dining room.

As soon as her mother was gone, Jessica turned to Sarah with an angry glare. "Just what did you mean by that remark? I've already warned you not to meddle. Nothing is going to stop this wedding. You try, and I promise you, you'll be very, very sorry."

"I didn't mean anything other than we all love Rand and want to be with him as long as we can. He was gone three years and only home a few days before coming out here." Sarah looked earnestly into Jessica's eyes. "I won't lie to you and tell you I don't still love him. But I want him to be happy, and if that means marriage to you, I'll try to accept that."

Jessica closed her mouth as her mother came back into the room. The look she cast at Sarah was full of venom, and Sarah could see the effort it took for her to control herself in her mother's presence.

The next hour was spent in light conversation over a delicious tea of dainty chicken salad sandwiches, tiny cakes, and cookies. It was all Sarah could do to ignore Jessica's seething anger just under her smooth surface.

"Do come again," Mrs. DuBois urged as she handed the girls their cloaks and bonnets. "I so enjoyed your company."

After promising they would return at their first opportunity, Amelia and Sarah made their escape. Amelia let out a sigh as soon as the door closed and they stepped down onto the path back home. "You've made a real enemy, Sarah. She seems capable of anything."

Sarah sighed. "I meant to try to be on friendly terms with her. I really want

God's will in this, even if it means I have to give Rand up." She swallowed the lump in her throat. "It will be the hardest thing I've ever done, though."

Amelia slipped an arm around her waist as they trudged through the snow toward home. "I pray about it all the time. God will work in Rand's heart."

"I think so too." Sarah hesitated, then continued slowly. "But if God chooses not to work this out—or if Rand won't let Him—I'll survive. That's one thing I've learned in these last few months. With God's help I can make it through anything."

Amelia smiled. "It's good to hear you talk like that." They reached their door, and Joel came tearing out.

Sarah caught him as he tried to rush past them. "Whoa. What's going on?" Before Joel could answer, Rand strolled out behind him.

"We're going ice fishing," Rand said. "With your permission, of course. I was going to ask before I took him, but I wasn't sure where you were, and he assured me you wouldn't mind."

"No, of course I don't mind. And we were at the DuBois's for tea," she added as he turned to go.

He stopped and gave her a quick look. "I see," was all he said. He cleared his throat. "Well, we'll be going now. He'll be back in time for supper."

"Have fun." Her heart ached as she watched him match his stride to Joel's shorter one. Her brother looked up at him adoringly as they walked away. Would things ever be right? Was it even possible to untangle this mess? She sighed and followed Amelia into the house. She'd try her best and leave it in God's hands. It was all she could do.

A couple days later, Rand was sleeping soundly when a timid hand shook him awake.

"Lieutenant Campbell, sir. Colonel Maynadier wants to see you right away," a young private told him.

He dismissed the private and pulled on his pants. What could the colonel want with him so early? Fifteen minutes later, he rapped at the door leading to his commander's office.

"Enter."

He stepped inside the room, taking in the piles of papers scattered over the old wooden desk before saluting smartly. "You wanted to see me, Sir?"

"Ah, yes, Lieutenant Campbell." The colonel looked up from his scrutiny of the document in front of him. He was a tall, spare man somewhere in his forties with blond, thinning hair and pale eyebrows. But there was nothing nondescript about his eyes. They were gray and eagle sharp. The soldiers under his command knew those eyes missed nothing that concerned the well-being of Fort Laramie.

Rand sometimes thought the colonel could see inside his soul with those eyes. "Camp rumor has it that a certain Lieutenant Jacob Campbell is your brother and that he arrived a few days ago with a wife and her companion. Is that correct?"

"Yes, Sir."

"Excellent. I have a proposition for you. Big Ribs and some of the other chiefs have asked for their children to be instructed in the basics of a white education. Learning English, a little reading and writing. I would like to request that Miss—" He peered at the paper in front of him. "That Miss Montgomery take over the task while she is here. Lieutenant Liddle informs me that she is a most gifted, intelligent young woman and not likely to be frightened by the Indian children."

"I'll ask her, Sir," Rand said, swallowing his dismay. The last thing he wanted was to get Sarah even more entangled in life at Fort Laramie. He kept his face impassive as the colonel outlined his plan for the school. The last few evenings had been pure torture. How long must he endure her presence? He'd decided to turn his life in a new direction, and he would stick with it.

"One other thing," Colonel Maynadier said as Rand saluted and turned to go. "There's a new authorized fur trader to the Sioux downriver. Please check in on him this afternoon and see that he understands the rules governing Indian trade."

"Yes, Sir." Another fur trader was the least of his worries, he fumed as he strode across the snow-covered parade ground. They were all alike anyway. All set on feathering their own nests at the expense of the Indians. They forced the Indians to pay for their own annuities with furs and made exorbitant profits when they sold the furs back east.

Sarah opened the door at his knock. Her eyes lit up when he repeated the colonel's request. "How lovely! It will help me feel as though I'm carrying my own weight. When does he want me to start?"

"Right away. You're to use the chapel for now, and next spring the colonel plans to build a small schoolhouse. You'll have to improvise, though. There are no schoolbooks here and probably won't be for months."

"Can I go too?" Joel asked.

"You actually *want* to learn something?" Sarah said in surprise.

Joel looked down at the floor. "There aren't any other boys to play with. I thought maybe I could teach some of them how to play baseball."

Sarah's face softened, and she nodded. "We need to get on with your studies too." She turned back to Rand. "Could you find me some slate? Or some paper to lay across boards?"

"There's plenty of slate in the cliffs across the river. I'll fetch some this afternoon. I have to go that direction anyway to check on a new fur trader."

The sun shone coldly on the glistening snow as Rand threaded his way through the massive snowdrifts along the rocky trail that led downriver to the trader's establishment. He was cold through and through by the time he reached the group of small buildings bustling with activity. The pure snow had been tramped to a muddy quagmire by the horses tied to posts along the front of the buildings. They stood with their heads down and their backsides to the cutting gale. Sioux and Cheyenne squaws huddled out of the wind in the doorway of the storage building. He caught a glimpse of crates piled nearly to the ceiling through the open doorway. Trying to ignore the stench of so many unwashed bodies, he pushed his way into the smoke-filled room and looked around for someone in charge.

A scrawny, red-necked young man with stringy blond hair seemed to be directing the dispersal of crates. Impatience was etched around his mouth as he argued with a young Sioux brave. "We ain't dispensin' no ammunition! You savages ain't to be trusted with gunshot and powder. Here. You can have some extra bean rations."

"Must have gunpowder! Need to hunt buffalo soon, or squaw and papoose go hungry! Beans, bah!" The brave spat for emphasis at the young man's feet.

"Well you won't get none from me. Learn to grow crops like normal folk, and you wouldn't have to worry about shootin' buffalo. Now either take your rations and go, or get out of the way so the rest can get their grub."

The young brave scowled and swept the rations into the skirt the squaw with him held ready. He gave the young man one last angry glare before stomping away.

Rand pushed his way up to the counter, and the man looked up. Rand noticed his eyes widen, and he looked around nervously.

"Lieutenant Rand Campbell. I was ordered to see if there's anything you need. You are the new trader, aren't you?"

The young man licked his lips, and his eyes darted toward a door to the side of the counter. "No, Sir. My name's Les Johnson, and I just work for him. He's in his office right now with some folks. I'll tell him you stopped by, though."

"You do that. I have another errand to run. I'll stop back later this afternoon." Rand turned to leave and almost ran into a familiar lanky figure. "Labe?" Rand stared, almost not believing his own eyes, but it was definitely Labe Croftner. What was he doing here? His blood pounded in his ears, and he swallowed the lump of rage in his throat. "Where's Ben?" He knew Labe would never roam this far from home without his brother.

"R–Rand!" Labe's eyes widened, and he started to back away, but Rand grabbed his arm so tightly he flinched.

"Where is he?"

His face white, Labe shook his head, but his eyes darted to the closed door to the right of the counter. Rand released his arm and strode toward the door.

"Wait, you can't go in there!" Les moved to intercept him, but Rand brushed by him and threw open the door.

Ben was seated at a makeshift desk with two rough-looking men dressed in buckskin sitting across from him on crates. He stared at Rand, then smiled and stood. "Well, well, if it isn't the illustrious Captain Campbell come to pay me a call. I didn't expect word of my arrival to reach you quite this soon."

"What are you doing here, Croftner?" Rand clenched his fists and took a step toward the desk.

"What does it look like? I'm the new trader, old friend. Thanks to you I was no longer welcome around Wabash. This opportunity was too good to pass up, so I decided to put up with the disagreeable thought of having to run into you occasionally and took the job." Ben offered Rand an insolent smile and sat back down. "And a very lucrative one too, I might add. Now if you don't mind, I have business to attend to."

Rand choked back his rage. He needed a clear head to deal with Croftner. There was some nefarious purpose to Ben's presence here, he was sure. "I'll be watching you, Croftner. You step out of line just one inch, and I'll be all over you like a wolf on a rabbit."

Ben smile indolently. "I'm terrified. Can't you see me shake?" The other men guffawed, and he leaned forward. "Give Sarah my love, and tell her I'll stop and see her real soon."

"You stay away from Sarah!"

"My, my. Does your lovely fiancée know how you still feel about Sarah? Perhaps I should inform her how you're still looking after the poor little orphan." He sat back and crossed his muddy boot over his knee. "But the beautiful Jessica doesn't have anything to worry about. Sarah belongs to me, and she's going to discover that real soon."

"You lay one finger on Sarah, and you'll be in the guardhouse so fast you won't know what happened."

"Hey, there's no law against calling on a lady."

"She doesn't want to see you." Rand wished he was as certain as he sounded.

"I think I'll just let her tell me that. I'm sure she'd be pretty cut up about discovering her precious Rand is about to marry someone else."

Tired of the exchange, Rand clenched his jaw. This wasn't getting him anywhere. "You just remember what I said." He turned and stalked out the door as the men behind him burst into raucous laughter.

His jaw tight and his chest pounding, Rand swung up into the saddle. Ranger danced a bit as if to ask what the trouble was. Rand patted his neck, then urged him down the trail back to the fort. Did Sarah know Ben would follow her out here? How much did she really care for Ben? After all, she had agreed to marry him.

When he arrived back at the fort, he marched over to see Sarah. She had her sleeves rolled up, and tendrils of hair had escaped her neat roll. He resisted an urge to wipe the smudge of flour from her cheek. "Did you know Ben is here?"

Her eyes widened. "Ben's here?" Her green eyes snapped. "He'd best leave me alone. I don't want to see him ever again."

"That's not what he says."

"You've talked to him?"

"He's a newly authorized Indian trader, and he's crooked enough to make a good one. He said to give you his love."

"The nerve of that man. I didn't have anything to do with this. You believe me, don't you?" She stared up at him anxiously.

He raked his hand through his hair. "I don't know what to believe." He started toward the door, then turned back. "By the way, I got your slate."

"Don't change the subject." She caught at his arm. "You have to believe me, Rand. I didn't know Ben would follow me. I don't want to have anything to do with him."

"It's nothing to me," he said, disengaging her grasp on his arm. "I'm engaged to another woman. Remember?" He felt a small stab of guilt when he saw the look of pain cross her face.

The next few days were full of getting ready for the school. By the time Monday came, Sarah felt she was ready for the new challenge. Joel carried the slate, and they set out for the chapel. As they approached the small building, a group of about thirty youngsters watched. She noticed one older girl of about fifteen. She was truly beautiful with soft, dark eyes, glossy black braids, and an eager look on her face.

The girl stepped forward as Sarah stopped in front of the door. "I am Morning Song, daughter of White Raven," she said softly. "I very glad to learn more English."

"You speak well already." Sarah smiled. "I'm very glad one of you can understand me." She opened the door and led them inside. Someone had already started a fire in the stove, and the room was warm and welcoming. She motioned for the children to be seated and waited until the rustling stopped. "I'm Sarah," she said. She didn't want them to have to start off with a difficult word like Montgomery. "Can you say Sarah?"

Dark eyes stared at her solemnly, then Morning Song spoke sharply. In unison they said, "Say-rah."

Sarah smiled. "Very good. This is my brother, Joel." Several of the youngsters had already been eyeing Joel. He smiled at them uncertainly. "Could you tell me the names of the children, Morning Song?"

The Indian girl stood and put a hand on the sleek head of each child as she spoke. "This Dark River. This Spotted Dove, this Spotted Buckskin Girl. She daughter of Chief Spotted Tail. Her Sioux name is Ah-ho-appa."

"How lovely." Sarah smiled.

The names went on and on. Sarah wondered how she'd keep them all straight. "Thank you," she said. "You'll have to help me for a few days until I can memorize them."

Morning Song nodded eagerly. "I very much like to help Say-rah."

The day went well with the children all eager to learn. Sarah was surprised how quickly they picked up the English words.

"That was fun." Joel's face shone with enthusiasm. "I even learned some Sioux."

Over the next few days, Sarah was almost completely consumed with her duties as a schoolteacher. Rand seemed to be avoiding her. He rushed in for a few minutes at night, then hurried away with some lame excuse of some kind. Ah-ho-appa, Morning Song, and her brother Red Hawk came by almost every day after school. Sarah felt as though the young Indian girls were the sisters she'd always longed for. Amelia loved them too. And Sarah was glad for Joel to have some company. He soon became best friends with Red Hawk.

Sarah and Amelia were clattering around in the kitchen and Joel was out playing with Red Hawk when the front door banged. "We're in the kitchen," Sarah called. She poured water from the wooden bucket into the kettle and set it on the stove as Rand came in. Amelia rinsed the last of the breakfast dishes and dried her hands on her voluminous apron before untying it and draping it over the back of a chair.

"Want some tea?" Sarah eyed his grim look with trepidation.

"Yeah." He pulled out a chair and sat down. "What's this I hear about you getting real friendly with some Indian kids? The whole garrison is talking about it."

"As a matter of fact, Morning Song and Ah-ho-appa will be here anytime. Wait 'til you meet them, especially Morning Song. She knows English, and she's the sweetest little thing." She waved good-bye to Amelia as she patted her hair into place and hurried to meet Jacob at the sutler's store.

"I'm not sure how smart it is to let yourself get too close to them. You may be doing a lot of harm."

"Whatever do you mean? They are my friends. I would never hurt them."

"Maybe not intentionally. But have you thought about how they may become discontented with their lives as Sioux? If you give them too many different ideas, they may not fit in with their own people."

"That's ridiculous! Ah-ho-appa is a chief's daughter. Maybe she can help her people climb up out of the primitive way of life they lead." She jumped to her feet and took the steaming kettle off the stove. "You soldiers would have them stay in squalor. One of the soldiers told Joel the only good Indian was a dead one!" She jerked her apron around her waist and tied it before spinning around to face him.

Rand sighed and ran his brown, muscular hand through his hair. "I know a lot of the army feels that way, but you surely don't believe I do. You know White Snake was one of my best friends back home." He and the Miami brave had been friends since Rand was five. "You're new out here, Sarah. There's a lot of prejudice and bitter feelings against Indians. You need to be careful about meddling in things you don't know anything about. I wish things were different. But I've seen too many Indian women taken advantage of in the short time I've been here. I wouldn't want anything to spoil Morning Song."

Sarah opened her mouth to defend herself, but there was a timid knock on the back door. She bit back the angry words and opened the door with a bright smile. She didn't want her friends to hear their discussion and think they shouldn't come back.

Morning Song peeked in the door, and Ah-ho-appa was behind her with timid, gentle eyes. Morning Song's eyes glowed with enthusiasm and joy. Behind them Sarah heard Rand suck in his breath when he saw Morning Song's beauty.

"Say-rah, I am too early?" Morning Song dropped her eyes as Rand rose to his feet.

"I was just going. Think about what I said, Sarah." He smiled at the Indian women and strode out the door.

"You're just in time, Morning Song, Ah-ho-appa. The tea is ready." Stiff with outrage, Sarah ignored Rand's departure. He hadn't given her a chance to explain her intentions. She wanted to show God's love to her Sioux friends. She swallowed her anger and poured them all a cup of tea. Ah-ho-appa ran a gentle brown hand around the gold rim of the bone-thin china and sighed in contentment as she took an eager sip.

"What we do today, Say-rah?" Morning Song asked.

"I thought we might go for a walk while the weather holds. Some of the men are predicting more cold weather within a few days, so we should take advantage of the sunshine while we can. I thought we might walk by the river."

Morning Song nodded. Her lovely face glowed with such joy and zest for life, Sarah found all her angry thoughts fading away. She untied her apron and hung it on the peg by the door, then went to fetch her bonnet and cloak from the front hall.

The wind was a gentle whisper instead of its usual gale force. Mountain chickadees chittered in the trees along the riverbank, and the sound was soothing. The last few days had been unusually warm, above freezing for a change. Morning Song skipped along beside Sarah, while Ah-ho-appa eagerly led the way. They passed several groups of soldiers felling trees for firewood, the heavy thunk of their axes comfortingly familiar. For Sarah, it brought back memories of her father and brothers clearing the back pasture the summer before the war began. Those were happy days, days of laughter and contentment, with Rand hurrying over every evening to take her for a buggy ride or just a walk by the river. A small sigh escaped her, and Morning Song looked up, her face clouding uncertainly.

"Why Say-rah so sad? Bluecoat with holes in cheeks make you unhappy?"

Sarah smiled at her friend's reference to Rand's dimples. "How did you know that?"

"Say-rah's cheeks red like apple, and she look like this when I come in." Morning Song scowled menacingly. "Eyes sparkle like dew on leaf. Say-rah love bluecoat?"

Sarah nodded. "Very much. But sometimes he makes me so mad."

"Say-rah marry bluecoat?" Ah-ho-appa asked.

"I want to, but first I have to convince Rand. He's being stubborn right now. I was engaged to him before the war, long before he ever met Jessica. Do you know what engaged is?"

Ah-ho-appa's sleek black head bobbed up and down. "Promised to marry. My mother wishes me to promise myself to Red Fox, but I say no. I want to marry bluecoat and live in fine house like Say-rah's."

Sarah looked at her in dismay. "Oh, Ah-ho-appa, you don't mean that. It would be best for you to marry one of your own people."

"You think I not good enough for bluecoat?"

"Of course not. But there are so many problems. Other people might not treat you well back in the East. And you would miss your own people."

"My friend River Flower marry bluecoat and live at edge of fort. She have baby boy."

Sarah knew she referred to the common-law marriages where the soldier paid the girl's father a few horses and "married" her. When he moved on to another fort, he generally left his squaw and any children behind. "You deserve more than that. Those marriages aren't legal in the sight of the white man's laws. You should look for a man who will love and take care of you always."

Ah-ho-appa shook her head, her face set with determination. "I marry blue-coat or no one." She turned and started back toward the cabin with Sarah and Morning Song trailing behind.

Morning Song looked at Sarah sadly. "I not know Say-rah not like Sioux." She turned and walked stiffly back toward the Indian encampment.

Sarah's heart sank. What had she done? And how was she going to fix it?

Chapter 11

S arah was quiet that evening as they all prepared for a dance at Old
Bedlam. She was worried about Morning Song and Ah-ho-appa. It certainly seemed as though Rand was right about her friends becoming
discontented with their lot as Sioux because of their friendship with her. The
thought of seeing Jessica with Rand only made her feel gloomier.

The place was full of smiling officers decked out in their dress uniforms, their
brass buttons and black boots shining. Sarah and Amelia were claimed for dances
immediately. As the awkward lieutenant whirled her around the dance floor,
Sarah found her eyes straying to Rand's dark head in the throng. He was so tall,
he was easy to spot. His chin rested on Jessica's gleaming red head, and she was
snuggled close to him.

Sarah dragged her eyes away and forced herself to make polite conversation
with poor Lieutenant Richards. The evening became a blur as one officer after
another claimed her for a dance. She wondered if Rand would ask her to dance,
then chided herself for her foolish hope. Jessica wouldn't allow him out of her
sight, she was sure. She danced twice with Isaac, Rand's bunky, and she was
tempted to ask him if he knew how Rand really felt, but she resisted. It would
be sure to get back to Rand, and she would look pathetic.

When there were only two more dances left, Jessica's father insisted on a
dance with his daughter. Rand glanced Sarah's way, then made his way determinedly through the throng.

"Are you promised for this dance?" he asked politely.

"Not really," Sarah said. "I don't think Joel will mind if he doesn't have to
dance. I told him he had to dance with me so he could begin to learn. But his
lesson will wait." She slid into his arms, and he guided her onto the floor.

"You were right," she admitted reluctantly.

"About what?"

"Ah-ho-appa wants to marry a soldier and live in a home like mine. When
I objected, she and Morning Song both thought I didn't think they were good
enough to marry a white."

He nodded. "I'd heard Ah-ho-appa refused her father's choice for her. But
don't beat yourself up over it. It may have happened anyway. There are a lot
of Indian squaws who jump at the chance to take a soldier. And their families

are well-paid for them."

"That's awful!"

"I know, but it's the way things are out here. A squaw doesn't have much value. Although, as pretty as your friends are, they'll probably fetch a high price," he said regretfully. "That will be a strong incentive to their fathers."

"Isn't there anything we can do?" Sarah couldn't stand the thought of her young friends sinking into that kind of life.

"Not really. Just be a friend to them. It's probably too late to do anything else."

The dance ended, and Rand escorted her to her chair. He stared down at her with a curious look on his face. It seemed almost tender. He opened his mouth but was interrupted by Jessica's arrival.

"There you are, Darling," she cooed. "Be a dear and fetch me some punch."

"Of course. Would you care for some, Sarah?"

"No, thank you," she said, turning before he could see the hurt in her eyes at his distant but polite tone.

As soon as he was out of earshot, Jessica turned to her furiously. "Just what do you think you're going to accomplish by staying here? I want you to stay away from Rand. He's mine now! You had your chance with him, and you let him slip away."

Sarah spread her hands placatingly. "Miss DuBois, we're just friends. And I'd like to be your friend too."

"Then stay away from Rand!"

Sarah bit her lip to keep back the hot retort. She breathed a sigh of thankfulness when Rand returned with Jessica's punch.

She was shaking as she hurried to find her cloak and go home. The party was over for her. She was tired and discouraged in spite of her bravado. Every-thing seemed so hopeless. Jessica was a formidable opponent.

Isaac stopped her at the door. "Leaving already?"

"I'm very tired," she said as she slipped the cloak over her shoulders.

"I was just coming to claim a dance. As compensation you must let me walk you home." Isaac grabbed his hat and greatcoat, then held open the door for her.

The cold air stung Sarah's cheeks as she took Isaac's arm on the front porch of Old Bedlam and walked across the parade ground with him. At her front door, she paused. "I'd ask you in for a cup of coffee, but it wouldn't be proper with no one else home."

He grinned. "That's all right. Maybe next time. And I really would like there to be a next time. I know you used to be engaged to Rand, but you need to get on with your life. With your permission, I'd like to call on you."

Sarah hid her surprise. She'd seen Isaac hovering close over the past few weeks, but she had thought he was just being kind because he knew how hurt she'd been. "I don't know, Isaac," she said. "You're a good friend, and I'd hate to ruin our friendship."

"How could we ruin it? We could have some Bible study together and become better friends."

Sarah was tempted. Isaac was a good Christian man, and she had a lot of respect for him. Were things with Rand really past hope? "All right," she said uncertainly. "But I can't make any promises, Isaac."

Isaac nodded. "I understand. But we both love God, and we shouldn't shut the door on something that may be His will. Let's just see where He leads." He touched her hand briefly and turned to go.

Sarah watched as he walked back toward Old Bedlam before going inside. He was right. God wouldn't want her to marry Rand unless he became a Christian. She had to be willing to walk through any open door He chose. No matter how hard it was.

Her heart was still heavy the next morning as she and Joel set out for the school. Ah-ho-appa was conspicuously absent, and Morning Song refused to even look at her. Sarah's heart ached as she saw the stiffness in her friend's demeanor.

She stopped Morning Song at the end of the week. "Don't go, Morning Song," she said. "I want to talk to you."

The girl almost seemed like her old self as she nodded and motioned her brother to go on without her.

"I'm sorry if I hurt your feelings. I really didn't mean I didn't think you were good enough for a soldier. Any man would be very lucky to get you or Ah-ho-appa."

Morning Song smiled. "I very angry, but no more. Say-rah my friend. I know you not wish to hurt me. And I have new friend."

Sarah's heart sank at the glow on the girl's lovely face. "A man?"

The girl nodded. "Him very handsome. Very light hair with eyes like stormy sky."

Sarah tried to think of a soldier who fit that description, but she couldn't think of who it might be. "What's his name?"

"Him new fur trader. Ben Croftner." Morning Song smiled a secret smile as she said his name.

Sarah stepped back as from a blow. "Oh, Morning Song. Not Ben. He's a very wicked, evil man." She caught the girl's arm. "Please, please stay away from him!"

Morning Song shook her hand off. "He tell me you will say this. But he loves me, Say-rah. Him good man. Give my father five horses for me. We marry tomorrow."

"Please, Morning Song. I beg you. Don't do this. It isn't a legal marriage.

Ben won't stay with you."

The girl just gave her an angry stare and stalked off. "I thought my friend be happy for me, but I wrong," she called back over her shoulder. "You my friend no more, Say-rah."

Sarah clasped her hands and paced the floor. What could she do? She couldn't just stand back and let Morning Song make a mistake like that. She caught up her cloak and hurried to the door.

She borrowed a horse from the stables and found the trail leading to the trading post across the river. Jacob and Rand would both be furious if they discovered what she was doing, so she kept a sharp eye out for them as she left the fort. Luckily no one was about as she forded the river and urged the horse up the trail. It was the first time she'd been outside the fort grounds on her own. She was a little fearful and kept looking around for signs of any Indians. But she was determined to do what she had to.

The trading post was almost deserted when she arrived. A few Sioux hunkered around a fire in the front and looked up as she approached the door. Labe was just coming out the door as she slid off her horse.

"Sarah! What are you doing here?"

"I'd hoped you hadn't followed Ben out here, Labe. I need to see him. Is he here?"

He nodded. "He's in his office. I'll show you." He opened the door and led her across the dirt floor to a battered door. He rapped on it once, then swung it open for her.

Ben looked up when he heard the door open. "Sarah?" He rose to his feet eagerly, but his smile faded as soon as he saw the look on her face. His expression masked, he motioned for her to sit down on the crate across from his crude table. "To what do I owe the honor of this call?"

"I want you to leave Morning Song alone," she said. What had she ever seen in this man? She struggled to control her rage.

He stroked his chin. "She'll be a lovely addition to my home, don't you think? And Indian women really know how to treat a man. I just don't see how I can agree with your request."

"Please, Ben. Don't do this." She hated to beg the likes of Ben Croftner, but she had to save Morning Song.

"You're begging now, are you? Well, I might agree under one condition." He smiled gently. "You could take her place."

Sarah flushed. She should have known he'd suggest something like this. "You're crazy. You know how I feel about you."

He stood and thrust his hands into his pockets. "You're just angry, and I'm not saying you don't have a right to be. But anything I did was only because I loved you. And you haven't had any luck with Rand, now have you?"

"Maybe not, but I couldn't marry a man I couldn't trust." Sarah stood. There was no more to say. She loved Morning Song, but it was out of her hands. Ben was the very antithesis of the kind of man God would have her marry.

"Then the wedding proceeds tomorrow as planned."

"You know it's not a real wedding! You'll just send her back to her family when you're tired of her."

Ben sneered. "She's just a savage, Sarah. That's all Indian women are good for."

"She's sweet and good and pure. You'll take that and destroy it!"

"My, my, you do have an exalted opinion of me, don't you? Well, you just run on back to your precious Rand and let me take care of my own affairs. But don't think this is the last of our discussion. I mean to have you, Sarah. One way or the other. Things will never be over between us."

She shivered as she made her way back to Fort Laramie, and not just from the cold. Ben seemed so cold and evil. She didn't know what he might try. The fort was in an uproar when she arrived. She found Rand and Jacob mounted and ready to leave when she reached the stables.

"Where have you been?" Rand looked upset. "We've looked all over the garrison. You know you're never to leave the grounds unaccompanied. The Indians are predicting a blizzard. What if you'd been caught in it? What if the Sioux had taken you? Don't you have any sense?"

She slid off her horse and lifted her head. He wasn't going to browbeat her! "You don't have any say over what I do. And what would you care, anyway?" She didn't wait for his answer as she led her horse into the stable. The odor of horses, straw, and manure struck her as she escaped from the avid stares of the soldiers and the incessant wind.

Rand jumped off Ranger and followed her into the stable. "I'd care, all right!" He grabbed her arm and pulled her around to face him. "Don't you ever do anything like that again."

Her heart stirred at the expression on his face. He almost looked as if he really did care.

Rand muttered an exclamation and pulled her close against his chest. "I don't know what I'd do if anything ever happened to you," he whispered.

Sarah could hear his heartbeat under her ear, and she was very conscious of his warm, male scent. He stroked her hair, then pulled her away from his chest and tilted her chin up. She held her breath. His eyes searched her face, and he lowered his head. Sarah closed her eyes and waited for his kiss, but it never came. Rand loosened his grip on her and stepped away just a moment before Jessica came rushing into the stables. Sarah was sure her face was scarlet, and she turned away quickly to tend to her horse.

"There you are, Rand. I've been looking all over Laramie for you. I see you found Sarah. Where was she?"

Sarah's irritation rose as Jessica continued to talk as though she weren't there. "I went for a ride," she interrupted.

"A ride? Are you mad? In the dead of winter with hostile savages around? I've wondered about you before, Sarah, but this borders on lunacy." Jessica's voice was acidic. "Well, no harm done, I suppose. But you caused a dreadful commotion. It seems to me you could have thought to inform someone of your plans. Unless, of course, you wanted to upset everyone."

"I didn't mean to cause any alarm. I thought I'd be back before anyone missed me. Now, if you'll excuse me, I really must get home." Sarah brushed by her and avoided Rand's anxious gaze. She just wanted to be alone. Rand did have feelings for her, but what difference did it make? Jessica wasn't about to give him up. And Rand wouldn't be the one to break the engagement. She knew him too well. And anyway, he still wasn't a Christian, no matter how much she prayed.

The next day, she watched from the window as Ben arrived with five horses to take possession of his bride. In a beautifully beaded dress bleached to a pale yellow, Morning Song was seated on a horse almost the color of her dress. Her unbound hair, rippling past her waist, gleamed in the weak sunshine as she followed her new husband back to their little cabin beside the fur post. Sarah wept as she saw her friend's glowing face look back one last time.

That night, the weather made one of its drastic changes. The temperature plummeted, and the wind picked up. Then the predicted blizzard struck in all its fury. The wind howled and blew snow through cracks around the windows. They all had to fight to keep the fires going in the fireplace. Jacob finally gave up the fight in the bedroom and dragged the bed and their belongings out into the kitchen.

They hung blankets over the doorway into the hall to try to block the flow of cold air. By the time the storm had vented its full fury, there were drifts of snow over the windows. Jacob opened the door only to be met with a column of snow completely covering the opening. They were effectively buried until the enlisted men dug them out. It was evening before they heard the scraping of shovels and friendly hellos from outside the door.

Sarah stood beside Jacob as he opened the door, and two half-frozen men stumbled inside, their faces, beards, hair, and clothing all packed with snow.

"Glad to see you're all right," the youngest private sputtered as he complied with Sarah's urging and took off his coat before staggering toward the fire. "The colonel said to tell you to stay inside tonight. We got a path dug out pert near all around the post so we can get from building to building. And the wood detail will be here with a load soon."

Amelia poured them all a cup of hot coffee and offered them bread and jam, which they accepted with alacrity. "Much obliged, Ma'am," the young private said, regretfully getting to his feet when the last crumb of bread was devoured. "We best be heading back to check with the colonel."

Jacob, Amelia, and Sarah saw their deliverers to the door and peered out the narrow path left by their busy shovels. "It looks like a maze," Sarah said, unable to believe what she saw. The snow towered over twelve feet in many places. The narrow path trailed down the steps and around the corner toward Old Bedlam.

Jacob saw her shivering and shut the door. "You girls had better stay in until the weather breaks. Feels like it's at least twenty below. Exposed skin freezes in seconds in this kind of temperature."

The weather didn't break for days. There would be a couple of days of bright sunshine, but the temperatures were way below zero, and the wind howled and blew the snow into ever-changing drifts. Those days would be followed by more snow and yet more snow. Sarah and Amelia took to pacing around the tiny quarters when Jacob and Rand were gone on duty. Jacob was sent out on telegraph duty several times, he was officer of the day three times, and he took his turn guarding the cattle and horse herds. They all tried to keep busy. Sarah played endless games of checkers with Joel and Amelia, while Jacob and Rand saw to their duties.

Mail hadn't been able to get through either. Sarah longed for news from home. Surely Rachel had delivered the baby by now.

Jacob kept them informed of the goings-on at the post. Big Ribs had returned with the Corn band of Brulé ready to make peace. Then Man-Afraid-of-His-Horses trudged in with his band of Oglala. The winter had been hard on all of them.

Sarah was forced to discontinue the lessons with the Indian children. The weather was too cold for the little ones to be out, but she intended to start again in the spring. Her thoughts turned often to Morning Song, and she wondered how Ben was treating her. And the confinement just made her dwell on the situation with Rand even more. Depression overwhelmed her all too easily.

Chapter 12

The weather finally broke and, with its usual capriciousness, turned unseasonably balmy. Sarah had dreamed about Morning Song again, and she was anxious about her friend.

"When will you be going to the trading post again?" she asked Jacob over breakfast.

"As a matter of fact, I have to run over there this morning. The colonel has a message to deliver. Why?"

"May I come along? I want to visit Morning Song."

He hesitated, then finally gave in to her pleas. "I'll have to take a couple more men along for protection. Make sure you dress warm."

She hurried to do his bidding. About an hour later, she hurried across the parade ground toward the Laramie River. Jacob and Isaac were waiting with five other soldiers and a mount for her by the ferry. She mounted, and they surrounded her as Isaac led the party up the trail to the trading post.

The little settlement was full of Indians and trappers when they arrived about a half an hour later. Squaws stood around smoky fires patiently, but Sarah didn't see her friend. Isaac pointed out Ben's cabin, set off in a grove of trees by itself.

"I'll keep Ben busy," he promised.

After glancing nervously around, Sarah dismounted and hurried toward the cabin. No one answered her first knock, so she rapped harder. Finally, the door opened, and Morning Song peered around the door.

"Say-rah," she gasped. She started to shut the door, but Sarah saw the marks on her face and pushed her way in.

"Oh, Morning Song," was all she could say for a moment. The young woman's face was marred by ugly purple and yellow bruises. One eye was swollen almost shut, and her lips were split and puffy. Morning Song cried softly as Sarah took her in her arms.

Morning Song pulled away and wiped at her eyes gingerly with the hem of her apron. "Do not look at me, Say-rah. I know what you say."

"Why have you stayed?" Sarah asked gently. "Didn't you know I would take you in?"

Morning Song lifted her hands, palms upward. "Ben watch close. And he say if I leave, he make me sorry. He say he hurt Say-rah."

With an exclamation, Sarah gathered the young woman back into her arms. "Don't you worry about Ben. He can't hurt me. The bluecoats won't let him." She released her. "Get your buffalo robe and any possessions you want. You're coming with me."

Morning Song looked at her doubtfully, then realized she was serious and hurried to do as her friend said. Sarah looked around as her friend tied all her belongings in a sheet. The cabin was furnished with crude wooden furniture for the most part, but there were a few surprising items. One was the ornately carved and lacquered bed, and the other was a silver picture frame that held a picture of Ben with his arm around Sarah. It had been taken at the county fair last summer. Sarah gasped at Ben's cruelty. Morning Song would have seen this picture every day.

Five minutes later, Morning Song was ready. Sarah opened the door cautiously and looked around. No one seemed to be paying any attention to the little cabin set off by itself. "You stay in the trees," she told her friend. "We'll meet you just over the knoll." Morning Song nodded and slipped away soundlessly. Sarah hurried along the path and quickly mounted her horse. She told one of the soldiers to wait for Jacob while she took the others and started for home. Her heart pounded. If Ben looked out and saw her, he'd know for sure that something was up.

She looked back as she rounded the bend. There was no hue and cry, so she began to breathe easier. When she crested the knoll, she heard a scuffle and a cry to her right. "Morning Song," she called. She urged her horse through the frozen brush with the soldiers following her. As she crashed through the thicket, she saw Morning Song struggling with Labe.

"Let go of her, Labe," she ordered.

He looked up, his eyes startled. "Ben will have my hide," he whined. "I'm s'posed to see she doesn't get away. It's nothing to you, Sarah."

"Look at her, Labe. Go on. Look at her. Do you honestly think Ben has a right to beat her like that?"

Labe glanced at the Indian girl's battered face and dropped his eyes. "I told him not to, but he wouldn't listen," he murmured. "You know how Ben can be."

"I know. Now let go of her."

Labe's hand fell away, and Morning Song picked up her bundle and scurried toward Sarah. Sarah reached out a hand and helped her swing up on the back of her horse.

"Ben ain't goin' to like it," Labe said.

"I don't care what Ben likes or doesn't like. You tell him to stay away from me and Morning Song, or I swear, I'll shoot him." She nodded to the privates who had followed her, and they all crashed back through the thicket to the trail.

Isaac and the detachment were just rounding the crest of the knoll as they arrived. Isaac whistled when he saw Morning Song's face. "Ben do that?"

Sarah nodded, her lips tight. "Thanks for keeping him busy."

"No problem. We'd better hurry, though. He'll be after us any minute. He said something about going home for lunch. As soon as he sees she's missing, he's going to be hunting for her."

"He'll know where to look. Labe saw us." She quickly told him and Jacob the full story as they kicked their horses and galloped toward the safety of the fort.

When they reached the fort, Morning Song insisted on going to the Indian encampment. "I must see my father. He will wish to know," she said.

Sarah agreed reluctantly and went to her quarters to wait for her friend's return. She wasn't at all sure Morning Song's father would be able to defend her if Ben showed up.

Morning Song was barely out of sight when the front door crashed open, and Ben stomped in. "Where is she?" he demanded.

Sarah rose from the chair. "Get out of here, Ben. I don't know how you have enough nerve to show your face here after what you did to Morning Song."

His face reddened. "She's just a squaw! And I can do anything I want with her. She belongs to me just like my horse! No one complains if I discipline my horse, now do they?"

"She's not a horse! She's a flesh and blood woman with a heart, which you've broken. Now get out of here."

Ben laughed derisively. He strode across the floor and caught her by the arms before she could even flinch away. He took her chin in his hand and tilted her head up as she struggled to get away. "I like it when you fight me," he whispered. She stopped her struggling instantly, and he laughed again before releasing her. "Run away, little rabbit. But you won't escape me. I have plans for you."

He leered at her, then stomped back out the door. "I'll find her, Sarah. She'll wish she'd stayed where she belonged. And you'll wish you'd stayed out of it."

Sarah let out a shaky breath as the door banged behind him. How had she ever thought he was attractive and kind? She shuddered. The door burst open again, and she flinched. But it was Rand.

"Are you all right?" he asked.

She nodded, close to tears. She hated to admit it, even to herself, but she was afraid of Ben. "He's looking for Morning Song," she stammered, then burst into tears.

Rand crossed the room in one stride and pulled her into his arms. "It's all right, Green Eyes," he said soothingly. "We won't let him take her." He caressed her hair until the storm of weeping was past.

"I'm sorry," she gulped. "I don't cry very often. I don't know what came over me." She was very aware of his hand on her hair. That hand tightened on the back of her neck when she looked up.

She saw Rand swallow hard when she put a hand on his cheek. She searched his face and saw confusion mixed with a tenderness she'd hoped to find for weeks. "Rand," she began. But the door opened, and Amelia rushed in. She'd heard the story at Suds Row, the laundry area.

Rand stepped away quickly, and the moment was lost. Again. Would there never be time for them to sort things out? Sarah sighed.

Ben's rage was overpowering as he stomped toward the Sioux camp. He hoped the Indians would try to stop him from taking Morning Song. He would love to smash a face or two. Although the face he really wanted to destroy was Captain Rand Campbell's. As he walked in front of the officers' quarters, he heard someone call his name. Startled, he saw a lovely red-haired woman motioning to him from her front porch.

"Mr. Croftner," she called.

It must be the lovely Miss DuBois, he thought. She certainly was beautiful, if you liked the type. Cool and remote. "At your service," he said, stopping at the foot of the porch steps.

"Won't you come in, Mr. Croftner? I think we have something in common."

He raised a questioning eyebrow but followed her inside to the elegant parlor. "And what would that something in common be?" he asked.

"We both want to keep Sarah Montgomery away from Rand," she said smoothly.

He stroked his chin. "Very true," he agreed.

"I have a plan," she said. Leaning forward, she explained her scheme, and he began to smile. It was superior in every way to his own. Sarah would learn his vengeance was terrible.

"Tell me more," he said.

The next morning, Sarah hurried over to the Indian camp to check on her friend, but the place was deserted. Every teepee, every pot was gone.

"They left," one soldier told her. "I think they were planning to meet up with Big Ribs."

Sarah breathed a sigh of relief. Ben wouldn't be able to get his hands on Morning Song again. She thanked God for that.

When she got back, Amelia and Jacob were still eating breakfast.

"What are you going to do today?" Amelia asked Jacob. Sarah sat beside them and took a small helping of biscuits and gravy. Joel was still asleep, with only a tuft of his hair showing above the blanket.

"Wagon train's due in this morning. Rand is leading a company to escort it as far as the Platte River bridge, then we'll spend the night to be ready to work on the telegraph tomorrow morning. Don't expect me back until suppertime tomorrow."

"I'll miss you."

Jacob grinned and kissed her. "No, you won't. You and Sarah have all kinds of things to do. It would be a good time to start on the stenciling around the doors and windows." He got to his feet and picked up his hat. "I've got to get moving before the captain reports me." He chucked her under the chin before striding out the door.

The girls followed him out onto the porch to watch the familiar scene of the guard mounting. The strains of the fort band playing drifted over to the porch, then the commander shouted, "Boots and saddles." The men swung up into their saddles in unison. The sun glittered off the men's brass buttons and weapons as they filed out of the fort. The girls watched until the troop crested the hill and was hidden from view. Sarah wished Rand would have stopped by to say good-bye. *He probably said good-bye to Jessica, though*, she thought, choking back tears.

Rand spent the day scanning for hostiles as he plodded along on Ranger beside the slow-moving wagon train. Most of the soldiers begged to be allowed on escort duty since most wagon trains had women emigrants, but it was just another duty to him. The last thing he needed was another female to worry about; he still didn't know what he was going to do about Sarah. Jessica seemed to sense his turmoil. She'd been after him to move up the wedding day to next month.

He must have been loco to have rushed into another relationship. Every time he looked at Sarah, his heart stirred and he knew he'd made a foolish mistake.

By the time they camped, Rand was bone-weary. They'd chased off a group of about fifteen Sioux, then followed them a short distance before turning back and continuing on toward their destination. At one point, Rand had one young brave in the sights of his Henry, then dropped his gun. He just couldn't do it. The youth was probably only fifteen, although he looked like he'd seen battle before—he had a livid scar running down one cheek. The brave had stared at him defiantly as Rand sighted down the barrel of his gun. When Rand let the muzzle fall, the brave lifted his spear in his hand and wheeled around with a bloodcurdling yell.

"That there was a mighty big mistake, young feller." Rooster, the scout, had seen the exchange. "You'll likely run into him again, and he won't be so charitable-like."

Rooster was probably right, Rand thought as he crawled into his bedroll. But the brave had reminded him of Shane. The same careless free spirit. Rand just couldn't kill him.

The weather turned frigid and stayed that way. Days went by with no relief. Finally, just before Christmas, Rand informed them all they could bundle up and attend a party at Old Bedlam. The mercury had crept up to twenty degrees—almost balmy compared to where it had hovered for weeks. The Laramie Minstrels band played, and Sarah danced until she thought her feet would fall off. Isaac claimed his share of dances as well as every other officer at the fort. Several times she saw Jacob glower as Amelia swept by on the arm of yet another soldier. She knew just how he felt when she saw Rand dancing with Jessica.

Halfway through the party, a sentry rushed in. "Colonel, Spotted Tail is at the Platte!"

Colonel Maynadier jumped up. "Raise the white flag and get my horse ready." He turned to Rand. "Lieutenant, I hate to drag you away from the festivities, but I need you to accompany me. We'll ride out to meet Spotted Tail and assure him of our good intentions. This is what I've been waiting and hoping for. He's been with Red Cloud. If Spotted Tail is ready for peace, perhaps Red Cloud is too."

Rand nodded. "I'll meet you at the corral, Sir." He pushed his way through the throng and found Sarah. "The party's over." She was pink-cheeked and breathless from a rousing round of the gallop. "I have to go," he told her.

"Not now! This is the first time we've been out of the quarters in weeks." Rand winced at the disappointment in her voice.

By the time Colonel Maynadier's group of officers had mounted, they could see the column of Brule' Sioux over the rise. The wind carried the chanting to them.

"Sounds like a death lament," the colonel said with a frown.

As they drew nearer, they could see Spotted Tail's face drawn with grief, and he dragged a travois with a shrouded body behind his horse.

A messenger rode forward and stated Spotted Tail's request. His daughter had died on the trail, and she'd begged to be buried in the white man's cemetery. Maynadier quickly agreed, and Spotted Tail rode forward to talk with the colonel.

"My heart grieves at your loss, my friend," Colonel Maynadier said as the sorrowing Indian pulled up in front of him.

Tears welled up in Spotted Tail's eyes. "My heart is very sad, and I cannot talk on business; I will wait and see the counselors."

Rand and Jacob looked at one another in dread as the chief turned away. Spotted Trail had only one daughter. It had to be Ah-ho-appa.

"You tell her," Jacob said.

Sarah was stitching on a lapful of quilting material when Rand strode into the parlor. The lamplight cast a soft glow over her glorious hair, and Rand caught his breath.

She heard him and looked up. "You're back sooner than I expected." Her welcoming smile made him feel even worse. He wished he could soften the blow.

He took her hand. "I don't quite know how to tell you except to just say it. It's Ah-ho-appa. She's dead, Sarah. Pneumonia." He cleared his throat. "It's been a hard winter, not enough food. She was too weak to fight the lung infection."

Sarah's eyes widened and she shook her head. "No."

"I'm sorry. I know you loved her."

Her eyes filled with tears. "There must be some mistake."

"There's no mistake. Her father has asked for her to be buried in the soldier cemetery. He said she wanted to marry a soldier." Rand hated to see her pain.

Sarah put her face in her hands and wept. "It's all my fault," she sobbed. "If she hadn't been friends with me, she would have been content with her life. She would have married some young brave who would have taken care of her."

Rand took her hands and drew her to her feet and into his arms. "I'm sorry, Green Eyes. But you did all you could for her. At least she didn't go through what Morning Song did." The feel of her in his arms, the sweet scent of her hair, made him more aware of everything he'd tossed away. What a fool he was. "The funeral's tomorrow. I'll take you if you want."

She nodded. "I must tell her parents how much I loved her."

The next day, several hundred mourners, consisting of Indians, off-duty soldiers, Colonel Maynadier, as well as Major O'Brien—who had arrived to take over command of Fort Laramie—attended the funeral.

Rand kept close to her side as she mourned the loss of the little Indian princess. His strength and concern lifted her spirits in spite of her grief. Maybe the Rand she knew and loved still existed inside the barrier he'd put up around him.

When the funeral was over, she pushed through the crowd, while Rand followed her. She touched the girl's mother on the arm. The squaw looked at her with pain-shocked eyes as Sarah fumbled with a ruby pin her father had given her on her fifteenth birthday. She pressed it into the mother's hand. "I'm so sorry," she whispered.

The woman stared at her, then slowly pinned the brooch to her shawl before pulling a row of beads from her own neck and placing them around Sarah's throat. *"Wash ta cola,"* Sarah whispered as the woman turned to go.

The Indian nodded, and a weary smile flitted across her face so quickly Sarah wondered if she imagined it. Then she followed her husband, both of their heads bowed in grief.

Rand was watching Sarah, his brown eyes warm with approval. "That was a nice thing to do. You've probably made a friend for life."

Her eyes filled again. "Ah-ho-appa was my friend. I'll never forget her. But I did tell her about Jesus, and she prayed for salvation. I can only hope she truly understood."

He nodded then shifted uncomfortably. "I know it's hard for you, Green Eyes. It's all so different out here. You're used to activity and fun. It's pretty dreary confined to those small rooms all the time and never being allowed to go outside the fort. If the weather holds, how about going skating on the Laramie River tomorrow after worship services?" An army chaplain had come to Fort Laramie two days ago, and they were looking forward to attending church on Sunday.

Sarah nodded eagerly. "I'd love to go!"

"Jessica's been wanting to go for weeks."

Sarah's elation died. Jessica's presence would spoil everything.

The next day was bright and sunny, with the mercury hovering near twenty-five degrees. "It feels almost balmy," Amelia said as they trooped across the parade ground to the tiny stucco chapel. Joel and Rand engaged in a snowball fight along the way, and they arrived breathless and laughing.

Inside were rows of backless benches and a rough pulpit in the front of the room. It was a familiar place to Sarah, since she had used the chapel for her classes, but Amelia had never seen it, since this was the first time a chaplain had been here to conduct services. Jessica motioned to Rand imperiously, and he left them to go sit with her.

Sarah drank in the words the minister spoke. She'd missed her little congregation from home so much. Until she'd come out here, she'd never realized how much the support and prayers of her friends had meant to her. A new thankfulness to God swelled up in her soul as she sang the hymns in her clear alto voice. Isaac sat beside her, and Jacob and Amelia sat on the other side. She glanced surreptitiously at Rand and Jessica. He seemed to be listening, which surprised her, because he didn't seem to have much use for God since the war. And he made it pretty clear he didn't think God had a hand in the day-to-day things of life. Jessica seemed bored, though.

Sarah dragged her eyes away from Rand's broad back and fixed her eyes on the chaplain. God would take care of everything. Nothing would be allowed to happen that He didn't know about. He had brought Rand through the war safely. If He could take care of Rand physically, surely He would care for Rand spiritually as well.

The service was over too soon for Sarah, and she had to force herself to hurry home to change for the skating party. What was the use? She dragged herself to the river but found no enjoyment in the fun around her. Every time she looked at Rand, he was smiling at Jessica.

Ah-ho-appa's death cast a pall over Christmas. Sarah could not really get into the festivities. Rand brought Jessica with him on Christmas Eve to the party at Jacob and Amelia's. She sat with a supercilious smile on her face while Jacob read the account of Christ's birth from Luke. Rand listened intently and even read a passage of Scripture himself.

Was he beginning to change? Sarah hoped so. Her eyes filled with tears as she heard again the old story. Only God had been able to keep her soul in peace through the difficult months here at Fort Laramie. She was close to giving up and trying to think about the future without Rand in it, but somehow she couldn't bring herself to let go yet—even though Isaac was sweet and would make a loving, God-fearing husband.

The long, hard winter gave up without a murmur in April. The nights were still cold, but the days warmed delightfully and melted the towering mounds of snow. Sarah looked eagerly for flowers, but all she saw was blowing sand and spindly brush. But Rand promised as soon as he had a break, he would take them on a picnic up the mountain where Rooster and Isaac told him was a spot full of violets.

When Rand left with a detachment heading for Fort Casper, Sarah took the opportunity to try to convince herself to go back home. It was almost time for Jacob and Amelia to move on. Sarah couldn't decide what to do, but for some reason, she wasn't at peace with the idea of leaving. Once Rand was back she would decide.

Chapter 13

Rand rolled over on his back and looked up at the dazzling display of stars above his head. They seemed closer and brighter out here. The long days on maneuvers and the free time in the evenings left a lot of time for thinking, and he'd been thinking a lot about God. Ever since Christmas there'd been a stirring in his soul. The sermon had started it. He'd tried to talk to Jessica about it, but she had looked at him as though he were mad. "Religion is for old people," she'd told him. "Going to church is fine. It's where one meets the best people. But don't take it too seriously."

A powerful wash of awe swept over him now as he gazed up at the glittering sky. It seemed he'd been fighting God for so long now. All his life. But now he just wanted to quit fighting, to trust in Someone bigger than himself. A quiet awakening to God's love had crept in over the past months, an awareness of His control. God was even in control of the mess his emotions were in. Surely He would tell him what to do about Sarah.

As he lay looking up into the night sky, he tried to really pray for the first time in his life. Oh, he'd prayed in prison, but it was more of a cry for help. Not a real understanding of who God was and what He wanted from him. "God, I know You're out there," he whispered. "And I want to belong to You and Your Son. I've made a mess of my life, but it's Yours if You want it—if You can forgive me." A sense of peace flooded him at these simple words, and he fought unfamiliar tears. God had heard him; he was sure of it! He could sense His presence as he drifted off to sleep, a thousand glad songs ringing in his head.

He awoke the next morning excited, but he couldn't remember at first why he was so happy. Then he remembered, and he whistled as he packed his bedroll.

"Yer awful chipper for so early in the morning," Rooster grumbled. "Keep yer whistles to yerself."

Rand laughed and trotted off to splash cold water from the creek on his face. Wouldn't Isaac be glad! He went about his tasks all that day with a cheerful expression and a kind word for everyone. Not that he'd been a grump before, but now he had a new reason to be joyful. His spirit was contagious, and soon the soldiers were working side by side singing as they restrung the telegraph wire. They had just finished when they heard loud yells from down in the ravine to their right.

"Injuns!" Rooster grabbed his rifle and vaulted onto his horse.

There was a wild scramble as the rest of the men clambered on their mounts and followed Rooster's mad charge.

"There's only three of them," Rand muttered as he fell into line. But the rest of the Sioux were hiding. As the main force leaped out from behind bushes and rocks, the charge of cavalry faltered. Instead of three, there were at least twenty-five.

"It's a trap," Captain Brown shouted. "Retreat! Retreat!"

But Rand was in the front line, and he knew retreat would just get him an arrow in the back. He slid off his horse and flung himself down behind a boulder. He took aim and began shooting desperately, pushing away the reality of his own situation. He just wanted to see his company get safely away, then he'd worry about how to get out himself.

"Git out of there, Boy," Rooster shouted, wheeling around on his horse and firing at a group of Indians crouching behind a rock. "It's better to say 'here's where he ran' than 'here's where he died'!" But Rand ignored him, and Rooster swore, then galloped away, still shouting for Rand to run.

Something bit into his flesh, and Rand grabbed his shoulder. His fingers were covered with blood when he pulled his hand away. A bullet? But these Indians just seemed to have bows and arrows. He heard another shot off to his left and felt a fiery sting on his left temple, then darkness claimed him.

When he awoke he was lying beside a fire. He groaned and tried to move, but his hands and feet were bound. "So you're finally awake."

He looked up at the familiar voice. Ben Croftner? Here? Where were the Indians? He shook his head to clear it. He must still be asleep. But a hard boot in his ribs convinced him he wasn't dreaming.

"So we meet again, old friend." Ben stooped and sneered in his face. "Did you really think I'd let you get away with taking my girl? But I'm going to do worse to you, Campbell. When I get through with you, you're going to wish that bullet had killed you outright."

"How—how did you get me away from the Indians?" Rand shook his head to clear it.

Ben smiled, but the expression was a cruel one. "I paid the Indians to stage an attack. They were just Laramie Loafers out for enough money to buy some liquor." He leaned forward and spat in Rand's face. "Are you ready to die, Campbell?"

"Yes. Are you?" Rand was surprised at his own calm assurance, but he *was* ready. Ever since last night.

Ben's gray eyes widened at Rand's gentle tone. "You'll pray for death before I'm through with you," he spat.

"You can't frighten me with heaven, Ben," Rand said softly.

Ben gaped at him, then stood with an angry oath. "Don't tell me you've gotten religion," he jeered. "If that doesn't beat all! Hey, Labe, Rand thinks he's going to heaven." He sneered and spat on the ground. "But he's going to find out what hell's really like before we're through."

Rand turned his head as Labe shuffled from behind a rock, fastening his suspenders. "Sorry to see you're mixed up in this, Labe," Rand said evenly.

Ben laughed again, an ugly laugh with no mirth in it. "Too bad you're mixed up with this, Labe," he mimicked. He tossed a shovel toward his younger brother. "Get digging."

Labe cast one agonized glance toward Rand's prone figure, then picked up the shovel and began to dig a small hole. He took a stake out of the knapsack beside the fire and pounded it into the hole, all the while keeping his eyes averted from Rand's gentle gaze.

Then Rand realized what Ben was planning. He was going to stake him out in the sun! A slow death, but a sure one in this deserted terrain. *Lord, help me to die with dignity,* he prayed silently. *And take care of Sarah.*

A few minutes later, Labe finished his task and threw the shovel down, then wiped the sweat from his face with his shirt sleeve. "I'm done, Ben," he said with a helpless look at Rand.

"I'm not blind. Grab his feet." Ben grabbed Rand by his wounded arm and dragged him toward the two posts.

Rand clenched his teeth to keep from crying out from the pain. Beads of sweat broke out on his forehead as he fought to retain consciousness.

Ben took a knife and began to cut his clothes off him. "Don't just stand there—help me, you fool," he snapped.

Labe shuffled forward and pulled off Rand's boots and socks. Ben grinned as he wound rawhide strips around Rand's wrists. "Think of me with Sarah as you're lying out here, old friend. Stage two of my plan is being put into action right now. You're little fiancée won't be too thrilled with this part of the plan, but her plan for Sarah was pure genius."

"What are you talking about?" Rand groaned as his wounded arm was wrenched above his head and bound to the stake. Sarah! What would become of her?

"Your little hussy cooked up a pretty good scheme to help me get Sarah. It's really what gave me the idea for this little rendezvous here."

"Jessica? What did she do?"

"You just stew about it while you're dying. But you can go knowing I'll take good care of Sarah."

Labe tied Rand's ankles to the stakes, then stood up, dusting his hands.

"You'll never get my blood off your hands if you leave me here, Labe," Rand whispered.

"Shut up." Ben kicked him in the side, then turned to his brother. "Get our things and let's get going."

Labe's mouth worked soundlessly, and he hesitated. For an instant, Rand thought he was going to defy his brother, but in the end, Labe dropped his head and shuffled off to obey Ben.

The two brothers swung onto their horses and stared down at Rand lying spread-eagled on the rocky ground. "So long, Rand." Ben smiled cruelly. "The best man always wins, you know. You were never ruthless enough."

Rand watched as they rode off, biting down on the pleading words struggling to escape. Wouldn't Ben love it if he begged for mercy? He turned his head away from the direct glare of the sun and began to pray for an early death.

After two days with no water, the burning sun scorching every inch of his exposed skin, Rand barely knew where he was. He muttered incoherently, sometimes shouting, sometimes screaming. The nights were bad too. The warm spring days plunged to cold nights, and Rand shuddered with the cold.

At one point he realized he was quoting the Twenty-third Psalm. " 'Yea, though I walk through the valley of the shadow of death, I will fear no evil.' " He was surprised he still remembered it after all these years. He'd learned it at his grandma's knee when he was eight. But this was the valley of the shadow of death, and somehow, he wasn't afraid to die. But something inside kept him from giving into the fever that racked his body, something stopped him from letting his spirit slip away.

The morning of the third day, he awoke relatively clearheaded after a night of blessed coolness. His lips felt thick, and his tongue filled his mouth. Today he would probably die, he knew. But at least he could see the land he loved with clear eyes one last time. His eyes closed tiredly several times, but he forced them open. This time when he fell asleep, he didn't think he would ever awaken. But the sun began to take its heavy toll, and he slipped into delirium for what must be the last time. His final thought was of Sarah, and he prayed for God to watch over her.

Chapter 14

It was a beautiful spring day. The girls were tired of being cooped up, and Sarah was too happy at the thought of Rand's imminent return to feel like doing any housework. She and Amelia decided to go for a stroll in the sunshine. They had barely stepped foot outside the door when Jessica hailed them.

"Sarah! Amelia!" She was dressed in a cream percale gown with cream lace lavished on it.

The girls stopped and waited as she came toward them. Sarah raised her eyebrows at Amelia. "Hello, Jessica," she said as the other girl stopped in front of them.

"I was hoping to find you," Jessica said. "I haven't seen much of you lately. Isaac has arranged for a detachment to escort Mother and I on a picnic. Would you like to come?"

Sarah and Amelia looked at one another. "Why?" Sarah asked. "You've made no secret of how you feel about me all winter. Why the change?"

Jessica smiled winningly. "I know, and I'm really sorry. I'd like us to be friends. Can't we start over? The fort is too small for enmity between us."

Sarah was silent a moment. There had to be some reason Jessica wasn't telling, but this might be an opportunity to get better acquainted. And she was weary of the tiny area she was allowed. She was not allowed off the fort premises without a guard of at least five soldiers. And it seemed the fort's parade ground got smaller and smaller every day.

"All right," she said. "We'll pack some food."

"Don't bother. Mother has packed enough for an entire troop." Jessica chatted easily as they strolled to the stable. Isaac had their mounts waiting for them, already saddled with sidesaddles. He helped them up, and they followed him west toward the purple mountains. A detail of twelve soldiers followed them.

Jessica kept up her smiling chatter, and gradually Sarah and Amelia relaxed. *It's just too bad she can't be like this all the time,* Sarah thought. They found a grassy area near an outcropping of rocks and spread out their blankets. The air was pungent with the scent of sage.

After lunch they decided to mount their horses and ride a bit over the rough terrain. Isaac was hoping to find some game.

Sarah let her horse pick its way up the winding trail, and breathing in the scent of sage, she reveled in the sense of well-being at being out of the confines of Fort Laramie. The men had been listening to Jessica tell a story about a ball in Boston and paid no attention as Sarah let her horse walk farther and farther away from them. Even Amelia didn't notice. At the top of the bluff, she slid down off her horse and sat down where she could look at the fort below her. She chuckled as she saw Isaac's sudden agitation when he discovered she was missing.

She raised a hand and opened her mouth to call to him, when she heard her horse whinny behind her. She stood quickly and turned to see an Indian brave, heavily painted, galloping toward her. She froze in sudden terror, then tried to put her foot into the stirrup and mount. But the Indian was upon her in an instant. He leaned down and scooped her up, his horse barely pausing as he caught her.

Sarah struggled to get away, gagging at the odor of bear grease and sweat, but his arm was like a steel band around her waist. She screamed, certain she was doomed. But the crack of a rifle sounded, and the Indian slumped against her, and his arm loosened. She wrenched free and fell from the horse. Stunned from the swiftness of both the attack and her rescue, she lay on the hard ground as the Indian wheeled away, his face glazed with pain, holding a hand to his bloody shoulder.

Rooster galloped out of a stand of trees, his cap gone and spiky red hair standing straight on end. "What's wrong with you, Gal? Don't you got no sense at all?" He slid down off his horse and pulled her to her feet. "Git on that horse now!" He shoved her up into the saddle. "There's prob'ly more of them sneakin' varmints around. We gotta git to the fort." He slapped her horse's rump, and they started down the bluff.

Isaac and Amelia, with the rest of the soldiers, met them at the bottom. Isaac's face was tight with anger. But before he could say anything, they heard a whoop behind them and turned to see a group of Indians charging toward them. "Get going!" Isaac fell back and began firing at the Indians to give Rooster time to get the girls to the safety of the fort.

Amelia and Sarah kicked their horses into a mad dash for the fort as Mrs. DuBois screamed and moved faster than Sarah had ever seen. Jessica kicked her horse into a gallop, her face calm, and the rest of the soldiers brought up the rear. Once Sarah heard a bullet whistle by her head as she clung to the horse's back. Then her horse stumbled, and she catapulted into a thornbush. Her skin was pierced in a dozen places, and she lay there too stunned to even move.

A young brave galloped up, brandishing a knife. Before she could even think to scream, he cut her loose from the thornbush and hauled her up in front of him. Sarah tried to struggle away, but her head was throbbing from the fall, and soon darkness descended.

Rand cried out and thrashed as the cooling temperature awoke him, shivering as the chill breeze swept over him. He vaguely remembered a dark face swimming before his eyes off and on and someone forcing water down his parched throat. He tried to move and found his hands and feet were unbound. He looked to his right and saw that Ranger was tied to a tree nearby. Rand sat up slowly, his head spinning. Beside him lay a skin plump with water. He took it and drank greedily, then wiped his mouth. A buffalo robe covered the lower half of his body. Puzzled, he looked around. Who had cut him free? He frowned and tried to concentrate on the dark face at the edge of his memory, but nothing more would come.

Where were Ben and Labe? He looked around slowly as his head continued to clear. The sun lay low in the sky. Only an hour or so of daylight was left. He swallowed another swig of water and shook his head to clear it, then stood to his feet. He swayed, then staggered toward his horse. A pile of soft buckskin lay at Ranger's feet. He stooped and picked up a pair of leather breeches and a calico shirt. Grimacing with pain, he pulled them on over his scorched skin. They were a little loose, which helped some, but they still chafed against his throbbing skin.

Some jerky was strung over the pommel of his saddle, and his mouth watered when he saw it. He stuffed some in his mouth as he leaned his head against Ranger's flank. Fortified with food and water, he forced himself to swing up into the saddle. He swayed weakly and caught at the pommel to steady himself. He had to make it. Sarah depended on it. He suddenly remembered what Ben had said about Jessica. What did Ben mean about Jessica's scheme? How could she be involved with a man like Croftner?

He urged Ranger to a trot and clung tightly to avoid slipping out of the saddle. Within an hour, he was in familiar territory. Maybe he could make Fort Laramie before it was fully dark. But his horse was exhausted, and he was forced to walk. He was still weak from his ordeal, and he had to stop often to catch his breath. He stopped for the night about five miles southwest of the fort on a bluff. Barely conscious, he crawled into his bedroll and was soon fast asleep.

The next morning, he awoke ravenous. His sunburn still throbbed, but he was stronger. His store of food was all gone, and his ammunition was low. But he was almost there, so he took his rifle and made his way down to the river. It wasn't long before he'd shot a jackrabbit. It was tough and stringy as he ate it hot from the spit, but it would do. At least it would give him the strength he needed to get home.

He saddled up Ranger and swung up onto the horse. In spite of the deceptive distances, he knew he'd be home soon. The fort drew nearer very quickly. Now he could make out the individual buildings. There was the commissary and the stable. The barracks and the hospital. Was he too late? He urged Ranger into a gallop.

Rand arrived about eight o'clock. There seemed to be an uncommon amount of activity going on as dozens of soldiers jostled one another in their hurry to catch a mount and saddle up. He heard Rooster, his voice shrill with emotion, calling for a fresh horse.

His heart pounding, Rand spotted Jacob and Isaac saddling horses beside the post headquarters. He kicked his mount into a canter and pulled up beside them. "What's going on?"

Jacob's voice was grim. "Indians got Sarah."

The clipped words hit Rand like a blow. Not Sarah! He felt light-headed with shock. "When?" And he'd been worried about Ben and Jessica's plan!

"Yesterday afternoon. We're just back for fresh horses and supplies. You coming?"

"Let me get a fresh mount." Outwardly he was calm, but inwardly he was churning with a cauldron of emotion. Anger, guilt, love. He realized in a blinding instant what a fool he'd been. He and Sarah had something precious, and he had treated it as something of inconsequence. And now it might be too late. He shuddered at the thought of what Sarah had perhaps already endured.

He followed Isaac and Jacob out of the fort as they caught up with Rooster on his way to pick up the trail.

Just before dusk they found a spot where a large group of horses had trampled the ground. "Some of these prints belong to white men," Rand said, kneeling in the dust. "Look here, Isaac. Shod horse prints and boot heels."

"Looks like two, maybe three, men," Isaac said with a frown.

Rooster came up behind them. "Sure am glad to see you, Boy. You look bad, though. Yer skin's blistered and peeling. What's happened to you? How'd you git away from them redskins?"

"I'll tell you later," Rand said. Finding Sarah was more important.

Rooster nodded. "What'd ya find, boys?" he asked, kneeling beside them.

"What do you make of this, Rooster?" Rand gestured to the telltale marks. "What would white men be doing with a pack of Indians?"

Rooster studied the ground for a moment without replying. "Don't look too good, young fellers. Don't look too good at all." He stood up and scratched his red hair. "Injuns and white men. Renegades, most likely." His brown eyes were compassionate as he turned to Rand. "Looks like maybe they got Sarah."

Rand shuddered. He felt as though his whole body turned suddenly to ice. Jacob clapped a hand on his brother's shoulder. "Don't give up hope yet, Rand.

We'll find her. White men move slower than Indians. We have a better chance of catching them now."

Rand nodded, but inside himself he knew Sarah was lost to him. And it was all his fault she was out there with depraved men in the wilderness far from her family and all she loved.

He felt almost mad with worry and grief as Rooster found the trail, and the detachment followed it up into the Laramie Mountains. The landscape grew more barren as loose rock over a bed of sand made travel more and more treacherous. As they rode, Rand told Rooster and Jacob about his ordeal and what Ben had said.

By the time it was too dark to follow the trail any longer, they were near the peak of the mountain. The night air was already cold, and a crisp tang to the air mingled with the scent of sage and the smoke from the fire as Rand unloaded his supplies and prepared to bed down near Jacob and Isaac.

"I'll take the first watch," Rooster said, taking his rifle out of its sling on his horse and walking over to a large boulder thrusting up through the thin soil.

Rand lay down on the hard ground and stared up at the sky, vaguely aware of the crackling fire to his right as he gazed at the bright panorama of stars above his head. The fire pushed back the blackness of the night, but nothing could push away the blackness in his soul as he thought about what Sarah might be going through right now. The plaintive howl of a pack of coyotes somewhere in the valley below him somehow added to his anguish. He prayed fervently for Sarah's safety, but he was so consumed with guilt, he couldn't keep his thoughts together. The fire died to embers before he finally slept.

When Sarah awoke, she found herself on a pallet on a hard, dirt-packed floor. She sat up slowly and looked around the tiny, one-room cabin. A rank odor rose from the grimy blanket over her, and she pushed it off with a shudder of disgust as she rose to get a better look at her surroundings.

Her head throbbed, and the room spun around as she took a step toward the small, oilskin-covered windows. She paused until her head cleared, then moved gingerly toward the door. She raised the latch and tugged at the door, but it refused to budge no matter how hard she pulled. She leaned her throbbing head against it and burst into tears.

Think, she had to think! Those savages would be back any minute. She could still see the painted face of the Indian who had grabbed her. But why wasn't she at an Indian camp? And whose old cabin was this anyway?

But there were no answers to her questions, so she pushed away the tears and looked around for another avenue of escape. Her body ached in a hundred places from her contact with the thornbush, and she limped as she picked through the debris on the dirt floor.

She found a small stool among the litter of papers, old tin cans, and rags and dragged it under the window. Standing on the stool, she pulled the torn oilcloth away from the window and tried to pull herself through.

But the tiny opening was much too small for even Sarah's slim shoulders, and the stool collapsed under her weight, one leg rolling useless across the floor, as she fell to the ground. She gave in to helpless tears again. *What am I going to do, Lord?* she prayed. She was hungry and thirsty and scared. Judging by the light, it was close to noon, so she must have been unconscious nearly twenty-four hours. It was no wonder her mouth was like cotton.

She sat there until the sun no longer shone through the east window, feeling more and more abandoned. What if she were left there to die with no food or water? Panic at the thought overwhelmed her, and she ran to the door and pounded on it. She heard the sound of horses, then the click of a lock being pulled back on the other side of the door.

Trembling, she rose to her feet and faced the door, so frightened she felt faint. *Help me, Lord,* she prayed as the door swung open.

The sudden flood of sunlight into the dark cabin blinded her momentarily, then she blinked in surprise as she recognized the two figures framed in the doorway.

"Be—Ben?" she croaked through her parched throat.

"You don't look too good, Love." Ben grinned.

Although she would rather anyone else rescue her, Ben was a welcome surprise from the savages she'd expected. She had opened her mouth to thank him when she noticed how unsurprised he seemed to see her.

"Been awake long?" he asked.

"You knew I was here?" Her voice was halting and incredulous.

"Of course." He kicked some refuse away from the door. "Shut the door, Labe." He reached out and touched a lock of her hair, and she flinched away. His lips tightened as he dropped his hand. "The Indians were eager for the guns I offered for the 'soldier girl with hair like the sun.' But I must give credit where credit's due. Jessica came up with the idea."

Sarah felt the blood drain from her face. Ben and Jessica had arranged for her kidnapping? But why? Her lips quivered as she forced back tears of weakness. She didn't want to give him the satisfaction of seeing her cry.

"Aren't you interested in why you're here?" The cruel light in Ben's eyes grew. "Well, let me tell you what I have planned. Remember that marriage we were supposed to have? You should have been my wife by now. Well, I aim to put that to rights." He pulled her to him and wrapped a hand in her hair.

A moan escaped Sarah's tight lips as he pulled her hair even tighter. "Too bad about your beloved Rand," he sneered.

A shudder shook Sarah's frame, and she closed her eyes. "Wha–what do you mean?"

"Just that your precious Rand is dead by now." He smiled unpleasantly.

Rand dead? She wouldn't believe it. After all, she'd believed Ben before— and look what had happened. She opened her eyes and stared into Ben's face. How had she ever considered marrying him?

The silence grew heavy as Ben stared back at her. Labe's nervous shuffle broke the silence. Sarah turned her eyes toward him. "Please," she whispered. "Please, Labe, help me."

Labe's eyes darted from his brother's set face back to Sarah's. "Come on, Ben. Let's take her back. She won't say nothin', will you, Sarah?"

"No. No, of course not." Sarah wet her dry lips with the tip of her tongue. "Just take me back to the fort, and I'll say you rescued me from the Indians. You'll be heroes."

Ben's lip curled in disgust. "You must take me for a fool!" He let go of Sarah's hair and shoved her off her feet, then spun toward Labe. "Get out!" He pushed his brother toward the door.

"Help me, Jesus," Sarah said under her breath. While Ben's back was turned, her hand groped along the dirty floor; her seeking fingers closed around the broken stool leg. As Ben bent over her, his hand gripping her shoulder, she twisted around, and with one last desperate effort, she smashed the stool leg against his head. He slumped against her without a sound.

Scrambling to her feet, she rushed to the door and pulled it open. She blinked as she surveyed her surroundings. The tiny cabin was in a small clearing surrounded by heavy forest. A meadow filled with wildflowers was in front of the door, and a narrow, barely discernible path ran through the middle of the meadow. She caught a glimpse of Labe's head over near a stand of aspen.

Watching to make sure Labe didn't see her, she stumbled along the path, casting furtive glances behind her to make sure neither Labe nor Ben was fol- lowing her. The path narrowed further, then disappeared at the bank of a small stream. Sarah sank to her knees and drank.

Birds twittered from the budding branches above her head, but that was the only sound as she followed the stream into the forest. The stream soon joined a larger river, and Sarah hurried along the bank. She wondered how long it would be before Ben regained consciousness. He would pursue her, she knew; she had to get as far away as she could.

When the sun told her it was midafternoon, Sarah stopped beside the river. Her head was light from lack of food, and she had to rest for a moment. She sank down to rest on a large rock and looked around, trying to think. She had to find something to eat, she realized, or she'd never make it. Wearily, she forced herself to her feet again and began searching the bushes, grateful for the forest lore Rand had taught her when they were growing up. After several minutes, she found some berries she knew were edible, despite their bitter taste, and she crammed handfuls into her mouth, grimacing at the flavor. Using her fingernails, she dug the roots of another edible plant out of the ground. She washed the soil off in the river, then crunched them down.

A little clearer headed, she stared along the riverbank again. She would make it. God was with her, no matter where she was. With His help, she would find her way back to her family.

But by the next morning, she was no longer so certain. The mosquitoes had swarmed around her all night, a living haze of biting misery. She was weak now from hunger and fatigue, and the night's noises had driven her nearly mad with fear. Coyotes had howled, their voices closer than she had ever heard them, and once a large animal had snuffled right next to her, causing her to freeze, too terrified to move for several long minutes.

Now, as the sun rose in the sky, her steps were slow and dragging. She rounded a curve in the river, forcing herself forward, then stood still.

She was face-to-face with a band of ten or so Sioux braves. Their faces were painted, and one young brave had a livid scar across his cheek. The blood drained from her face as they came toward her.

Chapter 15

A s the men rode silently through the woods, Rand was filled with a desperation that pushed him on.

Jacob reined his horse in suddenly and dismounted. He bent over and picked something off the ground.

"What is it?" Rand's voice was hoarse. He held out his hand, and Jacob dropped a brooch into it.

He'd seen it many times. The delicate filigree rose customarily adorned the bodice of Sarah's dress. Rand had given it to her for her birthday the year he left for the war. He stared at the dainty pin, and his face turned hard as he fought to control the pain that surged through him. "At least we know we're on the right trail," he said at last. He managed a tight smile. "Everyone always said Rooster could follow a wood tick on solid rock." He picked up the reins, gripped by a renewed sense of urgency. "Let's get going."

Rooster led the way, his keen eyes following the fresh trail. They splashed across the stream and picked their way up a steep hill. Rooster glanced around at the silent men as they paused at the top of the hill. "Reckon we all fell a little bit in love with that gal," he said morosely.

"Don't say it like she's gone!" Isaac's knuckles were white where they gripped the reins. "We can't be more than a few hours behind her." He urged his horse forward and took the lead through a line of trees.

Rand and Jacob, following close behind, reined in at the sound of a startled snort. Two bear cubs bleated and rolled toward their mother. She swung around from her perusal of a fallen tree trunk, ready to face the threat to her offspring.

Rand's eyes met the grizzly's, and he read the rage there. She roared angrily as she rose to her hind feet, a good seven feet tall. Her mouth wide with another roar, she dropped to all fours and charged toward them.

Jacob was closest, and his horse shied. Caught off guard, he fell to the ground. He grabbed for his gun, but it had fallen from his holster when he catapulted from the saddle. He scrabbled backward, away from the grizzly.

"Lay still, Boy!" Rooster said softly. He aimed his Winchester at the bear's head, just as Rand frantically aimed his own gun. The rifles barked, but not before the grizzly swiped at Jacob's leg with her claws. She swung her head in dull surprise, then crashed to the ground beside Jacob.

Blood was already pouring from Jacob's leg, soaking his torn pants. "Quick, hand me the canteen," Rand shouted, kneeling beside his brother.

Rooster handed him the canteen. "Clean it good, Boy, or it'll fester for sure. No telling where that bear's claws have been."

Rand ripped the fabric away from the wound and splashed it with water again and again. Jacob's flesh was flayed so badly that the bone gleamed through the shredded skin. Rand tried to keep the dismay from his face as he bound the wound with a clean handkerchief.

Jacob's face was pale, and sweat sheened his forehead as he gritted his teeth against the pain. "Sorry, Rand." His face contracted in pain and frustration. "We were so close."

Rand patted his brother's leg. Isaac crouched beside him and gave Jacob a sip of water. "How bad is it?" he asked Rand softly.

"Bad." Rand shook his head and turned away so Jacob wouldn't hear. "It's deep in his thigh muscle—to the bone. He'll be in even more pain when the shock wears off. We need to find someplace for him to hole up." He paused bleakly. "He won't be riding for awhile."

Isaac nodded. "I hunted this area last year. If I remember right, there's a small cabin just beyond the woods to our north. Let's make for there. It's almost dark anyway."

Rand fought despair as they made a rough travois to carry Jacob. This delay could be deadly for Sarah.

Isaac led the way through the trees. Rand spared a thought for the motherless bear cubs, but he knew there was nothing they could do for them. He found himself smiling, thinking that if Sarah were there, she would probably have insisted they catch the cubs and bring them with them to raise. His smile faded, turning to a frown of pain, as he was washed anew with fear for Sarah.

The light was murky by the time they stepped out of the forest and into a small meadow clearing. The cabin squatted against the sloping north side, and they hurried toward its meager haven.

The open door creaked in the gentle breeze as they swung down off their horses. "Me and the men will take care of the horses," Rooster said. "Git that boy inside. Better clean the wound again too."

Rand and Isaac carefully lifted Jacob off the travois and carried him into the dark cabin. "Light a lantern, Isaac," Rand said as they lay Jacob on a moldy mattress in the corner. Rand eased his brother's boots off and began to untie the handkerchief on Jacob's leg. Isaac lit the lantern, and the dim glow pushed the shadows back.

The wound had reopened from the jostling on the travois, and Jacob lay senseless. One of the other men came in with a small flask in his hand. "Rooster says he brought it along for medicinal purposes."

Rand uncapped the flask and poured a generous amount into Jacob's gaping wound. Jacob thrashed and cried out, then lapsed back into unconsciousness as Rand rebound the wound.

"I reckon that's all we can do," he said to Isaac.

"Except pray."

Rand looked at Isaac, then back at his brother. He nodded and knelt on the floor, Isaac beside him as they each asked God for His help. After a few minutes, Isaac got to his feet, but Rand stayed where he was. *Help me find Sarah, Lord. And once I do, please take things into Your own hands and clean up the mess I've made. I've been so selfish, following my own way. Please guide us now and show us what to do. Take care of Jacob and heal his leg. And take care of Sarah. You know where she is, and only You can lead us to her.*

At last he stood up, a new peace filling his heart. He felt his first real sense of hope that they might find Sarah alive and well.

They made up their beds on the dirt floor of the cabin. Rand checked on Jacob several times throughout the night, as his brother thrashed restlessly. Finally at dawn, he touched Jacob's forehead and found it cool. He breathed a sigh of relief as he pulled on his boots and woke the others.

They were eating a cold breakfast of hardtack and dried meat when Rooster burst into the cabin. "She was here! Our little gal was here!"

"What are you talking about?" Rand jumped up and gripped Rooster's arm.

"Our Sarah was here. Look!" He held out a scrap of familiar green and yellow calico.

"Where did you find it?" Rand wanted to dance with joy. God was already moving.

"Down by the stream. And I found her trail—she's alone!" Rooster said.

Rand smoothed the scrap of fabric, almost giddy with relief. She'd gotten away from whoever had held her captive. "Let's check Jacob," Rand said, impatient to be on their way.

Jacob was sitting up, sipping a thin gruel made of water and hardtack. He gave them a wan smile. "Sorry, Rand. Guess I won't be in any shape to travel for a few days."

Rand nodded. "I'm just thankful you're alive, Brother." He grinned, anxious to wipe the look of guilt off Jacob's face. "I have to wonder, though, if you didn't get in that bear's way just so you'd have a good story to tell back at Bedlam."

He waited until Jacob smiled weakly, then he turned to the group of privates who were leaning against the cabin. "I want you soldiers to stay with Jacob until he can travel; then get him back to the fort. Isaac and Rooster will come with me to find Sarah." He cocked an eyebrow at his two friends. "Okay with you?"

"Let's get going," Isaac said.

Rooster nodded. "I'll saddle up the horses."

"That gal will never make an Injun," Rooster muttered fifteen minutes later. "She leaves a path even a greenhorn could follow."

Rand grinned in agreement. *Thank You, Lord.*

Near noon, they rounded a bend in the river they were following, and Rooster stopped short. He whistled in dismay. Sarah's clear tracks were obliterated by unshod pony tracks and moccasin prints. "Bad news, fellows. Looks like the Injuns caught her."

Rand stood staring at the telltale marks, his heart pounding. So close to finding her, and now this! He swallowed hard as he fought to hold onto his new faith and hope. "Can you tell what kind of Indians?"

"Hard to say, but I'd guess Sioux."

They followed the trail for the rest of the afternoon. Rand struggled to pray, but despair kept rearing its head, coming between him and his sense of God's presence. *Dear Lord, please take care of her.*

Chapter 16

The band of Sioux gave Sarah jerky and fresh water before jabbering and pulling her to her feet. In spite of her terror, she was grateful for the food. She'd never been so hungry in her life. The jerky was tough, but she didn't know when anything had tasted so good.

The young brave with the scar on his face pulled her up behind him on his pony, and the entire band began to pick its way along a faint trail through the forest. Sarah would never have recognized it as a trail, but once they had followed it for awhile she was able to see the slight impression from other Indian ponies. Twilight was sending out long golden shadows by the time they turned the crest of a hill and saw campfires and tepee shapes below them in the valley beside a stream.

Children jabbered, and squaws stared at her with hostile eyes as the braves paraded through the camp, raising their bows and spears in triumphant shrieks. Sarah fought unconsciousness as she tried not to droop wearily against the young brave's back. Her vision blurred and doubled as the brave stopped beside a tepee and slid to the ground. He pulled her down, and she fought his grip on her arms.

"Let go of me."

He grinned at the tired anger in her voice, then thrust her inside the tepee and closed the flap, encasing her in darkness. She was too weary to do more than stumble wearily to a soft pile of furs and sink into instant sleep.

When Sarah awoke, she was in a dark, cool place. Strange chanting filled her head, and she heard the rumbles of unfamiliar voices. But the words were all jumbled together, and nothing made any sense. She tried to rise and was surprised to find she could move her hands and feet. She had thought the Indians would tie her up so she couldn't escape in the night. The sounds outside were distant and not threatening, so she snuggled back down in the furs and fell asleep again.

The next time she awoke, she was not alone. A beautiful Indian girl knelt beside her and offered her a bowl of stew that smelled wonderful. She took it and began to eat eagerly. It was flavored with unfamiliar herbs, but the meat and vegetables were tasty, and she ate it quickly. The young squaw smiled, then quickly stepped outside and closed the flap on the tepee behind her.

Sarah's shoulder protested as she got to her feet. Swaying weakly, she started toward the flap in the tepee, then staggered and sank back onto the ground. She was just too tired, she realized, to push herself any longer. She sat back down on the bearskin rug to await further developments.

While she was waiting, she looked around curiously. She'd always wondered what a tepee looked like inside, but she'd never been in one. Not even Morning Song's.

The tepee was large, at least ten feet in diameter. In the center was a tripod arrangement that supported a pot over what were now stone-cold ashes, although a pile of buffalo chips lay heaped to the side. Spears and knives hung from the lodge poles, and buffalo robes were piled to one side. Pelts of various animals—beaver, wolverine, raccoon, and antelope—were in various stages of tanning on a rack of some kind.

She dragged her eyes away from the furnishings of the lodge as the flap opened, and the Indian brave came in. There was a fierce scowl on his young face, and Sarah's heart pounded in trepidation. It was the youth with the terrible scar on his cheek she'd seen before. "He–hello," she stammered. Then she smiled as she remembered the Sioux Isaac had taught her. *"Wash ta cola,"* she stammered hopefully.

The brave merely grunted, his black eyes roaming over Sarah's bright, tangled hair. He reached out and touched a bright lock.

She forced herself not to flinch away. "Sarah." She gestured at herself. "My name is Sarah."

The brave nodded in sudden comprehension, a smile of delight winking across his face so quickly Sarah thought she'd imagined it.

The flap lifted again as the young Sioux maiden entered. She reminded Sarah of a young antelope, all long limbs yet curiously graceful. Sarah's heart clenched as she thought of Morning Song.

"You awake," she said, her dark eyes liquid with a hidden smile.

"You speak English." Sarah smiled in relief.

"Little. Little English. Live at mission one year." The girl squatted and offered her another bowl of stew. "You eat."

She wasn't really hungry any longer, but since she intended to escape at the first opportunity, she knew she needed to build up her strength as quickly as possible.

The brave grunted again and said something to the girl. "Little Wolverine say you belong to bluecoat with eyes like eagle. Soldier not kill Little Wolverine in battle. Why?"

Sarah searched her memory, but she couldn't remember Rand mentioning an incident like he described. "I don't know," she admitted reluctantly.

The girl translated to the young Indian, and he fired a volley of words back at her. "He say bluecoat with eagle eyes spare Little Wolverine. Little Wolverine save you." She pretended to weigh her hands until they were on an equal level.

"Yes. Even. Thank you." Sarah looked into the dark eyes beside her and thanked God for sending such an unlikely rescuer. They weren't going to hurt her.

Sarah's strength grew daily on the good food White Beaver, the Indian girl, brought. White Beaver gave her a beautifully beaded Indian dress to replace her torn dress and braided her hair.

She and the young maiden grew to be friends—she felt an almost uncanny sense of friendship and identification with her as if she'd known her all their lives—and by the third day, Sarah felt at home in the busy Sioux camp. The children were curious about her and soon lost their shyness when she appeared. White Beaver was happy to translate their innumerable questions.

But Sarah grew more anxious daily. Where was Rand? Was there any truth to what Ben had told her? Was he looking for her? She was filled with trepidation as she thought of having to explain that Ben had taken her and what his intentions had been. What if Rand blamed her? What if he thought she'd encouraged Ben to follow her out here?

"Why you so sad?" White Beaver asked as they waded in the stream fishing just after dawn on the fourth day.

Sarah's eyes filled with tears as she clambered out of the water and sat on a large rock, White Beaver following close behind her. "I miss my friends," she said simply. "And I worry about the bad man who tried to hurt me. He may be looking for me still."

White Beaver nodded slowly, her dark eyes compassionate. "Little Wolverine take you back soon. Then debt to bluecoat is paid. And Little Wolverine say Sarah cry no more. He know man who hurt Sarah. He make sure he not hurt Sarah again." She reached over and touched Sarah's arm shyly. "White Beaver miss Sarah."

"I'll miss you too," she said hoarsely. "Thank Little Wolverine for me. You are both good friends." Just a few days with the Indians had shown her how alike they all were. And she felt sad knowing their way of life would soon be no more. She knew Little Wolverine and the other braves had no idea how many settlers were clamoring to take away the Indian hunting grounds. And Rand might actually have to fight Little Wolverine someday. She couldn't stand the thought of the bright young brave lying dead on a field of battle.

She picked up her string of fish and followed White Beaver back to camp.

Why was life never simple?

Rand and his companions followed the trail as it led on through rocky hills and sagebrush-choked gullies. When they ran low on rations, Rand and Isaac brought down an antelope and cut it into jerky, smoking it overnight over a low fire. Rand alternated between worry for Sarah and concern for Jacob back at the cabin.

Four days from the fort, they awoke to a leaden sky with a stiff, moisture-laden breeze whipping across the stark landscape. Desperation clouded all three of their faces. If it rained, the trail would be washed away. And they were so close! They hurriedly saddled up and rode out.

But their haste was useless. The storm struck with its usual force in the mountains. Hail rained down on them, and they were forced to take shelter under an overhanging cliff wall. Then the thunder boomed around them as torrents of rain fell and lightning crackled overhead.

"We've got to git to high ground!" Rooster shouted above the crashing thunder. "This here's a real gully washer. There's liable to be a flash flood anytime!"

Staying as close to the rock wall as possible, they led their horses up the rocky hill. Halfway up the side of the slope, Rand looked down and saw a mountain of water sweep away the tangle of sagebrush and aspen in the gully where they'd been only minutes before.

"This here's prob'ly high enough," Rooster said, pausing under an overhang.

They crouched there, hugging the side of the rocky wall. The horses shifted restlessly, but the men managed to hang onto the reins.

Finally it was over. Steamy mist shimmered in the heat as the sun broke through the clouds, and they emerged from their sanctuary. Rand was appalled at the changed landscape. The flash flood had carved new gullies and filled in old low spots, as the raging water carried away everything in its path. He stood surveying the damage, as dawning dismay swept over him. The trail to Sarah would never have survived such rain.

Rooster saw his consternation. "Don't take on so, Boy. We ain't done by a long shot."

"What do you mean? How will we ever find her now?"

"I've scouted these parts before. Over yonder peak is one of the Injuns' favorite camping grounds. We'll just mosey on over there, and maybe we'll find your Sarah."

Galvanized, Rand leaped astride his horse as Rooster led the way, and Isaac brought up the rear. By nightfall they were in a line of trees overlooking an Indian campground. The tepees glowed with color from the sunset. They caught glimpses of dimly illuminated figures moving around the campfires.

"Now what?" Rand asked.

"Now we stay put 'til later when they're sleepin'." The old Indian fighter took off his hat and smoothed his red hair. "Then we sneak in and look around for your Miss Sarah."

They tied their horses to a tree and hunkered down to wait. Rand kept watch, while the other two tried to catch a little sleep. He was just about to wake Isaac for his turn at watch when he noticed a movement just below their lookout. He cocked his rifle, and the other two were awake in an instant.

"What is it?" Isaac whispered.

"Don't know. Thought I saw something." Rand searched the spot where he thought he'd seen the movement. But he froze when he heard a sound on the slope above them. He swiveled his head and faced a row of fiercely painted Indians holding spears, all pointed at him and his friends.

They were obviously outnumbered, so when one of the Indians motioned for them to drop their guns, they obeyed. The Sioux bound their hands with brutal efficiency, then marched them down the slope to the camp. They thrust them roughly into a large tepee and fastened the flap firmly behind them. Rand could see the outline of a guard through the teepee's buckskin.

The three men looked at one another with grim faces. Some rescuers they were. Now they were all in the same uncomfortable spot with Sarah, if she were even here. "Why didn't they kill us outright?" Rand asked.

"They're probably saving us for some special ceremony," Isaac said, sitting down on a buffalo robe. "We'd best get some sleep. They'll be on their guard tonight, but maybe tomorrow we can find a way to escape."

They sat down and tried to relax, but Rand couldn't sleep. Was Sarah here— maybe only a few feet away?.

Rand sat up just before dawn, too keyed up to lie down any longer. He sat listening to the sounds of the Indian camp beginning to stir around him. He understood none of the guttural language outside as he heard squaws light fires and call to one another.

Diffused light gradually lifted the darkness inside their tepee as the bustle outside increased. Finally, the flap lifted, and a young Indian brave stepped through, followed by an Indian girl. Rand immediately recognized him as the brave he had spared in the battle the week before. And he was the one whose face he'd seen in his delirium!

"I told you you'd be sorry." Rooster recognized the brave too.

But Rand felt no fear as he looked into the youth's calm, dark eyes. Then the Indian girl stepped forward and smiled at him. "Do not fear. Little Wolverine your friend. But he say, 'Why you not shoot him?' "

Rand hesitated. His reasons would probably sound silly, but there was no help for it. "Little Wolverine reminded me of my younger brother. You know the word *brother?*"

The girl nodded. "One who shares mother and father?"

Rand nodded. "I have a younger brother about the same age as Little Wolverine. I saw that same brave spirit in Little Wolverine."

The girl smiled as she translated. The youth's black eyes never left Rand's face as she explained. Then he nodded and barked an order to the girl. She gave Rand a slight smile, then slipped out the flap of the tepee. Moments later, Sarah stepped through the flap behind the Indian girl.

"Sarah!"

Sarah's green eyes widened, and she gasped as Rand shouted her name and started toward her. "Rand?" She ran into his open arms, and over his shoulder she saw Rooster and Isaac beaming at her.

"Who did this to you?" His fist clenched as he looked at her bruised and battered face. Whoever had hurt her would have to pay. "And how'd you get away from the renegades who had you?"

"I—I came to a cabin," she stammered. She flushed at Rooster's gaze, his curly red eyebrows cocked questioningly, but she wanted to talk to Rand about Ben when they were alone. "Later," she whispered to Rand. She turned to the two Sioux standing silent behind her. "I would have died if it weren't for my friends. I'd like you to meet Little Wolverine and White Beaver."

Rand held out his hand to the two Sioux. "I don't know what to say—how to thank you."

The girl smiled. "Sarah and Sioux friends. We miss her. You leave in morning for soldier fort, but first we have feast."

Rand could sense the goodwill coming from the two before him, and he thanked God in his heart for working all things out for good just as He'd promised. It was almost too much to take in that his impulsive act of mercy could have such far-reaching consequences.

They spent the day with their new friends. Sarah insisted on smearing a foul-smelling ointment White Beaver had given her on Rand's peeling skin. It soothed his sore and itchy burn amazingly well. As they sat beside the stream and talked, Rand told her about his salvation, and she wept tears of joy that God had answered her prayers.

As some of the women prepared a feast for the evening, others were kept busy taking down tepees and preparing to move camp. "What's going on?" Rand asked White Beaver. The girl drew him off to one side. "We go to make war with Red Cloud at Powder River."

Rand's face mirrored his shock. "Don't go, Little Wolverine. I don't want anything to happen to you. Tell him not to go," he appealed to White Beaver.

The Sioux brave drew himself up straight and taut as the Indian girl translated. "He say, 'Should Little Wolverine stay in camp like dog and let others fight for his family? Soon people have no hunting grounds. Whites take all. Red Cloud say Indians must fight or be forced to farm.' "

The brave spat in the dust. "He say, 'Braves not dirt diggers.' " Little Wolverine's face softened as he spoke again, and White Beaver continued to translate. "But he say, 'Rand and Little Wolverine brothers. They not fight.' "

"No, my brother." Rand laid a hand on Little Wolverine's shoulder. "We'll not fight. And someday I hope we meet again."

The brave clasped his hand over Rand's large, square hand on his shoulder as though he understood his words before White Beaver translated them. His dark eyes were warm with friendship.

Rand wasn't sure how the bond between them had come to be, but it was there as surely as the one between his real brothers, and he'd known it as soon as he looked into the Indian's eyes at their first confrontation. "May God keep you safe, my brother," he said.

The next morning, they said their good-byes to their new friends as soon as dawn broke.

Chapter 17

A melia watched the hills surrounding the fort every day, anxious for word of Sarah. The main detachment had returned, hauling Jacob home two days ago, but no one had heard a word from the three who pushed on after Sarah.

After breakfast on the third day of Jacob's return, Amelia sat on the porch railing, watching as the cavalry prepared for maneuvers. Joel sat listlessly beside her. "Boots and saddles." Captain Brown shouted the familiar command to mount, and the cavalry swung up on their horses and rode out of the fort.

Jacob limped across the parade ground to join her in her vigil. "The commander says there is still no word. They haven't shown up at Fort Casper or the Platte River Bridge Station."

Amelia burst into tears and buried her face against Jacob's chest. "I have a terrible feeling she's dead," she sobbed. "And we'll never know for sure."

Jacob patted and soothed her as best he could. Joel stood up suddenly and pointed west. "What's that?"

Jacob turned and looked, then grew suddenly still, his eyes scanning the slope to the west of the fort. He pulled away from Amelia. "Wait here."

"What is it?" she protested as he took off in a running limp for the stable. But then she saw four riders coming down the rocky incline toward the fort. And one of them, dressed in buckskin like a squaw, had sunny red-gold hair. With a sob of relief, she picked up her skirts and ran after Jacob.

"They've got her!" a sentry to the west of the fort shouted as soldiers ran from the mess hall and barracks to greet their beloved Sarah. Amelia wasn't the only one who had just about given up hope.

Soldiers lined the road and cheered as the four travelers, tired and dusty, rode into the fort.

Sarah had never been so tired in her life. Surrounded by the soldiers, she searched the crowd for Amelia. She wanted a bath and bed.

"Sarah!" Amelia waved to her from the stoop in front of the general store.

With a sob of joy, Sarah slipped off her mare and fell into Amelia's arms. Laughing and crying, she hugged Amelia, then Joel as soldiers cheered and whistled and slapped each other on the back in jubilation. Even the post commander was out to greet them.

Joel clung to her as Amelia led her home. She heard Rand laughing as he tried to tell their story. But the true story still had to be told.

Amelia sent Joel out with the men, then heated a kettle of water and poured it into a hip bath as Sarah peeled off the dusty, stained buckskin dress. Amelia poured cold water into the bath and tested to make sure it wasn't too hot, then as Sarah eased in with a sigh, she began to comb the tangles out of her friend's red-gold locks.

A half hour later, hair washed and clad in clean clothes, Sarah curled up on the sofa, while Amelia stood over her, plaiting Sarah's hair into a long braid. "You have so many bruises. But of course the Indians are notorious for their brutality." She'd been appalled at the dozens of bruises on Sarah's body.

Her friend's sympathetic touch and voice broke the dam on Sarah's emotions, and she burst into tears. She had to tell someone—she couldn't hold it inside any longer. "It wasn't the Indians, Amelia—they helped me. It was Ben!"

Amelia's fingers in Sarah's hair stilled. "Ben Croftner? He beat you?" Her voice was incredulous. She detested Ben, but he had always seemed a perfect gentleman, courteous and gentle.

In a flood, the horror of her ordeal gushed out. Amelia sat and held her as sobs ravaged her body, and she choked out the truth.

"Did you tell Rand?" White with shock and disbelief, Amelia pushed the hair out of Sarah's face, then held her close.

"No. But I know I have to." Sarah pulled back and laced her hands together. "I—I just couldn't face it. He'll hate me, I know it. You know how jealous he is of Ben." She shuddered. "What if he thinks I encouraged him? What if he doesn't believe me when I tell him I got away before Ben could—"

The words hung in the air as Amelia considered her friend's words. "Oh, Sarah, he'll believe you. He seems different, more like himself again. I'm sure he doesn't blame you anymore. It wasn't your fault."

The front door banged open, and they both turned as Rand, Joel, and Jacob hurried into the room. Rand's face brightened as he saw Sarah's scrubbed face and clean hair. "You look much better."

"Well, I'm starved. How 'bout you, Honey?" Jacob pulled Amelia to her feet. "Let's go get some grub at the mess hall." They started toward the door. "Come with us, Half-Pint," he told Joel. "We won't be late," he called back over his shoulder.

Sarah yawned hugely as the door banged shut. "I'll fix you some flapjacks," she said, struggling to keep her eyes open.

"I already ate." His gaze lingered on her bruises, and she pulled her sleeve down defensively. "You about ready to tell me how you got those?" he asked quietly.

Sarah's breath caught, and she nodded.

"Ben. He hired some Laramie Loafers to grab me." She blurted the words out in a rush, then hurried on as his face darkened. "When I came to, I was in a locked cabin by myself. Ben showed up—" She drew a ragged breath. "He–he said we should have been married by then. He. . ."

Her words trailed away. Sarah stared at Rand's face fearfully. Would he believe her this time?

"That no-good skunk. So that's what he meant." Rand spoke slowly and precisely. "He gave you those bruises? Did he—did he hurt you in any other way?"

She shook her head. "I hit him over the head with a stool leg and knocked him cold. Then I took off and got away while he was out. Labe was there too, but he wasn't watching the cabin. What did you mean, 'that's what he meant'? When did you talk to him?"

Rand drew a couple of deep breaths, then grabbed his hat.

"Where are you going?"

"To find Jessica. I have some unfinished business to take care of." He came back and kissed her quickly. "Don't go outside the grounds. I might not be lucky enough to find you a second time. Don't look so worried. I'll tell the whole story when I get back." He gazed down into her troubled eyes, then touched her cheek gently. "I know it wasn't your fault, Green Eyes."

She watched him go with some relief. He did trust her after all. "Be careful," she called after his retreating back.

❧

Jessica looked up as her mother ushered Rand into the parlor, then left them alone. "Darling," she said, rising to her feet. "I didn't know you were back." She lifted her face for a kiss, but Rand just stared at her impassively. "What is it? What's wrong?"

"Your little plan failed."

"Whatever do you mean?" Her blue eyes looked huge and innocent.

Rand had never wanted to slap a woman so badly in his life. "I know all about it, Jessica. Ben told me the whole story when he tried to kill me."

Her eyes widened. "Ben who? Who tried to kill you?"

Rand could see the pulse beating quickly in her throat. She was a smooth one all right, but he could see through her now. "Don't play the innocent with me. You and Ben schemed to kidnap Sarah to get her away from me. You knew I still loved her."

Jessica's face tightened. "How could you prefer that little milksop to me?" she spat. Then her eyes filled with tears. "I love you, Rand. I didn't want to lose you. Surely you can see I had to do something. I could see the hold she had over you."

"I love her. I always have." He saw her flinch but went on anyway. "I tried to deceive myself, but I can't any longer. How could you do such a thing? If people just knew the evil that hides behind that beautiful mask of yours! You can consider our engagement off, of course." He put his hat on and stalked toward the door.

"Wait, Rand!" Jessica ran after him and caught his sleeve. "I know you love me! We can work this out."

He shook her hand off. "All I feel for you is pity." He didn't wait to see the effect of his words but slammed the door behind him.

That was over. Now to find Croftner. He stopped to see Colonel Maynadier, who readily agreed to let him take six men out to look for Ben and try to bring him in.

After two days, he had no luck in picking up Ben's trail. Reluctantly, he turned toward Fort Laramie and home. He hated to face Sarah with his failure. He knew neither one of them could rest until they knew the threat Ben posed was eliminated.

He paused atop a bluff, took a swig from his canteen, then led the men down the slope. "Lieutenant, over here!" One of the men waved from the top of the bluff.

Rand trotted over to where the men stood. A body lay facedown in a ravine. He rolled the man over and gasped in shock. It was Labe! Labe groaned. He was alive!

"Get me my canteen," Rand shouted. He poured a little water into Labe's mouth. "Easy, now. Not too much," he cautioned as Labe tried to sit up to suck more water down.

"Indians!" Labe moaned and thrashed around as Rand drew the canteen away.

"They're gone. You're with friends now," Rand said.

"Rand?" Labe peered up at him. "I'm sorry 'bout poor little Sarah. I tried to talk Ben out of it, but he wouldn't listen to no reason."

"Where is Ben?"

Tears welled up in Labe's eyes. "Dead. Indians attacked us. Ben fought them, but he fell off his horse and hit his head. They took his body and buried it over there." He pointed to a long pile of stones.

Rand patted him gently. "How'd you get away?"

"They left me here." He touched his head gingerly. "They must have hit me on the head."

"You'll be all right. We just need to get you back to the fort." He helped Labe to his feet and up into the saddle. It was a long way back to Fort Laramie.

❦

The week flew by as Sarah immersed herself in activity. She tried to still the worry as she thought of Rand out looking for Ben. On Monday, Wednesday, and Friday morning she taught the Indian children. Living with the Sioux for those four days had given her a new love and tenderness for the dark-eyed youngsters who crowded into the small church. She delighted in seeing their solemn faces break into smiles.

She had just gotten back from school when Joel came bursting into the parlor. "Rand's back!" She jumped to her feet and followed him out onto the porch where she saw a familiar set of broad shoulders striding toward her across the parade ground. With a cry of relief, she ran into his open arms.

He hugged her tightly, then led her back inside the house. Joel jabbered excitedly as he followed them. "I need to talk to your sister for a few minutes alone, Half-Pint. Can you find something else to do for a little while?"

"Sure. Tommy Justice, the new lieutenant's son, said he'd play baseball with me."

"Thanks." Rand turned back to Sarah. "Sit down here with me. We have a lot to talk about."

Sarah sat down beside him, her heart pounding.

"Ben's dead." He told her what Labe had told him, then the entire story of Ben's plot.

Sarah was surprised at her own reaction. She felt unexplainable sadness over Ben's wasted life, although she knew he had received his just reward. "I read a verse this morning," she began. "It said, 'And He shall bring upon them their own iniquity, and shall cut them off in their own wickedness; yea, the Lord our God shall cut them off.' "

Rand nodded. "But Jessica was in on it too. And God hasn't cut her off."

"What? She didn't even know Ben."

"The whole thing was her idea." He raked a hand through his hair. "Not that Ben wouldn't have come up with something himself. But the kidnapping was her idea."

"Why would she do such a thing?"

"To get you away from me," he said simply. "She could sense I still had feelings for you." He shook his head. "I had no idea she was capable of such an act of vengeance."

Her heart surged at his admission in spite of her shock. He did still love her! "That's why she left Fort Laramie in such a hurry," she stammered. She saw his questioning look. "She left the day after you did, and her mother went to Boston for a visit."

"I see." He took a deep breath. "I wanted to tell you at the Sioux encampment, but I felt it was only right that I break things off with Jessica first. I've been a fool, Sarah. I never stopped loving you. I've never loved anyone but you."

She laid a hand on his cheek. "There's fault on both sides," Sarah said softly. "There's nothing to forgive. I've always loved you."

He caught her hand and brought her palm to his lips. "Will you marry me?"

"When?" Her stomach was playing mumblety-peg as he kissed her palm lingeringly.

"Today wouldn't be too soon." He put an arm around her and pulled her onto his lap. "I love you so much, Green Eyes. Even when I told myself I hated you, I knew better deep down." He traced a finger along the curve of her smooth cheek, then bent his head.

As his lips found hers, tears slipped out of Sarah's eyes. She put her arms around his neck as the kiss became more urgent. When he pulled away, she slid her fingers through the rough thatch of his hair.

"Let's not wait too long to marry," he whispered. "I want you all to myself."

"Me too," she said, blushing. "But what about Joel?"

"He'll live with us, of course. But I think my brother will keep him for a week or so while we settle into married life."

⚜

A crisp spring day three days later, Sarah and Rand stood before the post chaplain, Reverend Jameson. It seemed every soldier in the fort had crammed into the tiny church. In the front pew, their families smiled as they watched them step forward to say their vows. Joel's face glowed with joy, and Sarah knew hers had to carry the same expression.

After Rand and Sarah repeated their promises, the men behind them put up a rousing cheer as Rand, in his best uniform, kissed Sarah and turned to face the crowd. The officers formed a canopy of swords that he led his bride through and out into the spring sunshine.

Sarah slanted a tender glance up at her new husband. Her heart had truly led her home.

PLAINS OF PROMISE

For my brother, Rick Rhoads,
who never let me lose faith in myself.

Chapter 1

The ticking of the grandfather clock in the hallway echoed in the shrouded darkness of the parlor. Emmie Courtney sat on the black horsehair sofa, her hands clasped in the folds of her silk skirt. Her violet eyes stared into space as she desperately tried to imagine she was some other place, that the reason her friends and neighbors were gathered here in her house on this sultry August day was something else entirely. The clatter of carriage wheels on the fine plank streets outside the open window thumped in time with the beat of her heart pounding in her ears.

He can't be dead. I have to wake up. This is just a nightmare. A nightmare. She repeated the litany over and over to herself as she closed her eyes to avoid the pitying eyes of her friends. Only last week her life had been perfect. Married to a handsome, up-and-coming lawyer in the rapidly burgeoning town of Wabash, Indiana, her life had seemed like a fairy tale come true. The War between the States was over, and parties and gay life were everywhere. But now her dashing husband lay newly buried in a grave under the steamy rain drizzling down outside. The nearly overpowering scent of the flowers massed around the room couldn't quite cover the stench of decay that had wafted up from the casket and permeated the room for the last few days. That undeniable smell told her quite clearly that this wasn't just a nightmare.

Her neighbor, Lally Saylors, touched her shoulder gently, and Emmie looked up. "Do try to eat a bit, Emmie dear," Lally said with a coaxing smile. She handed her a cup of tea and a small plate with potato salad and a ham sandwich on it, then sat beside her.

Emmie took it and forced a sip of tea down her tight throat. "I still can't quite grasp it, you know. I keep expecting Monroe to come bursting in the door shouting for me to get my cloak and go for a drive or something. I don't think I'll ever forget the sound of the horses screaming as the carriage rolled over."

"You were lucky to get off with only a concussion," Lally said gently.

"But Monroe—" Emmie broke off, too choked up to continue.

Her eyes misting with tears, Lally patted Emmie's hand. "I know, Dear."

It had been three marvelous months. Emmie had lived securely in a love that she'd never before experienced, a love that shone out of Monroe's laughing brown eyes whenever he looked at her.

"Have you thought yet about what you will do?" Lally asked.

Emmie shook her head. "I haven't heard from Ben and Labe since they left for the Dakota Territory six months ago. I don't have any other family."

"I just hate it that you're here all alone so far from your kin at a time like this."

Emmie nodded wearily. She was used to it, though. She and her brother Ben had never been close; and after her mother died when she was twelve, her father was almost always drunk until his death three years ago. She'd grown up isolated and shy in a ramshackle country home just outside town, with the animals for friends. Her brother Labe had given her sporadic attention, but Ben ignored her except when he wanted something. He had always had dreams of making the name Croftner stand for something except the town drunk. He would have approved of Monroe.

She'd never even had a best friend and didn't really know how to have fun until Monroe swept into her life like a whirlwind. They'd married after a courtship of only six weeks, and after three months of marriage, she still felt she hadn't even begun to know her fascinating husband. Now she never would.

"I'll probably stay here at least for awhile," she told Lally. "The house is paid for, and we never seemed to want for money. Surely there is enough to live on for awhile if I'm careful. James is supposed to come out tomorrow to discuss my financial affairs." She cringed at the thought of facing Monroe's employer and his sympathy. All she wanted was to curl up here in the dark house and be left to probe her wounds alone.

Somehow she got through the funeral and the burial until all the well-meaning friends and neighbors left with promises to call again. She shut the front door wearily, then lay down on the sofa. Through the open window she heard the happy shouts of children playing hopscotch across the street and the gentle hum of the bees in the honeysuckle just under the window. The fecund scent of the Wabash River, just down the hill, wafted in with poignant memories of happy picnics with Monroe beside its placid waters. How could things seem so normal? She bit her lip as the hot tears coursed down her cheeks, then pulled the afghan down off the back of the sofa onto her shivering body. It was hot, but she couldn't stop shaking, a reaction to the trauma of seeing Monroe's casket lowered into that dark, forbidding hole in the ground.

She hadn't been able to sleep since the accident, but now she was so tired she couldn't keep her eyes open. The creaks and rattles of carriages outside on the busy street faded as she fell asleep, dreaming of Monroe's laughing brown eyes.

The parlor was deep in shadow when she awoke. She gazed around her in bewilderment, not sure what had awakened her. The clock still ticked in the hallway, and carriages still rattled over the street outside. Then someone on the front porch banged the knocker again, and brushing at the wrinkles in her silk skirt, she lurched to the door. She felt disoriented and fuzzy-headed as she pulled the door open.

"Emmaline Courtney?" A young woman stood on the porch with a small boy of about two in her arms. She was neatly dressed in a dark blue serge dress with a demure white collar. Gentle brown eyes looked out from beneath a stylish though modest bonnet with a single, drooping ostrich feather.

"Yes. May I help you?" The child reminded her of someone, but she was still too groggy from sleep and sorrow to place who it was he looked like. And the woman's calm appraisal put her hackles up in some indefinable way.

The woman looked away from her inquiring eyes, then set her small chin and looked straight into Emmie's eyes. "May I come in? I have something of the utmost importance to discuss with you. It's about Monroe."

Puzzled over the identity of her caller, Emmie nodded and led the way into the parlor. She lit two more lamps, seated the young woman on the sofa, and sank into the matching armchair facing her guest. Discarded china from the funeral dinner still littered the smooth walnut tables.

"I'm sorry for the mess," Emmie stammered. "The funeral and all—" She broke off on a choked sob and drew a ragged breath.

Her visitor nodded as she settled the little boy on her lap and drew off her gloves.

"I'm sorry, I didn't catch your name." Emmie's gaze was caught by the pity in the woman's eyes. She caught a whiff of a faint lilac sachet as the woman pleated the folds of her dress nervously. She used to wear the scent herself, but Monroe didn't like it, so she'd switched to lily of the valley.

The young woman drew a deep breath. "This is going to come as quite a shock to you, and I'm truly sorry for that. I'm Mrs. Monroe Courtney. Catherine Courtney. Monroe was my childhood sweetheart. We were married three years ago in Cleveland."

Emmie just looked at her in puzzlement. The words had no meaning to her. How odd that they were married to someone with the same name. Then the pity in the woman's gaze penetrated her stupor. Surely the woman didn't mean she was Monroe's wife! Beginning to tremble with an awful premonition, she stared at the woman.

"Surely you wondered why he never brought you to meet his family?"

"He said they were all dead. That they died in a train accident when he was seventeen." Emmie's lips barely moved as she spoke in a whisper.

Catherine's lips tightened, and a flush stained her pale cheeks. "He has four brothers and three sisters. His mother and father are both in excellent health. They've been very hurt by his silence." She opened her reticule and drew out a picture. "Here's a family portrait of Monroe with his father and the rest of the family. It was taken just before he disappeared."

Emmie took the picture and stared down into Monroe's familiar laughing eyes. An older man with a curling handlebar mustache sat in the middle of a group of young adults. There was a marked resemblance between him and the other people in the photograph. They all had the strong jawline that made Monroe so attractive, the same large, expressive eyes.

Catherine drew a deep breath and continued with her story. "We had an argument one day. It was silly—over nothing, really. But he'd been acting restless and short-tempered for several weeks. He took off, and I never heard from him again until I saw his obituary in the *Cleveland Plain Dealer*. He didn't even know about Richard here." She indicated the little boy, who had his thumb corked in his mouth. "He was never very good at responsibility. Even as a child, he enjoyed pretending to be someone he wasn't. There were spells when he'd take off, but he always returned in a few weeks. This was the longest he'd ever been gone. I heard he passed himself off as a lawyer here too. Actually, he only got about halfway through law school before he grew bored and quit."

"You have proof of this?" Emmie asked, the numbness beginning to wear off. Monroe already married? Where did that leave her? She couldn't seem to take in the horror of her situation. Bigamy. The very word brought a wave of shame and nausea. Monroe had always seemed mysterious. That had been part of his magnetism. And it was true he was easily bored. But his eagerness for new adventure was part of his charm.

"I have an affidavit from his father and my marriage lines, of course. I will present them to your lawyer tomorrow."

"Then this house, his possessions, it all belongs to you," Emmie said numbly.

Catherine nodded gently. "I wouldn't have come if it wasn't for Richard. But my family is poor, and Monroe's father has been supporting me and Richard. But he's struggling too. I heard that Monroe had amassed a small holding here. It's only Richard's due that he inherit his father's possessions. You're young, and you don't have a baby to worry about. And you can always go home to your family."

Emmie wanted to burst into tears and wail aloud. But she was too numb to react. There was a certain contempt mixed in with the pity in the woman's face. Emmie was sure Catherine thought she was a fool for believing Monroe's lies.

And I was, she thought with self-contempt.

Catherine stood and pulled her gloves back on. "I'll leave you to consider all I've told you. If you need to contact me, I'll be at the Blue Goose Inn." She stared down at Emmie's face. "I'm truly sorry."

The blood thundering in her ears, Emmie watched Catherine gather her son into her arms and leave with a last, pitying look. *That's who the child looks like,* she realized with a final horror. He was a younger version of Monroe right down to the pouting upper lip. She sat rigidly in the chair with her hands clenched. What was she going to do now? There was no way to contact Ben and Labe. No one to take her in. The townspeople were kind enough, but times were too hard in the aftermath of the war for any of them to consider taking on a new burden. She couldn't ask it. This was just another instance of the feckless Croftners. She shuddered in shame. What a heyday the gossips would have with this.

Well, it was too late to do anything tonight. Tomorrow she would talk to James about her options. She blew out the lamps and climbed the open stairway to the room she'd shared with Monroe. Repugnance overwhelmed her as she stepped into the familiar room and smelled the faint, sweet scent of Monroe's hair tonic. The big four-poster bed with its lace coverlet looked cold and alien. She couldn't sleep there, she decided. She took her nightgown and went down the hall to one of the spare rooms. The realization that she was ruined was beginning to sink in. But she couldn't think about it tonight. It would have to wait until tomorrow.

Two days later, as she sat in the overstuffed chair in the law office of Taylor and Eddingfield, Emmie felt as though she couldn't handle any more shocks. Catherine had left her documents with James Eddingfield, Monroe's employer, to check. James looked through his wire-rimmed glasses and pursed his thin lips as he studied the documents.

"These seem to all be in order," he said grudgingly.

"Do I have any rights at all?" Emmie asked.

"I'm afraid not. Only what you brought into the so-called marriage. Your personal belongings and any dowry."

"I didn't have a dowry yet. When Ben's bills were settled, he told Monroe he could have what was left. The house Ben promised us as my dowry is still tied up until his debts are paid. I don't have any money until then." Ben had fled town after Rand Campbell had returned from the War between the States and everyone discovered he had lied when he claimed Rand had died. Ben had wanted to marry Rand's fiancée, Sarah Montgomery. When the townspeople found out about his deceit, all his debts had been called in. Rather than face what he'd done, he had taken off out west.

"The law, unfortunately, is all on Catherine's side. And she does have a child to consider."

For just a moment, Emmie wondered what she would do if she discovered she were pregnant also. But the thought was too shameful to consider, so she pushed it away.

James took her hand. "Is there no one who would take you in? Your brothers, perhaps?"

She didn't like the feel of his moist hand or the way he was looking at her, and she tried to discreetly pull her hand away. "No one. I don't even know where Ben and Labe are."

James squeezed her hand tighter, then lifted it to his lips. "I've always admired you, my dear Emmie. And, uh, tendered a certain regard for you. I would consider it an honor to be allowed to take care of you. There's a lovely little house on Sherman Street I own. Secluded and private. I could visit you there and see to all your needs."

The meaning of his words eluded Emmie for a few moments, but the greedy look in his eyes didn't. She gasped when she realized at last what he meant. She dragged her hand out of his grasp and rose shakily. "I thought you were Monroe's friend—and mine!"

"You're soiled goods now, my dear. What I offer is the best you can hope for once everyone knows you lived with Monroe without benefit of marriage."

"That's not my fault—I thought I was married," she whispered. She felt shamed and unclean. Was there something about her looks that made men think she was a loose woman? She'd always wondered if she was truly a Croftner. Her raven black hair and violet eyes were so very different from her brothers' fair hair and eyes.

"Perhaps. Who can say for sure what you really believed? At least that's what people will say," he said with a tight smile.

She gathered up her reticule, nausea rising in her throat, and stumbled toward the door. She had to get out of here. "I'd scrub clothes before I degraded myself like that," she whispered.

"You'll come crawling back when you see no one in polite society will accept you," he shouted as she closed the door behind her.

A half hour later, drained and disheartened, she let herself inside the cool, dark house she'd called home for three months. Mrs. Matthew must have been here while she was gone—she could smell the faint scent of lemon and wax, and the house shone as it always did after her part-time housekeeper's ministrations. It would probably be the last time Mrs. Matthew deigned to work for her once the town knew about her shame. Not that she could afford her now, of course. Her steps echoed on the oak floor as she took off her bonnet and walked wearily to the parlor. The house seemed so empty and desolate. Was it just a week ago that the house rang with voices and laughter at the elegant dinner party they'd had?

She looked around at her home. She'd brought so few personal belongings. She wouldn't even be allowed to take enough to set up housekeeping elsewhere.

Just her mother's cedar chest packed with a few linens, her own clothing, and a Chippendale tea set that had belonged to her grandmother.

What was she to do? Where could she go? Could she find employment here somewhere? But she had no skills, no special training. And what if James was right and she was shunned by polite society, by the very people she'd thought were her friends? She buried her face in her hands and gave into the tears she'd managed to keep at bay for the past two days. She'd tried to be strong, stronger than she felt. But fate seemed determined to keep her down in the mire. She was just the daughter of the town drunk, after all.

After a few minutes, she raised her head and wiped her cheeks. There had to be an answer to her dilemma. She bolted upright as a sudden thought took hold. What about Sarah Montgomery? She'd married Rand Campbell and followed him out west somewhere. Emmie had been so excited when Ben became engaged to Sarah, hoping that her influence would temper Ben's violent mood swings. But, of course, once Rand returned alive from the war, that engagement ended.

She'd run into Sarah's mother-in-law, Margaret, at Beitman and Wolf's dry goods counter last week. Margaret had said her daughter-in-law was pining for some female companionship; she wished she knew of some young woman to send out to keep Sarah company, she had said.

Would Sarah welcome the sister of her ex-fiancé? Sarah had always treated her like an older sister and acted as though she genuinely cared about her. She'd even sent a congratulatory letter when she'd heard of her marriage to Monroe.

Emmie rose and went to fetch her bonnet. If she hurried, she could get to Margaret's in time for lunch.

Chapter 2

The stagecoach lurched and rolled its way across the arid landscape. Emmie clutched the seat to keep from falling across the lap of the soldier sitting next to her. She still could hardly believe she was out here in the Great American Desert. The soldier had told her earlier that they should arrive at Fort Laramie today.

Catherine Courtney had given her a month to find other living arrangements. After a flurry of telegrams and last-minute plans, Emmie had found herself standing in a train station about to leave for a far-off place she'd only vaguely heard of. Now, ten days later, her journey was about to end. She bit her lip and tried to still the nervous pounding of her heart.

The scenery was certainly nothing to get excited about. She peered out the open window. Dry buffalo grass, sage, and weeds undulated as far as she could see in every direction. She already missed the soft greens of Indiana. No towns or settlements, just endless plains of wilderness without much promise.

But there was no other option except James, and almost anything was better than that. She could surely stand the isolation for awhile. Then she could try to come up with another plan if this one didn't work out.

"Ever been west before, Miss?" A grizzled soldier in the seat across from her leaned forward and smiled a gap-toothed grin. His angular face was rough and reddened from the sun, and his uniform was none too clean. But he'd been friendly without being too familiar during the entire trip from Fort Leavenworth.

Emmie fanned her face and tried to keep her stomach from roiling at the stench of his breath mixed with the smell of rank, unwashed bodies and dusty leather in the tightly packed stagecoach. "Never," she said, forcing a faint smile to her pale lips.

"You ain't seen nothing until you seen them mountains out here. Lots of wide-open spaces."

The stage lurched again, and one of the soldiers up on top shouted, "Laramie up ahead!"

Emmie craned her head in a decidedly unlady-like way out the window and tried to see, but the laboring horses threw up too much dust. She drew her head back in as the driver cursed at the flagging horses and urged them toward their destination. They stopped briefly at a swiftly running river, then the driver cracked the whip again and urged the team onto a waiting ferry. Her heart pounded as the fort grew nearer.

She pulled a handkerchief out of her reticule and wiped her face with it. She knew she must look terrible. Her face and neck felt gritty with cinders from the train, and her scalp itched. Large patches of dust and mud clung to her skirts and shoes. She tied her blue bonnet firmly under her chin as the driver pulled the team to a halt beside a crude adobe building. Soldiers milled around outside, and just across a wide parade ground, Emmie could see a neat row of whitewashed adobe buildings. This was the famous fort? This nondescript assortment of rough buildings and barren wasteland? Her heart sank at the thought of living in this primitive place.

As she stepped off the stage, she gasped and almost fell when she caught sight of a throng of Indians outside the entrance to the building. She pulled her cloak tightly around her as a shield against the dangerous-looking natives. She'd heard of all the Indian atrocities just a few months ago. The papers had called 1865 "the Bloody Year."

Her garrulous soldier friend chuckled at her dismay. "They won't hurt you none. Those Injuns are Laramie Loafers. They're too dependent on gov'ment rations to cause a peep of trouble."

They looked plenty savage to Emmie. She gave them a wide berth as she hesitantly followed the soldiers into the building. Inside, even more Indians milled around. A counter made of rough wooden planks and piled with all kinds of necessities lined the back of the store, much like a general store back home. Barrels of sugar and flour and tea sat off to one side, and wide shelves behind the counter held a wide assortment of items from coffee grinders and Arbunkle coffee to ribbons and beads and boots. The smell of coffee, dust, and sweat was almost overpowering. A single kerosene lamp swung from the ceiling, and its sickly glow cast a yellowish pall over everything.

Suddenly aware that the overwhelming babble had ceased and every eye was staring at her, Emmie flushed and forced herself to approach the sutler standing behind the counter. "Excuse me, Sir, but could you tell me where I might find Lieutenant Rand Campbell?"

"That lucky lieutenant always has purty wimmenfolk lookin' for him." A scrawny soldier with bright red hair stepped up beside her before the sutler could answer. "I kin take you to Sarah." He thrust out a brown hand. "I'm Lieutenant Jackson Wheeler, but you kin call me Rooster. I'm the best scout you ever laid eyes on."

Emmie hesitated, then shook his hand gingerly. "I–I'm Emmie Croftner."

She'd debated about what name to use and had decided on her legal one. She wanted to try to forget all about Monroe, if she could.

"Let's git out of this-here crowd of buzzards. Rand and Sarah's little place is over yonder on the other side of the parade ground." Rooster opened the door for her and grabbed her satchel from her unresisting hand. "They'll be tickled pink to see you. You here to help with the wee one?"

"Yes." Emmie let the soldier ramble on. She was too tired to think or respond. She spared a quick glance around at her surroundings as she followed Rooster around the parade ground.

Soldiers stood in neat lines at attention on the parade ground as the trumpet blew a vaguely familiar tune. Two more soldiers lowered the flag from the flagpole in the middle of the field. Emmie was unable to quell the twinge of excitement and admiration at the rows of blue uniforms. There was something so masculine and attractive about a man in a uniform. Not that she was interested, of course. Between her shiftless brothers and her lying "husband," she'd had enough of men to last a lifetime. She just wanted a place to heal and a good friend to talk to.

She couldn't help gawking as she followed Rooster's spry steps. A surprising amount of activity seemed to be going on all around the fort. She could see a forest of tepees on the north side of the grounds, with squaws stooping over campfires and half-naked children shouting and running between the tepees. Beyond the barren, sage-dotted landscape stretched the edge of purple mountains in the distance.

Rooster stopped outside a white bungalow with a wide front porch. He bounded up the steps and pounded on the first of two doors.

Sarah opened the door with a squeal of delight and flung her arms around her. "Emmie! Oh, I'm so glad to see you. The stage must have been early—I intended to be there to meet you. Come in, come in." She drew her in and waved her thanks at Rooster before shutting the door.

Emmie hadn't seen Sarah for nearly a year. Not since she broke her engagement to Ben and followed Rand out here to this desolate place. The bright golden hair still gleamed, and her green eyes still sparkled with joy and excitement. She'd gained a little weight with her pregnancy, but Emmie thought the soft roundness suited Sarah's petite femininity.

"I'm chattering like a magpie, and you must be exhausted," Sarah said. "Would you like to freshen up while I fix us a cup of tea?"

"That would be lovely. I'm grimy from the trip." Emmie took off her bonnet and smiled at Sarah.

Sarah shuddered at the mention of the trip. "How well I remember the journey out here," she said. "Horrible food, no bathing facilities, no place to sleep.

Why don't I heat some water for a bath? Rand won't be home until supper-time. You can have a lovely soak."

"Sounds heavenly. But I'll get it ready if you show me where everything is. Shouldn't you be resting?"

"Now you sound like Rand." Sarah laughed. "I feel wonderful. I have a long way to go—almost four months. It will be a long wait. I'm so anxious already."

Emmie followed her through the tiny quarters. The small entry led to a parlor about ten feet square. It was a homey room with an army cot, obviously used as a sofa, that was covered with a colorful Ohio Star quilt in burgundy and blue calico and matching pillows. Warm burgundy calico curtains and matching table covers topped with lace doilies added more color. A crude table and two chairs stood under the front window and held a Bible, a copy of Shakespeare's plays, *David Copperfield,* and *Wuthering Heights.* A mantel over the fireplace held a delicate rose tea set and several small china figurines.

Just off the parlor was a small kitchen. The rough table and chairs were painted the same warm burgundy as the curtains in the parlor. Pots hung from pegs along one wall, and a small cookstove sat in the middle of the room. A dry sink with a plank counter sat in one corner.

The door in the left wall of the kitchen opened into a tiny bedroom with only room for a bed and small chest. Sarah started to lift the hip bath from its peg on the wall, but Emmie quickly stepped forward and took it down herself.

"I don't want to be a bother. I'm here to help you," she scolded.

Sarah laughed as she pointed out room in the corner for the bath. "I'll heat some water."

An hour later, Emmie felt like a new woman. Her dark hair shone, and the lavender dress deepened the violet in her eyes. The ladies drank their tea and ate warm bread with thick butter and jam as they chatted. The months since they last talked seemed to fall away.

Sarah sat down her teacup, and her lively smile faded. "I was sorry to hear about your husband. You were married such a short time."

Emmie carefully chewed the last bit of her jam and bread before answering. She knew she needed to tell Sarah the truth, but she didn't think she could face it yet. She'd told her she wanted to take back her maiden name since she'd been married such a short time. But Emmie was smart enough to know a secret of such magnitude never stayed hidden. There were already a few people who'd looked at her oddly in the last few days before she left Wabash.

Sarah patted her arm, her emerald eyes luminous with tears as she saw her friend's agitation. "We don't have to talk about it yet. Someday when the grief isn't so fresh and you want to tell me how wonderful Monroe was, I'll be ready to listen. It's still very difficult to talk about Papa. I still miss him so, and it's been almost a year." She dabbed at her eyes with a lace-trimmed handkerchief and quickly changed the subject.

By the time Rand came home, tired and dusty, the two young women were deep in gossip from home. "I'm starving, Woman," he shouted as he strode into the parlor followed by Joel, Sarah's younger brother.

Emmie didn't remember Rand very well from before the war, but she was impressed by him. He exuded a quiet strength and compassion that were unusual in a man. And he was very good looking. A shock of dark hair and expressive brown eyes, with dimples that made her want to smile with him. She'd worried all the way here that he would hold Ben's actions against her.

But her fears were groundless. Rand was the perfect host and teased her unmercifully about breaking the hearts of all the soldiers as Sarah put the delicious venison stew she'd prepared on the table. "Usually we go to officers' mess," she explained to Emmie. "But I didn't want to share you with the men your first night here. They'll be around soon enough when they hear there's a young, beautiful widow in their midst."

"They already know," Rand grinned. "I had at least ten men ask me about her. I had to tell them I hadn't seen her for years and she might be an ugly hag by now. I can see I was mistaken."

Emmie flushed. "I'm not interested in finding another husband," she said firmly. "Not ever." Any mention of her looks always made her uncomfortable. She knew she was very ordinary. Only Monroe had ever called her beautiful, and it was obvious now that he'd lied. Her real attraction had been the money Ben had promised.

Rand raised his eyebrows but said nothing. After supper the ladies cleared the table and washed the dishes, then followed him into the tiny parlor. He took down two harmonicas, handed one to Joel, and they began to play "Nearer My God to Thee," as Sarah sang the words in a clear, sweet alto. Emmie knew the song a bit; it was one her father had bellowed when he was drunk, so after a slight hesitation, she joined in with her clear soprano.

"That was wonderful," Sarah said, clapping her hands. "We like to have devotions together at night. We sing and Rand reads a passage of Scripture. Would you like to join us or are you too tired tonight?"

"I'd love to join you." Something about their simple, heartfelt faith pulled her. She'd always felt that God was too busy to pay any attention to someone like her. But Sarah and Rand acted like He was right there with them.

Rand picked up the worn Bible on the table by the window and flipped through the pages. "We're up to Psalms," he said, settling his broad-shouldered frame into the chair. He began to read Psalm 61 in his deep voice. " 'Hear my cry, O God; attend unto my prayer. From the end of the earth will I cry unto Thee, when my heart is overwhelmed: lead me to the rock that is higher than I. For Thou hast been a shelter for me, and a strong tower from the enemy.' " His voice faltered and fell silent as he saw the tears sliding noiselessly down Emmie's cheeks.

"No, no, go on," she choked. "It's what I needed to hear."

As he finished the psalm, she felt a curious peace. She wanted to find out more about this personal God her friends seemed to trust so completely. This was certainly the ends of the earth like the Scripture mentioned.

Chapter 3

T*a-dum-dum.* The shrill notes of the bugle pierced the dawn air, and Emmie bolted upright in the narrow bed Rand and Sarah had fixed her in the hallway. Without sliding out of bed, she looked out the window at the top of the door. Streaks of pink heralding the day lightened the dark sky. She slid out of bed, shivering as her bare feet touched the cold floor, and padded to the door. She could hear the shouts of men across the grounds as they groomed their horses. She pushed open the door and took a deep breath of sage-scented air.

She was here at Fort Laramie, that famous bastion of might against the hordes of savages threatening the settlers trekking along the Oregon Trail. Or so the men back home said. She herself hadn't seen any threatening hordes in the short time she'd been here, just those Laramie Loafers. But there were certainly a lot of impressive-looking soldiers. She shut the door and watched through the window as the men scurried toward the mess hall. The two-story barracks across the parade ground was alive with blue-coated men hurrying toward their breakfast, then on to saddle their horses or start their fatigue duties of the day.

She got dressed and went to the kitchen.

"Good morning," Sarah said as Emmie came toward her with a smile. "Did you sleep well?"

"I woke up a few times when somebody yelled 'All's well.' "

Sarah and Rand chuckled.

"Night watchman. You'll get used to it," Rand told her. He kissed Sarah and picked up his hat. "I'm going to be late for boots and saddles if I don't get a move on."

"Boots and saddles? What's that—some kind of war game?"

Rand grinned at the question. "That's the call to mount our horses and get on with our day. I've got to lead a detail to escort a wagon train coming in, then round up some beef for Cookie—that's what the cook's called at any fort I've ever been at. But I'll wager the men will be finding any excuse to come over here to meet you."

Rand's prediction came true. Nearly every man in the fort made some excuse to drop in over the next few days. Emmie felt strange even going outside for a walk or going to the sutler's store. Men stared at her with awe and deep respect in their eyes. It was very intimidating, especially when she felt as she did about all males. Except for Rand. He was a very nice man, God-fearing and honest to a fault. But there couldn't be two like him in the world.

Each soldier showed up hat in hand, his hair slicked back with a hair tonic that smelled of spice, blue uniform brushed and pressed. Emmie felt sorry for them, but she let Sarah deal with sending them away. Two even proposed marriage, practically in their first breath.

"I just can't stay inside another minute," Sarah announced one day after sending Joel off to school. "Can we go for a picnic?"

Rand shoveled the last bite of flapjacks into his mouth. "I guess you could. The weather has been warm, but it won't last long. You might as well enjoy it while you can. I'll see about an escort. I need to repair some telegraph line the Indians cut, but I'll send someone over. What time do you want to go?"

"About eleven. Could we go to the stream in the meadow?"

"Sure. Just don't wander off."

The girls took the laundry to Soapsuds Row, a line of tents at the edge of the fort where a couple of enlisted men lived with their wives, who acted as the fort laundresses. The women were visiting back east right now, and the men did the laundry while they were gone. After delivering their laundry, Sarah and Emmie scrubbed the tiny quarters and packed a lunch.

Promptly at eleven, someone pounded on the door and shouted in a deep baritone, "Open the door, Woman. Time's a wasting!"

Emmie swung open the door and looked up into the bluest eyes she'd ever seen. The man had a friendly, open face with a shock of auburn hair that fell down over his forehead from under his blue hat. His flowing mustache matched his hair, and he was quite tall, for she had to crane her neck to look up at him.

"You must be Emmie. Every man in the fort is already in love with you."

Emmie smiled in spite of her resolve to keep aloof from the soldiers. His grin was infectious. "They just haven't seen any women in awhile. Who are you?"

"Isaac Liddle at your service, Ma'am." He slapped the heels of his boots together and kissed her hand, then grinned again at her surprise.

She tried to place his soft accent. "I've heard a lot about you. You're Rand's best friend."

Sarah joined her at the door. "I see you've met Isaac. You behave yourself, Isaac. I don't want you scaring Emmie into leaving me."

His voice took on an injured tone. "Now, Sarah, one look at my handsome mug and she's sure to want to stay. Besides, I'm here to escort you two on your picnic. Every man in the fort clamored for the job, but I know how to get around your husband. All I had to do was promise to shine his boots for the next six months."

The girls laughed as he took the picnic basket from Sarah. "Come right this way, ladies. Your steeds await you."

The horse he selected for Emmie was a lovely buckskin with gentle eyes. "Molly's a darling, aren't you, Girl?" Isaac patted the insistent nose the mare thrust into his hand.

"Have you ridden much?"

"Not really, but I like horses. We had a pony when I was little. He was an old pinto and ornery." She tentatively held out her palm, and the mare gently snuffled her velvet nose against it.

"Well, Molly will be good for you. She's gentle and sweet-natured." He offered his linked hands. After a moment's hesitation, Emmie put her foot in his hands, and he helped her up onto the sidesaddle. She adjusted her skirts and gathered up the reins as he helped Sarah. Her friend's horse was a placid bay with a wide back. Rand had obviously instructed Isaac well.

Isaac led the way past the parade ground and the stables where four other soldiers joined them. As they crossed in front of the tepee village, Emmie was conscious of the black-eyed stares of the squaws and Indian children as they passed the Indian encampment. She wrinkled her nose at the pungent scent of some concoction bubbling in the pot over the open fire they skirted, mingled with dung from the numerous dogs roaming the fort area. She still hadn't been close enough to any Indians to get a good look at them. Sarah seemed to have a few friends in the group, for she waved and called to several Indian women.

The sun blazed down overhead in the brilliant blue canopy of sky. Fluffy white clouds drifted across the banner above them like lazy puffs of smoke. Emmie heard a bird cry out and looked up to see an eagle soar up into the brilliant haze above her. She felt almost as free herself. Oh, this west was a wonderful place.

The meadow where they stopped was a sunny glade with a cold, clear stream running through it. The scent of sage was heavy in the air, and Isaac pointed out a prickly pear cactus for them to avoid stepping in as they dismounted and followed him to a shady spot under a cottonwood tree beside the stream.

"It's lovely," Emmie said as she spread a blanket on the mossy ground beside the stream.

"You'll love it in the spring. There are bluebells and violets everywhere." He straightened the other side of the blanket and sat down, while she and Sarah opened the hamper of food. The four privates each took a separate spot in different directions and stood watch for hostile Indians. Sarah and Emmie took them a plate of food before settling down on the blanket with Isaac.

Emmie watched his face surreptitiously as they ate their lunch of cold sand-wiches and baked beans. He really was a most attractive man. But she wasn't interested in getting involved with anyone. Not ever. And to be perfectly hon-est, he didn't seem overly smitten with her, in spite of his flirtatious manner. It was probably how he treated all women. Teasing and indulgent like an older brother, which was fine with her.

Emmie soon fell into the pattern of fort life, listening almost unconsciously for the trumpet to sound out the various calls. She didn't need the little watch pinned to her bodice anymore. Her days were divided by reveille at 5:00 A.M., breakfast at 6:00, followed by stable call at 6:30, drill at 10:00 and 2:00, retreat at 6:00 P.M., tattoo at 8:30, and taps at 8:45. She loved to watch the boots and saddles call in the morning. At the order, the cavalry swung up into their saddles in unison, the sun dancing off their brass buttons and their sabers. Then they would ride out of the fort grounds onto the open plain to practice wheel-ing and charging imaginary foes. It was an exhilarating sight.

After she'd been there a month and was finally beginning to settle in and feel at home, Rand came bursting in with a big grin on his face and sat in a chair beside them.

"I received new orders today."

Sarah stopped eating the dumplings made with dried apples and put her fork down. "Oh, no, Rand. Where? I don't want to go anywhere else."

His grin widened at the dread in her voice. "We're going to Fort Phil Kearny."

Sarah shrieked and jumped to throw her arms around him. He almost toppled backwards in his chair. "I get to see Amelia!" she cried as she hugged him exuberantly.

He grinned and sat the chair forward with a thump. "I thought you didn't want to go," he said with a chuckle.

Emmie watched with a pensive smile. If she could have a marriage like her friend, she might consider it, but there weren't very many men like Rand Campbell around. She pushed away the stirring of envy. What made her think she even deserved such a fine man?

Emmie knew Amelia McCallister, of course. She was the daughter of Wabash's only doctor. It was the talk of the whole town when Amelia married Jake and moved out west with him. Sarah spoke often of how much she missed her best friend, and Emmie couldn't help a stab of jealousy. Would Sarah have time for her once Amelia was around?

"When do we leave?" Emmie asked.

"You've both got two days to pack."

"Two days! You must be joking."

"They wanted me to go tomorrow, but I talked the colonel into another day in deference to you ladies. And that's quite a feat with the army. They don't even officially recognize that the wives exist usually. In the army's eyes, you two are just camp followers like the ones across the river."

Emmie's cheeks grew hot at his oblique reference to the soiled doves on the other side of the Laramie River. Rand had tried unsuccessfully to get their place of business closed down, and it was a sore spot with him. Would he put her in the same class as the prostitutes if he knew about her false marriage? She desperately hoped she'd never have to find out. Her resolve to tell Sarah the truth had faded as the days went by. She didn't want to risk seeing her friend's love and respect change to repugnance.

By working late both nights, they managed to get everything packed. Rand brought them empty pickle barrels, and they packed most of their belongings in the pungent containers, with hay packed around the breakables. Joel chattered the entire time about seeing his friend, Jimmy Carrington, again.

Both women were almost sick with excitement and nerves as they pulled out of the fort two days later. Emmie was curious to see something of the countryside. She'd already begun to chafe at the restrictions on her movements in the fort. In thirty-five days, she'd only been out of the confines of the fort once on that picnic to the meadow.

They boarded the ambulance, a heavy wagon outfitted with a straw mattress and the canvas sides rolled up to let the breeze in. A canteen hung near the roof with the lid off to allow the water to cool in the breeze. Rand had rigged up a padded bench seat along each side for them to ride on, and the rest of their belongings were packed into every available inch of space. By the time they'd gone a mile, Emmie and Sarah wished they had a horse to ride. The ambulance had no springs, and they were jarred and thrown about with every pothole as they moved with the troop of nearly twenty men.

They stopped for lunch, and the girls got down thankfully. Emmie drew deep breaths of sage-scented air as she bolted down the beans and bacon the cook presented. The bacon was tough so she ate around it.

"Can you bring the blanket and come with me?" Sarah whispered. "I wish there was such a thing as a portable privy."

The girls hurried off a short distance on the far side of a scraggly cottonwood tree, and Emmie held the blanket up as a screen. Above their heads the branches swayed with the breeze, and Emmie caught a whiff of some sweetly scented autumn wildflower. The gurgle of the clear creek to their right muted the sounds of the army camp behind them.

"Hurry," Emmie said. "I think they're about ready to go, and I don't think they saw us leave."

By the time they started back, the ambulance was pulling away without them in it. They ran, shouting for the soldiers to stop. Rand saw them and halted the procession.

"Don't ever go off like that again without telling me," he said angrily. "We never know when we're going to run into hostiles this far from the fort. I would think you'd learned your lesson after last time, Sarah."

She flushed and tossed her head. "It didn't turn out so bad. I made some new friends."

"And almost got killed, and Jake too."

Sarah just compressed her lips as he wheeled and rode back to the front of the line.

"What's he talking about?" Emmie was shocked at the ruckus their little necessary errand had caused.

Sarah sighed, then picked up the knitting she'd been working on before lunch. The little yellow booties she was making were half finished. "I went off by myself on a ride and Indians took me," she admitted. "But they were Laramie Loafers, and it wouldn't have happened if your brother hadn't put them up to it." She stopped a moment, then sighed and went on. "They left me in a cabin for Ben, but I got away from him, and some hostile Sioux found me. Little Wolverine was a young Sioux who respected Rand because of an earlier battle, and he protected me until Rand found me." She shook her head and sighed again. "Jake was injured by a bear while they were out searching for me. So now, Rand keeps a close watch on me."

Emmie could tell her friend was uncomfortable talking about Ben, but this was as good a time as any to clear the air. The entire time since she'd arrived, she knew they both had been avoiding the subject of her brother. "So Ben did follow you. I often wondered if that's where he went." She noticed Sarah's downcast look. "I don't have any illusions about my brother's character, Sarah. I lived with him, remember?"

Sarah took a deep breath. "That's not all, Emmie. There's something I've put off telling you. I didn't want to hurt you after you'd been through so much."

"What is it?" Emmie asked after a long pause.

"I'm sorry to have to tell you that Ben was killed in a fall from his horse. Labe told Rand."

Emmie was silent. She wasn't sure how she felt about Ben, but she cared about Labe. He'd been good to her in his clumsy way. "Is Labe all right?"

Sarah nodded. "He joined up with a group of miners passing through here a couple of months ago. They were headed up the Bozeman Trail to the goldfields in Montana."

So much death. Everywhere she looked there was death. First Monroe and now Ben. She wasn't sure how she came to be there, but she suddenly found herself sobbing against Sarah's shoulder. She didn't know why she was crying. She'd never been close to Ben, but he was her older brother, and now that he was gone, she was even more alone in the world. She'd probably never see Labe again either.

By evening, the wind picked up and began to moan through overhanging rocks. Black thunderheads rolled in over the tops of the bluffs, and jagged flashes of lightning lit the roiling undersides.

"Get the horses tied down," Rand shouted after the supply train went into corral formation. He wheeled off on his horse, Ranger, shouting his instructions to the rest of the soldiers.

The wind struck with a fearful punch as Emmie struggled to unroll one side of the canvas covering for the ambulance while Sarah fought with the other side. Sharp needles of cold rain pelted them before they could get the bedding covered, and Emmie could barely see through her heavy wet hair hanging across her face. Looming out of the driving rain, Rand dashed to secure the canvas on Sarah's side. Emmie frantically pushed her wet hair from her eyes and fought the rope holding the canvas in place. She almost shrieked as strong hands gently pushed her out of the way and fastened the canvas down with deft, practiced movements.

"Isaac," she gasped. "Where did you come from?"

He grinned, his blue eyes dancing with merriment. "I've been on ahead scouting. You didn't think I would let a pretty gal like you get away, did you?"

She flushed. Was he making fun of her? She certainly didn't feel very pretty right now with her hair plastered to her head and her dress covered with mud. And he always seemed to put her at a disadvantage.

Isaac didn't seem to notice her embarrassment. He just patted the top of her head and strode off to help the rest of the men secure everything.

Emmie pulled her shawl around her protectively. He'd patted her like—like she was a dog or a child. Was that how he saw her? She pushed away the prick of hurt and climbed back into the ambulance.

The storm cleared quickly, and the procession moved on. Emmie found her gaze straying more often than she liked to Isaac's erect figure on the bay gelding. His burnished hair curled over his collar, and he was easy to pick out of the group. He seemed to have a kind and encouraging word for everyone. All the more reason for her not to believe him when he said she was beautiful. He was evidently one of those people who looked for the good in everyone. An admirable quality, she had to admit, but it made her more cautious.

"You ready to go back to Indiana?" Sarah asked when they took a short break in the middle of the afternoon.

"I thought about it," Emmie admitted. "This wilderness is a fearful place. Even the storms are wilder." Then she smiled. "But it is beautiful in a savage way. I love the scent of sage in the wind and the deep, rich reds and browns of the earth. And I can't wait to get a closer look at the mountains."

They saw wildlife everywhere. Elk, deer, jackrabbit, and once a small herd of buffalo off in the distance. Emmie wanted to get a closer look at the famous beasts, but they never came close enough to see them well.

"That's why the Indians are so set on keeping this area," Sarah told her when she mentioned the abundant game. "And since the Montana gold mines opened up and miners keep traipsing through on the Bozeman Trail, the game is beginning to thin out. Red Cloud is said to be gathering a large war band up in the Powder River area. He's promised a fight to the knife. Rand doesn't know where it will all end. He sees the Indians' point of view, but he knows we have to expand clear to the Pacific if this nation is going to thrive. We need the railroad completed and the telegraph to all cities. The Indians won't stand by and see it happen without a fight." She shivered. "It scares me when I think about it. Every time Rand goes out on detail, I'm terrified he won't come back."

Emmie hadn't realized it was so dangerous. So far she hadn't seen a single hostile Indian. It was hard to imagine that the problem was as severe as Sarah said.

Rand called a halt around six o'clock. After beating the brush for rattlesnakes, three men pitched a tepee-like structure called a Sibley tent for the ladies.

"What are you doing?" Emmie asked Rooster as he uncoiled a large horsehair rope.

"Snakes won't cross a horsehair rope," he said, laying it on the ground all around the tent and bedrolls. "Reckon they don't like them hairs ticklin' their bellies. Rattlers ain't nothin' to mess with, and we don't want to lose our only wimmenfolk. Course it's late in the year fer snakes, but it's so much warmer than usual, I don't 'tend to take any chances."

Emmie wasn't sure if he was telling the truth, but his words sounded comforting, so she and Sarah carried their clothes and blankets inside and tried to make the interior comfortable. When they came out of the tent, one of the men had gotten a blazing fire going. The aroma of stew made Emmie's mouth water. She had hardly touched her lunch, but now she was famished. She ate two plates of the delicious stew and washed it down with the water in the battered tin cup Rooster gave her.

While four of the men went off to stand guard duty after supper, Rand brought out the harmonicas. The plaintive notes of "Home Sweet Home" mingled with the crackle of the fire and the howl of some animal in the hills to their left.

"What's that?" Emmie knew her voice was too shrill when several of the soldiers snickered and Joel grinned.

"It's just a pack of coyotes," Isaac said. "They're more scared of you than you are of them."

Emmie shivered at another howl. "I wouldn't be too sure of that," she said shakily.

Rand played a couple of hymns, and the men joined in song. Rooster had a surprisingly deep bass voice, and Isaac sang tenor. But it had been a long day on the trail, and they were all yawning, so Rand sent them all off to find their bedrolls twenty minutes later.

As Emmie crawled beneath her own blanket, she wondered about this life she found herself in. The unknown was so scary, but it was exhilarating too. Was it perhaps her father's wanderlust blood coming to the fore? She'd always been content to stay close to hearth and home and had never dreamed she'd find herself in some wild land with rampaging coyotes and hostile savages. Maybe her father would finally be proud of her if he could see her now. Maybe he would even finally love her in spite of the fact that she wasn't a son. But to be honest, he hadn't had much use for Ben or Labe either. All he'd ever cared about was his whiskey. He was long buried anyway, so there was no use in thinking about it. She would just concentrate on the future.

Chapter 4

The landscape grew more wild and untamed as the procession turned north and trekked up toward Fort Phil Kearny. The mountains loomed in the distance, their purple peaks blending into the deep azure sky. Game flourished everywhere, and Rand had no trouble finding crack shots who could provide fresh meat to supplement the mess-chest fare. The rest of the section he ordered to keep close together as they all kept a sharp lookout for Indians.

E. B. Taylor had attempted to negotiate a constructive peace treaty in May 1866, but Red Cloud had angrily stomped out when Colonel Carrington showed up to establish three new forts in the last of the Sioux hunting grounds. Red Cloud objected that the army would be setting up forts without waiting for the agreement from the Indians to allow troops to patrol the Bozeman Trail. These last three months had been tense, with numerous skirmishes between soldiers and Indians. Red Cloud was said to be massing together not just Sioux but Cheyenne and Arapaho to fight the invasion of bluecoats. Along this very trail just a month earlier, three soldiers had been killed and several others wounded during an ambush, Rand told them. So he preached constant vigilance and caution.

If the girls had been allowed to travel on horseback instead of riding the lurching ambulance, they would have enjoyed the trip immensely. As it was, they alternated between enduring the jolting ride and getting out and walking along the dusty trail. Emmie longed for a brief respite, just long enough to take a bath when they crossed a stream or occasionally glimpsed the Powder River.

The nights were cool and clear. Once Isaac pointed out a pack of timber wolves on a bluff overlooking the camp. He assured the girls they were safe from attack, but Emmie hadn't slept well that night. She dreamed of wolves surrounding her with red eyes and slavering fangs before being driven off by Isaac. He disturbed her dreams way too often.

Sarah worried her too. Most mornings, Emmie held the cracked tin bowl while Sarah was sick. By ten o'clock, her friend was usually well enough to walk alongside the ambulance and laugh and joke with the men. But she grew paler, and her laughter seemed forced by the fifth day.

"Have you noticed how poorly Sarah looks?" she asked Rand finally while

Sarah was inside napping one afternoon.

He nodded, his brow crinkling with worry. "There's a post surgeon at Fort Phil Kearny. It's only another three days away or so. I just hope she can hold on. I've been thinking we might camp here an extra day. The horses could do with the rest too."

"I think it might help if you thought it would be safe," she said. "She keeps pushing herself so. Today is the first time she's agreed to take a nap. A bath in the river might be nice too."

Rand nodded slowly. "I'm anxious to get to the fort. The chance of meeting up with hostiles is pretty high, but I don't want Sarah to lose the baby. We'll just have to risk it. I'll post extra sentries and string up some blankets for privacy while you girls take a bath. I could use a bath and a shave myself." He rubbed his grizzled cheeks with a rueful grin.

A bath! Emmie almost skipped as she hurried to tell Sarah. Her friend was braiding her long red-gold hair when Emmie peeked in.

The afternoon sun still blazed by the time Emmie and Sarah wandered down to the stream to find Rand, but the air was brisk. True to his word, he'd rigged up a rope with blankets around a lovely pool of water. The water looked clear and inviting, and Emmie couldn't wait to strip her clothes off and plunge in.

"I'll go get us some clean clothes," she told Sarah.

By the time she got back, Sarah had pulled off her shoes and stockings. She sat with her skirt pulled up to her knees and her feet dangling in the water. Emmie looked all around, but the soldiers were busy about their other duties setting up camp. Reassured of their privacy, she slipped behind the curtain and pulled off her stained and dusty dress and tugged the pins from her hair. She plunged in and came up sputtering. "It's like ice," she gasped.

Sarah wasted no time in joining her. Birds chirped in the trees around them, and the breeze lapped the water into gentle waves and ripples as they quickly washed their hair. The water was too cold to stay long, and the air was chilly.

After they dressed, they left their hair down to dry as they washed their dirty clothes. Emmie thought Sarah looked better already. They spread their wet clothes out on the rocks and sat at the edge of the stream.

Emmie sighed, a sound of pure enjoyment as she felt the heat from the rock she was sitting on bake up through her chilled body. Almost dozing, she stretched out in the sun like a cat until a faint movement on the other side of the stream about fifty yards away caught her eye. "Oh, Sarah, look! Is that a buffalo?"

Sarah squinted against the glare of the sun as the movement came again. "Indians!" she screamed as she jumped to her feet.

Aware they'd been seen, the dim shapes rose to their feet and threw off their buffalo robes. Charging across the shallow creek with fierce yells, they headed straight toward the women with their tomahawks raised over their heads.

Emmie shrieked as she dashed toward the safety of the camp. She held tightly to Sarah's hand as they screamed for Rand.

Isaac and Rand, followed by four or five other soldiers, charged toward the Indians immediately. "Get under the wagon," Isaac ordered. Sarah grabbed Joel as he raced past them and dragged him under the wagon with them. Isaac dropped to one knee and aimed his rifle toward the advancing Indians. A fearsomely painted brave choked and fell seconds after the rifle cracked. Soldiers raced from all over the camp to join the fray. Emmie covered her ears at the booming gunfire and the terrifying screams and shouts. She was sure she and Sarah were about to die.

Rooster rolled in under the wagon beside the women. "Don't you fear, Missy," he panted to Emmie. "No redskins gonna git ya. I'll shoot ya first myself 'fore I let them red devils take ya." Unaware of the shock his words caused Emmie, he fired his rifle methodically at the faltering horde of Sioux.

A few minutes later, it was over. One man was dead and three were injured, including Rand, who had taken an arrow in the left arm.

"It's just a scratch," he said impatiently as Sarah fussed over him. "I'm all right, Green Eyes." He held her with his good arm as she burst into tears.

Emmie couldn't hold back the tears either. Isaac's vivid blue eyes met Emmie's, and she had to check the impulse to run to him. Turning away from his anxious gaze, she wiped her eyes and hurried toward the tent before she disgraced herself by begging Isaac to hold her. What was wrong with her anyway that she would have such a crazy thought? Men couldn't be trusted. She'd best not let herself forget that.

The next morning, Sarah looked much better. Rand had awakened them early and was even more eager to reach the safe haven of Fort Phil Kearny after the ambush the day before. As they rolled along, Isaac rode next to the ambulance and pointed out the majestic peaks in the distance.

"That's the Bighorn Mountains. Beautiful, aren't they? This Powder River country is the last of the Sioux hunting grounds. It's usually thick with buffalo, but they're already beginning to thin out from the white man hunting them. The Indians are afraid if they let us establish the Bozeman Trail along here that we'll drive away the last of the game. And they're right, as usual. It's already beginning to happen."

Emmie looked at Isaac's face, bright with awe and love for the land. His nose was peeling a bit from the sun, and his blue eyes stood out in sharp contrast to his tanned face. He seemed so solid and dependable mounted on his horse. She felt a tugging at her heartstrings and looked away.

Later that night, Emmie mentioned what Isaac had said. After the terror of the day before, Emmie thought it might be a good thing for the game to be driven away. Maybe the Indians would decide to be civilized if they couldn't find game.

"I lived with the Sioux for a few days," Sarah said. "It was a curiously peaceful life where we worked for our food and really lacked nothing important. Their ways aren't any different to us than our ways are to the Europeans. The Indian women do beautiful needlework. Sometime I'll show you my buckskin dress and let you see inside a Sioux tepee. My friend, White Beaver, taught me a lot about what's really important in life. Things like love and unity and self-sufficiency. You would like her."

"Where is she now?"

"With Little Wolverine in Red Cloud's resistance, as far as I know. Rand and I tried to talk them out of going, but they said they had to stand with their people before the Sioux are no more."

"How can Rand fight the Indians when he has friends among them? What if Little Wolverine were with the band who attacked?" Emmie asked.

"It would be Rand's worst nightmare to have to fight his friend. I don't know if he could or not. But Wolverine said they would always be friends, so I don't think he would ever attack us."

Their discussion was interrupted by shouts from the front of the procession. "Phil Kearny ahead!"

Sarah and Emmie both thrust their heads out under the rolled-up canvas on the sides of the wagon and looked eagerly for their destination. Emmie could see sentries on a hill ahead waving signal flags.

"They're signaling our arrival to the fort," Sarah told her. "The commander will send out an escort."

Rand had ordered the women to stay in the ambulance away from the possible eyes of hostiles, but Emmie longed to climb out of the lurching conveyance and run on ahead to the fort. The thought of sleeping in a real bed was enticing. As she and Sarah looked toward the fort, a wagon loaded with wood lumbered by. On the back of the wagon a bloodstained figure lolled, one arm flung down the back of the wagon. Emmie thought he looked like he had red hair like Isaac until Sarah gasped.

"That soldier's been scalped," Sarah choked out, her hand to her mouth.

Emmie shuddered and looked around fearfully for the Indians who had committed the atrocity. But the wooded hills around the fort looked peaceful. The ambulance jerked forward as the driver urged the horses to a trot. Rand had seen the dead soldier and motioned the troops to hurry toward the safety of the fort.

As they pulled inside the stockaded garrison, soldiers milled around shouting orders. "Do you see Amelia?" Sarah asked anxiously.

Emmie looked around but saw no other women. "It's around lunchtime," she said, consulting the gold watch pinned to her dress. "Maybe we could find her in the mess hall."

They climbed down out of the ambulance. Emmie was glad to be on solid ground again. She looked around the tiny fort. "It looks more like I thought Laramie would look," she said. "There are stockades and sentries along the blockhouses."

Sarah nodded. "If that murdered soldier is anything to go by, they need all the protection they can get. There's no telegraph line strung this far north, so if they've been having a lot of trouble with hostiles, they wouldn't be able to wire for reinforcements." Joel was dancing around impatiently, so she gave him permission to go look for his friend.

Rand stepped up and put an arm around Sarah. "I'll see if I can find Jake and Amelia. You look done in. While you're resting at Amelia's, I'll see the quartermaster and get our housing assignment." But before he could go look for his brother, he heard a familiar voice.

"Rand!" His brother Jake ran toward them, and seconds later, the brothers were hugging and slapping one another on the back. "I can't believe you're here. And Sarah too. Amelia will be ecstatic. She's been driving me crazy with missing Sarah." He pulled Sarah into a bear hug, then his handsome face sobered when he saw Emmie. Rand gave him one last clap on the back and hurried off to find the quartermaster.

Emmie knew Rand's brother Jacob—or Jake, as everyone called him—had never liked Ben. She hadn't had much occasion to talk to Jake herself, so she assumed his reserve was because of her brother. He would just have to find out she wasn't like her brother. She held out her hand. "Hello, Jake."

He smiled then and took her hand. "Emmie. What are you doing here? Did your husband join the army? Ma wrote when you got married."

Sarah rushed in as she saw Emmie bite her lip. "Emmie's a widow, and she's here to keep me company. But there's plenty of time for explanations later. I'm dying to see Amelia. Where is she?"

"I'll show you to our quarters. She's been feeling poorly, and I told her to rest this afternoon."

"What's wrong with her?" Sarah's voice was alarmed as she and Emmie hurried to keep up with Jake's long strides as he led them across the uncompleted parade ground toward a row of wooden houses.

He grinned. "You'll have to ask her."

"You don't mean—"

"Yeah. Can you believe I'm going to be a papa? Rand and I are going to make each other uncles within a few weeks of one another."

Sarah clapped her hands together. "Wait until Rand hears!"

"Here we are." He stopped beside a small wooden house.

Emmie looked around curiously. The home was tiny, and sap ran from the cuts and nicks in the logs. She touched a sticky lump. It smelled like pine. She'd noticed coming toward the fort that this area had a lot more trees than down around Laramie.

Jake pushed open the door and led them into a tiny parlor with a fireplace in one wall. It looked much like the home they'd left except it was even smaller. "It doesn't look like much now, I know," he said with an apologetic grin. "I haven't had time to knock together a table and chairs for the kitchen yet, so we've been eating in the parlor. It's pretty inconvenient for Amelia, but I told her I'd make sure I got to it this week. The Indians have been a constant nuisance. Even the wood detail has to be accompanied by armed troops. And that doesn't always stop Red Cloud's band, as I'm sure you noticed on the way in."

"Who was the murdered soldier?" Sarah asked as Jake led the way through the minuscule kitchen toward the closed door on the far side. "Did I know him?"

"No, he was a new recruit. Corporal Johnson was his name, and he was as hotheaded as they come. We're just lucky more weren't killed. Some of the men have been spoiling for a fight, but I thank the good Lord that Carrington has been able to restrain them so far." He pushed open the door to the bedroom and smiled when he saw his wife.

She lay on her side, one arm outflung and her face pink in sleep. Her black hair was unbound and fanned out on the pillow in a silken cloud. Emmie saw Jake's face soften in love and pride as he gazed at his sleeping wife.

"Honey. Look who's here." He spoke gently as he took her hand.

Her long lashes fluttered, and she opened her eyes blearily. She stared for a long minute into Sarah's eyes, then bolted upright. "Sarah?" She looked over at Jake, then back at Sarah.

Sarah bounded forward and jumped onto the bed. "It's me, Amelia. It's really me."

Jealousy, scalding and acrid, overwhelmed Emmie as she saw Sarah and Amelia fall into one another's arms with tears of joy. She'd always liked Amelia, but she'd grown to regard Sarah as her best friend over the past weeks. Bleakly, she knew she would have to settle for second place in Sarah's affections. Unconsciously, she squared her shoulders and pushed the hurt feelings away. She would not be like her brother Ben. He had allowed jealousy and possessiveness to ruin his life and Labe's too. She'd come here alone, and she could leave the same way if she had to. But she admitted to herself that she didn't want to leave.

It felt grand to laugh with friends like Sarah and Rand.

Amelia drew away and noticed Emmie standing unobtrusively to one side. "Why, dear Emmie too!" She slipped out of the bed and ran to give her a quick hug. "How wonderful to see you. I had no idea you were with Sarah. Is Monroe with you?"

Amelia seemed truly glad to see her. Emmie shook her head at Amelia's question. She glanced gratefully at Sarah, who rushed in with a quick explanation of Emmie's circumstances.

"You poor dear," Amelia said with another quick hug. "No wonder you look so peaked. I am glad you're here, though you may want to run screaming for home with two crotchety women in delicate condition for company."

"Well, I'll leave you three to get caught up on all the gossip and go find my brother," Jake put in.

The girls barely noticed his departure as they all three piled on the bed and began to talk at once. "We brought some fresh newspapers from back east with us—they're only two months old," Sarah said.

"And I brought a magazine of new fashions Margaret sent with me. I've been saving it until winter settled in, but we could get it out whenever you want," Emmie added.

"Let's save it until we can get together with the other ladies," Amelia said. "You'll love our little community. There's Mrs. Horton, the wife of our post surgeon and Surgeon in Chief of the Mountain District; Mrs. Carrington, the commander's wife; Mrs. Wands; Mrs. Bisbee; and Mrs. Grummond. They've been a wonderful help to me." She slipped off the bed and, picking up the hairbrush from the barrel that served as a nightstand, began to put her hair up. "Let's have some tea, then I'll introduce you to the ladies."

Chapter 5

Emmie put her teacup down as someone banged on the front door. "I'll get it," she told Amelia and Sarah. Emmie opened the door and stared into Isaac's face.

"Isaac. I thought it was Rand." Her heart jumped at the sight of him.

"He sent me to fetch you two ladies. Your quarters are ready for your inspection." He took out his large, white handkerchief and carefully wiped the corner of her mouth. "Jam," he said with a gentle smile.

Emmie's cheeks burned. Why did he always have to catch her at such a disadvantage? Besides, she wasn't interested in a flirtation with anyone, no matter how attractive. He looked particularly handsome with his auburn hair ruffled by the wind and his face tanned from the sun. He grinned at her discomfiture. "I'll get Sarah," she said abruptly. She left him standing at the open door as she went to fetch her friend.

"Are our quarters close to Amelia?" Sarah asked. She and Emmie snatched up their bonnets from the hook near the door and followed Isaac down the steps.

"The permanent ones will be next door."

"Permanent ones? Where are we going now?"

Isaac pointed toward a group of tents in a small open space near the quartermaster's yard.

"You're joking, right?" Sarah stopped and looked up at Isaac in dismay. "Amelia says we'll have snow soon. We can't live in a tent."

"It's just while your quarters are built. We've put a Sibley stove in for you to keep the cold away. Rand tried his best to get you something else. Jake even offered to let you stay with them, but you saw how small their place is. This is the best the quartermaster could do on short notice."

Sarah bit her lip. "Well, if it's the best he could do, then we have no choice. Please don't say anything to Rand about my being upset," she said.

Isaac gave her an approving smile. "Good girl." He glanced at Emmie. "Think you can stand it too?"

"Of course," she said with more certainty than she felt.

He smiled again, and Emmie thought she saw a hint of admiration in his blue eyes, but she pushed the thought away. She didn't want admiration or anything else from him. Not from him or any other man.

Rand was busy directing soldiers where to put the barrels of their belongings when they arrived. "I'm sorry, Green Eyes, but this will have to do for now. But it's not too bad. See, we've put three A tents together to make three rooms. We can store our trunks and mess chest in one. You and I can sleep in here, and Emmie can have the next one. Joel is going to stay with the Carringtons until our quarters are ready. There's a stove in Emmie's room too, as well as this one. Will you be all right?"

"Of course. This is very pleasant, Rand." Sarah walked through the interconnected tents with Emmie following close behind. Two army cots and the stove took up most of the area in the Campbells' room, but Emmie would have a bit more floor space for possessions.

"We could use my room as a parlor during the day," Emmie said with a quick look around. She was very conscious of Isaac's nearness as he hovered at her elbow. When he looked at her, she felt as though he were looking into her very soul.

"You'll probably spend most of your daylight hours with Amelia and the other ladies," Rand said. "But thanks for the offer."

The bugle sounded mess call, and Isaac took Emmie's arm to escort her to the mess hall. She could feel the smooth muscles of his forearm under his coat sleeve, and she wanted to draw her hand away. To do so would have been rude, though, and it wasn't Isaac's fault that she found him entirely too attractive for her own peace of mind. They followed Rand and Sarah across the parade ground.

By the time they ate the luncheon of ever-present salt pork and beans, reconstituted vegetables, and coffee, the first fat drops of rain had begun to fall. The clouds obscured the sun and cast a dark pall over the fort as the wind howled like a thousand banshees. The men had already left for their afternoon duties, and Emmie glanced at the sky nervously as she and Sarah left the mess hall. They ran for the safety of Amelia's quarters, with the wind driving sand and cold rain into their skin like a horde of vicious mosquitoes. Soaked and chilled, they burst through the door into Amelia's parlor. As they shook the water out of their clothes and hair, a horrendous pounding and clattering began all around them.

"What is it?" Emmie cried. She'd been terrified of storms ever since she'd been caught in the field during an Indiana thunderstorm once, cowering in terror in a ditch while a blackish-green tornado had whirled above her.

They all ran to the front window and looked out on a scene of utter pandemonium. Horses reared in terror and soldiers fought to control them as man and beast alike were pelted with hail the size of eggs. The white missiles fell so hard they left dents in the soft ground. Emmie saw several soldiers cringe beneath the blows as their hats went flying. It only lasted for a few minutes, but by the time the freakish weather was over, the post surgeon had several bleeding soldiers to attend to. One man was trampled beneath the hooves of a panicked horse. The three women worried about the men until Amelia spied her husband under the overhanging roof of the sutler's store. He waved at them cheerily and gave no evidence of dismay, so they assumed everyone was all right.

The next morning, Emmie awoke with something tickling her nose. She could hear the wind howling through the tent, but she had piled on so many blankets and buffalo robes, she was pleasantly warm and comfortable. She reached up to scratch her nose and touched cold, dry snow. During the night, the early snowstorm had arrived, and the wind blew the powdery fluff through the cracks in the tent openings. A thick layer of white stuff covered Emmie and all her possessions.

She sat up and shook the snow from her hair and bedclothes. Scrambling out of bed, she emptied the snow from her shoes. She felt oddly light-headed as she shook her dress thoroughly and pulled her nightgown over her head. By the time she was dressed, she was shivering almost uncontrollably. As she bent over to tie her boots, she almost tumbled to the floor as a wave of dizziness washed over her. Straightening up, she retched with a suddenly overwhelming attack of nausea. She hurriedly reached for the chamber pot at the end of her cot and vomited into it. What on earth was wrong with her? *I can't get sick now,* she thought frantically as she sank back on the bunk, clutching the chamber pot weakly. Not with Sarah and Amelia dependent on her. They both felt poorly so often; who would clean up and cook if she fell ill?

As she thought of their condition, a terrible thought assailed her. When did she have her last monthly? Another wave of nausea shook her as she lay weakly back against the pillow and thought about it. She hadn't had her monthly at all in August, and September's should have arrived last week. She closed her eyes as she contemplated the possibility that she might be pregnant. It could be, couldn't it? Weak tears trickled from beneath her closed eyes. Was there no end to her shame? Did she now have to bear an illegitimate child? Surely not. This was probably just a result of being chilled in the night—or perhaps the influenza, or maybe even cholera. Anything, even something deadly, would be preferable to what she suspected was true.

Sarah had evidently heard her retching, for she scratched at the opening between the two tents. "Emmie? Are you all right? I'm coming in." She didn't wait for an answer but pushed open the flap and entered. She hurried straight to the bed where Emmie lay bleakly contemplating how much to tell her friend.

"I'm fine. Just a little sick feeling. It's probably nothing."

"You look wretched," Sarah said. "Rand, please ask Dr. Horton to stop by," she called to her husband, who hovered near the doorway. "I don't like the way she looks. And get the fire going in the stove too, please." She turned briskly back to Emmie. "Now I want you to get back in your nightgown and into bed. It's my turn to take care of you."

"I'm feeling much better. Maybe if I had a cracker and some tea—" Emmie stammered.

"The very thing. That always helps me when I feel sick. I'll be right back with some, and I want to find you snuggled in the covers when I return." With a last admonishing wag of her finger, Sarah stepped through the tent flap.

Wearily, Emmie pulled off her clothes and tugged on her thick flannel nightgown. There was no use in protesting. Sarah could be implacable when she thought she was in the right.

Sarah returned with the steaming tea and a tin of crackers at the same time Dr. Horton arrived with his black bag. He was a tall, spare man in his forties, with a balding pate and a pleasant smile and demeanor. "Well, now, what seems to be the matter, young lady? You should be up and about. That pretty face of yours is good for morale." He set his bag down on the bed and drew out his stethoscope. Rand came in just behind him and began to poke at the coals in the stove.

Sarah handed the tea and crackers to Emmie. "I'll run over and get Amelia while the doctor's with you."

"There's really no need—" But Sarah was gone before Emmie could finish her protest. Rand followed her out after winking at Emmie kindly.

"When did you start feeling poorly?" the doctor asked, putting the cold stethoscope against her chest.

"Just this morning." She bent forward obediently as he placed the stethoscope on her back and listened intently. She answered the rest of his questions and lay back against the pillow as he probed around on her stomach.

"Ah," he said after a few moments.

"What is it?"

"When did you have your last monthly?"

Oh, no. She swallowed hard, then told him in a hoarse whisper.

He nodded. "I'd say you're increasing. The little one should arrive about mid-May." He frowned when he noticed her obvious distress. "You don't seem overjoyed."

"My husband is dead, Dr. Horton, and I have no family."

He nodded again. "Yes, I know. But at least you're among friends. And I'm sure in a fort full of eligible men you could find a father for your baby if you wished."

"I'm not interested in marrying again," she whispered. The doctor raised his eyebrows at her answer, and she laid a hand on his arm. "You've been very kind. How long will the morning sickness last?"

"Hard to say." He stood and began to put his things back in his bag. "It could only be for a few weeks or a few months. If you're really unlucky, it could last your entire pregnancy. But most women find it subsides after four or five weeks." He gestured at the crackers in her hand. "Those usually help if you keep some beside your bed and nibble on them before you even get out of bed. I would suggest you stay in bed today—you've had quite a shock, and I can see it's upset you. If you need me again, just send one of the men for me." He patted her hand kindly. "At least you won't be alone any longer. God knows best, my dear." With a final pat he hurried away.

Emmie closed her eyes, and a few tears slipped out from under her lashes. It was easy for him to say that God knew best. He wasn't alone in the world. She had no means of supporting herself, let alone a baby. What was she going to do? Rand and Sarah wouldn't throw her out, but she was supposed to be here to help Sarah, not be an additional burden on her friends who'd been so kind. She had no skills, no resources. She shuddered from the hopelessness of her situation. Why did she ever have to meet Monroe? Her life was in ruins.

She turned her head as Sarah and Amelia hurried into her tent. Amelia looked as anxious as Sarah did, and Emmie felt a wave of love for both friends. They truly did care about her. She didn't know why they should, but they did, and she was grateful to both of them.

"What did the doctor say?" Sarah laid a cool hand on Emmie's forehead.

Emmie bit her lip. There was no use trying to keep it from them. "I'm going to have a baby."

Sarah's eyes widened, and she gaped before she recovered her composure. "Oh, Emmie, that's wonderful! When?"

"May."

Amelia clapped her hands in delight. "It will be such fun for us to raise our babies together. We'll have all kinds of good advice for you by the time the wee one arrives."

Emmie was grateful for the way they were hiding the dismay they must both be feeling. "I'll be fine in a day or two, and I promise not to be a bother, Sarah. I'm supposed to be helping you."

"Oh, pish posh, I don't need any help. I just needed company. You'll be even better company now that you know what we're going through."

"But what will Rand say?"

"What do you mean?" Sarah seemed genuinely puzzled. "What could he say?

He loves kids." She fluffed up Emmie's pillow and pushed her down against it. "Now you just quit your fretting and get some rest. Everything is going to be just fine. You'll see."

Emmie allowed herself to be tucked into the quilts and furs as the fire in the stove threw out welcome warmth and cheeriness. She didn't know what the future might hold, but with friends like the Campbells, it would surely be all right.

Chapter 6

I ndeed, Emmie found that Rand treated her no differently than he always had over the days that followed. He was just as solicitous of her as he was Sarah. He truly did not seem to mind the change in the bargain they'd struck, and Emmie began to relax. She was not sure if Rand told Isaac, but he didn't stop by as often as before. As the days passed and the chilly October wind blew while the fort prepared for winter, she told herself she didn't care if he came by or not. All men were fickle at best and treacherous at worst.

Early one sunny day in late October, Rand announced their permanent quarters were ready to move into. Several soldiers showed up eager to be of service, and they soon had their few possessions hoisted on their shoulders and hauled across the parade ground to the three-room quarters. It was similar to what they'd left behind in Fort Laramie in layout but smaller in size. The fresh-cut pine boards still oozed sap and smelled of newly milled lumber. The fresh plaster walls looked clean but stark, with no trim around the windows or floor. The kitchen was bare of accessories but serviceable and clean. Emmie was so glad to be out of the tent, she didn't care how it looked.

"It's plain, I know, but I'll knock together a dry sink and corner cupboard as soon as I can," Rand said apologetically.

"Already done, Partner," Isaac's voice broke in. He grinned as he set a sturdy sawhorse down against the wall. "Be right back." He stepped outside and came right back in with another one, which he placed a couple of feet away from the first. Then he brought in four rough planks of wood and laid them over the sawhorses. "This is the very latest in Fort Phil's kitchen decor. All the best-dressed kitchens have one. And I have it on the best authority that it makes a dandy ironing board as well."

"Isaac, you darling!" Sarah exclaimed. She ran to hug him.

"Don't I get a hug from you too?" he asked Emmie with a grin.

Emmie felt the warm blood rush to her cheeks. He hadn't shown his face for days, and now he showed up talking about hugs. "Maybe when we get the chairs," she said awkwardly. She flushed again when he laughed. *What a stupid thing to say,* she told herself disgustedly. But he'd caught her off guard.

"I'll hold you to it." He chuckled as he walked away.

162

Emmie was amazed how easily she and Sarah adapted to their rough surroundings. She'd never had nice things growing up, but Monroe had insisted on the finest of everything, and she had found herself enjoying every luxury. Now she was content with the barest necessities.

They delighted in fixing up their tiny home over the next few days. They begged some wool blankets from the quartermaster and tacked them together to make rugs for the parlor and bedroom floors as well as for the small area in the hall that was partitioned off for Emmie. With Sarah's little knickknacks around, the place looked very homey. Several of the other ladies were very friendly and stopped by with invitations to tea and some small offerings of household items.

"I think I'll go for a walk," Emmie told Sarah one evening after the supper dishes were done. Rand had taken Joel and gone out to make some rounds, and things were too quiet for Emmie. She didn't like having time to think. "The wind isn't blowing for a change. I'm going crazy cooped up inside. Want to come along?"

"I don't think so. Rand tore his britches on some cactus yesterday, and I promised I'd mend them. Why don't you ask Isaac or one of the other officers to escort you? Any of them would jump at the chance."

"No, thanks. I don't mind going alone." Emmie shied away from the thought of Isaac. She had tried to avoid him ever since he brought by the camp chairs for the kitchen while she was taking their laundry to Soapsuds Row two days ago. *He's surely forgotten all about that stupid remark I made,* she told herself.

The cool night air felt invigorating, but Emmie shivered as wolves howled outside the stockade. She wrapped her cloak more tightly around her as she strolled along the sawdust path in front of the officers' quarters. She decided to wander in the direction of the front of the stockade.

"Mind if I join you?" A tall shadow came toward her, and she flinched back before she recognized Isaac's smiling face.

"There's really no need. I'm perfectly all right. I just wanted a walk." Her pulse quickened, and she took a step back.

"I could use a chance to stretch my legs myself." He fell into step beside her. "Did you have someplace special in mind to go or shall we just look in some windows?"

She chuckled in spite of herself, then glanced at him hesitantly. He probably wouldn't let her do what she planned. "I know Rand said to stay away from the stockade perimeter, but I wish I could climb up in the blockhouse and look out over the wall for just a minute. I'm so tired of seeing the same things day after day. I haven't been outside the confines of this fort in weeks."

Isaac was silent for a minute. She shivered again as she heard a pack of wolves howl off to her right, but Isaac relaxed at the sound. "Those are real wolves and not Indians. I guess it wouldn't hurt for just a minute. But you have to promise to get away from the wall the minute I say we have to leave."

"I promise," she said excitedly.

Isaac led her past the hospital and warehouses and through the tangle of hayricks and shops and quarters for wagon makers and saddlers. He stepped carefully and pointed out piles of manure and mud for her to avoid before stopping outside the blockhouse. "Let me tell the soldiers on duty what we're doing," he said. He disappeared inside the door and returned several moments later with a smile on his face.

"What's so funny?"

"I told Corporal Lengel I wanted to show you the moon on the Little Piney River."

"He'll think—"

"Well, I had to give him some reason."

Emmie flushed as she followed Isaac's broad back up the ladder. She didn't want anyone getting the wrong idea about her and Isaac. Rumors could run through their little community like a herd of thundering buffalo. The corporal grinned knowingly as they brushed past him to get to the window.

"Call when you're finished here, Captain," he said, his grin widening as he backed down the ladder.

"Now see what you've done," Emmie said. She was glad it was too dark for Isaac to see her hot cheeks.

Isaac just laughed. Ignoring her outburst, he pointed out the window. "Look at the river."

Emmie looked and caught her breath. The trees along the river looked as though they were made of diamonds. The moon glittered on their coating of heavy frost, and the iced-over river caught the shimmering reflection and bounced it back. She longed to run out and skate along its shining surface. She leaned out the window, but Isaac caught her arm and pulled her back.

"Don't do that! There could be Sioux out there just waiting to put an arrow through your pretty head."

Emmie swallowed hard and shrank back against his side. A warning bell rang inside her head as she realized how close he was. She straightened up and started to pull away, but he caught her and turned her to face him.

"A real lady always pays her debts, you know."

"What do you mean?" Her heart thundered in her ears. She knew what he intended and put up one hand against his chest. She could feel the thud of his heart under her fingers. She knew she should run as fast as she could, but his warm male scent was intoxicating.

His voice was husky as he leaned closer. "I distinctly remember you promising me a hug when I brought the kitchen chairs. It's been two days, and I haven't gotten my hug yet. I think I'd better charge you a little interest."

He gathered her closer. Emmie stared mesmerized as he bent his head. She smelled the warm scent of his skin as his lips found hers, and she found herself responding in spite of her resolve. His kiss was gentle at first but began to turn into something else as she finally gathered her strength and pulled away.

"That was more than a little interest!" She was trembling in spite of the warmth of her cloak.

"I think it was just perfect." He traced a finger along the curve of her cheek. "Just like you."

"I—I'd better get back." She swallowed hard. "Sarah will be wondering about me."

He nodded and let her go. She kept a wary eye on him as she took one last look out the window, then hurried down the ladder. She didn't wait for him but struck off toward the officers' quarters.

"Wait up, Emmie. What are you so scared of? I won't hurt you."

"I—I don't want you to think I'm the sort of girl who dallies in the moonlight," she gulped, her voice nearly inaudible. "Just because I'm a widow doesn't mean I'm looking for someone to fill in for Monroe."

"I never thought you were." Isaac's voice was cool. "That husband of yours must have been a piece of work for you to be so prickly, but you don't need to lump all of us men in the same pot of stew. I wouldn't want to do anything to dishonor you or my God."

"Don't you say anything about Monroe! You don't know anything about him." She was near tears. Isaac's mention of dishonor flooded her with shame and guilt. She'd had all she could bear of the soaring heights of love; she knew all too well how hard the blow was when the time came to come back to earth.

"I know he must have hurt you badly. When you arrived at Fort Laramie, you were like a stray dog everyone had kicked too often. I left you alone to lick your wounds, but it's time for you to put the past behind you and get on with your life." He swept his arm expansively. "This is a new country out here. You can forget Indiana. God sent you out here to make a new life for yourself. Don't throw His gift back in His face."

"I am making a new life. It just doesn't include kisses in the moonlight with you or anyone else," Emmie said softly, near tears. His tender kiss had awakened feelings she didn't want stirred.

"Maybe I'm rushing you a little," Isaac said. He stepped away from her. "But I'll be here when you decide to quit living in the past." He turned and strode back toward the officers' quarters.

Emmie's throat burned with unshed tears as she mounted the steps to the door. *I just don't want to be hurt again,* she thought, trying to compose herself. *He's only interested because there aren't any other unmarried women here,* she told herself firmly. *If we were in Indiana, he wouldn't give me a second glance.* She'd never felt she was a lovable person until Monroe came into her life. And after he'd done what he did, she was sure there was something inherently wrong with her. No one had ever loved her for herself. Not even her family.

Sarah looked up as she came in. "Did you have a nice walk? Oh—" She broke off when she saw the look on Emmie's face. "What's wrong?"

"Nothing. I'm just tired." Emmie forced a smile to her face. She felt Sarah's probing eyes, but she refused to meet her gaze. "I think I'll turn in early. I'll see you in the morning." She fled to the meager haven of her curtained-off bedroom. *Sarah wouldn't understand,* she told herself. She'd like to see her marry Isaac and settle down next door. *But that isn't going to happen,* she vowed as she slipped between the cold sheets. Men just couldn't be trusted. Under his exuberance and flattery, Monroe had been just like her brothers and father. Just as selfish and deceitful. Isaac was no different. He was just hiding it like Monroe had done. Monroe's kisses had seemed tender and loving too.

The next morning was Sunday. Emmie hummed as she donned her best dress and pulled her hair back in a ribbon. She'd managed to vanquish thoughts of Isaac in the night and was determined not to let him unsettle her. A church service would actually be held in the little post chapel today. A chaplain had arrived earlier in the week and would lead the little post's first service.

She'd never attended church in Wabash other than an occasional wedding. Her pa didn't hold with religion, even though he bellowed out hymns when he was drunk. Emmie always wondered where he'd learned them. He never talked much about how he was raised, and she never knew her grandparents. Her pa always said religion was a crutch for weak people, but personally, Emmie thought the liquor was more of a crutch. She wanted to know more about what made her friends so different. Maybe it was their religion. Church should be interesting.

Sarah looked at her sharply as she pushed the curtain back and stepped into the parlor. "You seem in a fine mood today."

"It's a beautiful morning for a church service," Emmie said. "I've never been to a real church service. Only weddings."

"Rand is so disappointed to miss it. He has orders to lead a squad to guard the wood detail. I promised to tell him all about it tonight."

The chapel was a small cabin with seats that were rough backless benches oozing sap. A small stove in one corner of the room belched out smoke along with a little warmth. Emmie, Sarah, and Joel sat on the second row beside Amelia.

The chaplain, Reverend Howard, was a nervous young man with thin, pale hair and a straggly mustache. He read from Isaiah 43:1–2: " 'Fear not: for I have redeemed thee, I have called thee by thy name; thou art Mine. When thou passest through the waters, I will be with thee; and through the rivers, they shall not overflow thee: when thou walkest through the fire, thou shalt not be burned; neither shall the flame kindle upon thee.' " He closed his large Bible and cleared his throat. "Though it seems we are compassed about by the enemy in this place, God tells us to fear not. He is with us, and He will be our shield and comfort."

Although he stammered occasionally as he spoke of God's protection, Emmie was drawn by the words. Was the minister right? And Isaac? She glanced at the back of his head in the row in front of her. He leaned slightly forward in his seat as he listened intently. Did God really care about her in a personal way? She'd never doubted the existence of God, but in her mind, He was a powerful Being who looked down on mere mortals with distant interest. Oh, He might deign to involve Himself in the moving of nations and history, but He wasn't concerned with the small day-to-day heartbreaks of an ordinary person like her. But was He? Did He send her out here to such good friends as the Campbells because He loved her and cared for her? The thought was comforting, and she wished she could believe it. It would be nice to be able to rest in His protection like the minister said. Emmie sighed. She'd have to think about it.

As the service ended and they stood to leave, Isaac's gaze caught hers for just a moment. She looked away quickly as Frances Grummond called to them. She was glad for an excuse to turn away from Isaac's warm eyes. The look in his gaze threatened to upset all her carefully laid plans to keep her distance.

"Yoo hoo, Emmie." Frances waved at them from across the room. She was a petite brunette with softly rounded curves and a delightful Southern accent. She, too, was expecting a baby soon. She hurried over when she saw she had Emmie's attention. "I'm having tea at my house. Won't you all join me?"

Sarah smiled and clapped her hands. "The very thing! I've gotten so tired of those same four walls. What can I bring?"

"I have everything prepared. I know my lack of cooking prowess is legendary, but my husband has secured the services of Private Brown as cook. His scones are exemplary."

"Sounds lovely," Amelia said with a gentle smile. "Our men are out on wood detail or guard duty. What time do you want us?"

"Oh, about three. Bring your mending or whatever, and we'll have a fine time of chatting. Mrs. Horton is joining us also."

The three thanked her again and hurried toward home, after waving good-bye to Joel, who went off quite happily with his friend, Jimmy Carrington. The fierce October wind whipped their cloaks about as they fought to keep their balance in the gale.

The fire was almost out as they stepped inside Amelia's quarters. "I'll get the fire going," Emmie said. The wind blew down the chimney and sent ashes fly-ing all over her and into the room as she opened the stove door. She quickly threw two logs in and shut the door again.

"Let's just have some soup, since we'll be having tea with Frances," Sarah said. "I'm really not that hungry, are you?"

"Not at all," Emmie said. "Soup would be lovely. I'll warm it up." She opened the back door and lifted the brick off the pan sitting on the ground. There were too many roving dogs to set the pan out without something heavy on the lid. She put the pan on the stove and turned to tie on an apron before she soiled her dress.

"I feel sorry for poor Frances," Amelia said.

"She seems happy enough," Emmie said. "Why should you feel sorry for her?"

"Her husband doesn't seem to give her much thought. He's always out play-ing poker at the sutler's store or trying to stir up some of the men to go on some confrontation with the Indians. Mrs. Horton says this is his second mar-riage. I have a feeling it won't be long before Lieutenant Grummond's hot blood brings him in harm's way. And poor little Frances is so loyal and sweet."

"But aren't most men a lot like that?" Emmie asked as she stirred the soup. "My brothers were, and so was Monroe."

Sarah and Amelia shared a long look.

"Rand and Jake are different, of course," Emmie said hastily. "But you two are luckier than most."

"Actually, Emmie, I'm glad you brought this up," Sarah said slowly. "I've wanted to talk to you about your view of men. I've seen the way you shy away from our male callers, even Isaac. I've found most soldiers to be loyal and kind to their wives. And Ben was—Ben was not a good example for you to look to. I hate to see you waste your life because of that distrust you carry around like a shield. I'm sorry to hear Monroe wasn't kind to you."

Emmie flushed. "It's not that he wasn't kind—" She gulped and sat down. She twisted her hands together in her lap as the other women sat beside her. *It's time for the truth*, she thought. But did she have the strength to tell it? She drew a shaky breath. "I've wanted to tell you about this," she said, slowly searching the faces of her friends. "But I was afraid you wouldn't care for me anymore when you knew the truth."

Amelia leaned forward and took her hand. "Nothing you say could possibly change how we feel about you, Emmie dear. You're our friend, and we love you. Your husband's character can't change yours. You're sweet and loyal and giving. I'm honored to be your friend, and I know Sarah is too. You can tell us anything, and we won't betray your confidence."

Tears welled up in Emmie's eyes. "I—I don't really know how to begin," she choked.

Sarah handed her a hanky. "Begin wherever you want," she said softly.

"You have to understand. Monroe was so—so alive when I met him. I'd never seen anyone with so much exuberance and energy. I couldn't resist that vitality. When he began to pay attention to me, I couldn't believe it. Me. The promiscuous daughter of the town drunk."

"Oh, Emmie, you were never that!" Sarah's voice was indignant.

"I heard Mrs. Lambert call me that once when I was thirteen. I've never forgotten it. I'd never even talked to a boy besides my brothers when I heard her say that, but I was so ashamed."

"My mother always talked about how sweet you were and what a shame it was you had to grow up with the father you had," Sarah said.

"Did she really?"

"Really. She would see you at Papa's store. When we'd get home, she'd tell me I should be more like you and not such a tomboy."

A tear slowly slid down Emmie's cheek. "She wouldn't say that now. Not if she knew the truth."

"What truth?" Sarah's voice was insistent.

Emmie took another deep breath. "After Monroe's funeral, a lady showed up at my door. Well-dressed and pretty with a small boy. She was Monroe's true wife, and the little boy was his son. He'd married me although he was already married to her. That's why I had to leave town. So you see," she finished bravely, "the baby I'm carrying is illegitimate. And Mrs. Lambert is saying she was right about me all along." The seconds seemed hours as the shock registered on the faces of her friends. Would they reject her too?

"You poor dear," Amelia said. She jumped to her feet and put her arms around Emmie.

At the compassion in her voice, Emmie burst into tears. Hot, scalding tears that she had kept pent up since she'd first learned the truth about Monroe. There had been no one who could hold her. No one who cared what happened to her.

"It's not your fault, Emmie," Sarah said gently, taking her hand. "You didn't know."

"That's not what they're saying back in Wabash, I'm sure. I was beginning to get some strange looks before I left." Hot blood rushed to her cheeks, and she bowed her head.

"But we know you too well to believe any lies," Amelia said. "Why didn't you tell us sooner? Surely you didn't think we wouldn't believe you?"

"I didn't know what to believe. It just hurt too much to talk about or even think about." She got to her feet and hurried to stir the stew before it burned. She turned around and scrubbed the tears from her cheeks with the back of her hand. "I can't tell you how much better it feels now that you know the truth. I've felt badly about deceiving you both. And now you know why I can never trust another man. It hurts too much to find out all their sweet talk is a lie."

Both girls kissed her cheek. "Emmie dear, God has someone very special in mind for you," Amelia said. "You'll see. But your secret is safe with us. Now let's have some of that stew."

By the time they ate lunch and cleaned up the kitchen, it was time to go to tea at Frances's. The sun shone weakly in a pale blue sky as they held onto their skirts and hurried across the parade ground. Frances met them at the door with tears in her eyes.

"Why, Frances dear. Whatever is the matter?" Amelia put an arm around the petite young woman, and Frances promptly burst into sobs.

"I was trying to fix some stew for my husband as a surprise. Our cook was late, and I thought I'd try a recipe Mrs. Horton gave me. She said it was fool-proof. But she didn't tell me how much of that hateful pressed vegetable cake to put in, so I broke off what I thought was the right amount." She sobbed pitifully and pointed to the kitchen. "Now, look. And I wanted it to be so perfect for my first tea party," she wailed.

Globs of stew ran over the big pot and lay deposited like a sticky surprise on the floor. The smell of scorched potatoes and carrots burned their throats with an acrid smoke.

Sarah made a strange, strangling noise, and Emmie looked at her in surprise. *Is she laughing?* She looked closer. Yes, she definitely was, although she was making a valiant attempt to suppress her mirth.

"I'm sorry," Sarah gasped finally, wiping the tears of laughter from her eyes. "I'm just so relieved to find out I'm not the only one who's done something like this. Ask Rand to tell you about my first attempt to cook with those desiccated vegetables."

Frances sobbed one last time, but a glimmer of smile appeared at the corners of her sweetly curving lips. "You did it too?"

"I did indeed. Only I made a much bigger mess. Don't fret. We'll help you clean it up, then we'll have tea by the fire."

"I just knew we were going to be good friends!" Frances clapped her hands in delight, then showed them to her rags and water.

"I hear another lady is joining our little band," Mrs. Horton, the doctor's plump and smiling wife, remarked later as she sipped her cup of tea. "Major DuBois is bringing his daughter, Jessica."

"Oh, no!" Sarah and Amelia spoke in unison, and Emmie frowned at their tone.

"Jessica DuBois is a bit of a problem," Sarah said hesitantly. "She set her cap for Rand, and she wasn't too pleasant about it. She had the nerve to tell me to go back to Indiana where I belonged. She said I was too starched to know how to deal with a real man. And for awhile I was afraid she was right," she added. "I've really tried to get over the way I felt about her, but she makes it hard for any woman to be a real friend to her."

"I'm sure she has her good points," Amelia said. "But Sarah is right—it's hard to find them. But maybe she's changed," she added hopefully.

"You are such an optimist," Sarah said with a loving look at her friend. "You can never seem to admit that some people are just plain rotten through and through. Like—" She broke off with an apologetic look at Emmie.

"Like Ben," Emmie finished for her. "You don't have to mince words on my account, Sarah. When is she coming?" she asked Frances.

"Any day," Mrs. Horton said.

"Wonderful," Sarah muttered, taking a bite of her coffee cake. "But it's probably for the best," she said with a shake of her head. "God has been telling me to forgive her, and as long as I didn't have to see her, I've been able to procrastinate. Now I'll have to obey."

"It's going to be a long winter." Amelia sighed.

Two days later, they heard that the young lady had indeed arrived. Even if they hadn't been told, they would have known by the way the men acted. They had fewer officers showing up on some pretext to talk with Emmie.

"I'm going to have to swallow my pride and go welcome her to Fort Phil Kearny in a day or two." Sarah groaned. "I'll have to pray for strength."

The next day was colder and more like they had expected late autumn to be. The wind blew ferociously, and the sky was overcast. Emmie offered to take the laundry to Suds Row. Amelia was feeling poorly and let herself be talked into some hot tea with Sarah, while Emmie ran across the parade ground to the laundress's cabin. As she passed the sutler's store on the way back, she saw a group of men all clustered around looking in the windows. Curious, she sidled up behind Rooster and tried to see around his scrawny neck.

"Howdy, Miss Emmie." He flushed and backed away from the window a bit.

"What's going on, Rooster?"

"Nothin' much. The men's jest curious about the new gal that come in with the supply train a couple of days ago. She's the daughter of Major DuBois and sure is a looker. Not that it matters to me, of course. She's in there with her pappy and Lieutenant Liddle."

Something squeezed tightly in Emmie's chest. Was Isaac interested in Miss DuBois? She stood on tiptoe and looked in the window. The young woman inside was a real beauty with deep red curls tied back at her long slim neck. Her dark blue gown enhanced her voluptuous figure, and the lace at the neck framed an exquisitely delicate face. She clung to Isaac's arm and gazed up at him adoringly with big blue eyes. Isaac was smiling down at her indulgently. He turned slightly and saw Emmie looking in the window. His eyes widened as they met hers, and he raised a hand involuntarily. Jessica turned to see what he was looking at. She clutched his arm tighter and said something that caused the other men to laugh.

Emmie turned and fled back to the safety of the Campbell quarters. She fought the tears prickling at the back of her throat. Jessica really was a beauty. And an aristocratic one. *With her father's help, a young officer could go far,* she thought. Why was she so upset, anyway? She had made it perfectly clear to Isaac that she wasn't interested.

For the next few days, Emmie threw herself into helping Sarah sew tiny garments for the coming babies. She didn't want to have any time to think. They spent their afternoons with the other women of the fort stitching tiny articles of clothing and learning about child care from the experienced mothers. They worked on Amelia's layette, since her baby was due first. They wanted to make sure everything was ready.

"I wonder where Isaac has been," Amelia remarked on a cold evening as they worked on the final quilt for her little one. "He hasn't been over in several days."

"I noticed that a couple of days ago and asked Rand about it," Sarah said. "He said he'd invited him several times, but Isaac always had an excuse. He's been acting strange, Rand said. Not his usual cheerful self. And Rand said he thought Jessica had set her cap at him now."

"Not Isaac!" Amelia's voice was alarmed. "We must do something, Sarah."

"What can we do? He has to see through her on his own just like Rand did." Sarah bit off the thread and smoothed the block she was sewing, then sighed. "I know we should stop by and call on her. God has been pressing me about it. I know she needs the Lord too, but it's so hard to imagine her ever bending her knee to anyone, even God."

Emmie kept her eyes on her needlework, but her heart thumped uncomfortably. Let him shower his attentions on the lovely Jessica! *It just goes to show all his pretty words meant nothing,* just as she'd known all along. *He is a typical man,* she told herself vehemently.

"Maybe if you invited him over, Emmie," Amelia said thoughtfully. "I thought he seemed to be sweet on you. If you were nice to him, maybe we could get him out of Jessica's clutches."

"Isaac will be fine by himself," Emmie said. "I've told you before I don't intend to get involved with any man."

"But Isaac is different," Sarah said. "He's like Rand and Jake. He has character and principles. And he's a Christian."

"Then he'll see through Jessica on his own." Emmie's tone did not invite further discussion.

"Maybe you're right," Amelia said with a sidelong glance at Sarah. "We'll just have to trust in his good sense. And do a lot of praying," she added.

Chapter 7

"Hurry up, Sarah. We're going to be late," Emmie called at the bedroom door. "Assembly sounded five minutes ago, and the post band is warming up."

"I'm coming!" Sarah rushed out in a flurry of rustling skirts and the wafting aroma of lilac. Emmie and Joel followed her out the door and across the parade ground toward the milling crowd in front of headquarters. It was an unseasonably warm day for the last day of October. The sun was so hot, Emmie wished she'd brought her parasol. They hurried up the platform that Colonel Carrington had ordered erected for the ladies and found a seat beside Amelia.

"I thought you were going to miss the opening assembly," Amelia whispered.

Lieutenant Adair, adjutant of the Eighteenth Company, had the adjutant's call sounded. The companies formed lines in front of their quarters, then moved to their battle positions. Colonel Carrington, short and round, stepped to the fore and addressed the men. He began a stirring address to dedicate the fort and the brave men who had lost their lives in the course of the fifteen weeks it took to erect the encampment.

Emmie found her eyes straying to Isaac's erect figure just to her left near the newly finished flagpole. He kept his eyes steadfastly on his commanding officer, and she felt a thrill of enjoyment that she could look at him without anyone noticing. He looked very fine with his new blue uniform pressed and the sun glinting off his brass epaulets and polished boots. She glanced to her right and saw Jessica DuBois glaring at her. Her cheeks warm, she looked away quickly and fastened her eyes on Colonel Carrington. The last thing she needed was for Jessica to think she was interested in Isaac!

The little colonel finished his speech by handing the halliards to William Daley, who had done most of the work on the flagpole. The men stood at parade rest with their right hands raised as the orders were barked out. "Attention! Present arms."

The rifles slapped in the hands of the soldiers, and the drum corps played a long roll, followed by the swell of the full band playing "The Star-Spangled Banner." Tears slid down Emmie's cheeks as the guns opened fire, and William Daley pulled the halliards and raised the twenty-by-thirty-six-foot flag slowly to the top of the mast. The warm, gentle breeze stretched it out to its full glory.

She waved her handkerchief in honor of the flag with the rest of the ladies and wept unashamedly. For the first time in her life, she felt part of something worthwhile, something good. She glanced involuntarily over at Isaac and found his steady gaze on her. He smiled and tipped his plumed hat. She smiled tremulously back at him. Glancing over at Jessica, she found the other woman engaged in a conversation with Colonel Carrington. Thank goodness she hadn't seen the exchange!

As the men marched off to their quarters to the tune of "Hail, Columbia," Isaac pushed his way through the melee and caught Emmie's hand.

"Will you save me a dance later? I have to take care of a few duties before I can join the party at headquarters."

"I don't think I'll be dancing. Besides, Jessica might be angry."

He frowned. "What's she got to do with us? Her father is my superior. I've just been helping her get settled in."

"I think she thinks it's more than that." Emmie glanced over and caught Jessica's stare.

Isaac shrugged. "She has nothing to do with us."

"There is no us!"

He sighed. "We'll talk about it later." He strode off in the direction of the barracks.

Emmie bit her lip. *Perhaps I shouldn't go to the party at all,* she thought. She just didn't know how to handle Isaac. Or her own turmoil. For just a moment, she longed to be free of the mistrust she felt about men. But it was the only defense she had. And she needed a defense when it came to Isaac.

Amelia grabbed her hand. "Wasn't it wonderful, Emmie? I was so overcome, I cried." She peered in Emmie's face. "You did too, I see!" She tugged her toward the line of ladies and officers heading toward the door to headquarters. "I don't want to miss a moment of the fun. Sarah went to find Rand and Jake. I told her we'd meet them there."

"I'm not sure I should go," Emmie began. "I'm still in mourning—" She broke off at Amelia's incredulous look.

"Don't be ridiculous, Emmie dear. Whatever do you have to mourn about? That rascal wasn't even your true husband."

"I don't think we've met yet," a soft voice behind them spoke. "Won't you introduce us, Amelia?"

Emmie turned to stare into Jessica's blue eyes. How much did she hear? Emmie's mouth went dry. Did she hear what Amelia said? But the beautiful face before her gave no clue.

"Hello, Jessica," Amelia said. Her voice sounded falsely gay to Emmie, but Jessica didn't seem to notice. "I heard you were here. Sarah and I had planned to stop in yesterday, but she was not feeling well."

"Oh?" The one word and upraised eyebrow spoke volumes. *Sure you were,* it said. *Just as I lost no time in coming to see you.*

Amelia flushed at her tone. "Uhm, this is our dear friend, Emmie Croftner."

"Croftner. Where have I heard that name?" Jessica frowned, a gentle ripple in the smooth perfection of her peaches and cream complexion. "You're not related to Ben?"

"I'm his sister."

"Oh, my." For a moment Jessica seemed flustered. "Do forgive me. I'm very pleased to meet you." She held out a tiny gloved hand, and Emmie clasped it briefly. "Well, I do hope to get to know you better in the future. Now I must go. I see Daddy motioning to me." She gave Emmie an enigmatic look before strolling over to her father.

"I wonder what she's up to," Sarah said as she hurried over to them. "It looked as though she was actually being nice."

"I really don't know," Amelia admitted. "Maybe she's changed, but she seemed quite sweet."

"We can pray," Sarah said with resignation. "God's been telling me to be friends with her, and I know I have to do it, but I haven't been able to gather up enough courage yet."

The furniture had been cleared out of the big meeting room and long tables piled with food lined the west end of the room. The wooden floor had been polished to a brilliant sheen that was a trifle slick to walk on. The band was already warming up at the makeshift bandstand at the other end of the room under the wide eyes of the post children clustered about them. Emmie noticed that Joel had his harmonica with him. She looked around the room and saw Jake wave to them from the food table.

"Trust that man to find the food." Amelia laughed as they threaded their way through the crowd. "Eating already?" she asked with a smile.

"Wait 'til you taste this apple pie," Jake said, taking an enthusiastic bite. "Mrs. Horton certainly has a way with dried apples."

Amelia pretended to be miffed. "Well, you can just eat at her table every night then. I won't inflict my poor attempt at culinary arts on you."

He put an arm around her. "Now you know I like your cooking just fine."

"Just fine, he says." She punched him gently in the stomach. "When I've been an army wife as long as Mrs. Horton, maybe I'll have a way with dried apples too."

Emmie gave a wistful chuckle. Sarah and Amelia were so lucky. She pushed the memory of Isaac's smiling eyes away. She would not think about him or any other man!

The band struck up a lively tune behind them, and Jake took Amelia into his arms. "Time's a-wasting, Gal." Amelia laughed as he swung her onto the dance floor.

Rand claimed Sarah a few moments later, and the officers began to line up for a dance with Emmie. She was exhausted within fifteen minutes. The men were so exuberant and determined to have a good time. When there was no lady available, they danced with one another. She passed from one set of arms to another until the faces all became a blur.

"I think this is my dance." Isaac cut in on a young lieutenant with a good-natured grin. He spun Emmie away from the disappointed young man. "You look very lovely tonight."

Emmie looked away, her cheeks burning. Why did he always have to embarrass her? "It was a very nice ceremony," she said awkwardly.

"Wasn't it?" He drew her closer as the music changed to a slower song and laid his chin on the top of her head. "You are just the right height," he said softly.

Emmie felt herself relaxing against his chest. She heard the thud of his heart under her ear and smelled the pine scent of his soap. *If I could just stay like this forever,* she thought dreamily before she caught herself. No! She pulled away slightly. That was how Monroe had trapped her before. Him with his sweet talk and tender arms. She was soiled goods now too. Isaac wouldn't be interested in her if he knew the truth.

"Isaac, I've been looking for you everywhere," a honeyed voice said. "Daddy wants to talk to you." Jessica laid a gloved hand on Isaac's arm and gazed up at him with an adorable pout on her lips.

"I'll be along in a moment," he said, pulling his arm away from Jessica's grasp. "Let me get Emmie some punch first."

"No, really, I'm fine," Emmie stammered. She stepped away from him hastily. "You go on along with Jessica. I've promised the next dance to Jake."

Isaac hesitated, then allowed Jessica to pull him away. Emmie looked after them with a faint film of tears in her eyes. *Why on earth am I crying?* she wondered. Isaac meant nothing to her and never could. She blinked the tears away just before Jake came to claim her for his dance.

"Amelia is determined not to let me sit by her all evening. She says she likes watching us dance as much as if she could dance every dance herself," Jake said as they swung into a rollicking galop.

Emmie was breathless by the time they finished the dance. Jake took her elbow and guided her toward the punch table. "I wanted a chance to tell you how much I appreciated the help you've been to Amelia," he said as he handed her a glass of punch. "She was so lonely and blue before you and Sarah came.

I haven't caught her crying once since the two of you arrived."

"I haven't done anything," Emmie said. "Sarah is the real miracle worker." She looked away and took a sip of punch. Sarah had told her it was just strong tea with citric acid in it, but it was really quite good.

"That's not true, you know," he said with a frown. "I've seen the way you hover in the background trying to make sure neither one are doing too much. You have a sweet, unassuming way of encouragement about you that has really helped Amelia."

His promise brought a warm glow to her heart. "I'm glad if I've been able to help her," Emmie stammered. "There's no one in the world like Amelia. She's so trusting of everyone and sees the best in everyone she meets. I wish I could be more like her."

Jake smiled. "She's too trusting sometimes. But you're right—there's no one like her."

"You love her very much."

He nodded. "She means everything in the world to me. I don't know what I'd do if anything ever happened to her." He looked over to where Amelia sat chatting with Mrs. Horton. "She seems so frail, sometimes it worries me."

Emmie laid a hand on his arm. "She'll be just fine. Dr. Horton is very pleased with her condition. Women have babies all the time, you know."

Jake squeezed her hand. "You're right, I'm sure. Anyway, thank you for all your help."

"You're very welcome." She watched him stride over to his wife, whose face lit up as she saw him coming. Emmie couldn't suppress the pang of envy that pierced her heart. Love like that would never be for her. She sighed and took the last sip of her punch before being claimed for another dance.

The next morning dawned bright and clear. Emmie slipped out of bed and poured cold water from the cracked pitcher into the bowl on the cloth-covered crate that passed as a nightstand. She shivered as she took a piece of flannel and quickly washed herself in the frigid water. She pulled on her blue wool dress and combed her hair up into a serviceable knot, then draped her shawl around her shoulders. She could hear Rand thumping around in the kitchen as he readied for his day. The clear notes of reveille sounded just as she pushed open the curtain from her bedroom and stepped into the small parlor.

Rand looked up as she entered. "Go on back to sleep. I wouldn't let Sarah get up either. I'll grab some grub at mess so you girls don't have to worry about fixing me breakfast."

"I don't mind," she protested.

He patted her shoulder as he strode by and seized his coat. "I know you don't, but I have a busy day today, and I might as well get to it. You get some rest." He opened the door and stepped out into the still-dark morning. "I'll see you tonight," he said before closing the door.

Now what was she supposed to do? She was already dressed and too wide awake to go back to sleep. She tiptoed past Joel, just a tuff of red hair showing above the blanket, to the bedroom door and peered in at Sarah.

"Rand wouldn't let me get up," Sarah murmured sleepily when she saw her at the door. "I really should, though. I need to take the laundry to Suds Row."

"I'll do it. I'm already dressed and not a bit sleepy. Would you like some breakfast before I go?"

"No, thanks." Sarah yawned and pulled the quilts up higher on her shoulders. "All I want to do is sleep."

"That's fine. You get some rest. I'll stop over and check on Amelia after I drop off the laundry." Emmie closed the door gently. She was so glad her own morning sickness had lasted such a short time, and she felt well enough to continue to be a help to Sarah. She threw some more wood in the fire, put a pot of coffee on to boil, and cut a slice of bread for breakfast. By the time she slathered jam on it and gulped it and two cups of coffee down, the bugle sounded fatigue call. She gathered up the laundry into a basket and stepped outside, as men from various parts of the fort hurried to fall in and find out what their duties would be for the morning.

The sun was just beginning to send pink streaks across the eastern sky as she skirted the parade ground and hurried toward Suds Row. Emmie stopped at the first tent she came to. A kettle of water belched out lye-scented steam, but the laundress was nowhere in sight. She set her burden down and rubbed her back, a bit sore from the previous evening's festivities.

As she looked around, she saw a pair of blue eyes regarding her seriously from behind the flap of the tent.

"Hello, what's your name?"

The child didn't answer but cautiously stepped out from the protecting flap of the tent. A small girl about two years old with a tangled mass of nearly black curls, big blue eyes, and chubby dimpled cheeks gazed up at her.

"Aren't you adorable!" Emmie exclaimed. "Won't you tell me your name?"

The little girl popped a thumb in her mouth, then took it out long enough to say, "Mary," before sticking it back in her mouth.

"Well, Mary, do you know where I might find your mama?" Emmie knelt in front of the tiny girl and touched the dark curls.

At that moment, a young woman scurried from behind the tent with an armload of uniforms. "Sorry I am if ye had to wait, Missy," she gasped in a broad Irish lilt. "I didn't know ye were here." Her face softened as she saw Emmie

179

kneeling before the little girl. "I be seeing you've made the acquaintance of me sister."

Sister? Emmie had assumed the child was the woman's daughter. They both possessed the same dark curls and deep blue eyes. But as she looked closer, she realized the young woman was hardly more than a child herself. Certainly no more than fifteen or sixteen. "Are you the laundress or should I talk to your mother?" she asked hesitantly.

The young woman dropped the uniforms beside the kettle of water. "Sure and it's myself, Maggie O'Donnell, you'll be wanting, Miss. Me mam, God rest her soul, has been with the angels these last two years. The childbed fever took her when Mary here was only six days old."

"I'm sorry." Emmie was intrigued with the energetic young woman. A child raising a child. From her accent, she wasn't too long out of the potato fields of Ireland. "How long have you been in America?"

Maggie dumped a uniform into a galvanized tub and proceeded to scrub it vigorously against the washboard. "Me da brought us to the wondrous city of New York just four months before Mary arrived. He took a job with the railroad and moved us to Chicago. But the Lord saw fit to take him of the consumption before he clapped eyes on Mary." She leaned forward and said in a whisper, "Between you and me, Miss, I think me mum died of a broken heart. She had no reason to go on with me da gone."

"And you've been all alone since?"

"Just me and Mary taking care of each other."

"How did you get out here in the wilderness?" Emmie was fascinated by the young woman's self-confidence and independence.

"A chum of me da's heard the army had a need for a washerwoman out here and arranged for me to have the job. It's hard work, it is, but honest." She saw the expression on Emmie's face. "But don't feel sorry for me, Miss. It's better work than I could get in Chicago. The only offer I had there was in a bawdry house. But I'd have taken even that if it meant the difference between watching young Mary starve or no." Maggie stood and pushed a stray black curl out of her eyes. "When you be needing your laundry done by?"

"Tomorrow is soon enough," Emmie said. The last thing she wanted to do was add to this young woman's burden.

"Won't be no problem at all. It's been real nice talking to you. Most ladies don't bother with the likes of me." Maggie grinned cheerfully. "Not that I'm complaining, mind you. I don't have nothing in common with those high-falutin' types anyhow. But you're different, Miss."

"Please call me Emmie." She held out her hand.

Maggie eyed her outstretched hand cautiously before wiping her own water-roughened hand against her apron and taking Emmie's fingers gingerly. "Pleased to meet you, Miss Emmie."

"Just Emmie. I'd like to be friends." She didn't know why it was so important to her, but it was. There was something about the young woman that drew her irresistibly. She didn't know if it was Maggie's indomitable spirit or harsh circumstances, but she just knew that she wanted to be able to call her a friend.

Maggie's eyes grew wide. "Friends with the likes of me," she said incredulously. Unexpectedly her eyes welled with tears. "Don't mind me," she sniffled. "Ever since we got here, it's like I'm a spirit or something. The other ladies all look through me, and I can tell they think Mary is me own lovely daughter and that I'm an indecent woman."

Emmie's throat grew thick with her own tears. What would everyone think of her if they knew the truth? "I'll be back tomorrow," she promised. Emmie waved to little Mary and set off toward Amelia's quarters. She was awed by Maggie's spirit and courage. At least Emmie had Sarah and Rand to look to for support. The young washerwoman had no one but was still able to smile at circumstances and find a way to support herself and her sister with honest, hard work. Emmie wondered if she was a Christian too, like the Campbells. Maggie's courage shamed her.

Amelia had insisted that she just let herself in whenever she wanted to stop by, so Emmie just rapped once on the door and slipped inside. Amelia looked up with a forced smile from her seat on the cot that served as a sofa in the parlor.

"I was hoping you'd stop by," she said. "I was just sitting here feeling sorry for myself." Her smile was gone and tears hung on her dark lashes.

"Why, whatever is wrong?" Emmie quickly crossed the room to put her arms around her.

"I'm just being a silly goose." Amelia sniffed. "For the first time I'm really frightened about having this baby. What if something's wrong with it? Or I could die and leave Jake all alone with a child to raise. Women do die in childbirth, you know."

Emmie hugged her. "You'll be fine, I know. You're strong and healthy," she said with more conviction than she felt. She and Sarah had discussed how fragile their friend had been looking the last few weeks.

"I'm not afraid to die, you know. I know I'll be with the Lord, but I just don't want to leave Jake all alone." Amelia scrubbed at her cheeks with the back of her hand, then turned and looked Emmie squarely in the face. "There is one thing you could do that would make me feel better."

"Anything. You want a cup of tea?" Emmie half rose to her feet, but Amelia pulled her back down and gripped her arms.

"I want you to promise that if anything happens to me, you'll marry Jake and take care of him and the baby."

Emmie caught her breath. What was Amelia saying? She tried to draw away, but Amelia kept a tight grip on her arms.

"I mean it, Emmie. I've thought about it a lot. It would solve your problems too. Jake would love your baby. He loves children, you know. It would make me feel so much better if I was sure they would be all right no matter what happens."

Emmie couldn't think with Amelia's beseeching blue eyes fastened on her. How could she ask such a thing? But Amelia had never been like other women. She always thought of others first and never seemed to consider her own feelings. "You can't just plan Jake's life for him like that," she said desperately.

"Jake has already agreed," Amelia said with a brave smile. "He pooh-poohed my fears, but he said he'd do whatever I wanted if the worst happened."

For an instant, a vague image of red hair and blue eyes swam across Emmie's vision, but she pushed it away. That wasn't reality. Her friend was reality. But really, what were the odds of anything happening to Amelia? She was just suffering from pregnancy jitters. Everything would be fine; she just needed a little assurance right now. "I promise," she said reluctantly.

Amelia smiled with relief. "I feel so much better. Now I'll take that cup of tea."

As Emmie put the kettle on the stove and threw more wood in the fire, she fought down a sense of panic at the thought of her promise. What about her promise to herself never to trust another man enough to marry? *But this is different*, she told herself. Amelia's God would not allow anything bad to happen to her. Besides, Jake was totally trustworthy. She just couldn't see herself married to him. *But I won't have to worry about that*, she told herself as she brought the cup of tea to Amelia. She would watch over her friend better than her own mother would. Another month and the baby would be born. Amelia would put these silly fears to rest.

Chapter 8

By the next day, both Amelia and Sarah had recovered their health and high spirits. Emmie couldn't wait to tell them about Maggie.

"I think it's lovely for you to befriend her," Amelia said after Emmie's explanation. "And we will certainly have her to tea. But you should know that the other women will disapprove. Army life is so regulated, and fraternizing with the enlisted men is frowned on here."

"But she's not an enlisted man," Emmie protested. "She's just a lonely young woman with no friends. I don't see how being a friend to her could hurt."

"I know it's hard to understand," Sarah said. "But there's a very rigid code of behavior in the army, and the laundresses are considered beyond polite society by most gentlewomen."

Emmie stared at them in bewilderment. "The one thing I've always noticed about army people is how friendly they are and how easily they welcome new people to the post. Why would they feel that way about someone who earns her living by her own hard work?"

"It's not that they don't believe in hard work," Amelia explained. "It really goes back to when laundresses were kept women who followed after the troops to see to the needs of their men. In the past many were—well, I don't like to say it—but they were scarlet women. Nowadays, many are wives of enlisted men too. Fraternizing with an enlisted man's wife is just the same as being friends with him."

So what does that say about me? Emmie wondered. *Does that mean the people who act so kind and friendly now would shun me if they knew the truth?*

Sarah saw the stricken look on Emmie's face. "I'm sorry if we upset you, Emmie. We just wanted you to know what the situation is like here. Of course, we don't feel that way, and we would love to meet young Maggie."

"It's not that," Emmie said. "I know you'll both like her as much as I did. It's just that my reputation would be much worse than hers if the people just knew about Monroe. Maybe I should leave. If your other friends would frown on associating with Maggie, they would really be disgusted with me. The truth will probably come out sooner or later. It always does."

"Oh, Emmie, anyone who knows you at all knows you're much too trusting and innocent. They would know you were just deceived by a scoundrel. No one would blame you." Amelia put her arms around her. "You put any thought of leaving us right out of your head. Besides, it's too dangerous now to even think about leaving the fort."

Emmie was unconvinced, although she let her friends lead her to the kitchen for a cup of tea and some bread with jam. The shame she'd pushed to the back of her mind swelled up again. No amount of love and acceptance would erase it. Maybe she should just confess it to the world instead of trying to pretend to be something she wasn't. She was sure Jessica wouldn't be as charitable about her innocence as Amelia and Sarah were.

That night as she crawled under her quilts and breathed in the scent of her hay-filled mattress, she tried to think about what she could do if she left here. She was still awake at the two o'clock sentry call. As she heard the familiar "All's well," tears leaked out of the corners of her eyes. All was not well for her. There was nothing else she could do but trust in the mercy of her friends for now. Maybe when spring came, she could think of some way to support herself and the baby. She felt so empty inside. How did her friends remain so calm and assured? Perhaps it was their faith in God. She shivered a little at the sudden thought. Could that be the reason? But God seemed very far away from her, beyond her reach. She was certainly undeserving of any attention from Him.

The next morning, Emmie was heavy-eyed and lethargic. She knew her friends were worried about her, but no one could help her with her private battle. The week sped by, and she was eager to attend the Sunday service. She'd thought often about what the minister had said about God caring for her. She didn't see how He could. Not after all the things she'd done.

This week he began by reading Isaiah 1:18. " 'Come now, and let us reason together, saith the Lord: though your sins be as scarlet, they shall be as white as snow; though they be red like crimson, they shall be as wool.' " The young minister cleared his throat, and his eyes seemed to look right into Emmie's. "No matter what you've done with your life, God can forgive it—He wants to forgive it. But you have to be ready to acknowledge your sin to Him. God is the only One you can truly tell your innermost thoughts, doubts, and fears. We all wrestle with our private doubts and troubles, but God can bring the peace and contentment you're longing for. Running away from a situation won't bring peace. Only Christ can do that."

He continued on with the sermon, but Emmie didn't hear anything else he said. Her throat burned with unshed tears as she considered his words. Peace and contentment. Was there such a thing for her? The very words seemed alien, meant for someone else. The home she'd grown up in was anything but peaceful. Her father had always been shouting and cursing; her brothers, especially Ben, had been filled with even more anger than her father. As the minister reached the end of his sermon, he asked the congregation to bow their heads. Emmie closed her eyes and felt her heart opening like a sponge, ready for the living water the preacher had spoken about. *Lord, if You'll have me, I want to give my life to You.* Tears slid silently down her cheeks. *Forgive my sins and make me as wool. You know how scarlet my sins are. Wash them away and bring me peace.*

As the preacher ended his closing prayer and the congregation rose, Emmie felt as though she was about to float off the floor. She felt new and clean. Was this what peace was?

After the service, she told her friends what she'd done, and they cried and rejoiced with her. She felt as though she could face anything with the Lord beside her. She'd always been so fearful. Of what, she didn't really know, but the terror had always been there. Ready to spring upon her like a cougar on an unwary doe. Now she felt strong and capable. Even the thought of the life stirring within her didn't fill her with gut-wrenching fear anymore. For the first time in her life, Emmie felt as though she mattered. She mattered enough for Jesus to die for her. That fact changed everything.

She and her friends spent most afternoons the next few weeks curled up by the fire in the parlor reading the Bible and discussing different passages. There was so much to learn, so much she'd never heard about. As soon as she read Philippians 4:13, she knew it had been written just for her. "I can do all things through Christ which strengtheneth me." The verse was a litany that sounded in her head all the time. Every time a twinge of doubt in herself would raise its ugly head, the comforting words would subdue all her fears.

Isaac stopped by every couple of nights, but she had no opportunity to talk with him alone. Not that she wanted to, of course. He rejoiced with them at the news of her salvation.

Emmie was so full of contagious joy and courage that Sarah was emboldened to go across the parade ground to the DuBois residence. Jessica had ushered her in, but she laughed when she'd asked her forgiveness, Sarah told Emmie later. Jessica told her she didn't want anything to do with God or Sarah's self-righteous pap and showed her the door. Sarah just seemed to pray for her more often. She told Emmie she thought she saw tears in Jessica's eyes for a moment.

❧

As November began, winter settled its icy claws more firmly into the little fort community. Cold, piercing winds, mountains of snowdrifts, and bitter cold kept the ladies constantly looking for ways to keep warm. The wood details, escorted by guards, went out every day but could barely keep up with the demand, even though wood had been stockpiled for several months. The ladies ventured out only when absolutely necessary. Even a brisk walk from quarters to quarters left them numb with cold.

Emmie couldn't remember a time when she didn't ache with cold. The wind howled around the tiny fort like a pack of ravenous wild dogs, poking icy fangs through her skirts that chilled her to the bone. Early one cold morning, she bundled her cloak around her as tightly as she could before picking up her basket and heading for the sutler's store. Sarah had been craving fruit, any fruit, so Emmie thought she would see what was available. The price would be dear, but Rand had told her to get whatever she could find. He worried a lot about his wife these days. Sarah seemed pale and listless, but Emmie thought it was the confinement of the tiny fort and the especially cold weather they'd been enduring that caused her friend's wan appearance. There had been constant skirmishes with the Indians, and the little graveyard beside the fort received a newly fallen soldier almost every day. The ever-present fear hung like black crepe over the encampment.

She staggered to keep her balance in the wind as she hurried as fast as she could toward the sutler's store. As she passed the DuBois residence, she saw Jessica motion to her. What now? She stopped for a moment before obeying her imperious summons. She had managed to avoid any contact with Jessica since the dance and since Sarah's encounter with her. The cold air followed her into the foyer as Jessica shut the door behind them. Emmie glanced around quickly as she followed Jessica into the parlor. The fireplace blazed with warmth and cast a golden glow over the gleaming mahogany furniture. The parlor looked lovely and welcoming, but the look on Jessica's face was just the opposite.

"I've been watching for you," Jessica said. "You haven't been out much." Her eyes swept contemptuously over Emmie's plain gray dress and bonnet.

"Sarah hasn't been well. I really can't stay. I need to get back to her as quickly as possible," Emmie said timidly. She shrank away from the cold smile on Jessica's face. She couldn't imagine what Jessica would want with her. And what did that triumphant glint in her eye mean? Her nervousness increased a notch as Jessica allowed a strained pause to drag out.

"This won't take long," she said finally with another chilly smile. "I just thought it was important that we get a few things settled between us."

"What kinds of things?" Emmie's agitation grew as Jessica stepped in closer. Her sweet, overpowering scent made Emmie's head swim.

"I've seen the way you look at Isaac. My father wants me to marry him, and I intend to do just that. Rand chose that chit of a girl over me, and I refuse to be humiliated again." She pushed her face into Emmie's. "I know all about you, Miss Croftner. I contacted a cousin who made some inquiries for me. I know that the child you're carrying is illegitimate, and you've never been married. If you force me to, I'll let everyone here know all about it."

Emmie felt faint. This was her nightmare come true. She couldn't stand for anyone to know about her shame. It would reflect on her friends too. She clutched icy hands in the folds of her cloak and swallowed hard.

Jessica smiled again. "You are to stay away from Isaac. Make it clear you have no interest in him at all. If you don't, I'll have no choice but to let everyone know you lived with a man out of wedlock."

"But I thought I was married!" Emmie protested. "It wasn't like you're making it sound."

"Look at you! Why would anyone marry you except for your money? If you were too stupid to figure out what the man was after, that's your problem." She flicked a disparaging hand at Emmie. "Oh, you're not unattractive, I suppose. That helpless look probably brings out the protective nature in some men. But the apple doesn't fall far from the tree, you know. You're no better than your brothers, and anyone who knows them would instantly know what kind of person you are behind that little-girl-lost facade."

Emmie gulped, and tears pooled in the corners of her eyes. She willed them not to fall with a fierce determination. She didn't want to let Jessica see how much her words had hurt her. Monroe had told her she was beautiful, but she'd always known it couldn't be true. She'd been so foolish. So easily swayed by Monroe's smooth words. She swallowed hard and stiffened her shoulders. "You needn't worry about me, Miss DuBois. I have no interest in Isaac. He is merely a friend."

Jessica's eyes narrowed as she stared at Emmie. "I certainly hope that's true. For your sake, it had better be." She opened the door and practically pushed Emmie through it. "And don't tell anyone about our conversation. Not if you want your little secret to remain between the two of us."

Emmie found herself staring at the brass knocker as the door slammed behind her. She gulped and forced herself to walk down the steps on shaky legs. She had always hated confrontation of any kind. It brought back too many bad memories of the constant barrage of abuse her father had heaped on her head. No matter what went wrong when she was growing up, it was always her fault. If Ben spilled his glass of milk, it was because Emmie filled it too full. If Labe forgot to feed the stock when it was his turn, it was because Emmie forgot to remind him. She swallowed the lump in her throat. No one must know. She couldn't bear it if Sarah and Amelia were hurt because of her foolishness over Monroe.

The walk in the cold wind stiffened her resolve, and she had quit shaking by the time she pushed open the door to the sutler's store.

She picked up the supplies she needed as quickly as possible, then hurried back to the Campbell quarters. Sarah looked up as she burst through the door. Emmie had intended to tell her friend about the confrontation with Jessica, but after one look at Sarah's pale, pinched face, she decided against it. Now was the perfect time to put into practice what she'd been learning the past few weeks. She whispered a silent prayer and turned the whole matter over to God. He would take care of it. He'd promised to take care of her and He would. She put on a bright smile as she closed the door behind her.

"I found some lovely apples at the sutler's store," she said proudly. "They're a little wrinkly, but they don't seem to have any bad spots. Here, smell." She put a small apple under Sarah's nose. "They should make delicious apple dumplings."

Sarah took the apple slowly and sniffed. A ghost of a smile brightened her face, then she lay back against the cushions on the parlor cot. "You are a dear." She handed the apple back to Emmie. "I don't know why I feel so poorly." She sighed. "The winter is just beginning, and already the wind is about to drive me mad."

Emmie sat beside her and put an arm around her slim shoulders. "God is here with you, though. I have so much peace since I realized that. Now the vastness that used to terrify me when I looked around outside just reminds me how powerful He is."

Sarah smiled at her. "You put me to shame sometimes, Emmie. You're right, of course. I shouldn't complain. At least I'm here with Rand and not stuck back east with my brother. God has been good to us. With all the fighting going on, Rand hasn't been wounded and neither has Jake. We should count our blessings."

Emmie hugged her again. "I think I'll get started on those apple dumplings. You rest awhile." She stood and went to the kitchen, all of three steps away. She hummed as she took down her apron and wrapped it around her waist. Hmm, it seemed her waist had thickened just since yesterday. She took down a tin of flour and dumped some into a bowl. "What time did Rand say to expect him?" she asked.

"He sent Joel by to tell us he'd be late. That reckless Lieutenant Fetterman has finally talked Colonel Carrington into letting him try an ambush. The colonel asked Rand to go along to keep Fetterman out of trouble. They're taking some mules as bait, but Joel said Rand thought it was a harebrained scheme. Red Cloud is no fool, but Fetterman is hotheaded and thinks all Indians are stupid and slow."

Emmie sighed. Always there was fighting. Every day, every hour they listened for the crack of rifles in the cold winter air and the war whoops of the Sioux. There was never a respite. As she kneaded the dough and sliced the apples, she and Sarah chatted about everything except the one thing they both listened for. Through the long afternoon and early evening, they waited and talked to fill the waiting. Only when they heard Rand's boot heels and Joel's excited chatter as they came up on the front porch did they relax.

Rand came in, stomping his feet in the entry and reminding Joel to do the same. Rand's face was pale and pinched with the cold. Sarah rushed to help him out of his snow-covered greatcoat. He shrugged it off and dropped onto the cot with a sigh. He held out his hands toward the roaring fire as Sarah sat beside him.

"I expected you before now," she said softly.

"You should have seen it," Joel put in excitedly. "I was watching from the blockhouse. The Sioux knew it was a trap. They just waited Fetterman out, then slipped behind the fort and stampeded the cattle. Fetterman looked as savage as a meat axe."

"Joel!" Sarah spoke sharply.

He looked sheepish. "Well, that's what Rooster said."

"You're not to talk disrespectful of your elders."

Her brother scuffed a toe on the floor. "He sure was mad, though. He told the colonel he wanted to go out after them right then and there, but the colonel wouldn't let him. He stomped off with Lieutenant Grummond. They were both grumbling."

Emmie broke in hurriedly. "Your supper's ready." She didn't want to hear about any more battles. She watched as Sarah put a hand on Rand's arm; then Emmie hurried to fix him a plate of thick stew and warm slices of bread with butter. She fixed a smaller plate for Joel.

"Joel's right," Rand said after a few bites of supper. "Fetterman is spoiling for a fight with the Sioux. He's going to wind up with his hair lifted if he isn't careful. He's rash, and I'm afraid he'll drag Lieutenant Grummond into a losing battle with him. Neither one of them have any respect for the way an Indian can fight. They haven't been out here long enough to have a little sense knocked into them."

Emmie shuddered. She'd seen Lieutenant Fetterman around. He usually had a group of starry-eyed soldiers around listening to stories of his exploits in the War between the States. His bragging and posturing repelled her and filled her with a strange foreboding. The tiny quarters seemed even more claustrophobic than usual. She desperately wished for a walk outside, but she could hear the wind howling around the windows. She jumped as someone pounded on the door, then hurried to open it.

Isaac's broad shoulders filled the doorway. The snow swirled around him like a thick, wet fog. "Come in," she gasped as the freezing wind took her breath away.

189

He pushed past her, and she shut the door. "We've got a visitor," he said to Sarah. "I told her to come in with me, but she insisted I come and ask if it's all right."

Sarah looked up at him anxiously. "Is Amelia all right?"

Isaac grinned. "It's got nothing to do with her. This is a visitor the Lord has blown our way. I think you'll be right happy to see her."

Sarah gave him a fierce look, and he laughed. "I think it should be a surprise in spite of what she says." He turned and opened the door again. "Come on in," he said gently.

A figure covered in a thick buffalo hide slowly stepped through the doorway. Emmie was startled to realize it was an Indian girl of about sixteen or seventeen. Her thick braids were coated with snow, and she looked pale and emaciated.

The young woman stared straight at Sarah, then smiled. "My Say-rah, do you not know me?"

Sarah gasped and jumped to her feet. "Morning Song!" She literally ran toward the young woman with her arms outstretched. "I didn't know if I'd ever see you again." She put her arms around the young woman and burst into tears.

Tears leaked from Morning Song's eyes as she shrugged off the buffalo robe and revealed a baby snuggled against her breast in an Indian carrier of some sort.

"Oh, Morning Song, you have a baby!" Sarah held out her hands. "May I?"

The Indian girl nodded and gently lifted her child out of the carrier and put him into Sarah's outstretched arms. "My son," she said proudly. Sarah cradled the baby and crooned to him softly.

Emmie noticed the child had light hair. *His father must be white*, she thought. She wondered who the young woman was. Sarah was obviously very fond of her. She'd heard Sarah talk about the time she'd spent in an Indian camp and her friends there, but the only Indian woman she'd heard her mention was one called White Beaver. Who was this girl? She had once been beautiful, Emmie was sure. Now her hair was dull and lifeless from hunger and deprivation, and the sparkle was gone from her large dark eyes.

The men stood around smiling foolishly. Rand seemed glad to see Morning Song as well. Joel was immediately pestering her about news of someone called Red Hawk. Emmie stood a little apart, feeling slightly left out. She had no idea who Morning Song was or why they were all so glad to see her. Isaac saw her confused look and stepped nearer.

"She was one of Sarah's first students back at Fort Laramie when Sarah taught reading and writing to the Indian youngsters," Isaac explained softly. A dawning look broke over his face, and he colored. "Um, your brother, Ben, was, uh, married. . . Well, not really married—" He broke off in embarrassment, then plunged ahead. "Anyway, Emmie, that baby is your nephew. Ben had mistreated Morning Song, and Sarah got her away from him. She disappeared shortly after that, and we haven't seen her since. She came in a little while ago with some friendly Shoshone."

The words didn't make sense. Her nephew. Emmie looked across the room at the child. Her feet drew her across the floor until she stood in front of Sarah. She gazed down into the face of the baby boy. Ben's son? He did have a certain look of her brother. His eyes were the same smoky gray. His hair was light like Ben's.

Sarah was suddenly aware of her standing there. The same dawning comprehension filled her face as had been on Isaac's. After a glance at her Indian friend, she gently placed the child into Emmie's arms. "What is his name, Morning Song?" Sarah asked.

"I call him John. I learn about John in Holy Book when I go to mission school. About how he teach others to love God. So I name him John Randall. My people, my father, call him White Buffalo."

Rand jerked his head up; then a delighted grin stole over his face. "You named him after me?"

Morning Song nodded slowly. "You and Say-rah my friends. I want for John to be fine man like you. Not like—" She broke off and took a deep breath.

Not like Ben, Emmie finished for her silently. She approached the young woman warily. Would she hate her when she knew she was sister to the man who'd used her? "I am your sister," she said gently. "Ben was my brother."

Morning Song flinched back as though Emmie had struck her. "You have her here?" she cried to Sarah. "Sister of my enemy?"

She whirled as though to flee before she remembered Emmie still held her child. She snatched her son from Emmie's arms, then realized Emmie was crying. She searched Emmie's eyes, probing secrets from her soul. The tension eased out of her shoulders, and she gently handed young John back to Emmie.

"You my sister. Ben hurt you too."

How did she know that? Emmie accepted the child again with wonder. What had Morning Song seen in her eyes? The baby played with strands of her hair that had escaped their confinement. She hugged him gently, then gave him back to Morning Song. "You have a beautiful son," she said softly.

Morning Song smiled and spoke softly to the baby as she eased him back into the carrier. "Ben is here?" she asked.

Sarah saw the fear and tension on her face and hurried to reassure her. "Oh, no, Morning Song. He's—" She broke off and bit her lip as she glanced at Emmie.

Emmie took a deep breath and finished Sarah's sentence for her. "He's dead.

Killed by Sioux." At least they thought that was true. And even if he wasn't, Morning Song would never have to worry about him again.

"When this happen?" Morning Song looked puzzled.

"Shortly after you left Fort Laramie. He was killed in a fall from a horse, Labe said."

Morning Song shook her head. "Then it not Ben. My brother see him at Sioux hunting grounds. Near the mountain where the white men take the yellow rock not many moons ago."

"You mean the gold mines in Montana?" Rand asked incredulously.

Morning Song nodded. "My brother want to kill him, but too many white men around with guns."

The only sound was the crackle from the fire as everyone digested the news. Ben was alive! *But he'd left Labe behind,* Emmie thought. Why would he do that?

"I can't believe it," Rand said finally. "All this time we were sure he was dead. Do you know if Labe found him in the goldfields?"

Morning Song shrugged. "I not know. Red Hawk only see Ben."

Sarah put her arm around Morning Song. "There's so much to tell you. Come over by the fire and rest. You'll stay here with us, of course."

Morning Song wilted visibly, and she began to tremble. "It is more than I hoped for, my Say-rah. I just wished to see you again. I go back to the camp."

"You'll do no such thing," Rand put in firmly. "You need to rest and get your strength back. We can make up a bed for you in the kitchen near the stove."

"She can have my place here in the parlor," Joel said eagerly. "I can stay with Jake and Amelia."

"Good idea," Rand said. "Is Red Hawk with you, Morning Song? He can stay with Joel."

The young woman bowed her head in sorrow. "He and my father are with Red Cloud."

They all fell silent at her announcement; then Rand said gently, "We'll pray for him that God will keep him safe."

Isaac left, and the others spent the rest of the evening curled around the fire talking. Baby John was passed from arm to arm and slept contentedly through it.

Rand stoked the fire for the night and yawned. "I'm ready for some shut-eye. You better head on over to Jacob's, Joel. Take some blankets with you so you don't have to wake them." Sarah was drooping with weariness as he led her off to bed. After Joel hurried out with an armload of blankets, Emmie made up the bed for Morning Song, then slipped away to her own bed. As she snuggled under the buffalo robe, she thought about how God had taken care of the young Indian woman. A sense of God's arms around her brought a smile to her face. He truly did care, didn't He? She could rest upon His promises. He would care for her just as He did Morning Song.

Chapter 9

The dawn brought a blizzard with it as snow joined the howling wind of the night before. The swirling snow blotted out the sun and blew through the cracks in the house. Emmie shivered as she lit her lamp and dressed in her blue wool gown. As she pulled her curtain back, she could hear Morning Song crooning to baby John. She was eager to see both Morning Song and the baby again.

Morning Song looked up from her seat by the kitchen stove as Emmie hurried toward her. "You up early," she said. "Say-rah still sleeping."

"Has Rand left?" Emmie asked as she poured hot water into the teapot.

Morning Song nodded as she went to lay the baby down in the parlor. She covered him with the edge of the buffalo robe and came back into the kitchen. "Baby up most of the night. Not used to house."

Emmie tried to imagine living out on the plains in a tepee and shivered. She poured herself and Morning Song a cup of tea.

Morning Song smiled as she spooned sugar into her tea and picked up her cup gently. "Many moons since I have tea with Say-rah." She sighed and took a sip of tea. "Many changes have come."

They both turned as Sarah opened the bedroom door and stepped into the room. Her eyes were sparkling with excitement. "I had to get up and make sure last night wasn't a dream," she said. "Rand and I talked about it after we went to bed, and we want you and John to stay with us, Morning Song. You can't go back to the Sioux. You said they didn't treat the baby or you very well. We love you and want you to become part of our family."

Morning Song swallowed hard as she visibly fought tears. "I do not wish to be burden for my friends," she said almost inaudibly. "Shoshone chief say I can stay at his encampment. But I wish to leave my son with you. Baby deserve to be accepted by whites."

Sarah nodded vigorously. "But we won't keep him without you, Morning Song. You must stay also. Rand has already gone to ask the commander for permission for you to stay. He's sure the commander will allow it. He is a very compassionate man."

Morning Song lost her battle against the tears, and they slid down her cheeks noiselessly. "I must help Say-rah if I stay," she said. "And baby is very good. We try not to disturb my friends."

Sarah smiled. "There will be plenty of crying in a few months anyway. My baby will be born in two months, and Emmie's baby should arrive in May."

Morning Song looked at Emmie quickly. "You not stay here all the time? You have husband here?"

Emmie shook her head slowly. *How much should I tell Morning Song?* she wondered. The suffering on the other girl's face convinced her. *She deserves the truth,* she thought. "No husband. Like you, I was not really married, although I thought I was. I am staying here with my friends, just like you."

A ghost of a smile flitted across Morning Song's face. "Rand will act like he eat loco weed after all babies come."

Sarah and Emmie chuckled. "He'll survive it," Sarah said. "Now let's see about getting you some other clothes. Then we'll go see Amelia. She'll be so glad you're here."

They scrounged through Sarah's and Emmie's wardrobes before deciding on a blue flannel dress of Emmie's. It was a little too small for Emmie now, but it fit Morning Song's too-thin frame loosely. They helped her bathe and dress, then arranged her hair in a coronet of braids around her head. Her moccasins were full of holes, but a pair of Sarah's boots fit fairly well. She looked like a modest young white woman with a suntan when they were finished with her.

Morning Song stared at herself in the small hand mirror and smiled in delight. The snow had finally stopped, so they donned warm cloaks and bonnets, bundled the baby up, and hurried across the parade ground to Amelia's.

The house was dark when they let themselves in. Emmie noticed the fire was almost out, so she threw some more logs on it, while Sarah hurried to the bedroom to check on Amelia.

"Emmie, come quickly!" Sarah called urgently from the bedroom. "The baby's coming!"

Emmie rushed to the bedroom with Morning Song close behind her. A slick sheen of sweat coated Amelia's pale face, and she moaned softly. She was so pale, Emmie felt a stab of pure terror. *Help her, Lord,* she prayed silently. *Give her strength in this hour.* She took Amelia's hand. "Your baby will be here soon," she said soothingly. "You're going to be a mama today."

Amelia moaned again.

"Sarah, I'll run and get Doc Horton," Emmie said. She knew by one look at Sarah's pale face that she was in no shape to take charge. "Morning Song, would you go find me some rags and boil some water? I'll send someone to go find Jake. This must have come on suddenly after he left."

At that moment, they heard the door bang, and Jake rushed in with Dr. Horton close behind. "I thank God you're here," Jake said. "I didn't want to leave her alone. I kept hoping someone would stop by, but no one was out with the weather so nasty."

They all stepped out of the room so the doctor could examine Amelia in private. Jake paced back and forth across the kitchen, pausing now and then to gaze into the bedroom. Beyond an initial look of recognition when he saw Morning Song, he withdrew into himself and said nothing to any of them.

Emmie finally took his arm. "Let's pray," she suggested.

He gave her a startled look. "You're right." He groaned as he dropped to his knees beside a kitchen chair.

Emmie knelt on one side of Jake and Sarah and Morning Song on the other.

"Lord, we know You're here with us right now," Jake said. "We know You love Amelia even more than we do. We pray that You would be with her in her hour of travail. Give her strength and endurance. Bring the baby quickly and ease her pain." He broke off with a choked sound that was half sob and half groan. He drew a shaky breath and continued. "And help us to endure watching her suffer. We leave her in Your hands, Father. In Jesus' name. Amen."

They all stayed on their knees for a few more moments, then rose as Dr. Horton came into the room. "She's in a bad way," the doctor said bluntly. "She's too weak to stand much of this, and the baby is coming the wrong way. Have any of you ladies helped deliver babies before?"

Sarah and Emmie looked at each other and shook their heads.

Morning Song nodded slowly. "I help many women in my village."

Dr. Horton looked at her for a moment, then evidently satisfied with what he saw, nodded. "Wash your hands and come with me. You too," he said to Emmie.

Morning Song and Emmie hurried to obey. They scrubbed their hands with lye soap and went into the bedroom.

"We've got to try to turn the baby," the doctor said. "Emmie, I need you to hold her down while I push on her stomach. Do you know what to do?" he asked Morning Song.

She nodded and knelt by Amelia.

Emmie thought she couldn't stand it as Amelia thrashed and cried out while Morning Song inserted her hand and began to turn the baby as gently as she could. Emmie was trembling and dripping with perspiration by the time the doctor stood up.

"You can let her go now," he said. "Things should move along now. You did very well," he told Morning Song approvingly. "Now both of you get out of here and try to calm Jake down."

Emmie closed the door behind her with a sense of relief. Jake was beside her instantly. "How is she?" he demanded in a shaky voice.

"We got the baby turned," she said. "The doctor says it should be all right now." That wasn't exactly what he said, but Emmie hoped it was true. She washed her hands at the wash bucket, then went to the stove on shaky legs and poured a cup of coffee.

Amelia cried out behind the closed door, and Jake shuddered convulsively. He sank to a chair and buried his face in his hands. "I can't stand it," he muttered.

The entry door opened, and his brother rushed in. "I heard the baby is coming," Rand said. He took in the grave faces in the kitchen. "She's going to be all right, isn't she?" he asked Sarah.

Sarah leaned against him and buried her face in his chest. "The doctor thinks so now. But she's very weak."

The afternoon dragged on as they paced outside the bedroom door. Finally, Amelia cried out again, then they heard the weak, wavering cry of a newborn baby. Jake shot to his feet and looked at the bedroom door wildly. Rand stepped forward and gripped his arm. "Calm down, little brother. You won't do Amelia any good in this state."

Just then the door opened, and Dr. Horton stepped through. He looked into Jake's agonized eyes and smiled reassuringly. "You have a beautiful daughter, Jake."

Jake's face was white. "How's my wife?"

"See for yourself." The doctor gestured toward the bedroom.

Jake jumped forward like he was shot out of a cannon. The rest of the family followed him eagerly. Amelia lay against the pillows with a little more color in her cheeks. A tiny face with a tuft of dark hair peeked out from under her arm. Jake sank to his knees beside his wife and daughter and stared at them with awe.

Amelia smiled up at them. "Isn't she beautiful? I'm glad we decided to name her Gabrielle. God's messenger. She really is a wonderful message from God."

"You're beautiful," Jake told her. He kissed her gently on the forehead, then turned his attention to his daughter. "She looks just like you," he said in wonder.

"Does she really?" Amelia looked up at her friends questioningly.

"Without a doubt," Rand said.

"Aren't you going to hold her, Jake?" Sarah said. "First you, then it's my turn."

Amelia lifted the baby, and Jake took her awkwardly. Her blue eyes, so like Amelia's, stared up at him, and he swallowed hard. After a few moments of mutual inspection, he handed the baby to Sarah.

She took her eagerly and snuggled her expertly. "Oh, Amelia, she's adorable!"

Amelia smiled, and her eyes closed wearily. Emmie saw her friend's exhaustion and motioned them all out. She was just about to shut the door when Amelia opened her eyes and motioned to her to come back.

"What is it, Amelia?" she said gently. "You need to get some rest."

"Thank you," Amelia said. "And thank Morning Song for me. You both saved my life. I was so surprised to see her. Tell her I want to have a long talk when I'm stronger."

Emmie smiled and smoothed Amelia's hair away from her forehead. "I'll tell her. I told you there was nothing to worry about. You're going to be here to take care of your own husband and baby."

Amelia smiled; then her eyes closed again, and Emmie tiptoed out.

By the time they had all exclaimed over the baby's perfection and had taken turns holding her, it was nearly time for supper. Emmie reluctantly handed the baby to Jake, and they all bundled up to head home. Weariness slowed her steps, and she lagged behind the others as they walked across the parade ground toward their tiny quarters. A figure loomed out of the shadows, and she choked back a scream before she realized it was Isaac.

He fell into step beside her. "Amelia and the baby okay?"

"Yes, thank God," Emmie said fervently.

"I heard you and Morning Song were the heroines of the hour. You're a gritty little thing." His tone was admiring.

"I didn't do anything but hold her down," she told him. "Morning Song and the doctor did it all."

"Doc Horton said he had you help because he knew you wouldn't faint. He was pretty sure Sarah would. He said you have a lot of backbone."

Emmie felt a warm glow at the words. "I didn't think I could stand it," she admitted.

Isaac stopped and took her arm. "You've gotten a lot more confident in the past few weeks. I think it's because of your faith. Don't you think God wants you to put the past behind you? You gave Him your fear. Can't you give Him your past and all its hurts?" His fingers grasped her chin, and he tilted her head up until he could look into her eyes. "I love you, Emmie. Can you look me in the eye and tell me you don't love me?"

Emmie tried to draw away, but his fingers under her chin were insistent. His usually smiling blue eyes were serious as he stared down at her.

"I—I don't know," she said unsteadily. "I don't want to love you." She burst into tears. "I don't want to be hurt again," she sobbed.

Isaac drew her into the shelter of his arms and rested his chin on her head. "I won't hurt you, my love. From the first moment I laid eyes on you, I knew you were the one I'd been waiting for. I want to be your baby's father. I've seen the gentle, loving spirit you have. You may not want to love me, but I think you do." He drew back and tilted her chin up again. "Don't you?" He bent his head and kissed her.

As his lips touched hers, Emmie felt all her resistance melt away. She did love Isaac. She'd tried to deny it to herself, but it was true. She loved his goodness, his devotion to God, his unwavering kindness to his friends, his sense of humor, everything about him. She gave a choked sob and wound her arms around his neck as she kissed him back.

When Isaac finally drew back, he was trembling. "Does this mean you'll marry me?" he asked with a teasing smile.

Tears hung on Emmie's lashes and she brushed them away. "Yes, I'll marry you," she whispered. *How can I tell him the truth about Monroe?* she thought. *I must wait for the right time.*

He put an arm around her and led her toward the Campbell quarters. "Let's go tell everyone."

The kitchen was bustling with activity when they arrived. Morning Song was cutting up venison while Sarah peeled potatoes. Rand and Joel were putting the bread and butter out and setting the table. Emmie and Isaac stood and watched for a few moments before Sarah looked up and saw them.

"Oh," Sarah breathed. "What's happened? You look so—" She broke off as she ran out of words.

"I've finally worn down Emmie's resistance," Isaac said. "She's going to be Mrs. Lieutenant Liddle."

Sarah shrieked and dropped her potatoes on the floor. She flung her arms around Emmie and danced her around the room. "I just knew you two were meant for each other," she crowed. "I knew God would work it out."

Rand slapped Isaac on the back. "I told you to keep trying." He grinned.

Sarah gaped at her husband. "You told me to stay out of it," she said with a merry scowl.

"He thought one meddling Campbell was enough." Grinning, Isaac chucked her under the chin.

Morning Song kissed Emmie on the cheek gently. "I am happy for my sister," she said. "I pray the Lord's blessings upon your life."

Emmie was touched. "Thank you, my friend," she said, near tears.

Joel gave a disgusted shake of his head, then shook Isaac's hand.

"You won't think it's so dumb in a few years," Isaac said as he ruffled Joel's hair.

"When's the wedding?" Rand asked a few minutes later as they sat around the table eating supper.

Emmie looked hesitantly at Isaac. "We haven't discussed it yet," she said. "It's all so sudden."

"Soon," Isaac put in. "I'll talk to the chaplain. How long will it take you to get ready?"

Emmie looked at Sarah helplessly. "How long?"

"A month, at least," Sarah said. "We have to make you a dress and get the food ready."

"Today's the seventeenth of December," Isaac said. "How about we plan it for January seventeenth?"

"Make it the eleventh. That's my birthday," Rand interrupted. "I'll give you a gift on my birthday. You couldn't ask for a better gift than a new wife. The Bible says, 'Whoso findeth a wife findeth a good thing.'"

Her head reeling from the speed of everything, Emmie nodded. As they cleaned up after supper and made plans, she felt as though it was all happening to someone else. She couldn't be this happy. It wasn't possible. She kept stealing glances at Isaac's profile in the parlor, where he talked with Rand. God was so good. He was giving her the desires of her heart, just like the Bible said. But what if Isaac didn't believe her about Monroe? What if he thought she had deceived him? Her mouth went dry. She had to tell him soon.

After he took his leave, she went to her bedroom and knelt. *Help me find the right words, Lord,* she prayed. *Help him understand.* As she snuggled under the buffalo robe, she suddenly remembered Jessica. What would her reaction be? Would she really tell Isaac her perverted version of the so-called marriage? She shivered in spite of the warmth of the buffalo robe. She must tell him tomorrow. If he heard the truth from her own lips, maybe he wouldn't believe Jessica's story.

Chapter 10

The smile on Isaac's face the next morning provoked much teasing among the men. The news of his engagement was all over the small fort encampment before he ever showed his face at officers' mess. Rooster just said, "When a woman starts draggin' a loop, there's always some man willin' to step in."

When Isaac reported for duty, Colonel Carrington congratulated him, then asked him to take a woodcutting detail out to the bend of Big Piney Creek. Although the sky was clear, the trek was slow going, with huge drifts of snow left by the blizzard. Several lines of enlisted men tramped the snow down for the horses; otherwise, the animals would have been walking through chest-high snow in some places. Isaac sat atop his horse and watched the surrounding hills for signs of trouble. The men had only felled one tree and begun to cut it up when he heard the whoops of a war band as they charged over the hill to his right.

"Take cover!" he shouted. He slid off his horse and flung himself down behind an outcropping of rock. "Lord, send help," he prayed as he saw the number of Sioux storming into the fray. The soldiers were outnumbered by at least three to one. Even with the repeating rifles some of them had, they would soon be overwhelmed. He knew the lookout on Pilot Knob could see the battle, but Carrington would need at least fifteen minutes to muster the men and come to the rescue.

❧

Morning Song had taken Joel to the sutler's store, while Emmie and Sarah cleaned the kitchen. Emmie lifted her head as she heard the volley of shots in the distance. She stopped and put a hand to her pounding heart. She knew Isaac was out with the wood detail. Men were milling around the parade ground and running frantically to saddle horses. She saw Rand and Jake ride past in the first company of cavalry led by Lieutenant Fetterman. Then Colonel Carrington led a small force of mounted men out across the creek.

Sarah put her arm around Emmie. "Let's pray for the men right now," she said. The women knelt together. Emmie couldn't stop the tears from flowing. She knew she should be trusting God, but it was so hard when she knew how dangerous the situation was. They had grown accustomed to the wagon bringing in dead and wounded men daily. She just couldn't bear the thought that it might be Isaac's body brought in bristling with arrows. Now that she had finally admitted how she felt, she couldn't help fearing that he would be taken from her.

"Lord, we put our loved ones in Your hands right now," Sarah prayed. "We know You love them even more than we do. Guard them with Your might; give them insight and wisdom on how to deal with this situation. Nevertheless, not our will, but Yours, Lord. In Jesus' name, we pray. Amen."

They continued to kneel beside the living room cot. Emmie felt her heart resume its normal beat, and peace flooded over her. She knew He was in control, and she felt her terror ease. She lifted her head and smiled at Sarah. "Let's go see if we can do anything for Amelia."

Sarah nodded. "I'm still worried about her. It was such a hard labor. She shouldn't be there alone."

But their fears were unfounded. Amelia was sitting up in bed with her hair brushed, a clean nightgown on, and the baby nestled in her arms. She looked up from her inspection of Baby Gabrielle as they tiptoed in the room.

"What is all the excitement about?" Amelia asked with a worried frown. "I heard the men shouting and the trumpet calling assembly."

"Nothing for you to worry about," Sarah said with a soothing hand on her friend's forehead. "Just a little skirmish with the Sioux." She frowned. "You seem a little warm. How are you feeling?"

"I'm fine," Amelia said. The frown eased off her face. Looking down at the sleeping infant, she said, "I can't believe she's really here. Isn't she the most beautiful thing you've ever seen? I just somehow knew I would have a baby girl."

Emmie leaned down beside her and touched the baby's face. "She's wonderful," she said. "You're so blessed. It's going to seem like such a long time before my baby comes now that you have her. Sarah and I will probably wear out our welcome in the first week."

"Don't count on it," Amelia said with a smile. "I can never see too much of you." She sat up in bed a little straighter and patted the side of the bed. "Sit down, both of you, and tell me all the fort news. Have you heard from home lately? What has Jessica been up to?"

Emmie sat on one side of the bed, and Sarah pulled the cracked straight-backed chair up closer to the bed and sat down. "Well, I do have some exciting news," Emmie said with a shy smile.

"Don't tell me. Let me guess," Amelia said. She looked into Emmie's shining face for a moment. "You're engaged to Isaac."

Emmie gaped at her, and Amelia burst out laughing. "I'm not a mind reader. Jake told me last night." She leaned forward and hugged Emmie. "I'm so happy for both of you. Isaac is a wonderful man."

"God is very good to me," Emmie said softly. "I just hope I don't disappoint Isaac." She stood and walked to the window. "How well do we really know someone else? I'm not very brave, you know. I'm just afraid that when Isaac gets to know me better, he'll wish he had married someone else. And how will he react when he knows I was never really married to Monroe?"

Sarah stepped quickly to the window and turned Emmie around to face her. "You're not to think like that anymore," she told her firmly. "God has not given us a spirit of fear but of power and a sound mind. Remember? Isaac is no fool. He knows you well enough now to know you aren't a loose woman."

Emmie smiled, then nodded. "I'll try to keep that in mind."

"When is the wedding?" Amelia asked.

"January eleventh. It's Rand's birthday. He'll give me away."

Amelia's face brightened. "I'll be back to normal by then. Too bad Gabrielle won't be bigger. She could be in the bridal party."

Emmie caressed the baby's face. "She'll be there, and that's good enough for me. You certainly had us frightened."

Amelia sighed and adjusted her blankets. "I had some kind of silly premonition that I was going to die. I'm just so thankful it's over and we're both all right."

Sarah took her friend's hand. "We wouldn't let anything happen to you. You're too special to us."

Amelia squeezed Sarah's hand. "Sometimes God decrees otherwise," she said softly.

Sarah gave one final pat to Amelia's hand, then leaned over and kissed the baby. "We'd better be getting back. We'll come back and bring you some nice soup for lunch. Do you need anything else before we go?"

Amelia shook her head. "I think I'll take a little nap while Gabrielle is sleeping." She snuggled down into the blankets.

"I'll put her in the cradle so you can rest better." Emmie gently took the baby and placed her in the cradle beside the bed. Jake had spent many evenings carving a woodland scene on it. Bunnies frolicked among flowers in a meadow, the carving beautifully done. She tucked the blankets around Gabrielle, then followed Sarah out of the room.

They checked the fire and made sure it had enough wood before they hurried across the parade ground toward the sutler's store. They'd been gone nearly an hour. Any news of the fate of the wood detail would be known at the store.

The store teemed with soldiers and other wives. Sarah saw Frances Grummond standing by the counter. Frances waved and immediately made her way toward them. She clutched at Emmie's arm and burst into tears.

"I'm so frightened," she sobbed. "Lieutenant Smith says Fetterman took a company of infantry and one of cavalry to the relief of the wood detail, while Colonel Carrington and George went with a small detail to cut off the Indians' retreat. But the scouts say our men were heavily outnumbered. At least one officer has been killed and several more men wounded. No one knows who yet."

The lump in Emmie's throat threatened to choke her. *Please keep our men safe*, she prayed silently. Sarah invited Frances back to their quarters to await any further news. The day passed in fitful periods of conversation. A pall of fear hung over all three women as they tried to keep up their spirits. They sang hymns, took meals to Amelia, worked with Joel on his studies, and above all, prayed. Finally, about nine o'clock in the evening, the bugle sounded the return of the troops. They hastily threw on cloaks and hats and hurried across the parade ground to greet the returning soldiers.

Emmie watched fearfully as the men filed through. Their faces were strained and red from the cold wind. Sarah cried out in relief as she spotted Rand, then Jake. Emmie strained her eyes in the dark, trying to see a familiar set of shoulders. Where was Isaac? She whispered another prayer and scanned the crowd again. There! There he was. She felt tears of thanksgiving well up in her eyes as he turned and saw her. He smiled and waved. The men couldn't speak with them for some time, but at least they were safe.

"No-o-o!"

Emmie turned at the drawn-out wail. Mrs. DuBois screamed and beat at her daughter's restraining arms that held her from rushing to the ambulance.

"Major DuBois must be the officer who was killed," Sarah whispered.

Emmie wanted to go offer her condolences, but she knew Jessica wouldn't welcome them. At least not yet. It was hard to believe that the strong, vibrant major had been felled by a Sioux arrow.

Isaac was exhausted and didn't stay long when he dropped in later that evening, so Emmie had no chance to talk to him about Monroe. It was only by God's grace that all the men hadn't been killed, Isaac told her before he left. If the Sioux had managed to surround them, all would have been lost. She fretted as she lay in bed again that night until she reminded herself that God was in control. He had taken care of Isaac, and He would take care of her.

The next day, Sarah and Emmie went to pay their respects to Mrs. DuBois and Jessica. Emmie's heart pounded, and her mouth was dry as she followed Sarah across the parade ground to the major's quarters. Jessica was sure to have heard the news of the engagement by now. How would she react? Emmie had not had an opportunity to tell Isaac about her "marriage."

Mrs. DuBois's striker answered the door and ushered them into the parlor.

Most of the officers employed "strikers," enlisted men who worked for them as servants on their off-duty hours for a small compensation. Emmie had asked why Rand hadn't done the same instead of taking in a homeless waif like her. It was probably more expensive to pay for her than to employ a striker. But Sarah had told her that Rand thought Sarah needed the company more than the physical help.

Jessica, sitting alone and staring out the window, looked up as they entered the room. Her eyes, swollen from crying, narrowed as she saw Emmie. "What do you want?" she burst out. "Did you come here to gloat? You have everything you want."

Emmie flinched. "We just want you to know how sorry we are about your father. I would like to be your friend, Jessica. Not your enemy. I never meant to hurt you."

Her face flushing with rage, Jessica rose and advanced toward them. "Get out!" she hissed. "I don't want your condolences, and I certainly don't need your friendship."

Emmie swallowed hard and put out a trembling hand to Jessica. "I've been praying for you, Jessica. I don't know what hurt drives you so, but God does. And He can heal your pain, if you let Him."

Jessica's eyes filled with tears, but then her face hardened, and she flushed a deeper red. "Get out!" She advanced toward them. "Get out, get out, get out!" She screamed the words at them. "I don't need your pity!"

Emmie and Sarah backed away hastily. "We truly are sorry," Sarah said as they slipped back out through the door. "We really didn't come just to be polite."

As the door shut in their faces, Emmie and Sarah looked at each other. Sarah was pale, Emmie noticed, and she was sure she looked just as ravaged as her friend did.

"You know, I think you have a lot of insight," Sarah said a few minutes later as they had a cup of tea back in their own kitchen. "I never really thought about why Jessica is like she is. There must be some hidden pain in her life that has shaped her. We really should pray for her. God could heal her."

They knelt beside their chairs and asked God to send peace and a sense of His love to Jessica. Instead of anger, they both felt a sense of compassion for Jessica DuBois. God alone knew what she needed to be whole.

The next day, Emmie spent most of the morning making pies and bread. She tried a recipe of Mrs. Horton's for mincemeat pie and decided to take a piece to Amelia. Morning Song was at the Indian encampment, so Sarah decided to accompany her.

The women bundled up in warm cloaks and hurried toward Amelia's quarters. The weather had been frigid, and the wind snatched their breath away

205

as soon as they stepped outside. As they approached Jake and Amelia's small cabin, they heard the baby's wail. The infant sounded frantic, and Emmie hastened her steps. What could be wrong with little Gabrielle?

They didn't bother to knock but opened the door and hurried to the bedroom, where the baby lay shrieking in her bed. Amelia lay on the floor beside the bed, one arm reaching toward the cradle where her tiny daughter lay.

"Quick, help me get her back into bed," Sarah said as she knelt beside their friend. She grasped Amelia's shoulders, and Emmie lifted her legs.

"She's burning up!" Emmie said as she touched Amelia's skin. The women managed to lift her into the bed. "You take care of the baby, and I'll fetch Dr. Horton."

Sarah hurried to pick up the baby as Emmie flew out the door and across the parade ground. By the time she and the doctor returned, Sarah had managed to calm the baby with a cloth dipped in sugar water. The baby was sucking on it vigorously and making mewing sounds of contentment.

Dr. Horton frowned at Amelia's condition. He quickly put his stethoscope to her chest and listened intently. Amelia muttered incoherently and moved restlessly in the bed.

"What is it?" Sarah asked anxiously as the doctor put his instruments away.

"Pneumonia, I'm afraid," Dr. Horton said. "Her condition is very grave. We must try to reduce the fever. You need to sponge her down with tepid water. She won't like it, but it must be done."

Emmie nodded. "I'll do it while you take care of the baby," she told Sarah. Sarah nodded. "When Morning Song gets back, we can send her to the sutler's store for some tinned milk."

Emmie warmed a pan of water to lukewarm and began to sponge Amelia's body. Wring, wipe, wring, wipe. Over and over, Emmie wiped the damp cloth over Amelia's body. After an hour, she felt as though her arms would fall off. But still Amelia drifted in and out of consciousness, calling for Jake and Baby Gabrielle. Morning Song and Sarah peeked in several times. Gabrielle was fretful, so finally Sarah asked Morning Song if she would mind acting as a wet nurse for the baby. After nursing the baby, Morning Song tucked her into her bed. The doctor checked back in also, but his expression grew more grave every time he saw Amelia's unchanged condition.

Around noon, Morning Song slipped in behind Emmie. She had a cup of steaming liquid in her hands. "I wish to try some Sioux medicine. It is from the bark of a tree you call white oak."

Emmie lifted Amelia's head and shoulders onto her lap, while Morning Song spooned the steaming liquid into her mouth. Some ran out the corners of her mouth, but she managed to swallow some. Emmie wiped Amelia's mouth and eased her back against the pillows.

"I wish Jake would get back," Sarah said as the afternoon wore on. "I'm so afraid."

Amelia moaned, and both women knelt beside her bed. She opened her eyes, and Emmie noticed how bright and blue they looked against the pure white of her face. Those blue eyes shone with love and a strange joy. Emmie swallowed hard and fought a rising sense of panic as Amelia smiled at someone just past Emmie's shoulder. Emmie almost turned around to look, but she knew there was no one there.

"Tell Jake I'll be waiting for him," Amelia whispered. "I'm sorry I have to leave him alone."

"No, no," Sarah said. "Don't talk like that. Jake will be here soon, and you'll be fine."

Amelia shook her head. "You must be strong, Sarah," she whispered. "Help Jake all you can and tell him I love him." She coughed violently, then lay gasping for air. She looked again at a spot just to the side of Emmie, stretched out her arms, and closed her eyes. She gave one last little sigh, a strange little hiccup, and her chest grew still. Baby Gabrielle wailed suddenly as though she somehow knew her mother was gone.

"No!" Sarah wailed. She tried to pull Amelia to a sitting position, but she was limp and unresponsive.

Emmie took Sarah by the shoulders and pulled her close. She swallowed hard past the tears burning in her throat. How could this be? She leaned her forehead against Sarah's head and closed her eyes as Sarah cried out in sudden comprehension of the loss of her best friend. Morning Song hurried to tend to the crying baby. Emmie heard her clucking noises of comfort through the dull veil of grief that squeezed her heart. "She's gone," she whispered against Sarah's hair. "But we know she's with Jesus."

"She can't be dead," Sarah said numbly. "She can't be. We've always been there for each other. This can't be true. Call the doctor." But the words were said without any real conviction. They clung together for several unbelieving minutes.

"We must pray," Emmie choked out. They both turned toward the bed. Emmie picked up Amelia's still hand and laid her lips against it. Sarah laid one hand on her friend's brow for the last time.

"Oh, Father, we hardly know what to pray because of the grief that overwhelms us. We pray for strength to see all of us through the coming days and nights. We ask especially for Your guiding hands to lead us through this valley of death. Jake and little Gabrielle are going to need Your love and mercy in these dark days even more than we do. We know that our sister is in Your presence, and we thank You for that. Let us sense Your loving arms as well."

They stayed in the same position for a few moments. Emmie felt a warmth steal through her limbs and a strange comfort enveloped her. She felt as though God was right beside her in a real and physical way. She could almost sense His touch on her shoulder. She looked at Sarah's white face and held out her hand.

Sarah shook her head. "I want to stay here for just a few minutes," she said with a pleading look. "I just want to remember the good times we had when we were growing up." Her words were choked with tears. "I still can't believe she's gone." Emmie touched her gently on the shoulder, then left her alone with Amelia.

Morning Song was in the kitchen with little Gabrielle. Emmie put water on to boil for some tea, then sat wearily beside Morning Song. Young John played happily on the floor with some wooden blocks. "I don't know how to tell Jake," Emmie whispered.

Jake. Emmie could only imagine the pain he would feel. And he had a new baby to care for. Of course they would all help, but it was still a huge responsibility to raise a child alone. Emmie gulped as she thought about the situation and her promise to Amelia. She'd promised Amelia she would marry Jake and care for Gabrielle if anything happened. *Surely Amelia wouldn't expect me to keep a promise like that now that I've found Isaac,* she told herself. She bit her lip and blinked back more tears. Just when life had seemed so perfect, everything fell apart. How could any of them even look forward to the wedding when Amelia was gone?

The day dragged by somehow. Morning Song took the children home to Sarah's, while Sarah and Emmie washed Amelia's cold, still body and dressed her in her favorite Sunday dress, the violet one that deepened the color of her eyes. Emmie couldn't bear the thought of those extraordinary eyes never widening in wonder again. Sarah combed and dressed her friend's long dark hair one last time as her tears gently bathed Amelia's white but still beautiful face. As the sad news traveled around the post, several ladies dropped by with whispers of condolences and offerings of food.

The bugle finally sounded the men's return to the fort, but it was nearly an hour before they heard the heavy tread of the men on the front porch. Isaac and Rand each held Jake's arms as they practically carried him through the door. His face was slack and glazed with disbelief and an overwhelming grief. All three men bore signs of the tears they'd shed. Isaac's eyes were full of sorrow as they met Emmie's, and he opened his arms to her. Sarah uttered a tiny cry and flew into Rand's arms, and they all wept together as Jake stumbled toward the room where his wife lay.

Moments later, they heard his harsh sobs as he sank to the floor beside Amelia. Emmie's eyes filled with tears again. Isaac pulled her closer and rested his chin on the top of her head as she sobbed against his chest. His shirt smelled of cold air and the warm musk of his male scent. She felt loved and comforted in the circle of his arms with his breath warm on her face. But the grief and aloneness poor Jake must be feeling!

After a little while, the four of them tiptoed into the bedroom to be with Jake. His sobs had stilled, but his fingers still traced the contours of Amelia's face. Rand put his hand on his brother's shoulder.

"I never got to say good-bye," Jake choked. "How could she leave without saying good-bye?"

Sarah knelt beside him. "Her last words were for you. She said, 'Tell Jake I'll be waiting for him. Tell him I love him.'"

Jake groaned and buried his face in his hands. His shoulders shook with the intensity of his grief. After a few moments, he lifted his head. "Where's the baby? Is she all right?"

"She's fine," Emmie said. "Morning Song took her to our house along with John and Joel."

"I want her. She's all I have left of Amelia now."

"I'll go get her," Emmie said.

"The wind is terrible. Let me go," Isaac said.

Emmie shook her head. "I want to. I'll be fine." She hurriedly wrapped her cloak about her and stepped out into the wind-whipped snow. She was numb from the emotions of the day as she hurried across the parade ground. The wind stung her cheeks, and the prickle of feeling brought a new wave of grief. How would they all bear this?

Morning Song looked up as Emmie stumbled into the parlor. Little Gabrielle and John slept contentedly on the cot. Joel dozed with his head against Morning Song's knee. Emmie looked at the baby, sleeping so peacefully. Her heart clenched with love for the motherless mite. Amelia would have been such a wonderful mother. Now little Gabrielle would never know the lovely person who had given her birth. Tears stung her eyes as the baby stirred and opened blue eyes so very like her mother's.

"Jake is back and wants to see the baby," Emmie said.

She knelt beside the cot and gently bundled the blankets around the baby. She lifted the baby into her arms and looked at Morning Song for a moment. "He's taking it very hard."

Morning Song nodded. "I knew it would be so. When one is cut, the other bleeds. I should come too?"

Emmie shook her head. "You stay with the boys. There's no sense in making them come out in this cold. When we get back, maybe you could go over and feed her."

"I come."

There was a thread of emotion Emmie didn't recognize in Morning Song's voice. The Indian woman was so stoical most of the time. It was hard to guess what she felt and how strongly Amelia's death was affecting her. With a last glance at her friend, she pulled the blanket over Gabrielle's face and tucked her under her cloak for added warmth. The wind caught the door out of her fingers, but Morning Song was behind her to grab it and pull it shut.

Jake was waiting at the door when she stomped the snow off her feet on the porch. He took the bundled baby out of her arms as soon as she extricated her from under the cloak. With tender hands, he pulled back the blankets and gazed into his daughter's tiny face. She yawned and opened her blue eyes.

"You look so much like your mama," Jake whispered. "Thank God." He pulled her close, then went to the bedroom and shut the door.

Emmie sank wearily onto the cot in the parlor. Isaac put a hand on her shoulder and squeezed gently.

"We'll get through this. God is here and in control."

Emmie nodded. She knew that it was so. But why would God allow such sorrow to come to them? She didn't know if she would ever understand.

Chapter 11

The next few days sped by as the entire fort rallied around the Campbell family. Ladies brought in mountains of food, and the men stood around ill at ease but unwilling to leave. The grave site had to be prepared, no easy task in the hard, frozen soil.

The day of the funeral dawned clear and cold. December twentieth, just five days before Christmas. The wind wasn't as fierce as usual, which was a mercy from God, Sarah told Emmie. Jake was insistent that the baby be at the service, although she was much too tiny to be out in the weather. Emmie bundled her carefully, then followed Sarah and Rand to the little chapel. Isaac was waiting for her outside the door.

"I've been praying for you all morning," he whispered as he opened the door for her. "For all of you." He squeezed her hand gently.

Emmie nodded gratefully. "We're going to need God's grace today," she said. "Rand was at Jake's all night. Morning Song too. She insisted she should be the one to go, since she is feeding the baby. Poor little John looks so bewildered. He doesn't understand what his mama is doing with that other baby all the time."

She eased onto the bench beside Sarah and Rand. Jake sat on the other side of his brother. He stared down at his hands with such a look of suffering on his face that Emmie's eyes filled with fresh tears. She ached to comfort his grief somehow, but she knew only God could give him the peace he needed. She offered a quick prayer for the minister as he made his way to the pulpit. *Give him the words that will comfort Jake,* she prayed. Isaac held her hand, and the warm press of his fingers gave her strength.

Reverend Howard cleared his throat nervously as he glanced around at the packed building. The entire garrison had turned out to see Amelia put to rest. "Today is a day of mourning for us gathered here to pay our final respects to Amelia Campbell." He leaned forward slightly over the pulpit. "But I say to all of you that it is a day of great rejoicing as well."

Jake glanced up sharply with a frown.

"No one could speak with Amelia for long without knowing about the great love she held for her Savior. If she could speak to us today, she would tell us not to mourn but to rejoice with her that she now sees her Jesus face-to-face."

He opened his Bible. "I want to read a passage that meant a great deal to me when my own beloved mother passed away. Listen to Psalm 15 and see if you agree with me that this so perfectly describes the Amelia Campbell we all knew and loved. 'Lord, who shall abide in Thy tabernacle? who shall dwell in Thy holy hill? He that walketh uprightly, and worketh righteousness, and speaketh the truth in his heart. He that backbiteth not with his tongue, nor doeth evil to his neighbour, nor taketh up a reproach against his neighbour. In whose eyes a vile person is contemned; but he honoureth them that fear the Lord. He that sweareth to his own hurt, and changeth not. He that putteth not out his money to usury, nor taketh reward against the innocent. He that doeth these things shall never be moved.' In Psalm 116:15 we are told, 'Precious in the sight of the Lord is the death of His saints.' This is not a punishment from God but a reward for our dear sister." He shut his Bible and looked out over the crowd. "Some of you may wish to tell about how Amelia demonstrated her love for her God in your own lives."

He sat down, and the chapel was silent, then one by one people stood and told of kindnesses that Amelia had done. Tears rained down Emmie's cheeks as she listened to the outpouring of love. Jake sobbed audibly when one soldier told how he had popped a button on his coat while carrying in a load of wood for Amelia, and she insisted on sewing it back on, then given him some tea and buttered bread.

"I'll never forget as long as I live listening to that little gal pray for the food," he said. "I was afeered to look over my shoulder for I was that sure I'd see God Hisself standing behind me."

The chapel was silent for a few moments, then Reverend Howard stood again. "The Bible tells that life is but a vapor and quickly passes away. We know not when God will call us home. We can only hope to live each day to His glory and make a difference with our fellowman. I think we can all heartily agree that Amelia Campbell lived her life to the fullest. She loved her family, and she loved her fellowman. I pray that each one of us can impact lives the way she did."

He prayed briefly for God's sustaining grace to be shown to the family, and the service was concluded. As Emmie, clinging to Isaac's arm, followed the procession to the grave, her heart was lighter than she would have dreamed possible. Someday she would also face her Savior. She could only imagine the joy Amelia was feeling at this moment. How could she mourn when she thought of her friend's unimaginable bliss? A glance at Jake's face showed he did not share her thoughts. Grief was etched deeply in his face as he carried his daughter through the ankle-deep snow.

The service at graveside was brief, just the traditional ashes to ashes, dust to dust eulogy. As they hurried home through the increasing wind, Emmie felt a sense of uneasiness as she followed Jake's broad back. He seemed hard and angry. She knew he blamed God. When the minister had tried to offer words of comfort, he had turned away with a harsh, "Don't talk to me of God's grace and mercy. My wife is dead, and my daughter is motherless." She had never expected an attitude like that from Jake. Amelia had said he had a strong faith. *But a blow like this could shake the strongest faith,* Emmie thought. Best to leave it in God's hands. He would show Jake He was still there for him.

"Emmie, would you mind coming in a moment?" Jake said as they reached his quarters. "I need to talk to you for a minute."

"Of course," she said and followed him inside after a quick wave at the rest of the Campbell clan. She hung her cloak on a hook in the hall and hurried to the kitchen to boil some water for tea. She was cold clear through and knew Jake had to be as well. Jake put little Gabrielle on the bed and sat at the kitchen table, while Emmie rummaged through the open shelves for some teacups. He sat silently while she finished preparing the tea. She glanced over at him once or twice and felt a little intimidated by his grim look.

"Sugar?" she asked. He shook his head and took the steaming cup. She dropped sugar in her own cup and sat beside him at the table.

"You aren't going to like what I have to say," he said abruptly. "I need your help."

Emmie smiled at him in relief. Was that all this was about? "You know I'll help in any way I can," she said. "I loved Amelia too. I know it will be hard to take care of Gabrielle by yourself."

"I need more than just occasional help," Jake said. "Gabrielle needs a full-time mother. I don't want her growing up shifted from place to place like a homeless puppy."

Emmie's smile faltered. "You want me to take her? Don't you want her to live with you?"

"I wouldn't give my daughter up for anything," Jake said with a scowl. "She's the only important thing in my life. I don't want you to take her to live with you. I want you to live here with me and take care of her."

"Jake, I would do anything I could to help, but I can't stay here alone with you. The entire fort would talk."

"Not if we were married. I want you to honor your promise to Amelia."

The words hammered into her brain, and Emmie sat back as though from a blow. Honor her promise? She couldn't marry Jake! She was going to marry Isaac. Kind, loving Isaac who was waiting for her at Sarah's. She shook her head. "You can't be serious. You know I'm going to marry Isaac."

"You made a promise. Amelia expects you to keep it. I expect you to keep it. I know you are a woman of your word, and Gabrielle needs a mother. You needn't worry about me bothering you or expecting anything else from you except to take care of my daughter. I'll never love another woman like I loved Amelia. You'll take care of Gabrielle, fix my meals, and take care of the house. That's all. You and the baby can have the bedroom. I'll sleep on the cot in the parlor."

He stared at her fiercely as he said the words. The stern look on his face seemed to dare her to contradict his demand. Emmie swallowed hard. What should she do? Didn't he know how unreasonable his demand was? Did he really expect her to give up her life and future with the man she loved to be an unloved nursemaid and housekeeper? *You made a promise,* a voice inside her head whispered. *A Christian honors her word.*

Jake stood up abruptly. "I know this is a shock, so I'm going to leave you and run over to talk to the colonel for a little while. You think it over. I know you'll do the right thing."

The right thing? This was supposed to be the right thing? Emmie stared at his back as he strode out the door. How could he ask such a thing of her? What should she do?

A timid knock at the door broke into her confused thoughts. "Come in," she called. She was relieved to see Morning Song slip inside and close the door gently.

"I have come to feed baby," Morning Song said.

"Gabrielle is still asleep," Emmie told her. "Would you like some tea while we wait for her to wake up?"

Morning Song nodded. "Tea sound good. Winter wind very bad." She looked into Emmie's eyes. "My friend is not happy. This place is sad for you."

Emmie nodded. "Yes, but that's not the only problem. I don't know what to do about Jake." She stood and put the kettle on the woodstove, then sat down and clenched her hands in her lap. "I made a promise to Amelia. One that I never thought I would have to keep."

"Promise very important. My father say if a brave cannot keep his word in the camp, do not trust him in battle with the enemy."

"But what if keeping the promise will ruin the person's life?" Emmie's eyes were full of unshed tears as she gazed pleadingly at Morning Song.

"Sometimes promise is hard, but man's word is how man is measured. Promise should never be made without thought. Remember what minister say today? About keeping oath even when it hurts?"

"I made the promise without thinking," Emmie admitted. "But it was only to ease Amelia's agitation. I never expected to have to keep it." The kettle began to whistle, and she went to the stove and poured the boiling water into the teapot and brought it to the table.

Morning Song watched her prepare the tea for a moment. "What is promise?" she asked. She touched Emmie's hand softly. "God will help you keep it."

"Several weeks ago, Amelia was distressed and convinced she wouldn't live through childbirth. She knew I was also expecting a child and was alone. So she asked me and Jake to marry so I could care for her baby and Jake. Then me and my baby would be provided for as well. Now Jake expects me to honor that promise." A strange look Emmie couldn't identify darkened Morning Song's features, then was gone as she listened to Emmie. Was it anger? Dismay?

Morning Song nodded slowly. "Your friend care for you even when she is afraid. I see her thoughts." Morning Song took a sip of tea, then set it down carefully. "You must honor your promise. A vow is most important when most hard."

Emmie sighed. "What about Isaac? I made a promise to him too."

"Promise to Amelia come first; is that not right?"

She nodded. "But I love Isaac. I've been so happy these past few days, happier than I've ever been!"

"I see this happiness. But there is still this promise you make."

The baby whimpered in the bedroom, and both women looked up. Morning Song rose to her feet. "You must pray to God to show you the choice you must make. Then you must be strong enough to follow His command." Leaving Emmie with her thoughts, she turned and went into the bedroom.

Everyone expected her to be strong, but she wasn't! How could she turn her back on her love for Isaac? Emmie rose and took her cloak from the hook by the stove. She would talk to Sarah and Rand. They would know what to do. "I'm going now," she called to Morning Song. She didn't wait for an answer but hurried out into the driving wind.

The wind took her breath away, and she had to battle to stay on her feet across the parade ground. Her bonnet lifted from her head for a moment before she yanked it down and tied it firmly in place. Drifts of snow were beginning to pile up against the steps as she hurried onto the porch.

Sarah was curled up with a quilt and a magazine on the cot by the fire. She looked up as Emmie came into the parlor. "Your face is so red! You shouldn't be out in this wind. Come join me under this quilt."

Emmie threw off her cloak and hung it by the fireplace, then dove under the quilt. Even with the fire going full blast, the heat couldn't keep up with the wind, and the room was chilly. Her teeth chattered as she nestled close to Sarah.

"You are frozen," Sarah scolded as she wrapped the quilt tightly around Emmie. "Where have you been? I expected you back long ago."

"Jake wanted to talk to me."

"All this time? What did he want?"

Emmie drew her legs up under the quilt and leaned against the wall behind her. "How important do you think a promise is?"

"Very important. That's why I try not to make any promises. I don't want to break my word. Papa was always very careful before he gave his word to someone. He said a man is only as good as his word. Why? Did Jake want you to promise him something?"

"I made a promise to Amelia before she died. It didn't seem important at the time, just a way of setting her mind at ease. She thought she was going to die."

"She never told me that! When was this?" Sarah asked.

"Several weeks ago when she wasn't feeling well. She asked me to give her my word that if anything happened to her I would marry Jake and take care of him and the baby."

Sarah sat up straight. "Jake would never go for that! He would never let someone else make such an important decision for him. Not even Amelia."

"He agreed before she ever asked me. And now he wants me to keep that promise."

Sarah was silenced for a moment. "I have to admit I'm shocked. But that was before you and Isaac were engaged. Amelia would never expect you to keep a promise like that now."

"I've been thinking about it, and I think she would. When she heard about my engagement after Gabrielle was born, she said it was a good thing she made it through the birth all right so I wouldn't have to keep my promise to her. And Jake expects me to honor it now. He wants me to marry him and take care of Gabrielle." She smiled a crooked smile, though she was near tears. "He says the baby and I can sleep in the bedroom, and he'll sleep on the cot. I wouldn't have to worry about any demands from him. Just take care of Gabrielle, cook, and clean."

"That's abominable! Does he just expect you to give up a full life with Isaac to become some kind of glorified nanny?" Sarah's voice rose in her agitation.

Emmie sighed again. "I know. I've been telling myself the same things for the past two hours. But I keep coming back to the fact that I promised Amelia. Doesn't God expect us to keep our word?"

Sarah wilted. "Yes," she admitted in a small voice. Then she brightened. "But you are free from the promise if Jake will release you."

"He won't," Emmie said with finality. "I don't know how I'm going to tell Isaac."

The front door burst open as Rand and Isaac came in stomping snow from their boots. Rand slammed the door shut against the wind. He glanced from Sarah to Emmie, then bent to kiss his wife. "I'm cold clear down to my socks," he said. "Any stew left?"

"It's on the stove. I'll get it." Sarah scrambled from beneath the quilt and started toward the kitchen. "Uh, why don't you help me get it ready, Rand?" she said with a sidelong look at Emmie.

Rand looked surprised, but he followed her into the kitchen.

Isaac grinned. "Looks like Sarah wanted to leave us alone," he said as he sat beside Emmie on the cot. "She must have thought we wanted to do some spoonin'." He slipped an arm around her and pulled her close.

Emmie sighed and nestled in the crook of his arm. She turned her face up to him, and he bent his head. As his lips found hers, Emmie closed her eyes and kissed him back with all the love in her heart. This might be the last time she felt his arms around her. She smelled the clean, crisp cold on his jacket mingled with the good scent of horse and hay. This moment would have to last the rest of her life. This one moment she could know how it felt to be embraced by a man who really loved her, one she loved with her whole being.

Isaac's arms tightened at her ardent response. He grinned as he drew back moments later. "Are you sure we can't get married sooner?" he asked.

Emmie swallowed hard and began to tremble. How could she tell him?

Isaac noticed her darkened look. "What's wrong?" he asked.

Emmie clenched her hands in her lap and silently prayed for strength. She knew she couldn't throw away everything she had ever wanted in her own strength. "I must tell you something, and I don't know how," she began.

Isaac frowned. "If it's about how that no-good Monroe committed bigamy, don't bother. Jessica gave me some perverted version of it, but I knew it wasn't true. Rand had already told me about it."

Emmie was glad to delay the awful news for a moment. "Rand told you? When?"

"This morning after Jessica's little bombshell. I knew she was lying, of course, but Rand told me how Monroe had deceived you." He clenched his fists. "If he weren't already dead, I'd make sure he paid for his treachery."

Emmie smiled slightly at his fierce tone, then sighed again. "That's not what I have to tell you," she said softly. "It's much worse."

"Just say it," Isaac prompted. "I love you, and nothing will change that."

"I love you too. That's what makes this so hard." Emmie looked into his dear blue eyes, and her own filled with tears at the blow she must give him. "I made a promise to Amelia, one I never expected to have to keep."

Isaac smiled in relief. "I would be glad to take her baby and love her. But I doubt that Jake would allow it."

"That's only part of it," Emmie said. "Just let me finish. Amelia thought she wouldn't survive childbirth several weeks ago. This was before you and I were engaged, before I would admit even to myself how much I loved you. She asked me to give her my word that if something happened to her I would take care of the baby and marry Jake."

The only sound for a moment was the crackling of the fire and the banging of pots in the kitchen. Isaac just stared at her as all the color drained from his face. "You promised to marry Jake?"

Emmie nodded. "And he intends to hold me to my promise." She took Isaac's hand in a desperate grip. "But I love you! What should I do?" In her heart she knew what she must do, but she prayed that he could find some way out for them both.

Isaac was silent and pain darkened his face; then he pulled his hand away and stood up. "You must honor your promise to Amelia," he said. "Only Jake could release you from it." He pulled on his greatcoat and went out the door without another word.

As soon as the door slammed shut, Rand strode into the room. "I don't know what that brother of mine has in his head, but I intend to have a talk with him," he said. "He can't ruin both your lives like this. I know he's grieving, but he just isn't thinking clearly. Don't lose hope until I can get to him." He patted Emmie's hand as the tears slipped down her cheeks. "Why don't the three of us spend some time with our heavenly Father about this matter? We can trust Him to work things out for the best."

The three of them knelt by the cot. Emmie let her tears flow unchecked while she listened to Rand's deep voice as he prayed for guidance and God's intervention. As they rose several minutes later, she felt strong enough to do whatever the Lord deemed right. If she had to honor her promise, she felt sure the Lord would care for her even in the midst of a loveless marriage. There could be joy in serving Jake. She had always liked and respected him. She'd even envied Amelia and Sarah because of the fine husbands they had. At least there would be peace in doing God's will.

"We'll let God talk to Jake first," Rand said. "Then I'll see what he has to say. You get some rest. Things will look different tomorrow."

Chapter 12

Isaac's thoughts were in turmoil as he strode across the windswept parade ground. His first inclination was to find Jake and shake some sense into him, but he didn't want to do anything rash. Jake wasn't thinking past his grief. "I need to pray," Isaac muttered to himself. "I need a quiet place to turn this over to God."

The small chapel at the other end of the parade ground beckoned, and he wrapped his greatcoat around him tightly and bent into the wind. The chapel was dark and cold as he shoved the door closed against the push of the gale. He lit a lantern by the door and carried it with him to the kneeling bench at the front of the chapel. As he sank to his knees on the cold wooden floorboards, he felt a sense of relief that he could turn it all over to the Lord.

His heart felt bruised and broken, and he didn't try to hide his pain from God. "Help me to understand this and deal with it if it truly is Your will, Lord," he prayed. "And be with Emmie. I know she feels the pain as I do. Help us both to follow You no matter what the consequences are." He stayed on his knees a few minutes longer, then rose and blew out the lantern. He would leave it in God's hands. He'd always told God that he wouldn't marry against His will. If it meant he wouldn't marry at all, so be it. He closed the door gently behind him and headed toward the officers' quarters. If the opportunity arose, maybe God would give him the right words to say to reach Jake. He knew his friend was hurting or he wouldn't be doing this thing. Tomorrow was a new day, and God was in control.

Isaac woke the next morning with a heavy heart as he remembered the events of the night before. *I'm not going to worry about it,* he told himself as he pulled on his boots and strapped his saber to his belt. Reveille was already sounding as he strode toward the stables after bolting down some hardtack in the mess hall. He saddled Buck, his buckskin gelding, and made it to the parade ground just in time for boots and saddles. He was on guard duty for the wood detail. He caught a glimpse of Rand ahead, with Jake trailing behind several other soldiers. If the Lord put the right circumstances in his way, perhaps he would get a chance to talk to Jake.

There had been so many skirmishes with the Sioux lately that the guard detail numbered nearly ninety men to protect the wood detail. The detail followed the river, then veered off on the trail to the Pinery cutting area. They had gone only a hundred yards or so when he heard a man in front of him yell as an arrow whistled by his ear. Rand shouted for the men to form the corral formation, and Isaac raced to form a protective circle with the other soldiers. He saw Indians massed on the hills all around and sighed in relief as he heard the picket on Pilot Knob blow the signal that told the fort there were many Indians. Relief would come from the fort soon. They just had to hold on.

Emmie heard the signal from Pilot Knob, then the sound of the bugle calling men together, but she tried not to worry. It was an almost everyday occurrence lately. A few minutes later, she heard the boom of the mountain howitzer. Joel looked up at the sound, but it, too, was almost commonplace these days. The Sioux feared the "gun that shoots twice" and almost always scattered after its use. She washed and dried the dishes, while Sarah dusted and made the beds. Joel carried in wood for the fire, then ran off to play with Jimmy Carrington.

Emmie was deep in her thoughts when a knock at the door startled her. "I'll get it," she called to Sarah. Morning Song had gone to care for Baby Gabrielle first thing this morning, and she wouldn't knock anyway, so Emmie wondered who could be out this morning as she hurried to the door.

Frances Grummond's tearstained face peered out of a fur bonnet. "Oh, Emmie, I'm so frightened," she sobbed as Emmie pulled her inside, and Sarah hovered consolingly. "George volunteered to go to the rescue of the wood detail, and I have such an uncanny dread on my soul. He was almost killed two weeks ago. Would you go with me to Mrs. Wands's? The other ladies are gathered there too."

"Of course we will," Emmie said, her heart sinking. Isaac, Rand, and Jake were all with the wood detail, she knew. "Would you like some tea first?"

"No, no. I just need to be with someone. Could we go now?" Frances's voice broke as she wrung her hands.

Sarah and Emmie grabbed their cloaks and bonnets and followed Frances outside. The wind still whistled, but a weak, watery sunshine brightened the day. Frances's baby was due in just a few weeks, and Emmie worried that the strain would bring on her friend's labor. She sent up a quick prayer for Frances.

The assembled ladies looked up when Emmie, Sarah, and Frances entered the Wandses' parlor. Mrs. Carrington hurried to take Frances in her arms. "My dear, don't fret so. There is no more cause for concern than usual. We both heard my husband tell George not to cross Lodge Trail Ridge, where the Indians are likely to lie in ambush. Your husband will be all right."

"I have such a strange foreboding," Frances sobbed as she let Mrs. Carrington lead her to a chair. Sarah and Emmie followed and sat on the sofa beside her. They all soon had a steaming cup of tea, and Frances began to calm down.

The door pounded again, and Mrs. Wands hurried to answer it. A sergeant stood nervously twisting his cap in his hands. "Colonel Carrington sent me to tell you ladies that a man has come in to tell us that the wood detail has broken corral and reached the Pinery safely. But Fetterman's detail went beyond Lodge Trail Ridge."

Frances cried out at the news of the detail's disobedience of orders, and Mrs. Carrington patted her hand. "George will be all right." Frances relaxed a bit, but she still sat on the edge of her seat. Emmie could tell she was listening to the sounds outside.

The six women chatted and talked about babies and recipes and anything else they could think of. They had a lunch of small sandwiches and stew, but tension still filled the room. They jumped when they heard a shout and a horse go thundering past outside, and they all grabbed their cloaks and went out to the porch. Colonel Carrington dashed down from the lookout and ordered for a howitzer to be readied and gave the order for a general alarm. Men ran in all directions as every man in the garrison reported to the position assigned to him in an extreme emergency.

"What does it mean?" Frances cried out.

"Probably the Indians have been repulsed," Mrs. Carrington said soothingly.

Rooster came scurrying up the steps to the ladies clustered on the porch. "No need to fret, ladies," he said. "Them Sioux bucks won't get ya, I promise."

Then one of the men shouted to open the gate, and the colonel's orderly came thundering through on one of the commander's horses. "Reno Valley is full of Indians!" he shouted. "There are several hundred on the road and to the west of it. It was a trap!"

Emmie was standing beside Frances and caught her as she sagged to the ground. "Help me!" Emmie cried to Sarah. The rest of the women clustered around, and they got Frances inside and on Mrs. Wands's bed. Mrs. Carrington put a cold cloth to Frances's forehead, and she soon came around.

She sat up with a start and burst into tears. "He's dead, I know it," she sobbed.

"Have faith," Mrs. Carrington urged. "Henry sent Captain Ten Eyck out with every man who could be spared. They'll get there in time."

They all went back to the porch. The silence was so intense it was almost painful, then suddenly several shots rang out. They listened as the shots increased to a frantic pitch, followed by a few rapid volleys, then scattering shots, and finally a dead silence.

"Captain Ten Eyck has repulsed the Indians," Mrs. Carrington said.

Colonel Carrington dashed down from the lookout. Emmie shuddered at the look of dread on his face. She looked at Sarah and saw the same dread reflected on her face. What was happening to their men?

Isaac lay behind an outcropping of rock. They had made it safely to the Pinery, but without reinforcements, they would never make it back to the fort. Rand lay a dozen feet away behind his own rock and Jake several yards beyond his brother behind a tree. Dozens of Indians hid just beyond the rise to the west. They were too well hidden to waste his precious ammunition on. He kept a close eye on the slope as he prayed for reinforcements to be quick. He wasn't quite sure what the Sioux were waiting on. Were they playing a game? It would be dark soon, and Indians didn't make war at night.

A volley of shots in the distance rang out. They increased in ferocity for several frantic minutes, then tapered off to an occasional shot before silence descended. Isaac knew that a horrific battle had just taken place, but which side had won? He lifted his head cautiously, then ducked as an arrow sailed by overhead. The arrow was followed by fierce war cries as a band of Sioux rushed toward them.

Rand cried, "Hold your fire until my signal!" Several moments passed. As the band came closer, he gasped, then yelled, "Wolverine!"

The lead Sioux faltered, then pulled his pony to a stop. He shouted something at the rest of the Sioux, and they stopped behind him. He gazed at the rock where Rand lay.

Isaac saw Rand slowly get to his feet. "No, Rand, don't," he whispered.

Rand raised a hand. "Greetings, old friend. I did not think to see you again."

The Sioux dismounted and approached Rand.

"Hold your fire," Rand said again to his fellow soldiers. He stepped forward with his hand outstretched as the young warrior came closer.

Isaac noticed a livid scar running down the cheek of the Sioux as he stopped in front of Rand. *This must be the young brave who rescued Sarah when she was lost in the wilderness after Ben Croftner abducted her,* he thought. He'd heard Sarah talk about Wolverine and White Beaver, the young woman he was pledged to marry. Rand had spared Wolverine's life during a battle once, and the two became blood brothers after that.

"I, too, did not think to see my friend again," Wolverine said. The two men gazed at one another for a long moment. "I think many times of my friend with the blue coat and my vow. I watch always in battle to make sure I honor my vow never to fight with my friend."

Rand nodded. "I also watch for my warrior friend. It is good to see you."

The brave grunted. "You in much danger. We will drive the bluecoats from the fort by the river. Already many dead beyond the hills." He gestured toward Lodge Trail Ridge.

Isaac looked over at Jake and saw the same alarm on his face. Many killed? Was the relief party dead? What about the fort? Was Emmie safe?

Rand put a hand on Wolverine's shoulder. "What of the fort? Sarah is in the fort."

Wolverine shook his head. "We not attack fort yet. But soon. You go back to fort. Other men come soon to bring you back. Then you must leave fort. I not fight with my brother."

Rand was silent a moment. "I will not fight my brother. But I cannot leave the fort unless my commander tells me to."

"Then you must tell him that the Sioux will destroy the fort. We will fight to the last blade and never stop until the bluecoats leave our hunting ground."

Rand's hand slid down and gripped Wolverine's hand. "God keep you safe, my brother."

Wolverine gazed into Rand's eyes. "And you, my brother." He turned and walked back to his pony. He vaulted onto his pony, then raised a hand before turning and galloping away. The rest of the band followed.

Isaac got to his feet, and he and Jake reached Rand's side at the same time. "The Lord works in strange ways sometimes," Rand said with a distant look on his face. "I knew Wolverine was with Red Cloud, and I always have watched for him. I didn't want to ever break my vow of peace with him."

"Do you think he told you the truth about the rescue party? Could they really be dead?" Jake asked.

The rest of the men were slowly beginning to gather around them. "Don't say anything," Rand said quietly.

A lieutenant slapped Rand on the back. "You must have done some fancy palavering with those savages," he said. "Congratulations."

"I knew him," Rand said shortly. "God worked it all out."

"I don't know about God. Looks like they hightailed it because of reinforcements." He nodded toward the hill, and they turned as Captain Ten Eyck and his men thundered up to them.

Ten Eyck dismounted and ran toward them. "We drove off a band just over the hill. Is everyone all right?"

"Just fine, thanks to you," the lieutenant said. He turned and ordered the men to round up the horses.

"Just be glad you're getting back in one piece," Captain Ten Eyck said quietly. "Fetterman's command wasn't so lucky."

"The relief party?" Rand asked.

Ten Eyck nodded. "Eighty-one men slaughtered, and not one left alive.

We drove off some Indians and recovered a few bodies, but there are nearly half still out there. The attack on the wood train was a decoy to draw another force out. Thousands of Sioux were hiding just over Lodge Trail Ridge."

The news was so horrific no one responded for several long moments. Eighty-one men! It was almost beyond comprehension. There had never been a slaughter like that in the Indian Wars. And thousands of Sioux! Isaac couldn't imagine such a large force of Indians. Two or three hundred was usually considered a large band.

"May God have mercy on their souls," Isaac said finally. "What of the fort?"

"Safe, but we don't know for how long," Captain Ten Eyck said. "Colonel Carrington has readied every mountain howitzer and every available man. But we've been operating with a minimal force, and you know how low our ammunition is. So we'd better mount up and get back as quick as we can."

They all hurried off to mount up and get back to the fort. Isaac just wanted to see Emmie with his own eyes and make sure she was safe, and he knew Rand felt the same about Sarah. He glanced at Jake riding beside him. Did he worry about Emmie at all?

The ladies sat around the fire in Mrs. Wands's quarters as night drew on. The evening gun sounded, but the men still weren't back. The colonel's orderly, Sample, had come in some time ago with the news that Reno Valley was full of Indians and nothing could be seen of Fetterman. The entire fort knew some terrible disaster had taken place, but no one knew just what it was.

Emmie wondered what the ladies would do if she suddenly jumped to her feet and shrieked as loud as she could. It was all she could do to hold her terror in check. What if Isaac had been killed? She vaguely wondered how Morning Song was getting along with the baby, but her fear for Isaac's safety wouldn't allow her to leave the little knot of ladies clustered together in a camaraderie of fearful waiting.

The wind whistled outside as the temperature dropped. Rooster had been predicting a blizzard all day, and the weather seemed to be trying to prove him right. Only a few flakes had fallen so far, but the wind was already whipping the existing snow into drifts.

Emmie started to her feet at the sound of a shout outside. She threw her cloak around her and rushed to the door, followed by the rest of the ladies. They all ran toward the gate as doors opened and wagons creaked inside. She saw dead bodies heaped on the wagons and nearly fainted as she searched the mounted men for a glimpse of Isaac's dear face. She breathed a prayer of thanksgiving when she saw Rand, Jake, and Isaac clustered near the last wagon.

The ladies were standing near the flagpole, and Captain Ten Eyck stopped just a few feet away from them where Colonel Carrington stood. His salute was a short, tired wave. "Sir, I'm sorry to report that Fetterman's entire command has been massacred. I brought in all I could, about forty-nine, but there are still more to be claimed."

Frances gasped and started to slide to the ground in a near faint as the ladies overheard Captain Ten Eyck's words. Emmie caught her by the elbow, and she rallied before bursting into tears.

"I knew it," she sobbed. "I just knew he was dead."

Mrs. Carrington put her arms around Frances. "You're coming home with me, Dear," she murmured gently as she led her away.

Sarah tugged Emmie's arm. "Let's go home," she said.

Emmie gasped when she saw the dark circles under Sarah's eyes. Her pallor was so pronounced Emmie thought she looked as though she might pass out at any moment. "You're going right home to bed," she said firmly. She took Sarah's arm and steadied her against the wind as they made their way toward their home.

The fire was out when they finally pushed the door shut against the wind. Emmie hurried to start one, while Sarah poked the fire in the kitchen stove to life. "I'm going to put on some water for tea," Sarah said. "I can't go to bed until Rand gets home. I couldn't rest anyway until I know what happened."

Joel came in moments later, his young face sober. He silently heaped wood in the fireplace for Emmie, then sat on the floor with his knees drawn up to his chin. The news had quenched even his high spirits.

By the time the men arrived, warm currents from the fire warmed the room, and the aroma of steeping tea filled the kitchen. Emmie cut some thick slabs of bread and spread butter and jam on them. She was suddenly ravenous and knew the men would be too. Morning Song was still at Jake's. Emmie knew the weather was much too cold to have the baby out, but she wished for Morning Song's calming presence. Did she know what had happened?

The door opened, and Rand and Isaac dashed in before slamming it against the howling wind. Sarah uttered a little cry and flew into Rand's arms. Emmie was right behind her as she ran to Isaac. She buried her face in the rough wool of his coat and burst into tears.

He put his lips against her hair and patted her on the back. "It's okay," he murmured. "The Lord was looking out for us."

Emmie pulled away and looked up at him. "I'm sorry," she said as she pulled away. What was she thinking of? Unless the Lord intervened, she would be marrying Jake. She had no right to be in Isaac's arms.

Isaac held on a moment, then let her go. "It's not over yet," he said softly as he saw the defeat in her face. "God's in control, you know."

Emmie nodded. "Want some tea and bread?"

"I thought you'd never ask," Isaac said. "I could eat the whole loaf and not know it."

"Me too," Rand said as he walked toward the kitchen with his arm around his wife.

"Where's Jake?" Sarah asked. "I thought he would come to see that Emmie was all right. After all, he says he wants to marry her."

"He wanted to see about Gabrielle," Rand said.

Emmie glanced quickly at Isaac. He had come to find her as soon as he could. This was just a taste of what it would be like to be married to a man who didn't love her. Not that she wanted Jake to love her. She couldn't imagine dealing with that problem too.

Sarah sniffed. "Is he coming over later?"

"No," Rand said. "He said he'd see us in the morning. We're all beat."

Sarah's fierce look softened. "Tell us about it," she invited.

They spent the next hour exclaiming over the harrowing adventure as Rand and Isaac related the day's events.

"I wish you would have asked Wolverine about White Beaver," Sarah said. "I would love to see her again."

"And what about Red Hawk?" Joel put in eagerly. "Did you see him?"

Rand shook his head. "I didn't see Red Hawk, and it would have done no good to ask about White Beaver. Even if she were close, you couldn't see her, Sweetheart. It's too dangerous to set foot outside the fort. You know that. You haven't been outside the gate since we got here."

Sarah nodded in resignation. "I still wish you'd asked."

Rand grinned. "Well, if we ever get in that situation, I'll be sure to say that my wife has insisted on knowing where his woman is. He'll be very impressed."

Sarah chuckled, then stood. "I'm going to bed. I'll fall asleep right here in this chair if I don't go now. You'd better get to bed too, Joel," she told her brother. Joel didn't complain but went off to his cot in the parlor.

Rand yawned. "Me too. See you all tomorrow." He stood and followed his wife into the bedroom and shut the door.

"I should be going too," Isaac said. "It's been a long day."

Emmie stood and followed him to the door.

"Try not to worry," he said. He bent and kissed her on the forehead. "Things will be all right."

Emmie didn't think so as she shut the door behind him. She just didn't see any way out.

Chapter 13

The next morning, Emmie hurried across the parade ground toward the Carrington residence. It was hard to keep her balance in the driving wind. Already four inches of snow had fallen, and if she didn't check on Frances soon, she knew she wouldn't be able to get through the drifts. A pall of dread and foreboding hung over the little fort. She saw sober faces everywhere she looked. The biggest danger, Rand said, was that the Sioux would attack the fort itself. Only the Indians' fear of the big howitzers kept them at bay. If they did attack, all would be lost, because the soldiers were outnumbered and low on ammunition.

Frances was huddled in a quilt on the sofa by the fire when Mrs. Carrington ushered Emmie into the parlor. Frances was pale, but she seemed composed with a strange peace.

"I somehow knew it would come to this," she told Emmie. "George seemed determined to force a fight with the Indians. He idolized Fetterman, but I knew his rashness would come to a bad end. George just wouldn't see it."

Someone knocked at the door again, and Sample, the Carringtons' orderly, led in a bearded man in his thirties. He was dressed in civilian clothes, so he obviously wasn't a soldier. Emmie thought he might be a scout. He had a wolf robe over his shoulder. He took off his hat and stood turning it in his hands in front of Frances.

"Miz Grummond," he began. "My name is John Phillips. I been a miner and a scout, but I ain't never seen such a bad thing. You been through enough. I'm goin' to Laramie for help for your sake if it costs me my life." He pulled the robe from his shoulder and laid it across Frances's lap. "Here is my wolf robe. I want you to have it to remember me by if I don't make it back."

Frances was nearly speechless, but then she thanked him with tears in her eyes as she stroked the robe.

"Are you going alone?" Emmie asked him.

He shook his head. "Lieutenant Liddle has asked to go too. We're setting out at different times, though. If one of us don't make it, maybe the other one will get through."

Isaac was going out through a blinding blizzard surrounded by hostile Indians? Why didn't he tell her that last night? "I must go," Emmie said as she

227

fought to keep her composure.

Everyone was assembled in the parlor when she arrived. Jake glanced at her when she came in, then quickly looked away. Isaac, his face set in a stubborn mask, stood stiffly with his back against the fireplace mantel. Sarah looked as though she had been crying.

"So it's true!" Emmie burst out. "You're going to Fort Laramie."

"Someone has to go," Isaac said. "We can't just send Phillips and hope he makes it. Too much is at stake. We have to have reinforcements and ammo. If the Sioux attack, we'll lose the fort itself and everyone in it."

"He's right," Rand said. "Wolverine said the Sioux were planning to attack soon. We can't afford to wait and just hope headquarters will send the reinforcements Colonel Carrington has requested for months now."

"But why does it have to be you?" Emmie asked near tears.

"Why not me?" Isaac said. "I don't have a wife and children here like some of the other men. And I know this terrain. Besides, I have the Lord on my side." He said this last with a grin in Emmie's direction.

A bugle sounded at the other end of the fort. "That's assembly," Isaac said. "We have to go." The men all put on their coats and filed out the door. Emmie wanted to run and fling her arms around Isaac one last time, but how could she with Jake there? What if she never saw Isaac again? She struggled against the tears as the door shut against the howling wind. She must not give in to despair! God was in control. She must trust Him no matter what happened. She whispered a prayer for Isaac's safety as she watched his retreating back through the window.

The blizzard had intensified as Isaac, followed by Rand and Jake, fought the wind all the way across the parade ground. The little colonel stood stiffly in front of the assembling men. "I don't have to tell you the urgency of the hour," he said after all the men had fallen into formation. "I need some volunteers to go retrieve our dead comrades. I will not allow the Indians to think we care so little for our fallen that we would leave them for the wolves. They always retrieve their dead no matter what the cost."

Men everywhere lifted their hands eagerly, and he picked out Rand and Jake and ordered them to choose eighty more men to accompany the detail. "I will lead it myself," he said. "It is my duty."

By the time Isaac had assembled his supplies for the trip, the detail to retrieve the dead was nearly ready to leave. John Phillips had already gone ahead, and Isaac wanted to get on his way. He was about to mount up when Jake approached him with a determined look on his face.

"I need to speak with you before you go," Jake said.

Isaac turned and faced his friend. He had tried to hate him for what Jake was doing to him and Emmie, but he couldn't. All Isaac could feel was compassion and pity.

"I know I've been acting like a fool," Jake said. "My brother has been none too gentle about pointing it out to me. I want you to know before you go that I'm releasing Emmie from her promise—if you make it back." He grinned and thrust out his hand. "That's a good incentive for you to fight to get through."

Isaac let out the breath he had been holding. It was just as he'd told Emmie: Be still and let God work it out. "Thank God." He took Jake's hand and pumped it. "It's been hard for me to shut up and let God handle it."

A shadow darkened Jake's face. "Yeah, I've been fighting God. Amelia would be ashamed of me. I've struggled with this thing every night. God wouldn't let me sleep or eat. He just kept telling me like He told Job, 'Where were you when I laid the foundations of the earth?' I don't understand why He would take the one person who gave my life meaning without even letting me say good-bye." Tears glistened in his eyes, and he swallowed hard. "But I can't fight Him. He knows best, and I just have to trust Him, as hard as it is."

"What will you do with Gabrielle?" Isaac asked. "She still needs a mother." He hesitated, then plunged ahead. "We would be willing to raise her."

"No, but thanks," Jake said firmly. "I'm going to marry Morning Song."

Isaac's eyes widened. "Have you asked her?" he asked slowly.

"No, but I think she'll agree. She loves Gabrielle." He smiled. "You should see Morning Song with her. And her John needs a father." He clapped Isaac on the back. "I don't want to say anything until you get back. If you don't make it, Emmie's baby will need a father, and I will honor my promise to Amelia." He said this last with a defiant determination.

"Agreed," Isaac said. "I would want her taken care of." He gripped Jake's hand again. "Whatever happens, will you promise me that you will try to learn to love your new wife? Amelia wouldn't want you to marry just for convenience. She intended for you to be happy."

Jake was silent a moment, then returned the pressure of Isaac's fingers. "All I can say is I'll try. I don't see how I can ever love anyone but Amelia, but I will try."

"That's all I ask," Isaac said. The two men looked at one another a moment. "Take care, Jake. You're not going on any picnic yourself. We don't want a repeat of yesterday."

Jake nodded. "I'll be careful. And Godspeed, my friend. I'll be praying for you."

With a last handshake, Isaac swung up onto Buck and urged him toward the gate. A soldier opened the gate and saluted as he slipped outside into the blinding snow. He had thought long and hard about what would be the best way to accomplish his mission. He decided to avoid obvious trails and travel by night as much as possible. That would help keep him warm during the frigid nights, and with the Lord's help, he could avoid confrontation with the Indians. He had left by a back gate and counted on the Sioux being occupied with celebrating their victory. The detail of men riding out to retrieve the dead would also divert the Indians.

The blizzard intensified out on the plain with no fort walls to block the wind. Isaac's mustache was soon coated with snow and ice, and he wished he had a full beard like many of the men wore. He had to stop often and walk his horse through the snowdrifts. Several hours from the fort, he came to a rock outcropping that offered some protection from the wind, and he decided to try to sleep there until nightfall. He and his horse were both exhausted. Leaving a robe on Buck, he pulled a buffalo robe over himself and fell into a deep sleep punctuated by nightmares of Emmie being dragged away by Sioux hordes. Her eyes were wide with terror, and she screamed his name over and over. When he awoke it was nearly dark. He ate a meal of hardtack and water, then mounted up and started out again.

The blizzard howled around him, and the temperature plummeted. Isaac knew it had to be at least twenty or thirty below zero even without the wind. He couldn't feel his fingers or toes, and by morning he could only slump numbly in the saddle. He was so cold and weary he couldn't think, but he forced himself to keep going. The morning only brought a lightening of the gloom as the snow continued to whirl around him. He wasn't even sure he was going in the right direction. He had tried to follow his compass, but the numbing cold made it hard to concentrate. He saw a forlorn cluster of trees to his right and turned Buck's head toward it. A huge snowdrift had formed around the trees, and he thankfully slid to his feet and stumbled toward it. Out of the wind it felt almost warm. He pulled his buffalo robe about him and fell into a dreamless sleep.

When he awoke, the moon was high in the sky, and he could see the stars. The snow had quit falling, but the wind still howled. He felt warm, though, and he knew he had to get up and get moving, for he was in danger of freezing. He made himself eat a couple of the crackers he'd brought with him and fed Buck some meager provender. He knocked the ice from his horse's eyes and tail and mounted up.

He found it hard to stay awake as he clung to his saddle pommel. The wind cut through even his buffalo robe, and he swayed in the saddle. *Hang on,* he told himself. *You have to get help for Emmie.* He clutched the saddle pommel with both hands and fought to stay mounted. As his horse rounded a grove of trees, he lost his tenuous grip and pitched sideways from the saddle into a drift. He felt nice and warm away from the wind. *I'll just lay here for a few minutes and rest,* he thought. He closed his eyes and slid into unconsciousness.

December twenty-fourth, Emmie thought as she awoke near dawn. Isaac had been gone three days. She felt an overwhelming need to pray for him. She slipped out of bed and knelt on the cold, hard floor. She shivered as the wind whistled under the door and through her flannel nightgown. If she was cold, what must Isaac be facing? *God, take care of him,* she prayed over and over again. *Only You know where he is and what he needs.*

She was stiff and cold clear through when she finally got up from her knees. She slipped back beneath the covers for a few minutes until she heard the sentry cry, "Five o'clock and all's well."

All's well. No one really believed that. The mood at the fort had been a peculiar one the last few days. Everyone seemed on edge, as though they were listening for some sound beyond the log walls of the stockade. Rand and Jake and their detachment had come back two days ago with the rest of the bodies of the slain soldiers. The Indians hadn't bothered them at all. Rand said he wasn't sure if they were holed up in camp because of the blizzard or simply too busy celebrating their victory.

Jake told them that before they left to recover the bodies, Colonel Carrington had opened the magazine and cut the Boorman fuses of round case shot. He opened the boxes of ammunition and adjusted them so that by lighting a single match, the whole lot would go up. His instructions were that if the Indians attacked in overwhelming numbers, the women and children were to be put in the magazine and blown up rather than have any captured alive. Thankfully, that had not happened, but Emmie couldn't forget that the magazine was still readied for such an eventuality.

It had taken several days to dig the grave site in the frozen ground for the slain men. It was so cold the men could only work in fifteen-minute shifts. Joel voiced all their fears when he innocently remarked, "How come they can only work for fifteen minutes when Isaac and John are out in the wind all the time?"

Emmie wondered the same thing. The snowstorm would subside for a few hours, then the snow would swirl down again in a blinding curtain. The soldiers had done all they could to keep a ten-foot trench dug around the stockade. If they had allowed the drifts to pile up, the Indians could have walked right over the tops of the logs in the stockade.

Now here it is Christmas Eve, she thought as she listened to the "All's well." Normally they would be wrapping presents and preparing food for a feast on Christmas Day. She sighed and slipped out of bed again. She pulled on her warmest dress, a worn blue wool one, and quickly combed her hair and washed her face in the cracked bowl on the stand by her bed.

She could try to make Christmas a little festive for Joel and Sarah, she decided. She would go to Jake's and check on Gabrielle, then see about what she could use for a tree. There were none on the fort grounds, but maybe Joel could find her a branch or something. Joel had been staying at Jake's for appearances' sake, so Morning Song could take care of the baby.

By the time Sarah and Rand came into the kitchen, Emmie had the fire going, and the room was beginning to lose its chill. She looked up as Sarah sat down next to her and pulled the teapot over to pour a cup of tea. Rand sat down next to her to pull on his boots.

"Are you all right?" she asked her friend. "You look as though you haven't slept all night."

Sarah sighed. "I'm feeling a bit poorly," she admitted. "My back hurts strangely. The pain seems to come and go."

Emmie narrowed her eyes and looked Sarah over. "I think perhaps Dr. Horton ought to take a look at you," she said. "It could be the baby."

Rand reared his head abruptly. "The baby? It isn't time yet."

"Not quite," Emmie said. "But it's not unusual for one to make his appearance a few weeks early."

"I'll get the doc." Rand didn't argue any more but grabbed his greatcoat and hurried out the door.

"I did wonder," Sarah admitted. "But I didn't want it to be the baby yet. I'm afraid, Emmie." She had tears in her eyes as she looked up. "I don't want to leave Rand and my baby. What if something goes wrong?"

"Don't talk like that," Emmie scolded. "Nothing is going to go wrong. Now you go get undressed and get into bed so the doctor can check you."

Sarah nodded and went to the bedroom. A few minutes later, Rand and Dr. Horton opened the door and hurried inside. Both were red-faced from the biting wind. Rand's mustache and the doctor's beard were coated with snow.

Dr. Horton tapped on the bedroom door and went right in. Rand stared blankly at the shut door, then sank down onto a chair. "I'm so afraid, Emmie," he said. "What if—" He broke off his words in midsentence.

Emmie took his hand. "I'll pray with you," she suggested.

Rand smiled wanly. "You are the newest Christian among us, but you sometimes seem like the strongest. I should have thought of that myself."

"I don't have anyone but the Lord," Emmie said softly. "So He's the only One I can turn to."

Rand nodded. "He's our only rock. And He is in control."

They both knelt beside their chairs. "Lord," Rand prayed, "I know we are so undeserving of Your love and care. We sometimes forget how You are always watching out for us and nothing comes to us that doesn't pass through Your hands first. Give us strength to go through what lies before us. Give Sarah strength and courage. If the baby is to come now, guide the doctor's hands and grant us a safe delivery both for Sarah and our baby. Be with me and Emmie that we may be a help and not a hindrance. Amen."

"Amen," Emmie echoed. They got to their feet just as the doctor opened the door and came back into the kitchen.

"The baby's coming," Dr. Horton said. "Unfortunately, Sarah is having back labor, so it could be awhile. It may help to rub her back, or she may not want you to touch her. It varies with different women. I'll check back in a couple of hours. If the situation changes, send for me."

He left a small bottle of laudanum with them in case the pain got worse. When the door closed behind him, Emmie and Rand went to the bedroom.

Sarah smiled wanly at them. "You were right," she told Emmie.

Emmie smiled and patted Sarah's hand. "Everything will be fine," she told her. "The doctor says it will be awhile yet, so why don't you try to rest while you can. We all may have a wonderful Christmas present after all."

"Oh, I hope it doesn't take that long," Sarah moaned as she burrowed deeper under the covers.

Rand and Emmie tiptoed out of the room and shut the door behind them. "I think I'll run over and tell Jake and Joel," Rand said. "Morning Song will want to be here too. And we may need her."

Emmie nodded. "It wouldn't hurt for Jake to keep you company."

Rand grimaced. "He may not be able to stand it after losing Amelia." He went toward the door. "If Sarah wakes up and asks for me, tell her I'll be right back."

"Try not to worry," Emmie called to his retreating back. She sighed and sat at the table. She was going to need every ounce of strength the Lord could give her. A thousand what-ifs rang in her head. What if she lost both Isaac and Sarah? She shuddered at the thought. Even losing one would devastate her. She just couldn't think about it. She stood up determinedly. She would keep busy, and the day would soon be over. The baby would be here, and soon there would be news of Isaac.

By the time she had cleaned the kitchen, Rand was back. Jake, Morning Song, and Joel were with him. Jake had Baby Gabrielle wrapped up in a buffalo robe, and her blue eyes peered up at her surroundings as soon as Jake unwrapped her. Joel had carried John over and set him down to play by a bucket of toys on the rug near the fire.

Morning Song took off her cloak and hurried to the bedroom to check on Sarah. "She still sleeping," she announced when she came back out. "That is good. She will need strength."

Emmie walked over to Jake and held out her arms for the baby. Jake kissed his daughter's fuzzy head, then handed her to Emmie and went to sit beside his brother. Everyone seemed quiet and subdued, and Amelia's spirit seemed to hover very near. Emmie knew no one could forget the terrible outcome of Gabrielle's birth. As she cuddled the baby, her own baby moved for the first time in her womb. She gulped and pressed a hand to her stomach. *No one noticed,* she thought with relief as she glanced around the room. Tears pricked her eyes as she thought about what the future held for her and her baby. Everything was such a mess. How could even God work out such a tangled web? She sighed and stood with the baby held close. As she laid her in the cradle near the kitchen stove, she asked God again for strength to face whatever the future held for her and her baby. And for Isaac. Always a prayer for Isaac lay on her heart.

Through the long day, Sarah's pains gradually intensified. Joel kept little John occupied, while Morning Song and Emmie took turns caring for Gabrielle and tending to Sarah. Dr. Horton popped in several times to check on Sarah's progress. "It will be awhile," he kept saying.

Rand and Jake grew quieter and more strained as the day wore on. Several times when Emmie came out of the bedroom, she saw them with their heads bent in prayer. The wind, howling around the corners of the house and whistling through the cracks around the doors and windows, put everyone on edge.

After supper, Sarah's labor began in real earnest. Dr. Horton tried to give her a small dose of laudanum, but she refused. She didn't want to risk any harm to the baby, she told him. He snorted, but he put his bottle away without protest.

Emmie was amazed at Sarah's strength and determination. She did not let out one cry when the pains came but only gripped Emmie's hand tighter. Only an occasional soft groan passed her lips. By ten o'clock the doctor had settled in with them for the night. "It could be anytime," he said finally.

Morning Song fed Gabrielle one last time and put her down for the night, then pulled up a chair beside her friend's bed. "Baby come soon now," she announced. She and Emmie took turns bathing Sarah's face with a wet cloth and rubbing her back during the contractions.

Just after midnight on Christmas Day, Sarah gave one last mighty push and a tiny baby boy slid into the world. He squalled in protest when Dr. Horton wiped the mucus away from his nose and mouth. Emmie grinned at the strong, lusty protest. She wrapped him in a bit of flannel and laid him in Sarah's arms.

"Isn't he beautiful?" Sarah asked. She stroked a tender finger down his cheek. "He looks just like his daddy."

"I'll get Rand now," Emmie said. She closed the door behind her and found

Rand just outside the door. Joel and John were asleep on a rug by the fire. Jake was sitting at the table with his head in his hands. He and Rand looked pale and haggard. "You have a beautiful son," Emmie said with a smile. "Do you want to see him?"

"How's Sarah?" Rand asked urgently.

"Tired, but just as beautiful as ever," Emmie said.

"Thank God," Jake murmured.

Rand shot through the door, and Sarah cried out and held out her arms to him. He went down on his knees by the bed and buried his face in her hair. She patted him and winked at Emmie as she closed the door behind Morning Song and the doctor.

Jake's knuckles were white as he gripped the table. "I have to go now," he muttered almost incoherently. He grabbed his greatcoat and ran out into the howling wind.

"Wait, Jake," Emmie called, but he just kept on going. She blinked back tears—there was such pain and grief in his eyes.

Morning Song looked at the door for a moment, then bundled the baby up. "I go home with baby," she announced. She wrapped her cloak around her. "Send John home with Joel in morning," she said.

Emmie was too tired to protest at the way it would look if Morning Song spent the night at Jake's alone. *He probably won't be there, anyway,* she told herself as Morning Song slipped out the door.

Rand opened the door and stepped into the kitchen with his small son in his arms. Emmie hurried to him and held out her arms for the tiny scrap. "I think he needs to be cleaned up a bit." She smiled. She had readied some warm water and strips of soft flannel. She had Rand pull the kitchen table close to the stove to keep the baby warm and quickly cleaned the little one and popped him into a gown. He was awake but made no protest at her ministrations. She wrapped him in a flannel blanket and handed him back to his father, who took him eagerly.

Rand gazed down into the face of his son with a look of awe and pride. "Sarah says he looks like me," he said. "But I don't see it."

"Then you must be blind," Emmie said with a laugh. "Look at that nose. And he has your dimples."

Just then the baby yawned and moved his mouth in such a way that Rand saw his dimples for the first time. "You're right," he said excitedly. "Ma will be so excited to hear about him."

"Maybe your family can come for a visit soon," Emmie said. "This may be all it takes to heal the breach with your father."

A shadow darkened Rand's brow. "I wouldn't hold my breath," he said shortly.

"Pa is determined that I give up what he calls my foolishness and come back to the farm. Ma says he doesn't mention my name."

"A grandchild can change everything," Emmie said.

"Maybe," Rand said with a shrug.

There was a sound from the parlor; then Joel came flying into the kitchen. His red hair stood on end as he slid to a stop in front of Rand and the baby. "Let me see," he begged.

Rand grinned and pulled back the blanket to reveal the baby. "Meet your new nephew."

Joel gave a sigh of awe. "Can I hold him?"

Rand passed him over to the young boy. "He's going to be pestering you unmercifully before you know it," he teased.

"I'm going to be the best uncle there ever was," Joel promised in a hushed tone. "I'm going to teach him all kinds of things, like where the best fishing spot is and how to play baseball." He looked up from his perusal of his nephew with a sudden look of alarm. "How's Sarah? She's all right, isn't she?"

Rand nodded toward the bedroom door. "See for yourself."

Joel carried the baby to the bedroom as Emmie opened the door for him. Sarah looked asleep, but she opened her eyes as soon as Joel stepped into the room. She smiled when she saw her brother with her baby. "Did Rand tell you what we named him?" she asked.

Joel shook his head. "I forgot to ask," he said with a sheepish look.

Sarah laughed. "His name is Joshua Joel Campbell," she said.

Joel gaped, then his chest swelled with importance. "Man alive," was all he could say. "If that don't beat the Dutch."

Rand clapped a hand on his shoulder. "If he turns out as good a boy as his namesake, we'll be very pleased."

Tears welled up in Joel's eyes at such praise from the man he adored. "I'll try to be a good example," he promised.

Sarah yawned, and Emmie saw the weariness behind her friend's smile. "It's time for the new mama to get some rest," she said. She shooed everyone out of the bedroom and put little Joshua in his cradle.

Sarah smiled sleepily at her as she plumped the pillows and straightened the covers. "I did good, didn't I?" she asked.

"You did good," Emmie assured her. "We're all very proud of you."

Sarah smiled again and was asleep before Emmie could close the door behind her. Rand and Joel were asleep in the parlor, Rand on the cot and Joel on the rug by the fire. As Emmie crawled into her cold bed, she thanked God that He had brought them safely through and asked again that He watch over Isaac.

Chapter 14

The next few days were the oddest Emmie could ever remember. On one hand they were all so excited and relieved that Sarah and the baby were all right, and on the other they held their breath as they waited for the Sioux to make their next move. No one had to tell the women that if the Sioux chose to attack, the fort would fall. Ammunition was dangerously low, and no one ventured outside the stockade except for the detail of men to keep the trench around the wall clear.

One night around midnight, a general alarm sounded, and Rand rushed out into the night. They had huddled around the fire and prayed for nearly an hour as they listened to the shouts and the boom of the howitzer as the soldiers rallied to the rescue of a corralled wagon train. When Rand returned, he grimly told them the train had brought an official notice of perfected peace, with instructions to freely make presents to the Indians. No wonder headquarters had not sent ammunition and extra troops when the colonel had requested it weeks earlier. Everyone evidently believed that falsehood.

The weather continued to hover between minus twenty-five and minus forty. Emmie and Sarah both longed for the company of the other women in the fort, but beyond a brief visit from Frances and Mrs. Horton the day after Joshua made his appearance, no one ventured beyond their own four walls. Finally, New Year's Day ushered in a slight break in the weather, and the entire fort gathered for a brief memorial service for the slain men. As Emmie looked at the faces gathered around the parade ground, the gravity of their situation was evident on every countenance. No one knew if they would all end up as the poor massacred men but with no one left to bury their remains and speak a last prayer over them. Mrs. Horton had to support poor Frances, who was nearly fainting from the stress and grief.

Two days into the new year, Emmie sat at the kitchen table up to her elbows in flour as she kneaded bread. Sarah, nursing the baby at the kitchen table, looked up as a bugle call sounded. Emmie, her fingers deep in bread dough, froze as the bugle sounded the long roll that meant troops had been spotted. Her hand to her breast, she held her breath as she rose and listened more closely. The bugle sounded again, and she bolted toward the door.

"Stay there," she told Sarah as she threw her cloak around her and ran out the door. From every home, people poured out the doors with looks of dawning hope. Jake ran past her, and she grabbed at his arm.

"Fresh troops are almost here," he told her. "Phillips or Isaac made it through!"

Tears of relief flooded her eyes as she ran to stand beside Frances. Even Jessica and her mother were out, she noticed. Jessica saw her stare and turned her back. The troops flooded through the gates. Emmie thought they all looked nearly frozen. Most had frostbite patches of white on their cheeks, their mustaches and beards were thickly caked with snow and ice, and they all wore a look of intense suffering. Desperate to find Isaac, she looked frantically through the milling men and horses, but there was no familiar grin or shock of red hair.

Colonel Carrington stood off to one side, talking to the major who had led the men. After several minutes, he came to where the women were. "Phillips made it through on Christmas Day," he told them. "It has taken this long for them to get through the blizzard."

"What about Isaac?" Emmie asked anxiously.

Colonel Carrington shook his head. "I'm sorry, my dear. He never showed up at the fort."

Emmie caught her breath. She clenched her hands beneath the folds of her cloak. He must be mistaken! Of course Isaac made it through. He was wrong. She searched the colonel's face, but she saw only compassion and understanding. He thought Isaac was dead. She took a step back.

"No, you're wrong," she stammered. She turned and ran across the parade ground. She'd find Rand. He'd know the truth. She found him giving directions to the men assigned to unpack the stores of supplies the troops had brought.

"Rand, I can't find any news of Isaac," she told him.

He put an arm around her and drew her off to one side. She looked up into his brown eyes and saw grief. She put her hands on his chest and pushed. "No, you're wrong," she said. "He's not dead. I'd know if he were dead."

Rand pulled her to him and held her. "You're strong now, Emmie, and you've got to face the facts. He didn't make it. He was a brave soldier, and he'd want you to be brave now too."

She wept against the rough wool of his jacket, but everything felt unreal. Isaac couldn't be dead. She couldn't accept that.

"Let me take you home," Rand said. He led her across the parade ground as she walked woodenly back to their quarters. Sarah saw the look of desolation in her eyes as she came in and stood up with a cry. She held out her arms and Emmie flew into them.

The next few days passed in a haze of grief and bewilderment. *How could it all end this way?* she wondered. She knew now how Jake felt when he lost Amelia. When Jake told her grimly that the plans for their marriage were moving ahead, she just nodded numbly. What did any of it matter now that Isaac was gone?

Isaac stirred and licked his lips. He was so very thirsty. He sat up and stared at the fireplace across the room. Where was he? The last thing he clearly remembered was pitching into a snowbank. He had vague impressions of the dark face of an old man that swam in and out of sight and dim memories of tossing and crying out feverishly.

A door opened, and the man in Isaac's dreams came through it. He was short and husky with a beard clear to his chest and black matted hair. He wore a faded red flannel shirt, stained and patched in numerous places, and trousers so dirty it was hard to tell what their original color had been. He squinted at Isaac, then spat a stream of tobacco juice on the floor.

"Awake, are ye?" he said with a scowl. "What in creation were ye doing wandering around in a blizzard?"

"What day is it?" Isaac struggled to swing his feet over the edge of the cot.

"Don't believe in answering questions?" the man asked. "That ain't polite."

"I've got to get to Fort Laramie. It's a matter of life and death." Isaac stood and swayed weakly. He leaned against the wall until his head stopped spinning.

"It was pert near your death," the man remarked. "Ye was as close to freezing to death as I'd ever seen. And the fever that followed about finished the job. It's a ways to Laramie. What's so all-fired important? I can see ye is a soldier."

Isaac nodded. "There's been a bloody massacre at Fort Phil Kearney. We need ammo and men, or we'll lose the fort itself and every man, woman, and child in it." He sat back down on the edge of the cot and leaned over to pull on his boots. "Where's my horse?"

"Not so fast. Ye can't light out again without some vittles. All ye've eaten is a little broth I was able to get down ye. Ye would never make it past the corral." He pointed to the table. "Sit down and fill your belly. The wind is still screaming like a banshee. The soup will warm ye."

Isaac eyed the steaming bowl. He was ravenous, he discovered. He started toward the table and staggered weakly. What was wrong with him? He sat down and bowed his head and thanked God for the food and for saving his life.

When he looked up, the man was staring at him. "Ye are a God-fearing man," he said. "I ain't seen nobody pray since my mam pert near forty years ago." He was silent a moment, then said, "My name's Pete Sweeney, but folks call me Hardtack." He cackled and pushed the bowl of stew toward Isaac. "I reckon 'cause they think I'm as tough as old shoe leather."

Isaac picked up a bent and tarnished spoon and dug into the stew. The smell made his mouth water. "Lieutenant Liddle," he mumbled between bites. "How far are we from Fort Laramie?"

" 'Bout a day's ride on a fresh horse," Hardtack said. "Which yer horse ain't. He was as near dead as you. Just now startin' to perk up some."

"You got a fresh horse?" Isaac wiped the last of the stew with a crust of bread and stood up.

"Naw. I got an old mule named Bertha, but she ain't good for much but carrying a light load downhill," the old man said.

"What day is it?" Isaac asked again.

Hardtack scratched his grizzled head. "I don't rightly know," he said. "The days all run together out here." He stood and walked to a faded dirty calendar nailed to the wall by the door. "Let's see, this is the day I went for supplies and it took me seven days coming back. I found you here and that were six days ago."

"Six days!" Isaac broke in. "I've been here six days?"

The old man continued as though Isaac had not interrupted. "January second," Hardtack said. "Near as I can figure."

"I've got to get to Laramie." Isaac jumped to his feet and looked around him. "Where're my boots?"

"Under the bed." Hardtack pointed a gnarled finger.

Isaac grabbed his boots and feverishly began to pull them on. "I even missed Christmas," he muttered to himself. He'd had such special plans for Emmie. His mother's engagement ring was hidden back in his room, waiting for the right moment to give it to her.

"Christmas, huh?" the old man said. "I ain't thought about Christmas since I were a boy. Ain't no one to give no presents to out prospecting anyhow." He shook his finger at Isaac. "Now I'm telling ye, ye can't go nowhere just yet. Ye need to get your strength back."

"I can't wait that long," Isaac said frantically. "I have to get reinforcements." He began to search for his greatcoat and buffalo robe.

Hardtack sighed and pointed to the other side of the bed, where he'd piled Isaac's belongings. "If ye are bent on killing yourself and your horse, I reckon I can't stop ye."

Isaac looked at the old man a moment, then, at an inner urging, rummaged through his knapsack and found his small New Testament. "Can you read?" he asked the old man.

Hardtack bristled. "Course I can read. What ye take me for? Some kind of half-wit? My mam was very particular 'bout all us young 'uns knowing about reading and writing."

"Then I'd like to say thanks for saving my life, with this." Isaac gently handed him the small black Book. "It's the most precious thing I own."

Hardtack blinked, then slowly reached out a hand and took the Book. "My mam had one like this," he said in a quavering voice. He stroked the battered cover. "Why would ye give me such a thing?"

"God told me to," Isaac said.

The old man blinked back tears. "Thank ye kindly," he said. "I'll take good care of it."

By the time Isaac left, Hardtack had pulled a chair near the fire and sat engrossed in the contents of the small black Book.

Isaac staggered weakly through the drifts of snow to the shed surrounded by a rickety corral. How was he going to get through when he was so weak? He grimly pushed on. He had to make it. God would give him the strength somehow.

He found Buck bedded down in a heap of straw with an old blanket thrown over him. "Sorry, Boy," he said. "We've got to get on the road again." He slipped the bit into Buck's mouth and hurriedly saddled him. He led him out the door into the wind-driven snow. After swinging up into the saddle, he tucked his buffalo robe securely around him, checked his compass, and dug his heels into Buck's flank.

He felt he was close enough to Fort Laramie to travel in the daylight. This close to the fort most of the Indians were friendly Brulé Sioux. It was still slow going in the drifting snow, but Isaac felt a new strength coursing through him, a new optimism. He was going to make it! He just prayed that God would protect the fort with His mighty right hand until help could arrive.

After riding nearly three hours, he began to recognize the terrain. He was almost to Fort Reno! Maybe they would have news of Fort Phil Kearny. A sentry stopped him as he rode up, then opened the gate. He made his way to the commanding officer's headquarters and knocked on the door.

"Enter," the commander called.

He stepped inside and saluted the major seated behind a scarred, makeshift desk. "Sir, I come with a dispatch from Colonel Carrington at Fort Phil Kearny. There's been a terrible battle, and we desperately need reinforcements and ammunition."

The major waved his hand. "Where have you been, Lieutenant? We got word of the massacre days ago. Troops should just about be there by now."

Isaac sagged in relief. The fort was saved! "I had some bad luck, Major. I'm just thankful Phillips made it through."

The major nodded. "You don't look well, Lieutenant. You'd better head to mess and get some chow."

Isaac opened his mouth to object and say he was going back to Fort Phil

Kearny, when the major interrupted him.

"That's an order, Lieutenant."

Isaac sighed. It seemed he didn't have a choice. He saluted, then left head-quarters and made his way across the tiny parade ground to the mess hall. After a bowl of stew and a stringy piece of meat, he mounted up and pointed Buck's head back to Fort Phil Kearny.

Sarah coaxed Emmie's hair into soft ringlets with the aid of the hot tongs. "You're going to be a beautiful bride," she told her.

Emmie forced a smile. "I doubt if Jake really cares how I look," she told her. "As long as I show up, he'll be content."

Morning Song peeked in the bedroom where the other two women were. "There you are, my friend. I bring you something for luck." She held out a beautifully beaded belt.

"Oh, Morning Song, it's lovely," Emmie said. She took the belt and examined it. The belt had tiny eagle designs with exquisite detailing. She hugged her friend and slipped the belt around her waist. It looked beautiful against the cream of her dress.

Morning Song sat on the edge of the bed. "Jake tell me to go make woman talk," she said with a shy smile. "He walk and pace like a panther."

The women chuckled. "Rand said Jake was nervous," Sarah said. "You wouldn't think so since he's been through it before."

They all fell silent at the oblique reference to Amelia. Emmie felt tears prick her eyes. She still missed Amelia and knew the pain was a never-ending one for Sarah too. Poor Jake. She knew she could never make up to him all he'd lost, but perhaps they could find some measure of happiness together in raising Gabrielle and the baby Emmie carried.

"I wish you much happiness, my sister," Morning Song said with downcast eyes.

Emmie looked at her lovely face and wished things could have been different. She had felt for some time that Morning Song harbored warm feelings for Jake. And sometimes she saw a softness in Jake when he looked at Morning Song. *Not love yet, but it could have blossomed,* Emmie thought. If there had just been the opportunity.

She finished her toilet, and the three women pulled on their cloaks, bundled up the baby, and hurried across the parade ground to the little chapel. Once inside the foyer, Sarah handed Joshua to Morning Song, then repaired the damage the wind had wrought to Emmie's hair and put the filmy veil on Emmie's head. Morning Song slipped inside the door and sat at the back of the chapel with Baby John.

Sarah looked into the chapel and motioned for the post band to begin the music, then stepped out and took Rand's arm as he escorted her to front of the chapel where they would stand up with Emmie and Jake.

Emmie took a deep breath and walked slowly down the aisle. She didn't look to the left or the right as she fixed her eyes on the preacher, but she was aware of the many eyes on her. Most of the fort, including Maggie, the laundress, and the enlisted men, had turned out for the wedding. Everyone was grateful for a chance to forget the bad time they'd all been through. She didn't look at the broad back of the man who waited for her. She knew she would burst into tears when she saw Jake there where Isaac was supposed to be. She stopped in front of the preacher with her head down. Warm fingers clasped hers, and she jumped a little at the gentle pressure. Perhaps Jake was beginning to feel some small affection for her.

"Dearly beloved," the pastor began. His voice droned on as Emmie blocked most of it out. Then he said, "Emmaline Croftner, do you take this man to be your wedded husband? Will you love him, honor and obey him, and cling to him only as long as you both shall live?"

The words pounded in her head, and she turned to meet the gaze of the man who would be her husband. Familiar blue eyes met hers, and she gasped and closed her eyes. She was hallucinating, for sure. She opened one eye cautiously to see a familiar grin.

Isaac caught her as she started to slide to the floor. "I thought you'd be glad to see me," he said.

It was Isaac! She looked around to see the smiling faces of her friends. Even Jake was grinning. She couldn't remember the last time she'd seen him smile.

"Surprise!" Sarah hugged her. "He made it back late this morning, just in time to switch places with Jake. I just found out myself. Aren't you going to answer the preacher?"

Emmie looked in bewilderment at the minister, who smiled complacently back at her.

"Well, are you going to marry me or not?" Isaac asked.

Jake nodded at her. "I've released you from your promise," he said. "And if Morning Song is agreeable, we'll make it a double wedding." He looked back at Morning Song and held out his hand. Her eyes never leaving his, she stood and handed John to Frances Grummond before walking to Jake and putting her small brown hand in his. Jake turned and faced the minister again. "Let's get this wedding moving along. I'm ready for some cake."

With her hand in Isaac's, looking into his warm blue eyes, Emmie knew the Lord her God had done this wondrous thing. Her heart overflowing with love and joy, she repeated her vows, then stepped into Isaac's arms.

Epilogue

Emmie looked around the nearly bare rooms where she'd spent the last two years. Was she leaving anything behind? This would be the last time she would ever see these rooms again. Sap no longer oozed from the rough logs, and the tiny rooms looked barren without their gay calico curtains and tablecloths. Dust motes danced in the hot summer sunshine that filled the parlor.

Because of the treaty of 1868, the army had agreed to abandon Forts Reno, C. F. Smith, and Phil Kearny to the Indians. No one would ever inhabit these walls again. Isaac said the Indians likely would burn the fort as soon as the soldiers were out of sight.

She looked down at a tug on her skirt. Tiny Amelia, just over two, lifted her arms up to be held. Smiling, Emmie knelt and took the child in her arms. She buried her face in her daughter's sweet-smelling hair. God had blessed her so much. Amelia's birth had been easy, and the joy the little girl brought to both her and Isaac was simply amazing. Who would have thought that she would have so much just three years after she had heard the shriek of the overturning carriage that day in Wabash?

Life was good. Even Jake seemed to have finally put the past behind him. He looked at Morning Song with love in his eyes now. They were expecting an addition to their little family in October. Sarah had given Rand another son last year and was also expecting a new baby around Christmas. She and Rand had said they wanted a large family, and they were well on their way to having their dreams fulfilled. Emmie had even had an opportunity to tell her brother Labe about how God had changed her life when he'd stopped by three months ago on his way back to the goldfields of Bozeman.

He had brought news about Ben's death in a shooting during a poker game with other miners. Emmie had been sad but not surprised. Ben had too much pride to ever bend his knee to God.

Emmie whirled now as the front door banged shut, and her husband strode in. Isaac smiled as he caught sight of her with Amelia in her arms.

"It won't be long before you won't be able to pick her up," he said, glancing at the gentle bulge where their new baby grew. Amelia held out her arms to him, and he took her and tossed her into the air.

She giggled. "Again, Daddy," she cried.

Emmie watched as Isaac played with Amelia. He was never too busy to take a moment to bring a smile to the little girl's face. He had certainly kept his promise to be a good father. And husband. She loved him with a fierce, almost painful, love.

His deep voice interrupted her introspection. "Are you ready to leave?"

Emmie linked her arm through his and gazed up into his blue eyes. "I'm ready," she said. He opened the door, and they walked across the parade ground for the last time.

"Bye, bye, house," little Amelia called, waving her chubby hands.

Emmie echoed the sentiment in her heart as Isaac helped her up into their wagon, then handed Amelia to her. A new fort and a new home awaited them in Arizona. She remembered the words of Ruth, *"Whither thou goest, I will go; and where thou lodgest, I will lodge: thy people shall be my people, and thy God my God: where thou diest, will I die, and there will I be buried."*

She would follow Isaac wherever the army sent them, and she would go happily. It was more than she'd ever hoped for and it was good.

THE HEART
ANSWERS

For my parents, George and Peggy Rhoads,
who have always believed I could do anything.
Thanks for always being there for me.
And for my "other" parents, Carroll and Lena Coble,
who adopted me as their own the first time their youngest son
brought me through the door.
I would not have written the first word
without the love and support of all four of you.
I love you bunches!

Chapter 1

You're what?!" Jessica DuBois raised her normally well-modulated voice to a near shriek.

"A lady never raises her voice, Dear," her mother admonished. She dotted a few crumbs of toast and jam from her lips and rose to her feet. "Your uncle Samuel is alone with three young children who need a mother. You and I need a home, and Samuel has graciously offered us one. I haven't wanted to worry you, but I really was at my wits' end when I learned there would be so little money for us to live on."

"But what about Boston?" Jessica jumped to her feet and nearly tripped over her blue wool gown. She tugged at it, impatient with her unaccustomed clumsiness. "Papa has only been dead a month! How can you even think about marrying another man so quickly? What would Papa say?" In truth, she cared less about what her father would say than about her spoiled plans.

"He would be glad you and I were provided for," her mother said gently. "Now I really must begin to pack. The troop leaves in two days, and I promised Samuel we would get to Fort Bridger as quickly as we could."

Jessica watched in disbelief as her mother gathered her skirt in her hand and swished from the room. Fort Bridger! She wanted the bright lights of Boston, concerts, social life, and teas with her friends.

What friends? She shrugged the thought away. Her mother couldn't do this to her! She didn't want to be buried in some backwater ever again. She'd had all she could stand of soldiers and dust and months-old news. *And humiliation.* Until coming to this wilderness, she'd had no shortage of admirers all fighting for the chance to spend some time with her. Not that there was a shortage now. But until coming west, no man had ever rejected her. Her lips tightened at the unpleasant memories.

Men were so gullible. First Rand Campbell, then Isaac Liddle had thrown her over for some namby-pamby woman. Why couldn't they see how much more beautiful and desirable *she* was? Jessica tossed her head and scowled.

She walked restlessly to the front window and looked out on Fort Phil Kearny's snow-covered parade ground. The March sunshine was beginning to melt some of the snow, but the incessant wind still poked icy fingers into everything. A few soldiers bent into the gale as they hurried to the warmth of the sutler's store across the way.

She would be glad to get out of this place. She didn't want to run into Rand or Isaac ever again. And she hated the pity in their wives' eyes whenever they met. Emmie Liddle, in particular, irritated her beyond all reason.

A new thought occurred to her, and her eyes widened. Why couldn't she go to Boston without her mother? She could stay with her aunt, as distasteful as that might be.

She hurried across the hall and interrupted her mother's packing. "I'm going to stay with Aunt Penelope," she announced without preamble.

Her mother sighed and turned to face her. "I'm sorry, Dear, but that just is not possible."

"Why not?" Jessica allowed her lower lip to tremble, a technique that usually worked wonders on her parents. A single tear escaped from her lashes. She saw her mother wince, and Jessica suppressed a smile of triumph.

Her mother bit her lip. "There just isn't enough money to send you back to Boston. I'm afraid your father—" She put her hand to her mouth. "Perhaps by spring I can save enough from your father's pension to purchase a stage ticket."

Jessica stamped her foot. "I can't go to Fort Bridger, Mama! I just can't!" She felt near panic at the thought of continuing to live in this desert.

Her mother put out a placating hand. "I'm sure it won't be for long, Darling. And Samuel says Fort Bridger is very pleasant. Lovely mountains, clear streams, and no dangerous natives. The only Indians he has seen since he arrived are friendly Shoshone. Please try to make the best of it."

But Jessica wasn't about to give in graciously. "Well, don't expect me to help with those brats of Uncle Samuel's! Especially Miriam. I told you and Papa years ago I didn't want to ever see her again!" She whirled and stormed out of the room, slamming the door behind her. How dare her mother force her to go even further west than this desolate place? What could have possessed her to agree to such a harebrained scheme?

Jessica remembered the last time she had seen Uncle Samuel and his family. His three children had teased her unmercifully, especially Miriam. She knew Jessica had been adopted, and Miriam had poked fun at her.

Jessica flinched at the painful memories, the nightmares that had plagued her for years. She would never forget the years of cold and hunger in the small shanty with her brother Jasper. One cold December night her mother had gone out partying and never returned. The police had come and taken her and Jasper away to an orphanage. She'd never seen her brother or her mother again.

Then her adoptive parents had arrived, taken one look at her beautiful face and red curls, and claimed her as their own. She swallowed past the lump in her throat. Papa had always told her he was a sucker for a beautiful woman.

He'd made such a big thing of her beauty that she had always wondered if he would have picked her if she were plain.

Jessica threw herself across her bed and buried her face in her arms. She wanted to go to Boston! She needed activity to keep the memories at bay. Her father had always told her she was beautiful, and now she needed to find someone else to tell her. She had to think of a way to get out of this place. Surely she would be able to get around her mother; she had always been able to get her mother to give in to her wishes in the past. She would surely think of something.

But two days later, Jessica found herself standing outside an army ambulance wagon with the wind and snow blowing about their little, well-guarded convoy. The trip would be long and dangerous. Several of the wives and daughters had gathered to say good-bye to them.

Jessica glimpsed Sarah Campbell and Emmie Liddle and turned her head. She didn't want to have to speak to them, but she didn't have any choice. Sarah touched her arm, and she steeled herself to face them. Both Sarah and Emmie wore identical expressions of concern on their faces.

"Jessica, I just wanted to ask you to forgive me for any hurt I've caused you in the past," Sarah said gently.

"Me too," Emmie put in. "We don't want to part as enemies. We just want you to know that we'll be praying for you."

Jessica narrowed her eyes and stared at them. Pray for her? What made them think she needed their prayers? Did they think they were so much better than an orphanage foundling that their prayers mattered more than her own? "I don't need your prayers," she spat. "I'll be just fine." She pointedly turned away from them as other ladies came to say good-bye.

When she turned around, she was relieved to see that they had gone. The nerve of those two! How dare they sit in judgment on her! Pray for her, indeed. She didn't need any prayers, especially from them. She was beautiful, and she would make her own way in the world. She swallowed hard past a sudden lump in her throat, then gathered her skirts and climbed into the ambulance.

Clay Cole reined in Misty, his bay mare, and looked back over the trail he had just covered. The wind tried to tease his wide-brimmed hat from his head, but it was jammed on too tightly. He took out his red bandanna and wiped his face and neck. After traveling mostly at night, he was nearly to Fort Casper; now he could finally begin to travel in the light of day. Most of the Sioux were north, terrorizing the forts along the Bozeman Trail. Throughout the entire year of 1866, they had carried out a war against forts like Fort Phil Kearny and then up to Fort C. F. Smith farther north in Montana. The region had buzzed with the news of over eighty men slaughtered at Fort Phil Kearny two and a half months ago.

He yawned mightily and stretched his cramped muscles, then turned his mare's head into the wind and started down the trail again. At least the spring thaw had set in early this year. A few days ago, the snow had begun to melt, though the wind still blew. He rounded a curve and came to a sudden halt.

The sound of shots and shrieks made him dig his heels into his mare's flank and pull his rifle loose. About a dozen Indians circled an army train just ahead. The soldiers had formed a protective circle and were firing methodically at the war tribe. Clay let out a whoop of his own and shot his rifle into the air.

A fearsomely painted Sioux turned. When he saw Clay's thundering approach, he wheeled, signaling to his band to retreat. Clay knew they thought he was bringing reinforcements. He howled again, and his charge scattered the last of the Sioux. He reined in Misty and cantered on into the circle of wagons.

A woman with red curls peered fearfully from the back of an ambulance, and he waved at her. After a moment, she waved hesitantly and withdrew back inside the ambulance.

A young lieutenant with thin brown hair cantered up to him. "Howdy, Preacher. You showed up in the nick of time. I was a bit surprised you fired on them, though. I thought you didn't believe in violence."

Clay grinned. "I can fight when I have to, Tom. Today wasn't one of those times, though. I just gave them a good excuse to leave."

The lieutenant raised his eyebrows. "Whatever you did worked. Thanks."

"Thank God, Tom."

Tom reddened and cut his gaze to the left of Clay's ear. "You can do the praying, Preacher. I don't have the knack for it." He turned his horse's head and galloped back to the front of the wagon train.

Clay watched him go with a ruefully. He'd been witnessing to young Tom Harris for over a year now. He was discouraged that he wasn't seeing more fruit from his ministry yet. But here was where the Lord had called him, and here he would stay unless God decreed otherwise.

He fell into line with the convoy, and the remainder of the trip into Fort Casper was uneventful. The wind cut through his coat in spite of the weak sunshine, and Clay longed for the warmth of a fire and a hot cup of coffee.

Just before dusk, he saw the smoke from Fort Casper ahead and breathed a sigh of relief. He knew the soldiers felt the same. He wondered briefly about the young woman he'd seen in the ambulance. What was she doing traveling in the middle of March? Perhaps she'd lost a husband recently; he made a mental note to check on her tomorrow and offer her some comfort from God's Word.

The mess hall was crowded when he made his way inside. He heard a shout and turned to see a young tornado running across the room. "Uncle Clay!" Three-year-old Franny hurtled toward him. She always called him uncle, although they were actually cousins.

He swung her into his arms and turned to look for Franny's parents, Ellen and Martin, his closest friends. He saw Ellen seated near the stove and made his way to her side, with Franny clinging to his neck.

Ellen rose with a gentle smile as he neared. "I didn't expect to see you back from Montana so quickly, Clay. But I'm glad you're here." Her words were low and choked with emotion.

Clay searched her eyes, and his heart jumped at the grief he found there. "What's happened?" He didn't think he really wanted to hear the answer.

Ellen swallowed hard, and her lips trembled. "Martin was killed in a skirmish last week."

Clay went very still. He and Martin were first cousins, but their relationship had always been that of brothers. He tried to speak past the lump in his throat, but all that came out was a choking sound.

Ellen touched his arm. "Let's go to our quarters. I shouldn't have blurted it out like that."

A few minutes later, he was seated at their kitchen table with a cup of steaming coffee in his trembling hand and Franny on his knee. His eyes blurring, he stared into the dark liquid and tried to get his thoughts around the fact of Martin's death. He would never see Martin's gap-toothed smile again, or the way his hair stuck up in a funny cowlick. He raised his head and looked into Ellen's grief-stricken eyes. "What will you and Franny do now?"

She sighed heavily. "I really don't know. I have to vacate these quarters next week. I suppose I could go home, but I love it out here. I can't quite bear the thought of going back to Indiana and leaving Martin in the cemetery on the hill. If I could just find some kind of job, I'd stay." She gave him a tremulous smile. "I even asked about taking on the post laundry, but Major Larson wouldn't hear of it. Maybe at another fort where no one knew Martin I'd have better luck."

"I could get you on at Bridger," Clay said impulsively. He hated to see her take on such a hard task, but he knew there weren't many jobs around for a woman. Not decent women, anyway. At least at Bridger he could check on Ellen and Franny occasionally.

Ellen immediately brightened. "Oh, Clay, that would be wonderful!"

Before he could respond, someone knocked on the door. Ellen rose and hurried to see who it was. The wind howled through the open door and nearly knocked over the two women standing in the doorway.

"Oh, you poor dears." Ellen's soft voice was full of concern. "Come in by the fire." She ushered them inside and took their wraps.

Clay raised his eyebrows at the sight of the young woman he'd seen in the back of the ambulance. Big blue eyes shone from a face with skin so translucent it looked like porcelain. But Clay was immune to her lustrous red curls and shapely figure. His five sisters had plagued him with their constant preoccupation with their looks, and now he found himself more drawn to a beautiful inner character than to outward looks. Still, there was something about the beautiful redhead that was intriguing.

Jessica was so glad to be out of the ambulance with her feet on solid ground, she didn't even mind the rude accommodations. The tiny cabin was hardly any bigger than her bedroom back in Fort Phil Kearny, but it was warm and homey and smelled wonderfully of coffee and yeast from the fresh bread on the table. Her mouth watered at the smell.

Her gaze traveled to the figure standing behind their hostess, and her eyes widened when she realized it was the same man who had driven off the Indians earlier in the day. Now there was a man! He was very tall, with massive arms, broad shoulders, and a narrowed waist, dark hair, and hazel eyes above a Roman nose. He held a tiny blond girl in his arms, and she felt a pang of disappointment at the thought that the child might be his. If he was unattached, he might be a pleasant diversion for the evening. She sent him a tiny smile, but he just nodded politely.

Her mother fluttered her hands. "My dear Mrs. Branson, we do so apologize for barging in this way. The commanding officer, Major Larson, assured us that you were used to taking in strays. We do beg your hospitality. I'm Letty DuBois, and this is my daughter Jessica."

Jessica fixed her blue eyes on Ellen and tossed her head imperiously. "I wouldn't turn down some of that coffee I smell." Why did her mother always sound so apologetic? One must take charge of a situation or be taken advantage of. And Jessica wasn't about to let anyone take advantage of her. She was used to having the best of everything.

Letty colored at her daughter's tone, then bobbed her head. "Your coffee does smell wonderful," she admitted. "We could smell it from the porch."

Ellen smiled. "Sit down at the table, and I'll bring you both a cup of coffee and some bread. It's still warm." She led the way to the kitchen and grabbed two coffee cups. "This is Clay Cole and my daughter Franny. Say hello, Franny."

" 'Lo," the little girl mumbled. Her eyes were round with astonishment as she gazed at Jessica. She wiggled, and Clay set her on the floor. She hesitantly drew closer to Jessica and touched the soft material of her gown. "You're pretty," she announced.

Jessica had never had another female besides her mother compliment her, not even one as tiny as this one. "Thank you," she said, a bit at a loss. "So are you." She was surprised to find she meant those words. The little girl looked angelic with her soft blond curls tied back in a blue bow and her big blue eyes round with admiration.

The little girl's eyes grew even bigger. "I am?"

Jessica nodded. "Very pretty. Would you like to sit on my lap?" She wanted to catch the words back as soon as she spoke them. What if the child had jam on her fingers? But it was too late to back down now. Even Letty looked astonished as Franny climbed onto Jessica's lap and settled there contentedly.

Jessica was surprised at how comforting the warmth of that small body felt pressed against her. She'd never had time for children. Actually, she'd never been around many small children. She awkwardly shifted Franny into the crook of her arm and took the coffee Ellen handed her.

"What brings the two of you to Fort Casper?" Ellen asked.

Letty glanced sideways at Jessica. "We're on our way to Fort Bridger. My husband died in the Fetterman disaster, and I'm going to care for his brother's children."

Jessica tossed her head. "Tell them the truth, Mama! You're marrying another man, and my father isn't even cold in his grave yet." She didn't care if she embarrassed her mother. She deserved to be embarrassed. How could Mama be so heartless? Had she really even loved Papa? She gave a mental shrug. What was love, anyway? A temporary madness that enabled a woman to get a man to do what she wanted. Jessica herself had never been in love. She doubted if there was such a thing.

She eyed Clay surreptitiously from under her lashes. He was quite amazingly good-looking. A fine male specimen, actually. He wasn't in uniform, so he wasn't a soldier. Perhaps he was a settler or a guide? It didn't really matter. All that mattered was that he wasn't married to timid Ellen. A mild flirtation to relieve the boredom was all Jessica wanted.

Ellen was no competition. She was short and pudgy with thin, flyaway brown hair and a mouth too wide for her face. Jessica dismissed her after a cursory look. She must find out more about Mr. Clay Cole.

"Do you live here at Fort Casper?" she asked him.

Clay gave her a glance from his hazel eyes and shook his head. "Just passing through on my way to Bridger."

Before Jessica could respond, Franny slid to the floor. "Uncle Clay, you haven't seen my new dolly. Daddy gave it to me." She took Clay's hand and tugged. "Come see."

"Okay, Angel Face," he said with an indulgent smile. "Show me your dolly."

"May I come too?" Jessica asked. What a perfect opportunity to get Clay to herself!

Franny nodded. "But you can't hold her. Only Mommy and me can hold her." She led the way to a tiny room, more a closet than a bedroom, with a small bed pushed up against the wall. She picked up a rag doll from the bed and held it up proudly. "This is Molly."

Clay squatted in front of the little girl. "She's very pretty, Franny. Almost as pretty as you."

Jessica admired the doll too, then stood close to Clay and looked up into his eyes. "I'm so glad you're going to be going to Fort Bridger. I do hope you'll find the time to come see me after we arrive. I'd really like to get to know the brave man who saved us from the Indians." She laid a hand on his arm as she spoke and gave him a tiny smile that she knew showed her perfect white teeth to advantage.

Clay looked down at her for a moment, then gently pried her hand from his arm. "I'm immune to beautiful women, Miss DuBois. But I'm sure there are plenty of men in Bridger who will be glad to dance attendance on you. I have better things to do." He swept Franny up into his arms, then turned and strode from the room without a backward glance.

"You, you—" How dare he speak to her like that! Jessica couldn't think of a suitable word to express just what she thought of him. She stamped her foot, but there was no one left in the room to see. She put her hands to her hot cheeks. He had snubbed her! Her! No man had ever snubbed her before in her entire life. There had been men who had walked away later, but never a man who had been immune to her beauty right from the first meeting.

She swallowed her anger and arranged her face into a bored smile. He mustn't see that his words had bothered her one bit. She'd had years of practice at hiding pain and disappointment. No backwoods cowboy was going to have the satisfaction of hurting her now. She took a deep breath and walked back into the kitchen.

Everyone was seated at the table once again, chattering animatedly.

"Oh, there you are, Dear," her mother said. "I was just telling Ellen she must travel in the ambulance with us tomorrow. It will be so pleasant to have another woman to talk to."

"You're going to Bridger?" Jessica sat back down in her chair without a glance at Clay. "Is your husband being transferred?"

A look of pain passed over Ellen's face. "My husband was killed last week," she said quietly. "Clay is arranging for me to work at Fort Bridger."

Uh-oh. Maybe she was competition after all. Not that Jessica cared after the way Clay had talked to her. But what satisfaction there would be to have Clay Cole eating out of her hand before she tossed him over! She knew exactly what she would say too. *But, Clay dear, you can't possibly want to marry a beautiful woman. You're immune. Remember? Run along and see if Ellen will have you. I certainly won't.*

Jessica was so lost in her pleasant daydream of crushing Clay under her heel that she missed what else Ellen had to say about her job. "That's nice," she said absently. "We'll be glad to have you to tea when we get settled."

She saw the strange glances both her mother and Clay gave her. What was wrong with them? She shrugged mentally and fixed a bright smile on her face. "Franny can spend some time with me while you're working."

"You'll be much to busy to bother with Franny," Ellen said with a nervous laugh. "She can help me with the laundry."

Laundry? Ellen did her own laundry? How odd. But Jessica was too full of plans to humiliate Clay to give it much thought. Revenge was such a sweet word.

Chapter 2

Over the next few days, Jessica did not find much opportunity to put her plans into action. She only caught occasional glimpses of Clay when she got out of the ambulance to stretch her legs and walk.

Ellen and Franny often joined her, and she found herself relaxing in Ellen's company. She'd never had a girlfriend before. She didn't trust women, and she trusted men even less. But Ellen was different. She didn't seem to have a bad word to say about anyone; she always had time to listen to her little girl, and she shared her thoughts and feelings with Jessica. Jessica still hadn't shared anything meaningful about herself, but it was pleasant to feel as though she could, and Ellen would keep her confidences private. Maybe someday she would tell Ellen about her childhood.

One bright morning, Jessica saw Clay walking his mare behind the ambulance. He didn't seem in any hurry to leave, so she decided it was a perfect opportunity to pique his interest. She knew sunshine enhanced the sheen of her red hair, so she loosened the ribbon that tied it back and climbed out the back of the wagon.

Clay looked up with a wary expression as she fell into step beside him. "Where is Ellen?" he asked.

"Taking a nap with Franny," she said. "She needs the rest. Martin's loss has been hard on her."

"I'm surprised someone like you would notice."

Jessica bristled. "Like me? You have no idea what I'm like. We only exchanged a few words, and that was days ago. What makes you think you know anything about me?" She realized she was scowling and quickly rearranged her face. Why did the man bring out the worst in her?

He smiled. "It certainly looks as though you've had everything you've ever wanted. Riches, adoration. I'm not the kind of man a woman like you would normally notice."

Rich! If he only knew. But still, at least he was talking to her. "My father didn't leave much money." She tossed her head and saw his eyes stray to her cascading hair. She suppressed a smile of triumph.

Clay raised his eyebrows, and his smile widened. "Oh? A little poverty is good for the soul. You might learn something." He broke off when a soldier from the front of the procession hailed him. He swung up onto his mare and cantered away without a backward glance.

Jessica gritted her teeth and stared after him. What a beautiful man. She *would* make him fall in love with her. She had to figure out what he admired in a woman. She looked thoughtfully toward the back of the ambulance. Maybe when Ellen awakened, they would have a little talk about "cousin" Clay.

Hoping Clay might come back, she walked along a few more minutes, then shrugged her shoulders and climbed back into the ambulance. Ellen and Franny were both awake and chatting with Letty. Jessica tied the canvas flap in place and joined them on the seats along the outside walls of the wagon.

"Your cheeks are pink," her mother said. "I do wish you'd take your parasol when you're out in this bright sun. Your skin will burn if you're not careful."

Jessica shrugged. "I forgot it. Ellen, I saw Clay just now. He seems so aloof, and I was wondering about his background."

Ellen laughed. "Clay, aloof? You just don't know him well enough yet. With five sisters, he learned early on how to hold his own with women. He's actually Martin's cousin, you know. But he's been a good friend to me. Whenever he passes through our area, he always spends a few days with us."

"Has he ever married?"

"Not Clay. He doesn't think it would be fair to a woman to ask her to share his nomadic life. But he is attractive, isn't he? He wouldn't have any trouble finding a wife, if he were so inclined."

Just then the shout of "Bridger ahead!" brought their conversation to an end.

Letty fluttered her hands and lurched to her feet. "Oh my," she whispered. "My hair is a rat's nest. What will Samuel think?"

"You look fine, Mother," Jessica said impatiently. "Uncle Samuel isn't expecting a fashion plate after a trip across the wilderness." Grabbing up her ribbon, she tied her hair back, then sighed and clasped her hands in her lap. Another fort. Each one was almost like the last one; it was such a boring life. Why couldn't she be arriving in Boston instead? Why couldn't she be looking forward to parties instead of dealing with her cousins?

The ambulance wagon lurched to a halt, and moments later, she heard Uncle Samuel's familiar gruff voice. He sounded so much like her father that a lump grew in Jessica's throat. Life was so unfair! Why couldn't it be Papa's voice outside the wagon? *Why, why, why?* The questions had no answers.

Her mother hurried to untie the canvas flap at the back of the wagon, and Samuel climbed aboard. He smelled of fresh air, tobacco, and the cloves he was always sucking. His broad shoulders made the tiny space seem even smaller. The lump in her throat grew larger; her uncle had the same silky, dark hair and square-jawed face her father had had. Her father's jawline had enhanced his air of authority, while Uncle Samuel's jaw was a bit softer and more blurred. He looked genial, prosperous, and good-natured.

And why shouldn't he look good-natured? Jessica sniffed and bit her lip. He was getting her mother as a drudge to cook and clean and take care of his brood. But not her. *She* wasn't about to kowtow to a man like that. She couldn't imagine a worse fate than laundry and cooking and cleaning up after other people.

"I've been watching the horizon for days," Samuel said in a hearty voice. "The kids are excited too."

I'll bet. Jessica bit her lip to prevent it from curling. If she knew Miriam, she wasn't any more eager to spend time together than she was. She gazed past her uncle's burly form, but all she could see were milling soldiers and rough log cabins. Where were the cousins, anyway? She and her mother began to gather their possessions and hand them to Samuel.

He turned and bellowed out the back of the ambulance wagon, "Caleb!"

Jessica's eyebrows raised as her cousin Caleb appeared. At fifteen he was already taller than his father and looked nothing like the eight-year-old boy she remembered. He was scrawny, but with the promise of slender good looks to come. He nodded to her and her mother, then stood and accepted the bundles his father passed to him.

"Where are your sisters?" Samuel demanded. "They should be here to greet their new family."

Caleb shrugged. "Miriam said something about baking bread, and Bridie was reading."

Samuel sighed. "You'll have to take them in hand, Letty. They've been on their own too long and don't mind the niceties much."

Letty fluttered her hands and nodded. "I shall enjoy it, Samuel. We always wanted more children." She glanced at Jessica's expression and fell silent, then gave a cheery wave to Ellen and Franny. Samuel lifted her down from the wagon, and she smoothed her skirts and smiled up at him.

Jessica wanted to throw something and scream at the look of devotion on her mother's face. How could she look like that at another man? Uncle Samuel might look a bit like Papa, but he was a stranger to both of them. Her mother had only seen him two or three times and Jessica only once. And that talk of wanting more children! Papa had always said Jessica was all the family they had ever wanted.

She followed them slowly and looked around. Fort Bridger had neat log cabins laid out around the usual parade ground, where the soldiers practiced their maneuvers and gathered for roll call. The stream gurgling through the center of this parade ground was a bit unusual. Across the way she could see the warren of tradesmen establishments. A couple of emigrants argued with a short, stocky blacksmith, and farther down, several horses milled in the stable. A wagon train sat curled in its circle of protection just beyond the fort proper. Perhaps there would be more than just soldiers here. Ellen had told her that Bridger was a favorite stopping-off place for emigrants on their way further west.

"Where are our quarters, Samuel?" Letty asked in a timid voice.

Samuel hesitated. "If you're agreeable, I thought we would be married this afternoon, and you and Jessica could move in right away."

Letty blushed and bobbed her head. "Is there a preacher on the grounds?"

"Supposed to be one come in with you," he said. "I'll go check and see if he came."

Jessica waited until his broad back disappeared around a wagon, then turned to her mother. "Mama, don't let him railroad you into a hasty marriage! You don't even know him all that well. He's not Papa! I want to spend a little time in our own place before we move in with him."

Letty shot a sidelong look at Caleb standing a few feet away, then whispered, "Don't make a scene, Dear. I've already agreed to marry him. What difference does it make if the wedding takes place today or next week? I'm not going back on my word."

Jessica sniffed and turned away. There was nothing more she could say. But the minute she could, she was getting out of this place. She would put up with her uncle and her cousins since she didn't have a choice at the moment, but surely it wouldn't be for long.

Samuel appeared a few minutes later. "The reverend is here. He'll come to our home in about an hour to perform the ceremony. Let's take your things to our quarters, and you can both freshen up."

They followed him across the parade ground. Jessica noticed this fort didn't seem to have the air of gloom that had hung over Fort Phil Kearny. She glanced back toward the wagons and waved at little Franny. The little girl started to run to her, but Ellen stopped her, then waved at Jessica too. Warmed by the exchange, Jessica squared her shoulders and prepared to meet Miriam and Bridie again.

The small home was surprisingly comfortable. The walls were lath and plaster, decorated with cheerful garden prints. A rug in soft greens and golds covered most of the floor. The fire blazed in the fireplace, and the aroma of some sort of stew greeted them as they stepped into the parlor.

Miriam sat on the sofa with her feet up. She looked up when they entered, then swung her feet to the floor. "So you're here," she said matter-of-factly. She turned and yelled down the hall, "Bridie! Aunt Letty and Jessica have arrived."

Miriam hadn't changed much. And when Jessica looked into her cousin's gray eyes, she knew the old animosity was still there. The girls were only a year apart in age, and Miriam had always been jealous of Jessica's beauty. Jessica gave a tiny sigh. She was too tired for her cousin's attitudes today, but she wasn't about to let her know. Never give an inch to the enemy was her motto. Put on a stiff upper lip, and don't let anyone see your weakness. But sometimes it got awfully lonely.

Bridie came in then, a pretty girl of thirteen with a wide smile and shiny brown hair. "Aunt Letty!" She kissed her aunt warmly and turned to kiss Jessica. Jessica offered her cheek and stepped back quickly. She didn't like being touched by someone she didn't know well. It was all right if *she* did the touching, but she didn't want someone else to touch her. Still, Bridie seemed nice enough. Better than Miriam, at any rate.

"You can freshen up in, uh, in our room," Samuel said hesitantly.

Letty blushed, and Jessica gritted her teeth. Couldn't the man give her mother even a night or two on her own to get to know him? She followed her mother into the small bedroom and closed the door behind them. She couldn't do anything about it; she was just too tired to make any more objections tonight.

The small bedroom was furnished with a beautiful sleigh bed covered with a burgundy comforter. A hip bath hung on the wall and several hooks for clothes were spaced around the room. Jessica gave a sniff, took off her bonnet, and shook her hair free. The curls were limp and dull from the dust of the trail. Thank goodness she wasn't seeing Clay again today. She ran a brush through her hair and pinned it up again.

"Aren't you going to change your dress?" Letty asked when she saw Jessica put on her bonnet.

"I just want to get this farce over with," Jessica said flatly. "I don't need to impress my dear *stepfather* or his horrid children. I'll wait until after the wedding for a good long soak." She wanted to cry.

"Whatever you say, Dear."

Jessica glanced at her mother sharply and noticed her pale cheeks. "Are you all right, Mama?"

"Of course, of course." She turned her back to Jessica and began to unpack. "You go on out and get to know your new family a bit. I'll be right out."

My new family. Jessica would never consider them her family; she would never feel close to any of them. Shutting the door behind her, she entered the parlor. Never before had she shared her parents with anyone, not even a sibling, and she didn't want to share her mother now. She would have to find a way to get them away from Fort Bridger.

Bridie smiled when she entered and scooted over to make room for her on the sofa. Miriam gave her a disdainful look from her almond-shaped gray eyes and looked pointedly in the other direction. Jessica sat down between her two cousins and smoothed her wrinkled skirt.

"Where am I sleeping?" she asked. "On the sofa?" She didn't see how there would be any room for her. Although comfortable, the quarters weren't large.

Samuel rubbed his hands together nervously. "Of course not, my dear. You'll share a room with Bridie and Miriam."

Jessica sucked in her breath and nearly groaned aloud. She hadn't considered that she might be in such close proximity to Miriam. How was she going to endure it until she could get out of this place? She had never shared a room in her life. She would have to endure Miriam's snipes after bedtime as well as before.

"The preacher should be here any minute. Is your mama about ready?" Samuel pulled out his pocket watch and peered at it. He raked a hand through his thick hair nervously.

Jessica nodded. "She said she'd be right out." His nervousness was obvious, but the fact didn't endear him to her. What did he have to be nervous about? She and her mother were the ones taking all the risk. Especially Mama.

Jessica jumped when the door knocker clattered. Samuel stopped his pacing and hurried to open the door. "Come in, Reverend," he said eagerly.

Jessica looked up, then gulped when Clay Cole came through the door, followed by Ellen and Franny.

"Jessie!" Franny ran to her and lifted up her arms to be picked up.

Jessica lifted her into her arms, but her eyes strayed to Clay's massive shoulders. Reverend? Clay was a *minister*? She couldn't believe it. She thought ministers were studious and soft-spoken. Clay was rugged and outspoken. He looked more like a lumberjack than a man of the cloth.

Her lips thinned, and she considered whether his profession changed her desire to humiliate him. She decided it didn't; in fact, it added an extra fillip to the chase. Did a preacher fall as hard as an ordinary mortal? She looked down at her dust-stained dress, and her smile faded. Why hadn't she changed her clothes? She must look a dreadful sight!

The bedroom door opened, and her mother appeared. She looked uncertainly around the parlor.

"The minister is here, my dear," Samuel said.

Letty looked at Clay, then back to Samuel. "Oh dear," she said faintly, biting her lip in distress. "Please forgive me, Reverend Clay—I mean, Reverend Cole. I had no idea you were a minister. I've not been addressing you properly the entire trip."

Clay smiled reassuringly. "I've always disliked being called Reverend," he said. "It makes me sound so pious and holy when I'm just a normal man like any other."

That was for sure, and Jessica intended to prove it. She squelched a smile.

"God has called me to preach His Word, but I fail Him just as much as anyone else. Just call me Clay or even Preacher like the men do." Clay turned to Samuel. "Are you both ready, Sir?"

Samuel nodded enthusiastically and reached out to draw Letty to his side. Letty swallowed hard, then took Samuel's hand. "I'm ready."

Jessica looked at her sharply and thought she saw tears in her mother's eyes. For the first time in her life, Jessica felt protective of someone else. She wanted to tear her mother's hand from her uncle's arm and drag her from the house. She wanted to cry for her father and beg him to stop this travesty. But in the end, she did neither. She took her place beside her mother and listened to Clay's deep voice read the marriage vows.

Funny how she'd never really listened to the vows before. *Love, honor, cherish, obey. In sickness and in health. 'Til death do us part.* The words seemed so sacred and final. There was no way she would ever repeat those words and mean them. No man could be trusted to honor them.

She buried her face in Franny's silky hair and hugged her tightly. Her life had changed so much in the past few months, and she had never liked change. She'd had enough change in her childhood, being dragged from one roach-infested hovel to the next. Predictability was her only security, but now as she looked toward the future, she had no idea what would happen next.

At the conclusion of the ceremony, Samuel bent his head and kissed his new wife. Jessica didn't like the gleam in his eye one bit. *What has Mama done?* Her uncle then turned to kiss her, and she offered up her cheek reluctantly.

"We're a family now," he said. "I want to take your father's place as much as I can."

Jessica managed a tight smile, but she couldn't speak past the lump in her throat. Take Papa's place? Impossible! How could he even suggest such a thing? She turned away before she could say anything hurtful. She couldn't stand the happy look on her mother's face, but she didn't want to spoil it either.

Clay was deep in conversation with Miriam, and Jessica felt a shaft of anger. He snubbed her, then hung on Miriam's every word! The simpering smile on Miriam's face turned her stomach. Could Clay really like that kind of woman? She *was* beautiful, if one liked the pale, fragile type. Jessica forced a smile to her face and sauntered over toward them.

"Miriam dear, your father wants you to get the refreshments ready," she said in a sweet voice.

Miriam flashed her a look of anger. "I'll talk to you later, Reverend Cole."

She gave him an adoring smile. "Jessica and I have duties to attend to."

"Your father said you and Bridie," Jessica said casually.

"You're part of the family now too, *Sister.*" Miriam took her arm and practically dragged her to the kitchen.

Rather than struggle in front of Clay, Jessica allowed herself to be pulled away, but she seethed with anger. She didn't like being touched.

"Don't you dare try to horn in now!" Miriam hissed once they were in the kitchen. "I saw him first."

"I don't think so, dear cousin." Jessica tossed her head. "Clay and I became very well acquainted on the trip here. Didn't you notice how Franny ran right to me?" For just a moment, she felt guilty about using the little girl, but this was war.

Miriam gave a tiny gasp of remembrance. "Well, it doesn't matter. You stay out of my way." She flounced over to the table and began to cut slices of bread with jerky, fierce movements.

Jessica watched her for a moment, then shrugged and went back to the parlor. She wasn't about to let her cousin tell her what to do. Clay was standing beside Ellen with Franny in his arms, and the little girl reached out for Jessica when she approached. A strange look crossed Clay's face, but he handed the little girl over to her.

"Why didn't you tell me you were a preacher?" Jessica went straight to the point.

"The subject never came up."

Jessica forced a smile to her face. "I do so admire men of the cloth," she cooed. "I knew you were brave, but I didn't realize how brave."

He looked at her with surprise in his eyes. "I would think you would have nothing but contempt for a minister. I don't even make enough money to keep you in hair ribbons."

Jessica pouted prettily. "That just shows you how little you know me. But I intend to change that in the next few weeks." She smiled up into his eyes. Out of the corner of her eye, she saw Miriam scowling in the doorway.

Jessica smiled to herself. His attention was important to her, more important than she could explain. But it was just a game, wasn't it?

Chapter 3

Clay saddled his mare and swung onto the horse. He'd been at Fort Bridger for a week and was getting itchy feet to move on to Colorado. He wanted to see how Private Lester Michaels was doing since he accepted the Lord two months ago. That was the bad thing about being an itinerant preacher—the constant worry about the spiritual condition of the men. They were sometimes like children, like the newborn babes the Bible called them, easily drawn back into their previous life of drinking and gambling. He knew how Paul had felt when he'd worried about the different churches. But it was all part of what God had called Clay to do.

He cantered out of the fort for a bit of exercise. Misty was feeling frisky this morning too, and she broke into a run when they cleared the gates. He sniffed the early April air and took a deep fragrant breath of sage and creosote. He loved this land with a fierceness that surprised him. It was so different from Ohio, and at first he had missed the green hills and budding trees. Soon, though, he had come to love the starkness and strange beauty of this Great American Desert, as the papers called it.

He stopped under a low-hanging tree by a rock formation. There was a cave in the rock, and this was a favorite spot of his to spend some time with the Lord. He took his worn leather Bible and hunkered down on the rock. His Bible fell open to Matthew 7.

Judge not, that ye be not judged. For with what judgment ye judge, ye shall be judged: and with what measure ye mete, it shall be measured to you again. And why beholdest thou the mote that is in thy brother's eye, but considerest not the beam that is in thine own eye?

Jessica's face came to mind, and he frowned. What was it about her, anyway? She seemed to dog his every step. He had no inclination to get tangled up with a woman like her. She was spoiled, willful, and vain. And yet there was something in her eyes that surprised him from time to time. Her little-girl-lost quality puzzled him. His eyes turned back to the Scripture. Okay, so maybe he shouldn't judge Jessica too harshly; maybe there was more to her background than he knew. But even as the thought crossed his mind, he dismissed it. She was just what she seemed: beautiful, spoiled, and willful. She had everything a woman could want, didn't she?

Except the Lord.

She wouldn't be interested, he argued with the inner conviction.

Have you tried? Have you really tried to show her real love, God's love? Or have you been too eager to demonstrate how immune you are to her charms?

"She's dangerous, Lord," he said aloud.

She's a lost child. She needs Me.

"All right, fine," Clay said. "I'll try, but don't expect too much."

I expect your all.

Clay bowed his head in resignation. The woman scared him for some reason, but it was his duty to do all he could to win her to Christ. It wouldn't be pleasant or easy, though.

After his prayer time, he rode back to the fort and headed toward Ellen's quarters, where she was to begin her duties as post laundress today. He stifled a laugh, wondering if Jessica had figured out what Ellen's new job was. Jessica was so concerned about her own self that she didn't seem to understand a lot of what was going on around her. She would probably drop her new friend and Franny the minute she realized Ellen's position. The officers' ladies didn't associate with laundresses.

His heart lightened, and he frowned. Was he glad about that? He was chagrined to discover he was jealous of Franny's attachment to Jessica. He shook his head and resolved to be glad for any pleasure his two precious cousins could find in Jessica's company. Some man of God he was. His attitude reminded him of Jonah's reluctance to go to the people of Ninevah. He didn't intend for the Lord to have to punish him for his lack of obedience.

Ellen came to the door when he knocked. She was dressed in an old cotton dress, and her hair was done up in a kerchief. She opened the door wide and gave him a welcoming smile. "Did you bring me some laundry?"

"I don't want to add to your work."

Ellen chuckled. "And here I thought you'd be my first customer."

"Where's Franny?"

"Jessica came and took her for a walk."

Clay raised an eyebrow. "Has she figured out what your duties are yet? I'm not so sure she'll associate with you when she knows you're a laundress."

"Clay, you do the poor girl an injustice," Ellen rebuked him gently. "She's not as bad as you think. She seems to genuinely care about Franny, and she's been a friend to me. In fact, I think I'm the first real friend she's had."

Clay fell silent. For all his high resolve earlier, he was certainly failing already. He decided to change the subject. "Can I help you with anything?"

She shook her head. "I have my fire blazing, and my pot of water set over it. It's about hot enough. Several men have already dropped off their laundry, and I'm about to get started. It helps having Franny out from underfoot. My biggest fear is that she will get burned by the boiling water."

"I've worried about that too. I'll try to take her with me some when I'm here." He turned back toward the door. "Guess I'll let you get to your work. I want to get a chance to talk to some of the men."

"When are you heading down to Colorado?"

"Not for a couple of weeks. I want to hold some services here first."

"Wonderful! I know Franny will be thrilled too." She waved and shut the door behind him.

The weak sunshine felt good on his arms as he strolled through the fort talking to the men. He held the reins for the blacksmith, Winston Claver, while he shod a skittish black stallion, and he helped some privates stack wood outside the sutler's store. The men were always surprised that a preacher would put his back into physical labor, but after he proved himself to them, they would usually at least listen when he talked about God.

He caught a glimpse of Jessica once or twice as she and Franny strolled about the fort under a pink lace parasol. He had to admit they made a pretty picture. Jessica had on a green dress and bonnet, and she had fixed Franny's hair just like hers. When he saw that, he felt a shaft of disquiet. Would she ignore Franny when she realized she wasn't a little doll to dress up?

Jessica held Franny's hand and swung it as they walked along the path. She felt happy and content for some reason. Franny was a darling, and she was glad to be able to help Ellen. She'd been appalled when she realized what Ellen's job was, but she was beginning to get used to the idea now. She looked at her own soft, white hands and couldn't imagine doing something like that herself. Ellen's skin would be chapped and red by the time the day was over.

At lunchtime, she and Franny walked back to the DuBois quarters. "Mama, we're home," she called. She shut the door behind them and found her mother in the kitchen preparing lunch.

Letty smiled. "I was just about to send Caleb out looking for you. Would you mind setting the table?"

Jessica looked at her sharply. Her mother had never before asked her to do any physical labor. Never. She thought about protesting; then she saw the weary strain on her mother's face. Reluctantly, Jessica went to the table, feeling strange as she laid out the plates and forks. The last time she'd done this she was eight years old, still living in the shanty by the river. She didn't like the feelings or the memories the small task aroused.

"Why doesn't Uncle Samuel employ a striker to help you?" Most officers employed enlisted men, called strikers, to help with the housework and cooking. Her mother had always had some kind of help. Resentment choked Jessica's throat when she realized how much work her mother had been doing the past few days without any servants. Did Uncle Samuel intend to turn her into a drudge?

"I want to earn our keep." Her mother pushed a stray strand of hair out of her eyes with the back of her hand. "Samuel already has a large household to support. I don't want to add to his burden. It was good of him to offer us a home. Besides, if Charlotte could do it, so can I."

Jessica compressed her lips. She was in too good a mood to fight with her mother, so she struggled to keep from blurting out what she thought about her new stepfather. If he was already making her mother compare herself with his first wife, it didn't bode well for the future of the marriage. Besides, how could one compare the love of a first marriage with a marriage of convenience? It seemed so unfair. She changed the subject. "Where are the cousins?"

"Miriam went to pick up some vegetables for me at the sutler's store, Bridie is in her room, and Caleb is at the stables. They should all be here for lunch any minute." Her mother gave her a tired smile. "Don't look so glum, Dear. I know it's an adjustment right now, but we'll soon feel a part of the family. Now, why don't you set this pretty little girl in a chair and give her some lunch?"

After the meal, Jessica walked back across the parade ground with Franny. The stink of lye stung her eyes as they neared Suds Row. She found Ellen bending over a steaming pot of clothing, her red face streaming with perspiration, while her hair fell onto her shoulders in damp strands. She plunged her hands, red and raw from the soap, into the steaming heap of laundry and began to rub a shirt against the washboard.

Jessica winced just watching her. How could Ellen do it? Jessica couldn't do such a menial task if her life depended on it. "Are you almost done?"

Ellen straightened up with a hand to her back and a tired smile on her face. "Almost. Maybe another hour's work before I can quit for the day." She held out a chapped, red hand to Franny. "How's my girl? Did you enjoy your day with Jessica?"

Franny nodded and ran to cling to her mother's leg. "Jessie bought me a licorice stick, and one of the soldiers whistled at us."

Jessica's face grew hot, and she dropped her eyes. She thought the child hadn't heard the whistle. She shuffled her feet, realizing she'd exposed little Franny to something like that. And she'd done it deliberately, now that she thought of it; she'd batted her lashes at the officers and smiled her best smile. Why did she feel such a need for approval from men? She bit her lip and forced the thoughts away.

The little girl preened. "Jessie fixed my hair just like hers."

"I see that. You look like twins." Her mother's lips twitched with suppressed amusement as she turned to Jessica. "Thanks so much for spending the day with Franny. She already loves you."

A lump came to Jessica's throat. "I'll pick her up in the morning again. I enjoy having her around." She stayed and chatted a few moments, but Ellen seemed distracted by the laundry still piled beside her tub. With a final promise to call for Franny tomorrow, she waved good-bye and set off for home.

Jessica felt like skipping as she walked away from the little cabin. She actually had a friend. It felt so strange. Why had she never had a friend before? Trust was hard for her, but for some reason, Ellen made it easy. Jessica had always thought if she had a friend it would be someone beautiful, but Ellen was plain and plump; her beauty was all on the inside.

Jessica rounded the corner of the sutler's store and was almost knocked over by Clay.

"Whoa!" He reached out a hand to steady her.

When his hand touched her, a peculiar tingle went up her arm. Her mouth went dry, and her heart skipped a beat. She'd never felt anything like it. Was she getting sick? She drew back from Clay a bit and looked up at him.

"Sorry," he said. "I didn't look where I was going." He settled his Stetson on his head a bit more securely and turned in the direction she was heading. "I'll walk you to your quarters."

Jessica looked at him surreptitiously from under her lashes. Was he beginning to be interested? Why else would he offer to walk her home? "I'd like that," she said with the smile that usually fetched men from miles away.

He showed no sign of being fetched. He casually took her hand and tucked it into the crook of his arm as he escorted her across the parade ground. Her hand felt warm, and she flushed. What on earth was wrong with her?

"Did Franny give you any trouble?"

"Hardly. She was a perfect little angel all day." She could feel the muscles in his arm move as they strolled toward Officers' Row. Why was her mouth so dry? Her heart pounded like a Sioux drum too. Was she flushed with a fever maybe?

"I really appreciate your taking time with her. It's been so hard for her to lose her daddy. They were very close."

"She doesn't talk about him very much. What was he like?" She didn't really want to know; she just wanted to keep him with her a bit longer. They were almost to the porch of the DuBois quarters.

"Martin was a great guy. He would give his last dime to you if you needed it. He and I were more like brothers than cousins. When we were kids, I was always the daredevil, and he was the levelheaded one. He kept me out of more trouble. When we came west, he told my mama that he'd take care of me. I never expected that he would be called home before me."

Jessica felt uncomfortable at the vague mention of religion. She could hardly believe that the strong, virile man beside her was a preacher. Personally, she avoided the thought of God as much as she could. In her mind, God was just a vague Being out there in the heavens somewhere, waiting to smash people like bugs if they got out of line. And she'd never been one for being told what to do. Orders just made her defiant.

They reached the steps to the porch, and Clay paused. Jessica slipped her hand from his elbow and started up the steps. She turned back a moment and gave him her best smile. "Thank you for escorting me. I'm taking Franny on a picnic tomorrow. Would you like to come?"

Clay hesitated a moment, then nodded. "I haven't seen Franny much in the last few days. What time?"

"About eleven."

"Why don't you invite your cousins? I haven't gotten a chance to get to know them very well yet."

Jessica's complacent smile faltered, and she could feel the mortified heat rise in her cheeks. "Are you interested in Miriam?" She might as well learn what her obstacles were right now.

Clay chuckled. "I don't even know her. I just thought it would be a good time to get acquainted with all of them. Your mama too."

"That's not an answer." Jessica could hear the outrage in her voice, and she softened her tone. She didn't want him to think his answer was actually important to her. "You won't think much of Miriam when you get to know her. She's a spoiled child."

"Kind of like her cousin?" Clay's voice was amused.

Jessica gave him a slow smile. "A little judgmental for a preacher, aren't we? Maybe I'll change your opinion of me." She smiled again, showing her dimple deliberately, then opened the door.

"You can begin by making an effort to be part of your new family," he called after her. "They'd probably love a picnic."

She didn't answer but shrugged and shut the door behind her. She didn't want him to see how his words had wounded her. How dare he sit in judgment on her? He didn't know what it was like to be thrust into a family with no warning, to be made to feel like an unwelcome guest. She sniffed back tears of outrage and stalked down the hall to her bedroom.

Thankfully, her cousins weren't in the room. She flung herself across her bed and buried her hot face in her down pillow. Clay deserved every bit of the humiliation coming his way. She'd show him he wasn't immune to her beauty.

After supper, her cousins began to clear the table while she enjoyed a final cup of coffee. Uncle Samuel frowned when he saw her still seated at the table. She ignored his scowl and took another sip of coffee. She didn't know what was bothering him now, but she didn't care.

He cleared his throat. "I've tried to give you some space, Jessica, but I think it's time we laid down some rules around here."

"Rules?" Jessica didn't like the sound of that. She'd never had any rules, and she wasn't about to let this red-faced man in front of her give her any now.

"It has been pointed out to me that you never help with the dishes or the housework around here. You need to carry your share of the load and not leave it all for your mother and sisters. From now on, you three girls will take turns clearing and washing the supper dishes while your mother rests."

Jessica clenched her hands in her lap. "I think not, dear *uncle!* If you want to spare my mother some work, you can hire a striker like most caring husbands. You may have managed to get my mother as a drudge, but I will not be one for you or any man!" She stood regally to her feet. "You are not my father; your daughters are not my sisters, and I will not be told what to do." She gathered her skirts in one hand and started from the room.

"Stop!" he thundered. "I will not be spoken to this way in my own house! You will do as you are told, or you will leave my home and protection."

Beyond his angry glare, Jessica could see the pale oval of her mother's distressed face, but nothing could stop her white-hot rage now. "Nothing would please me more!" she spat. "I didn't want to come here in the first place. Feel free to send me back to Boston." She gave him a final contemptuous look, then went to her room.

Even with the door shut, she could hear his raised voice in the kitchen and her mother's soft pleading tones. The nerve of the man! Did he think he could order her around when her own father had never so much as raised his voice to her? She paced the room and thought about all the other things she should have said.

After a few minutes, she sighed and sat down on the faded quilt that covered the bed. Truth be told, she really wasn't all that eager to go back to Boston just yet. She was enjoying her friendship with Ellen and her pursuit of Clay. Not that she was making much headway with Clay, but the chase was enjoyable. She couldn't let her uncle tell her what to do, though. The angry voices had stilled in the kitchen, but she could still hear soft murmurs.

She picked up a book of Miriam's and leafed through it carelessly. It was a wild tale about Indians—did her father know she read trashy dime novels?—but at least if someone came in the room, they would see she was so unconcerned about the confrontation in the kitchen that she was reading instead of worrying. She didn't want to appear to care what her uncle had to say.

After a few moments, she heard a soft knock at the door.

"Jessica, may I come in?" Her mother's voice was fraught with tension.

"Of course, Mama." Jessica put the book down beside her and folded her hands in her lap.

Her mother stepped into the room and closed the door behind her. She stood looking at Jessica, then cleared her throat. "Darling, surely you must see that everyone must help out just a bit. Couldn't you agree to at least help clear away the supper dishes twice a week? It would only take you a few minutes. I told Samuel that I really couldn't condone forcing you to do dishes, but he insists you must do something."

"And what will he do if I don't?"

Her mother fluttered her hands helplessly. "He will turn you out."

"Oh, really?" Jessica gave a short, mirthless laugh. "Just turn me out into the street? I think the commanding officer would have something to say about that." She knew that would terrify her uncle. He knew the colonel was enamored with her.

Her mother's white face paled even more. "You wouldn't speak to Colonel Edwards? Samuel wouldn't like that at all."

"Well, then you tell dear Uncle Samuel that I will do no more than help you set the table for supper. Otherwise, I will have to speak to Colonel Edwards about this situation." She felt sorry for her mother when she saw the way she gulped and swallowed, but she would hold to her guns now. Maybe, though, she could help her mother in small ways without Uncle Samuel finding out.

"Of course, Dear. You've been doing that anyway. I'll tell your uncle." She fluttered her hands again and hurried from the room.

Jessica let out a sigh of relief. She'd won that skirmish. For now. But if she knew her uncle, and she felt she was beginning to, it wasn't the end of the war. With Miriam keeping him stirred up, the next battle wouldn't be far away.

She thought again about Clay's request for her to invite her cousins on their picnic tomorrow. Maybe she could work out some kind of truce with Miriam if she made the effort. The very thought made her grit her teeth, but she had to do something. She sighed and went to find her cousins.

At least she wasn't going back to Boston just yet. She pushed away the image of Clay's face. Her desire to stay at Fort Bridger had nothing to do with him, not really.

Chapter 4

B y the time morning boots and saddles, the bugle call for the cavalry
to mount their horses, rang out, Clay was already dressed and striding toward the mess hall. He wanted to stop in and see how Ellen's
first day had gone. The lantern glowed softly from her quarters, and he
bounded up the steps to the door.

She opened the door and smiled when she saw his anxious face. "I'm fine.
You worry too much."

"Someone has to worry about you. You don't worry about yourself." Clay
shut the door behind him and followed her to the kitchen table. The laundress quarters were modest by any standards: a tiny, one-room cabin furnished with a crude wooden table, a small bed she shared with Franny, and a
battered bench. A small fire burned in the fireplace, scenting the air with
pine. He noticed a tuft of Franny's blond hair peeking out of the bedcovers,
and he felt a pang of remorse that he hadn't been able to do better for them.
The position of post laundress wasn't held in much esteem by most people,
and these quarters were much more sparse than those they had been used to
as the dependents of an army officer. When he'd asked the post commander
for the job for Ellen, the senior officer had been astonished that anyone
would request such a menial job for a relative.

"Coffee?" she asked him.

"Sure." He watched her pour the coffee into a cracked cup.

"You had breakfast?"

"Probably before you were out of bed." He took a gulp of hot coffee. "You
ready to quit yet? There'll be a stage through here tomorrow heading east."

Ellen smiled gently. "You know better than that. It's hard work, but I'll get
used to it. And once I get enough money put by for a small ranch somewhere,
we'll move on."

"I hear Jessica is taking Franny on a picnic today."

She nodded. "I don't know how I'd ever do this job without Jessica. It is such
a blessing to not have to look after Franny or worry about her being scorched by
the water. I think you've misjudged our friend. She really is a sweetheart."

Clay snorted. "Sweet is not how I would describe her. I would choose
words more like hard and calculating."

Ellen lifted her eyebrows at his tone. "I've never known you to take such a dislike to someone before. Her uncaring attitude is just a wall of protection. You should get to know her better."

Clay flushed at the gentle reprimand. What was it about Jessica? Ellen was right; it was odd for him to be so antagonistic to someone. Where were all of his lofty intentions from yesterday? How could he show her God's love when he couldn't even bring himself to say a nice word about the woman? "I'm going on the picnic with them today."

Ellen brightened. "Wonderful! Franny will have her two favorite people in the world dancing attendance on her."

He laughed. "When do you suppose her highness will wake up?"

"Anytime now. I'm surprised she's still sleeping. Probably all the excitement from yesterday. And she hasn't been sleeping well since Martin died. She still cries out for him in the night."

Clay winced at the words. He had wanted to make up for the loss of her father, but he'd been foolish to think his presence could remove that pain.

Ellen touched his hand. "Don't worry, Clay. We'll be fine eventually. We just have to get through one day at a time. God's provision has been wonderful." She dropped her hand and turned away. "Now why don't you wake her up? I need to get her dressed anyway. I'll have to get started on my work pretty soon."

Clay walked to the bed and gently peeled the covers off his young cousin. With her pink cheeks and tousled blond hair, she was a beautiful sight. He swallowed past the lump in his throat, remembering the day she was born. Martin had been so proud and happy, but now he would never watch his darling little girl grow to womanhood. Clay vowed in his heart to do all he could to help and protect her. After all, he doubted he would ever have any children of his own. What woman would ever want to take second place to his calling?

By the time Ellen had dressed Franny, they heard Jessica calling from the front porch. When Ellen opened the front door, Clay caught his breath at Jessica's beauty. Her blue gown emphasized her eyes, and the way she'd caught her curls back in a bow revealed the perfection of her face. Clay reminded himself he didn't have any use for beautiful women. They never had any thoughts beyond their looks and what they wanted. This woman was certainly no exception.

Jessica smiled. "Is Franny ready?"

"I'll get her," Ellen said. "You'll never know how much it means to me for you to take time with her."

Jessica smiled up at Clay while Ellen left to get Franny. "I've decided to take on Franny's education," she said.

"Oh?" he said. "Bored?"

She flushed. "Don't you think Franny needs an education? When would Ellen have time with all the work she does?"

"Sure, Franny needs an education, but so do the other children in camp. You could start a school for all of them."

Her color deepened. "Why do you persist in baiting me? I thought we were going to have a nice picnic and enjoy the day."

Clay shuffled uncomfortably. He had to watch his tongue if he had any chance of winning her to the Lord. "You're right. I'm sorry."

She lifted her eyebrows in surprise at his apology, then smiled sweetly. "You're forgiven. Where would be a good place to go for lunch? I'm going to start lessons with Franny until eleven or so, then we can meet for our picnic."

"There's a grassy knoll overlooking the river just a half mile from the fort. I'll pick you up at eleven. Will you be at your house?"

Jessica nodded, then tilted her head to look up at him. "I did what you asked."

Clay frowned. What had he asked her?

She smiled at his puzzlement. "I invited my cousins on the picnic."

Clay was surprised but managed to hide it. "Now that wasn't too painful, was it?"

She tossed her red curls. "Of course not," she said airily. "They were delighted to accept. But don't say I didn't warn you. Miriam will probably spend the afternoon flirting outrageously with you; Bridie will have her nose stuck in a book, and Caleb will pester you with questions about Indians."

Clay grinned. "I think I can handle it." He gave her a wave and went to make his visits with a couple of ill soldiers. He had to admit he was surprised she'd actually followed his suggestion. It must suit her schemes somehow. He judged her to be a woman who always knew exactly what she wanted and how to get it.

By the time Jessica got back to her home, she had managed to stop seething. He really was a most infuriating man! Not even a word of appreciation that she'd done as he asked. But she was determined to get through that indifferent shell of his somehow.

She took Franny to the bedroom and sat her down at a small table with a beginning primer she'd found in her mother's trunk. The morning passed quickly, and Franny had begun to recognize some of her letters by eleven.

Jessica closed the book and went to change her clothes. She dressed carefully in a sky-blue dress lavished with cream lace and tied her hair back with cream lace that matched the dress. She pinched her cheeks to redden them and wet her lips. Turning this way and that in the mirror, she didn't see how Clay would be able to resist her. She turned at a knock on the door.

"Jessica, Dear, that lovely Reverend Cole is here for your picnic. The rest of the children are in the kitchen waiting."

"We're coming." She took Franny's hand and followed her mother to the kitchen, where Miriam stood laughing up into Clay's face. Jessica struggled against her jealousy. She didn't care what he did or who he flirted with!

Franny flung herself against Clay's legs.

"Hey, Muffin." He scooped her into his arms and hugged her. "Are you ready for a picnic?"

She nodded vigorously. "Jessie taught me my letters," she said importantly. "I'm gonna learn to write my name and read."

Clay looked suitably impressed. "I didn't learn to read until I was five, and you won't even be four until next month."

She preened, then slid down to the floor and ran to Jessica and hugged her skirts. "Jessie is my friend."

Jessica felt a warm glow. "Are we ready to go?" She stroked Franny's silken hair.

"I brought the fishing poles," Clay said.

Fishing poles? Jessica frowned. She'd never been fishing in her life, and the thought didn't appeal to her now.

Miriam clapped her hands. "I love fishing!"

Jessica swallowed her dismay; she couldn't let her cousin best her. "Then fishing it is," she said with a shrug. She wanted to groan in dismay and think of a reason to stay home. This was not the day she'd planned.

"I packed you some boiled eggs and potato salad," her mother said. "I'll put in a skillet and lard to fry up the fish you catch."

Jessica suppressed a grimace; the thought of frying fish herself was not appealing, though she supposed she could do it if she had to. She'd watched her mother often enough, but she hated the way frying fish made her hair smell. Would she be expected to clean the fish too?

Her mother handed Caleb the lunch basket, and they all filed out the door to the waiting two-seat wagon. Clay tossed the gear in the back, then helped Miriam onto the front seat. He lifted Jessica, Franny, and Bridie into the back before he swung up beside Miriam and Caleb.

Jessica ground her teeth as she watched her cousin flirt with Clay all the way to the river. Meanwhile, Bridie kept up a steady stream of questions, and Jessica found it hard to keep from snapping at her. Why had she ever let herself be talked into inviting her cousins? They were just in the way. They were never going to be a family.

When Clay stopped the wagon, the fort was only a blur in the distance. Blackbirds circled overhead, and the air smelled fresh and moist from the

Black River gurgling its way down the mountain. Small, puffy clouds drifted lazily across the blue sky.

In the shade of a large tree along the riverbank, Clay tethered the horses and lifted the ladies down from the wagon. "Find us a likely fishing hole, Caleb," he said. "I'm starved."

While Caleb scrambled to do as he was asked, Clay spread the blankets under the protective canopy of the trees, then handed the fishing poles to Jessica. "Why don't you get these baited?"

Baited? Trying to hide her dismay, Jessica took the poles and the can of bait from him. She thought about refusing, but the look of challenge in his eyes stopped her. She eyed the sharp and dangerous-looking fishhooks, then handed the bait can to Franny, and they carried them over to the riverbank. Miriam stayed with Clay, but Bridie followed Jessica.

"Over here!" Caleb waved to her from farther down the river.

Reluctantly, she led the way to where Caleb stood peering into the clear water. She laid the fishing poles on a rock and took the can of bait from Franny. "Um, Caleb, would you like to bait the poles?"

"Naw; Pa says everyone should bait his own hook. Here, I'll show you." He grabbed the can of bait and opened it. He poked around in it for a moment, then extracted a large squirming worm. A night crawler, she remembered her brother Jasper calling them. Taking the sharp hook, Caleb poked it into the worm's body in several places and tossed the hook and worm into the river. "Nothing to it."

Jessica felt nauseated. How disgusting! She glanced at Bridie and saw her take a worm and thread it on the hook the same way Caleb had done. She bit her lip; she was not going to pick up a worm.

"I can do it," Franny said importantly. "My daddy showed me how." She poked her small fingers into the can and drew out a worm.

"Be careful with the hook," Jessica warned.

Franny nodded. "Daddy told me." She took a few moments longer than the other two, but she managed to get the worm on the hook. She looked at Jessica expectantly.

Jessica fought the panic rising in her throat. She just couldn't touch a worm! She swallowed hard. Maybe she could get Franny to do it for her when no one was looking. . . . She jumped when she heard Clay's deep voice behind her.

"Ready?" He stepped up behind her, and she shivered at his warm breath on her neck. She didn't understand these strange sensations she felt whenever she was close to him, but she didn't like them. She pushed away the shivery feeling and turned to face him. She would just tell him she couldn't touch a worm. But when she saw the amused look on his face, the words died in her throat.

Miriam was only steps behind him. Jessica's cousin took a fishing pole and a worm and went to sit on a warm rock. Her hook and worm went into the river with a gentle splash, and she rinsed her fingers off in the water.

Jessica looked at Clay, then down at the pole and bait can. She had to do it. Somehow she just had to do it. She swallowed the bile in her throat. "Take yours, then I'll go on downriver."

With a knowing look, Clay took a pole, pulled a worm from the can, and walked over to a nearby rock. Jessica looked at his broad back as she picked up the last pole. She took the bait can and walked a bit downstream from the others. Glancing behind her to make sure no one was watching, she shook the worm out of the can and onto the warm rock. She nearly screamed when she saw the fat, wriggling body. She bit her lip until she tasted blood, then took her hook with determination. Holding the hook firmly between her thumb and index finger, she stabbed the barbed end into the middle of the worm's body. As the hook sank into the soft body, the cold flesh of the worm touched her finger, and she dropped the hook with a soft moan.

"Need some help?"

She stood up quickly at Clay's deep voice. "Not at all." She was surprised by the steadiness of her voice. "I'm ready to start fishing." She hurriedly tossed the hook and worm into the water before Clay could see how poorly the worm was attached to the hook. She knew she should poke the hook through in another spot, but she could not let that cold body touch her fingers again.

"I'll fish here beside you for awhile," he said. "Franny is with Bridie."

Jessica nearly groaned aloud. His presence was the last thing she needed. She didn't want him to realize she'd never been fishing in her life. She glanced upriver to make sure Franny was doing all right, then sat gingerly on the rock and stared at the bobber floating in the water. How was she supposed to know when she got a stupid fish, anyway? She felt Clay sit beside her, but she didn't look at him. If she did, he would surely be able to read her expression. She kept her eyes fixed on the bobber and gripped the pole tightly.

After about five minutes, she felt a tug on the pole, and the bobber ducked under the surface of the water. She looked again at the bobber. Was the worm trying to get away? What would she do if it did? She just couldn't put another worm on that hook. The bobber jerked again and stayed under the surface of the water.

Clay jumped to his feet. "Hey, are you sleeping? You've got a bite!"

A bite? Did that mean the fish had teeth? She shuddered at the thought just as the pole jerked again and almost went flying out of her hands. She stood and gingerly pulled on the fishing pole. The fish pulled back. She scowled and jerked up on the pole. A large trout, dripping and wriggling, came straight for her head. She shrieked and swung the pole to the left. Before Clay could react, the wet fish slapped him in the face. He shoved it away, and Jessica swung the pole again.

"Watch out!" he shouted.

Jessica swung the pole again, and this time it landed in his armpit. He jumped away, but she threw the pole and fish into the sand at his feet. "Why didn't you stay out of my way?" She dared a glance at him. A single fish scale clung to the tip of his nose and shimmered in the sunlight.

Slowly, Clay brushed at the sand and water on his face. "I didn't know fishing with you would be dangerous. What were you trying to do—behead me?"

Jessica drew herself up to her full five feet four inches. "I was doing just fine until you came over here breathing down my neck. Why don't you go stare at Miriam? She would welcome your attentions, but I do not."

Clay's lips twitched, and he made a strange sound. Was he laughing at her? Suspiciously, she glared at him.

He choked again, then roared with laughter. "Red, you should see your face! You've never had a fishing pole in your hand before, have you?"

"Don't call me Red. I hate that name!" She chose to ignore his question about her fishing experience.

"What's wrong with Red? It suits you. In fact, I think I'll call you that from now on." Clay grinned again at the scowl on her face.

She stamped her foot and turned to storm away.

"Hey, Red."

She whirled, but Clay interrupted before she could say anything.

"You forgot your fish. You'll want to clean it and get it ready to cook."

Jessica gulped. Clean it? She didn't have any idea how to do that. She slowly walked back to the fish and looked down at it. She looked back up into Clay's expectant face. "I'm not in the mood for fish," she said lamely.

"Well, I am. That's a nice trout you caught. We can't waste it. Besides, I should have something for my trials. I've never had a cold, wet fish in my armpit before, and I can't say as I recommend the experience." He knelt and removed the fish from the hook with a practiced jerk, then stood and held it out to her. "Here you go. But pardon me if I don't stand too close while you have the knife in your hand."

She managed a feeble smile and swallowed hard as she reached out an unsteady hand to gingerly take the fish by the tail. The cold, slimy feel of it raised a bubble of nausea in her throat, and she couldn't look in its staring eye. With it held out in front of her, she walked over to the rock where Clay had laid out his fillet knife and some newspaper. She put the fish on the paper and picked up the knife. What did she do next?

"Hey, you need some help?" Caleb's hair stood up in spikes where he'd swiped a wet hand through it, and he carried a string of four fish.

Jessica thought she'd never seen a more welcome sight than his eager smile. He wasn't making fun of her; he seemed to really want to help. Her smile was tinged with relief. "Don't tell anyone, but I've never cleaned fish before."

His grin widened. "You think we don't know that? It's nothing to be chicken about. I'll show you." He took the knife from her unresisting fingers and proceeded to scrape the scales off all five fish, then showed her how to gut and fillet them.

Jessica didn't really want to watch, but she felt it was the least she could do. In spite of the mess, she found herself actually interested in the deft way he handled the knife and how quickly he dispatched the process of preparing the fish for cooking.

When he was done, he handed the fillets to her with a big grin. "I get the biggest piece."

"You can have two. Why did you help me?" she asked with narrowed eyes. "I haven't been exactly warm to you."

Caleb hesitated and gave her a shy grin. "Last Sunday at church, Clay told us to do something nice for someone you don't much cotton to, so I picked you. But you know what? You ain't so bad. When you first came here, you were like a bear with a sore head, always snarlin' and uppity. But once I seen you don't know everything, you were okay. I guess I could stand having another sister." He blushed bright red and ducked his head.

He left Jessica with her mouth open. The heat rose in her face, but whether it was from pleasure because he had decided he liked her or because of how he had seen her before today, she wasn't really sure. She looked down at the fish fillets in her hand and smiled. At least she knew how to cook them, even if she hated doing it.

Clay had made a fire beside the water and stacked some rocks as a ledge for the skillet to rest on. As she cooked the fish, she thought about what Caleb had said. Was that really how people saw her? Cross and uppity? She wanted to be thought of as a force to be reckoned with but not as someone who snarled at people and was totally unapproachable. She'd always wanted people to see her as beautiful and cultured but likable.

Clay thought she was frivolous, without any real purpose in life. What *was* her purpose in life? Did she even know herself? What could fill this void, this insatiable hunger inside her? Her eyes smarted, and she tried to tell herself it was from the smoke of the fire, but deep inside, she knew better. She wasn't happy, and she had never really been settled and content with herself or her life. She was good at putting on a facade, a beautiful and smiling face to fool everyone. But now it seemed no one had been fooled after all. No one at all.

Chapter 5

For several days after the picnic, Jessica kept pretty much to herself. She began to notice how the others tiptoed around her as if afraid of incurring her wrath. Was that what she wanted? To be feared? As she watched her cousins interact with their father and her mother, she often felt like an outsider. She realized she had never had that kind of loving relationship with anyone, not even her own parents or her biological mother. She'd never felt she was a real, necessary part of a whole. Even her doting parents had seemed to stand together as a unit, loving her as a separate entity. She didn't know how to even go about becoming part of a family.

Morose, she decided to wander over and talk to Ellen about her feelings. She'd never really bared her soul to anyone before, but maybe it was time.

Ellen had just put Franny to bed. The little girl sat up with a delighted smile when Jessica came into the cabin. "Jessie!" She reached out her arms. "Will you tell me a story?"

Jessica gulped. She didn't know any stories, but she walked slowly to the side of the bed and sat down. "What kind of story?"

Franny looked up at her and thought for a moment. "How about one with a little girl with red hair like yours?" She reached up and touched one of Jessica's curls.

"Well," Jessica said slowly, "once upon a time there was a little girl named Ruth. She had red hair, but she hated it."

"Oh, no, Jessie, she couldn't hate it," Franny interrupted.

Jessica tickled her. "Am I telling the story or are you?"

Franny squealed and giggled. "You are, you are. But any little girl would want hair like yours."

Jessica smiled. "This little girl didn't. She hated her hair. She wanted beautiful blond hair like her friend Alice. Anyway, Ruth lived in a tiny house with her younger brother Jasper and her mother Mary. It was dirty and there were bugs, but they had each other."

"What about her daddy?" Franny wanted to know.

"Her daddy, uh, he ran—I mean, he didn't live there anymore. He went out west to find some land for his family and was gone a long time. Anyway, Jasper had a tadpole he'd caught in the creek behind the house, and, my, how he loved that tadpole. Ruth did too. One day she decided to surprise Jasper and find him another tadpole to keep the first one company. She took off her shoes and socks and waded in the creek with an old tin cup, trying to find a tadpole. She stepped into a hole in the creek and got all muddy. But she found that tadpole. She was so happy when she walked home because she just knew Jasper was going to be happy to have another tadpole. When she got home and her mother saw how muddy she was, she was sent to bed without supper."

"How mean," Franny said with a pout. "You would never do that to me, would you, Mommy?"

Ellen shook her head. She looked as engrossed in the story as her daughter.

Jessica glanced at Ellen and smiled. "Well, your mommy is a special kind of mommy. But back to the story. Ruth went along to the little room she shared with Jasper. She didn't care about supper, since she got the tadpole. She hurried to the jar where Jasper's tadpole was, and guess what she found?"

"What?" Franny asked breathlessly.

"There was a *frog* in the jar. It was trying to keep its head above water and looking kind of sickly. Ruth was shocked. Where had the frog come from? She got it out of the jar before it could drown, then looked all over for the tadpole. She couldn't find it anywhere, so she figured the frog somehow got in the jar and ate the tadpole. She put her new tadpole in the jar and screwed the lid on tight so the frog couldn't get back in and eat it. Just then Jasper came home. When she told him what had happened, he laughed at her and told her that the frog used to be the tadpole but had grown up and changed."

"Really? It really changed?"

"It sure did. Ruth was surprised too. But the more she thought about it, the more excited she got. Because that meant that maybe she could change too. Maybe she was just a tadpole now, but someday she could be somebody special. And she decided she *would* be someone special."

Franny frowned when Jessica fell silent. "That's not the end of the story, is it?"

Jessica laughed. "It is for tonight. I'll finish it some other time." She tucked the covers around Franny and kissed her on the nose. "Now you go to sleep, little tadpole, and dream about what kind of frog you want to be when you grow up."

"I want to be just like you," Franny murmured sleepily. She snuggled down into the covers and closed her eyes.

Just like you. The words rang in her ears. Was she any kind of person a little girl should emulate? She was afraid she wouldn't like the honest answer to that question.

"Would you like some tea?" Ellen asked.

"That sounds wonderful." She was glad for the interruption of her thoughts. She followed Ellen to the kitchen table and sat down while her friend put the kettle on to boil. She leaned her chin into her hand and watched Ellen's quick movements. Where did she get all her energy? Surely she must be exhausted from doing laundry all day.

Ellen sat in a chair and gave her a penetrating look. "That story sounded true. Was it?"

Jessica smiled slightly. "Yes. That really happened."

"Who was Ruth? A friend?"

Jessica felt sudden tears well up in her eyes. What was wrong with her lately? She *never* cried. "No, it was me," she admitted.

Ellen looked at her sharply. "You had a brother? Your mother never mentioned it."

Jessica felt tongue-tied for a moment. "I was adopted," she said finally. She had never told anyone outside the family the story. "My father went off out west and never came back. My mother took up with different men until she was killed when I was eight. The police came and took me and Jasper. Several weeks later, I was adopted by Mama and Papa DuBois."

Ellen was silent for a moment, but her eyes were wet. "What happened to Jasper?"

Tears spilled down Jessica's cheeks, and she scrubbed at them furiously. "I don't know. I never saw him again." The constant pain had been with her all these years. She just wished she knew Jasper was okay.

"Oh, my dear Jessica, I'm so sorry you had to go through such pain, especially at such a young age. Life can be hard. But you can thank God that He put you into such a warm and loving family."

"But I'm not happy," Jessica admitted. "I know I should be. I have everything a woman could want. What's wrong with me?" The cry came from her heart. Was this all there was to life? Her lips trembled, and she swallowed hard.

Ellen took her hand. "Happiness is something different from real joy and peace, Jess. God gives us joy and peace through good times and bad. He's what keeps us stable through whatever life throws our way."

Jessica shook her head. "Where was God when my family was ripped apart? Where was God when Papa died? God doesn't care about me now. He never has."

"Oh, you're so wrong, Jessie. God has always loved you. He's there for you if you will just turn to Him and ask for His help."

"What do you mean? If He's there, why should I have to ask?" Jessica drew her hand out of Ellen's grasp. She had never begged in her life, and she wasn't about to start now.

"God never forces His presence on His children. How would you like it if your mother was always butting in and telling you how to do things and never letting you learn anything on your own? God wants to be your comfort and your strength. But you have to come to the end of yourself, where you realize you are helpless and that the only way to heaven and God's peace is by what Jesus did on the cross for you. He took your punishment for everything you've done wrong in your life. He reconciled you to God—but you have to receive His free gift of grace."

Jessica shook her head. It made no sense to her. But she did envy Ellen's peace and contentment. Even through her bereavement, she had been strong and somehow secure.

"I can see you don't understand. Why don't you come to church with me and Franny on Sunday? Clay explains it so well."

Clay. Just the mention of his name set her heart to pounding. "What do you think Clay really thinks of me?" she asked slowly.

Ellen was silent for a moment, and Jessica could read the answer on her face. "He thinks I'm a frivolous, spoiled brat, doesn't he?"

"He doesn't know you as well as I do," Ellen said. "You have to understand something about Clay. He grew up with sisters who never had a thought in their heads about anything but their looks. And because of them, he doesn't think any woman with beauty could have any real depth of character." She touched Jessica's hand again. "But he'll see who you really are someday."

Jessica's mouth twisted into a wry smile. "Maybe a vain, selfish woman is all I am, Ellen. Maybe you're the one who will see the real me someday." She stood and stretched. "I'd better get home and let you get to bed. Thanks for listening. I've never had a friend before. It's nice." She bent and kissed Ellen's cheek. "You're a peach."

The next morning when she went to pick up Franny, the day was warm and lovely. Spring was here in full bloom. When she saw wisps of thistledown floating in the wind, she realized that's all her life was: a bit of will-o'-the-wisp pulled in any direction the wind blew. But she didn't want to be like that. She wanted to have real purpose in life.

When she knocked on the door, she could hear Franny's piping voice reciting her ABCs. Jessica swallowed the lump in her throat. Franny had remembered what she'd been taught so far; that was at least one good thing she had done in her life, if God was keeping score.

Ellen opened the door, and her face crinkled into a smile. "It's about time you got here. Franny has been driving me crazy wondering where you were."

The room was pleasantly perfumed with smoke from the woodstove and toasting bread. Jessica felt a pang of wistfulness for the simple pleasures Ellen enjoyed with Franny. She herself had never felt the contentment that glowed on Ellen's face. That happiness seemed so elusive. Would she ever feel it herself? How did one go about finding it?

Franny looked up from her perch on Clay's lap. "Jessie!" she cried. Dimples flashing, she slid to the floor and hurtled toward Jessica.

Jessica knelt and held out her arms. "You're doing very well with your ABCs," she said, sweeping her up. The feel of that small, warm body brought a lump to her throat. It was a strange feeling, one she wasn't sure she liked. It was safer not to get involved with other people, safer not to open herself up to pain and disappointment. But she'd already done it now.

Clay stood and thrust his hands in his pockets. "Run out of things to do?"

Jessica thrust her chin in the air. "Did you?"

He laughed. "Touché. Truce?" He held out his hand.

"Truce." She shook his hand and quickly let go when her heart for some strange reason began to race. She just didn't understand these reactions she had to him. The wisest thing would be to avoid him altogether, but she was determined not to let him get the upper hand in their relationship.

"Have you had breakfast?" Ellen cut fresh slices of bread and reached for the jam.

Jessica's stomach rumbled before she could answer.

"I guess that's a no." Ellen laughed. "That was a hungry stomach if I ever heard one."

"It does smell good," Jessica admitted. "But are you sure you have enough?"

"She means are you sure you have enough to feed a hungry man as well as the rest of you," Clay put in. "Just to set your minds at ease, I had breakfast—but I wouldn't turn down a bit of toast."

Jessica carried Franny over to the table and sat down in the chair beside Clay. She thought about asking if she could help Ellen, but Ellen might ask her to do something she didn't know how to do, and Jessica didn't want to betray any more ignorance to Clay. Besides, since when was what a woman could *do* important? All that mattered was that she was beautiful and cultured—and on that basis, she was a success. She tilted her chin and straightened her shoulders, proud of her beauty and culture; no one had the right to mold her into something she wasn't. Just because Clay's sisters had prejudiced him against beautiful women didn't mean she had to be ashamed of being beautiful.

They spent a pleasant breakfast laughing and talking about nothing and everything. She flirted with Clay, and although he showed no sign of responding, she enjoyed the challenge in his hazel eyes. She was careful to keep her complacency from her expression, though. There was something about Clay.

Something that made her want him to see beyond her outer beauty. She wanted him to see what she saw in Ellen, that inner loveliness that seemed to emanate from within.

❧

Clay was thoughtful as he walked away from the tiny laundress cabin. He didn't know what to make of Jessica. He had thought he knew just what kind of person she was from the moment he met her; then she would do something that seemed so out of character for the spoiled, willful woman he thought she was. Like the challenge he'd given her to invite her cousins, for instance; he'd been shocked when she actually did it; then she had obviously managed to make friends with Caleb. After lunch she had even laughed and talked with Miriam and Bridie. And he had thought she would soon lose interest in Franny, especially once she realized the officers' wives wouldn't associate with Ellen. But instead of being embarrassed to be associated with a laundress and her child, she faithfully took Franny for lessons every day and often dropped in after supper to visit with Ellen.

She had even come to some services at the fort. For some reason, though, her big blue eyes gazing at him all through the service had been distracting. There was no way he was going to let himself get involved with someone like Jessica DuBois. Someone like her would never play second fiddle to God.

He spent the day working on his Sunday message, but Jessica's beautiful face kept intruding on his concentration. He finally threw down his pen in disgust and stretched. His two weeks at Fort Bridger were almost up, and it was time to be thinking about moving on to Colorado. Maybe the day after tomorrow would be a good time to head out.

He made his plans and left two days later. Jessica wished him a quiet goodbye, and he wondered what she was thinking. Sometimes he surprised a strange look in her eyes, and he wasn't sure what it meant. A haunted, hungry look full of pain and longing.

❧

Most of the summer passed before he knew it. He alternated his time between three different forts, but he found himself looking forward to his visits at Fort Bridger. For one thing, the men there were beginning to respond to his message, and three of them had accepted Christ on his last visit. But if he was honest, he would have to admit that he looked forward most to the verbal sparring with Jessica. She was an intriguing woman, and he had to keep reminding himself to protect his emotions. The last thing he wanted to do was develop any tender feelings for her. The man who fell into her clutches would rue the day.

In early September, he arrived back at Fort Bridger, feeling restless and at odds with himself. He grabbed his jacket and strolled toward Ellen's cabin, but to his surprise she wasn't out beside her tub of laundry. The fire was out; obviously, she hadn't done any laundry today. He rapped his knuckles against the door and waited. After a few minutes, he knocked again, then turned to go. Maybe she had taken Franny for a walk.

He'd taken only one step when the door creaked open behind him. He turned around and saw Ellen leaning against the doorjamb. Alarm raced through him at the sight of her white face and labored breathing.

"Clay. Thank God," she whispered. "I've prayed and prayed for you to come."

In two quick steps he was at her side and caught her just as she staggered and nearly fell. "Ellen! Here, let me get you to bed."

The heat radiating off her body made his mouth go dry with dread. Sweat had plastered her hair to her head, and she smelled of dried sweat and vomit. How long had she been sick? He half carried, half dragged her to her bed. Glancing around for Franny, he found her asleep at the foot of the bed. She looked okay, and he breathed a sigh of relief that she'd been spared whatever illness had struck Ellen.

He laid Ellen on the bed and pulled a thin blanket over her. "I'll be right back with the doctor."

"Franny," Ellen whispered. "You must get Franny away from me."

"She's asleep right now. She'll be fine until I get back with the doctor."

"No! Get her out of here now!" Ellen pushed herself up and pulled on Clay's arm urgently.

"Okay, okay." He gently forced her back against the pillow, then scooped Franny up. She didn't even awaken. "I'll take her with me. You rest, and I'll be right back."

He hurried across the parade ground to the infirmary, almost colliding with Jessica as she and Bridie came out of the sutler's store. "Here." He handed Franny to Jessica. "Ellen's sick, and I've got to get the doctor."

Jessica's mouth opened, but Clay didn't wait for her questions. He barreled through the door to the infirmary, shouting for the doctor.

Dr. Harold Mason stood washing his hands at a table on the far side of the room, a tall, well-built man with dark hair. With a weary shrug, he turned to face Clay. "No need to make such a ruckus, Preacher," he said. "I'm not deaf."

"My cousin Ellen is real sick, Doc," Clay began. The door opened behind him, and he caught a whiff of Jessica's familiar honeysuckle sachet. "You've got to come with me right now."

Dr. Mason sighed. "Cholera, most likely," he said with a frown. "It's spreading like wildfire."

Cholera. The very word struck terror to Clay's heart, and he heard Jessica catch her breath behind him. Clay figured now she'd give Franny right back to him for fear of catching the disease herself. When he turned toward her, though, he saw her hand Franny to Bridie.

"Take Franny home with you and tell Mama what's happened," she said in a firm, no-nonsense voice. "I've got to take care of Ellen."

Clay raised his eyebrows, but he wasn't about to look a gift horse in the mouth. Dr. Mason grabbed his bag and followed them out into the street. Clay led the way back to Suds Row.

When he entered the cabin this time, the strong odor of sickness hit him in the face. He felt a rising ball of dread in his gut and hurried to the bed. Ellen was lying on her side with her legs drawn up to her chest.

Dr. Mason pushed him out of the way. "Go fix some coffee or something, and let me look at her," he ordered. He bent over Ellen's inert form and opened his bag.

Clay turned away and sank bonelessly into a chair. The feeling of dread grew, and he swallowed hard. He bowed his head and prayed fervently for Ellen. How could little Franny survive without her mother? Ellen *had* to pull through. He sensed Jessica moving around him and raised his eyes to see what she was doing. Her face set in concentration, she was trying to make coffee. She frowned at the coffeepot, and he could tell she had never made coffee before. He stood and gently moved her to one side. "Here, let me show you."

Surprisingly, she didn't come back with her usual sharp comment but let him demonstrate what to do. "Thank you," she said softly. "I'll remember next time."

He raised an eyebrow at her mild response, suddenly overwhelmed with gratitude for her presence. Her concern surprised him. He turned to see what the doctor was doing, but the other man's bulky form blocked Ellen from view. He sat in the chair again and buried his face in his hands. Cholera was deadly. He'd had a good friend die from it back in '64. It took him fast too.

Dr. Mason cleared his throat, and Clay looked up. The doctor put his instruments in his bag and walked to the table.

"That coffee done yet? I haven't had a minute to even eat today. The first case of cholera showed up last night. It's sweeping through Fort Bridger like a herd of stampeding buffalo."

Jessica poured them all a cup of coffee and sat down beside the doctor. "What do we need to do for Ellen?" She cut the doctor a slice of bread, buttered it, and spread it with jam.

Dr. Mason bit appreciatively into the jam and bread. He swallowed and sighed. "That does hit the spot." He shook his head. "It will just have to run its course. I gave her laudanum, but anything I do is like barkin' at a knot. Only thing you can do is give her plenty of fluids, keep her clean, and stay alert in case she chokes when she vomits."

Jessica nodded. "I can do that."

"I'll help too," Clay said.

The doctor finished his coffee and bread. "Send for me if you need me. There's not much any of us can do but pray, though. She'll either pull through on her own or she won't." He picked up his bag and headed for the door. "I have other patients to check on. I'll try to stop back later tonight."

When he'd shut the door behind him, Jessica stood. "I'll take the first watch. Why don't you go check on Franny while I get Ellen cleaned up? We need to make sure Franny isn't getting sick too."

Clay hesitated, but what she said made sense. He wasn't sure if he trusted her to care for Ellen by herself, but she should be the one to clean her up. And he was worried about Franny. He picked up his hat and jammed it on his head. "I'll be back in a little while." He stopped when he reached the door. "Why are you doing this?" He still found it hard to believe Jessica would risk her own health for Ellen.

"She's my friend," Jessica said simply. "I've never had a friend before." She stood and went to the little chest against the wall where spare clothing was kept. "Go check on Franny. I can handle getting Ellen cleaned up."

Clay shrugged and went out to see Franny. Letty met him at the door with soft words of concern. He told her what the doctor had said and that he and Jessica would be caring for Ellen. She promised to help in any way she could, then showed him into the bedroom where Franny lay sleeping. He touched her head, but she felt cool. Her color looked good, and she was breathing evenly. Satisfied that she wasn't getting sick, he closed the door softly behind him and went across the parade ground to Ellen's cabin.

When he let himself in, Jessica was holding Ellen upright, trying to force some tea down her throat. Ellen's head lolled back, and the tea dribbled down her chin. "Let me help." He sat on the edge of the bed and leaned Ellen against his chest so her head stayed up. Jessica pinched her cheeks to get her mouth to open and managed to dribble a bit of tea down her throat.

"Maybe if you got a cloth and let her suck the tea up," Clay suggested.

Jessica brightened. "Good idea." She went to the kitchen and tore a strip of cotton from a clean dishcloth, dipped it in water, and brought it back to the bed. She twisted it and dunked it into the tea, then put it between Ellen's lips.

Ellen sucked on it feebly. "Good," she gasped.

Through the long night they held the basin while she vomited; they cleaned her and the sheets as often as the diarrhea came; and they got as much tea and water down her as they could. The doctor checked on her twice and seemed satisfied with her care.

By dawn they were both exhausted. Jessica's eyes looked bruised from lack of sleep and worry, and Clay figured he looked just as bad. But he thought Ellen looked a little better. He hoped it wasn't wishful thinking.

"Why don't you go home and lie down for a few hours?" he suggested to Jessica. "When you come back, I'll catch a few winks."

Jessica hesitated, then nodded. "I want to check on Franny, anyway." She stood and wearily stretched. "I'll be back in a couple of hours."

When she opened the door to leave, he called out, "Hey, Red."

She didn't even glare at him when he said the hated nickname. She just looked back with a question in her eyes.

"You're all right. I guess I was wrong about you. Thanks."

Her face lit with a weary smile. "That's the first time I ever heard a man admit he was wrong."

Clay grinned. "Treasure it then. It may be a long time before you hear it again." He watched her close the door behind her, then turned back to Ellen. She was sleeping peacefully with a bit of color in her cheeks, and he felt a surge of hope.

A few minutes later, Dr. Mason opened the door and walked into the room with dragging feet. Clay could tell he was totally exhausted.

"I think she looks better," Clay said hopefully.

The doctor bent over her and put his stethoscope to her chest. "Lungs are clear," he grunted. He straightened up and put his stethoscope away. "Today will be crucial if she's going to make it."

Clay's heart sank. He'd hoped they were through the worst of it. "When can we know?"

"When she starts sitting up and taking a bit of food and is able to keep it down, then she'll be through the worst of it." Dr. Mason picked up his black bag and headed for the door. "I'm going home to try to get a couple of hours sleep. Send someone for me if she gets worse."

After the door closed behind the doctor, Clay sank to his knees and bowed his head. He pleaded for Ellen's life again and listed all the reasons why God shouldn't take her now. But he couldn't help an overwhelming sense of foreboding. He stayed on his knees beside her bed and watched her sleep. She breathed easily and deeply; surely she was going to be all right. He was worrying needlessly. When he heard the door open behind him, he turned to see Jessica enter. He glanced at his pocket watch. She'd come back in exactly two hours, just as she'd promised.

"Franny is fine," she said. "Caleb and Bridie are taking her to play at Burts's."

"Good." He got to his feet and stretched.

"Has the doctor been back?"

He nodded. "He said she wasn't through the woods yet. Today should tell."

Jessica sighed and went to fix some coffee. "I thought she was better. It's going to be a long day. You'd better get some rest while she's sleeping."

Clay nodded. "I will soon." He grinned wearily as he watched her carefully fix the coffee just the way he'd showed her. Maybe he'd misjudged the selfish beauty. Maybe she really did love Ellen.

Ellen groaned, and Jessica turned and hurried to her side. She held the basin while Ellen was sick again, then wiped her friend's mouth and coaxed a bit more tepid tea down her.

Ellen opened her eyes and looked from Clay to Jessica. "You two been here all night?"

"Where else would we be?" Jessica smoothed Ellen's tangled hair back from her face. "How do you feel?"

"Pretty awful." Her face was nearly as white as the pillow and a yellow pallor lurked behind the white. "What's wrong with me?"

Clay looked at Jessica, then back at Ellen. He didn't want to tell her, but he couldn't lie to her. "Cholera," he said reluctantly.

Ellen winced as cramps gripped her stomach. "How's Franny?"

"She's fine," Jessica told her. "She was on her way fishing with Caleb and Bridie when I left her a few minutes ago."

Ellen nodded and closed her eyes with a grimace of pain on her face.

"Go get some sleep." Jessica pushed Clay toward the door.

The touch of her hand against his chest made his mouth go dry. He surely wasn't beginning to get attached to her, was he? The light through the window set her hair aflame, and he longed to reach out and touch a shining curl. He could smell the fresh scent of the soap she'd used and the honeysuckle scent she wore. She smelled like sunshine. She stared up at him with those amazingly blue eyes, and he saw the pulse in her throat begin to hammer. *She feels it too,* he thought in amazement. She parted her lips, and he bent his head.

As his lips touched hers, Clay felt a jolt of lightning run clear through him. He gripped her shoulders and pulled her closer. The soft feel of her in his arms made him dizzy. He tore his mouth from hers and looked into her bemused face. Her eyes were still half closed. "I have to go," he gasped. He pushed her away and ran out the door as though a thousand demons were after him. He had to get away and get his thoughts together. He couldn't love her. She wasn't a Christian. Surely it was just the stress of their shared situation that made him feel such crazy things. They both just needed a little comfort.

Chapter 6

Jessica stared at the closed door in disbelief, then touched her fingers to her lips. Clay had actually kissed her! She still felt the shock of his lips on hers. She had flirted with many men, had held their hands and gazed into their eyes, and she had even done the kissing necessary to make another woman jealous. But she'd never *been* kissed where it was a mutual touching of lips and souls. She smiled and spun around the room.

I love him. The thought was overwhelming. So this was what love felt like. That's what the difference in the kiss meant. And surely he must love her, or his kiss would not have felt so amazing. She felt giddy from the revelation of her feelings.

What should she say when he came back? Would he ask her to marry him? She frowned at the thought. She wouldn't like him to be gone a lot. And that's what a traveling preacher did—travel. Perhaps she could contact some of Papa's friends back east and find him a position in a large church somewhere. He was too imposing of a man to be stuck in this backwater. Her head was filled with visions of a socially prominent life as Clay's wife, and she smiled. She could learn to adjust to hearing about God all the time too. She was a great pretender; no one would ever know she wasn't a true believer herself.

She rinsed the coffee cups, then went to sit beside Ellen's bed. After a few minutes of daydreaming, her head began to nod. She slid to the floor and leaned her head against the bed. If Ellen needed anything, she would hear her. She drifted to sleep with sweet visions of being in Clay's arms again.

She awoke when the front door banged. Clay came toward her with a frown. "If you were too tired to watch her, you should have said so." He helped her to her feet, and they both turned to check Ellen.

Her mouth and eyes were both open, and a dribble of vomit trailed down her chin. Jessica stared in horror, then reached out and touched her. She was cold. A scream rose in her throat, and she backed away from the bed.

She'd killed her! She had killed her only friend! She put a hand to her mouth, strangling the cry that burst from her lips, then sank bonelessly to the floor and buried her face in her hands.

Clay made a queer, choked sound in his throat and gently closed Ellen's eyes. Tears leaked from his eyes, and he struggled to control his emotions.

"I killed her," Jessica sobbed. "If I'd been awake, she wouldn't have died."

"You don't know that," Clay said woodenly. He sat in the chair and leaned his head into his hands. "The doc said it would be touch and go. God decided it was her time. I don't know why. Why would He take Franny's mother and father both within a few months of each other? How do we tell Franny?" It was a cry from the heart.

Jessica sobbed aloud again. How could she bear this pain? Poor Franny. She loved her mother so much.

They stayed motionless, stunned with grief for several long minutes; then Clay got to his feet and started toward the door. "I'd better notify the doctor. Can you stay with her?"

She nodded. "I'm sorry, Clay. So sorry. It's my fault. All my fault." Grief and guilt gnawed at her insides. She'd never felt such remorse. If she could take her friend's place, she gladly would. How could Clay bear to look at her now? How could she bear to see the accusation in his eyes? "Why wasn't it me? I have nothing. Nobody would care if I died. Why Ellen?"

He turned and looked at her. "Don't blame yourself, Red. We can't know God's ways sometimes. We just have to trust Him even when it hurts." He closed the door behind him.

Jessica dragged her skirts behind her as she crawled to the bed where Ellen lay. Ellen's skin was beginning to take on the waxy pallor of death. Just a few days ago they'd sat in this room and laughed. She had told Ellen things she hadn't told anyone before. Why had she never realized before what a blessing it was to have a friend? She didn't think she would ever have another one. It hurt too much to lose one.

Clay came back soon with the doctor, and they wrapped Ellen's body in a sheet and carried it out. The doctor touched her shoulder briefly. "There will be five other funerals tomorrow, Miss DuBois. You did all you could."

Did he think it would comfort her to know others had died too? Well, it didn't. She didn't care about the others; she only cared about Ellen. And she *hadn't* done all she could. That's what hurt so much. If she had been awake to help Ellen when she vomited, she would still be alive.

Numbly, Jessica gathered up the soiled clothing and bedding and took them out to the pile of laundry in the yard. She looked around at the stacks of clothing and the pot for boiling the clothes. Someone else would take this little cabin and the job Ellen had been so thrilled to get. A sob burst again from her throat, and she hurried across the parade ground toward home. She wanted to fling herself across her bed and weep until she had no more tears.

Her mother looked up when she burst into the house. She put her hand to her mouth when she saw Jessica's tearstained face. "Oh, my dear girl," she said in a faltering voice. "I feared she wouldn't make it."

Jessica burst into fresh tears, and her mother held her as she sobbed out her grief and misery. Poor Franny. The little girl knew more about loss already than any child should know. She lifted her wet face from her mother's shoulder. "Can we take care of Franny, Mama?"

Her mother hesitated a moment, then nodded. "Of course, Darling. I'm sure you're Uncle Samuel won't mind if she stays with us for a bit."

"Not just a bit. Always. I want to keep her." Until she spoke the words, she didn't realize she felt that way. She didn't see how she could love Franny any more if she were her own daughter. "Please, Mama."

Her mother bit her lip. "We have no room, Jessica. You know we're already cramped."

"We can put up a small bed in my room, or she can even sleep with me." But even as she argued, she knew it was no use. Her mother was right. There was barely room for all of them as it was. Franny was just a little girl right now, but she wouldn't stay little forever. But there had to be a way to keep her. Somehow, she would find a way.

"I'll ask your uncle," her mother promised.

But Jessica knew what he would say. He was a stingy man and would see no need to take in Franny when she had a blood relative right here in Fort Bridger. But how could Clay care for a little girl? He was gone for weeks at a time. It would be too hard on Franny if he took her from fort to fort. Maybe an arrangement where they shared her care would work. She bit her lip. But where would Clay keep her? He lived in a cabin even smaller than Ellen's when he was here; there was no place for Franny there.

Jessica went to her room wearily. She was too tired to think of a solution now, but surely some idea would come to her. She lay down across the top of the bed without bothering to get undressed, thinking she would just close her eyes for a few minutes. Her head throbbed from stress and tears, but every time she closed her eyes, she saw Ellen's face.

She had been lying there for what seemed like only a few minutes when she heard Franny's voice. She got quickly to her feet, smoothed her hair, and went to the parlor.

Clay was there too with Franny on his lap. He was listening as Franny recounted the day's events to him.

"I tried to find a tadpole for Jessie, but I couldn't find none," she said. When she saw Jessica come into the room, she gave a squeal of delight and slid from Clay's lap. She ran across the floor and flung herself against Jessica's skirts.

Jessica kneeled and gathered her close. "Hey, Muffin, did you get muddy like I. . .I mean, Ruth did?"

Franny shook her blond curls. "I stayed clean." She patted Jessica's hair, then touched her face. "Why are you crying? I really tried to find you a tadpole."

The tears rained down Jessica's cheeks harder. "I know you did, Muffin," she said, muffling a sob. She took a deep breath and looked at Clay helplessly.

He saw the plea in her eyes and stepped forward. He took Franny from Jessica and brought her to the sofa. Jessica sank beside him and clasped her hands in her lap. "We need to talk to you, Franny," Clay said.

The little girl touched his face and looked over at Jessica. Her eyes welled with tears. "Is it Mommy? Did she go to see Jesus too?" Her lips trembled, and there was fear in her eyes.

Jessica's gaze flew to Clay's face. He looked as astonished as she felt. How had Franny known? She caressed her blond curls. "Yes, Darling. Yes, she did."

Franny's lips trembled, and she buried her face in Clay's chest. "I want my mommy," she wailed. "I don't want Mommy to go to see Daddy and Jesus without me." She ground her tiny fists in her eyes and sobbed. "Mommy! Mommy!"

Jessica wanted to sob aloud with her, but she bit her lip and forced back the tears.

Clay hugged her close, and Jessica could hear the tears in his voice. "We didn't want her to go either. But Jesus wanted to see your mommy real bad, and Daddy was missing her so much. Just think how happy they are together again." He hoisted her up so he could look in her face. "And you know, we're going to see them again someday."

"When?" she cried. "I want to see them now!"

"We can't go now," he told her. "But someday we will. Whenever God says it's time."

She cried softly for awhile, then rubbed her eyes. "Where will I sleep? Where will I live?"

"With me," Jessica and Clay answered simultaneously. They each stopped and eyed the other.

"We'll talk about this later," Clay said under his breath to Jessica. He ran his palm over Franny's head consolingly. "You can stay here with Jessica for now."

"I want my mommy," she cried again. Her cries became wails of anguish.

Tears streaming down his own face, Clay rocked her back and forth in his arms until she finally cried herself to sleep. He carried her to the bedroom and laid her in the middle of Jessica's bed.

While he was gone from the room, Jessica marshaled all the reasons she had for keeping Franny with her. She had to make him see reason. Franny needed a woman. She *had* to make him see that somehow.

"Let's sit on the porch," she suggested when he returned.

He inclined his head in agreement and let her lead the way. Neither of them said anything until they were seated on the porch rocking chairs.

"Franny is my cousin," Clay began. "You're no blood relation at all. She needs someone who will love her no matter what. I don't mean to be unkind, but you really have had very little experience with children. You've mostly seen her at her best. The next few months are going to be rough for her while she deals with the loss of both her parents. And I love her. She belongs with me."

She just had to make him understand. "I know that everything you say is true. But I love Franny too. I don't see how anyone could love her more than I do." Clay's face softened at her admission, and she took hope as she plunged on. "You have to understand, Clay. I was always afraid to open myself up to care about anyone else. I'd been hurt at a young age, and I didn't trust other people. Ellen and Franny changed all that. Ellen was the first and only friend I've ever had. I will never hurt Franny. Never. I would give my life for her." Tears stood in her eyes after her impassioned speech, but she didn't care. She didn't care about anything but keeping Franny with her. A small part of her wondered why he didn't see the obvious solution. If they married, they could both keep Franny. Did that kiss mean nothing to him?

Clay was silent a moment. "She belongs with me," he repeated stubbornly.

"You travel so much—who's going to care for her when you're not here? And you don't have room for her in that tiny cabin, anyway."

His restless movements stilled. She could see he hadn't really thought the whole thing through. "Just think about it," she pleaded. "A decision doesn't have to be made yet. Let's get through the funeral, and we'll talk about it some more."

He stood and paced the length of the porch. "All right," he said abruptly. "But I'm not promising anything."

"Fair enough. Do we know when the funeral is?"

"Tomorrow morning at ten. Ellen's will be first; then I have five more to do in the afternoon. Do you want to pick out a dress for her to buried in?"

Tears blurred her vision again, and she nodded.

"Fine. I'll be in the infirmary. Bring it there as soon as you can." He turned and walked down the steps.

She watched his long strides across the parade ground. She hoped he might turn and wave, but he just walked to the infirmary and disappeared inside. What had the kiss earlier meant to him? Nothing at all? Or had she killed any affection he might feel for her with her negligence? She was suddenly fiercely glad she had never felt like this before about a man. It hurt. It hurt more than anything she had ever experienced. She swallowed the lump in her throat and got to her feet. She'd better find a dress for Ellen before Franny awoke.

Ellen's cabin still smelled of sickness and death when she opened the door. She walked to the window and threw it open to let in the fresh air. Rummaging through Ellen's few dresses, she couldn't find anything she thought was appropriate. Maybe one of her own dresses could be altered to fit. Ellen was shorter and plumper, but surely something would work.

She went back home and sorted through her own things. At the bottom of her chest, she found a blue silk dress she had been saving for a dance or some other special occasion. The seams were wide and could easily be let out. The length wouldn't matter. She carried it out to the parlor and showed it to her mother, who agreed to see what she could do with it.

Miriam looked on with a supercilious smile. "Useless is what you are," she said. "Can't you do anything for yourself?"

Jessica ignored her, but the words hurt. "Can I help do anything?" she asked her mother.

"I do need to put supper on, Dear. Could you let the seams out if I show you how?"

Jessica frowned uncertainly. She felt all thumbs with a needle. "I can try," she said reluctantly. At least it was better than trying to cook supper herself.

Her mother gave her a pair of tiny scissors and showed her how to snip the threads without harming the delicate fabric, but Jessica still spent an hour just letting out all the seams in the bodice, waist, and arms. At last, she laid the dress across the sofa and went to the kitchen. "Thanks, Mama," she said. "Is there anything I can do to help you?"

"Ooh, Madame is willing to soil her lily-white hands in the kitchen," Miriam sneered.

Jessica was too tired to think of a good answer, so she just shrugged and took the plates her mother held out to her. She began to set the table, all the while aware of Miriam's resentful glare. She had thought they were getting along better. Why was her cousin acting like this now? She didn't need this aggravation today.

"I know what you're planning, and it won't work," Miriam said finally.

"I don't have any idea what you're talking about." Jessica picked up the silverware and began to set it beside the plates.

"You think you'll catch Clay by taking in Franny. But he won't be trapped that easily." Miriam tossed her head. "He told Caleb you weren't his type."

Fresh tears clogged Jessica's throat, and she swallowed hard. She wasn't about to let Miriam see how her words hurt. Rather then risk having her voice quiver, she said nothing at all but continued with her chore. Irritated that her taunt had gone unanswered, Miriam muttered under her breath and stormed from the room.

"That's really not why you want Franny, is it, Dear?" Her mother's face was creased with worry.

Carefully, Jessica laid the last setting on the table and turned to face her mother. "Would you really believe that I would do something like that, Mama?"

She had her answer in the flash of uncertainty that crossed her mother's face. "I'm going for a walk," Jessica said. She whirled and practically ran from the room. Was that how everyone saw her? As a conniver and deceiver? She hurried across the parade ground to Ellen's cabin, where she sat at the familiar battered kitchen table. In the peace and quiet there she faced her own nature.

She *had* done things like that before. No wonder that's what people thought now. She remembered her unholy alliance with Ben Croftner and how they had arranged for Sarah Campbell to be handed over to the Sioux. How she had investigated Emmie's background and threatened to tell Isaac all about how she hadn't really been married to her first husband. She had done a lot of bad—even evil—things in her life. She wasn't proud of them, and she didn't really know why she had done them. At the time, it had just seemed important to win. Saving face and getting what she wanted had once been the most important things to her.

She wasn't even sure how or when the change in her had begun. Papa's death had probably been the beginning. Seeing the goodness in Emmie and Sarah back at Fort Phil Kearny had made her yearn to be better herself, even though she had hated to admit it. But the main relationship that had changed her was her friendship with Ellen and Franny. Ellen had been so good, so caring. Jessica wished she could be like her, but no amount of good intentions would bring about such a miraculous transformation. But she would try to be a better person. She would care for Franny and perhaps somehow atone for Ellen's death.

She gave a heavy sigh. Life was so complicated, so hard. Where was her relationship with Clay going? That kiss was another thing that had changed her. But apparently it had meant nothing to Clay; he showed no sign that the moment had even touched him. She squeezed her eyes shut, then got to her feet and slowly went back home.

The next morning, the leaden sky looked as heavy as Jessica's heart felt. She curled Franny's hair and dressed her in her best dress. The little girl's face was peaked and woeful, and Jessica's heart broke for this small child who had to face such sorrow. She clung to Jessica's hand, and they made their way to the officers' rec room where the funeral would be held.

The small room was packed with enlisted men. None of the officers' wives had come, though, except Jessica's mother, and Jessica felt a sharp stab of anger that they would continue with their snobbery in the face of this tragedy. Her cousins and uncle's presence gave her a warm glow of gratitude, though.

Maybe this was what family was all about—sticking by one another in times of tragedy and heartache.

The funeral was brief. Jessica tried not to watch Clay, but his grief was evident. He almost broke down several times during the service. Franny cried the entire time. After the service, Jessica took Franny back to the house and tucked her into bed for a nap. Clay had said he would be over after the other funerals. There would be just one mass funeral for the men who had died of cholera, so he shouldn't be more than an hour or so.

She found it hard to wait. She wanted to keep Franny so badly, but what if Clay said no? Restlessly, she followed her mother into the kitchen. "Did you talk to Uncle Samuel about Franny?" She had a feeling she already knew what he had said. Her mother had been uncharacteristically quiet since they got back from the funeral.

Her mother bit her lip. "I'm sorry, Darling, but there just isn't room to keep Franny permanently. Of course, she can stay until Reverend Cole can make arrangements for her."

Jessica blinked furiously to keep the tears at bay. She had to make them see how important this was to her. But before she could marshal her arguments, someone knocked on the front door. Her heart pounding, she raced to the front door and flung it open.

"Jessica." Clay took off his hat. His eyes were grave and shadowed with grief. He followed her into the parlor. "Where's Franny?"

"Napping. She was exhausted from crying." She showed him to a seat and went to fetch them both a cup of coffee.

"I'll let you discuss Franny's situation with Reverend Cole alone," her mother whispered. "I need to make a call on Mrs. McNeil. She's feeling a bit poorly. I'll be back in about an hour." She took her bonnet and left to make her call.

Jessica took the coffee and slowly walked back to the parlor. She felt a sense of futility and trepidation. Clay wasn't going to let her keep Franny. She tried to tell herself she was jumping to conclusions, but somehow she just knew. She handed Clay a cup of coffee, then sat down in the chair facing him.

Clay took a gulp of coffee and stared down into it morosely. "I wish Ellen had some family I could notify about her death, but her parents are both dead, and I have no idea where her brother is." He took another gulp of coffee and finally raised his gaze to her face. "I've prayed about your request to keep Franny," he said after a long moment of staring into her eyes. He set his cup down on the table beside him and stood. "I have a lot of reservations about it." He paced from the fireplace to the sofa and back again.

"Why? Surely you can see that a little girl needs a woman around." Perhaps he hadn't decided against her plans after all. Her heart began to pound in hope.

Clay nodded. "I know you love her, Red, but love isn't everything." He took a deep breath. "She also needs a Christian upbringing, to be taught solid spiritual values, to be introduced to Jesus when she's ready. Franny needs to know that if she wants to see her mother again, only Jesus can do that for her. Can you teach her those things?"

Jessica tried to speak, but what could she say? She swallowed hard.

He gave a slight smile. "I know you don't have much use for God, and that's a very important issue. I don't want Franny to grow up thinking God doesn't matter." He stared at his hands a moment and raked his fingers through his hair. "Another thing is the matter of her support. If you keep her, your stepfather would be the one providing her support. I could help, but he would have the ultimate responsibility. She'd be a charity case, and I really don't want that for her. So I've come up with a plan that might solve all of our problems, but I don't think you'll agree. I'm not sure you could even do it." His tone was ominous.

Jessica jumped to her feet. "I can do anything if it means I can keep Franny with me!"

Clay gave a wry grin. "I don't think so, Red. The only way I can agree to let Franny stay with you is if *you* provide her support yourself by taking over Ellen's job as post laundress. We would have family devotions when I'm here, and when I'm not here, you'll teach her about God yourself with some lessons I'll leave for you."

Jessica gaped at him. "Me? Post laundress?" Her voice rose and ended in a squeak. It was ludicrous! How could he even ask her to do such a thing? "You must be mad!" The strength left her legs, and she sank back into the chair.

"I didn't think you'd agree, but those are my terms. It's the only way I'll agree to let you raise Franny."

His tone was inflexible, and Jessica knew he wouldn't budge from his position. But it was ridiculous! Even if she agreed, which she wouldn't, she didn't even know *how* to do laundry!

"If she stayed here, she would just be another burden on your mother. If you want her, *you* have to be the one who does the work. This is a job you can't pass off on someone else."

Suddenly furious, Jessica leaped to her feet and pointed her finger at him. "Now I understand! This is just your way of pointing out how worthless you think I am! You had no intention of letting me keep Franny, did you? You just wanted to humiliate me!" Tears choked her, and she was so angry, she couldn't think of anything else to say.

"I'm sorry you see it that way," Clay said mildly. "But those are my terms."

She put her hands on her hips. "Well, I won't do it! And I still intend to keep Franny!" *Just let him try to take her.*

Clay shrugged. "I'm sorry, Red. I'll take Franny now."

"You will not! She's sleeping."

But she wasn't. Her blond head peeked around the corner, then she ran to Clay. Her face was screwed with grief as he gathered her against his chest. "Hey, Muffin. You ready to go home with me?"

She gave a sob and nodded. "I want Molly." Her voice was muffled against his chest.

"When I left her she was lying on the bed waiting for you to come play with her." He turned around and started for the door.

There was nothing Jessica could do, short of dragging Franny from him bodily. She watched helplessly as he gave her one last penetrating glance before he carried Franny out the door. She stared after him in disbelief, then burst into tears.

She hated to cry. It made her feel weak and out of control, but she couldn't seem to help herself lately. She suddenly hated Clay with a fierce passion. How dare he sit in judgment of her? This was all because she was beautiful, and he didn't trust beautiful women. She would be a good mother to Franny. Why couldn't he see that?

She refused supper and stayed in her room when the family came home. Lying on the bed, she stared at the crack in the ceiling above the bed, and she was still wide awake when her cousins came to bed later. She pretended to be sleeping, though, because she didn't want to hear Miriam's smug comments about Clay refusing to let her raise Franny.

When morning came, she hadn't slept at all. She heard the six o'clock call for reveille and slipped out of bed. She would do it. There was simply no other way. Clay wasn't about to change his mind, but she would show him what kind of backbone she had. She quietly dressed and slipped out of the house to find him. She thought he would be at Ellen's cabin, and the light shining through the window proved she was right.

Clay opened the door almost instantly at her knock. He stared at her for a moment, then gave her a slow smile. "Couldn't sleep, Red?"

She brushed by him without answering, then turned to face him. "I'll do it."

His jaw dropped, but he quickly recovered. "It won't be easy," he warned.

"I don't have any choice."

"Sure you do." He frowned and thrust his hands in his pockets. "You can be sensible and go back to your mother's house and forget all about this nonsense."

"That's what you'd hoped I'd do, wasn't it? You thought I'd never agree to your little test, and you could just do as you pleased with Franny." She poked a finger in his chest. "But I can take anything you throw my way, Clay Cole. I'll prove to you that I can do whatever it takes to provide a home for Franny." She shoved past him and poured herself a cup of coffee. "Now get out of my house and leave me in peace."

Clay stared at her, consternation written across his face. He closed his mouth, picked up his hat, and turned to the door. "Franny didn't get much sleep last night, so you might let her sleep in this morning. I'll notify Colonel Edwards that you will be accepting the position. There's plenty of laundry waiting to be done, so you'd better get to work." He clapped his hat on his head and shut the door behind him.

Jessica stared at the closed door, then around her at the tiny cabin and the duffel bags full of dirty laundry heaped in the corner. What had she done?

Chapter 7

The strong smell of lye and soap hung like a moist veil in the heavy air. Jessica blinked against the sting of the fumes and tried to encourage the fire by poking at it with a stick. It responded momentarily with a flare of flame, then settled down to a dull glow again. How did one go about getting the stupid thing to burn, anyway? She blew a strand of hair out of her eyes and sighed as she turned toward the door to check on Franny.

The little girl still slept, and Jessica breathed another sigh, this one of relief. Since Clay had left an hour ago, she'd piled the logs in the stove and fetched bucket after bucket of water. But the fire refused to burn hot enough to dissolve the soap properly, and her determination was fast deserting her. She felt like bursting into tears at the enormity of the task. She had never washed a single article of clothing in her life and really didn't know the first thing about how to start. She wasn't even sure she had put the right amount of soap in the water; she had just dumped until she thought it smelled strong enough to clean. She wished she could consult her mother, but Franny was still asleep, and she couldn't leave her alone.

How had she let Clay manipulate her into this fix? She poked at the fire again. It responded this time by sending out small flames that began to lick eagerly at the piled wood. She gave a smile of triumph and dumped the first gunny sack of clothing out onto the ground. She'd seen Ellen soak the clothing in the big tub, but other times she'd seen her scrubbing things on an old washboard in the smaller tub. Which came first?

While she stood contemplating her chore, Miriam came by with Anne Dials, the young wife of Lieutenant Billy Dials. Both young women stopped and looked at Jessica in amazement.

"What on earth are you doing?" Miriam demanded, leaning against the fence.

"What does it look like?" Jessica pushed the hair out of her eyes again. "I'm the newest laundress for Fort Bridger. I told you yesterday I was going to do this."

Miriam's mouth opened like a fish, but no sound came out. "I didn't believe you were serious!" she gasped finally.

Jessica looked at her with irritation. "Does it look like I'm joking?"

Anne giggled behind her hand, and Miriam reddened. "Wait until your mother and my father hear about this," she announced with a toss of her head. "You can't do this. It's embarrassing!" She whirled and stalked away. Anne followed with a last pitying glance toward Jessica.

"Tell Mama I need to see her!" Jessica shouted after them. The contempt in Anne's eyes had stung. Jessica had been too defiant and angry with Clay earlier to remember how lowly a laundress was in the eyes of the women here. Angry heat rose in her face. She didn't care what someone like Anne Dials thought about her.

The water was bath-warm when her mother came hurrying across the parade ground. "Miriam told me what was going on over here," she gasped. "You can't do this, Jessica. It's much too hard for you. You've never even washed a single article of clothing!"

"I'll learn." Jessica stirred the soap and explained the deal she had struck with Clay. Her mother was silent throughout her narrative, but Jessica thought a hint of a smile might have come and gone on her mother's face. What was there to smile about? There was nothing remotely funny about this situation. She scowled at her mother and turned abruptly toward the pile of laundry.

"Can you explain how I'm supposed to do this wash?" She kicked at a pair of dungarees at her feet. They were heavily stained with grass and mud. How was she supposed to get those stains out?

Letty fluttered her hands. "Oh dear. Let me see what to tell you first. Put the clothes in the pot to soak some of the soil loose. Then you agitate them with this." She pointed to a paddle against the wall. "Other stains have to be scrubbed on the washboard." She stayed for about an hour and showed Jessica what to do.

A sentry shouted the time, and Letty put her hand to her mouth. "I must go. Samuel will be home for his lunch soon. I'll check back this afternoon to see if you're having any problems."

She scurried away, pausing once to look back with a strange look on her face, a mixture of pride and exasperation. But Jessica certainly didn't feel any pride in what she'd agreed to do, although she felt plenty of exasperation.

She had just hung the first batch of clothes on the line when Franny came out the door, rubbing her eyes sleepily. She stumbled across the muddy yard and hooked her hand in Jessica's skirt. "Where's Uncle Clay?" she asked.

"He had to go to work, Sweetheart," Jessica told her. "He'll be back after supper. I'm going to stay here with you and take care of you."

The little girl's blue eyes grew enormous in her face. "Forever and ever?" she whispered. "Just like Mommy did?" Two giant tears rolled down her cheeks.

Answering tears stung Jessica's eyes. "Forever and ever," she promised. She knelt and took Franny in her arms. "Your mommy was a wonderful mommy, and I know I can't be as good a mommy as she was, but I'm going to try to take care of you like she would have wanted." The feel of those chubby arms around her neck made the last hour's work worthwhile, she decided.

She put Franny back on the ground and took her hand. "How about some lunch?" They walked back to the cabin, and Jessica sat the little girl down on a chair at the table. "What sounds good for lunch?"

She looked at the meager supplies and realized she would have to see about getting some food. There were some dried beans which she could cook for supper, a bit of salt pork, two slices of bread, and a few shriveled potatoes. "How about some jam and bread?" There didn't seem to be much else to fix.

"I love jam." Franny leaned her chin against her hand and watched as Jessica spread butter and jam on the last remaining bread slices.

As they ate their lunch, Jessica watched the dimples in Franny's cheeks come and go and felt content. After she finished with the laundry, she would try her hand at baking some bread. Mama had promised to come back, and maybe she could take time to show her how.

After their meager lunch, she put the beans in a pan and covered them with water the way she had seen her mother do. She put the pot on the cookstove and got the fire going, relieved that it was a bit more cooperative than the one in the yard. Feeling pleased with herself, she took Franny and her doll out to the yard and settled her in a corner of the laundry tent while she tackled another load of dirty clothing.

A mere hour later she wasn't feeling so complacent. Her back and arms ached from bending over the tub, and her head hurt from the fumes. Red, chapped areas on her hands itched almost unbearably, and Franny was beginning to whine from boredom. Her mother had stopped by, but only briefly, and Jessica felt abandoned and alone. How was she supposed to get all this work done? The thought of doing this every day made her shudder. She was thankful for the meager protection from the sun offered by the tent, although she still had to stand in the sun to stir the clothes in the tub over the fire.

She straightened wearily and put a hand to her back. After fetching Franny some blocks, she hung clothes on the line and gathered up another armload of laundry.

"Hey, Red, you look tired." Clay's wide grin was insufferably smug. "Ready to give up this crazy idea?"

Although that was exactly what she'd been thinking, Jessica straightened her shoulders and lifted her chin. "Of course not," she said loftily. "I'm getting along just fine. You really don't need to check up on me."

His grin widened. "You look done in. Want some help?"

Torn between her pride and her common sense, Jessica hesitated. She was relieved when Franny ran up to Clay and distracted him.

"Did you finally wake up?" He picked her up and tossed her into the air. "How would you and Molly like to go to the sutler's store for a piece of licorice?" He cocked an eyebrow at Jessica. "That okay with you?"

"Of course. I was about to suggest you spend some time with her. Watching me do laundry isn't much fun for her." So much for his offer of help. Not that she would have let him know she could use the assistance, of course.

"Now you know why Ellen was so grateful for those days you took Franny with you." He settled his hat more firmly on his head and turned to go, then turned back toward her. "I'll be over about seven for devotions with you and Franny. That should give you time to get supper done and Franny bathed and settled."

"Why don't you come for supper?" As soon as the words were out, she wished them back. What had possessed her to invite him? She was exhausted, her back hurt, and this was her first attempt at cooking a meal. She bit her lip and looked away. Maybe he would refuse.

But he grinned again, that devastating smile that did funny things to her stomach, and nodded. "It's a deal." He gave her a small wave and left her alone with her thoughts.

She squeezed her eyes shut, and two lone tears trickled from behind her closed eyelids. She would get through this. There were men here, lots of men. She needed to think about finding one who would get her out of this situation. It shouldn't be too hard. Her thoughts strayed to that single kiss she'd shared with Clay. If only he loved her as she loved him, but that was just a trap. Love meant nothing. She needed to find a man before this work destroyed her beauty.

Clay shook his head in amazement as he strode across the parade ground. He had been shocked when Jessica agreed to his demands and even more amazed when she started actually doing the dirty laundry. He hadn't realized how incongruous the picture of her bending over a tub of laundry was until he saw her do it. The sleeves of her expensive gown had been pushed up to reveal the smooth, white skin of her arms, and her hair, usually so carefully coifed, hung in strings around her flushed face. Her flawless complexion was now dusted with freckles from the sun. Red had a lot more gumption than he'd given her credit for. He had actually felt sorry for her when he saw her bending over that tub, but he had hardened his heart. She needed to learn this lesson. He didn't want Franny raised by a high-society debutante.

A memory of the way she had felt in his arms stirred him, and he pushed it away. It was a never-to-be-repeated moment of madness, a temporary wave of insanity. They had too many differences, and the main one was her lack of faith in God. If she ever thought she could twist him around her finger, she'd have him tucking his tail between his legs and meekly agreeing to pastor some high-society church back east somewhere. She didn't understand his calling, and she never would.

He and Franny bought a stick of licorice, then strolled around the fort. Several soldiers hailed him, and he stopped for a chat several times. He helped one soldier upright an overturned wagon, then took Franny to visit Lieutenant Brown's wife, Charlotte. She had recently given birth to a daughter, and Franny was fascinated with the red-faced, wrinkled baby. He had to admit it was a cute little mite, and he found himself remembering when Franny looked like that. For a moment a vision of Jessica with a baby—his baby—in her arms swept over him, but he quickly dismissed it. *That* would certainly never happen. Mrs. Brown insisted they stay for tea, and it was nearly six when he took Franny and hurried across the grassy knoll to Suds Row.

The acrid smell of burned beans escaped from under the closed door, and he could hear Jessica banging pots. He suppressed a grin. Good thing he wasn't really hungry after eating with Mrs. Brown. He knocked on the door and waited several minutes, then knocked again when she didn't answer the door. After another long moment, the door swung open, and she motioned him in. She had made an attempt to make herself presentable, but she was still flushed and a bit bedraggled. Dried soap speckled her dress, and freckles stood out on her sunburned face and arms.

"Smells like supper is done," he said with a grin.

She glared at him, then burst into tears. "You're making fun of me, and I've tried so hard today," she wailed. She scrubbed at her eyes like a child and turned her back to him.

For just a moment he wanted to turn her around and hold her against his chest. What a crazy thought. There was no way he was letting his emotions get involved with her. A beauty like her could take a man's heart and rip it to shreds; she couldn't be as vulnerable as she seemed. He tried to think of something funny to say to diffuse the tears, but his mind went blank.

Franny tugged on Jessica's skirt. "Don't cry, Jessie. I brought you a piece of licorice." She held up the candy with a bright smile on her face. "See?"

Jessica looked down at the little girl, then sniffed back the tears. She took the licorice and attempted a watery smile. "How did you know licorice is my favorite candy?"

Clay grinned at the quick recovery of her composure, but his eyes watered from the smoke in the cabin, and he wanted to get away from it. "Let's go for a walk while the cabin clears of smoke," he suggested.

Her blue eyes filled with tears again, but she just nodded. "I need to go by my mother's and get my things." She followed him out the door, and they turned toward the row of officers' quarters.

Clay felt tongue-tied in her presence. The sharp-tongued, confident Jessica he could handle, but he wasn't so sure about this weepy, uncertain one. This was what he wanted, though, wasn't it? To humble her a bit and make her take a good hard look at herself? But this new Jessica was more intriguing than the other one, and he wasn't sure he dared to know her better.

They stopped at the DuBois quarters, and Clay and Franny sat on the porch while Jessica went inside to get her things. They were joined a few minutes later by Miriam and Bridie.

Miriam gave him a flirtatious smile and swished her skirts as she sat down beside him. "I haven't seen you for ages," she said with a reproachful look.

"I've been pretty busy," he said. "And you won't see me at all for the next few weeks. I leave tomorrow for Utah."

She pouted prettily. "Will you miss me at all?"

He grinned. "I'll be too busy to miss anyone."

Bridie interrupted. "Is Jessica really going to be a washerwoman? Miriam said she saw her doing laundry, but I didn't believe her."

Clay grinned. "I don't think she'd like that title very well, but yeah, she is going to be doing laundry."

Bridie's green eyes danced with amusement. "I'll have to stop by and see this for myself."

Jessica came out of the house with an armload of clothing. "I have a trunk of things too. Do you think you could get it to the cabin for me?"

"No problem." He found the small trunk just inside the door and hoisted it to his shoulder. "What you got in here? Books?"

Jessica smiled. "Actually, there are some books in there. I wanted to continue Franny's education."

"Just when do you think you'll have time for that? Even Ellen didn't have time to do everything."

She spun around to face him and put her hands on her hips. "Are you insinuating that I can't do the things Ellen did?"

He started across the parade ground without answering her. She would just get more riled if he told her what he really thought. She was a high-society do-gooder and would soon tire of this role. In the meantime, he would take the help she offered and let Franny enjoy her company. He had to admit that she'd stuck it out longer than he thought she would. She definitely had pluck. He had thought he'd find her and Franny back at the DuBois quarters by nightfall. He felt a little uneasy at the thought of leaving her for two weeks. He didn't think she would do anything to hurt Franny, but still, he felt a bit of trepidation.

He heard her scurrying to catch up with him. Pausing when he reached the little bridge across the stream in the middle of the parade ground, he shifted the trunk to the other shoulder and hurried on toward Suds Row. He just wanted to get her settled and leave before he weakened and kissed her again. He thought about that kiss a lot. Too much for his own peace of mind.

The sharp smell of smoke had dissipated some when he shoved open the door and deposited his burden in the corner of the room. Jessica laid her arm-load of clothing on the bed and eyed him warily. She bit her full lower lip, and he thought again about that kiss. What was wrong with him? Why couldn't he forget it? He stepped away and turned his back on her. These sudden surges of attraction had to stop. She was not anywhere near the ideal he had in his head of a suitable wife. He was suddenly glad he would be leaving for a few weeks; maybe by the time he came back these compelling bouts of tenderness would be gone.

He cleared his throat, then held out his arms to Franny. "Give me a kiss, Moppet. I have to go away for a little while."

Franny's eyes filled with tears, and her lips trembled. She flung herself into his arms and wound her arms around his neck. "You can't leave me, Uncle Clay!" she sobbed. "Please, please, don't go!" Heart-wrenching sobs racked her shoulders, and her tears soaked through his shirt.

"Hey, don't take on so." He smoothed her hair back from her forehead. "I won't be gone long. And Jessica will be here with you. She'll take good care of you."

But his comforting words did little to still the storm of tears. He patted her and looked helplessly at Jessica. She moved to his side and caressed Franny's back.

"How about if Uncle Clay reads you a story before he goes?"

Slowly, Franny lifted her face, red and blotched with tearstains. "The one about the little red hen?"

"I can cluck with the best of them," Clay said solemnly. "You get in your nightie first, and when you're ready for bed, I'll demonstrate my wondrous hen imitation."

She giggled and slid out of his arms to the floor. "Can Molly listen too?"

"If you promise she won't laugh at my clucking."

She laughed again and ran off to change. Clay gave Jessica a grin and a mock sigh. "Now look what you've gotten me into, Red."

"I'm not the one who offered to cluck." Her lips twitched. She looked weary, but her blue eyes were full of mischief. "I wouldn't miss this for anything."

He read two stories to Franny, then took out his Bible. "Time for devotions," he said.

He saw Jessica's eyes widen, and she looked away. It was easy to see that spiritual things made her uneasy. He was curious about her background. Her mother faithfully attended the services and seemed truly interested in learning all she could about God. How had that spiritual hunger missed Jessica? Ellen had hinted that he should get to know her better before judging her. Was there some secret from Jessica's childhood that had shaped her?

He shook the musings away and opened his well-thumbed Bible. He decided to start with something easy and turned to Psalm 23. He read the psalm to Franny and helped her learn the first two verses.

Jessica listened closely and seemed determined to participate in this facet of Franny's upbringing. "Is there such a thing as still waters in this life?" she asked him after they put Franny to bed. "My experience has been that turbulence and trouble follow us everywhere we go. Look at what happened to Ellen."

"True," Clay admitted. "But when we have God, we can rest in Him and know that He has everything under control even when we can't see it."

She was silent a moment. "Did God want Franny to be orphaned?"

"You ask hard questions," he said. "God never promised we wouldn't have trouble and problems in this life. He just promised to go with us through them. As parents we would like to spare our children any hardship and trials, but if we were able to shield our child from any hard blow, she would grow up spoiled and selfish with no idea how to take care of herself, with no compassion for the pain of other people, and with the thought that the world revolved around her. God is much too wise and loves us too much to ever make that mistake. The hard things in life shape us and mold us into a closer picture of Jesus. Our goal here should be to become more like Him. We can't do that if God shields us from every bump and bruise."

He could see her thinking about his words. "You're describing me, aren't you?" she said finally. "You think I'm spoiled and selfish and that my parents coddled me too much. You really don't know about the bruises and bumps I had early in life."

Clay was quiet for a moment. "We can choose to let those bruises shape us into someone better, or we can use them as an excuse for willful, selfish behavior."

Jessica stood and turned her back to him. "At least now I know what you really think about me," she said. "I think you'd better go. I'm tired, and I need to go to bed."

He picked up his hat and jammed it on his head, then took his Bible and rose to his feet. "Just remember what I said, Red. Only you can decide whether to let those painful memories help you or heal you."

Her eyes were shadowed with fatigue and defiance, but she followed him to the door.

"I'll be back in a few weeks, and I'll try to take Franny off your hands as much as possible during the day," he told her. "If you need anything, you can send a telegram to Fort Hall."

She didn't answer him but only inclined her head. He looked at her stiff shoulders and sighed. He hadn't meant to hurt her, but maybe she was beginning to see herself. She had at least recognized that she was spoiled and selfish. Maybe when he got back they could talk more.

Chapter 8

Jessica slammed the shirt she was washing against the side of the tub, then scrubbed it viciously against the washboard. The hapless shirt was taking the brunt of the anger and hurt she felt after her talk with Clay. He'd been gone a month, but his remarks still rankled. She couldn't seem to get them out of her mind. She'd show him! There were plenty of men around here who admired both her beauty and her spirit. Why was she pining away for a man who cared for neither? Officers and enlisted men stopped by daily, and the fort thronged with men stopping through on their way to the goldfields or the West Coast, men who had cast appreciative glances her way. She could snap her fingers and have any of them.

The trouble was none of them made her breath catch in her throat the way Clay did. None of them stimulated her thinking and made her yearn to be better than she was. Only Clay did that.

She looked down at her hands. After years of wearing gloves and lanolin to keep her hands soft and white, they now looked like they belonged to someone else. They were red and freckled, with itchy red patches. Her nails were broken and ragged. Someday when she was back in Boston, this would be like a dream. She and Franny would wear gloves and take tea with people of culture. Her heart ached at the knowledge that her future would not include Clay. He might make it back east once in awhile to see Franny, but he had made it clear that his future didn't include Jessica.

She hung the last of the clothing on the line and went to the cabin with lagging steps. Franny followed her with her doll Molly. She had been unusually quiet today, and Jessica knew she missed her mother. Jessica spent a little extra time cuddling her after supper, then read her a story and put her to bed.

She thought again about her situation. What she should do is find a man to marry her, one who would be willing to be a father to Franny. Once the idea took root, she smiled. That wouldn't be hard to do. But not a soldier! Perhaps one of the emigrants on their way to California or Oregon. She'd heard it was beautiful along the coast. Suddenly, Boston didn't seem so attractive. A man would solve all her problems.

The next morning, she awoke determined to put her plan into action. She slipped her best dress over her head, arranged her hair in becoming curls, and applied a discreet touch of rouge to her cheeks. Franny watched in fascination as Jessica transformed herself.

"Now it's your turn, Sweetie," Jessica told the little girl. She put a ruffled blue dress on her and pulled the soft blond curls back in a ribbon. How long had it been since she'd taken the time to attend to Franny like this? She bit her lip guiltily. So much for being the perfect mother.

She took Franny's hand and went to the door. "Let's go to the bakery and buy you a sticky bun."

Franny's eyes grew wide. "Just for me?"

"All for you," Jessica agreed.

Quite a little town had sprung up in recent months. Fort Bridger had turned into a major stopping-off place for emigrants and prospectors. Jessica almost felt as though she didn't know the place anymore. Clay had said it wouldn't be long until it was a regular town. She was aware of people's stares as they walked past the various shops and businesses.

A tall, middle-aged gentleman took off his hat and bowed as she passed. "Ma'am," he said.

"It's miss," Jessica said with her most fetching smile.

He was immediately fetched. "Robert Ketcham, at your service, Miss, er?" He ended with a question in his voice.

Jessica held out her gloved hand. "Miss Jessica DuBois," she said with a demure flutter of her lashes. "I'm so pleased to meet you, Mr. Ketcham. This is my ward, Franny."

Robert knelt and took Franny's small hand. "Hello, Franny. Would you like a licorice stick?"

Franny looked up at Jessica, then shook her head. "We're going to get me a sticky bun. One just for me."

"A sticky bun it will be then," he said solemnly. He offered Jessica his elbow. "May I?"

She smiled again in a way to make her dimple appear. "Why, thank you, Sir. How kind."

"Please, call me Robert." He escorted her down the street to the bakery and held open the door for her.

Robert was attentive throughout their breakfast. He was a businessman on his way to California, and he told Jessica all about his factories in New York and Pennsylvania. "When my wife died, I decided to expand my concerns to the West," he said. "It seemed a good time to see something of the world while profiting at the same time. Unfortunately, we had no children, so there was nothing to keep me back east."

He's perfect, Jessica decided. She debated about how much to tell him and finally decided on the truth. He would have to know about her circumstances sooner or later.

"My father, Major DuBois, was killed in the Fetterman disaster last December. Mama was forced to marry his brother when Papa died without enough money for her to support us." She told him all about Ellen and how much she loved Franny and just what she'd agreed to do to keep her. Robert's eyes were fixed on her face through her entire explanation. She could see the admiration intensify as her tale unfolded. Just as she'd hoped.

"You're a remarkable woman, my dear," he said. "You deserve a bit of enjoyment after all you've been through. May I take you and young Franny to dinner tonight?"

She allowed herself just a moment of hesitation so he wouldn't realize his invitation was exactly what she'd been waiting for. "Why, that's very kind of you, Robert. I think we can squeeze that in. It sounds delightful."

His face reddened with pleasure. "Shall I call for you about six?"

She inclined her head. "We'll be ready."

He took her gloved hand and pressed his lips to it. "I look forward to it with great anticipation." His dark eyes gleamed as he escorted her to the door.

She could feel his eyes on her all the way down the street, but she resisted the impulse to turn to make sure. Smiling to herself, she forced herself to walk sedately, even though she felt like skipping. She had known it would be easy, but she hadn't expected to find someone so cultured and rich the very first day.

When they reached the cabin, she changed her clothes and popped Franny into a play dress. "Did you like Mr. Ketcham?" she asked her.

Franny nodded. "But I like Uncle Clay more. When is he coming back to see us?"

When, indeed? Jessica had expected him last week. But when he finally showed his face, she was determined that he would not find her pining away for him. When he saw her on Robert's arm, he'd realize what he'd lost.

Since she was anticipating the pleasure of an evening out with an admiring man, the day flew by. Even the daunting task of the laundry didn't dampen her spirits. Franny played happily in the shade of the tent while Jessica scrubbed the clothes. October was almost here, and winter wouldn't be far off. She would need to move quickly with Robert in order to get out of here before the snows fell in the mountains to the west. She tried not to think about Clay. She was determined to put that madness behind her. Somehow she would forget him and go on with her life.

She finished her day's work around five and hurried inside with Franny to get cleaned up for their evening out. She hauled and heated water for the small hip bath by the fire, then bathed herself and Franny before dumping the water out the back door. She dressed Franny as she had this morning, then surveyed her own wardrobe, debating for a few minutes over what to wear. She wanted to look demure yet alluring, because she had to hook Robert quickly. She finally settled on a blue satin dress with a daring neckline, pearl buttons running up the sleeves, and a flounced hemline. She curled her hair again and applied rouge to both her cheeks and her lips. After peering in the hand mirror, she was satisfied with her appearance.

She turned at a knock on the door. He was early! Luckily, she was ready. She smoothed one last stray hair and hurried to the door. Her welcoming smile froze when she swung open the door and stared into Clay's hazel eyes. Her heart clenched with the shock even as Franny shrieked and flung herself against his legs.

"Uncle Clay, Uncle Clay!" She tried to climb his pant leg, and he scooped her up and held her high.

"How's my girl? Did you miss me?" He settled her against his shoulder and stared down at Jessica.

"We missed you most awfully, didn't we, Jessie?" Franny patted his cheeks. "I don't want you to ever go away again."

He patted her absently while his gaze probed Jessica's face. She flushed at his appraisal. Why did he affect her like this? She didn't like the feeling. Men were the ones who were supposed to gasp at the sight of her. She wanted to be the one in control. She swallowed the lump in her throat.

"When did you get in?" She stepped aside so he could enter.

"Just now. I came straight here. I thought I might catch you before you fixed supper and take you both to Bridger Inn for dinner."

"We already have a dinner engagement."

A tiny muscle tightened in his jaw, but he nodded. "That explains the finery. I thought maybe you'd heard I was back." He looked down at Franny. "It looks like it's just you and me, Muffin. May I have the honor of your presence at dinner?"

Franny squeezed him around the neck. "I told Jessie I liked you better than Mr. Ketcham." She planted a kiss on his chin. "I missed you."

"I missed you too." He looked at Jessica. "Who's Mr. Ketcham, Red?"

She tossed her head. "Robert is a very wealthy gentleman from New York," she said loftily. "He's due here any minute. I'd appreciate it if you would leave before he arrives."

"Ashamed of him?"

"Of course not!" she snapped. "I just don't relish the thought of having you look down your nose at my friends."

"I don't care who you see as long as you realize that Franny's welfare comes first. I should have expected you to cave in as soon as my back was turned. You're not the type to stick with anything for long. I can find other arrangements for Franny."

"What do you mean? I have no intention of giving up Franny!" Her heart began to pound. Surely he wouldn't go back on their agreement.

"The deal was that you would stay here and care for Franny with money you'd earned with your own hands, that you would raise her by Christian standards." He turned to the door. "We'll talk about this later. I'm disappointed in you, Red." He wheeled with Franny in his arms and stalked out the door.

Jessica stared at the shut door and swallowed hard. Tears pricked her eyes, and she blinked them back fiercely. She wouldn't cry. He wasn't worth it. He obviously cared nothing about her if he would insist that she work such long, hard hours. Most men coddled and protected women. But not Reverend Clay Cole. Oh, no! He thought a woman should work at a humiliating job that left her sweaty and exhausted. Well, she'd had enough of him and his strange ideas for one day!

She lifted her head at the knock on the door and fixed a smile on her face. Some men knew how to treat a woman, so why was she wasting her tears on a man like Clay? He wasn't worth it.

Furious, Clay strode toward the hotel with Franny in his arms. As soon as his back was turned, Jessica had reverted to her old ways. A man was always the solution for a woman like her. Just when he was beginning to hope she might really have some inner beauty inside that pretty head, she proved him wrong. He knew he seemed cruel and uncaring, but she had some lessons to learn. She would never grow if all she had to do was bat her beautiful blue eyes and some man would fall all over himself to meet her every wish. How would she ever realize her need for God when she never went without her slightest whim?

"Are you mad at me, Uncle Clay?"

Franny's sad little voice interrupted his thoughts. "Of course not, Muffin. I'm just thinking." He gave her a little squeeze.

"Oh. You were frowning. Are you mad at Jessie? She tooked really good care of me." She peered anxiously into his face. "I don't want you to be mad at Jessie. She cries at night sometimes."

He smiled at her matter-of-fact tone. "She does, huh?"

Franny nodded. "I asked her one time why she was crying, and she said she missed her brother, but that I made everything all better."

"That's 'cause you're a special little girl. You make everything better for me too. I didn't know Jessie had a brother."

"His name is Jasper, and he had a tadpole in his bedroom. The policeman came and took him, and Jessie never saw him again." Woe was in her voice when she told him the story. "He was just a little boy. Can the policeman take me away from you and Jessie?"

"Of course not," Clay assured her. "You'll always be with me." He couldn't speak for Jessica. He felt unutterably weary. They had reached the boardwalk, so he set her down and took her hand. "Are you hungry?"

"Uh-huh. Can I have some chicken?"

"Chicken it is."

The restaurant was filled with the appetizing aromas of fried chicken, beef roast, coffee, and bread. Clay's mouth watered when he saw a waitress go by with plates of fried chicken. It sounded good to him too. He found a table near the window and ordered chicken for both of them, then turned to look around the room.

Several soldiers waved to him, and a couple stopped by his table to welcome him back to the fort. The place was mostly filled with miners and soldiers, but he caught an occasional glimpse of an emigrant family. The waitress had just brought them their food when he saw Jessica come in the door accompanied by a good-looking man of about forty-five. He had dark hair with wings of gray, and he seemed very attentive to Jessica.

The noise in the hotel stilled suddenly as the other men stared at her too, but she seemed oblivious to the attention. *She's probably used to it,* Clay thought morosely. A woman with her beauty was used to being ogled and cosseted wherever she went. That was probably another reason this past month had been so hard for her. Maybe he was expecting too much from her. How did he expect her to suddenly change who she was overnight?

He was surprised by the jealousy that burned in his chest. He felt a shaft of panic. When had he begun to care about her? He thought back to the kiss they had shared just before Ellen's death. Jessica's lips had been soft and pliant under his own, and she'd not shown the experience he had expected. His pulse raced at the memory, and he determinedly stared down at his plate. He couldn't let his feelings get the best of him. She wasn't a Christian.

As he ate his supper, he tried to pay attention to Franny's chatter, but his eyes kept straying to Jessica's red curls. She talked animatedly with the man, who kept his gaze fastened on her face. The fellow was obviously smitten. Clay watched as Jessica threw back her head and laughed. Her melodious laughter made other heads turn. Even Franny turned around in her seat at the familiar sound.

"It's Jessie!" She slid from her chair and evaded Clay's restraining hand. "Jessie!"

Jessica turned at the sound and opened her arms. Clay saw the way her face lit up at the sight of Franny. *She really does love her.* He'd never been totally sure of her motives before, but the adoration on her face was obvious. Franny hurtled into her arms, and Jessica kissed her, while the man looked on with an indulgent smile on his face. It was a proprietary smile, as though he were looking at his own wife and child. Maybe that's what Jessica and Franny needed: stability with someone who could provide for them. Did he have the right to deny them that?

He rose slowly to his feet and sauntered toward the other table. "Sorry; I couldn't stop her when she realized you were here."

Jessica gazed up at him with a look on her face that made his heart leap. It almost seemed like the same look she gave Franny. *Stop it!* She was a master at making men fall in love with her. She played with men's hearts like men played with cards. He needed to keep her character well in mind.

"Enjoying your supper?"

"Very much."

Her companion stood, and she smiled at him. "I'd like you to meet Robert Ketcham. Robert, this is Franny's cousin and coguardian, Reverend Clay Cole."

Clay shook the man's hand and was impressed with his direct gaze and firm shake. He wanted to find a reason to dislike him, but if first impressions were anything to go by, he wouldn't find a thing wrong with the other man.

"Please join us," Robert said politely. "We were just about to enjoy a piece of Martha's famous apple pie." He gestured at the two empty seats.

Clay wanted to refuse, but he also didn't want to seem churlish. He smiled his thanks and took Franny from Jessica, then placed her on a chair and scooted her up to the table before sitting down across from Robert. He might as well find out as much as possible about the situation while he was here.

"What do you do?" he asked Robert. He listened as Robert explained his business and his desire to discover new markets and horizons. He seemed like a nice guy. Clay didn't want to like him, but he couldn't help himself.

As soon as they finished their pie, Clay took his leave and left Franny with Jessica. She was heading back to the cabin anyway, and he needed to get away somewhere and think. He was shocked at how much the thought of Jessica being interested in another man shook him. He walked slowly through the dusty streets, looking up at the stars. The whine of the sawmill had stilled, and he heard frogs croaking in the stillness.

His cabin was cold and lonely when he shut the door behind him. He lit a lantern, then started a small fire to take the edge off the chill and looked around his cold, empty room. This was likely all his life would be: a series of empty rooms where he hung his hat for a few days or weeks before he moved on to the next place. Would the Lord ever give him a home of his own, his own family, and his own church? Did he even want that? Jessica stirred a sense of longing he'd never thought to have. He poked the fire dejectedly, then picked up his Bible. He was never alone, and he knew it. There was no sense in wallowing in self-pity.

He thumbed through the pages and found Psalm 84:10, one of his favorite verses.

> For a day in Thy courts is better than a thousand. I had rather be a door-keeper in the house of my God, than to dwell in the tents of wickedness.

Instead of stopping there, he read the next verse. He didn't remember reading the verses with quite the same meaning he saw now.

> For the Lord God is a sun and shield: the Lord will give grace and glory: no good thing will He withhold from them that walk uprightly.

No good thing. Did that mean a family someday, a godly wife, and a house-ful of children? He closed the Bible with finality. Why was he thinking like this now? He bowed his head and asked God to take these feelings from him. Whatever the future held, he was sure of one thing: Jessica DuBois wasn't part of it.

Robert pressed Jessica's hand and wished her a good night before slipping off into the dark night. She stood for a moment on the front stoop with Franny in her arms and listened to the crickets. It was a peaceful night, but she felt far from settled. Clay had ruined everything. One look at those broad shoulders and warm gray eyes had shattered her resolve to leave Fort Bridger by whatever means it took. Oh, she still intended to leave with Robert if she could, but her courage was gone. It would be so much harder with Clay here. She would have to fight her feelings for him every minute as well as focus on winning Robert's affections. Of course, that deed was already well on its way to accomplishment. He had been an easy target.

She had been conscious of Clay's gaze all evening. She'd tried to act gay and uncaring, but it had all been a facade. She was so tired of playacting, tired of living up to everyone else's expectations of who and what she should be. She suddenly wanted to sit and talk with her mother, but there never seemed to be any time for just the two of them anymore. One member or the other of her mother's new family was always demanding her attention. *Maybe I should make more of an effort to be friendly with my cousins,* she mused. She needed someone to fill this empty ache inside her.

She undressed Franny and slipped her into her nightgown, then read her the Bible verses Clay had prescribed for the night. Every night it got harder and harder to read those verses. They seemed to mock her. She could never hope to be good enough to understand what they meant. Tonight's verse, John 3:3, was a good example: *"Verily, verily, I say unto thee, Except a man be born again, he cannot see the kingdom of God."* She wasn't sure exactly what being born again meant, but it sounded life-changing and alarming. She hated being confronted every night by these Scriptures, but she had promised Clay to teach Franny. The problem was it was hard to explain something she didn't understand herself.

She kissed Franny good night, then went to the stove and heated some water for tea. She missed Ellen. Ellen always seemed to know what to do about everything. She needed a friend. But there was no one.

She jumped when someone knocked at the door. Her heart pounded. Was it Clay? She hurried to the door, but it was Miriam who stood scowling at her when she opened the door. Her cousin pushed past her without a word, then stood and glared at her with her arms folded in front of her.

"Your mother sent me to fetch you," she said abruptly.

"What's wrong?" She couldn't keep the alarm from her voice.

"We've been ranked out and have until eight o'clock tomorrow morning to get out!"

"Oh, no!" It was a common practice in the army for a superior officer to demand a lower officer's quarters on short notice. "Where will you go? The fort is filled to capacity." Jessica's thoughts raced as she tried to think of any empty buildings or cabins she'd seen.

"That's why your mother wants to talk to you. I'm supposed to stay here with Franny."

Jessica glanced at the little girl and saw she hadn't been disturbed by the knock on the door. "All right," she said reluctantly. "I shouldn't be long. Thanks for staying."

Miriam looked surprised at the thanks but nodded.

As she hurried across the parade ground, Jessica wondered if the tension between her and Miriam was her fault. Had she been so prickly and unapproachable that the other girl had retaliated in kind? It was something to consider.

The DuBois residence was a bustle of activity when she entered. Caleb and Uncle Samuel were piling boxes and crates in the hall while her mother and Bridie packed breakables in wooden crates filled with hay. Her mother looked up and saw her, then burst into tears.

"Jessica, you must help us!" She fluttered her hands. "We've no one else to turn to."

Jessica was bewildered. "What can I do, Mama? Do you want me to talk to the colonel?" It probably wouldn't help. He'd lost his interest in her since Major Adams had brought his daughter to the fort.

"We need a place to stay, Darling. Can we stay with you?" She saw Jessica begin to frown and hastened to add, "Just for a little while. Something else will open up soon."

"But. . .but, Mama, my cabin is tiny!" Her thoughts whirled as she tried to think where she could put all of them.

"I know, Darling, but there is nowhere else for us to go." Her mother looked at her piteously, and more tears trickled down her cheeks. "We can't sleep on the streets."

Uncle Samuel cleared his throat gruffly. "Your mother is right. I've searched high and low for a place for us. It's either your cabin or a tent."

Jessica couldn't imagine her mother in a tent. "I don't suppose I have a choice," she said grudgingly. "But I have no idea where we can put your things."

"I've already thought about that," Uncle Samuel said. "I've arranged for some tents for the majority of our things. We'll set up camp outside your back door for easy access to our possessions. All we'll bring inside are the beds and necessities."

"I suppose that will work." She still wasn't happy about it. The freedom of her own place was one of her only compensations for her new life. Now she would have to put up with Miriam and the rest of them. She sighed.

Her uncle didn't wait for her to change her mind. "Caleb, come with me and we'll see about setting up the tents. Bridie, you go spell Miriam with little Franny, and let Miriam help Letty with the packing for awhile. Once the tents are set up, Caleb and I will bring the beds over. Jessica, you rearrange your things to find room for us, and we'll be over soon."

She bristled at his order but said nothing. She knew he was right. But if he thought he could talk to her like that all the time, he would find out he was wrong. She sighed again and went to make room for her unwelcome visitors.

Chapter 9

The tiny cabin was packed with beds and people. Clothing hung from nails on nearly every available bit of wall space. A three-quarter-sized bed was pushed into one corner for Bridie and Miriam to sleep on; a small cot for Caleb crouched behind the front door, and Uncle Samuel's four-poster bed hid behind a makeshift screen in the corner farthest from the door. Jessica had taken down Franny's cot, knowing that the little girl slept with her much of the time anyway. Their bed was repositioned along the wall by the bed for Bridie and Miriam. There was barely enough room to walk around all the beds.

Franny had awakened during the commotion of moving but soon fell back to sleep when everything settled down. No one else had slept much, though. Breakfast had been a fiasco with everyone cross and irritated with one another. Jessica had barely had enough bread to feed them all toast. She seethed with resentment when her uncle made a pointed comment about a good housewife always being prepared. How was she supposed to know she would suddenly be feeding an additional five people? She held her tongue, though, knowing they were all tired. She didn't want to add to her mother's burden.

After breakfast, she stood and tied her hair back in a kerchief. "I'd better get to work. Bridie, would you want to help Franny with her lessons this morning?"

Bridie looked up in surprise, but she didn't object. "Where are her books?"

Jessica sighed. "I have no idea. The last time I saw them, they were under her cot, but I don't remember where we moved them last night when we took the cot down. She'll help you find them." She looked around at the rest of the family. "Anyone want to help with the laundry?"

Miriam sniffed disdainfully. "Not me. I'm meeting my friends at the millinery shop about ten."

Her father frowned. "I think not, young lady. Your mother will need your help to get all this stuff sorted out."

"She's *not* my mother. She's my aunt." Miriam scowled.

Jessica's mother fluttered her hands. "That's fine, Samuel," she murmured. "I can get things done by myself."

Jessica's simmering temper boiled over. "Mama, there is no reason for you to have to do everything by yourself! Everyone lives together, and everyone needs to share in the responsibility." She began to angrily push boxes out of the middle of the floor. "Miriam, you start unpacking these boxes. Caleb, get some money from your father and run to the sutler's store for some more flour and any other supplies Mama thinks we need." She turned to Bridie. "We'll forget Franny's lessons for today. I wasn't thinking about just how much needed to be done."

Miriam put her hands on her hips and tossed her head. "You can't tell me what to do. You unpack the boxes yourself."

"Fine," Jessica said sweetly. "You do the men's laundry, then."

Miriam stared at her for a moment, then turned and began to empty the nearest box with angry, jerky motions.

Uncle Samuel cocked an eyebrow. "Changing your tune a bit, aren't you, Missy? Where were you when your mother and cousins were doing everything without your help?"

Jessica shrugged. "We were living under your roof then, but now we're under mine. I've realized how hard a household is to run. I've grown up some, I guess."

"It's about time." He turned and went toward the back door.

Jessica flushed hotly at the reprimand. "You've got a lot of nerve criticizing me when you married my mother just to have a servant. Why don't you try treating her like a wife for a change?"

Her uncle turned scarlet with rage, but she didn't wait for a response. She had work to do. Her back stiff with anger, she slammed the door behind her and went to the laundry tent.

She had just hung up her first load of laundry when Clay strolled up. Her mouth grew dry at the sight of his broad shoulders.

"Hey, Red, what's going on at your place?" He took his hat off and raked a hand through his hair.

"Mama and Uncle Samuel were ranked out last night." She turned her back to him and proceeded to dump another load of dirty clothes into the steaming tub of hot water. Her hands were trembling, and she hoped he didn't notice. She wished she didn't feel like this every time he was near.

He whistled softly. "Bet your uncle is madder than a bear with a sore foot. Where'd you put them all?" He put his hat back on his head and followed her when she ducked inside the tent for more soap.

She sighed. "It was hard to find room. We're all falling over one another."

"I can imagine."

His intent gaze made her flush, but hopefully he'd assume it was from the fire. "Robert seems like a nice guy. How long have you known him?"

"What is this, an inquisition?" she snapped. She brushed past him abruptly.

He held up a placating hand. "I didn't mean it to sound that way. I was just interested."

"Well, get uninterested. My relationship with Robert is my own business! You can keep your nose out of it." She saw his nostrils flare, but he managed to control himself. Jessica was impressed with his restraint. Why was she trying to goad him into losing his temper? Was it because she wanted him to show some sort of jealousy? She almost laughed out loud at the thought. There wasn't much chance of that.

"Let's start this conversation over," he said finally. "I really wanted to just come by and see how things went with Franny while I was gone. Did you have any problems? How are you for money?"

"Fine," she said shortly. She softened her sharp tone. "Franny can say all the alphabet and seems to be sleeping better. She doesn't cry out for her mother in the night as much as she did." She snapped a wet sheet briskly and hung it on the line. "As far as money goes, I'm about out, but I get my first army paycheck tomorrow. We're doing fine."

"What about her spiritual education?"

She glanced up at his anxious tone and was snared by the warm look in his eyes. She was lost in the depth of his gaze for a few long moments. Did he feel anything for her? Anything at all? She swallowed the lump in her throat and dropped her eyes.

"I've read the verses you picked out every night. Now that you're back, we'll attend the service tomorrow." She looked up and was surprised at the look of amazed happiness on his face.

He dropped his gaze and hooded that expression of incredulous joy. "I thought I might have to threaten and beg to get you to come."

"I'm not a complete heathen," she said. "I may have trouble believing all that stuff myself, but I want Franny to have the best of everything."

His expectant look faded. "I'll see you tomorrow then." He stepped toward her and tucked a stray curl back up into her kerchief.

Her breathing quickened at his nearness. She inhaled the clean, male scent of him. For just a moment, she thought he might kiss her, but he stepped back and tipped his hat. "Sit in the front row. It will inspire me."

As he walked away, her breathing returned to normal. She was determined not to let him see how much he affected her. She'd better invite Robert to attend the service with her so Clay wouldn't suspect how much she cared. She'd had all the humiliation she could take.

❦

Clay straightened his cravat and slicked down a stray cowlick. The last few services he had held before he had to go on to Colorado had been well attended, and he hoped this one would follow the same pattern. What he was nervous about was whether Jessica would really come with Franny. He wanted her to love and know his God so badly. He shied away from examining just why it was so important to him. He loved sharing God's love with people, but he wanted this for Jessica even more than usual. He tried to tell himself it was for Franny's sake, but was that the only reason? He shook the thought away, clapped his hat on his head, picked up his Bible, and walked across the parade ground to the unmarried officers' quarters. The meeting room already had soldiers milling around near the door. He tipped his hat as he entered the room.

He walked up the aisle created by the benches the men had hauled in. *Please, Lord. Please let her come today. Let her hear something that creates a hunger in her heart to know and love You.*

When he looked up, Jessica was coming down the aisle on Robert's arm. They looked like a happy, prosperous family with little Franny in tow. Clay's insides clenched strangely, but he wouldn't let himself think about how he felt. He had to put those feelings behind him. They sat right in the middle of the front row, but he couldn't read Jessica's face at all this morning. She looked like the cool, self-possessed young lady he'd first met all those months ago. Perhaps it was only wishful thinking to imagine he saw a change in her.

He welcomed the worshipers to the service. As he looked around, he estimated the group at about twenty-five, a respectable showing for a busy fort like Bridger. He led the group in two hymns, then opened his Bible. "Turn to Proverbs 6," he told them and began to read. " 'These six things doth the Lord hate; yea, seven are an abomination unto Him: a proud look, a lying tongue, and hands that shed innocent blood, an heart that deviseth wicked imaginations, feet that be swift in running to mischief, a false witness that speaketh lies, and he that soweth discord among brethren.' " He saw Jessica's eyes widen as he read the verses.

He plunged into his sermon, and it was as though he preached to her only. As he talked of sin and forgiveness offered by God through Jesus Christ, he felt a connection with her he'd never felt with anyone before. It was almost as though he could see right into her soul and see the pain and longing she had to be clean and forgiven. Her eyes grew huge in her face, and he thought there might be tears hiding there. When the service ended, he tried to make his way to her, but several soldiers hurried forward to talk to him, and she left before he was finished. He rejoiced at the soldiers' response to his message, but he was frustrated that he couldn't talk seriously with Jessica. Maybe he could catch her alone after lunch.

Jessica could barely keep her face in order following the sermon. She trembled all over but was careful to hide it from Robert and her family. She just wanted some time alone, but where could she find it? Every square inch of her cabin was filled. Her mother began to prepare lunch while Jessica got Franny out of her good dress and into her everyday one. Her mother urged Robert to stay for the meal, and he accepted quickly. Jessica was almost glad for an excuse to avoid dealing with her thoughts for awhile.

After the meal, Robert asked her to take a walk. She caught up her wrap as a barrier against the autumn wind and followed him out the door.

They left the confines of the fort and followed the river past the old corral. Robert took her hand and stopped in the middle of the path. He raised her hand to his lips and looked at her intently.

"We haven't known one another very long, my dear girl, but my time here is short, and I feel I must speak. I believe we would deal very well together. I could provide a good home for you and Franny." He pressed her hand ardently. "I have the highest regard for you, and I'm asking you to consider becoming my wife."

This was exactly what she'd hoped for—a man who would care for her and Franny, someone with wealth and prestige, someone kind and easygoing she could manipulate to her will. She regarded him thoughtfully.

He hastened to sweeten the deal. "I plan to build us a lovely home by the sea in San Francisco where you can entertain whenever you want. As my wife, you'll be respected and revered. Please say you'll come with me."

Why was she even hesitating? She smiled at him. "Let me think about it."

He frowned. "Of course. I know this is very sudden, but surely you must have had some idea of my intentions."

"I can't say I'm surprised, but marriage is a big step."

"True," he admitted. "But winter will be here in a few weeks, and we must move quickly."

"Give me until tomorrow." She knew she was going to accept; it was the only solution for her and Franny, but she saw no reason to give Robert the upper hand. She must begin as she intended to go on. If she accepted his proposal, she intended to be firmly in control.

"Very well. Until tomorrow." He bent his head to kiss her, but she turned her head, and his lips landed on her cheek. The touch of his lips didn't stir her as Clay's did, but she would have to learn to deal with that.

When Robert left her at her door, she couldn't bring herself to go inside the cabin. She knew she would walk in on a scene of utter bedlam, so as soon as Robert's back disappeared from view, she cut through the yard and around the back of the cabin. A creek angled through the property, and she had always wanted to take time to follow it for a ways. She knew Bridie would keep Franny entertained, and she just needed a few minutes to herself.

The cold air whipped through her wrap. Winter came early to the mountains, and she wasn't looking forward to it. The thought of hanging clothes to dry in the frigid air was not appealing. The other laundresses didn't associate with her, or she would have asked one of them how they managed. She smiled wryly. She no longer fit in with any group. The officers' wives felt they were too good for her, and the other women thought she was above them.

The trail beside the creek suddenly petered out, and she sat on a flat rock overlooking the gurgling brook. Alone with her thoughts, Clay's words from his sermon came back to her mind. That Scripture he'd read about the seven things God hated had described her perfectly. She had done every single one of the those things, even the shedding of blood. Although she hadn't actually killed anyone, she *had* tried to arrange Sarah Campbell's elimination. Clay had explained how such a person might be forgiven, but she didn't think it was really possible. Not for someone as uncaring about other people as she'd been.

Tears filled her eyes, and she stooped and picked up a flat stone and tossed it across the water. It skipped three times before sinking beneath the water. That was just how she felt sometimes: No matter how hard she tried to keep her head above water, she always ended up sinking.

She swallowed the lump in her throat. Robert's offer seemed like an answer to her, but it was really more of her own manipulation of events. What was it Clay had said? Oh, yes, something about a heart devising wicked imaginations. That's what she'd done all her life—schemed and planned to get her own way.

Suddenly, the thought of leaving that kind of life behind and becoming someone with character on the inside was overwhelmingly appealing. Fear clamped her chest, and she felt like she couldn't breathe. It was a terrifying moment just imagining what it would be like to turn loose the reins of her life and trust an unseen God for her future. She didn't know if she could do that. She wasn't very good at trust.

Trembling, she sank to her knees. "Oh, God, I'm tired of running, tired of messing up my life. I know I've done a lot of things You hate, but I'm going to try to change. Maybe then I'll be good enough for You to think about forgiving me. I want to be more like Ellen was." She could change. Once she was a better person, maybe God would forgive her.

She started back toward the cabin. A few flakes of snow drifted down, and the wind was stronger than before. Before she'd gone ten feet, the snow was swirling down heavily. Unfamiliar with the path, she found herself stumbling over rocks and branches. Minutes later, she wasn't sure where she was.

Was this a blizzard? It was only October. Panicked, she began to run but tripped over an uprooted tree. Which way was home? She stopped running and shouted, "Help!" The snow muffled her voice, and her panic rose. What if no one could hear her? The wind penetrated her wrap, and she shivered, realizing that the temperature had plummeted in the last fifteen minutes. Already the snow covered the tops of her boots. She'd never seen snow come down so fast and thick.

She was near tears when she saw the dark outline of a building ahead. Eagerly, she hurried toward it. It wasn't until she was nearly at the door that she recognized her own cabin. She let herself in the back door and found Uncle Samuel pacing the floor, her mother in tears, and Miriam sitting sullenly in the corner.

"It's about time you got back," her uncle barked. Worry creased his forehead.

"What's happened?" Her voice rose in alarm. She glanced around the room. "Where's Franny?" A ball of foreboding curled in the pit of her stomach.

"Bridie took Franny for a walk, and they aren't back yet."

She put a hand to her throat. "I have to find Clay." She knew he would want to be out there looking.

"Caleb went to get him." Her uncle went to the door and threw it open. "I can't even see across the parade ground! I don't know how we'll find them."

Dread rose in her throat again, but she forced it down. "Clay will find some soldiers to help look for them. I'm going too." She took her heavy coat from a nail on the wall and pulled it on. It was made of beaver and fairly warm, but the matching muff wasn't practical for the search. She wound a scarf around her throat and followed Uncle Samuel out into the driving snow. What did Franny have on? Surely it was only her thin wrap.

In the stifling white again, she was immediately disoriented. All she could do was follow her uncle's burly form through the drifts. The snow was already nearly knee-deep in places, and it was hard plodding through it. They stopped outside the corral, and Uncle Samuel shouted for his horse to be brought.

"You can't accomplish anything here," he told her. "Go back with your mother. We'll find them."

She knew he was right. If she insisted on mounting a horse and following him, they would soon be searching for her as well as Bridie and Franny. She didn't know her way around the countryside well enough to be of any use in this white wilderness. She wasn't even sure she could make it back to the cabin without help. But how could she go back to the warmth and safety of the cabin with Franny out here somewhere?

Uncle Samuel swung up onto his gelding, and both man and horse disappeared from view almost instantly. She turned and began to follow her tracks back to the cabin. New snow had already nearly filled them, so she hurried as fast as she dared. By the time she reached her cabin door, the tracks were nearly impossible to see.

She stumbled in the door and nearly fell into her mother's arms. The blazing fire was a welcome sight. Her mother helped her out of her coat and settled her near the fire.

"I'll get you a cup of tea, Dear." She put the kettle on the stove to heat and sat beside Jessica.

"I should never have let them go," her mother fretted. "I'm so sorry, Darling."

"It wasn't your fault," Jessica said. "None of us realized this storm was blowing up. I almost didn't make it back from my walk." It did no good to blame them. It was entirely her fault. "I'm the one responsible for Franny," she told her mother. "I should have been here."

Her mother looked up in astonishment at her words. The surprise on her face would have been comical if they weren't all so frightened.

The teakettle began to whistle, and her mother jumped to fetch it, but Jessica restrained her. "I'll get it, Mama. You've waited on everyone today. Sit here and rest." She got to her feet and took the teakettle from the stove. *I have to be a better person,* she told herself. Maybe then God would save Franny.

When she handed her mother a cup of tea, she could see her mother didn't know what to think of her actions. Had she really been that thoughtless and domineering that her mother would show such astonishment over a simple cup of tea? The thought was disquieting. Did anyone ever really know how others perceived them?

She took a cup across the room to Miriam. "Why don't you join us by the fire?" she asked.

Her eyes narrowed in suspicion, Miriam took the proffered cup of tea. After studying Jessica's face a moment, she grudgingly took her stool and moved it beside her aunt.

"Are you feeling all right, Dear?" her mother asked.

"Just worried," Jessica said.

"You should be worried all the time then," Miriam said snidely. "You'd be easier to live with."

Jessica was silent for a moment. "I know I've been difficult, but I've grown up some in the past few months. I hope you'll both give me another chance." It was as close as she could come to an apology right now.

"Of course," her mother said faintly.

Miriam scowled but said nothing. Her face showed her skepticism.

Jessica put her cup on the hearth and went to the door. Opening it, she peered through the snow again, but the heavy snow continued to block any view of even the officers' row across the parade ground. She was trying to cling desperately to the hope that God wouldn't allow anything to happen to Franny. Or Bridie. She'd barely spared a thought for her younger cousin, she realized. Bridie must be terrified, especially knowing she was responsible for Franny as well. If the men didn't find them soon, they would freeze.

Chapter 10

Plodding through the snow, Clay swayed from weariness. He couldn't feel his fingers any longer, and he longed for a warm fire and dry clothes. But Franny was still out there somewhere. Even with the snow muffling everything, he would have heard a shot announcing the girls had been found. He'd prayed and begged with all his strength for God to spare both girls, but he was beginning to lose hope. He didn't see any way they could have survived this blizzard. It would take a miracle for him to ever feel Franny's arms around his neck.

He should never have allowed Jessica to keep her. She'd been out gallivanting with Robert instead of taking care of her responsibilities. When would he learn never to trust a beautiful woman? He had thought she was beginning to change, but it was just wishful thinking.

Drifts of snow came nearly to his horse's belly in spots, and Misty had trouble breaking her way through. He knew she was exhausted too. She was used to carrying him long hours, but this kind of weather was hard on man and beast both. The trouble was that with the heavy snowfall, the girls' bodies would be buried beneath the drifts, and they wouldn't find them until spring. He pushed the thought away. He would look until there was no longer any hope.

He stopped near an outcropping of rock and slid to the ground. The snow came up to his knees, and he staggered toward the shelter of the rock face. Misty followed, her head down to avoid the wind. Just around a straggly pine, he saw a small cave in the rock face. Was it possible they could have found shelter there? Hope rising in his chest, he knelt, brushed the snow from the entrance, and peered inside.

His heartbeat slowed when he saw the empty spot. Discouraged, he mounted Misty and turned her head toward the fort. The snowfall grew steadily lighter, and he could actually see the stockade ahead. He would let Misty get some rest and borrow someone else's horse for the morning.

When he dismounted, he found Samuel preparing to go out again himself. "Any sign at all?" he asked the older man.

Samuel shook his head. "Not a trace."

Neither man looked the other in the eye. Clay knew his hopelessness would show on his face. The girls had spent the entire night out in this blizzard, and he didn't see any way they could have survived. Even if they had found a cave to huddle in, the mercury had fallen below zero. They surely would have frozen to death by now.

The snow had completely stopped, though. Clay asked for a fresh horse and swung into the saddle, then turned the horse's head toward the gate. Before he got more than a couple of steps, Jessica called to him.

She looked much different than she had a mere twenty-four hours ago. Her tangled hair had obviously not been combed, and her tearstained face was white. She put her hand on the horse's bridle.

"You have to find them, Clay." A sob caught in her throat.

He stared down at her. "Your concern is a little late, Jessica. Where were you when she wandered off into the snow? It's a little like Ellen's death, isn't it? You're always too busy thinking of yourself to worry about other people."

She was crying in earnest now. "I deserve everything you say to me, Clay. But please, you must keep searching. I just know she's still alive." She put a hand against her breast. "I can feel it here, in my mother's heart. You can't give up."

"Oh, I'm not giving up on Franny. But I'm giving up on you. God will have to reach you in His own time. I can't handle anymore." He wheeled his horse around and took off as quickly as the drifts would allow. He only caught a glimpse of her stricken face before she turned and went back the way she'd come.

Sobs racked Jessica's body, and she struggled not to fall in the drifts along the parade ground. She couldn't blame Clay for giving up on her. She had been willful and headstrong, without a care in her head for what anyone else wanted. She should have been home caring for Franny instead of leaving it to Bridie to do. And his reference to Ellen hurt badly, because she knew it was true. If she hadn't fallen asleep, she could have kept Ellen from choking on her own vomit.

How could You let her die, God? It was my fault, not Ellen's. She wanted to raise her fists in the air and scream. Staggering from both the weight of her guilt and the thick snow, she fell facedown in a huge drift. "God, why?" she screamed. The wind caught her words and flung them away like so much chaff. "Take me instead! You always take the ones I love. What about me, God? Take me and spare my Franny."

The cold wet from the snow seeped through her clothing, but she welcomed the discomfort. She wanted to die, to just lie there and let the icy grip of the snow take her away from the pain here. She had never felt such despair, not even when she had lost Jasper and their mother.

"God, help me," she moaned. "I can't take anymore. I want to believe in something better than this life, in Someone who loves me no matter what I do. Why is it so hard?" She sobbed aloud again and burrowed deeper into the snowdrift. "Forgive me, Lord, forgive me."

Memories of the things she'd done and the people she'd hurt paraded through her memory like accusing judges. Belinda Cramer who had snubbed her at a party, and Jessica had found revenge by stealing her fiancé, Richard Drewy, until she tossed him aside for the next handsome face; the parade went on and on, culminating in her behavior at Fort Laramie with Sarah Montgomery and again at Fort Phil Kearny with Emmie Croftner. How could even a loving God forgive such terrible behavior? What were those sins again? Oh, yes, a proud look, a lying tongue, hands that shed innocent blood, a heart that devises wicked imaginations, feet that run to mischief, a false witness that speaks lies, and sowing discord. She'd done them all and more.

"Can you forgive me, God? Will You forgive me and accept me as Your child? I know I'm not worthy, but Clay said Jesus took my punishment. I have nowhere else to turn, Lord. No one but You."

A quiet peace stole into her heart.

I am here, Beloved. I have always been here, waiting for you to turn and acknowledge Me.

She felt the sense of God's presence with a sense of wonder. Everything Clay had said was true! She pushed her hands into the snowdrift and levered her way out of the clinging snow enough to sit up. Managing to get her feet under her, she stood up and brushed the wet, caked snow from her coat. She took a deep breath.

She had some terrible things to face in the next few days, but she could sense the bedrock of God under her feet, holding her up. She would have to live with her guilt for not caring for Franny properly, but since God had forgiven her, maybe someday she could forgive herself, despite her grief. Clay was right about everything. She had killed Ellen and now Franny, but wonder of wonders, God loved her anyway. Gratitude, a totally unfamiliar emotion, welled up in her heart.

Clay knew he'd been out of line with Jessica, but he hadn't been able to hold his temper in check. It was his own fault for allowing her to get under his skin. But no more. He had only been telling her the truth when he said he was giving up on her. He was going to dig out and destroy the root of love that kept springing up in his heart. He didn't want to love a woman like her; moreover, he *would not* love her. And when he pulled little Franny's body out of the snowdrift she was lying in, it shouldn't be too hard to muster up dislike for the one responsible.

Plodding through the heavy snow, he found no sign of the missing girls. Growing more and more discouraged, by lunchtime he decided to check in at the fort. The crack of a rifle pierced the cold air, and he craned his head in the direction of the blast. Was it a signal? He rode in the direction of the shot and found three soldiers milling around a rock face about a quarter of a mile from the fort.

One of them waved to him. "Over here, Preacher! We found them!"

Lord, help me to get through this. He braced himself to see Franny's lifeless little body, forcing himself to go forward. He reined in his horse about five feet from the men and slid to the ground, then fought his way through the drifts. The snow was piled high in this section because of the way the rock formation angled. One of the soldiers moved, and he saw Franny's blond head. She was *standing!*

Clay ran the remaining few steps and scooped her up into his arms. Tears came to his eyes, and he let them fall unashamedly. Her face was white and pinched with the cold, but she seemed unhurt. How had she survived? He looked at Bridie. Her skirt hem was wet and dirty, and her hair hung on her shoulders in matted tangles, but they were both all right. He put an arm around her and hugged her too.

She burst into tears. "I was so scared, Clay," she sobbed. "The storm came up so fast; then I couldn't see anything. I didn't know what to do."

"Whatever you did, it was the right thing. You kept Franny and yourself alive."

"We found a cave, but it was just so cold. We huddled together at the back of the cave, but I started feeling really strange and sleepy and not cold anymore. Then Buster showed up." She pointed at the golden retriever a few feet away. Buster belonged to the post commander and everyone loved him. "Me and Franny curled up with him. He saved our lives, I know."

"I'm going to find him some meat when we get back to the fort." He knelt and patted the dog. "Good boy, Buster."

Buster woofed and thrust his nose into Clay's hands. It was almost as though he knew he'd done good. Clay swallowed hard and got control of his emotions. He had been so certain the girls had died in the storm. God had to have protected them. There was no other explanation.

"Let's get you both home. You need a hot bath and some food." He swung up into the saddle, and one of the soldiers handed Franny up to him. He settled her against his chest and gave his hand to Bridie. She swung up behind him and put her arms around his waist.

The trip back to the fort seemed long. Clay was eager to get Franny to a warm place and into dry clothes. News of the rescue had already spread throughout the fort by the time they rode through the gate.

Jessica's face was the first thing Clay saw when he stopped at the stable. Although pale and strained, she gave a glad cry when she saw his precious bundle perched in front of him.

"Franny!" Jessica stumbled forward and held up her arms.

The little girl practically fell into her embrace. "Jessie, I waited for you and Uncle Clay to come find me," she said reproachfully. "Me and Bridie was scared."

Jessica covered her face with kisses. "Sweetheart, we were so worried! Uncle Clay looked and looked for you. He looked for you all night."

Franny wound her arms around her neck and kissed her. "I missed you."

"I missed you too. Now let's get you home and into a hot bath and clean clothes." She carried her off toward the cabin.

Franny waved to Clay. "Bye, Uncle Clay!"

Clay lifted his hand, then dropped it to his side as soon as Franny was out of sight. He was going to have to make other arrangements for Franny. Things couldn't go on like they were. He just didn't trust Jessica. When her own interests were at stake, she forgot everything and everyone else.

He plodded through the snow to his quarters, where he looked around the room as if seeing it for the first time. He'd never noticed before how stark and unwelcoming his tiny room was, holding only a bed, a battered stove with two pots, a rickety table he'd dragged out of the trash heap when an officer had moved on, and a chair with one leg missing that was propped up with a piece of wood. It was not a very welcoming environment for a little girl, but it would have to do. He'd see about adding a few furnishings.

What about when he was traveling? For the first time, he wondered if the Lord was telling him it was time to settle somewhere and build a ministry in one place. But where? And how did he know for sure? He decided he would spend some time in study and prayer and listen to what God was saying. Franny was his family now, and he had a responsibility to her.

He closed his Bible and drew his pocket watch out. Nearly four o'clock. He sighed and picked up his coat. He wasn't looking forward to the coming confrontation. He didn't like hurting Jessica, but it had to be done. She had to know he couldn't let her negligence continue.

Knocking on the door, he wondered how he would manage talking to her alone. He owed her that much. Taking Franny would be humiliating enough without having her family witness it.

Miriam opened the door and smiled when she saw him. "Clay, did you come to join the party?"

"Party?"

"Aunt Letty baked a cake, and we're celebrating the safe recovery of Bridie and Franny. You have to join us." She took his arm and pulled him inside.

Jessica was sitting on the edge of the bed reading Franny a story. Franny's hair curled around her shoulder in shiny ringlets, and she was snuggled with her favorite blanket against Jessica's side. She looked happy and contented. They both looked up when they heard him stomp the snow from his boots.

Jessica's smile brightened when she saw him, and Franny hopped to the floor and ran to him.

"Uncle Clay, Grandma Letty bakeded me a cake. It's chocolate. But I can't eat any 'til after supper. I'll share with you."

Grandma Letty. Franny was being assimilated into the DuBois family more every day. Before too long she would be calling Jessica Mama. He had better do something quickly. He looked at Jessica and said abruptly, "Can we talk?"

Her smile faded, and she looked apprehensive. "Of course."

"Not here. Would you care to join me for dinner at Bridger Inn?" The impersonal inn would be good.

"What about Franny's party?"

"We'll be back in about an hour."

Her gaze probed his face; then she nodded. "I'll tell Mama and get my coat."

While she explained to Letty, he told Franny they were going out for a bit but would be back in time to share her chocolate cake. The little girl wanted to come with them, but he promised her a licorice stick if she was good.

The only sound as they walked to the inn was the crunch of their boots in the snow. Clay wanted to wait until they were seated to tell her his decision. Jessica kept her head down as she tried to keep up with him. He realized he was going too fast and slowed his steps.

It was early yet for the inn's supper crowd, so they were able to be seated in a corner table away from other customers. Jessica slipped off her coat, and he took it and hung it up on the hook behind her chair, then sat across from her. She sat and folded her hands in her lap, her blue eyes fixed on his face as she waited.

He had to admit she looked lovely tonight. Her hair was up in a mass of curls with a few escaping to caress the smooth skin of her neck and cheeks. It was too bad she wasn't the angel she looked on the outside. Clay clenched his jaw. *Get on with it,* he told himself. *Waiting is not going to make it any easier.*

He took a deep breath. "I've been doing a lot of thinking since last night," he began.

"So have I," she said softly. "About more than you know."

"Ellen expected me to take care of her daughter," he said. "I've neglected that responsibility and palmed it off on you. I can't do that any longer."

"What do you mean? You haven't asked me to do anything. I asked for Franny." Her voice rose a bit, and he heard the alarm in it. Grimly, he went on.

"I'm going to have to cancel our arrangement. I'm taking Franny to live with me."

"You can't do that! We agreed this was best for Franny!" She gripped the edge of the table and leaned forward. "She needs a mother; you can't just rip her away from me. She loves me, and I love her!" Her lips trembled, and tears pooled in her eyes.

"I'm sorry, Red, but I really feel this is for the best." It took all his resolve not to back down. "It's really too much for you."

"You think I neglect Franny?" Fire sparked in her eyes, and she started to rise from her chair but sank back down with an obvious effort at control.

"You can't just have someone else watch her every time you want to flirt with a man."

"Is that what this is all about? You're angry because Bridie watched her while I went for a walk? Robert had already brought me home; then I went for a walk alone. I wanted to think."

Was that really what was bugging him? That Jessica was seeing another man? He hated to think he might be that petty. "I just don't think you realize what a responsibility raising a child is. I think she needs to be with me. You're trying; I can see that. But I want Franny to have a firm spiritual foundation. Almost losing her made me realize how vital it is that she know and understand about God. Life is precarious. I couldn't live with myself if someday Franny slips away into eternity without Jesus. Right now she's too young to totally understand, but it won't be long before she'll be able to choose to follow Christ or the world. It's better to wean her away from you before she gets any more attached."

The tears finally spilled over onto her cheeks. "Please, Clay, you can't take Franny. It would be devastating to her! Give me one more chance."

"I'm sorry, Red. Someday you'll see this is for the best. You'll marry and have your own children. Franny would just be in the way."

Mattie brought their food, and they both fell silent. Jessica kept her gaze down and chewed on her lip. As soon as the waitress walked away, she began again.

"Give me just until Christmas. You said you had to get to three other forts by Christmas. Finish your trips for the year, and we'll reevaluate at the beginning of the year."

He hardened his heart against her entreaty. "I've made up my mind, and there's nothing you can say to persuade me differently. It really is for the best."

Fresh tears poured from her eyes, and she jumped to her feet. "I won't let you! You can't take her away!" She grabbed her coat and ran from the dining room. The other customers in the room stared, then went back to their meals. Clay threw his money on the table and grabbed his coat too. Suddenly, he wasn't very hungry.

Jessica sobbed as she hurried across the parade ground. The tears were of anger and pain both. How could he do this to her or to Franny? Didn't he understand how traumatic it would be? And how could he take Franny into danger when he traveled? He'd have to find someone to care for her, and there was no one else to do it but Jessica.

What could she do? Could she ask the colonel to intervene? But he had no real authority over Clay. Would he listen to Robert? As soon as the thought struck her, she discarded it. In spite of what Clay had said, her relationship with Robert was how this all began. He might say he thought Robert was a good man, but she doubted he really believed it. Could he be jealous? Did he care anything about her at all? He was just too hard to read.

She had gotten control of her emotions by the time she got back home. Franny looked up with a bright smile when she came in.

"Where's Uncle Clay? He promised to come for my party."

"He'll probably be here soon," she said. Would he insist on taking Franny tonight? She gave herself a mental shake. He wouldn't want to upset her right after her ordeal in the blizzard. Perhaps she could think of something in the next few hours to change his mind. She couldn't give Franny up.

Clay showed up for a few minutes and ate a piece of cake with Franny. When he finished, he asked Jessica to walk him to the door. A ball of dread formed in her stomach, but she followed him to the door.

"You need to tell her tomorrow," he said. "I'll pick her up tomorrow night. I have a few things to do to get ready for her."

"Please don't do this, Clay," she whispered.

His jaw tightened. "I'm sorry, Jessica. I have to think of Franny."

The funny thing was, she believed he was sincere. She couldn't fault him for not loving Franny. She knew what kind of man he was. He wouldn't be doing this if he weren't totally convinced it was best. But there had to be a way to convince him he was wrong. She stared into his eyes and saw no reason to hope. She struggled not to cry, to beg, but the only way she could hold her tongue was to walk away and let him see himself out.

She lay awake long into the night, considering her options. She could let Franny go without raising any more arguments; she could go to the commander and hope he could change Clay's mind; she could marry Robert and ask him to leave tomorrow with her and Franny before Clay could find out and stop them. The last option held the most appeal. It would be just what he deserved for his pigheaded refusal to see reason. She and Franny would have a good life with Robert.

Trust Me, Beloved.

Her eyes widened. Trust God with something this important? Where had that idea come from? How could she just sit back and do nothing? What if He didn't have the same idea about what was best as she did?

Trust Me.

The persuasion to do just that tugged at her again. This was a chance to put her new faith to the test. If God proved His faithfulness in something so important to her, He could be trusted with anything. But did she really believe that? How could she go about finding the courage to take her hands off the situation and leave it in God's hands?

"God, help me," she whispered. "Help me to trust You enough to allow You to work. It's going to be hard. I don't know if I have enough faith."

She would do it. She would tell Robert she couldn't marry him. Once that safeguard was removed, she would have no one to depend on but God. She would have to trust Him. A sense of peace stole over her, and she finally fell asleep, but her dreams were haunted by images of Franny clinging to her in tears.

Her mother was already banging pots at the stove when she awoke. Franny still slept, and Jessica breathed a sigh of relief. She wanted to tell her mother what was happening first and ask her to help. She slid out of bed and slipped behind the makeshift screen to wash and dress. When she emerged, she was determined to hold to her resolve from the night before. With God's help, she would hold her temper in check, allow Clay to take Franny, continue her work as laundress, and stand back to see God work. She knew it would be the hardest thing she had ever done.

Chapter 11

Clay had managed to find a cot for Franny from Mrs. Captain Berry, some pots from the quartermaster, and he had bought some extra supplies from the sutler's store. He set the cot up in a corner of his room and roped off a partition around it with an old blanket. Mrs. Berry had also given him a flat but still serviceable pillow and a faded pink quilt he spread over the bed. He thought the little "room" looked welcoming with a gingham-covered barrel sitting beside the cot as a washstand. He put a battered trunk at the foot of the bed for Franny's clothes, and on the floor beside the bed he threw a hooked rug he'd bought from an emigrant family passing through Bridger. Not a bad day's work. He hoped Franny would like it.

At six o'clock, he made a final inspection, then grabbed his coat and headed toward Suds Row. At least Jessica wouldn't have to wash clothes anymore. She could marry her rich suitor and go off to a life of leisure. He had been out of his mind to try to change her.

The door was opened almost immediately at his knock. He had expected to find Jessica and Franny both in tears, but Jessica was smiling when she opened the door.

"You're a bit late," she said cheerfully. "Franny was beginning to fret."

Had she told Franny yet? Did she think he'd changed his mind?

Franny squealed and ran to him. "Uncle Clay, Jessie said I get to go stay with you for a little bit."

He picked her up and kissed her. "I'm real excited about it too."

She patted his face. "I'll try not to let you be sad," she said. "Mommy and Daddy are in heaven together. They aren't sad, and Jessie says we shouldn't be too sad either. We can miss them, but we should be happy they are with Jesus. That's what Jessie says."

His mouth dropped open, and he quickly shut it. He shot a look at Jessica, but she just looked serenely back. "Jessie said that?"

Franny nodded. "Jessie is going to learn me to read in the evenings after she's done working. I told her she could stay for supper sometimes. She can, can't she, Uncle Clay?"

He heard the anxiety in her voice and hastily reassured her. "Jessie can come and see us anytime she wants."

"And I can spend the night with her sometimes, and she can sleep over with me sometimes."

He wanted to laugh but kept his face sober. "Well, you can spend the night with her sometimes."

Franny frowned, but before she could argue, Jessica interrupted.

"You'll want to come stay here so you can see Bridie."

The little girl nodded vigorously.

"Her things are all ready," Jessica put in before Franny could come up with anything else.

Franny was delighted with her "room." She put her doll, Molly, on the faded pink quilt and helped Jessica pack her clothes away in the trunk. Clay was astonished at how easily the transition was accomplished. Jessica must have handled the explanation very well. He had to admit to himself that he was surprised by how amenable she had been. He'd expected another argument at least, and maybe a downright screaming fit. Something was different about her, but he couldn't put his finger on what it was.

Jessica kissed Franny good-bye, then quickly left, but not before Clay saw tears in her eyes. She had been braver than he would ever have believed.

The next morning, he took Franny with him and went to see Colonel Edwards. The post commander's office was empty, an unusual occurrence for which he was glad.

Colonel Edwards rose when he saw Clay. "Preacher! I haven't seen you in awhile. How long are you in town for?" He indicated for Clay to have a seat. "Franny, would you like a licorice stick?" Anticipating her response, he was already reaching for one in the glass container on his desk. "What can I do for you, Preacher?"

"Circumstances have changed a bit for me, Colonel, and I need your help."

Colonel Edwards leaned back in his chair. "Shoot."

"I would like to establish a church here at Fort Bridger. A real church, not just services that meet in the officers' quarters. Fort Bridger is becoming a stopping-off place and is growing fast. We need to have a spiritual base before immorality and drunkenness get out of hand. I'd like some help getting a spot and having a building erected." This was a subject close to the commander's heart, Clay knew. He'd asked Clay to consider making his home here several months ago.

The commander didn't disappoint him. "That's wonderful news, my boy. I've had a spot in mind for some time now. It's at the end of the main commercial district, and it should prove to be a good location for discouraging the drunken carousing from the bars. Let me show you what I have in mind." He rose, grabbed his coat, and led the way out the door.

Clay was impressed with the site. When he and the commander parted,

Colonel Edwards had promised to put some men on construction right away. Clay walked away with a sense of peace that he was following the Lord's leading. He had asked the Lord for an open door if this was what He wanted, and it wasn't just cracked open, it was wide open. He would be able to have a stable home for Franny as well as minister to those traveling through on their way west.

When he and Franny stopped at Bridger Inn for lunch, he saw Robert eating alone at a table. Clay hesitated, then walked back to see him.

Robert looked up and pointed to the other chairs. "Join me."

Clay sat Franny down on a chair and dropped into the one beside her. "When are you and Jessica leaving?" he asked Robert.

Robert looked at him blankly. "What are you talking about? I'm leaving tomorrow morning, but Jessica isn't coming with me."

"I didn't know," Clay said lamely, unable to stem the tide of relief that washed over him. She wasn't marrying Robert! He forced down his elation. It changed nothing. She was still the same person, self-centered and willful. He wished she could be different, that he could be free to love her, but it was not to be.

Clay prayed over the food, and as they ate their lunch, Clay had an opportunity to talk to Robert about his soul. Robert promised to think about it. As they parted, Robert shook his hand. "Take good care of her," he said.

Clay looked down and put his hand on Franny's golden curls. "I will."

"I mean Jessica," Robert corrected. "She's more fragile than she seems."

Clay's gaze met that of the other man. "Things will sort themselves out."

"She loves you, you know."

Shock rippled through Clay's chest. Jessica loved him? He frowned. Had she told Robert a lie to get out of going with him?

Robert answered his unspoken question. "She didn't tell me, but it was obvious. You must be blind if you can't see it." He cleared his throat with an embarrassed cough. "Take care, Preacher. Pray for me sometimes." He gave a small wave and stepped out into the melting snow.

Clay was still in shock. What made Robert think Jessica loved him? Could it be possible? Much as he'd tried to forget it, he still remembered that kiss. He shook his head to clear the memory. Robert had to be just rationalizing Jessica's rejection of his proposal.

Jessica pushed the hair from her face and thrust her hands back into the hot water. Only two more pairs of pants, and she was done for the day. She missed Franny's chatter with a fierce ache. The past two weeks had seemed interminable.

One good thing had come from the storm's enforced togetherness: She had finally seen that most of the fault with her cousins had been on her side. The Lord opened her eyes to her attitudes, and she softened her tone to Miriam. Miriam began to respond, just as Jessica had once responded to Ellen. With time, Jessica felt she might be able to share her faith with her cousin.

Her uncle had even seemed to be kinder to her mother. She wasn't sure if he had actually taken a look at himself after Jessica and his sharp disagreement the morning he and his family were ranked out, but he had told her mother he would begin to look for a striker to help once they got in quarters of their own again. The pinched look around her mother's eyes had eased, and she looked almost happy lately.

Jessica still saw Franny three nights a week and taught her lessons, and last weekend Clay had allowed Franny to spend the night on Saturday, but the tiny cabin echoed with silence most of the time. Jessica could only continue to bring her pain to God, trusting that He would somehow work everything out.

She still hadn't told anyone that she had accepted Christ. She wanted them to see a difference in her and ask if she had become a Christian. She'd gotten some strange looks, but so far no one had asked.

"Help me hold onto Your promise to work all things out for my good," Jessica whispered. She hung the last pair of pants up to dry and dumped out her water. Her hands throbbed like a sore tooth. The cold coupled with the soap and water had left them cracked and bleeding.

She put a bleeding knuckle in her mouth and dashed through the rain from the tent to the cabin. It had rained for three days now. First the weather had warmed enough to melt the snow, then the rain had started. She was heartily sick of waking to gray, dreary skies every day.

Her second paycheck had come last week, and she had considered catching a stage to Boston, but she just couldn't leave Franny. It would be like leaving part of herself behind, so she had grimly continued on with her duties. She was determined to stick it out until God showed her another direction. He seemed to want her here, and here she would stay as long as she had breath and courage left. It was already nearly Thanksgiving, and she thanked God daily that He had helped her make it this far.

She put a kettle on the stove to boil water for tea, chilled to the bone from the damp. The sound of several shouts outside made her turn, and when the shouts changed to screams, she ran and threw open the door. The sight that greeted her made her stagger back.

A wall of water roared down the swollen river that ran through the middle of the parade ground. She saw Lieutenant Sanders clinging to a splintered piece of tree before the roaring wave carried him from her sight. Barrels and household goods were carried along by the crest of the water and on past her. When the wave passed, the water lapped at her doorstep and rushed down the sides of the cabin. *The back door!* She slammed the front door shut and raced to the back, but when she threw the door open, water gushed across the threshold and over her boots. No way out there. She slammed the door shut and went to the front door again. She had to get to Franny!

She grabbed her shawl and opened the door again. Water rushed in, and before she could move, it was up to her ankles. She waded out onto the stoop and across the yard. The water was cold, and soon its icy grip lapped at her knees. The current made it hard to keep to her feet. She heard someone shout her name and turned.

Clay waved to her from a small boat. "Stay there! I'll come get you!"

"Franny?"

"Safe!"

Swaying from the fierce current, she nodded and waited for him to reach her. She saw a movement out of the corner of her eye and turned to look. Miriam, her eyes wide with terror, swept past her on the crest of a fresh wave. Miriam screamed, then her head slammed against an uprooted tree. Her eyes closed, and her head sank beneath the waves.

"No!" Jessica dove into the waves and frantically swam toward her cousin. "Hold on, Miriam!" She had to get to her. Her cousin wasn't ready to face eternity yet.

Miriam's body tumbled with the rest of the flotsam in the flood. Her head went underwater, and she floated limply; then another wave tumbled her again, and she floated faceup, her eyes closed. A barrel floated by, and Jessica grabbed it. Kicking her feet, she used it as a float and managed to get to Miriam's side. Holding one arm around the barrel, Jessica tried to reach her. Her fingers stretched as far as she could, but Miriam's sleeve evaded her. She tried again, leaning out as far as she dared without losing her grasp on the barrel.

"God, help me!" An infinitesimal stretch farther, and she snagged Miriam's sleeve. Quickly she pulled her toward the barrel. Was she dead? Jessica pulled her against her chest and held on until Clay could come.

Where was he? She sobbed with the effort of hanging onto Miriam's dead weight. Just when she thought she couldn't hold on a moment longer, she felt strong arms grab hold of her.

"I've got you, Red." He guided her hands to the side of the boat. "Hold on while I get Miriam in the boat."

He seized Miriam and dragged her into the boat; then Jessica was lifted free of the frigid water and pulled to safety. He threw a blanket over her, and she huddled into it gratefully. She coughed up the water she'd inhaled as she looked down at Miriam lying on the bottom of the boat. Her eyes were still closed, and blood ran from a cut on her forehead, but her chest rose and fell with her breathing. She was alive! Jessica breathed a prayer of thanksgiving.

She looked up and met Clay's anxious eyes. As their gazes locked, her breath caught in her throat. Surely that was love she saw blazing there! She swallowed hard and reached up to touch his face with a trembling hand.

"You're different. What's happened to you? The old Jessica would never have risked her life for someone else." He caught her hand and kissed her palm.

"I've found Christ," she said simply.

"You've become a Christian without telling me," he whispered. "I saw how much you'd changed, but I was afraid to hope it meant anything but willful determination." His thumb traced the contours of her lip. "Why didn't you tell me?"

"I wanted you to notice by yourself. I told God it was in His hands and He would have to work it out." She leaned her cheek into his palm.

"I love you, you know." He put his other hand against the other side of her face and leaned forward. His lips touched hers, and the warmth drove the last remnants of the cold from her limbs. Leaning into his embrace, she gave a sob and lurched forward, nearly tipping the boat.

As the boat steadied, Miriam opened her eyes. "I may have looked as cold as a wagon tire, but I'm very much alive. While I'm grateful you saved my life, Jessica, I've played dead all I'm going to. Will you two get on with the marriage proposal before we end up in the drink again? Just remember; I get to play bridesmaid."

Clay grinned, and Jessica made a noise that was half sob and half laugh.

"Guess we'd better make Franny a happy girl and give her the mama she wants. You game, Red?"

She put her hands around his face and kissed him very deliberately. "Just try to get away now," she warned with a glint in her eye.

Epilogue

December 16, 1867

What a wonderful day it is, Jessica mused. Her wedding day. They'd had to wait until another preacher could make it to Bridger to marry them, or they would have been wed already. As it was, the delay had allowed the men to throw up the small church building, so they actually had a real church to be married in. It had also given her time to write to Sarah Campbell and Emmie Liddle. She had wanted to thank them for their prayers and tell them about her accepting Christ. Although they had been unable to come to the wedding, she had received warm letters from both of them.

Miriam fluffed her hair and grumbled. "No one will notice me with you in the room."

"I'm the bride. It's supposed to be that way." Jessica laughed.

"I suppose." Miriam turned and looked toward the door. "What's keeping Clay?"

Jessica frowned. "I don't know. He said he was picking up a wedding gift for me." She sighed. "Silly man. I told him I was getting all I wanted with him and Franny."

Outside the door they heard the wedding music start up. "He must be back," Jessica said. "Do I look all right?" She pulled the veil over her face and adjusted it quickly.

"You'd put an angel to shame," her cousin said. "Let's go." She opened the door for Jessica and followed her out the door.

The seats were packed in the small church. Jessica smiled at her mother as she passed her, then fixed her eyes to the front of the church where the man she loved waited. Reverend Slagel, his bald head shining in the light, stood to the left of Clay. Another man stood beside him, but Jessica didn't pay any attention to either one of them. She drank in the sight of Clay in his black suit, his marrying and burying suit, only now he was the one getting married. She suppressed a smile. She was almost to his side when she spared a glance at the stranger.

Red-haired and freckled, the man looked vaguely familiar. Then he smiled at her, and she saw the small gap in his front teeth. She stopped short in the aisle. With a trembling hand, she raised her veil and stared.

"Sissy." He took a step toward her and smiled that gap-toothed smile again.

"Jasper?" She took a step closer. "Jasper!" With a cry she threw herself into his waiting arms and burst into tears. "Jasper, is it really you?"

The entire congregation stood and began to clap and cheer. Tears poured down her cheeks. Was this real? If it was a dream, she didn't want to ever wake up. Clay took her in his arms, and she buried her face in his chest. "How, where?" she began.

He grinned and kissed her tenderly. "God helped," was all he said.

Jessica finally composed herself and gazed into the smiling eyes of the most wonderful man in the world. With a deep breath, she put her hand in his and raised her expectant gaze to the preacher. Love had called, and her heart had finally answered.

TO LOVE
A STRANGER

For my beloved husband, David Coble,
whose many qualities serve as a model for all my heroes.
I love you, Dave!

Prologue

Fort Bridger, Wyoming, 1868

Y ou are not going to marry some chit you've never set eyes on, Jasper! I don't care what kind of promise you made."

Jasper Mendenhall winced at the strident tone in his sister's voice. Still, he was glad to hear her say his name in any kind of voice. Just a few months ago, he was certain he had no hope of ever seeing her again. Sent to different homes from the orphanage, their reunion had seemed a lost dream. But now at long last they had found each other.

He glanced at his sister. Her face had flushed bright with the intensity of her emotions and nearly matched her red hair. He resisted an urge to tell her to mind her own business. She was just showing sisterly concern, but it still grated a bit. He wasn't some callow sixteen-year-old youth. "I know her quite well, Jessie," he said calmly. "We've been corresponding for over six months. I appreciate your concern, but I must ask you to stay out of this."

Clay Cole, Jessica's husband, put a restraining hand on her arm. "Calm down, Sweetheart. It's not good for the baby for you to get upset." He guided his wife to a nearby chair. Once she was seated, he turned to Jasper.

"I can't say I'm in favor of this idea either. What do you really know about this woman? She could say anything in a letter. What is her name again?"

"Bessie. Bessie Randall. She's twenty-five and lives in Boston."

Jessica sniffed in disdain. "Huh! A spinster. She's probably homely as a fishwife, Jasper."

Jasper took a picture from the pocket of his uniform jacket. "See for yourself." He handed the picture to Clay. He glanced at it, then gave it to Jessica.

She stared at it and sniffed again. "All right, she's beautiful, and that makes it even worse. How can you even contemplate taking a lovely young woman out to the Arizona Territory? She looks refined and gently reared. Have you even told her what kind of conditions she'll be facing at Fort Bowie? Besides, something must be wrong with her if she's so beautiful and still unmarried. That pretty face probably hides a shrew."

Jasper and Clay looked at one another and grinned.

Jessica's flushed cheeks darkened even more, and she had the grace to look embarrassed. "I can see what you're thinking. And if it was once true in my case, that just goes to prove what I was saying. Now answer my question. Did you tell her where you were going to be stationed?"

Jasper shifted his gaze from Jessica's accusing glare. He hadn't told Bessie everything; he wanted to surprise her. He knew her well enough from her letters to know she craved adventure and would welcome the challenge. But what if Jessica were right? Was it proper to take his beloved to such a wild and untamed place?

"I thought not." Jessica's voice held a trace of satisfaction. "Jasper, think about this before you do it." Her voice softened. "You should wait until you find the right woman. I want you to have what Clay and I have. Don't settle for second best." She sent a tender glance toward Clay, and he smiled back just as tenderly.

Jasper wanted what they had too. And he was certain he and Bessie would have that, given time. He already loved her fire and spirit, the tenderness he found in her letters. He longed for a home and children. "It's already done, Jessie."

Clay and Jessica both looked at him sharply. He shrugged and looked away. They might as well hear it all. "She went through a proxy marriage and sent me the papers. I did the same and sent her the marriage lines and tickets last week. She's my wife, and I expect you to make her welcome when she gets here. I expect her within the month." He said the last firmly. Jessica could still be a bit of a termagant if she thought someone was taking advantage of her precious family.

Jessica rose to her feet and stared at him. The color drained out of her face. "Jasper, what have you done?"

Chapter 1

W hat are you doing in my room, Bessie?"

Bessie Randall heard Lenore's shrill voice as though from a great distance. The lines of writing wavered before her eyes, and the hand that held the letter shook violently. This letter couldn't mean what it said. It just wasn't possible. She stared at the words again, then closed her eyes briefly before turning to face her sister.

She held out the letter. "Can you tell me what this means, Lenore?"

Lenore's pale, lovely skin flushed with color. She shifted her gaze guiltily and swallowed hard. "What are you doing going through my things?" Her tone of outrage didn't ring true. Her blue eyes filled with tears, and she bit her lip.

"Don't try to change the subject. I was looking for my ostrich fan you borrowed for church last week." Bessie waved the letter in the air. "And it's a good thing I did. I would have never known about this. What is the meaning of this?" She desperately hoped there was some explanation other than the obvious.

Lenore gulped. "It's rather difficult to explain," she began. She wound a raven lock around her finger and avoided her sister's gaze.

"I should say so! There seems to be train and stage tickets here with the letter too. Tickets to Fort Bridger, Wyoming Territory—in my name." Bessie gave an incredulous laugh. Wyoming Territory! That was the last place she would want to go. She had heard about the Indian uprisings and bloodshed out there.

"If you would just let me explain," Lenore said with a pleading glance. "It started so innocently." She took a deep breath, then blurted it all out. "Jasper Mendenhall sent a letter to Marjorie's agency six months ago. I had just started volunteering there, and it seemed so romantic to help lonely bachelors in the West find mates. Jasper wanted to correspond with a young woman who was interested in marriage. I saw his picture and was quite taken with him."

Bessie took several deep breaths. It wouldn't do to get angry. "I knew no good would come of you helping out at that agency. Our cousin never had a lick of sense, and you can be just as bad."

Lenore colored and bit her lip at the reprimand. "I knew Mother and Father would never allow me to correspond with a man, especially a soldier. . .so I used your name." She wrung her hands and turned away from her sister's accusing glare. "I know it was wrong, but it seemed harmless at the time. I intended to break it off. Truly, I did. But it just escalated. He asked me to go through a proxy marriage and join him. It sounded so exciting, Bessie. I didn't think. I just did it." She turned back and stared at Bessie with pleading eyes. "You know how I've longed for adventure, how I've dreamed of going west."

"But this, Lenore!" Bessie's heart pounded, and dread congealed her stomach. She didn't want to think about this tangle or how on earth she was going to get her madcap sister out of this scrap.

Lenore glanced at her sister anxiously. "Since then I met Richard. I want to marry him, not some man I've never met."

Lenore had done some thoughtless things, but this was beyond the pale. To lead a man on like this—and a soldier serving his country, no less! It was despicable. Tears burned in Bessie's eyes. Would Lenore never learn to think before she leapt into things? "Are you telling me that you married this man? And falsely too, since you aren't Bessie Randall."

Lenore couldn't meet her gaze. "No, Bessie. It means you are married to Jasper. If you contest it, I—I think I could be arrested for forging your name."

Bessie gasped. The strength drained from her legs, and she sat on the bed. Taking a deep breath, she looked from her sister back down to the tickets and letter. She drew another shuddering breath. How was she to extricate Lenore and herself from this predicament? "I see," she said tonelessly. "You didn't want to marry a man you've never met, but you've married me to someone I've never heard of before today." She shuddered. "What am I to do?" she whispered. "What can be done?"

"Please don't tell Mother and Father about this," Lenore said. "Father said if I got in any more trouble, he would ship me off to Uncle Matthew's in Rhode Island. I can't leave now that I've met Richard. I intend to marry him."

Did Lenore ever think of anyone but herself? Bessie loved her younger sister, but this was too much. She didn't know if she could forgive her this. "How could you, Lenore? How could you bind me to some man I've never met?" She scarcely heard her own words, though. Her thoughts raced, trying to uncover a plan, any plan, to unravel this tangle.

Lenore burst into noisy sobs. "You hate me!"

Bessie pressed her fingers between her eyes where the persistent throbbing pulsed. "Oh, do hush, Lenore, and let me think."

Her sister's sobs tapered off, but Bessie could still feel her anxious gaze. Lenore turned away finally and began to fuss with her hair. Bessie stared at her sister. She was so lovely. Translucent skin, thick black hair, and a tremulous mouth that drew men like bees to honey.

Bessie paled in comparison. Her own hair was merely mousy brown, and the rest of her features were only echoes of Lenore's beauty. Lenore had beaus by the dozen, and although already twenty-five, Bessie had yet to receive her first proposal of marriage. And she might never receive one. She wasn't ugly, she thought. Just ordinary. Quiet and ordinary.

Lenore turned from the looking glass and gave her a coaxing smile. "I know you would like Jasper, Bessie. And you'd make a much better soldier's wife than I would." She crossed the room and sat on the bed beside Bessie. "You know Father says I shall not be allowed to marry until you do. What if you never marry? Richard may weary of waiting for me." She bit her lip, and tears hung on her lashes. "I don't mean to be cruel, but you're already twenty-five. Perhaps this is your opportunity."

And perhaps it was. How picky could he be if he were willing to marry by proxy? Maybe he would not really be expecting a beauty; simply a wife. He was expecting Bessie Randall, and she was Bessie Randall, not Lenore. If she didn't go, she would be breaking a promise made in her name. Her reputation and honor would be smirched. She supposed the marriage could be annulled or whatever one did in this kind of situation, but she had to be honest with herself. She longed for a husband and children of her own. Lately, she had questioned whether it would ever happen—or if she would die a spinster.

"I shall never marry a nonbeliever, Lenore. What of this Jasper? Have you inquired about his faith?" That was the most important thing. She could deal with other problems, but marriage to a nonbeliever would be intolerable.

Her sister brightened. "Indeed I did, Bessie. Jasper is a fine Christian man. His brother-in-law is a minister at Fort Bridger." Hope gave a sparkle to her eyes.

A minister's brother-in-law. It sounded good. Bessie pressed her fingers against the bridge of her nose again. Was this the Lord's will for her? She couldn't decide now. "I shall pray about it, Lenore. Say nothing to our parents until I make my decision." She started toward the door, then hesitated. "Have you a picture of this man? And might I see a letter or two?" Not that his looks were really important, but ill humor often showed in the expression.

"Of course." Lenore hastened to her dressing table and opened her jewel box. She extracted a photo and a bundle of letters tied with pink ribbon. "He is really a very nice man, Bessie. I think the two of you would deal splendidly together."

Bessie took the packet of letters and the photograph. "I shall be the judge of that, Lenore," she said. "Your judgment leaves much to be desired." She hardened her heart against the hurt expression on her sister's face and hurried to her own room.

Shutting the door behind her, she opened the balcony door and stepped onto the small porch overlooking the ocean. Settling onto the single chair, she turned her attention first to the photograph. Jasper was not what Bessie would call handsome, but his face was interesting. A nose a bit too large for his face with a hump in the middle as though it had been broken, thick brows, and a square jaw gave his face character. And there seemed to be a bit of humor in his eyes and in the tilt of his lips. The rapid pace of her heart stilled a bit. Character was all-important. She laid the photo on the table, then untied the ribbon on the letters. She began with the oldest.

By the time she was halfway through the letters, she knew she had to go. She could not disappoint this man. She had a heart of love to give, and this man seemed willing to accept a wife with open arms. Besides, the deed was already done. She was bound to this man, and she would see it through. If he chose to put her away once he saw her, that decision would be upon his head. She would go west.

Jasper paced the rough boardwalk outside the stage depot. The stage was never on time, and today was no exception. It should have arrived early this morning, and here it was nearly five. His heart pounded at the thought of finally meeting his lovely bride. Her letters had filled him with delight, for she had a fire and passion for life. He flipped the cover from his pocket watch again, then sighed and slipped it back inside his pocket.

Stepping into the street, he looked down the rough trail to the east. Was that a cloud of dust? Shading his eyes with one hand, he squinted. It was the stage. He stepped back onto the boardwalk and slapped the dust from his breeches with his hat. What would Bessie think when she saw him? Would she be disappointed?

The lathered horses stopped in front of him, and the stagecoach driver began to toss luggage from the top of the stage to the numerous waiting hands. Someone opened the stage door, and the passengers began to disembark. A corpulent man with a handlebar mustache climbed out first, while the stage springs groaned in protest at his weight. Next came an older woman with a baby in her arms, followed by a slight young woman in drab brown.

Jasper waited eagerly for several minutes, but no one else came out. He approached the stage door and peered in; two men in black suits were the only occupants. His heart fell. *She didn't come!* The telegram she had sent had said she would be on this stage. He felt a stab of alarm. Was she all right?

The young woman in brown averted her eyes when he turned back around. She had been staring at him, and the flush on her cheeks told Jasper she was aware of her bad manners. He had to pass her to reach the telegraph office next to the stage depot, and she cleared her throat when he reached her side.

"Excuse me, Sir. Are you—" She raised grave eyes and searched his face. "Are you Jasper Mendenhall?"

He stared down at her. She was a tiny thing, barely five feet tall, and slightly built. She wore a striking hat with an ostrich feather that dangled over one eye, but such an elegant hat looked out of place on such an ordinary woman. A tendril of light brown hair had escaped its pins and straggled against her pale cheek. Her gray eyes were enormous in her pinched face.

How did she know his name? A sense of unease swept over him. "Yes, Ma'am. I'm Jasper Mendenhall. May I assist you in some way?"

Her lips trembled, and her face became even more colorless. She swallowed hard. "I—I'm Bessie. B—Bessie Mendenhall. Your wife."

Jasper blinked; then the breath left his lungs. This couldn't be his Bessie! This little mouse of a woman? His Bessie was vibrant with life. She was dark and striking; she wasn't this little brown wren. Was this some kind of terrible joke?

The young woman saw his shock, and tears flooded her gray eyes. She fished in her reticule but couldn't seem to find what she was looking for. "I am so sorry," she whispered. "Have you a handkerchief?"

Dazed, he pulled a handkerchief from his pocket and handed it to her. He looked her over again, trying to find some resemblance to the photo he carried next to his heart. Perhaps the nose and mouth were similar?

She dabbed her pale cheeks, then straightened slim shoulders and craned her head to look into his face. "Is there someplace more private we can go to discuss this matter?"

Still speechless, he nodded. He was afraid to say anything; the hot, clamoring words rushing through his head would crush this pale bird. But he longed to shout them. Duped. He'd been duped. What a fool he was! Jessica and Clay had been right. How could he have been so foolish? He thought he knew his Bessie, but he was obviously wrong. As he led the way down the street to Clay's church, he couldn't bear to look at her.

When he realized Bessie was nearly running to keep up with his long stride, he slowed his pace and offered her his arm. The touch of her hand on his arm was loathsome to him, but he forced himself to accept it. Just what kind of woman would deceive a man the way she'd done? Contempt curled his lip, but he kept his mouth clamped shut. He didn't dare give vent to his feelings.

He opened the church door and ushered her into the cool interior. The calming atmosphere had an immediate effect on his temper. His breathing slowed, and he seated her in a pew and stood gazing down at her.

She fiddled with the tassels on her reticule. "I know how this looks," she began.

"Do you?"

She glanced up at his tight words. "Please, sit down. You'll give me a crick in my neck. You're very tall. Taller than I expected."

He sat beside her. "And you're not at all as I expected you."

She bit her lip. "I know. You were expecting Lenore. I didn't think to ask if she'd sent a picture of herself. When I saw your reaction, I knew she had."

"What on earth are you talking about?" he asked impatiently. "Who is Lenore? I don't understand anything except the fact that you deceived me."

She laid a small hand on his arm, and he had to resist the impulse to shake it off. "Lenore is my sister. My baby sister. She's twenty-one and should have known better, but she's the one who has been writing to you, using my name. I discovered these contretemps by accident, and I have come to honor the promise made in my name."

He stared into her face. Had she seriously thought that she could take the place of her lovely sister? Did she think him so desperate he would marry a bride sight unseen? Why hadn't this sister she called Lenore come? Twenty-one was of an age for marriage.

"I know how it looks," she said, nervously pleating the folds of her dusty, brown dress.

"I don't think you do," he said slowly. "If you did, you wouldn't have come. You would have written and explained the situation and given me the chance to set this tangle straight. Did you think that one woman was the same as the next to me?"

"Well, you did write to the agency looking for a wife," she began timidly.

"Yes, but I had the opportunity to choose for myself," he said hotly. "You had a picture of me, didn't you?"

She nodded uncertainly.

"How would you have felt if you had arrived and found you'd married a man of fifty with gray hair and whiskers?"

Bessie's face whitened as his words penetrated. "I see what you mean," she said softly. "You are displeased with my appearance." Tears swam in her gray eyes again. "Please forgive me, Lieutenant. If I'd realized you had a picture of Lenore, I can assure you I would never have come unannounced this way."

He folded his arms across his chest. "I find that hard to believe, Miss Randall." She had trapped him. Perhaps her younger sister had done it deliberately, since it was obvious this woman would never find a husband on her own. This woman had to have known what her sister was doing.

"Mrs. Mendenhall," she corrected softly. "We are legally wed. That is why I have come."

Jasper stared at her. He wanted to groan in frustration. What was he to do?

How could he untangle this mess? "That may be true, but under the circumstances, we may not be wed long. I will consult an attorney as soon as I can and see just where we stand."

Bessie's face paled even more, if that were possible. "You would send me home?"

He sighed and rubbed his chin. Against his will, pity stirred his heart. Perhaps this monstrous trick was not her doing. She didn't seem conniving enough for such a scheme. "You must be tired. Let me take you to my sister's home. She likely has supper waiting."

Chapter 2

Bessie saw every knothole, every nail in the boardwalk as she followed her new husband across the fort to meet his family. New husband. What if he set the marriage aside; what if she had come all this way only to be sent back in disgrace? He had done nothing to endear himself to her, but she couldn't bear the thought of going back to Boston. What would people think?

Fort Bridger bustled with activity. Men tipped their hats at her as they passed on the wide boardwalk, and several women stared inquisitively at her. They seemed especially taken with her hat. It was new and the height of fashion, but Bessie wanted to fling the hat away so she could creep through town without being noticed. Did they all know Jasper was expecting a beautiful wife?

"Jasper!"

She turned at the sound of a feminine voice. A dark-haired young woman stepped from the nearby general store and waved her hand in their direction.

"Miriam." Jasper tipped his hat at the vision in blue.

Her hat was perched atop a cluster of dark curls, and her gown, although last year's fashion, enhanced her slim figure. Bessie smiled at her uncertainly.

"Bessie, this is my cousin, Miriam," Jasper said.

Miriam tapped him on the arm with her fan. "Why do you insist on pretending we are related?" she pouted. "Jessica is my cousin only by adoption. You and I are not."

Jasper ignored the question. "Miriam, I'd like you to meet Bessie, my wife."

Miriam's eyes widened, and she shot a venomous glare at Bessie. Then her blue eyes filled with tears, and she took a step back. She whirled and practically ran down the boardwalk.

"She cares for you," Bessie said. She felt sorry for the girl.

Jasper sighed. "Perhaps, but the feeling is not mutual. She is too much like a younger sister. I never intended to hurt her, though."

He sounded grieved, and she realized he had a softer heart than she had imagined. Heartened, she took his arm again, and they continued down the boardwalk. Her mouth was dry at the thought of meeting his family. They would surely be just as astonished at her appearance as Jasper had been. Her heart fluttered in her chest like a frightened bird. At least he hadn't denounced

360

her and cast her off at first sight, but she had seen the disappointment in his eyes when he looked at her. And who could blame him? Lenore was a scarlet cardinal; she was a brown wren.

She drew her shawl around her shoulders to ward off both the chill of the wind and the coldness of his rejection. Had she really expected he would take one look at her and forget Lenore? She blinked back tears and squared her shoulders. She might not be a beauty, but there was more to being a good wife than beauty, wasn't there? Or was that truly the only important thing to men? She hadn't had enough experience to know.

Fort Bridger was an attractive place, she realized. The walk they were on led past neatly whitewashed homes with wide front porches and small yards with spring flowers poking up through the soil. Bessie liked what she saw. It was so different from Boston. They stopped outside a small, whitewashed cabin with a curl of smoke escaping from the chimney. The front stoop was barely large enough for them both to stand on.

Jasper rapped once on the door, then pushed it open. "Jessica, we're here."

The tantalizing aroma of beef stew wafted down the hall, and Bessie's stomach rumbled hungrily. The fare had been poor on the stage route; she'd eaten mostly hard bread and bits of salt pork. Now she was suddenly ravenous, but the thought of eating in front of Jasper and his family unsettled her.

A lovely red-haired woman hurried toward them. The gentle bulge under her skirt proclaimed the imminent arrival of a new baby. She had to be Jessica, Jasper's sister; they both had those vivid green eyes that tilted up at the corners. Her smile was welcoming, but it seemed to hold a touch of reserve at the same time.

She looked at Bessie, then turned to Jasper with a question in her eyes.

He cleared his throat. "Jessica, this is Bessie. Bessie, my sister, Jessica."

Jessica's mouth dropped open, but she quickly recovered and held out her hand. "Welcome, Bessie. I always wanted a sister. I look forward to getting acquainted. Come into the kitchen. We're about to sit down for supper, but we were waiting for you."

Bessie could sense the discomfort emanating from her husband. He hadn't introduced her as his wife. She had to wonder why, when he had told Miriam. Obviously, Jessica had seen the picture of Lenore as well. Oh, why hadn't she thought to ask Lenore if she had sent a photograph? Tears pricked the backs of her eyes, but she bit her lip and forced them away. She would take one step at a time.

A blond giant of a man stood when they came through the door. Unlike his wife's, his welcoming smile held no trace of surprise or wariness. Bessie warmed to him instantly.

"So, this is my new sister! Welcome to Fort Bridger, Bessie." His large hand enveloped hers.

A little dark-haired girl was seated at the far end of the table. "Hello. My name is Franny. What's yours? I'm four."

Bessie smiled at her in relief. She loved children. "I'm Bessie." She wanted to tell the child she was her new aunt, but what if Jasper didn't let her stay? "I'm very glad to meet you, Franny. I've heard lots about you from your uncle Jasper."

She sensed Jasper's start of surprise and realized how her words sounded. Like she had been corresponding with him. He would be convinced she had been a part of the deception. She swallowed the tears burning in the back of her throat.

Jessica interrupted before she could continue. "Sit down. You can tell us all about yourself over supper."

Bessie slid reluctantly into the seat beside Franny, and Jasper sat beside her. In spite of her hunger, she didn't know how she could force a morsel of food down with all of them looking at her.

Clay said grace, then passed around the stew. "Have you always lived in Boston?"

Bessie nodded. "All my life. This is very different from what I'm used to. It's lovely, though. Even the terrain looks wild and untamed."

Jessica glanced at her brother. "So you two have been writing to one another over six months, Jasper says. I must say, you don't look quite like your picture."

Bessie gulped and drew a deep breath. What should she say? The silence drew out for a long moment before Jasper cleared his throat.

"I mistakenly showed you a picture of Bessie's sister, Lenore." He turned to his brother-in-law and changed the subject. "Did you hear about the Sioux attack up north yesterday?"

Bessie was glad to let the men talk while she gathered her composure. Her cheeks burned with mortification, and she could barely hold the tears at bay. She thought she had done the right thing to come, but now she would give anything to be back in her home in Boston. This tangle became worse every moment. At least Jasper had made it seem as though it were his fault about the picture. That was kind of him. She sent him a smile, and he smiled briefly before he frowned and turned away.

She was aware of Jessica's probing gaze all through dinner, and although it was kindly, it still discomfited her. She knew her sister-in-law was full of questions. After supper the men retired to the parlor while she helped Jessica clear away the supper dishes. Franny helped them and kept up a steady chatter. Bessie was thankful for the distraction; she dreaded more questions from Jessica.

Just before they joined the men, Jessica put her hand on Bessie's arm. "I don't quite know what's gone on in this courtship, Bessie, but I want to tell you I think you'll be very good for Jasper." She hesitated, then continued with a sparkle in her eyes. "I was afraid he was getting some hothouse society beauty from the East who would lead him on a merry chase. If there's ever anything I can do to help, just ask. I'm here for you both."

Bessie lost the struggle against her tears. "Thank you, Jessica. I'll do my best to be a good wife." She struggled to stifle her sobs. What would Jasper think if he came in and saw her crying to his sister? He would despise her all the more.

"My goodness, don't cry. Jasper will think I've been asking nosy questions in here, and Clay will scold me." She gave her a handkerchief. "Things will work out. Do your best and trust God for the rest."

"Thank you," Bessie managed.

When the women entered the parlor, Clay smiled at his wife and patted the seat beside him on the threadbare sofa. Jasper gave Bessie a stiff smile and moved over so she could join him on the settee. She sat gingerly on the edge and tried not to crowd him too much. This was the closest she had been to him since she arrived, and she felt a flush warm her cheeks.

"I have some news for all of you," he announced once they'd all gotten settled. "The column leaves for Fort Bowie Tuesday."

"No, Jasper, not so soon!" Jessica wailed. "We haven't had enough time to get reacquainted, and Bessie and I have hardly even had a chance to talk."

What does he mean? Bessie wondered. *Where is Fort Bowie?*

He turned toward her. "I've been reassigned to Fort Bowie, Arizona Territory."

Bessie felt the blood drain from her face, and she felt light-headed. Apaches were in the Arizona Territory; she had heard many stories about the feared Indians. Did he expect her to go into a place like that? She wasn't going there; she would just refuse. She could either go home or stay here until he returned. He questioned the truth of their marriage, anyway. She opened her mouth to tell him so, but Jessica beat him to it.

"You can't take Bessie there."

"Bessie came all this way for a husband. I don't imagine she would allow me to leave her behind."

Was that a touch of mockery in his voice? He surely didn't really want her to go, did he? This would be the perfect opportunity for him to get rid of her. He smiled, a slight upturn of his firm lips, but his expression decided Bessie. If this marriage had any hope at all, she had to try. She knew he still questioned her motives, but perhaps on the long trip to Arizona Territory, she would have a chance to answer his doubts.

The candles had burned low by the time Jasper stood and announced it was time for bed. Bessie's heavy eyelids popped open at the mention of bed. Where was she to sleep? She couldn't share a bed with him yet. She just couldn't. Since he questioned the marriage, he surely didn't expect her to. Her mouth dry, she clenched her fists in the folds of her dress and frantically tried to think of an excuse.

"I've put a bed in the hall for Bessie, Jasper. Are you staying at Officer's Row for now?" Jessica asked.

Jasper nodded. "There was no reason to request quarters for just a few days." He laid a hand on Bessie's shoulder. "I'll see you in the morning."

Bessie breathed a sigh of relief when he turned and left the house. At least God had spared her that problem.

"I expect you're exhausted," Jessica said. "Let me show you to your bed."

She showed Bessie to her tiny curtained-off alcove in the hall and left her alone. Bessie sat on the edge of the bed and took off her ridiculous hat. She disrobed quickly and pulled her nightgown on, glad to be alone even though lonely tears burned her eyes. She missed her large room with the familiar quilt her grandmother had made. Why hadn't she told her parents the entire story? Her father would have found some way to fix it. Instead, she had allowed herself to be swayed by her sister's tears and her own thoughts of a husband and children. At this moment, she saw no way she and Jasper would ever have the kind of marriage she'd hoped to have. If Lenore had been here, she could have cheerfully throttled her.

Ever since Lenore was born, Bessie had been compared to her lovely sister. Bessie longed for someone to love her, to think she was wonderful. If she had only known Jasper had seen a picture of Lenore, she would have handled this very differently. She squeezed her eyes shut and whispered a prayer. *Please, Lord. Please make him love me.* It was her last thought before the long trip took its toll and sleep claimed her.

She awoke to the sounds of bugles and the shouts of men. Her eyes felt gritty, and she was reluctant to leave the warmth of her bed. For a moment, she wondered where she was, until she heard a deep voice call, "Six o'clock and all's well."

She was at Fort Bridger, and all was not well. Her new husband and his family would be looking her over again today. She sighed and sat up. Today was a new day, a fresh start. Lenore would have given up and gone home, but Bessie hadn't come this far to turn tail and run. She had always stayed in the background, but this was her only opportunity to prove to herself and to Jasper that she could be a good wife. Gathering her courage, she slipped out of bed and quickly washed. She pulled on a blue chintz dress, then pushed aside the blankets that curtained off her partition.

Her new husband sat beside the fire with Franny on his lap. Bessie could smell the aroma of coffee and fresh-made bread. For just an instant, she fantasized this was her home and Franny was her daughter. Her face burned at the thought.

Jasper was dressed in his blue uniform, his red hair slicked down with hair tonic. Bessie thought he looked very appealing. Not handsome, exactly, but strong and competent. His broad shoulders filled out his jacket nicely, and the tenderness in his face when he looked at Franny tugged at Bessie's heartstrings. Would he ever look at her like that?

Jasper looked up, and his gaze locked with hers. A slight hint of color rose on his cheeks.

He stood and sat Franny on her feet. "Run and tell Mama that Bessie is ready for her breakfast." He continued to regard her gravely for a moment. "Did you sleep well?"

"I don't remember," she said with a smile.

He grinned. "That's a good sign."

They stared at one another for a long moment, then Bessie flushed and looked down. "When do we leave for Arizona Territory?"

"Actually, the departure has been moved up. We leave tomorrow." His green eyes searched her face. "Are you sure you want to do this, Bessie? I have to be honest. It's a hard place to live. You seem—" He broke off and looked away.

"I seem what?"

His gaze caught hers again. "Frail, timid, shy. I'm not at all sure you are up to the challenge."

Bessie pressed her lips together. Appearances could be deceiving. Would a frail, timid woman even have come this far? She thought not. "Why are you saying this now? Why didn't you mention it in your letters?"

"The Bessie I thought I knew would have relished the challenge. I wanted to surprise her."

Bessie's temper flared at the condescension in his tone. "I'm not the frail bird you seem to think I am," she said hotly. "I may be small and plain, but I have grit and determination. I can see you're disappointed, but you're not what I expected, either. Your letters seemed to reveal a man with humor and good nature."

Jasper flushed and raised an eyebrow. "I never deceived you—I mean, Lenore. I never pretended to be someone I was not."

"I didn't either," she said. "The deed was done by the time I found out about it. What do you intend? Divorce?"

The ugly word hung in the air between them. "It might be an annulment," he said slowly. "When we reach Arizona Territory, I'll consult an attorney and see where we stand. We can then make a decision on what to do." He smiled. "If you're with me, at least I'll have someone to talk to when the wolves are howling outside the door and the scorpions are trying to get in."

The blood drained from her face at the word picture he drew. Then she saw the mirth in his eyes and realized he was teasing. She sent him a feeble grin. "I shall just invite them in for supper. That will frighten them away."

A look of surprise raced across his face, and he grinned. "Is your cooking that bad?"

"Well, let me put it this way. Indigestion would be the least of your worries."

He laughed, and Bessie liked the sound of his deep chuckle.

"We'll get along somehow," he said. "I'm a pretty fair cook myself." His smile faded, and he turned toward the door. "Be ready to leave at six."

She nodded and watched him leave. This was her first glimpse of the humor and wit she had seen in his letters. But what did it matter if he intended to find a way out of their marriage? She went to the kitchen to find some breakfast.

Jessica smiled in welcome. "Are you hungry? There's hot coffee and bread with jam."

"I'd love some. I'm famished." Bessie sat at the table and took the cup of coffee Jessica handed her. She was already beginning to feel Jessica could be a friend. She spread some blackberry jam on a slice of warm bread and bit into it, but her hands trembled.

Jessica sat beside her. "What's wrong? You seem distressed."

Bessie forced a smile. "Everything is so new and strange."

Jessica smiled. "I felt the same way!" She hesitated, and her gaze probed Bessie's face. "But I feel you're upset about something more. Do you want to talk about it?"

Tears burned Bessie's eyes. She longed to pour her heart out to this woman, but she was Jasper's sister; her loyalties would lie with her brother. Bessie bit her lip and shook her head. "I'll be fine in a few days," she whispered. "I thank you for caring, though."

Jessica smiled. "I want to help, if I can. I've so recently found Jasper, I want to do all in my power to ensure his happiness. And yours too, of course."

Bessie looked up curiously. "What do you mean, you recently found Jasper? The two of you seem so close."

Jessica smiled. "Our mother died when we were small, and we were adopted by different families. Neither of us knew what had happened to the other. Clay knew I had a brother and decided he would find him and surprise me. Clay's mother supported an orphanage in Texas and had some connections with the one in Ohio where Jasper and I were taken when Mama died. Clay's mother made some inquiries for him and found out Jasper's new name. Clay then tracked him down. He was stationed at Fort Laramie when Clay contacted him. At our wedding he was waiting at the altar as Clay's best man. It was the most wonderful surprise of my life." Her eyes were misty with remembered emotion.

Tears filled Bessie's eyes. Perhaps that was why Jasper was willing to take a mail-order bride: He had been deprived of a loving home when he was small, and now he craved a family and stability. She would do her best to fill that need. Lenore wouldn't have been capable of the selfless love Jasper needed—but Bessie was. She knew she could fill the void in his heart, if he would only let her in.

Chapter 3

The horses and wagons kicked up so much dust, Jasper could barely see. He glanced back and saw his new wife peering from the back of the covered ambulance wagon. Her small, pinched face was pale with fright, and she clung to the side of the ambulance with white fingers. His lips tightened. Her terror did not bode well for the rest of the trip. He should have sent her back to Boston. Let her family untangle this mess. If the noise and commotion frightened her now, what would she be like in the wilderness of Arizona Territory? He wasn't sure he wanted to find out.

But she had shown more grit than he had expected. He had thought she would insist on staying with Jessica or going back to Boston. Jessica seemed quite taken with her; she had even sent her precious seed packets along for Bessie. Jasper decided he would withhold judgment until he got to know Bessie better. And he had to admit he wanted to get to know her.

She was no beauty, but she was attractive in a quiet sort of way. And something about her spirit drew him. Some indefinable integrity and honesty was in her eyes—which was strange, considering how she had come to be his wife. But he didn't want to think of that. It hurt to know the woman he had thought he loved had duped him like that.

He dug his heels into his mare's flank and cantered back to the ambulance. Bessie smiled when he stopped beside the ambulance, and his spirits lifted.

"You doing okay?" he shouted above the commotion.

She nodded. "Are we leaving soon?"

"Any minute."

A wave of pity for her washed over him. What was he doing dragging a frail woman like Bessie to the deprivation they faced? "You can stay here with Jessica if you want," he told her. "At least until I see what Arizona Territory is like. I can decide what to do and let you know later."

Alarm raced over her features, and she shook her head. "I shall go with you," she said.

He nodded. "As you wish." He looked to the front of the column as the band struck up the familiar departure tune of "The Girl I Left Behind Me." He tipped his hat to her and wheeled his horse to fall in line with the rest of the officers. The die was cast now. It was too late to change anything. Bessie would just have to make the best of it.

Bessie clung to the side of the wagon ambulance as the conveyance lurched its way across the trail. She hadn't seen much of Jasper since they had started. She was the only woman traveling with the column, and the commander had graciously allowed her to make the ambulance her home for the trip. She shared it with an occasional soldier sent over for ointment for his feet or some such minor complaint, but for the most part, she was alone. Dr. Richter rode his horse and only stopped in if his services were needed.

She was thankful to not have to sleep on the ground. At night the wagons were put into a protective circle and tents were quickly erected. She had shuddered when she heard that several rattlesnakes were killed every night.

The spring sunshine brightened her spirits, and when the detachment stopped for a break, she decided she would get out of the ambulance and walk a bit. She could use the exercise since they had been on the trail a week now. Besides, she was lonely. She climbed down from the back of the wagon and tied her bonnet firmly under her chin. The band started its familiar tune, and the column began to move forward. She walked briskly along, but she soon began to cough from the dust.

She was about to give in and get back in the ambulance when Jasper saw her and cantered up to her side. "Tired of the wagon?" he asked.

"There are no springs in that thing. And there is no one with whom to talk," she told him.

His green eyes looked her over; then he sighed. "You want to ride with me for awhile? I can look for a spare horse."

His sigh stung, but she was determined not to go back to the wagon yet. Besides, how could they ever hope to make something of their marriage if they never spent any time together?

"I'd like that," she said. She had never ridden a horse in her life, but she wasn't about to tell him that. It would just reinforce his opinion that she was a frail, useless female. And how hard could it be to ride a horse, anyway? It looked easy enough.

He nodded and left her. A few minutes later, he returned with a golden-colored horse with black markings. She thought it was called it a buckskin, but she wasn't sure.

"Hop on," he told her. "We don't have a sidesaddle, but I think your skirt is full enough to allow you to straddle modestly."

She eyed the stirrups. Hop on? How exactly did one do that? The horse was so big. Her head barely came to the top of the horse's back. Tentatively, she grasped the pommel and forced her boot into the stirrup. She heaved her weight up with her hands while pushing with her foot and found herself standing in the stirrup. Unfortunately, she didn't have the least idea how to get into the saddle from there. She glanced at Jasper, and the corners of his mouth twitched.

"Wrong foot," he said gently. "You've never ridden before, have you?"

She felt the tide of heat on her cheeks and averted her gaze. She wasn't about to admit anything to a man who would laugh at her predicament. "I think I'll go back to the wagon after all," she muttered. She eased down, feeling for solid ground with the toe of her boot.

"I don't think so," Jasper said. "I got this horse for you, and now you're going to ride her. Put your other foot in the stirrup and try again." He slid to the ground and tied his reins to the side of the ambulance wagon. "I'll help you."

Bessie bit her lip and put her right foot into the stirrup. She pulled up again, and Jasper grasped her around the waist and helped her slide her left leg across the saddle. He seemed to touch her so matter-of-factly, but the warmth of his fingers brought heat to her cheeks.

He rearranged her skirt to make sure her legs were covered. "That wasn't so hard, was it?" He handed her the reins. "Think you can handle it from here?"

"Of course," she said loftily. What should she do with the reins? She would not ask Jasper. He already thought she was useless. Suddenly dizzy at the height, she clutched the reins in her hands and swallowed hard. She hadn't realized a horse was so tall. What if she fell off? But if Lenore could ride, she could too. She tried to remember how she had seen her sister handle the reins and moved them experimentally.

Jasper jogged ahead and caught the wagon. He untied his horse and swung into the saddle. "Follow me, and we'll go to the head to get out of this dust!" he shouted above the racket of wagons and horses. He wheeled his horse and started toward the front of the column.

Bessie tried to follow, but her horse didn't want to go in that direction. The mare tossed her head and jerked the reins from her hands, then took off at a dead run toward a grove of trees to the left of the wagons. Clinging to the pommel with both hands, she was jarred and jerked on the back of the mare. She knew she was going to go flying off at any moment. Would death be painful? She would find out soon enough. Frightened, all she could pray was a whispered, "Jesus, help me."

She thought she heard Jasper shout behind her, but she wasn't sure. She was going to die; she knew it. The trees closed in on her, and she shut her eyes. Before the tree limbs could crash into her, she heard Jasper shout.

"I've got you! Kick your feet free of the stirrups!"

She opened her eyes and hunched farther down onto the neck of her mare. She managed to work her boots free of the stirrups, then turned to look at

Jasper. Leaning out of the saddle toward her, his hand grasped for the reins and missed. Then his arm snaked around her waist, and he dragged her from the saddle and across his lap.

In the ignominious position of lying facedown across his saddle, she clutched his leg with both hands. The sweaty horsehair under her cheek made her wrinkle her nose in disgust, but she was too thankful to be alive to complain about the odor or her position.

"Whoa." Jasper pulled his horse to a stop.

Bessie took a deep breath and struggled to sit up, but she was trapped with the pommel digging into her stomach. Firm hands grasped her shoulders, flipped her over, and sat her up. There was little room for both of them in the saddle, and she was forced to hang onto him as he stared into her face.

"You could have been killed!" Dust streaked his face, and red spots of color marked his cheeks. His green eyes sparked with temper.

She coughed dust from her lungs. She had lost her bonnet somewhere, and her hair hung down her back and in her face. With trembling hands, she pushed strands of hair out of her eyes. She looked around and saw her mare drinking from the river under the trees. She looked back up at Jasper. He glowered at her. She hated for anyone to be angry with her. Perhaps a little humor would diffuse him. She tried a tentative smile. "Chirk up," she said. "I was just taking my horse for a drink. She got a little eager, but there was no need to overreact."

He stared at her, and his lips twitched. She smiled again, and his grin broadened. He pulled her against his chest and rested his chin on her head. She heard the thud of his heart under her ear and breathed in the musky male scent of him. When he pulled her away, she felt bereft.

He shook her gently. "I'm sorry I got so angry. It was really my fault. I should have led your horse. You look a little peaked. Are you sure you're all right?"

She smiled. "I will be if I can just lean against your chest again."

He laughed aloud then. "I think you got knocked on the head. You're behaving a bit strangely."

She had to admit to herself that she had never imagined she could be so bold. Maybe she had been hit on the head. She smiled up at him again. Maybe they could just stay like this forever.

He cupped her cheek with his hand, and she thought he was going to kiss her. But he jerked his hand away at a shout from the column.

"Lieutenant! Indians ahead!" A private waved to him from near the trees.

"Get the horse!" Jasper shouted at the private.

Bessie cowered against his chest. Indians! Her mouth dry with dread, she clutched his shirt in her fists and buried her face against him. He clutched her to his chest and urged his horse to a run.

She raised her head as they reached the wagons. The commander had already ordered the troops to get the wagons into a protective circle. They stopped at the ambulance, and Jasper handed her down to another soldier.

"Get her to safety," he told the sergeant.

Jasper looked for a long moment into her eyes, then wheeled his horse and dashed away. Bessie watched until he was lost from sight in the milling horses and men. Sergeant Crandall hurried her under the ambulance and covered her with a blanket. He lay on his belly beside her with his gun ready. Within moments, unnerving shrieks rent the air, and Bessie cowered and tried to look invisible. She had heard of the cries Indians made in battle, but she had never thought she would hear them herself.

She buried her head in her arms and prayed. *Keep him safe, Lord. Don't take him when we're just now starting to get to know one another.* The battle seemed to rage forever, then suddenly the shrieks died away until the only sounds were the shouts of the soldiers and the sharp reports of the cavalry rifles.

She got to her knees and began to crawl from under the blanket.

"Wait, Mrs. Mendenhall," the sergeant said. "I'm not sure it's safe yet."

"I've got to see if my husband is all right." Bessie crawled from under the blanket and the wagon. She just wanted to look into Jasper's green eyes again.

Pandemonium reigned in the camp. Dr. Richter saw her and motioned her over. "I have wounded and need your help."

She tried to protest; she had to find Jasper. But the doctor requested her assistance again, and she had no choice but to follow him inside the ambulance. It seemed like hours that she held compresses to bleeding wounds and soothed pain-racked soldiers. They all seemed to still at her ministrations, and Dr. Richter told her she had a healing touch.

When the last one had been tended to, she washed the blood from her hands and climbed out of the ambulance. Where was Jasper? At least he hadn't been among the wounded. But was he among the dead? She had asked about him, but no one seemed to know.

Her hair still hung down her back, and she knew she was a dreadful sight, but she didn't care. She had to find Jasper. Everywhere she looked she saw overturned wagons and crowds of soldiers standing around discussing the battle. When she asked several soldiers if they had seen Lieutenant Jasper Mendenhall, no one seemed to know where he was. She was beginning to panic when she caught sight of his familiar red hair.

He stood talking to a group of officers. His hat was missing, and he was dirty, but he seemed to be in one piece. Bessie paused, uncertain about disturbing him when he seemed to be busy. Then one of the soldiers nodded in her direction, and he turned and saw her. Their gazes locked, and she saw the same concern she felt mirrored in his green eyes.

He smiled then and hurried toward her. "I heard you were helping the doctor with the wounded. It was good of you to help." He took her hands.

She clung to his fingers. The touch of his warm hands calmed her, and a sense of belonging swept over her. She wanted to be his wife, and she was fast on her way to learning to love him. The thought frightened her. What if he didn't feel the same about her? But she pushed the thought away. This felt right; it felt as though God had put His hand of blessing on them.

"You're shivering." He took off his jacket and put it around her shoulders. Guiding her in the direction of the ambulance, he took her hand and walked with her. When they reached the ambulance, he peered inside. "I'm not sure where you'll be able to sleep tonight." He paused and looked down at her. "You could stay in my tent."

Her heart pounded in her throat at his words. In his tent? What did that mean? What did he expect? Was he ready to accept their marriage as true and binding?

As though he could read her thoughts, he brushed his knuckles against her chin and gazed into her eyes. "No strings," he whispered. "I'll get an extra cot. It will give us a chance to get better acquainted."

Wasn't that what she wanted? Then why was she so afraid? She swallowed her fear and nodded. "I'll get my things."

Chapter 4

J asper pushed the cot up against the wall. An empty cot like his empty marriage. What was the right thing? What was he to do? He didn't believe in divorce, but what about annulment, especially when he had been deceived? What would God expect? When he had first invited Bessie to stay tonight, he had been appalled at his own invitation. It was best not to get too close yet.

He saw her shadow hesitate outside the door to the tent. Was she going to turn and leave? He stepped forward and pushed up the tent flap. "I'm here. Come on in." He took her small valise and put it on the floor by her bed. She looked like a bird who might take flight at any time. The fading light silhouetted her slim figure and illuminated her hair like a halo. She had certainly acted like an angel of mercy today. The doctor had been very impressed with her.

"Shall we go to mess?" She needed fattening up. A strong wind would carry her to Arizona Territory by itself.

Bessie nodded. "Do you know what we're having?"

"Beans."

Her lips curved upward. "That's all we ever have. Do we ever get vegetables or fruit?"

"You mean like potatoes and apples? Is that what they're called? It's been so long since I've seen one, I'm not sure anymore. I don't think the army knows what they are either." He took her arm and guided her toward the tent opening.

He joked with her during mess and noticed how often other soldiers stopped by to talk to her. She talked easily with them and seemed genuinely interested in each of them. He was surprised to find he was jealous. He wanted those gray eyes to light up at the sight of him like they had earlier today, he realized as he watched her thoughtfully. Was there more to her than he had first thought?

Dusk had begun to fall when they strolled back to his tent. She was obviously nervous, and he admitted he was a bit uneasy himself. He needed to keep the fact firmly in mind that she might soon be on her way back to Boston. And he needed to keep his distance so an annulment would be possible.

Jasper shut the flap on the tent and lit the candle on the crate by the opening. He lit another and handed it to Bessie. She smiled her thanks and perched on the edge of her cot. It was too early to go to bed. What were they to do all evening?

She filled in the silence. "Tell me about yourself, Jasper. We hardly know one another."

He seated himself on his cot across from her. "I'm a boring subject."

"You've seen a lot of the world. This is my first time out of Boston."

"You've never been to Texas, then."

She shook her head. "Was that where you grew up?"

"There and Ohio. Jessica and I lived in Toledo, Ohio, until our real mother died. I don't remember our father. When we were put in the orphanage, we tried to stay together, but we didn't have any choice. Jessica was adopted by the DuBois family while I was sent west on an orphan train. That was the hardest day of my life. I knew I'd never see my sister again. And I wouldn't have, if it hadn't been for Clay." He smiled, remembering how he felt when he got the telegram from Clay.

"I remember standing on the siding in Abilene while the train blew its horn and pulled away. All my friends were on that train, and it left me behind with a gruff man and sober woman who said they were my new parents. I was terrified. But the Mendenhalls were great folks. It wasn't their fault they were never able to make me feel I belonged. They tried, but I could never quit waiting for them to throw me out or scream at me for spilling my milk the way my real mom did."

He hadn't realized he had drifted into reliving the past until Bessie touched his hand. Her soft gray eyes were tender with compassion.

She glanced at her hand on his arm, and a wave of pink stained her cheeks. She left her hand where it was, though. "I'm sorry," she said softly. "You've gone through a lot. But hasn't God been good to reunite you and Jessica?"

She was so right. He laid a hand over hers. "I thank Him for it every day," he told her soberly. "What about you? What was it like growing up for you?"

Her color deepened. She pulled her hand away and looked down. *There's some mystery here,* he realized, wondering what her real reason was for coming out as a wife to someone she had never met. Sure, it was already done when she found out about it, but she could have written and had it annulled or questioned the legality of it. She would have never had to meet him. Why had she?

"What's Lenore really like?" As soon as he asked the question, he wished he could snatch it back.

The light in her eyes died, and she sat back on her cot. "She's a wonderful girl," she said slowly. "Everyone says so. Beautiful, cultured, adventurous. Everything I'm not," she finished abruptly. She stood and turned her back to him as she stared down at his tiny cache of three books that sat atop his mess chest.

He rose and looked over her shoulder. He turned her to face him. "I didn't mean to hurt you. I wasn't comparing the two of you. I just wondered about the sadness in your eyes. Let's talk about something else."

She gave him a slight smile and picked up a tiny carved buffalo. "This is exquisite. Wherever did you get it?"

"I made it."

She turned and smiled. "You carved this? Do you have others you've done?"

"Sure." He felt a little strange showing them to her. His hobby of whittling sometimes seemed useless and embarrassing to him. But he carried his knife along wherever he went, and whittling helped calm his mind. No one had ever seemed to think this talent remarkable. With a warm wave of affection for her, he opened his mess chest and pulled out the small gunnysack that held his work.

Her delight in the tiny carved animals washed away the last of his self-consciousness. "This is Lollie, the golden retriever I had as a kid. She died three years ago." He ran his fingers over the smooth surface, then handed it to her.

"Oh, Jasper, look at the devotion on her face." She gave him such a smile of approval, he had to grin. Her joy was contagious.

She took his hand and rubbed her fingers over the scars. "I wondered where these nicks and cuts came from."

The touch of her small hand did funny things to his heart. Was this normal? He hadn't been around women much. "Sometimes I get so intent on what I'm doing, the knife gets away from me."

She released his hand, and he felt oddly forlorn. He had liked the feel of her small hand in his. He mentally shook himself and dug into the bag again. "Do you know who this is?"

She looked at the figurine a moment. "Is it Jessica as a child?"

He nodded. "How did you know without the red hair as a flag?"

She stared at it again. "The slant of the eyes and the imperious expression."

He chuckled, and she joined him. "She's a lot more mellow than she used to be, according to Clay. Jessica admits it too. God has changed her."

"He changes us all." Bessie sighed and put the figurines back in the bag. "Do you ever wonder why He fashioned you as He did?"

"What do you mean?" Was there something about him she didn't like?

"Nothing. Forget it." She yawned and sat on the cot.

All his confidence evaporated. Did she hate red hair?

"I'm really tired. Do you suppose I could go to bed now?"

"Of course." He suddenly realized she had no privacy to get ready for bed. Looking around, he grabbed a blanket. "Let me fix an area for you." He dug some twine out of his mess chest and strung off a section in the corner, then draped the blanket over it. "I've got a couple of things to do before bed. I'll be back in a little while."

She took her valise and started to her privacy corner. Before she slipped the blanket back, she turned to him and smiled. "Thank you for a lovely evening, Jasper. I enjoyed getting to know you better."

He almost sighed with relief. She didn't seem angry with him. What had caused the barrier between them just now? "You're welcome. Call me if you need anything."

"I will."

With Jasper gone, Bessie felt like weeping. Things had gone so well until he mentioned Lenore. Would she live in the shadow of her beautiful sister even in marriage? Jasper could never have Lenore now. Did he still pine for the spirited girl with whom he had corresponded? Bessie knew she wasn't as beautiful as Lenore, but that didn't make her own desires less important. She was just quieter about it. With Lenore, everything was done with fanfare and a flurry of activity. Bessie liked to accomplish things quietly in the background.

He had seemed curious when she asked if he ever wondered why God had fashioned him as He did. Was she the only one who ever wondered about that? Why had He chosen to give Lenore all the physical beauty in the family? Did He love her more than Bessie? She knew the Bible had called David a man after God's own heart, and David had been handsome and sought after. Did that mean He loved others less? Often Bessie pondered these questions.

She sniffed away the tears in the back of her throat and undressed. She pulled on her flannel, high-necked nightgown and took down her hair. Pushing aside the blanket, she took out her brush and sat on the edge of her cot. *One, two, three.* Counting each stroke of the brush, she didn't hear Jasper come in until he cleared his throat.

Her head jerked up, and her mouth went dry at the expression on his face. No man had ever looked at her like that. Could it be that he actually liked the way she looked? She swallowed and stared into his eyes. "I—I'm almost ready for bed," she said nervously. Her fingers felt as though they could barely hang onto the brush.

He cleared his throat again, and his gaze followed the brush as it flowed through her hair. "Could I do that for you?"

It was all Bessie could do to keep her mouth from dropping open. "If—if you like." She handed him the brush and turned so her back was to him. He touched her hair so gently at first, she could barely feel it. "You won't hurt me," she said.

He ran the brush through her hair, his hands following behind the strokes. It felt almost like a caress to Bessie. Did he mean it as one? The pulse hammered in her throat.

"You have lovely hair." His voice was husky. "Like silk."

If she had tried to answer, she would not have been able to say a word. She closed her eyes and shivered at the sensation of his hands in her hair. She couldn't even remember the last time her mother had brushed her hair. It must have been years ago when she was a child. She tried not to think about what Lenore's hair looked like. Jasper didn't know Lenore's hair was as black as a raven's wing and just as glossy, that Bessie's own waist-length locks were only a pale reflection of her sister's. And Bessie was fiercely glad of that. If he never actually saw Lenore, maybe someday he could grow to love his wife.

He abruptly dropped the brush in her lap. "I'd better let you get some sleep."

She opened her eyes reluctantly. The dream was over. It was back to reality. He would think back and regret he had touched her when it was Lenore he really wanted. She put the brush back into her valise, then slipped beneath the rough woolen blanket. "Good night, Jasper."

She could sense his gaze on her for several long moments. "Good night, Bessie. Sleep well." He blew out the candle, and she heard him slide into bed. Within a few minutes, she heard his breathing deepen. How could he sleep? She didn't think she would be able to sleep at all. The sentry called the time every hour, and the last one she heard was two o'clock.

She awoke to the sound of reveille and the shouts of soldiers packing the column for departure.

"I was about to wake you. We need to pack so I can get our tent down." Jasper was fully dressed with his hair slicked back. The dim glow of the candle cast shadows on his face.

Bessie sat up groggily and pushed her hair out of her face. That searching expression was on his face again. She flushed self-consciously. "I must look a fright."

"You look lovely," Jasper said. "I'm sorry to rush you. I'll be outside when you're ready."

She waited until he closed the flap on the tent behind him, then slipped out of bed. He had called her lovely. Could he really think that?

A battered tin pitcher held the water he had brought in for her. How thoughtful. A flush raced up her cheeks at the dreamlike remembrance of his hands in her hair last night. More shouts echoed through the tent wall, and she hurriedly washed and dressed, then pushed the flap aside and stepped outside. Dawn was just beginning to cast rosy fingers across the horizon, and she was chagrined that she had slept so late. What must Jasper think of her?

"Do you want to ride in the ambulance today, or would you like to try the horse again?" The teasing note in Jasper's voice brought the heat to her cheeks again.

"I'd better ride in the ambulance until you have time to teach me to handle a horse."

He grinned. "That's probably a good idea. Maybe we'll have a chance for your first lesson tonight." He touched her arm, then went to help take down the remaining tents.

Her skin tingled where his fingers had been. She rubbed her arm absent-mindedly. Sighing, she took her valise and hurried to the ambulance. Several of her patients from yesterday were up and gone after a night of rest. She scolded herself for her disappointment that she would not spend the night in Jasper's tent again.

His handlebar mustache quivering with pleasure, Dr. Richter smiled and waved her over. "Ah, Mrs. Mendenhall, I was wondering if I would have your assistance today. As you can see, our patient load has dwindled overnight."

"How is Private Brindle doing this morning?" Bessie knelt beside the young man who had taken a bullet through the shoulder. He winked at her, and she felt the heat of a flush on her face. She wasn't used to such attention.

"Better," he answered at the same time as Dr. Richter.

His fever was down, and his color was better. Bessie gave him a smile and patted his shoulder before moving on to the next patient.

While she followed the doctor from patient to patient, her thoughts kept drifting to Jasper. What was he doing? Was he thinking of her at all? She shook her head at her thoughts. He was likely thinking about Lenore.

The day stretched out interminably. As evening approached, Bessie kept glancing out the back of the covered wagon and watching for Jasper. Would he come to take her riding, or was he already regretting his invitation?

Just before supper mess, he appeared at the back of the wagon. He looked tired, but his face brightened when he saw her. "Would you care to walk with me to supper? Afterwards, we can go riding." He picked up her valise. "We might as well drop this in our tent on the way."

Our tent. Her heart pounded. *He said* our *tent.* Did he expect them to be together from now on? She smiled at the thought. Perhaps last night had meant something to him after all. She followed him past the huddled tents and campfires. The smoke stung her eyes, but she liked the scent. He tossed her valise into a tent near the center of the encampment, then took her hand. His fingers were warm and comforting. She curled her fingers around his and smiled at him.

After supper they went to the corral, and he picked out a gentle mare for her. He instructed her on mounting and dismounting, using the reins, and saddling the horse. Then he helped her mount. She clung to the pommel and tried not to remember her last disastrous ride. But this time they were both prepared for her inexperience. First Jasper led her on the horse around the encampment. Several soldiers called out encouragement, and Bessie flushed with embarrassment. Did they all know she was a total novice? But the teasing was good-natured, and she soon relaxed.

Then Jasper gave her the reins and walked beside her while she practiced guiding the mare. "You're doing great!" he told her.

Was that pride on his face? She sat taller in the saddle. She wanted Jasper to always look at her with that air of pride and proprietorship.

They stopped at dusk, and Jasper lifted her off the saddle. Bessie's stomach fluttered at the touch of his strong hands on her waist. He held her a few moments longer than necessary, then smiled slightly and released her. As they walked back to the tent, he took her hand.

He tied the flap behind them while she lit the candles, and she felt as though they were a loving married couple settling in for the night. Did he feel anything for her at all? Even if he did, would the memory of Lenore's deception always be between them?

Chapter 5

Jasper picked up the envelope and stared at the familiar writing. Bessie's writing. The Bessie he had thought he had known, anyway. The real Bessie was back at the tent waiting for him to join her. His mouth dry, he opened Lenore's letter and unfolded the pages inside. At least she signed her real name this time. He leaned against the wagon and quickly scanned the pages, then folded them up and put them in his pocket. His gaze thoughtful, he strode toward the tent.

He didn't know what to do about the contents of the letter. Just reading the letter brought back his feelings of betrayal. He had been so foolish. Shame burned in his belly and resentment flared against Bessie. Could she really have been innocent of any involvement in Lenore's duplicity? It seemed hard to believe that.

Bessie smiled when he entered the tent, but he frowned instead, and her smile faltered. "Is something wrong?"

"I need some time to think, Bessie." He took off his hat and raked a hand through his hair. Why did Lenore write to him now? What did she expect from him?

"Some time? What do you mean?"

"I just wonder if this can ever work out. The deceit this began with is too much to overcome. Maybe it would be best if you went back to the ambulance." He wanted to add that any repercussions would be on her head, but he bit back the words. He steeled himself for tears. Hardening his heart, he told himself she deserved a bit of suffering for all she had done.

At first her reaction was what he expected. Her gray eyes filled with tears, and she rose to her feet and stared at him. She started toward the door, then stopped and whirled around to face him, her hands on her slim hips as she glared at him. "I shall do no such thing, Jasper! How can you even ask such a thing? What would the soldiers think if you cast me off after two nights together? It would leave me open to unkind comments and even actions. I am your wife. You may not love me, but I must insist on the same respect you would give your sister or any female under your protection."

His anger flared, but with it came a sense of shame. He nodded stiffly. "Very well. You may continue to abide in my tent for the time being. When we get to

Arizona Territory, we shall discuss what to do with this so-called marriage." He turned and walked out. He would wait until she was asleep before he went back.

Bessie's eyes burned as she watched him go. What had changed? He had been so gentle and sweet today when they were riding. She just didn't understand. Her high hopes had sunk into despair. Maybe it would be best to let him annul the marriage and just end this struggle. She shook her head. No, she couldn't bear the shame of going back to Boston after being cast off. Out here, no one would think anything about it, but in Boston there would be titters and jokes. She wouldn't be able to hold up her head.

She had been the one left sitting in a chair along the wall at coming-out parties and balls; she had overheard myriad comments from sour dowagers about how she was not the beauty her sister was; their parents had fussed over Lenore and relegated Bessie to a position more like that of the younger daughter instead of the elder. She had accepted all these snubs, but she would not sit in the shadows again. Now was the time to stand and fight.

She closed her eyes, then pressed her lips together and straightened her shoulders. Jasper was a decent man, and in her mind, he was her husband. He might want to find a loophole, but she did not. She would not make it easy for him to set her aside. Her throat tightened with panic, but she had to make it work. What could she do out here with no husband?

Her only hope was in showing him she was a proper wife, but she had little time to show him what kind of wife she could be. They would be to the new post in another two weeks. She doubted an attorney could be found there, so Jasper would have to write one back east. He would not hear back for some time. Her advantage was the shortage of women in the West. Perhaps that consideration would be enough to slow him down.

She pulled her nightgown on and crawled under the blanket. After she had cried for a few minutes, she told herself not to be a ninny. She needed a plan, not tears. But when she finally fell asleep, she was no closer to knowing how to prove to Jasper that he needed her.

The tenseness of the next few days began to drain Bessie's drive and determination. Jasper avoided her as much as possible, and the times they were together, he was cool and remote. They had no more hair-brushing moments. As the days dragged by, she began to long for the wagon train to reach Fort Bowie. Maybe in their own home they would be able to find common ground again.

When they were almost to Arizona Territory, their last obstacle was a forty-foot gorge they had to cross by means of a rope-and-board bridge. The gorge fell so deep, Bessie couldn't see the bottom. Another wagon rattled along the planks toward them, but instead of waiting until it passed, her driver lashed his horse and started across too. There might be room for them to pass, but a sense of panic choked her, and she shouted to the driver. "Stop! I'm getting out." She scrambled to the back of the ambulance and pushed back the flap.

The private looked back and shook his head. "I ain't stoppin', Missus. Hang tight."

"You either stop, or I'll jump out with it moving. What will my husband do if I'm hurt because you refused to stop?" Most likely he would be glad, but Bessie didn't let herself think about that. She wanted out of this wagon.

Still grumbling, the private shrugged his shoulders. "Whoa." He pulled on the reins and got down to help her out.

She didn't wait for assistance but scrambled out the back. The bridge swayed in the wind, and she felt sick. She couldn't look over the side, or she knew she would humiliate herself and Jasper.

As if the thought of him had summoned his presence, he rode up. "What's going on? Why have you stopped?"

She answered before the private could. "I will walk across. It's not safe with the other wagon coming."

He looked toward the swaying bridge. "I think you might be right." He nodded to the private. "Back up and wait until the way is clear. We'd rather get there late than have a disaster."

The soldier shot Bessie a glare of contempt, then did as he was told.

A prospector who had been riding with the army detachment muttered an oath and swung his wagon past the ambulance. Jasper shouted at him to wait, but he ignored the warning. His mule trotted briskly toward the approaching wagon. Bessie watched in horror as the prospector came abreast of the other wagon, and the front wheel of one caught the rear wheel of the other. She shuddered at the squeal of metal grating against metal. The mule reared, and the next moment both the mule and wagon, along with the prospector, vanished over the edge. The mule and the man both screamed a bloodcurdling sound that brought bile to Bessie's throat.

She seized the edge of the ambulance and hung on as her vision blurred and went dark. She mustn't faint. Jasper grabbed her, and she clung to him with all her strength. Other soldiers rushed past them. The pounding of Jasper's heart under her ear calmed her, and she finally pulled away. "I'm fine," she said, wiping her eyes.

"That could have been you," he said gravely. "Thank God you stopped the ambulance and got out."

One of the patients poked his head out the back of the ambulance. "You saved our lives, Ma'am." His face was pale beneath his grizzled beard, and he stared at her with an expression approaching awe. "You must be pretty close to God."

She smiled faintly. "Not close enough, Private."

Jasper put an arm around her shoulders. "Why don't you ride with me for awhile?"

"I'm not sure I can get on the horse," she said honestly. She still felt weak and shaky.

"I'll help you."

Did he actually want to spend time with her? He had been avoiding her for days. "I'll try," she said.

He kept his arm around her as they found the remuda, and he picked out the same mare she had ridden before. He helped her mount, and she felt a bit better with the wind in her face and the warm sun on her arms. Vaulting into his saddle, he took the reins and led her horse across the bridge. She kept her eyes averted when they passed the spot where the prospector had gone over.

"Can we recover his body?"

Jasper shook his head. "Too dangerous."

She fell silent. This was a harsh country where a man could fall to his death and his bones be left for the birds to pick. Did she even want to stay? One look at the man beside her convinced her she did. No matter how hard it was.

On the other side of the bridge, the terrain grew even more desolate. Jasper picked his way through prickly pear cactus and mesquite brush. When they neared a grove of gnarled creosote bushes, she heard a faint sound. "What is that?"

Jasper paused. "I didn't hear anything."

It came again. "There. Did you hear?"

He listened again. "It's the wind."

"I don't think so." She turned her horse's head and proceeded toward the bushes.

"Bessie, we need to move along. It's nothing but the wind."

It sounded like a baby. She knew that was impossible; the accident had made her skittish, but she had to know for sure. When she reached the bushes, she slid to the ground. She could see Jasper was impatient, and she sent him a coaxing smile. After a moment, he returned the smile and shrugged.

A dark bundle lay beneath the nearest bush. At first she had thought it was a rock, but it moved, and she rushed forward. A gaunt Indian woman lay nearly hidden beneath the brush. Was she dead? Bessie touched her and found her cold. Yes, she was dead. Poor woman. What had moved? She turned to call to Jasper, when she heard that mewling sound again. Crawling beneath the scrub, she moved the blanket and found a newborn child sucking on her fist.

She gasped, and Jasper was at her side at once.

He took her arm and started to move her out of the way, but she darted forward and picked up the baby. "Oh, poor thing!"

"Is she dead?"

"The mother is. Can you see to a proper burial for her? I need to get this baby to the doctor."

"I'll call some of the men. I should check with our Indian scouts too and see if they have any idea who she is or what tribe she is from."

Bessie sent him a grateful smile, then hurried to the ambulance with the baby.

The doctor raised his great, bushy eyebrows when she came rushing into the ambulance with a naked baby in her arms. "A baby! Yours?"

"Of course not," she said impatiently. "I found her in the desert."

He took the infant from Bessie and laid her on a cot. He pinched a fold of skin between his fingers. "She's very dehydrated. She likely won't live, Mrs. Mendenhall."

"She will live," Bessie said fiercely. "I'll take care of her."

The doctor shrugged. "What will she eat? We have no nursing woman here."

Bessie thought fast. "The goat. I can feed her goat's milk."

He nodded grudgingly. "Might work if you can rig up some way of getting enough down her."

For the next few days, Bessie fought for the life of the tiny Indian girl. She dipped a rag in milk and fed the baby nearly around the clock. Jasper checked in every few hours, and Bessie thought he was getting attached to the tiny baby too. Finally the doctor pronounced the infant out of danger.

What was she going to do with the baby? Bessie fiercely wanted to keep her, but she was almost afraid to ask Jasper. She wrapped the infant in a scrap of blanket and took her to their tent. Perhaps if Jasper became attached to her, he would suggest it.

She felt as though she hadn't been in their tent in days, and she smiled at the curious sense of homecoming. Placing the baby on the cot, she took off her bonnet and washed her face. She'd scarcely taken time for herself since the baby's discovery, but now she took down her hair. Before she could comb it and put it back up, Jasper came in.

A gentle expression came over his features when he saw her. Bessie wondered if he cared for her more than he would admit. It was probably just wishful thinking on her part.

"You're back." He glanced toward the cot and frowned. "What are we to do with her? I'm not sure what tribe she's from, but I would suspect Navajo or Apache."

"What do you think we should do?" *Please say we can keep her.* Her heart pounded as she waited for his answer.

His frown deepened. "It would be hard, if not impossible, to find her family. I don't know if there are any orphanages in Phoenix or Tucson. I suppose we could try to locate one."

Her eyes blurred with tears. She couldn't give the baby up. She tried to speak but found she could not get any words out past the lump in her throat. She kept her head down, but Jasper put his fingertips on her chin and lifted her face.

"You want to keep her, don't you?"

"Yes," she whispered.

"What if we end this marriage? Will you take her back to Boston? Will people there accept her?"

His words were gentle, but she sensed the steely purpose behind them. He still wanted to get rid of her. Tears flooded her eyes again, and she jerked her chin away. He didn't need to gloat over her pain. She turned her back to him. "Can't we worry about that if and when it happens?"

He sighed. "You'll get so attached to her, it will be impossible to give her up."

"I already am." She identified with the baby, for she had often felt like an unwanted waif herself. She wanted the child to feel the love and acceptance she had craved all her life.

Jasper was silent, and she risked a glance at him from under her lashes. He was still frowning, and her heart sank.

"Very well. But don't blame me when you have to find her another adoptive family when you go back to Boston."

She felt a mixture of pain and joy at his words. He still intended to send her back to Boston, but at least she would have the baby. She turned and focused the full force of her smile on him.

"She needs a name," she said.

"What do you have in mind?"

"Ruth. She followed Naomi away from her own people the way this baby will follow us from her tribe."

Jasper nodded. "Good choice of name, but we may regret this decision."

"I won't."

He sighed. "I guess I'd better get started on a cradle for her. She'll have to have somewhere to sleep." He pushed open the flap and went outside.

Bessie sank onto the floor and stared at little Ruth in relief. "Mama will take care of you, Sweetheart. I won't let anyone hurt you." She took the baby's hand, and the tiny fingers closed around hers. Now the stakes for preserving the marriage were higher. She couldn't let Ruth down.

By evening, Jasper had knocked together a cradle for Ruth. He had even carved bunnies and her name on the headboard. Bessie hugged him when he brought it in. He looked like a little boy who had brought his mother a fistful of flowers, pleased and embarrassed at the same time. Ruth seemed to know it belonged to her, for she put her thumb in her mouth and went to sleep almost immediately once she was in the cradle.

The weather turned unbearably hot as they plunged deeper into the heart of Arizona Territory. Bessie and the baby were both lethargic from the heat. They stopped for a day in Phoenix, a small settlement of nearly fifty people. Bessie saw several other women and yearned to spend some time with them, but the army wagons moved forward before she could get the courage to approach them. The trail led south through rocky outcroppings and saguaro cactus.

"Fort Bowie ahead!" the scout at the head of the column shouted.

Bessie made sure Ruth was asleep in her cradle in the ambulance; then she climbed out. She scanned the horizon for a look at her new home. All she saw was a small cluster of ramshackle adobe buildings surrounded by an adobe wall. Her heart sank. It was even worse than she had imagined.

Jasper grinned at her from near the front of the column. She could see his excitement even from a distance. She smiled back feebly. If he would smile at her like that every day, it would be adequate compensation for what she would have to endure.

The gates swung open, and the wagons rolled into the fort. Bessie jumped onto the ambulance as it came past and climbed back inside. When the wagon finally stopped, she picked Ruth up and went to see where they would live. She didn't know if she was ready to see it, but there was no choice. They were here, and they must make the best of it.

Bessie stared in dismay. There were nearly as many wagons as there were buildings. The windows of most of the buildings were open holes, and many of the roofs were gone. Dust and sand made a dismal backdrop to the tiny fort. She clutched Ruth and gazed around in numb horror.

She saw Jasper directing the soldiers as they unpacked and stowed the supplies they had brought. She shuddered and climbed back inside the ambulance. She could wait to see their quarters. They were likely much worse than the wagon.

It was nearly dusk when Jasper finally came for them. Dust had crept into the lines of exhaustion around his mouth and nose. His uniform was covered with a fine coating of dust and sand too. A wave of pity washed over Bessie when she saw him. She would not complain and make it worse.

"Ready? I haven't had a chance to check out our quarters, but I'm heading there now. Most of the buildings will need to be rebuilt, but at least our place has a roof."

Bessie picked Ruth up from her cradle, and Jasper lifted Bessie's valise. He led her across the dusty ground to a small adobe building on the south end. There was no stoop, and sand covered the threshold.

Jasper pushed the door open and stepped inside. Bessie followed him eagerly. As her eyes adjusted to the dim interior, her gaze traveled around the room. Their quarters consisted of three rooms. A tiny parlor led into a minuscule kitchen. Off the kitchen was a tiny bedroom. There was no furniture, and thick dust covered the rough plank floor. Her heart sank at the filthy condition of the home.

"We can't sleep here tonight," Jasper said.

Bessie heard the dismay in his voice and mustered every ounce of courage she possessed. "If you can find me a broom and some cleaning supplies, I'll see what I can do."

He stared at her. "You'll clean it yourself?"

"It's a typical chore for a wife," she reminded him.

She saw admiration as he smiled at her. "I'll be back with your supplies."

When he was gone, she wanted to sink to the floor and weep in dismay. For all her brave words, she didn't know how she could clean this in a week, let alone an hour. But she had to try. This was her first real opportunity to demonstrate to Jasper just what kind of wife she could be. Her entire future and that of Ruth's hung in the balance.

Chapter 6

When Jasper had been told the troops would rebuild the fort, he had expected to find more to work with than what was available. He knew speed was of the utmost importance; Cochise had begun a reign of terror along the Butterfield Trail nearly two years ago, and the nation had endured it as long as it intended. The army's job was to provide protection to travelers and homesteaders in the area; but until they had somewhere to stay, that would have to wait. He regretted bringing Bessie and Ruth here. The crumbling stockade was little protection against the fearsome Apache tribe.

He didn't know what to tell Bessie. He still couldn't believe the army had sent them all this way to rebuild the fort but had sent no lye or soap. If he could just find a broom, Bessie might be able to make a beginning, but there were none. He found a stick and whittled it down to a semismooth shape. Then he attached some brush to the end with twine. It would have to do.

When he returned to the house, Bessie had found an empty crate. She had dragged it to the center of the room and sat on it with Ruth in her arms. Jasper felt a pang of regret they weren't the happy family they appeared. He pushed the thought away. He didn't have time to think about that now. There was too much work to do.

Bessie sent him a gentle smile. "What is that? It looks like a porcupine on a stick."

He grinned. "I know my broom-making skills leave much to be desired, but I thought you'd at least recognize it."

Her mouth dropped open, but she recovered quickly. "You made me a broom? Were the rest gone?" She stood, handed the baby to him, and took the broom. "Can you watch her? It would probably be best to take her out of here while I'm sweeping so she doesn't breathe the dust."

The baby was wet, and he grimaced. "She's wet."

"There are clean clothes in the ambulance. I'll go get them." She dropped the broom and started toward the door.

"No, no. I'll do it. It can't be that hard."

She smiled and picked up the broom again. Dust flew, and he coughed and backed away. Ruth's wet bottom began to soak through his coat, and he shuddered. He had already offered, though, so holding the baby at arm's length, he hurried to the ambulance.

He laid the baby on the seat in the ambulance and rummaged through Bessie's small chest until he found a square of soft cloth he assumed was a diaper. This couldn't be that hard. Gingerly, he unwrapped the baby's blanket and grimaced. He unpinned the wet diaper and dragged it from under her bottom. Wiping his hand hastily on his pant leg, he slid the clean diaper under the baby. How did this thing connect? After several tries, he managed to get it hooked together, but the diaper drooped.

He found a dry blanket scrap. Bessie had evidently cut a blanket into squares for Ruth. He respected her resourcefulness; what would have become of Ruth if Bessie had not been part of their detachment?

The baby would be dead in the desert like her mother, he realized. Bessie was the one who heard the infant's cries. Did it take a woman to hear a baby's weak wails? If he had even heard it, he would have dismissed the sound as a bird or some other kind of animal. Bessie's curiosity had saved this little life.

He stared into the baby's innocent dark eyes. She stared back and gave him a slow, tiny smile that tugged at his heartstrings. He waggled a finger at her, and she wrapped her tiny fingers around it. She was going to be a charmer, all right. When he wrapped her in the blanket, she popped her thumb in her mouth and promptly fell asleep. Weren't babies supposed to cry more? She hadn't let out a peep while he cared for her, and she didn't seem to mind a sagging diaper at all.

Such a cute baby with a thick head of black hair and smooth, soft skin. He nestled her against his chest and walked across the dusty parade ground to the quartermaster's tent, where he arranged for cots and kitchen supplies. By the time he concluded his business and went back across the barren yard, nearly an hour and a half had passed. He wasn't expecting much improvement in their quarters, since Bessie didn't have anything to work with. They would have to stay in a tent tonight.

Pushing open the door, he stopped in amazement. Instead of sand and dirt crunching beneath his feet, the rough floorboards were clean and scrubbed. It looked like they had even been mopped, which meant Bessie would have had to do that on her hands and knees. The dirty fireplace hearth had been swept and new logs laid. Cobwebs no longer festooned the corners of the ceilings, and the rooms even smelled cleaner. How did she do it? Suddenly, changing the diaper didn't seem to be something worth bragging about.

He walked through the parlor and the kitchen until he found Bessie in the tiny bedroom. She was on her hands and knees, scrubbing the floors with what looked like wet sand. A little pile of sand was heaped about four feet from her where she had swept it up. Dark smudges of dirt marred the silky white perfection of her skin, and Jasper thought she looked tired. No wonder! She had worked the entire time he was gone.

Unnoticed, he stood observing her for a few minutes. Her hair covered with a kerchief, she knelt to her task, while her slim shoulders flexed with the force of her scrubbing. When she stopped to push a stray hair out of her eyes, she saw him standing in the doorway. Her eyes widened, and she got to her feet. Hurrying to his side, she held out her arms for the baby.

Jasper handed over Ruth. "This place looks splendid. I have some cots on their way. If you can keep the baby now, I'll knock together some kind of kitchen table and benches."

"Did you bring her cradle?" The blanket fell open as she took the infant, and Ruth's sagging diaper was exposed. Bessie looked startled, then smiled. "I see you managed to get her changed."

"It's not as easy as it looks," he admitted gruffly. "The cradle is on its way with the rest of our things." He put his hand on her shoulder. "You worked hard here. Thank you."

Her expression of surprise and delight shamed him. He didn't want her to think he was an ogre who didn't appreciate her efforts. Startled at how much he wanted her good opinion, he backed away. "You've done enough for tonight. At least the bugs and sand are gone."

"What about the open windows? I'd feel better if they were covered with something. Would the quartermaster have some thin cloth we could tack up? I don't want anything heavy enough to block out the breeze, just the bugs."

"I'll see what I can find. There are only three windows, so it won't take a lot of fabric. It's almost dark, though. It may have to wait until morning. Can you bear it for one night?"

"Of course. We just need to make sure Ruth isn't bitten by a spider or scorpion. I'll have to be vigilant."

"We'll be careful." He was surprised to find her frail appearance hid a competent woman.

The quartermaster had already closed shop when he walked back across the parade ground. They would have to deal with the open windows tonight. Looking out over the dark hills, he shivered. Cochise was out there, and they had little protection here. He had a responsibility to Bessie and Ruth now. Bugs were the least of their worries.

Bessie rocked Ruth in her arms and crooned to her. She was exhausted, but the admiration on Jasper's face had been worth all her hard work. Was he beginning to see her differently? It certainly seemed so, but she was almost afraid to hope. Maybe it was her own wishful thinking.

Two privates had brought their belongings, but the three small rooms still looked bare. Could this ever be a home? She had to try, but it seemed an impossible task. With a sigh, she wearily put the baby into her cradle and went to make up the cots. The privates had placed two in the tiny bedroom and pushed them together. That would never do. In fact, she thought she would ask Jasper to sleep in the parlor while she and Ruth took the bedroom. She made the beds and began to unpack the crates and barrels.

"I thought you'd be in bed by now."

She jumped at the sound of Jasper's voice. "I was just trying to put the last of our things away."

He took the crate lid from her hand. "You're done for the day," he said firmly.

The way he was staring at her brought the blood pounding to her cheeks.

He touched her cheek gently. "You're tired. I'll take the cot in the parlor. You and Ruth can have the bedroom."

She felt a sense of gratitude for his perception. She didn't even need to ask him. "Are you sure you'll be all right out here? This room has the biggest window."

"You are more worried about the windows than I am," he said with a chuckle. "I've slept outside without even a tent over my head more times than I can count."

She smiled. "Very well. Good night." He didn't answer but continued to stare at her as though he had never seen her before. Did she have a smudge on her nose? She didn't know whether to walk away or stay. Her heart pounded, and her mouth went dry.

From the bedroom came an angry wail. "The baby," she whispered. "I must tend to her."

"Yes," he said, but he touched her cheek again, and she couldn't move.

He finally dropped his hand and smiled. "She sounds outraged."

"She's probably hungry again. She eats better since we got the bottle in Phoenix, but she's making up for lost time now."

He nodded. "See you tomorrow."

She took a calming breath and hurried to the kitchen. Taking the bottle of milk from the cooling water bucket, she prepared Ruth's meal. While she prepared the bottle, Bessie felt Jasper's gaze upon her, and the knowledge made her curiously clumsy. She breathed a sigh of relief when she was finally able to close the bedroom door behind her and focus on the baby. She didn't know what to think. What had happened? Perhaps he was simply grateful for the cleaning she had done.

She fed the baby, then she took her Bible from the makeshift table beside the cot. She needed all the wisdom she could get on how to deal with this situation. Was she feeling love for Jasper? She just didn't know, but she decided to spend every night finding out what God had to say about love.

The sun beat brightly through the tiny window and awakened Bessie. She sat up groggily. When she saw how bright it was, she slid to the floor and grabbed her dress. She should have been up hours ago. And why hadn't Ruth cried and wakened her? When she looked into the cradle, she found it empty. She gasped, then smiled slowly. Jasper must have taken her.

When she had finished her ablutions, she hurried into the kitchen and found Jasper sitting at a rough plank table on a crude wooden bench. Ruth was in his arms, sucking greedily at the bottle. Bessie felt a pang at the homey picture. Would they ever be the happy family she longed for?

She cleared her throat, and Jasper looked up.

"Good morning, Sleepyhead. I see you finally decided to join us." His green eyes were warm.

"Why didn't you wake me?" She stepped farther into the room.

"When this little mite's complaining didn't do the trick, I decided you must need the sleep." He pulled the bottle out of Ruth's mouth and stood. "You can play mommy. I need to get back to work."

"I'm sorry I slept so late."

Was he angry with her? But he smiled and touched her cheek like he did the night before. "I'll try to be back for lunch."

The next few days flew by. Bessie cared for the baby while trying to make a home in the ramshackle quarters. At times it seemed a losing battle. Dust blew under the door and through the cloth at the windows almost as fast as she could clean it up. Around the fort the men were trying to rebuild the stockade as quickly as possible. Cochise was to the south of the fort, but no one knew when he would be back up this way. Most of the men still slept in tents, but they would soon be under roofs.

The soldiers hired Mexicans and friendly Indians who showed them how to mix adobe and make bricks. One of the Indians, a young brave about twenty-five, was fascinated with Bessie and Ruth. Jasper kept an eye on him, but he was harmless and curious.

Within a week, Fort Bowie began to look like a very different place. Jasper organized groups to begin to roof the buildings once the stockade was repaired and they were in a safer position. Bessie worried about him; he often came home looking tired and dirty.

"Those curtains look so sweet and homey," he told her when she finally got them finished and up on the windows. "Even Major Daniels remarked on it.

He's thinking about sending for his wife since you're here."

Bessie felt a sense of jubilation. Was he beginning to think of them as a family? How she longed to be what they seemed. Would he ever look at her with that special look in his eyes he had had that night on the trail? She was beginning to wonder if she had imagined it all.

"What's for supper?"

She suppressed a smile at the mirth on his face. So far they had eaten at mess every night, but she knew she needed to get started on learning to cook. She dreaded letting Jasper know she wasn't joking when she said she didn't know how. Although she had brought her grandmother's cookbook with her, some of the directions seemed incomprehensible to her. If another woman came to the fort, Bessie could talk to her about cooking and other concerns. Sometimes she felt lonely surrounded by men, even though the soldiers were kind and considerate. One private, Rooster Wheeler, a grizzled red-haired man who reminded her of a banty rooster, especially looked after her.

"Probably beans again," she said at last, answering Jasper's question.

"Nope," he said. He rummaged in the gunnysack he had laid on the table and produced a small package. "Rooster bagged an antelope this morning. He gave me this roast for 'the little woman,' as he called you." He grinned hugely and handed her the meat. "You do know how to cook it, don't you?"

"Is there anything to go with it?" What was she going to do? She had no idea how to cook this hunk of meat, but she couldn't face the humiliation of telling Jasper. He was beginning to think she was competent as a wife. Would Rooster know how to cook it? He caught the antelope, after all.

Jasper grinned again and produced two wrinkled potatoes filled with eyes. "These were worth their weight in gold, but I gave Corporal Myers the scouting assignment he wanted, so I got them. I also got some canned peaches. We shall feast like kings tonight."

What was she to do? She turned away to care for the baby so Jasper couldn't see her face. *How hard could it be to cook this roast, anyway? Toss it in a pot with some water and these potatoes and it could be a kind of stew.* That sounded good. Her mouth watered at the thought of real meat. Beans grew tiresome after weeks of eating little else. She would consult her cookbook and see what it suggested. At least she could read.

Chapter 7

Jasper reread the letter and frowned. He didn't know whether to be happy or mad. He would have to discuss this with Bessie tonight. The thought of his wife brought a smile to his face. Supper should be ready by now. Would she have fixed a stew with the meat or just roasted it? Thinking of the possibilities made his mouth water. He bounded across the parade ground as he hurried home.

The curtains blew in the hot desert wind as he approached their quarters. The adobe looked clean and scrubbed. He had caught Bessie brushing the debris from the walls of the house the other day. Barely five feet tall, she was standing on one of the benches he had made for the kitchen, and he grinned at the picture she made. The soldiers called her "Angel." He had asked Rooster where the nickname came from, and the old soldier had said she was their angel of mercy. She was always there to listen to a problem or to pull out a splinter. It made Jasper see her in a whole new light. Physically, she was tiny, but her spirit was mighty.

He could smell supper cooking through the open window, and his grin widened. Stew and fresh-baked bread. He threw open the door and found his way to the kitchen. Bessie stood over the woodstove stirring the pot. She tasted the stew and grimaced.

"Something wrong?" he asked. "It sure smells good."

She turned slowly. "I guess it's ready."

She didn't seem very enthusiastic. Maybe she wasn't hungry. He took off his hat and poured water into the pitcher to wash his hands. "Ruthie sleeping?"

"She should be waking anytime."

"I reckon we should eat before she does. Then you won't have to be hopping up and down." He dried his hands and sat on the bench expectantly.

Bessie took a cup and ladled stew into the two waiting bowls. She sat them on the table, then turned back to the stove. "The biscuits should be done too. I'll get them." Taking a cloth, she pulled the biscuits from the oven and put them on the table.

Jasper's mouth watered just looking at them. They were golden brown and looked delicious.

"Thomas was overseeing supplies today. I talked him out of some jam for the biscuits," she told him. She sat on the other bench and folded her hands while Jasper said grace.

He picked up his spoon. He couldn't wait to eat something other than the usual mess slop. He took a big spoonful of stew and shoveled it into his mouth. It was so hot it was hard to really taste it for a minute, then the gamy flavor hit his taste buds. His gaze shot to Bessie. Her eyes down, she chewed slowly. The expression on her face looked as though she were in pain. He swallowed and reached for a biscuit. That ought to kill the gamy flavor.

Ladling jam onto a biscuit, he bit into it with appreciation, then spit it back out. "What did you make these out of?" he asked before he could stop the words. "They taste salty."

She frowned and took a biscuit. "I just followed the directions." She broke off a piece of biscuit and put it in her mouth. Shuddering, she discreetly spit it back out again. She folded her hands in her lap again and bent her head. "I don't understand it," she murmured.

Jasper got up and looked at the ingredients she had on the stove. "How much saleratus did you use? Sour milk and molasses usually work better."

Her eyes filled with tears. "I didn't have any molasses, so I just guessed. I used too much?"

He felt sorry for her. She had tried so hard. He would just eat the stew and not say anything until later about the spices she should have used. There was no reason to make her feel any worse. "You'll learn," he said. He put a hand on her shoulder. "It's better than mess hall food." He sat down and quickly ate the stew.

She took another bite of the stew and burst into sobs. "It's terrible!" She threw down her spoon with a clatter and buried her face in her hands. "I so wanted to impress you," she wailed.

He knelt beside her. "Don't cry. It's no big deal. It's my fault; I should have showed you how to do it. Antelope is tricky. There are special herbs you can use to take the gamy flavor out." He stroked her hair. Her tears made him feel helpless. He pulled her to his chest. "Shh. It's all right."

Her sobs stilled, and her hand crept up his chest and nestled at his neck. A wave of protective tenderness swept over him, and he suddenly realized how much he liked the feel of her in his arms. She was small and compact and fit neatly against him—like she belonged. When she lifted her head, he stared into her gray eyes. Was that fear in her eyes? He cupped her cheek in his hand. After a moment, she closed her eyes, and he kissed her. The shock of her soft lips against his was like the kick of a mule.

He didn't want it to end, but she finally pulled away from him. He saw the fear in her eyes, the uncertainty. She had good reason. Neither one of them knew where they stood.

Tears were in her eyes again, and he wanted to ask her why, but he was afraid to speak, afraid of seeing that soft expression fade from her face. Did she love him? Did he love her? He enjoyed the kiss, but was that love? What was love, really? He didn't think he even knew.

From the bedroom they heard Ruth's cry. "She's hungry," Bessie whispered. "I must feed her."

"All right. When she's settled again, I wish to speak with you. There is something we must discuss." The letter burned in his pocket, and he felt like a traitor knowing what he had to say to her.

He released her, and she got slowly to her feet, then hurried to the bedroom. The frightened expression was back on her face, and he knew there was reason for it this time.

Ruth's cries soon stilled as she sucked eagerly at the bottle. What was it she had seen in Jasper's eyes. She was afraid she didn't want to know what he wanted to talk about. Was he going to send her home now? She couldn't go, she just couldn't. She loved her baby, and she was starting to love Jasper as well. She hadn't wanted to lose her heart until she knew it was safe, but she had been helpless to prevent it. She sniffled and rubbed her eyes. Well, if that's what he wanted, she wouldn't agree. She would stay and fight if she had to.

Ruth's eyelids soon drooped again, and Bessie put her back into her cradle. Before she went to the parlor, she peered into the little handheld mirror on the nightstand and smoothed her hair. Her gray eyes looked fearful. She pinched a little color into her cheeks and bit her lips. Straightening her shoulders, she marched into the parlor.

Jasper sprang to his feet when she entered the room. He patted his coat pocket as if to check that something was there, then raked a hand through his hair. "Sit down, Bessie," he said, indicating the cot that served as their sofa.

She sat gingerly on the edge of the cot and looked up at him expectantly. Her heart pounded.

He put his hand in his pocket and drew out a letter. "I hadn't mentioned it yet, but I wrote to an attorney in California about our situation. I received his answer today." He avoided her eyes as he pulled the letter out of its envelope and opened it.

She clenched her fists in the folds of her dress. "Why didn't you talk to me about it first? You didn't give me a chance to say anything."

"What is there to say? We needed to find out where we stand in this marriage."

"Very well." She forced herself to sit back and look at him as though she didn't care, when inside she felt as though her heart were literally breaking.

Jasper leaned against the fireplace. "He says that I signed the papers and married myself to Bessie Randall no matter who she was. The fact that she wasn't the person I thought was Bessie didn't matter. You, however, were not involved on your end until it was done. If anyone has grounds for an annulment, it would be you. So if we are to set aside this marriage, you will have to be the one who does it."

"Then it will not be done, because I will not. When I came out here, it was to be your wife. I have not changed my opinion on that because of your disappointment in me."

"I did not say I was disappointed." Jasper finally met her gaze. He sighed and looked away. "I didn't say I wanted you to set it aside. I just wanted you to know you had that option."

"It is no option. Marriage is sacred before God. I would not break my vow."

"That's just the issue, Bessie. It was not your vow, it was Lenore's. Why do you feel you must honor your sister's deception?"

Was that disappointment in his voice? In spite of his assertion that he just wanted her to know she could set the marriage aside if she so desired, had he really thought she would do so? She couldn't answer his question. She couldn't look into his green eyes and tell him she loved him, not when he did not love her. In her heart she knew he didn't. But he might one day. She stood and walked to the window.

When she didn't answer his question, he sighed. "I would like us to begin to make some progress toward a real marriage, Bessie. Would you be agreeable to studying what God says about love and marriage? I don't feel I really know what love is or how to love you as a husband should love his wife."

It was such an unexpected request that Bessie froze where she was. He wanted to learn to love her. That realization filled her with joy. Perhaps one day she would see genuine love in his face. "That would be lovely." For just a moment Bessie allowed herself to hope.

He picked up the Bible from the top of his mess chest, then sat on the cot and patted the spot beside him. "Sit with me."

She settled in next to him, and he opened the Bible. "May I?"

She found her voice. "Of course." She was afraid to say more, afraid her heart would betray her.

"I asked Clay once what Scripture a husband and wife should read together. He suggested 1 Corinthians 13 to discover what love really is. He told me to beware of thinking love was just a feeling. Shall I begin?"

"Please do."

"Clay said to remember the word charity means love." He began to read. The words poured into her heart. She had never heard these words quite like this. Had she ever loved someone this unselfishly? Could she learn to love Jasper like this? It was a bit daunting.

" 'Charity suffereth long, and is kind; charity envieth not; charity vaunteth not itself, is not puffed up, doth not behave itself unseemly, seeketh not her own, is not easily provoked, thinketh no evil.' "

Jasper closed the Bible. "Let's pray." He took Bessie's hand. "Lord, we ask You to show us how to love one another as You would have a husband and wife love. Give us grace and patience, and bind our hearts together as one. In Jesus' name, amen."

Tears pooled in Bessie's eyes when she raised her head. His prayer had seemed so heartfelt. Did he really intend to try? And even if he did, could he ever love her? She wasn't a beauty; she couldn't cook a decent meal; she wasn't anything special. Perhaps she could love him enough to make up for those deficiencies.

He smiled at her. "God has given us a pretty big list. I think we should just work on one characteristic at a time. After that meal, long-suffering will be my first goal."

She stared at him, then slowly began to smile as his words penetrated. "At least you got to eat it in the privacy of your own home," she said. "And what about the rest of that sentence?" She opened the Bible to Corinthians. "To paraphrase, love suffers long and is kind. How about a little kindness? You could eat those biscuits anyway."

"I'm not that kind," he told her with a grin. "But a stray dog came into the fort today. He would probably consider it a kindness to eat them."

She burst into delighted laughter. "You get the dog; I'll get the biscuits."

She couldn't believe the difference in their relationship over the next few days. Jasper went out of his way to do small things for her. They spent the evenings reading together from the Bible or the small stash of books she had brought west with her, or they discussed dreams and goals. She discovered Jasper wanted to open a general store in a small town when he was out of the army, and she confessed to him how much she had always wanted a sewing machine.

He sometimes kissed her before she went to the tiny bedroom with Ruth, and she wondered when he would begin to demand his husbandly rights. She so longed to hear him say he loved her, but he never did. Perhaps he never would. If not, she must learn to deal with that fact. They could raise a family on mutual respect and consideration. She wanted a family, a large family. Much as she loved Lenore, she had always regretted having only one sibling.

They were trapped inside one day while a sandstorm blew through. The wind howled and blew sand through every crack and crevice, but they spent the time playing checkers on a battered board with painted rocks Jasper had scrounged. Bessie loved the time together and was almost glad for the storm.

When he went off on patrol the next day, Bessie knew she had her work cut out for her. A thick layer of sand covered everything, even their clothes. After sweeping and dusting, she asked one of the privates to haul her some water for washing. The supply train had come with cleaning supplies, and she was ready to give the house a good cleaning. She filled the tub with soap and water, took down the scrub board from the kitchen wall, rolled up her sleeves, and got to work.

Jasper had left his mess chest open, so she decided to clean everything in it too. She was almost to the bottom of the chest when she found a letter with familiar handwriting. Her throat closed up as she recognized Lenore's familiar flamboyant penmanship. Kneeling on the hard wooden floor with the letter in her hand, her chest felt heavy as though she couldn't breathe; she wanted to crumple the letter into a ball and toss it into the stove.

When had Jasper gotten this letter? Why hadn't he told her he was still corresponding with Lenore? And Lenore. How could she write to her sister's husband behind her back? The sting of betrayal brought tears of pain and rage to her eyes. She had known her sister was selfish, but how could she do something like this? Had Lenore's relationship with Richard soured, and so she thought to resume her long-distance romance with Jasper? He was a married man now. He was her husband, not Lenore's.

Bessie had thought things were going so well, but now she discovered he had kept this secret. Her hands shook, and she put the letter down as though it might bite her. She wouldn't read it. She couldn't. She couldn't bear to see words of endearment. Jasper would be home soon, but she didn't want to see him. How could she hide her feelings? But hide them she must. He must not have the satisfaction of knowing she loved him.

She had never known she could feel such jealousy and anger. How could she face him? He would surely read her pain and betrayal in her eyes. She slowly buried the letter in the bottom of the mess chest and piled the rest of Jasper's things on top. Closing the lid, she got to her feet as though she were an old woman. She felt old and used and hurt.

Taking a deep breath, she leaned her forehead against the wall, then straightened her shoulders and forced back tears. She would weather this somehow. She still had Ruth, even if her husband's heart would never be hers. How could he ever love her when Lenore waited for him?

The baby wailed, and she hurried to care for her. She felt like wailing herself, but she was an adult and her responsibilities waited for her. She wished she could just sit in the middle of the floor and weep until she had no more tears.

Chapter 8

Ruth was crying when Jasper got home. He felt irritable and out of sorts, and a crying baby did nothing to ease his mood. Bessie had been acting oddly for the past week too. He had tried to get her to tell him what was wrong, but she refused to answer him. He had enjoyed coming home to a smiling wife, but this solemn little wife with the stiff back disconcerted him. She still did everything she had done before. The house was spotless with supper on the table when he arrived, but he missed the light in her eyes when she saw him and her ready smile. He had to find out what was wrong.

He picked Ruth up and walked through the kitchen, looking for Bessie. Supper was cooking; it smelled like beans and corn bread, and his stomach rumbled hungrily. He finally found her just outside the back door with a pile of wood in her arms.

"Why didn't you wait until I got home?" he asked. "Ruthie was awake and crying."

"I just left her a moment. Rooster brought the wood right up to the back of our quarters. She couldn't have been crying long."

He held the door open while she carried the wood in. He would have done it for her, but he could tell by her expression it would be best not to offer. She dropped the wood in the box by the stove, then she rinsed her hands in the bowl of water on the dry sink. Holding her arms out for the baby, she didn't meet his gaze.

He sighed and handed Ruth over to her. How was a man supposed to know how he had transgressed with a woman? What man understood women? He wished Clay and Jessica were there. Clay had plenty of experience in dealing with a temperamental woman.

"I'm going to be gone for three or four days," he told her. "I've been assigned patrol duty. Word is Cochise is headed this way. He attacked a wagon train over by Lordsburg, then killed a settler and his family near San Simon."

Her head jerked up, and he could read the fear in her eyes. He felt a sense of relief. Whatever was eating her, at least she still cared about his safety. "I'll be fine," he said. He gave her a smile, and she returned it tentatively.

"The officers are hosting a party at their quarters tonight. You want to go?"

She hesitated, then nodded. "These four walls get tiresome. I wish I could plant a garden, but headquarters did not send any seeds."

"What kind of garden? Vegetables or flowers?"

"Both, really."

"It would be difficult. We would have to haul water."

"I know, but the acequia isn't far."

"It would take more water than you realize."

"A small garden wouldn't take that much."

He smiled and went to the parlor, glad he could surprise her. When he opened his mess chest, he sensed her stiffen. Puzzled, he glanced at her. What was eating at her? Rummaging through his chest, he found a box in the very bottom and pulled it out. "Jessica sent these with me. I had forgotten about them until now."

She gave a cry of delight at the seed packets in his hand. "Bless you!" She snatched the packets from him and rifled through them. "Carrots, green beans, beets, even a packet of flower seeds." She stood on her tiptoes and kissed his chin. "Thank you, Jasper. I'll get started tomorrow."

"Wait until I can help you," he advised. "The ground will be hard as brick. I doubt you can break it up by yourself." Her enthusiasm pleased him. He wanted things back the way they were. Even their Bible reading at night was tense. He hoped she would get over whatever was bothering her by the time he came back in a few days.

❦

Bessie pushed on the shovel with all her might, but she didn't have the strength to shove more than the tip into the ground. She sighed at her own ineptitude. If she couldn't do something as simple as turning over sod, how could she ever prove to Jasper she was a better wife than Lenore ever could have been for him?

She didn't want to wait to plant the garden until Jasper came home. She needed something to occupy her time now. If she had too much spare time, her mind went round and round her problems. Thoughts of her husband's betrayal were just under the surface of her mind, like an itch that needed to be scratched. The more she tried to ignore it, the more it nagged at her. Would she ever be able to erase the memory of her sister's bold writing on the envelope of that letter?

"Missus, you ought not to be doin' this by yourself. I'm off duty now. Yer husband would have my hide if he knew I'd let you dig this-here dirt." Rooster plucked the shovel from her hands and shooed her out of the way. He jammed the shovel to its hilt into the dirt and turned it over.

He might look like a scrawny banty rooster, but he was stronger than he looked. She backed away to where Ruth lay under a blanket canopy and watched. Rooster made it look so easy.

A strange rattling noise made her look down. She froze. A snake! Its coils glistened in the sunshine, its flat, triangular-shaped head low to its body. She tried to call out to Rooster, but before she could get a sound past her tight throat, it struck. Its fangs sank into her leg, and she screamed.

Before she fainted, she heard Rooster shout; then the ground rose to meet her.

"Ruthie." Bessie tried to raise her head. Where was she, and where was the baby? Her right leg throbbed and burned, and she felt light-headed and weak.

"Lie still, Missus. You been bit." Rooster's voice seemed far away.

"My baby."

"I got the little one right here. She's fine. You gotta lie still, Missus."

Gentle hands pushed her down. She gasped, struggling to breathe. A rattlesnake. It had bitten her. She shuddered as a wave of nausea washed over her. Rooster held a pail while she vomited.

He muttered clucking noises and patted her shoulder awkwardly when she began to cry. "You'll be all right. I done sucked out the poison."

She shuddered and turned her head, seeking for sight of the baby. When she saw her sleeping in the cradle, she closed her eyes and slept too. She awakened off and on and cried out for water, for Jasper or for Ruth, but Rooster was always there to hold the pail or give her a drink. Once she thought she saw Lenore sitting on the edge of the bed, but she told her to go away. She had already spoiled things enough; Bessie didn't want her there.

Jasper drooped tiredly in the saddle. He wondered how Bessie and Ruth were getting along without him. Maybe Bessie was glad to have him out of the way.

Twenty-three men rode with him. So far they had seen no Apache Indians, only a few friendly Navajo who had strayed off their reservation. Jasper was beginning to wonder if their information was correct. Cochise might have headed back into the Dragoon Mountains. He had been a formidable foe, striking small parties and settlers, then fading back to his hideaway in the mountains, but now that the fort was operational again, he would be even more cautious. Most tribes avoided the white man's forts and the "guns that shoot twice," as they called the army's howitzers.

Jasper came over the rise of a mesa and signaled the men to stop. He took the spyglass and searched the countryside. Nothing. He led out again, and the troop started down the rocky slope. If he saw nothing by evening, tomorrow they would turn around and head home.

A war cry interrupted his thoughts. Seeing the war tribe hurtling toward them from the right, he shouted for his men to dismount and take cover behind the boulders. The exchange only lasted a few minutes, but by the time the Apache withdrew, he had lost two men and two more were wounded.

The next two days the Apache eluded them, and Jasper had no choice but to assume they had gone to hole. He turned the troop toward home. Eager to see Bessie, he kept a brisk pace back to the fort.

Facing the Apache braves had been an illuminating experience. He wanted children, part of his own flesh and blood to leave behind him. If he had died in the skirmish, would anyone have cared? He thought of Bessie, of his strange marriage. Enough was enough. It was time he was a husband to her.

He didn't think Bessie would object if he asked to move his cot beside hers in the bedroom. But did she love him? He wasn't sure how he felt about her. He admired her and felt a strong liking for her, but was that love?

He was trying to show her biblical love, but it was hard. That was all action, mutual submission, and consideration. Would he ever feel the emotion of strong love, the feeling of being caught up in something bigger than himself? Would he be willing to die for Bessie? The Bible talked about a man loving his wife as Christ loved the church, of offering himself for her. That was a daunting thought.

If they ever hoped to achieve that ideal, they had to make a beginning for a real marriage. He hoped Bessie agreed. The thought of their children around the dinner table, running to greet him when he came home was heartwarming. He wanted lots of children around—little boys with red hair like his own and little girls with Bessie's gray eyes.

The fort seemed unusually quiet when the troops rode in. Several soldiers waved laconically, but most stayed in the few patches of shade. The temperatures were already hovering near one hundred degrees Fahrenheit, and it was only May. What would midsummer be like? He sighed as he rode into the stable.

"I'm home," he called, shutting the door behind him. The dim, cooler interior was a welcome relief from the bright heat outside.

The bedroom door opened, and his smile faded when Rooster came out instead of Bessie. "What's wrong? Where's my wife?"

"Settle down, Lieutenant. A rattler took a liking to your missus, and she's been mighty sick. She's yonder in the bed."

A rattler! His heart sank. She was such a tiny thing. Rattlesnake bites could be deadly to children and small or weak adults. He hurried to the bedroom.

Her head propped on pillows, Bessie lay in the bed, her face turned toward the window. She looked so small even though the cot wasn't large. Translucent skin so white and fine he thought he could almost see through it. Small drops of perspiration beaded her forehead, and her breathing was erratic. He had seen men bitten before in Texas; she wasn't out of danger yet.

Still asleep, she turned her head, and he sat beside the bed. When he took her hand, it was hot and dry. So small and delicate, but when he turned it over, he saw the calluses there. She had never had calluses in Boston, had she? He studied her sleeping face and realized she didn't have that dusting of freckles back at Fort Bridger. She had been a good wife, and she was trying so hard.

He bent his head and prayed for God to spare her. Ruth needed her, and so did he. If this wasn't love, it was as close as he had ever felt. Maybe he wasn't capable of more. The way he had been shifted from pillar to post as a child could have stunted his capacity for love, but he felt more for this small woman on the bed than for any other woman who had ever come into his life. She had tried so hard to make a life and a home for him. For the first time he thanked God He had sent Bessie instead of Lenore.

Jasper stayed beside the bed through the long night. Just before dawn she thrashed in the bedclothes and called his name. "Jasper, don't leave me."

"I'm here, Bessie."

With great effort she opened her eyes and managed to focus on his face. "Don't leave me, Jasper," she whispered. "Please don't send me back to Boston."

He smoothed the hair back from her face. "I wouldn't do that. You're my wife, and we belong together."

"Lenore couldn't love you, you know." Her eyes were bright with fever.

"I know. I'm not interested in Lenore. You are a much better wife."

She seemed to relax at his words, and with an indistinguishable murmur, she fell back asleep. Was that what had been bothering her? Did she think he cared anything about Lenore? From what he had heard of her, he couldn't see Lenore sticking it out in a place like this.

He gazed into Bessie's face. In spite of his intentions to make their marriage a real one, the circumstances prohibited that. Maybe when she was better, they would talk about it.

Bessie winced and shaded her eyes from the sun. Her gaze traveled around the room and came to rest on Jasper. His red head lay inches from her arm. His breathing was deep and regular, and her right hand lay in his. When had he arrived?

For the first time in days she felt clearheaded, though she was still weak and dizzy. She was just glad Ruth was all right. At the thought of her daughter, she glanced around the room again. Where was the baby?

For a moment, she panicked. Then she remembered Rooster's presence earlier. He had surely taken the baby. She put her hand on Jasper's hair and twined her fingers in its thick, coarse texture, smiling at her audacity.

He muttered, and his eyes opened. The sparkling green depth of his gaze made her mouth even drier. She pulled her hand away quickly, and he sat up.

He touched her forehead and smiled. "You're better."

Her heart fluttered at the relief in his voice. "I think so, yes. Where is Ruthie?"

"Rooster has her."

She nodded, then another thought struck her. "Was she bitten?" Agitated, she raised up on the pillows.

He pushed her gently back. "She's fine. Happy as the soldiers who are spoiling her. I checked on her last night. She was cooing and gurgling with her fist in Rooster's hair."

She relaxed and smiled at the picture.

"The soldiers even got your garden planted." He smoothed her hair. "All you have to do is worry about getting well."

"I'm well," she told him. She sat up and ran a hand through her tangled hair. "I must look a sight."

"You're a sight for sore eyes," he told her. "I missed you and Ruthie while I was gone. We're a family now."

Did he really feel that way? She searched his earnest gaze and saw no deceit. Was this a new beginning for them? She pushed away the specter of her sister.

Chapter 9

Jasper insisted Bessie rest for a few days. She was relieved at his insistence, for she still felt dizzy and light-headed. He brought her the watercolors she had brought with her, and she and Ruth spent daytime hours under the trees along the acequia. She painted scenes of fort life and thought they were pretty good. She captured Rooster and several of the other soldiers practicing drills on the parade ground, the small post band playing their instruments in the cool of the day under the trees near her, and the Indians moving to and from the sutler's store.

For the first time since she had come west, she had time to stop and savor the sights and smells of the fort: the licorice smell of the tobacco plugs the men chewed, the mix-and-match uniforms they wore, and the fragrance of creosote bushes and sagebrush. She tried to get all that flavor of life down on canvas and was amazed at her own paintings. Her uncle in Boston had urged her to send him some of her work; perhaps she would send him some of these.

Jasper sometimes joined her with a block of wood and his whittling knife. They seemed to have made an uneasy truce, uneasy on her end, anyway. He seemed relaxed and content.

"What are you doing up? I can get my own breakfast," Jasper said.

Bessie jumped. Sometimes he was so noiseless, like a cat. "It's time things got back to normal," she said firmly. "I've spent too much time relaxing as it is. The laundry is piled up, this house is filthy with dust and sand, and we're out of bread."

He grinned. "You could always make more biscuits."

"They might even be edible this time now that I know how to make them."

He put a hand on her shoulder. "You're doing a fine job. You might make a fair-to-middlin' cook yet." His green eyes twinkled. "I'm in the mood for beans and corn bread."

She smiled. "That's exactly what I was planning for supper. Where are you going today?"

"We're building new latrines. The commander wants the heavy digging and hard work done before it gets any hotter. Which reminds me. I've arranged for some help for you."

She frowned. "I don't need any help. I'm managing just fine." Did he feel she was failing in some way as a wife? She was trying so hard, but she knew her cooking still wasn't great. Jasper ate it without complaint, but maybe he longed for better cooking than she could muster.

"Yes, but I don't want to turn you into a drudge. I want my wife fresh and lively when I come home at night. You have plenty to do just caring for Ruthie. You'll like Eve."

"Who?" she called after him as he walked toward the door.

"Eve. She'll be here soon."

"Another woman?" She couldn't believe it. She had seen no other women since they went through Tucson on the way to Fort Bowie. She felt a sense of excitement tinged with jealousy. Where had he seen this woman, and what had been his true motive in asking for her help?

A soft knock interrupted his answer, and Jasper moved quickly to answer the door. When he opened the door, all Bessie could see over his shoulder was a shining cap of black hair. She smoothed her own brown locks down and hurried forward.

A lovely Indian woman stood on the stoop. Her soft brown eyes were full of trepidation, and her gaze darted from Jasper to Bessie and back again.

"Missus." She bobbed her head and cast her gaze to the ground. "I come to help you with your work." Her English was nearly flawless, as was the smooth brown perfection of her skin.

Bessie immediately felt dowdy and unattractive. How could Jasper fail to see how lovely this girl was? Something about her reminded Bessie of Lenore. Perhaps it was the raven hair or the smile, but if she thought of Lenore when she saw Eve, did Jasper think of her also? In her mind's eye, she could see Jasper and Eve with Ruth. The perfect little family. He had to have hired her because of her beauty. *Stop it!* She was behaving like a half-wit.

Jasper frowned and glanced her way, and she realized she was behaving poorly. "Welcome, Eve. Please come in. My husband was just telling me of you." She stepped back from the doorway and motioned her in.

Eve gave Jasper another glance, and she walked past him.

"I'm going now." He brushed Bessie's cheek with his lips and closed the door behind him.

Her cheek burned from the touch of his lips. He did not usually kiss her good-bye in the morning. Was this an attempt to throw her off the rabbit trail her thoughts had taken? Could there be anything between Jasper and this young woman?

Bessie forced a smile to her lips. "What do you know how to do, Eve?"

"I can do laundry, clean, cook—anything you need, Missus."

"Where did you learn to speak English so well?"

"My mother was white, Missus. She met my father, a Navajo chief, when her parents came through on their way to California. My father stole her away, and they were very happy for many years."

"I see." Bessie couldn't imagine such a life for herself. But the woman had evidently never forgotten her roots. She had made sure her daughter spoke English.

"She and your father are still living?"

A shadow crossed Eve's face. "My father died last year. Mother still grieves."

"Where does she live?"

"With my brother and his wife on the reservation."

"I would have thought perhaps she would try to find her white family in California."

Eve shook her head. "She would not be accepted after marrying a Navajo." She said the words matter-of-factly, without a trace of self-pity. "She tried once to write them, but the letter came back. Her parents had rejected it. She threw it away and never spoke of them again."

Bessie felt a stab of pity for the unknown woman. How terrible it would be never to hear from her parents and family again, to give up a way of life for another and never be able to go back again. "Perhaps you should try to contact them, Eve."

Eve gave her a slight smile. "I think I should begin my work, Missus."

In other words, mind your own business. Bessie felt the sting of rebuke. She had been meddling. Flushing, she led the way to the kitchen.

She showed Eve the washtub and scrub board, but before she could instruct her further, Ruth began to cry. Bessie left Eve in the kitchen and hurried to the baby. "Why is Mama's girl so sad?" she cooed, picking up the infant.

Ruth stopped crying and smiled, reaching out a chubby hand to grasp a tendril of hair.

A wave of tenderness washed over Bessie. She wanted so much for Ruth, but after talking with Eve, she was fearful. Would people accept her adopted daughter? She snuggled her close and frowned. She could fight some of Ruth's battles, but the child faced a great many more.

Kissing the top of the baby's downy head, she carried her into the kitchen and began to prepare a bottle for her.

Eve stopped what she was doing and stared at the baby. "She is not white."

Bessie flushed. "No. I found her with her dead mother in the desert. She is mine now. I love her."

Eve nodded. "It will not be easy, Missus."

"Call me Bessie. I would like to be friends." She was surprised to find she no longer felt jealous toward Eve. She knew Jasper would never betray her with this girl. What had she been thinking? Her husband was a man of integrity. Being out in the desert with a man who wanted her sister was making her think unreasonably.

Surprise and pleasure vied for Eve's expression. "I am your servant, Missus," she said with downcast eyes.

"I need a friend more." Bessie touched Eve's shoulder.

Eve bit her lip. She raised her eyes and met Bessie's gaze. "I, too, need a friend."

"Then let us do our work together, and we can talk as we work. It will make the day go faster."

The day flew by. Eve left before Jasper returned for the evening. She lived with her brother about a mile out of Fort Bowie, and she needed to prepare his supper. When Bessie shut the door behind her new friend, she felt as though she had turned some kind of corner in her acceptance of her new life. Just having a friend made all the difference.

After supper, Jasper took out his Bible and studied it while Bessie did the dishes. She stopped and stared at him through the open doorway. Would she ever get to really know her husband? She knew she loved him now, knew it in every fiber of her being. She loved everything about him. The way his hair grew in a cowlick, the way he played so gently with Ruthie, the sweet, kind things he did for her. Just like hiring Eve. He had only been thinking of her, but her first thought had been of suspicion. He had shown concern by finding Eve for her; he was solicitous of her health and well-being, but what did he really feel? Did he still think of Lenore?

Bessie thought again of the letter hidden in the bottom of his mess chest. She desired to know its contents but feared to read it. So far she had resisted the temptation and hoped she was strong enough to continue.

Drying her hands on her apron, she took it off and hung it on a peg on the wall. She smoothed her hair and joined Jasper in the parlor.

He smiled when she sat beside him. "Ruthie sleeping already?"

"Like a lamb. She won't wake until morning."

He stretched out his legs and sighed. "I'm bushed."

"Hard day?"

He nodded. "That sun saps me. But the latrines are dug. How did it go with Eve today?"

Bessie could feel her spirits lift at the mere mention of her friend. "Wonderfully! Did you know her mother is white?"

Jasper looked surprised. "I had no idea. Did she tell you that?"

Bessie nodded. "She doesn't have to live on the reservation because she is part white. Her mother still lives there, though, even though her father is dead."

Jasper nodded. "Understandable. She would be ostracized back east."

"Even out here?"

"People might be polite to her face, but they would likely talk about her behind her back. Men would think she was fair game, and women would think she was no better than a common street girl. She's better to stay where she is."

Bessie frowned. "What about Ruthie?"

Jasper sighed. "It won't be easy, Bessie. I hope and pray things change by the time Ruthie grows up." He put an arm around her and hugged her. "Let's not borrow trouble yet. We'll do the best we can, pray, and leave it in God's hands."

She leaned against him and marveled at how safe she felt in his arms. He pulled her closer and propped his chin on her head. She could hear his heart beating under her ear and smell the scent of horse and leather on his uniform.

"Hey, I almost forgot to tell you. The stage brought news about the impeachment. President Johnson was acquitted because the Senate didn't have a two-thirds majority. The vote was thirty-five for impeachment and nineteen for acquittal."

She didn't care about politics. It seemed very far away, especially tonight. Back in Boston her father would be arguing with his cronies over the vote, and papers would be full of screaming headlines. Her world had shrunk to this man and the baby in the other room. It seemed a fair trade to Bessie. And even if Jasper never loved her, she could be contented.

"Are you ready for our study tonight?"

His grip around her shoulders relaxed, and she pulled away reluctantly. "What are we looking at tonight?" They were still going through 1 Corinthians 13 and cross-referencing it with other verses.

"Verse 7 says, 'Beareth all things, believeth all things, hopeth all things, endureth all things.' I found a reference there to Galatians 6, verse 2. 'Bear ye one another's burdens, and so fulfil the law of Christ.' " He cupped her cheek with his hand. "Can you share any of your burdens with me, Bessie? I'll try my best to help you carry them. You've seemed distant for awhile. Is it something I've done or failed to do?"

She longed to tell him she had found that letter, but she couldn't. She just couldn't bear to bring Lenore into this house by talking about her. Jasper never mentioned her, but did he still think of Lenore? Did he find his wife a poor substitute? She suspected he did, but she didn't want her fears confirmed. She smiled into his green eyes.

"It's been an adjustment." Which was true. It had been hard to make the transition from Boston to here. She hoped he would accept that.

He did. His expression softened, and he nodded. "You've been gently reared, and dealing with scorpions, snakes, and spiders has not been fun. Have you written your family lately? I know you haven't received any letters. Would you like to go visit them for the summer?"

Was he trying to get rid of her? She swallowed past the lump in her throat. "No. My place is with you. Mother promised they would try to visit next year. I'll be fine. I want to be here."

He smiled, and Bessie saw the relief in his face. Her heart sped up at the realization that he didn't want her to go.

"What do you want out of our marriage and our life together, Bessie?"

Did she dare tell him? Did she dare say she wanted his love and his children, the joy of teaching their children about Jesus and growing old together? The words stuck in her throat. He would think her forward if she mentioned children now. But where was her courage? She had always been timid and unsure, but out here she was more courageous than she had ever been.

She took a deep breath. "I want—" She broke off at the wail from the bedroom.

"Uh-oh. I thought you said she was out for the night."

"She had to prove me wrong, didn't she?" She stood and walked toward the bedroom. "I won't be long. I'm sure she'll go right back to sleep."

Bessie laid a soothing hand on Ruth and sang to her gently. The baby corked her thumb in her mouth and went right back to sleep. What had disturbed her? Was it a sign from God that she shouldn't tell Jasper how she felt yet? Tears burned her eyes. She didn't know how much longer she could go on the way things were. Even if Jasper never loved her, she could have the comfort of raising their children if she could just muster the courage to speak.

She straightened her shoulders and made her way back to the parlor. Jasper looked up from his perusal of his Bible and smiled.

"Everything all right?"

"Fine. I don't know what woke her."

He patted the space beside him. "Come finish our conversation."

His green eyes followed her every movement, and she felt self-conscious as she walked to the cot and sat next to him. He immediately put his arm around her, and she forced her shoulders to relax. Together they leaned against the wall.

"Do you have anything to say about my question?" he asked, his words muffled by his lips in her hair.

Her heart pounded. She swallowed past the lump in her throat. It was now or never. An opportunity might not come this way again.

"I want to have a family, children that we raise for God." A whisper was all her dry throat could manage. "What do you want from our marriage?"

Jasper stilled. His heart beat beneath her ear, and now it sped up. She heard him catch his breath, then he tilted her face and gazed into her eyes. "Children? You want children too?"

Did he mean he wanted children? Her gaze searched his. Did she dare ask him how he really felt about her? He was doing all the right things, but was it out of a sense of duty or out of genuine emotion? She opened her mouth to ask, but the impetuous words were stilled by a knock on the door.

"Lieutenant Mendenhall!" Someone pounded on their door.

Jasper gave her a rueful glance and got up to answer the door. He came back moments later. "I have to go. There's been an attack on some settlers south of here. I'll probably be gone a few days." He knelt and took her face in his hands. "We'll talk of this when I return." He kissed her briefly and took his hat.

Bessie willed him to look back and smile just one last time; but without looking at her, he shut the door behind him.

Chapter 10

The stars twinkled in the night like pinpoints of hope against the dark velvet sky. Jasper led the detachment along the rocky trail and thought about what had just happened with Bessie. He was glad of the interruption. Her admission that she wanted children had rocked him. It was what he wanted too, but to hear her admit it seemed like a gift from God.

They came over a rise and saw the orange flames still smoldering in the burned and blackened cabin below them. Grimly, Jasper led the way to the cabin. He didn't want to see what condition the settlers would be in. They were probably dead.

They were almost to the cabin when he heard a wail off to his right. He wheeled his mare and spurred her toward the sound. Beside a small stream gleaming in the moonlight, he found a woman crouched over the body of a man and a child. Keening in grief, she rocked back and forth on her heels.

He touched her shoulder, and she whipped around with a long-bladed knife in her hand.

"You're safe, Ma'am!" He sprang back, then grappled with her and finally succeeded in wresting the knife from her grasp. She fell atop the two bodies and resumed her wailing.

He pulled her away, and she didn't resist this time. Leading her away from the carnage, he motioned to Rooster to bring him the spare horse they had brought with them. Her head rolled back as he lifted her onto the horse, and he saw with shock that she could have been Lenore's twin. He almost snatched his fingers away but scolded himself for his flight of fancy. This poor lady had just lost her entire family, and he was letting a simple resemblance get in the way of his compassion.

He would take her to Bessie before pursuing the savages who did this. His wife's gentle touch would help this lady. He told Rooster to load the bodies and bring them back to the fort for burial. He then helped the woman into the saddle. She slumped against the gelding's neck, and he swung into his own saddle and started back to Fort Bowie.

Their quarters were dark when he helped the woman inside. He shut the door and fumbled as he lit the lantern. "Bessie," he called.

The woman started when he spoke, and he laid a soothing hand on her arm. "It's all right. My wife will be here in a moment."

Moments later, Bessie came running from the bedroom, her hair falling to her waist and her eyes frightened. "Jasper? What's wrong?"

Her gaze went to his hand on the woman's arm, and he withdrew it hastily. "This woman has lost her family to Cochise and his band. Can you care for her? I have to go after them."

Bessie stepped closer, and her face blanched. "Lenore?" she asked in a trembling voice.

"No, Bessie. Not Lenore, but I saw the resemblance too." He stepped away, and Bessie stepped closer. "I must go." He stared at his wife uneasily and saw the color begin to come back into her cheeks.

"You poor dear," she said softly. She went to the woman and put her arm around her shoulders. "Come with me. I'll fix you some tea."

The woman allowed Bessie to lead her to the kitchen, and Jasper sighed in relief. He would have the men give the bodies a decent burial, and Bessie would take care of the woman.

Bessie's hands trembled as she poured the boiling water into the teapot. The woman's resemblance to her sister was uncanny! Why would God bring such a reminder into her home when Lenore's memory was finally dulling in Jasper's mind? She bit her lip at her uncharitable thought. This poor woman had no control over her appearance. How could Bessie be thinking such things when this woman had just lost everything? She was ashamed of herself.

She set the cup in front of the woman. The poor lady stared into space vacantly, then tears began to flow, leaving clean rivulets in her smoke-blackened face.

Bessie touched her hand gently. "Have some tea," she urged. "You don't have to talk about what happened."

The woman began to sob softly. "Oh, it was terrible! My poor little Danny! And James." Her sobs grew louder, and she rocked back and forth in her grief.

Tears flooded Bessie's eyes. She could feel this woman's pain. If something happened to Ruthie or Jasper, how could she bear it? What could she say now to comfort this woman?

After nearly an hour of racking sobs, the woman began to bring herself under control. She took several deep breaths and raised reddened eyes to meet Bessie's gaze. "You're very kind. Was that your husband who brought me here? I don't remember much." She bit her lip and closed her eyes with the strain of trying to control her emotions.

"Yes, that was my husband. I'm Bessie Mendenhall, and my husband is Jasper."

"I'm Myra Trimble." Tears flooded her eyes again. "James always said my name didn't fit me. It means tearful, and he had never seen me cry. Now, he never will." She bowed her head in a fresh spasm of weeping.

Bessie knelt and put her arms around Myra. "I know it hurts," she murmured. "Let it out." She patted her back and cried with her. She could only imagine her pain. What if it were Jasper lying beneath that sandy soil with Ruthie? The mere thought brought a hard knot to her stomach.

Myra finally pulled away and fished in her sleeve for her handkerchief. "I've always been so stoic and strong. Now I can't seem to stop crying." She took a deep breath. "The vision of my son lying beside his father burns in my brain. I can't get it out."

"God has your husband and son in the palm of His hand," Bessie said. "You can rest in that."

Myra's lips tightened. "Don't talk to me of a God who would allow my two-year-old son to be slaughtered! I want nothing to do with a God like that." Hectic spots of color stained her cheeks, and she took her cold tea and swallowed a gulp.

The poor woman didn't even have faith to help her through this. Bessie felt an overwhelming wave of pity for Myra. How did one deal with a tragedy of this magnitude without faith? But she wouldn't argue with her. Maybe her short stay with them would open her eyes to eternal things. Bessie prayed for wisdom to say the right things in the next few days.

After she got Myra situated on the couch cot, Bessie went to bed. She tossed and turned for a long time before sleep claimed her exhausted body.

When Ruth whimpered and cried out, Bessie groaned and opened her eyes to the dawn light. She wasn't ready for morning. It had to have been after two o'clock before she got to bed. She reached over and put her hand in the cradle. Ruth grabbed her finger and brought it to her mouth. She sucked on it greedily, and Bessie laughed.

"All right, you slave driver, I'm getting your breakfast." Eve would be there soon too. The thought of her friend lightened her heart. She had two women today. She wouldn't call Myra a friend yet, though. The woman's bitterness against God separated her from Bessie. But Bessie determined in her heart to be the best friend she could to the bereaved woman.

She climbed out of bed and quickly dressed in her lightest dress. July was almost here, and the day already promised to be a scorcher. She picked up Ruth and went to the kitchen. By the time she had fed her and put her on the floor on a blanket, Eve was knocking gently on the back door.

"We have a guest," Bessie warned her quietly when she let her in. "A widow from an attack last night."

A shadow crossed Eve's face. "Perhaps I should go. She will not wish to see me today after such a thing."

"She can't possibly blame you. You had nothing to do with an attack by Apache braves."

Eve shrugged. "I see it many times, my friend. To some whites, the only good Indian is a dead one."

Bessie had heard that expression many times, but it still pained her. "Don't go. I was so looking forward to seeing you."

Eve smiled. "I too. Very well, if you wish it, I will stay. But do not say I did not warn you."

They soon had the kitchen and bedroom cleaned as they waited for Myra to awaken. It was nearly ten o'clock before they heard her stirring. Bessie went to the parlor to greet her.

"Good morning," she said with a smile. "We have tea and biscuits for breakfast. Are you hungry?"

Myra sat up and pushed her hair back from her face. In the daylight, she didn't look quite so much like Lenore, but the resemblance was still there. The same raven hair, sultry eyes, and pouting mouth.

"That sounds lovely." Her expression wooden and grave, she slipped out of bed and followed Bessie to the kitchen. She stopped short when she saw Eve and little Ruth. Venom and rage chased one another over her face. "Indians!" she spat. Her hands curved like claws, and she started toward Eve.

Bessie sprang after her and only succeeded in stopping her with great difficulty. "Eve is my friend. She had nothing to do with your loss."

"All savages are the same," Myra said, glaring at Eve. "If she didn't do this one, she likely had a hand in others."

"No, you must calm down, Myra. Have some tea." Bessie forced her into a chair and hurried to get the tea and biscuits.

Myra pointed a shaking finger at Eve. "You wouldn't be telling me to calm down if that were your husband and child she and those murderers had butchered." She glared at Eve again, then slumped back in her chair.

Bessie gave a sigh of relief when she saw the agitation seep out of Myra's manner. She set the tea and biscuits on the table in front of her guest. "Is there someone we can telegraph for you? Family somewhere?"

Myra didn't look at Eve again. She picked up a biscuit. "I should let my brother know. He has a ranch near Tucson. And our parents, I suppose. They live in Boston."

"I'm from Boston!"

Myra looked her fully in the face for the first time. "You are? We lived in Boston until a year ago when James decided to come out here. I tried to warn him, but he wouldn't listen." She sighed and stared into her teacup.

The similarities choked Bessie for a moment. Did tragedy await her somewhere down the road? She hadn't wanted to come here either. For a moment, she felt as though a heavy weight lay on her chest. She wanted to run out of the house, find the nearest stage, and head for home. She took a deep breath and sat cautiously beside Myra.

She must not let Myra realize how much her words had shaken her. They chatted about Boston for a few minutes, but she could sense the rage in Myra just below the surface. Bessie pitied her, but she did not really like her. The rage she sensed unsettled her.

Ruth gave a mewling gurgle, and Myra's head swiveled toward the sound. Her eyes narrowed, and she looked at Eve. "Your brat?"

Bessie's throat tightened. Their brief truce was obviously over. "She's mine," she said before Eve had to answer. "She's a darling. I found her with her dead mother in the desert and adopted her."

"You should have left her to die," Myra spat. "To lie out under the blazing sun just like my Danny." She began to weep again and left the room with a last venomous look over her shoulder.

Shaken, Bessie looked at Eve. "What should we do?" she mouthed. She didn't want Myra to hear her and launch into another tirade.

Eve shrugged. "She will have to deal with this in her own way," she said softly. "Do not fret over my feelings. I am used to it." She turned and began to get out the ingredients for the stew they had decided to prepare for supper.

The next morning, she and Myra filed to the burial of Myra's husband and son. She left Ruthie in Eve's care. Myra's eyes glared balefully from a face devoid of color. She didn't cry, not even when the small wooden coffin containing the remains of her son was lowered into the scarred earth. Bessie wept for her, though. She could only imagine how much pain cried to be released from the other woman's heart.

The next few days were like living in an armed camp. Bessie felt she had to watch everything Myra did. She didn't trust her around Eve or Ruth. Ruth cried every time she came near, as if she sensed her animosity.

Bessie longed for Jasper to return. She needed his strength and wisdom to handle this situation. Meanwhile, Myra made no mention of leaving. Why couldn't she go to her brother in Tucson? What held her here? For just a moment, she wondered if Myra wanted to see Jasper again, but she pushed the thought away. What was she thinking? The woman had just lost her husband and small son.

After waiting in expectation for nearly a week, Bessie heard the commotion of the returning detachment. She hurried to the door. "Jasper is back," she said excitedly.

"Newlyweds, are you?" Myra said with a sly smile. "Don't worry, Honey, that excitement will wear off soon enough. You'll soon be looking forward to times away from him."

Bessie didn't bother answering. She knew she would always long to be with Jasper. When she heard the back door close, she was glad Myra had the sense to leave so she could greet Jasper alone.

The baby didn't give a peep either in the half hour Bessie waited for Jasper. Finally, she heard his step on the front stoop and hurried to open the door.

He looked dusty and tired, but he smiled when he saw her. He held out his arms, and she rushed into them. "I missed my girls," he said.

"We missed you," she told him. "Did you find Cochise?"

He shook his head. "Not a trace. He hides in those Dragoon Mountains like a snake." He removed his hat and followed her inside. "How did you get along with the widow? I don't even know her name."

"It's Myra Trimble. She's still very distressed." She wanted to blurt out her fear of the woman, but what if he thought she was being foolish? It would be better if he saw for himself.

"Is she still here?" Jasper looked past her into the kitchen.

"Yes. She has a brother in Tucson, but she hasn't seemed in any hurry to go to her family. I'm not sure why. She hates Eve."

He frowned then. "Because she's Navajo? Not surprising under the circumstances, I guess. What about Ruthie? Is she all right with her?"

"I'm not comfortable with the way she looks at the baby," Bessie admitted. "She's so strange, Jasper. Full of bitterness and anger. She hates God."

He hugged her. "Sounds like you've been under siege."

"It's felt like it at times."

"Where's my girl? Sleeping?"

Bessie nodded. "I'll get her."

"No, don't wake her up. I just was wondering if she'll recognize me. She'll be cranky if you wake her."

She laughed. "That baby doesn't have a cranky bone in her body. She's outgrown that cradle too. Her feet were sticking out the ends, and her poor little head bumped the headboard. I've had her sleeping with me. I pushed the cot up against the wall so she won't fall out."

"I'll have her another bed by tomorrow," he said.

His gaze brought the heat to her cheeks. Did he mean to begin their marriage in earnest tomorrow? Her mouth went dry. Surely not. Myra would be in the next room. It would be too embarrassing. But soon, his expression promised. She smiled uncertainly.

"I think I'll check on Ruthie." She could sense his gaze on her as she hurried from the room. Why did she always run when things got too intense? She was a coward. She should have stayed, melted in his arms, and kissed him.

She opened the door to the bedroom and stared at the bed blankly. Was Ruth covered by the blanket? She couldn't see even her little rump sticking up through the bedclothes. Bessie went to the bed and felt it. Empty. She whirled and looked around. Had Ruthie fallen out? Bessie looked under the bed and over every inch of floor space before she began to panic.

"Jasper!"

He came immediately. "What is it? What's wrong?"

"I can't find Ruthie," she gasped. "She isn't anywhere in the bedroom."

"She has to be," he said reasonably. "Let's look again. Was she in the bed?"

Bessie nodded. Perhaps she was mistaken, and she had put Ruthie down for her nap on the cot in the parlor. But the tiny parlor was as empty as the bedroom. No Ruthie.

"She has to be here. No one would take her." Jasper joined her in the parlor.

At his words, the blood drained from Bessie's face, and she felt faint. "Myra!"

Chapter 11

J asper tried to tell himself that no woman would harm a child, even her worst enemy's. But Bessie's terror soon communicated itself to him. He sent for Eve. She could help keep Bessie calm while he mounted a search.

"It's my fault, my fault," Bessie wailed. "I knew she was unbalanced. I didn't like the way she looked at Ruthie. I should have known to keep the baby with me at all times."

"It's not your fault," he told her. "You couldn't have known she would take the baby with you right there in the house."

"Lieutenant."

They both looked up at the sound. Rooster stood in the doorway, his face filled with concern. "I've found tracks, Sir. They're heading toward the Dragoon Mountains."

"On foot?" Would Myra be so crazy?

"No, Sir. She's mounted. She stole a horse from the corral while Private Montel took a siesta."

Which just proved her craziness. What person in her right mind would head off into the desert during the worst heat of the day in the hottest month of the year? Jasper's fear for his adopted daughter increased. What did the woman plan to do? And why head right into Cochise's territory? It *was* madness.

Eve rushed in the door, and Bessie threw herself into her arms. "She's taken my baby," she sobbed.

Eve patted her back and soothed her. "I was with my brother when Jasper sent for me. My brother has gathered some braves, and they are searching too. He will find her." Eve's eyes met Jasper's, and he saw fear. The desert was a big place, and Ruth was just a tiny baby at the mercy of a madwoman. What if Myra got it into her head to leave the baby somewhere to die in the heat? The thought tormented him. He thought of his and Bessie's laughter the day she learned to roll over, the little birthmark shaped like a butterfly on the inside of one chubby knee, and the way her brown eyes widened when she saw him, followed by her slow smile and reaching hands. He had to find their baby.

Bessie followed Jasper to the door. She thrust a full pillowcase in his hands. "Here, take this. There are diapers, clean clothes, and her bottle. It's full."

She buried her face in his shirt, and he hugged her fiercely. "Pray, Bessie. Pray for all you're worth." He kissed the top of her head and left her with Eve.

The scorching sun beat down, and he flinched at the heat. How could a frail woman withstand hours of this with no shade? She did not even have a hat. He found his mare already saddled and led the detachment toward the Dragoon Mountains. Rooster could follow a hawk's shadow where it fell on the sand, or at least that's how Jasper felt sometimes. The old man was the best tracker Jasper knew.

They had followed the trail for fifteen minutes when Rooster pointed. "Sandstorm coming."

"We have to find them before it hits!" Jasper was frantic. The storm would wipe away any trace of prints. It would likely kill Myra and the baby too. She didn't have enough sense to seek shelter, what little shelter there was.

Rooster pointed again. "We can shelter there, behind the horses."

Jasper knew Rooster was right. He was responsible for the safety of his men, but his heart was almost unbearably heavy as he turned his mare's face and led the men to the rock face Rooster had pointed out. All hope was lost. What could he tell Bessie?

They positioned the horses in front of them and knelt and covered their faces with their coats. The wind was upon them in moments, driving the sand into any exposed skin like tiny biting insects. Jasper prayed as he knelt there. All he could see was Bessie's face when she realized the baby was gone. She would blame herself if he didn't find Ruth. He didn't think she could live with that.

The storm was over nearly as quickly as it started. The sun came out and the wind died down. Jasper stood and ordered the men to saddle up and get ready to ride.

"Where to, Lieutenant?"

Rooster's eyes met his, and he nearly flinched at the resignation he saw there. They might never even find the small corpse. "All we can do is go in the direction we last saw her tracks," he told Rooster.

Rooster sighed. "Even the biggest ball of twine unravels," he said. "But with the good Lord's help, maybe we can rewind this one."

Jasper looked at him askance. "This was a small storm. With a bit of luck we may pick up their trail on the other side."

Jasper didn't think Rooster thought it a likely occurrence, but it was better than no hope at all.

They plodded through the rocky sand but found no trace of a trail. At dusk, Jasper knew he had no choice but to call off the search for the night. The thought of little Ruth spending the night in the desert was almost more than he could bear. Dangerous creatures came out at night. Rattlesnakes and scorpions.

He prayed for her safety as he unrolled his bedroll and lay out under the stars.

Starting at every sound, Bessie paced the floor restlessly. How could Ruth still be alive? But the tiny flame of hope refused to die. Jasper would find her. He loved her too. So did the men. Rooster could track anything, and they had some of their best men with them. If anyone could bring back her baby, that detachment could.

Eve refused to leave her, although Bessie urged her to go home. Several of the soldiers stopped by to see if they could do anything for her. Even Major Saunders sent over a note urging her to call on him if she needed anything. She knew many of them thought she should not have kept Ruth, but in this hour of need, they rallied around her.

Four days and nights had dragged by. Bessie couldn't eat, couldn't sleep. If she just knew what was happening. If only Jasper had allowed her to go! She understood, of course, that it simply was too dangerous. But that fact did not make the wait any easier. Eve talked her into going to bed, but all she did was doze off and on.

The morning after the sandstorm, Jasper awoke gritty-eyed and discouraged. He dumped the spoiled milk, and they quickly broke camp and mounted up. As dusk fell for the second night, he knew they would have to start back if they did not find sign of Myra tomorrow. They were almost to the Dragoon Mountains, and he didn't have enough men to hold off Cochise's warriors.

As they were saddling up the next morning, the scout gave a shout. "Indians, Lieutenant!"

Jasper vaulted into his saddle and grabbed his rifle. As he wheeled to face the charge, he realized they weren't hostile Indians. The Indians plodded toward them without weapons drawn. He shielded his eyes and tried to see what they were up to.

As they came nearer, one held up a hand. "Lieutenant Mendenhall!"

They knew his name? This one spoke perfect English. Jasper squinted in the bright morning sun. The man looked vaguely familiar. With a start, Jasper realized the Indian reminded him of Eve. This must be her brother. As they came closer, he saw the man was holding something. A glimpse of dark hair brought his heart to his throat. Was that Ruthie?

He urged his horse toward the band and stopped in front of the leader. The man was smiling, and Jasper could see the resemblance to Eve even more clearly.

The man reined in his horse and held out the baby. "Is this small one what you searched for?"

Jasper took her and snuggled her close. She opened her eyes and smiled her slow smile and gurgled. Tears pricked his eyes, and he struggled to thank the other man. "How can I thank you?"

The man smiled. "I am Ben, brother to Eve. You have been kind to my sister. We always pay our debts."

"What about the woman Myra?"

A mask of stone came down over Ben's face. "She is no more. Cochise and his warriors found her before I did. She resides beneath the earth with her husband and son now."

Jasper searched for the capacity to feel pity for the woman and was surprised to find himself capable of it. She had been driven mad by grief. "How did you get Ruthie?"

"I told Cochise she had been stolen from her mother, and I would return her. She cried, and he was glad to give her to me." Ben grinned and patted Ruth's silky head. "He did not ask about the mother, and I did not tell him."

Jasper held out his hand. "Thank you, my friend."

Ben shook it. "You will need this for the trip." He handed a sheepskin of milk and a cup made out of a gourd.

"Can she drink from the cup?" Jasper asked doubtfully.

"She does not like it, but she drinks," Ben said. "It will do until she is in her mother's arms." He nodded to the Navajo braves with him, and they all filed away.

Jasper tucked Ruth in his left arm. The sooner they got to the fort, the better.

❧

Bessie woke when the sentry called the midnight hour. She sat up and looked around. Something had awakened her. What was it? Not the sentry; she was used to that. She listened closely, then went to the door. It sounded like horses and voices.

At her first movement, Eve opened her eyes on her pallet on the floor and joined her at the door. Bessie opened the door, and they both stepped out onto the front stoop. The moon was so bright it was almost as light as dusk.

"What is it?" Eve whispered.

Bessie squinted through the moonlit night and thought she saw horses milling around in front of the stagecoach station. She was still dressed, even down to her boots, so she started across the parade ground. Eve followed her.

As she neared the group, she heard a familiar cry, then Jasper's voice. Her pulse beat wildly in her throat, and a sob burst from her lips. Jasper heard and turned with Ruth in his arms. He grinned from ear to ear.

She leaped forward with arms outstretched. "Ruthie!"

The baby gurgled and reached out chubby fingers for her. "Mummm, mummm," she chortled.

Bessie gathered her into her arms and buried her face in the baby's chubby neck. She reeked of sweat, urine, and sour milk, but Bessie had never smelled a flower or a sachet more wonderful. She kissed her over and over again, while Jasper looked on with an indulgent smile. Ruthie soon tired of the attention and began to fuss.

Bessie turned to Jasper with shining eyes. "I knew you would find her." Her smile encompassed all the tired men. "Thank you all so much. I'll never forget what you've done."

"I wish I could take the credit, but you have to thank someone else." Jasper nodded to Eve. "Her brother Ben found her. Cochise's braves had already killed Myra, and they had Ruthie. They'd been taking good care of her; she was clean and well fed. They even sent back some milk for her, but it's all gone now, and I ran out of clean clothes. She's probably hungry. Ben managed to talk Cochise into letting him take the baby."

This was a debt she could never repay. Bessie turned to Eve. "My friend, what can I say?"

Eve smiled. "There are no words necessary with friends."

Bessie kissed her on the cheek. "Thank you, my friend." She turned back to Jasper. "She needs a bath and bed."

He grimaced. "I know. So do I."

She was stricken with conscience. She hadn't even thought of how tired he must be. The lines of exhaustion around his nose and mouth smote her like a blow. "I'll heat some water," she told him.

He gave her another tired smile. "I'll be along in a minute." He turned to thank his men again.

Bessie hurried back home. Home. It truly was home again. Their little family was safe and complete once more. She saw the Indian who worked with the soldiers making adobe and waved. He had always taken a special interest in Ruth; he would be glad to know the baby was safely home. He nodded gravely. Several soldiers had come out to see what the commotion was, and they clapped when she walked by with the baby.

After Bessie fed the baby, she fetched the bathtub down from the wall in the bedroom and poured hot water into it, while Eve hauled more water from the acequia. They filled the washtub for Ruth and the bathtub for Jasper. She stripped Ruth and plunked her into the warm water. The baby gurgled and kicked, and Bessie laughed. Everything seemed so normal again.

Although she didn't want to let the baby out of her sight, she handed her to Eve to dress and went to lay out a towel for Jasper. She heard him come in while she was in the bedroom.

She was testing the water when he shut the door behind him.

"I'm bushed," he said. "All I want is a hot bath and bed."

"Are you hungry?"

He shook his head. "Too tired to be hungry. I wouldn't turn down a cup of coffee, though."

"I'll make some." She turned to go, but he laid his hand on her arm.

"We're a family now, aren't we, Bessie?"

"Yes," she said softly. "We're a family now."

Was a near disaster needed to make them both see the treasure found in these four walls? She felt an overwhelming sense of gratitude to God that they finally had seen it.

She sensed his eyes on her as she let herself out and shut the door behind her. By the time the coffee was ready, Jasper should be done with his bath. Ruthie was already asleep on the cot in the parlor with Eve.

Bessie's cheeks went hot. Eve evidently had assumed Jasper slept in the bed with her and thought it would be okay to go to bed with the baby. What was she to do? Her mouth dry, she poured Jasper a cup of coffee and tapped on the bedroom door.

"Come on in. I'm decent."

She cautiously pushed open the door and found him dressed in long johns, his hair sticking up on end. "Here's your coffee."

He took it with a smile of thanks that faded when he looked at her. "What's wrong?"

Was she that easy to read? She gulped. "Eve and Ruthie are already asleep on the cot in the parlor."

His gaze grew soft, but he didn't say anything for a long moment. "The sun took everything out of me. You're safe. It will be a squeeze, but that cot will hold both of us, if you don't mind." His words were gentle.

Her face burned with humiliation. Did he think she planned it this way? They had never had a chance to finish their discussion of her desire for children. He stared at her, but she couldn't read his expression. "I don't mind," she said softly.

His expression softened further. "I'll be asleep before you ever get ready for bed," he promised.

She nodded, not daring to meet his gaze. She quickly gathered her things and went to the kitchen. She shivered as she took off her dress, hung it on a hook by the door, and pulled on her nightdress. Then she took her hair down and slipped back inside the bedroom.

Jasper lay along the edge, exhaustion etched in his face. He breathed deeply, already sleeping. Bessie blew out the candle and felt the end of the bed. She crept along the wall to the pillow, then slipped beneath the bedclothes. The desert night was cool, but her shivering wasn't just from the chill. Her husband's warmth spread toward her like a welcoming hug, and she snuggled inside.

It felt strange and wonderful at the same time. She allowed herself to relax. Reaching out a tentative hand, she touched his arm. Knowing he was sleeping, she gathered her courage and slid closer and pillowed her head on his shoulder. The sound of his deep breaths relaxed her further, and it wasn't long before she slipped into the welcome arms of sleep.

Chapter 12

Jasper yawned. Every bone in his body ached, and his eyes felt swollen from hours of staring in the hot sun. He started to move and discovered his arm was trapped. Startled, he looked down and saw Bessie sleeping with her head on his shoulder. He smiled.

He stared at his sleeping wife. She looked so lovely, so peaceful. And she was his. Why had he ever thought she didn't compare to the picture of Lenore? Her sister's image had dimmed in his mind, and he could barely remember what she looked like. Her hair was darker, wasn't it? He picked up a lock of Bessie's fine light brown hair and rubbed it between his fingers. It felt like strands of silk. He brought it to his nose and inhaled the fresh scent. Eve had shown her how to make shampoo from yucca, and they had added some flowers.

Her skin was white and fine-pored with a hint of pink to her cheeks. And she was so small. He felt a wave of protectiveness as he touched her face gently before slipping out of bed. He glanced at Bessie's sleeping face once more while he pulled on his clothes, then reluctantly opened the door and stepped into the kitchen.

Eve was feeding Ruth, and he patted the infant on the head before moving to the stove. Pouring a cup of coffee, he took it back to the table and sat across from Eve.

"Bessie is exhausted. Please let her sleep."

"Of course." Eve pulled the bottle from Ruth's slack mouth. The infant sighed but didn't awaken. "She will not sleep long, though. She will wish to see Ruthie soon."

Eve was right, and he nodded. Bessie was a good mother. And a good wife. She tried so hard, and he didn't always appreciate her efforts. God had given them a miracle by preserving little Ruth through this ordeal.

The door opened, and Bessie came out from the bedroom rubbing the sleep from her eyes. Her hair was tousled, and she still wore her nightgown. Her gaze skittered away from Jasper, and he realized she was embarrassed. She quickly went to Ruth and knelt beside the chair.

Touching the baby's soft head, she laid her lips on her forehead. "Is she all right?"

"Just sleeping," Eve reassured her. She handed the baby to Bessie and rose. "I would like to return home and thank my brother for finding Ruth. Is that all right?"

Bessie gripped her hand. "I would like to thank him myself," she told her. "Please convey my heartfelt gratitude."

"And mine," Jasper added. He knew he would have come home bereaved and empty-handed if it hadn't been for Ben. He would not have been able to bear the grief in Bessie's eyes.

Eve smiled and squeezed her hand. "I will be back this afternoon."

"Take the entire day," Bessie urged her. "You haven't slept in days either. None of us will do much today. I'm not going to let Ruthie out of my sight."

Eve nodded. "In the morning, then." She smiled once more and hurried away.

Jasper stared at Bessie until she finally looked up and met his gaze. "Did you sleep well?" he asked.

Color tinged her fair skin, and she looked away. "Very well, thank you. You?"

"I didn't move all night." How did he go about bringing up the fact that he wanted their sleeping arrangements to continue? It was so awkward. Perhaps he would wait until tonight. He shook his head inwardly at his cowardice.

"What are your plans for the day?"

She smiled and looked down at the baby. "Nothing except spending time with Ruthie."

"I think I'll do the same. My eyes still burn from the sun, and last night the colonel told me to take the day off. Is there any heavy lifting or something special you're needing done that I can help you with?"

"Well, I have been wanting to move the furniture out and clean under it and behind it. Your mess chest is heavy."

"I can do that." He was happy there was something she needed from him. He wished he knew how she really felt. But did it matter? They were married, and they would build a life together. It was as simple as that. He enjoyed the thought of spending the day with his small family.

She put Ruth on the cot, and Jasper made a mental note to get a crib made for her.

"Well, Boss, what do we do first?" he asked when she came back.

"Let's move your mess chest underneath the window. Then we can use it as a window seat."

He nodded and went to shove it across the parlor floor. As he put his hand behind it, he felt a sticky substance and jerked his hand away. A shiny black spider raced toward his fingers. Bessie screamed, and he jumped farther away. The spider disappeared behind the chest.

"It was a black widow, wasn't it?" Bessie said fearfully.

He nodded. "I knew as soon as I felt that sticky web. That's why I pulled my hand away so fast."

"We have to kill it," she said. "What if it should bite Ruthie?"

"Get me a shoe," he told her. "I'll get a shovel to pull the chest out with."

She bit her lip and hurried to the bedroom, while he went out the back door and grabbed a shovel. He hated spiders. Back in Texas he had seen his share of tarantulas, and they never failed to spook him. Black widows were more dangerous and fast. This one would have nailed him if he had hesitated at all. But he was glad he had been there. If Bessie had tried to move the chest herself, she would have been bitten.

Bessie wasn't in the parlor when he returned. "Hey, where are you?" he called.

Her muffled voice floated through the bedroom door. "I'm getting dressed. I want all the layers of clothing possible between me and that spider. And I'm trying to decide which shoe to use. I don't want to use one of mine. I would probably never wear it again."

He chuckled. "I'll protect you," he called.

She opened the door. Her hair was still disheveled, but she had her boots on and wore a determined expression. She carried one of his work boots in one hand and the broom in the other.

"You look like you're loaded for bear," he said with a grin. "Have you had experience in spider hunting before?"

"Many times. And I've killed more scorpions than I can count since we've been here." Her shoulders stiff with purpose, she advanced into the room.

"You've never mentioned it," he said in surprise. But why was he surprised? She had proven herself more than equal to any task so far.

"I knew I had to learn to handle these kinds of things if I expected to be a helpmeet," she said with a shrug.

An altogether remarkable woman. He smiled and moved to the mess chest again. "Maybe you'd better move Ruthie to the bedroom. If that thing decides to run, there's no telling where it may end up."

Bessie looked alarmed and snatched the baby up. Ruth stirred but didn't awaken as Bessie took her to the bedroom.

Jasper waited until she returned. "Ready? I'm going to use the shovel to pull the chest out. When the spider comes out, smack it with the broom to stun it enough so I can kill it."

Her face was white, but she nodded. "Ready."

If he didn't hate them so much, Jasper would have felt pity for the spider. Bessie held the broom between both hands like a bat, and he suspected she would deliver a mighty whop with it. He thrust the shovel behind the mess chest and pushed it out from the wall with one strong shove. He saw several black blobs race up the back of the chest. "Here they come," he shouted.

"They?"

Her eyes widened in horror, but she stood like a miniature Valkyrie, her feet planted with the broom ready to strike. He would have laughed if the situation hadn't been so intense. Two spiders reached the top of the chest, and she brought the broom down with a thump that rattled the doors. She raised the broom wildly again, and he saw the blow had either killed or severely stunned the spiders. Two more reached the top, and again the broom came down with amazing force from such a small woman.

He peered behind the chest and saw there were no more spiders. They all lay motionless atop the mess chest. He took the shoe and pounded them to black pulps. He held out his hand. "Give me the broom a minute."

For a second, he thought she wouldn't relinquish it. "They're all dead," he said. "I just want to clean out the web. I don't want to get it all over my hand when I move the chest."

She nodded and handed him the broom. "You're sure they're all dead?" she asked in a quavering voice.

He laughed. "After that attack, how could they survive? You've mastered the art of death by broom, but I flattened them to be sure."

She gave a laugh, but it was a shaky, unconvincing one, and he realized just how terrified she had been. He put an arm around her and hugged her gently. "You're really terrified of spiders, aren't you?"

"All my life. I would never even kill them at home, just run screaming for my father. But I knew these had to be eliminated for Ruthie to be safe." She smiled slightly. "Love conquers fear, I guess."

Love conquers fear. The words struck a chord in his heart. Was it fear that had been holding him back from allowing himself to fall in love with his wife? What was the other verse? *Perfect love casts out fear.* He had to figure out how to allow God to create perfect love in his life.

❦

Bessie had never had a man's attention the way she had today. Jasper was so attentive and sweet all day. After they killed the spiders, he helped her rearrange the furniture, then he went to the quartermaster for some wool blankets. She stitched them together and made a rug for the parlor to cover the bare floors. The room looked so warm and cozy that she felt as though she had a real home now, a home of her own.

They baked oatmeal cookies together and played with Ruth in the afternoon. Ruthie enjoyed her first cookie immensely, and they had laughed at the expression on her face. Jasper asked Bessie to read from his book of Walt Whitman poetry, and they studied more about love from the Bible after Ruth went to bed for the evening. Jasper had built her a crib out of two crates that would suffice for a few months.

The candle burned down, and Bessie knew it was time for bed, but she was reluctant for the day to end. Tomorrow their life would resume as normal. Jasper would go back to work, and Eve would come again to help with the pile of laundry that waited. But today had been a day Bessie would not soon forget.

"I think I'll haul in some water for morning before we turn in," Jasper said. How thoughtful of him. He kissed her cheek.

"I'll be right back."

She watched him go out the back door with the pitcher. He left the back door open, and just before he came back in, she saw a black shape fly in. A bird or a moth? She couldn't tell what it was, but it would have to be shooed back outside. Sighing in resignation, she got to her feet and went to fetch the broom. That ratty broom Jasper had made had come in handy today.

By the time she found the broom, the bird or whatever it was had managed to hide. Where had it gone?

"Another spider?"

She hadn't heard Jasper come back in. "No, a bird got in. I was going to shoo it out, but I don't know where it's gone."

Jasper helped her look for it, but neither one of them could see it.

"Let me get the lantern," Jasper said. He went to the parlor and fetched the lantern. Its bright light illuminated the dark corners.

"There it is!" Bessie pointed to the corner near the fireplace in the parlor.

"I see it." Jasper approached the shadow on the ceiling. He touched the broom to it, and it took off flying, then dove directly at Bessie's head.

She ducked. "It's a bat!" She had seen them occasionally in the attic at home but had never had one fly directly at her. Once one had gotten trapped in Lenore's hair. She had to be revived with smelling salts.

Bessie covered her hair with her hands and cowered on the floor. Jasper chased the bat around and around the room. He fell over furniture and banged his shin against the doorway, but the bat still eluded him.

"Open the front and back doors, and I'll see if I can chase it out."

She didn't want to get up, so she crawled to the front door and swung it open. She ran outside, around to the back, and opened the back door. The door to the bedroom was shut, so Ruthie was safe. Bessie would stay outside until the thing was gone. She could hear Jasper whacking the broom as he tried to get the bat to fly out. Suddenly, a black shape came zipping out the back door, and she screamed and cowered again.

"What is it, Missus?" The soldier on guard duty appeared at her side almost immediately.

"Just a bat," she admitted.

He shuddered and hurried away. She guessed she wasn't the only one who hated bats.

"It's gone," she called to Jasper. She closed the door behind her and went to the parlor to find him.

He appeared at the front door. His hair stuck up in spikes, his shirt had come untucked, and he looked wild-eyed. She chuckled. The chuckle turned into a giggle, then full-blown laughter. Jasper stared at her, then his own chuckle started. It fed Bessie's mirth, and holding her stomach, she sat on the cot. She laughed so hard she cried.

"It's not that funny," Jasper protested between his own laughter. He dropped beside her and tickled her. "I'll give you something to laugh about."

He grabbed her ribs, and she shrieked. "No, I'm ticklish!"

"That's the whole point." He pulled her onto his lap and poked her a couple of more times until she begged for mercy.

"You don't deserve mercy," he pointed out. "You deserted me in my hour of need."

"It was only a bat. I thought you could handle it on your own," she laughed.

"I'll let you off this time, but don't let it happen again." He stopped tickling her but kept his arms around her.

"I hope we don't have a bat in here again. If we do, I can't promise anything." Her smile died at the expression in his eyes. She gravely searched his gaze and closed her eyes as his lips came down on hers.

"I don't want to sleep in the parlor anymore," he whispered. "What do you say to that? We'll take it slow, Bessie. I won't share your bed yet, just the room."

What did she say to that? Her heart beat wildly in her throat. She was suddenly terrified.

He kissed her again, and her terror melted. This was right, and God had joined them. It didn't matter if he didn't love her. She had enough love for both of them. She smiled shyly and nodded.

Chapter 13

Bessie hummed as she prepared a bottle for Ruth. Bessie felt love and contentment in their predictable routine. Jasper seemed happy too. Several times she had been tempted to tell him she loved him, but somehow the words always stuck in her throat. She wanted to hear him say those words first. She wondered if she would wait the rest of her life.

She knew he cared for her. She saw it in the way he provided for them—giving of his money and possessions willingly, hauling wood so she wouldn't have to carry it, taking Ruthie while Bessie washed the supper dishes. All the little things he did shouted his regard. But was it love? Would Jasper ever call it love? She didn't know, but she longed to hear him say it.

Ruth tugged on her skirt, and Bessie looked down. At seven months old, Ruth was trying to learn to crawl. She would get on her hands and knees and rock back and forth until she lunged forward. Bessie noticed Ruth had something in her mouth.

"Spit it out," Bessie commanded. She felt around and pulled out a sliver of wood. "Silly baby." She picked her up and kissed her soft neck, delighting in the soft warmth of the baby. It was hard to imagine how life could be better.

She heard the front door shut. That was odd. Eve usually came through the back door. "I'm in the kitchen," she called.

"It's me," Jasper said.

Her welcoming smile died when she saw the white strain on his face. "What is it? What's wrong?"

He reached her in two strides and took her in his arms. "Sit down. I need to talk to you."

Numbly, she let him lead her to the table. Once she was seated, he knelt beside her and took her hand. "I have news—" He broke off, and his throat worked convulsively. "I don't know how to say this."

Terror seized her. Whatever it was, it was very bad. "Just tell me," she whispered.

He drew a deep breath. "The colonel called me into his office. It seems Ruthie's relatives have found out where she is, and they are laying claim to her."

In her worst nightmares she had imagined this. But how could anyone know where Ruthie was? And how could anyone ask her to give up her baby?

"I'm the only mother she's ever known," she whispered. "I can't give her up."

Jasper struggled to control himself. He loved Ruth too. "There will be a hearing next week when all the evidence will be brought. But we must be prepared, Bessie. We may lose her."

"No!" Denial burst from her lips. "We'll take her east. Today, right now." She rose and paced wildly. "No one can find us there. They wouldn't even look. No one would care."

"What kind of life do you think our Ruthie would have back east with the prejudice she would have to endure?" Jasper said gently. "Can we do that to her to save ourselves now? Even living here with us will be difficult. When she is grown, she'll have trouble fitting in. We both know this."

"We would protect her from it," Bessie said. "No one would dare say a word to the granddaughter of Thomas Randall."

"Would your father claim her as his granddaughter?"

Bessie fell silent. No, he would not, nor her mother. They were as snobbish as any others in Boston. But how could anyone not love Ruthie?

Jasper took Bessie in his arms and stroked her hair. "We must be strong and pray for God's will to be done."

Did she want God's will? What if His will was that she give up her daughter? Could she do that? No, that couldn't be His will. He had to work it out. He just had to.

"Do you know who is claiming her?" Perhaps it was a grandparent or an aunt or uncle. In that case, perhaps her own claim would be stronger.

"Her father."

Bessie's heart sank. "You are the only father she knows!"

"I know." There was a world of heartbreak in the heavy words.

She clutched him. "You have to think of something, Jasper."

"There is nothing, Bessie. We have to go to the hearing and present the strongest case we're able to make. We'll gather witnesses who will testify of our love for her and the care we've given. We will leave it in God's hands. His will be done."

His will be done. The words sounded final and frightening. She tried to pray, but the words wouldn't come. Was it only moments ago she had been reflecting on how very blessed and fortunate she was? Tears burned her eyes.

Jasper pressed his lips against her forehead. "We'll get through this, Bessie. Somehow, we'll get through this."

When he left her, she tried to think, to plan, but she was too numb. Tears finally fell, and when Eve came, Bessie was sitting at the table sobbing.

Eve shut the door behind her. "Bessie, what is wrong?" At the concern in her friend's voice, the tears began again.

"Ruthie's father is laying claim to her."

Eve was silent. "I feared this would happen. It has become common knowledge that a white woman at Fort Bowie found a baby in the desert and adopted her. Children are precious to the Navajo."

"We need people who will testify that we love her and have cared well for her. Would you be our advocate?"

"Of course, my friend. And I know Ben will also say how he found Ruthie and how your Jasper was searching for her." She laid a hand on Bessie's shoulder. "Do not despair. Our God is in control of this. We will pray for His will."

"But what if His will is to take Ruthie from us?"

"Then that is what is best for Ruthie."

Bessie couldn't accept that. What was best for Ruthie, for all of them, was for their family to stay together.

The week dragged by. Bessie spent every moment with Ruth and drank in every expression of delight, every moment of joy. It was a bittersweet time that made her appreciate her daughter even more.

A pall seemed to hang over the fort too. The men loved the baby, and they stopped by at odd times to offer their help if there was anything they could do. Bessie or Jasper thanked them and even asked one or two to testify on their behalf. Rooster would testify, as would the colonel.

Bessie dressed carefully in her best dress. The blue fabric brought out the color of her gray eyes. She wanted to look competent enough to care for the needs of a child. Jasper looked splendid in his freshly brushed uniform, but his eyes were sober. She knew hers were full of fear. She had seen it when she brushed her hair.

Jasper handed her up onto the buckboard, and a group of twelve soldiers escorted them out of the fort. The Indian agent's office was about five miles away.

If the circumstances had been different, Bessie would have enjoyed her first excursion outside the confines of Fort Bowie in six months. Just to see different cactus and scrub was a treat. They bounced along the rutted track, and she tried to remember all she wanted to say. She must not lose her temper or her composure. She had to convince them that the baby would be better with her.

She snuggled Ruthie close and tried not to imagine the return trip if she had to give her up. It couldn't happen. There was no way any man would require Ruth to return to a father she had never known.

All too soon they stopped in front of the agent's quarters, a square adobe structure with several Indians milling around. Bessie caught sight of Eve and raised her hand in greeting. The man beside her must be Ben. They both gave her a lopsided smile.

Jasper took the baby and helped Bessie down from the buckboard. She took Ruth from him and followed him inside. There were several Indians inside as well as a man in his fifties with graying hair and a handlebar mustache.

"McCloskey, the Indian agent," Jasper whispered.

He looked like a reasonable man. Bessie sent him a tiny smile, which he returned. She didn't have many feminine wiles, but she intended to use what few she had to keep her baby.

Glancing around the room, she was surprised to see Black Will, the young Navajo who had taught the men construction techniques. He stood with a group of three other Navajo men and two women. One of the women, a beautiful young woman of about twenty-five, sent her a glare of dislike. The other, an older woman with graying hair, nodded politely in her direction.

"I think we're all here now," McCloskey said ponderously. "Please be seated, all of you, until you are called to tell your side of the story. Let's hear from the man laying claim to the child."

One of the young men with Black Will stepped up. "I am called Thomas by the white man. The child is mine." He was tall and well-built with a self-confidence unusual in an Indian.

His quiet, confident demeanor caused Bessie's heart to sink. She should have known the man who would father a darling like Ruth would be someone with whom to reckon.

"What proof do you have?"

"I have those who will testify where the child was found as well as the family birthmark she carries on the inside of her knee. It matches the one on mine. My mother is here to swear that the woman was my wife and that we were legally wed according to our laws and lived together as man and wife."

How did he come to speak such perfect English? Bessie had to wonder about him.

"Bring forward your witnesses."

His mother testified first of her son's marriage and his wife and the love they shared. She told of their joy when they found they would have a child.

"How did the mother come to give birth in the desert?" Agent McCloskey asked.

"She was on her way to gather supplies and was set upon by Apaches. They took her wagon and left her in the desert. The shock brought on her labor," Thomas explained quietly.

"How do you know this?"

"My brother found my wagon and persuaded the thief to tell the story." He smiled grimly as he gestured to Black Will. "Black Will is my brother."

The agent cleared his throat gruffly. "I see."

Then the Navajo who had been their guide told how the baby had been found by Jasper and Bessie. He had seen the dead woman with his own eyes and testified as to the clothing she had been wearing. He had taken the grieving husband to her grave, and he had identified the clothing as belonging to his wife. "My brother saw the child's birthmark with his own eyes."

The chips were stacking up against them. Bessie could feel the panic rising. When did she get to plead for her daughter?

Abruptly, the agent turned to Jasper. "Have you anything to add to this, Lieutenant? The evidence seems pretty clear."

Jasper stood and cleared his throat. "Yes, Sir. We freely admit we found Ruth. We have loved and cared for her these seven months as if she were our own child. Indeed, we feel she is our own child. We could not love her more if she was our own flesh and blood. We ask you to think of her welfare also. We can give her many advantages and much love. We have several witnesses who can testify that we have given her excellent care."

Agent McCloskey waved his hand. "That won't be necessary, Lieutenant. I'm sure you and your wife have been good caretakers. But this child belongs to her father, and since you are not disputing that fact, I have no choice but to order her to be given back to him."

"No!" Bessie sprang to her feet. "You can't. Think of Ruth. We're the only parents she knows. She's too young to understand. Please, you must not do this." She began to weep, wringing her hands. How could she make them understand? She turned imploring eyes to the young father. She thought she saw compassion in his eyes, and she took a step toward him.

Jasper put a restraining hand on her arm. "Bessie, don't. It's no use."

She shook off his hand. "I can't let them take her. Please, Jasper." She turned back to the agent. "Please don't do this, Sir. She's our baby. We love her so much." Sobs racked her body, and she held Ruth close.

"I'm sorry, Ma'am. I have no choice." He turned back to Thomas and his family. "You may take the child."

Bessie whirled and would have fled with Ruth, but Jasper stopped her. Thomas walked slowly toward them, then turned back and faced agent McCloskey. "I will give Lieutenant Mendenhall and his wife two days to say their good-byes to my daughter and prepare for the separation. I do not wish to cause them any more harm. I am grateful for their care of my daughter." His eyes were full of compassion when he turned and faced them. "I will come for her in two days. Please have her ready."

He walked away, and Jasper took Bessie's arm and half carried her to the waiting buckboard. She was dazed. This couldn't be happening. She fought the feeling of light-headedness and stumbled along as best as she could. She saw the shocked faces of her friends as she passed. Eve moved as if to go to her, but Ben restrained her.

Jasper helped Bessie into the buckboard and climbed up beside her. They were silent with shock and sorrow as the buckboard lurched along. Bessie stole a glance at her husband. His jaw was set, and his face was white.

"How could he do this, Jasper? I don't understand how this could happen."

"I feared the worst. I think the agent felt he had to keep the Indians appeased. We have enough trouble with the Apache without riling the Navajo. And as her father, he does have a right to her. Think how we would feel in his place."

Bessie shook her head. "Let's just go, Jasper. Just keep driving until we reach the stage stop. We'll go to California or back to Fort Bridger. Somewhere they'll never find us."

"The army would find me, Bessie. I would be a deserter."

She had forgotten that. But there must be somewhere they could go.

"What are we going to do?"

He sighed heavily. "We have no choice, Bessie. We must give Ruthie back to her father."

She was shaking her head before he even finished. "You've never been a quitter, Jasper. Why are you giving up now? We can't give her back. We just can't."

He stopped the buckboard and turned to face her. "You have to stop this, Bessie. We have no choice. None. I would give anything if we could keep her with us. But the fact is that she is that man's daughter, the child of his own body. What if your true child had been lost to you and you found she was alive and living with another family. Would you want her back?"

She stared at him. She would want her child back. Could she blame Ruth's father for wanting what any father would desire? Hopeless tears leaked from her eyes, and she buried her face in her hands.

They finished the trip in silence. Bessie wished she could just die. How was she to face that man when he came to her door? How could she hand Ruthie into his arms? She closed her eyes and moaned.

When they reached their quarters, Jasper helped her down. "I need to report the decision to the colonel. I'll be in shortly." He hugged her gently and hurried across the parade ground.

She carried Ruth inside and laid the sleeping child in her crib. Soon that crib would be empty; soon her arms would be even emptier. She dropped onto the cot in the living room and buried her head in her hands. She couldn't bear it. Why did God allow something like this to happen? Could this really be His will? She didn't understand; she couldn't begin to think of any way this could be the right thing. Was it only her own will that made her so certain?

Neither one of them could eat supper. Jasper just picked at his stew, and

Bessie didn't even try to eat. She felt if a single morsel passed her lips, she would throw up. Ruthie was particularly adorable that evening. She giggled and pulled on Jasper's pant leg. She blew bubbles at Bessie and gurgled. Every time she babbled what sounded like Mama or Dada, they winced. It was all Bessie could do to keep her composure throughout the evening.

The next two days were bittersweet. The fort commander gave Jasper the time off to spend with his family. They took Ruth for walks, gathered the clothes Bessie had so lovingly made, and spent time just holding the baby. Bessie told her she was going for a nice visit with her daddy but that they would always love her.

The knock on the door came too soon. Bessie held Ruth's soft body against hers and trembled. She couldn't do it. Praying for strength, she nodded to Jasper to open the door. His face white, he walked to the door and opened it. Thomas and his mother stood on the stoop.

"Come in," Jasper said. "The baby is ready, but I can't say we are."

The Navajos did not answer that comment but stepped inside. Ruth's grandmother smiled at the baby, then her grave eyes met Bessie's.

"Again, I thank you for all you have done for my daughter," Thomas said. He approached Bessie with Ruth in her arms and spoke softly to her in Navajo.

Ruth buried her face against Bessie and didn't look at him. Bessie tightened her arms around her, and tears spurted from her eyes. "Please don't do this," she begged softly.

Thomas's eyes met hers. "She is my daughter. I have searched for her for seven months. Would you deny me the right to raise her in the traditions of her people? What can you give her that I cannot? Love? I love her more than you know. Money? I have my own ranch and am not a poor man. I have enough to see to her needs."

"She loves us," Bessie whispered. "Can't you see that? We are her parents now. I don't mean to hurt you, but she doesn't know you."

"She will learn. It will be hard for a few days, but she is just a baby. She will adjust. My mother and sister look forward to teaching her." There was no compromise in his eyes. She could sense his compassion, but she knew he would not change his mind. He would take Ruth, walk through the front door, and she would never see her again.

"Could I visit her?" She found it almost impossible to speak past the tears in her throat.

He hesitated. "Perhaps someday. But not now. She needs time to accept us and for us to accept her. She will be happy with us. She would never be truly accepted in your world. I think you know this in your heart."

She tightened her arms around Ruth and backed away a step. She saw tears in Jasper's eyes as he came toward her and stood beside her.

Thomas held out his arms. "My daughter, please."

Bessie searched his eyes, then looked at Jasper. The pain she saw reflected there almost broke her composure totally. She buried her nose in Ruth's neck and inhaled her baby scent for the last time.

Jasper bent his head and kissed Ruth's cheek. "Take her quickly," he muttered brokenly.

Bessie thrust the baby into her father's arms, then turned and ran from the room.

Chapter 14

The bright sun shone most of the time in Arizona Territory, but Jasper knew that Bessie never saw it for days. A dark cloud of despair seemed to have wrapped itself around her heart and colored everything she said and did. Jasper was helpless to penetrate her depression. He missed her gentle smiles and thoughtful gestures. He didn't recognize this hollow-eyed stranger who never laughed.

He was dealing with his own grief too. The house echoed with memories of Ruthie, her laughter, her smiling eyes, and childish voice. How would they ever find their way out of this maze of despair? Perhaps if he were a real husband to her and there was the possibility of a child, Bessie could throw off this depression. But now was not the time to discuss that subject.

He stopped Eve on her way to his house nearly two weeks after Ruth was returned to her father. "What am I to do about Bessie?" he asked her. "Does she talk to you at all?"

Eve's eyes were filled with grief. "She does not speak. It is as if the laughing part has died."

Jasper raked a hand through his hair. "The evenings are like sitting alone. She stares into space and only answers my questions when she has no choice."

Eve nodded. "Could she go home for a visit? Perhaps it would help her to see her own people."

His heart sank. He hated to think about being without her. But he didn't have his Bessie now. The woman sharing his home was not the Bessie he had come to admire and love. And he did love her. He knew that now when she had left him in spirit. Several times he had tried to tell her, but the words stuck in his throat.

He thanked Eve, and with lagging steps he went to check on a ticket. This was the only thing he could think to do. Once he checked the stage schedule and the cost of a ticket, he headed back across the parade ground to tell Bessie.

Bessie didn't bother to give Eve any instructions. Her friend knew the house as well as she did. Besides, none of it seemed very important. Their quarters could have been covered in dust and cobwebs, and she wouldn't have noticed. What reason did she have to keep it clean? No precious baby would crawl across its floors; no pudgy fingers would reach to put stray dirt into her mouth.

She thought of Boston. The emerald lawns and trees, the parties and laughter. What would Jasper say if she told him she wanted to go home? She longed for green grass, for parties to take her mind off her loss. She wanted to share with her family what a lovely child Ruthie was. Surely they would understand her loss if she told them in person, wouldn't they? She wanted to get away from this house filled with memories of her smiling baby.

If Lenore were no longer seeing Richard, perhaps Bessie should step aside and let Jasper have the woman he really wanted. Although it would mean her own ruin, Bessie would have some satisfaction in seeing another's happiness. What did it matter if her reputation was in tatters now? Her daughter was gone. She stared at the bright spot of sunshine on the kitchen floor. Why did the sun continue to rise each day when in her heart she felt only darkness?

She knew Jasper was concerned for her. He stared at her when he thought she wasn't looking. First he was saddled with a wife he didn't know, then he was left with this shell. And that's how she felt. A shell. All the joy and happiness had fled from her spirit. Jasper deserved better. She thought she still loved him, but any emotion was hidden deep inside. It hurt too much to care. If she went away, he would soon forget her.

The front door banged, and she jumped. Jasper smiled at her anxiously.

"What are you doing home? You just left," she said.

He took her hands in his. "How would you like to go home, to Boston, for awhile?"

How had he known? She stared at him silently. Did he want to be rid of her? She knew she had been nothing like a wife to him lately. Though she knew it, she couldn't help herself, couldn't shake the grief that hung over her like a shroud.

He rushed on as if he thought he had to convince her. "I've checked on stage tickets, and you could leave tomorrow or Friday. You could stay as long as you like, get caught up on all the news with your sister. She would be delighted to see you. The autumn balls will be in full swing soon."

"I'll go," she said. "I have been thinking about it."

His face lit up, and he hugged her. Her heart clenched with pain. Had he been looking for an excuse to send her home all this time? "I want to go tomorrow," she said.

His smile dimmed, but he nodded and kissed her forehead. "I'll buy the ticket."

Eve stared at her from the kitchen where she had begun the laundry. "I will pack your valise," she told her.

"I'd rather do it," Bessie said. "I know what I want to take." She would take everything important just in case she never returned.

Eve nodded and returned to her chores. Bessie went to the bedroom to pack. The sooner she was gone from this house of painful memories, the better.

While standing at the stage stop the next day, Bessie felt as though she were in a cocoon of cotton; she couldn't feel anything. No pain, no joy, no feelings of any kind. She hugged Jasper and allowed him to kiss her, but her heart felt like wood in her chest. His green eyes stared at her worriedly, then he helped her aboard the stage. Did he suspect she might not return?

"Write when you arrive safely," he told her.

"I will."

He looked as though he had more he wanted to say, but in the end, he shut the stage door and stepped away. She lifted a gloved hand and waved at him gravely; then she fixed her gaze straight ahead. She wouldn't allow herself to feel regret.

The days aboard the stagecoach were an ordeal, but Bessie loved the train. The train whistle blew, and Boston was just ahead. She felt the most excitement she had felt since before Ruthie had been ripped from her. Leaning out the train window, she breathed in the moist air. How she had missed the green grass and leafy trees!

When Jasper had kissed her at the stage stop, she had tried to tell him she wouldn't be back, but the words wouldn't come. Had that been relief on his face when he waved good-bye?

The train jerked to a halt, and she gathered her valise and reticule. Tying her bonnet firmly under her chin, she pushed her way through the throng and looked anxiously around for a familiar face.

"Bessie!"

She whirled and saw Lenore hurtling toward her at a most unlady-like pace. Behind her came her parents. "Lenore." Tears pricked her eyes, and she flung herself into her sister's embrace. Her parents arrived, and she hugged them.

"Let me look at you." Her father held her at arm's length. "What are these dark circles?" he demanded. "Isn't that new husband taking care of you?"

She bristled at the criticism of Jasper. "Of course he is. It's just been a long trip."

Her father snorted. "I thought you said you wanted adventure." He linked his arm with hers. Her mother looped her arm through her other elbow, and they strolled toward the waiting carriage. She knew they looked the picture of a happy family. Appearances were so important to her parents.

Lenore kept up a steady stream of comments as she followed them. "Your letters said you were bitten by a rattlesnake. Do you have a scar? What's it like living in a place that hot? Is it true there is no green grass?"

Bessie laughed and was surprised at the sound. She thought she would never laugh again. This trip had been a good idea.

Her room looked just the same. Her clothes were still in the wardrobe, and her extra shoes lined the end of her bed. Her room was the same, but why did it all feel so different? She gazed at her reflection in the mirrored dresser. Her appearance was unaltered, but she knew she was not the same young woman who had stood there eight months before. It was like trying to fit into a dress a size too small. Not impossible, but not comfortable either.

Lenore pecked on the door. "Dinner, Bessie. Emma made your favorite. Fried chicken."

She grabbed her shawl and joined her sister in the hall. Their parents were already seated at the dining room table. Her father rose politely until his daughters were seated; then he rang for Emma to serve the meal.

As they ate their meal, Bessie was conscious of the stares the three of them sent her way when they thought she wasn't looking. She knew the inquisition would begin after dinner. When the last plates were cleared away, her mother suggested they retire to the game room. Bessie laid down her napkin and followed her family.

"You look terrible, Bessie. I want to know what's been going on out there in the desert. Is your husband kind?"

"Oh, Mother, of course he is. Jasper is the sweetest, kindest man I've ever met." Bessie was shocked they would think anything different. She had written them of her husband's many fine qualities.

"Your sister finally confessed her part in your hasty marriage," her father began ponderously. "I must say your mother and I were shocked you didn't confide the truth to us."

"I wanted to go, Father," Bessie began timidly.

He waved his large hand. "That is beside the point. Your sister acted irresponsibly, and so did you."

Bessie couldn't argue with that. She glanced at Lenore, but her sister avoided her gaze.

"Have you left your husband?"

How had they guessed? She took a deep breath. "I haven't decided. Don't think it's Jasper's fault." She pressed her hands together. "We lost the child we'd adopted, and I'm afraid I haven't dealt well with the loss."

Her father frowned, and she saw Lenore lean forward, her eyes sparkling. Was she still yearning after Jasper?

"Whose child was it?" Her mother sounded bewildered.

"An Indian child, Mother." Bessie burst into tears and sobbed out the story of Ruthie.

When she raised her head, she saw her mother's face pursed in disapproval. "You should have searched for the child's parents immediately, Bessie, and you would not have gotten attached to her."

She knew they would react this way. Why had she tried to deceive herself? She straightened her shoulders and got to her feet. "I'm tired," she said. "May I be excused?"

Her father's expression darkened, but he nodded curtly. "We will discuss this tomorrow," he said ominously.

As Bessie fled for the sanctuary of her room, she heard Lenore demanding to know what she intended to do. She shut the door behind her and threw herself across the bed. Lenore wanted Jasper. Bessie had seen Lenore's acquisitive expression when she heard Bessie might be annulling the marriage. But hearing her father ask the question had made Bessie realize how impossible the very thought of it was.

She didn't belong here. This large brick structure with fine furniture and more room than they knew what to do with was no longer her home. Her home was an adobe three-room building with a cot for a sofa and a handmade kitchen table. Jasper was her family. She belonged with her husband.

Her parents would tell her they loved her, but real love was what Jasper had been showing her for months. He might not have said the words, but he told her with his actions, just like the Bible said he should. She saw his love in the way he saw to her needs, his kind words, and tender care. Why had she doubted?

She had been hurt and confused, but now she realized she was on the verge of a huge mistake. She thanked God He had guarded her from herself. What would Jasper say when she got home? Would he even expect to see her again? Had he realized the finality of her good-bye?

She looked up at the knock on the door.

"Can I come in, Bessie?" Her sister's voice was soft as though she feared their father would hear.

Bessie opened the door. "I'm not giving up Jasper," she announced. "You can come in, but if you're here to try to convince me to leave him, you're wasting your breath."

Lenore stared at her and shook her head. She brushed past her and shut the door. "I don't want your Jasper, Bessie. You should know better. I can see you love him. All I've ever wanted was for you to be happy."

Bessie searched her sister's eyes and nodded. What had she been thinking? Lenore was sometimes irresponsible and thoughtless, but she would never deliberately harm her.

"I just want to hear about the West. Do you think I could come for a visit?

My hopes for marriage here have not materialized. I'm so sick of Boston society, of Father's determination to find me a man of substance." She shook her head. "I don't care about money. I want a man who is a real man, not my father's paid lackey." Her eyes gleamed. "I've thought about writing and asking, but I was afraid you'd say no. But now that you're here and I can tell you I have no designs on your husband, maybe you'll take pity on me."

Bessie laughed. She felt as though a huge weight had been lifted from her shoulders. Lenore didn't want Jasper. Her smile faded. What if he still yearned for her? The last thing she needed was for Jasper to be around Lenore. She knew the comparison would be devastating to her marriage. "Are you sure you don't still care for Jasper, Lenore? You wrote to him even after I went west."

A guilty expression raced across her sister's face. "Yes, I did," she admitted. "I'm surprised he told you."

"He didn't. I saw the letter."

"Did you read it?" Lenore's question was casual. Too casual.

"No. I couldn't betray Jasper like that." She frowned at the relief on Lenore's face.

Her sister got to her feet. "I must get to bed," she said airily. "Don't worry about the letter, Bessie. It meant nothing. Not to me nor to Jasper."

Her eyes narrowed, Bessie watched her sister's hurried departure. What had been in the letter?

The days were lonely for Jasper without Bessie, and the nights even lonelier. The little house echoed with silence. The laundry was neatly folded and put away, and the house was spotless after Eve's visits, but it lacked Bessie's touch. Several times Jasper had been tempted to send Bessie a letter begging her to come home, but he managed to restrain himself. He wanted the old Bessie back, and if he forced her hand, he feared he would never see his laughing wife again, just her empty shell.

October was drawing to a close; soon the welcome monsoon would arrive. Would she be home for Thanksgiving, for Christmas? Would she come home at all? He forced himself to face the possibility that she might not. Her goodbye had seemed so final. As she had clung to him with a strange desperation, she had searched his eyes with her grave gaze, as though imprinting his likeness on her mind. Why had he never realized before just how precious she was to him? Was it too late to tell her?

He thought of Ruthie. How was she getting along with her father? He was tempted to ask Black Will several times, but he didn't want to speak with the man who had been responsible for this turn of events. He told himself he was being unfair; after all, Black Will was Ruthie's uncle, but he couldn't seem to rid himself of the animosity.

It was late when he let himself in the house one night. How odd. The lamp in the bedroom was lit. Frowning, he walked through the parlor and kitchen and pushed open the bedroom door.

Bessie lay in the bed fast asleep. His mouth gaped. She must have come in on the stage late this afternoon. He had heard the normal stage commotion, but he hadn't thought anything about it. She couldn't have been in Boston longer than a few days. What had caused her to come back so quickly? He wished he could believe it was because she missed him.

Relief flooded him. If she hadn't come soon, he knew he would have been compelled to go after her. In spite of the strange circumstances of their marriage, Bessie was his wife. He knelt by the bed and just drank in the sight of her. Her light brown hair spread over the pillow, and he buried his face in it. He kissed her gently, but she didn't awaken, and he saw the shadows of exhaustion under her eyes. What a grueling trip she had to have endured. He ran his fingers over her lower lip and kissed her.

"Bessie," he said softly.

She opened her eyes and stared at him. Then she smiled and opened her arms.

Jasper gathered her close. "Don't ever leave me again, Bessie. You're all I have. We can have a baby together and build our family from tonight forward." He kissed her gently at first, then with mounting passion. "I love the way your hair smells as fresh as sunshine, the way you tilt your head when you smile," he muttered against her neck. "Promise you'll never leave me again."

"I promise," Bessie whispered. Then she moved over for him to join her in their bed.

Chapter 15

The smell of coffee awakened Bessie. For just a moment, she forgot where she was. Then she smelled the scent of sage wafting through the open window and saw the bathtub hanging on the wall. She smiled and stretched. She was home.

She heard Jasper moving around the kitchen, and she got up and quickly dressed. He whistled as he banged the coffeepot back down on the stove.

She pinched some color into her cheeks and opened the door. Everything had changed last night. She felt shy at the thought of facing him this morning.

He turned at the sound and grinned. "Couldn't stand a place with no snakes or spiders, huh?"

She smiled. "And no bats." She drank in the sight of him with his silly grin and tender eyes.

"I missed you," he said softly.

"I knew as soon as I arrived in Boston that I had made a mistake. There's nothing left back there for me."

"And here you have sagebrush and sand, rattlesnakes and scorpions. What more could you want?"

"Ruthie," she said without thinking.

His mirth faded. "I know," he said.

"Have you heard anything about her at all?"

He looked away and sighed heavily.

"Tell me!" She panicked at the look of resignation on his face.

"It's nothing bad," he said quickly. "It's just—" He broke off and sighed again. "I'm not sure it's the best thing for either of us, but her uncle said we would be permitted to visit her."

Joy flooded her heart. To see her baby again, to touch her. "When?" she asked eagerly.

"Whenever you want. The family is still in the area right now. They will be leaving next week to go back north."

"Can we go today?" She wanted to go right now, this minute. She couldn't wait to feel Ruthie's chubby arms around her neck, to smell the sweet baby scent of her.

"I've already asked for the day off."

"Let me comb my hair." She hurried to the bedroom, brushed her hair, and put it up. She picked up her bonnet and rushed toward the front door, but Jasper stopped her. "You must eat something, Bessie. You're white with fatigue."

"I'm not hungry." She smiled. "Let's just go. I can eat later." But when she swayed, she realized he might be right. When had she eaten last? She hadn't been able to force down much at the stage stops.

Jasper guided her to a seat and pushed her down gently. "You have to take care of yourself. You're all I have."

Bessie was touched at his admission. She searched his tender gaze. "All right," she said. "I'll have some bread and jam. That coffee smells wonderful too." She started to get up, but he shook his head firmly.

"I'll get it. You look like a stiff wind would blow you over. I don't think much of the care your family has given you."

She smiled but didn't tell him they had said the same thing about him. "How's Eve?"

"She's taken good care of the house, as you can see. She'll be glad you're back."

Why were they talking about such mundane things? Why didn't he sweep her into his arms and tell her never to leave again? Had he really missed her? What had last night meant to him? The questions stuck in her throat.

"I'll get the buckboard while you finish your breakfast," he told her.

By the time she was done, he was back. "Ready?"

She took a last gulp of coffee. "Ready."

Several of the soldiers waved and welcomed her home. The buckboard bounced over the ruts and scrub, and she clung to Jasper's arm to keep from being thrown from the seat. The scent of creosote and sage was like a tonic. How good it was to be home!

They headed toward the small encampment west of the fort. Several ramshackle adobe buildings squatted amidst the cactus and yucca. She saw half-clothed children playing in the dirt with several dogs, and her heart sank. Was this the kind of life her Ruthie would have?

Jasper stopped the buckboard at the first building and asked where he might find Thomas. The somber woman pointed to the last building in the row. He tipped his hat, and they went on. The building looked deserted, and Bessie frowned in disappointment. What if the family had already left? Jasper helped her down, and they went to the door.

Bessie felt as though she could barely breathe. The door finally opened, and Thomas's mother stared at them impassively.

"We've come to see Ruth," Jasper said.

The woman motioned them inside. It took several moments for Bessie's eyes to adjust to the dim interior; then she saw Ruthie lying on a blanket.

The baby slept with her thumb corked in her mouth as usual. She was clean, her hair neatly done in tiny braids.

Bessie went onto her knees with a soft cry. Ruthie opened her eyes and stared at her. Her mouth puckered, and she sought her grandmother's face.

Her grandmother went to her with soft clucking sounds of comfort, and the little girl held up her arms. She stared soberly at Bessie and Jasper from the sanctuary of her grandmother's arms.

Bessie thought her heart would break. How could Ruthie have forgotten them so quickly? It had only been six weeks. "Hello, Darling," she said softly. She touched her soft hair, then patted her cheek. "Have you forgotten me?"

"Ma-ma-ma," Ruthie chanted. She reached up a chubby hand and grasped an escaping tendril of Bessie's hair.

Tears of relief flooded Bessie's eyes. Perhaps she hadn't forgotten them totally. Did she think they had deserted her? She touched her soft cheek again, so engrossed in the baby, she didn't hear Thomas come in until he spoke.

"You have come."

She and Jasper both turned. Thomas stood in the doorway, his feet apart, his arms crossed on his chest.

He gave Ruth a fond gaze. "You see she has adjusted well. I wanted to set your minds at ease before we go home."

"She looks very happy," Bessie said grudgingly. "She obviously loves her grandmother."

Thomas nodded. "She cried the first day, then no longer. This will be the last time we meet. I wished you to see she was well. You love her and saved her from death. Now you can rest knowing she will be happy."

"Where are you going?" Jasper asked.

"I cannot tell you," Thomas said. "Wherever the Lord leads."

Bessie stared at him in shock. What did he mean? Her heart pounded in sudden hope. Her worst nightmare had been that Ruthie was going into spiritual darkness.

He smiled at her expression. "I was raised by missionaries near the Colorado border," he told her. "The Lord called me as His own when I was ten years old. I will do my best to raise my daughter in the ways of Jesus as we travel among my people to tell them of His love."

Tears flooded her eyes, and she gave Thomas her hand. "I can go now," she said softly. "I was wrong to question God's purposes. My faith was small. May God go with you."

He took her hand and pressed her fingers gently. "You allowed the Lord to work a miracle through you," he said. "I will tell Ruth of the woman with the eyes of love who saved her from the desert. Your reward will be great in heaven."

Tears spurted from her eyes at his words. Had God truly used her? Was there some greater purpose in these events? Only God knew, but Bessie thanked Him for allowing her to have the joy of knowing Ruthie just those few short months.

Jasper put an arm around her and led her from the shanty. They both took one long, last look at Ruth. She stared at them, then smiled at her grandmother.

"Come, Bessie," Jasper said softly. "There's no need for us here."

Bessie's arms were empty, but her heart was full as they rode home. She had been so foolish to doubt God's provision and to question His will. She cast a sidelong glance at Jasper. The relief was evident on his face too.

Although she still missed the baby, after several weeks Bessie was able to finally let go in her heart. She would accept God's will. The walls came tumbling down in her relationship with Jasper too, now that they were truly man and wife—more than just in name. The tender light in her husband's eyes made her forget the disappointment she had seen there the day they met. Then something would remind her of Lenore, and she would still wonder how he would feel when he met her sister for the first time. They were certain to meet someday.

"I'll be gone all day," Jasper told her one morning over breakfast. "We have a lead about Cochise's whereabouts. There's a dance at the officers' quarters tonight. I'll make sure I'm back to take my best girl out on the town. Such as it is." He grinned at his own joke.

"I'll save every dance for you," she told him.

"We can eat at the mess hall tonight." He kissed her good-bye, and she got up to wash the dishes. A wave of nausea struck her, and she rushed to the bedroom for the chamber pot. She vomited and sat back weakly. What was wrong with her? She felt so light-headed. A sense of unease struck her, and she went to the kitchen and looked at the cloth calendar hanging on the wall. Counting back, she smiled incredulously. Today was her birthday, and she had forgotten all about it. If what she suspected were true, the Lord had presented them with the most perfect gift she could imagine.

Dr. Richter confirmed her suspicions. "You'll probably deliver in late July," he said. "I want you to get plenty of rest. You don't look well. Eve will be glad to come more often, I'm sure."

In a daze of joy, she hurried back home. For a moment, she almost felt guilty. No other child could replace Ruthie; she would always love her, but God had seen fit to fill the empty hole in her heart. She hoped this would heal Jasper's heart as much as it did hers. He would be a wonderful father to this baby.

Her heart full of hope, she sat on the cot and waited for Jasper to come home. She would wait until after supper to tell him. The joy of savoring his anticipated reaction was sweet. A baby! It was almost beyond belief.

When Jasper came through the front door, she was still smiling. She stood, and he put his arm around her.

"My sweet Bessie," he said, kissing her. "I missed seeing your smile today. You hungry?"

"Starved."

He chuckled. "I think it's beans and salt pork."

She smiled and gave a small shrug. "At least I don't have to cook it."

He held her hand as they crossed the parade ground. When they entered the mess hall, a rousing cheer went up.

"Happy birthday, Bessie!" the assembled soldiers shouted.

"Bessie!"

She turned. Was that Lenore's voice?

Lenore beamed at her sister's amazement. "Surprised?"

As they hugged each other, the gentle fragrance of Lenore's lilac sachet slipped up Bessie's nose. "I'm speechless."

Lenore giggled. "I wrote Jasper months ago to plan this."

The hall was decorated with crudely painted signs, and a birthday cake sat on a center table surrounded with packages. Confetti, obviously hand cut from old newspapers, showered over her. Beaming with pride, Jasper led her to the table and had her open her gifts.

Rooster gave her a small leather-bound diary. "It was my mother's," he told her. "I can't read, so I'll never use it. It would make me right proud to know you was writing in it."

Some gifts were homemade, like Private Bechtol's gift of a small dulcimer. Bessie was overwhelmed at the show of love.

"There's no gift here from me," Jasper whispered. "I'll give it to you at home later."

She wondered what it could be. Whatever it was, her gift to him would be even more joyous. She smiled at the thought.

"What's that smile about?" he asked while he spun her around the room when the band started playing.

"I'll tell you later," she whispered.

Jasper refused to let any other soldier cut in, but the high-spirited men didn't care. They partnered Lenore when they could and danced with each other when they couldn't.

Bessie was exhausted by the time Jasper led her and Lenore back across the dark parade ground. He lit the lantern on the mess chest, while Bessie dropped onto the cot in the parlor.

"I'm just exhausted," Lenore said. "Can I go to bed? We can talk tomorrow."

"Do you mind sleeping out here?"

"Of course not."

"See you in the morning." Bessie rose and followed Jasper to their bedroom and shut the door behind them.

"My feet hurt," she moaned. "You stepped on them twice."

He grinned and slipped her feet out of her boots. "Let me rub them," he said. "I never claimed to be a dancer."

She sighed at the touch of his strong fingers on her sore feet. She gazed at his bent head and savored the news she was about to tell him. They would be a true family now. Nothing could part them.

"Better?"

"Much." She tucked her bare feet under her skirt and smiled at him. "I have a present for you."

He cocked a quizzical eyebrow. "It's *your* birthday."

"That reminds me. How long have you been planning this party? I don't even know when your birthday is."

"Lenore and I planned it months ago," he said with a proud grin. He set the lantern on the floor and pulled a letter out of his pocket. Bessie recognized it immediately. It was the letter from Lenore. "She wrote me shortly after you arrived to apologize for her deceit. She wanted me to know what a wonderful wife you would make and told me all kinds of things about you—your birthday, how much you love cats, the way you care for other people, the fact that you hate onions." He grinned. "She admitted you didn't know how to cook but assured me you would soon learn."

Bessie's face flamed. Why had she assumed the worst? She met his gaze shamefacedly. "I saw the letter, but I didn't read it," she admitted. She wanted no secrets between them any longer. "I thought you still loved Lenore and were writing to her." A weight rolled off her heart. She had longed to speak to him of this pain and uncertainty she felt.

His mouth dropped open. "How could you think that?" he asked incredulously. "We've been studying about love, and I thought I was doing a good job of showing you I love you."

Did he just say he loved her? Tears flooded her eyes, and she smiled at him tremulously. "You never told me," she said. "I saw you cared, but you never said you loved me. You said you loved things about me, but you never said you loved me. Lenore is the beauty, and I've lived so long in her shadow it's been hard to stop." Joy flooded her heart at the love that shone out of his eyes.

He shook his head. "My silly Bessie." He knelt beside her and took her hands. "I love you so much it hurts sometimes. I see your spirit, your gentleness, and the way you give of yourself to others, and it humbles me. You are more beautiful than any woman I've ever met."

"Not more beautiful than Lenore," she said sadly.

"All Lenore is to me is your sister. I forgot Lenore when you insisted on keeping Ruthie. I saw your heart that day and couldn't help but love it. I know I don't deserve you, but with God's help, I'll try my best to make you happy."

She had been so blind. She would never doubt him again. He was a man of integrity, a man who loved and honored her. He would be a wonderful father.

He pressed his lips against the palm of her hand. "I know it's been hard lately, Bessie, but we'll get through it. Someday God will bless us with more children, but until then we have each other."

Tears coursed down her cheeks. "I love you so much," she whispered. "I read your letters and knew you were the man I'd longed for all my life." She smoothed his hair back from his forehead and gazed into his green eyes. "God has blessed us so much. More than you know."

"I know He has," he said.

The tenderness in his eyes made her heart sing. Why had she allowed her insecurities to make her doubt him? "You don't know about this blessing," she said. "We're going to have a baby." She almost hated to tell him. The anticipation had been sweet.

He stared at her; then his eyes widened. "A baby? Us?" He whooped and stood, swinging her up into his arms.

He whirled around the room with her until she was dizzy and laughing. "Stop or I'll throw up. And besides, you'll have Lenore in here any minute."

He stopped immediately and stared into her eyes. "I thought I loved you before, Bessie, but it was nothing compared to how I feel right now." He set her back onto the cot and put his hand in his pocket. Drawing out a small box, he opened it and took out a gold wedding band.

Bessie caught her breath at the sight of the ring. How did he know she had longed for a tangible sign of his love, a visible announcement to all that she belonged to him?

He knelt again and took her left hand. "You are my precious treasure, Bessie. I want you to wear this and always remember that I will never leave your side until God takes me home." He pronounced the words solemnly, his green eyes full of promise and commitment. Slipping the ring on her finger, he pressed his lips to it and sealed it in place.

Bessie felt she finally saw his heart. He was a stranger no longer and never would be again. She was flesh of his flesh and bone of his bone. He opened his arms, and she went into them with an overwhelming joy in her heart. No matter where the Lord led, she knew her heart was safe with this man, her beloved husband.

Epilogue

Jasper looked up at the sound of a baby's cry. Pacing the kitchen floor, he waited for the doctor to announce whether he had a son or a daughter. He didn't care which it was as long as Bessie and the baby were safe and well. He was glad to be back in Wyoming for this occasion. Back among friends.

She hadn't cried out at all but had endured her labor with the same courage he had first loved about her. He heard a murmur; then the baby cried again.

A few minutes later, the door opened, and a very disheveled Dr. Richter motioned him in. Propped in the bed, Bessie smiled at him wearily. His gaze traveled over her anxiously. She was pale, but she seemed to be all right. Only then did he glance down to see the baby. His jaw dropped. There were two babies. And they both had red hair.

Bessie chuckled at the expression on his face. "Do you want to hold Cassie or Charles first?"

Jasper began to laugh. Bessie's eyes met his, and she joined him in laughter. He knelt beside the bed and kissed his wife, his son, and his daughter. "God said He would give us blessings beyond all we could dream or imagine," he told her. "I think this is what He meant."

A Letter to Our Readers

Dear Readers:

In order that we might better contribute to your reading enjoyment, we would appreciate you taking a few minutes to respond to the following questions. When completed, please return to the following: Fiction Editor, Barbour Publishing, Inc., P.O. Box 719, Uhrichsville, OH 44683.

1. Did you enjoy reading *Wyoming?*
   ❏ Very much—I would like to see more books like this.
   ❏ Moderately—I would have enjoyed it more if _____
   _____
   _____

2. What influenced your decision to purchase this book?
   (Check those that apply.)
   ❏ Cover   ❏ Back cover copy   ❏ Title   ❏ Price
   ❏ Friends   ❏ Publicity   ❏ Other

3. Which story was your favorite?
   ❏ *Where Leads the Heart*   ❏ *The Heart Answers*
   ❏ *Plains of Promise*   ❏ *To Love a Stranger*

4. Please check your age range:
   ❏ Under 18   ❏ 18–24   ❏ 25–34
   ❏ 35–45   ❏ 46–55   ❏ Over 55

5. How many hours per week do you read? _____

Name _____

Occupation _____

Address _____

City _____ State _____ Zip _____